MISRULE

A DEATH DWELLER'S MC NOVEL

KATHRYN C. KELLY

Misrule
A Death Dwellers MC Novel
By Kathryn C. Kelly

Cover design by Mayhem Cover Creations
Formatted by Mayhem Cover Creations
Cover Image ©2019 Wander Aguiar Photography
Cover Model: Nathan Van Dyken

ISBN: 978-1-7325889-7-4

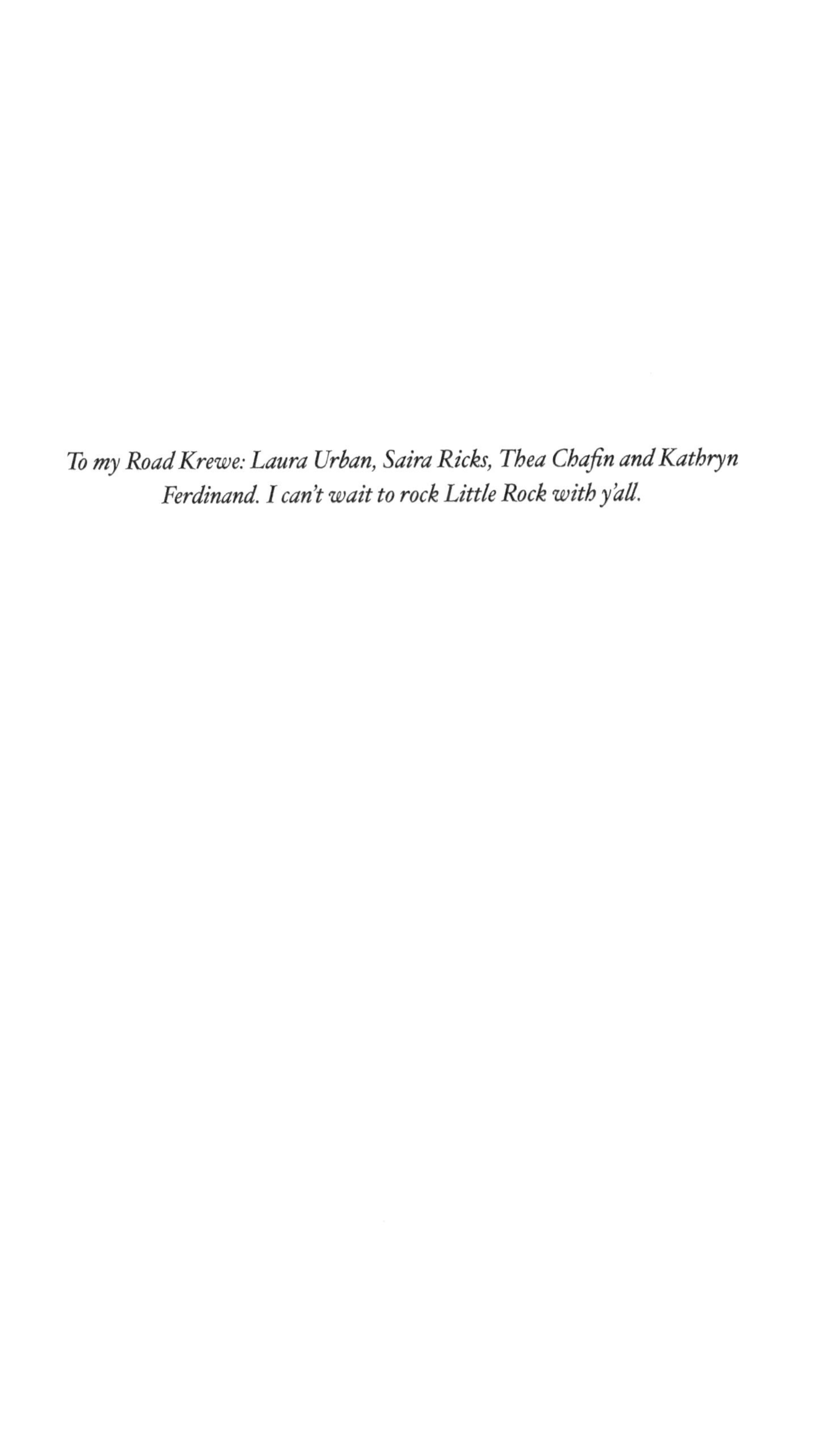

To my Road Krewe: Laura Urban, Saira Ricks, Thea Chafin and Kathryn Ferdinand. I can't wait to rock Little Rock with y'all.

ACKNOWLEDGMENTS

Misrule wouldn't have been possible without the assistance of many. It took a village to see the conclusion to the Death Dweller's saga completed. As always, I want to thank my mother, Memaw Kelly, for her support and championing of the Dweller boys and of me throughout my life. Zoey, Kate, and Alegra, thank you for all the kitchen duty so I could write. Melissa Kulis, you rock at getting the word out about my books. Crystal Cuffley, you will always be my Mistress Dibs. Danni, thank you for your keen eye and editorial skills. Kristin Inselman, thank you for keeping in touch with me and loving the books in spite of Outlaw. Melanie Cooper, thank you for your fabulous beta reading. Wander Aguiar and Nathan Van Dyken, I saw the photo and had to have it in my life, which meant Knox had to have tattoos. Finally, thanks to Mayhem Cover Creations for your fabulous designs.

They've been Misled. They've been Misunderstood. They've been Misguided.
Now it's time to put the past aside and focus on new beginnings.
Knox and Roxy have finally set the date for their wedding, but things won't go smoothly. There are too many people within the Club who won't accept Knox—and one woman in particular whose day of reckoning has been a long time coming.
Not to mention the outside interference from family.
But the deadliest threat of all will come from an unexpected enemy.
Can the Club put aside differences long enough to defeat the looming threat against them?
Or will Knox and Roxy's wedding turn into a funeral...?

CONTENTS

Knox

"When you intend to make a honest woman out of my momma-in-law?"

For the past two months, Mortician had been posing that question to Knox Harrington on an increasingly regular basis. He felt the pressure. Truth be told, he wanted to marry Roxanne Doucette, Mortician's "momma-in-law", and something of a mother figure to not only the women of the Death Dwellers Motorcycle Club, but the men, too.

Knox shrugged, his usual answer. The other men at the table sent him various looks of disapproval and displeasure. The club president, Outlaw, lifted a brow at him, the silent question screaming *DANGER* to Knox.

Outlaw discarded three cards, then replaced them in his hand with three from the deck. They were at their weekly get-together, this time held at Mortician and his wife, Bailey's, house. Roxanne lived in the mother-in-law quarters, where Knox also lived now. The place was small, nothing he was used to; however, it made Roxanne happy so he was more than willing to ignore the lack of space.

A burst of female laughter emanated from the den, two doors down the hall from where the men sat in the game room. Knox picked out Roxanne's robust laughter and couldn't help but smile. She was such a beautiful, intelligent, vivacious woman. She brought meaning and sunshine to his life. He should want to jump at the chance to marry her.

So what was stopping him?

He glanced around the table, focusing first on Mortician, the club enforcer, who loved his dreads, the club, and family, and not necessarily in that order. If something made Bailey unhappy, Mortician went out of his way to change that. And, if Roxanne was unhappy, then most assuredly Bailey would be. The girl simply adored her mother.

Knox looked at Johnnie, club VP. He was educated and easy-going, so above the rest of the club—on Knox's level actually—that Knox wondered why Johnnie didn't turn in his patch. Recently, he'd separated from his wife. Which pleased Knox to no end. He *hated* Kendall, and was glad he didn't have to suffer her presence at the family dinners anymore.

Next, he spied on Val, the club's Road Captain. He was an idiot. Period.

Knox turned his attention to Digger, sergeant-at-arms and Mortician's blood brother. Another idiot, who, so far, hadn't packed on the pounds with all the eating he'd become known for.

Knox moved on to Cash and Stretch, the explosive's technician and secretary/treasurer respectively, as well as husbands to each other, and boyfriends to Outlaw's sister, Ophelia. And her baby daddies to her two kids. Cash might've been on-level with Knox and Johnnie, except he'd tied himself to Ophelia and Stretch, Pushover One and Pushover Two.

And, finally, there was Outlaw. King of Criminals, Jerks, and Assholes...

There was his answer, Knox realized. He hadn't proposed to Roxanne because of *them*.

"A perfect time to propose might be at Meggie Valentine Ball," Val offered into the silence, not dropping the subject as they usually did once Knox gave his shrug-answer.

Mortician studied the cards in his hand. "What you think about that, Knox?"

Placing his cards in front of him, Knox squeezed the bridge of his nose. He had to say something to get them off this track. "We're living together," he blurted. "We don't need to marry."

"What? You planning on ducking out on my momma-in-law or some shit?"

Frustrated, Knox growled. "Of course not! But why get legalities involved if she's perfectly happy with our arrangement?"

Mortician opened his mouth to put up another argument.

Irritation surged into Knox. "If she was so concerned about marriage, she wouldn't have invited me to live with her beforehand," he snapped. "Why pay for something when I'm getting it for free?"

Dark ire lit Mortician's eyes. Throwing his cards aside, he got to his feet, his hand going to his cut where he kept his gun.

"You can't bully me into marrying her," Knox pointed out.

"I can do whatever the fuck I want to, son," Mortician sneered.

Deciding this moment wasn't the time to back down, Knox stood, too. "You want me to propose? Fine. I'll ask her to marry me, then have the longest engagement in history. That's *if* she even accepts."

"She going to accept," Mortician stated. "She love you."

The words did something to Knox's heart. Made it swell. Beat faster. Melt. And whatever other flowery idiom he could think of. He cleared his throat. "And I love her."

"She been through enough," Digger inserted. "Cancer, kidnapping, fucking with your uppity ass."

Knox glared at Digger, although he continued, unperturbed.

"She deserve to know you belong to her and she belong to you."

Outlaw released smoke from the cigarette he'd just lit. "That's what the fuck the motherfucker sayin', Digger. They be-fuckin-long to each other but it just easier if they ever wanna split the fuck up."

"And you okay with that, Prez?" Mortician asked, outraged.

"Ain't sayin' that shit, Mort," Outlaw corrected. He studied Knox.

"Listen the fuck up, assfuck. You either gonna marry Roxanne, and soon, or you gonna lose your fuckin' cock."

"Is that so?" Knox sneered, losing his patience *and* his temper. "Why should I go through with a fucking wedding to her, even if I propose? She's driving a *purple* vehicle that screams ignorance. Not to mention it being a gift from another man. *Outlaw!*" Before any of them commented on that, Knox changed the subject and continued, lost in his self-righteous anger. "My parents might accept her as my live-in lady but as a wife? I don't think so. And she insists on showing all of you allegiance. She's definitely not wife material for me! But if it makes you happy, I'll ask her to marry me, fuck her a month or two as my betrothed, then walk out. And I'll do you all a favor. I'll never tell her you fucking forced me into a corner and ruined our relationship..."

Even before Mortician pressed his .380 in the center of Knox's forehead, his mouth caught up to his brain and his stomach turned. He hadn't meant most of what he said. But these men frustrated him so much with their bullying tactics. Worse, there was no indication *from Roxanne herself* that she hoped to marry him.

"Mort, if you pull the fucking trigger, Roxanne might have a problem with you." Johnnie spoke as if he talked of which type of Scotch he preferred.

Hearing patience the situation didn't call for, Knox feared Mortician *would* shoot. A frisson of sympathy for the men Mortician visited as the club's enforcer went through Knox.

"You marrying her or you leaving her, dead or alive," Mortician snarled, twisting the barrel into Knox's skin before yanking the gun away and shoving it back into his cut. "You got until Valentine Day to decide."

Straightening his jacket lapels and brushing off the sleeves, Knox reseated himself. It would be a cold day in hell before any of these ignoramuses outsmarted him. He'd propose to Roxanne, but if they *ever* ended up at the altar it would be on *his* terms and no one else's.

Period.

～

Roxy

Slipping into bed, later that night, Roxy slid closer to Knox, who welcomed her with open arms. The red mark on his forehead grabbed her attention again and she caressed it.

"What happened, sugar?"

Knox readjusted and settled her in the crook of his arms. "Nothing much," he answered, noncommittal. "Just goofing off with the guys."

For a time, all the boys had accepted Knox into their fold, allowing her to breathe a sigh of relief. Her concern for her man's safety had lessened. Knox had had a rough adjustment. Most of the men of the motorcycle club and Knox came from two different worlds, but they'd adapted and accepted each other for her. That bliss lasted a few months before some hostility on both sides returned.

Knox kissed the top of her head. "What are your thoughts on marriage, Roxanne?"

Roxy stilled. She'd say she was a progressive, twenty-first century woman, who didn't need marriage to have a committed relationship. Yet, she was a romantic, if nothing else, and she loved Knox so much.

"What do you mean?" she asked, wanting clarity before she answered. She didn't want to jump to conclusions about where this might lead. "My general thoughts on marriage or specifics, particularly between us?"

He chuckled, and she joined him in laughter.

"Subtle, right?" she said.

He scooted down and turned on his side, meeting her eyes. "Very."

"Knox, baby, what do you want me to say?" She traced the outline of his lips. He was so handsome and upstanding. "I mean I get why somebody like you wouldn't want to marry an ignorant—" She paused and her voice trailed off, before she swallowed and continued. "Ghetto slut like me."

Those words, in her son's voice, spoken a couple of months ago, still echoed in her head. She hadn't even called Duke. She'd just happened to walk in when Bailey was talking to him and their sisters. Her girls all greeted Roxy with enthusiasm. Duke had been pure venom.

"Say that again," Knox said. "I don't think I heard you right."

Tears rushing to her eyes, Roxy's nostrils flared. She sighed. "You heard me just fine. Ignore—"

Knox narrowed his eyes. "You're about to cry!" he accused. "What's...fuck! It's Duke, isn't it? He's the only person in the world who brings you to tears."

After a moment's hesitation, she nodded. "He's my child."

"He's a disrespectful little asshole," Knox snarled. "I should fly to New Orleans and teach him a lesson."

She gave him a watery smile and caressed his stubbly jaw. "You don't even know the context in which he said it."

"It doesn't fucking matter, Roxanne," Knox fumed. "You're his mother and you're owed his every respect."

"Bailey was talking on speakerphone to Carissa and Alexia. You know she's about to marry her girlfriend? They were discussing details. I walked in, heard that part of the conversation, and added my two cents. I didn't know Duke was even on the phone. He really went for the jugular and said I'd only be relegated to looking in from the outside for long-term commitment since a man like Knox Harrington would never marry an ignorant, *ghetto* slut like me." She tried to laugh it off, but the attempt sounded as hollow as it felt. "Mortician threatened to go to New Orleans and box Duke up. It took me and Bailey to talk him down. No matter what Duke does, I'll never sanction his murder. It was such a mess, Knox. After we talked him down from Duke, the boy wanted to confront you about putting a ring on my finger. Part of it was I was so upset that it affected Bailey. To keep shit from blowing up too much more, I just lied and said you and me were talking about marriage. I was just waiting for you to propose."

"Now, I understand," Knox mumbled, more to himself than to her, but Roxy heard anyway.

"Understand what?"

"What are you talking about?"

"What you just said. What do you understand now?"

"It isn't important," he brushed off. "What *is* is how you feel about marriage. Is that what you want? For us to marry eventually?"

"I don't know," she admitted with soft honesty. "I love you and want to spend the rest of my life with you, but suppose you want more children?"

"I have all the children I want, sweetheart," Knox said gruffly. "My son and your three daughters."

Though his words made her swoon, she couldn't allow a certain slight to pass. "What about Duke?"

"I make no claim to him unless I'm free to kick his ass."

"Knox," she chided.

"And," he went on as if she hadn't spoken, "I would be the luckiest man alive if I ever proposed and you agreed to marry me."

She smiled at him. "Then we'd both be pretty fucking lucky because you're the kindest, smartest, handsomest man I know."

He brushed her lips with his own. "Mmmm. Compliments like that might just get you ravished."

"I'm yours for the ravishing." She chuckled and turned on her back, desire racing through her at his sheer sexiness. He was one fine motherfucker.

Knox rolled over onto her and slid his fingers through her hair, staring deeply into her eyes, his amber ones mesmerizing her. Slowly, he lowered his mouth to hers and kissed her with slow, exquisite tenderness.

Opening her mouth to him, Roxy wrapped her arms around Knox's neck, relishing his scent and his weight. He wasn't rushing inside of her, despite how his heavy erection throbbed against her belly.

Still kissing her, Knox readjusted and began to slide her nightgown up, running his fingers along her thighs, her hips, and her stomach. His touch ignited fire within her and sent goosebumps rushing along her skin. Her nipples hardened and her pussy heated.

With her nightgown above her waist, Roxy spread her thighs. Knox brought his hand to her clit and massaged it.

"Knox," Roxy groaned, lifting her hips.

"I'm here, sweetheart," he whispered, putting more pressure on her sensitive clit.

She arched her back. "Keep doing that, baby," she breathed. "That feels wonderful."

"This will feel even better," he responded, closing his lips around her covered nipple.

The thin material of her nightgown allowed Roxy to feel every sensation. She gripped his shoulders, moved to the rhythm of his fingers, and gasped at each little sensation she felt.

She moved her hips faster. He sped up his fingers, necessary to end her agony.

"Oh God!" she cried, shaking in her ecstasy.

For the briefest moment, Knox pulled away. Through her haze, she heard his nightstand drawer open and close. A moment later, she felt the coolness of the lubricant as he spread it in and around her pussy.

When he entered her, they moaned together.

Duke's hateful words flashed through Roxy's head, but she shoved them aside. Knox loved her and, when they mutually decided the time was right, she was sure they'd walk down the aisle.

CHAPTER ONE

Roxy

"Happy Valentine's Day, everyone."

A few days later, the sound of Knox's voice caught Roxy off-guard. They'd just witnessed vow renewals between Outlaw and Meggie. Once Outlaw grabbed Meggie's hand and walked from where they'd stood at the DJ's booth, Roxy had turned away to find food. Now, Knox had recaptured everyone's attention with his greeting.

"Roxanne, if I can have a moment of your time?" he asked politely, lasering her with a smoldering gaze.

Swallowing, Roxy grinned as everybody's focus turned her way. She didn't want to get all googly-eyed and jump to conclusions...but, fuck it, she was getting all fucking googly-eyed and jumping to conclusions that Knox was about to propose to her.

Her heart hammering, she sashayed her way to where her man stood, so extraordinarily handsome, tall, and fine looking in his tuxedo. The moment she reached him, he bent and brushed his lips over hers.

"From the moment we met, you've captivated me," he said gruffly into the microphone.

She opened her mouth to respond, but he placed a finger over her lips.

"You bring excitement and passion to my life. You mean the world to me. I love you with all my heart and soul." He dropped down on one knee.

Roxy's hands flew to her mouth, and she felt light-headed. She'd been married three fucking times and not one of her previous husbands ever got down on one knee. To her, that was a romantic dream that happened to other women.

Knox dug into his jacket pocket and produced a princess cut diamond engagement ring.

Tears rushed to Roxy's eyes. Her hands dropped from her mouth; one fluttered to her chest.

"Will you do me the great honor of becoming my wife?"

She released a sob-laugh and nodded. "Yes," she said in a low, watery voice.

"She said yes, everyone," Knox spoke into the microphone.

Amidst cheers and whoops, he laid the microphone on the floor, took Roxy's hand into his own and held the ring up.

"This was my father's great-grandmother's ring," he told her. "I picked it up just yesterday after having it adjusted for you. My great-great-grandparents had a happy, long-lasting marriage, so wearing this ring will bring us nothing but happiness."

He raised the ring for onlookers to view. The light hitting the diamond made it gleam and revealed the culet underneath.

A premonition of doom hit Roxy, speeding her heartbeat up. His words were based in lore and myth, she knew, but she had a few of her own that seemed to prick her with unease.

He'd picked up her ring on a Friday. Strike one against their future union. Fuck Friday the 13th. For whatever reason—probably a fucked up one where a bride and her wedding party had been slaughtered—purchasing a ring on a Friday was bad luck.

"Do you like it?" he asked with uncertainty as she stood in silence, staring at the ring.

"I love it, Knox," she told him, the truth. Yet, somewhere, she'd read or heard that having such a prominent culet invited evil spirits to enter the ring and put a curse on the wearer.

Logic told her it was just old New Orleans legend, where voodoo queens and ghost legends featured as prominently in the city's history as real people. But each of Roxy's previous marriages had failed and she'd prefer not to invite catastrophe into her union with Knox.

She loved him so very much.

"Sweetheart, if you would prefer your own ring..."

The swift kiss she pressed against his lips interrupted him. "No, Knox. It is beautiful. I'm honored to wear it." He still held her hand, so she pulled free from his grasp, to hold her hand up.

Taking the hint, Knox offered his heart-stopping smile and slid the beautiful ring onto her finger. He stood, and Roxy stepped into his embrace.

"I love you, Knox," she said, shaking from all the emotion flowing through her. Despite her overwhelming happiness, she couldn't shake her sense of foreboding.

He kissed her temple. "And I love you, sweetheart."

"Oh my God, Momma!" Bailey squealed as she rushed up to Roxy. "Let me see the ring."

Mortician held his hand out to Knox. "About time you make an honest woman out my momma-in-law."

Roxy had no choice but to step out of Knox's hold. "We'll celebrate later," she whispered with a wink.

He smiled at her.

"We have a wedding to plan," Bailey said as the other girls rushed up to view the engagement ring.

"Chile, please," Roxy said. "I've been married three times already. There's no way in hell I'm having a big wedding. All it would be is a big goddamn party. Who the fuck would bring us wedding gifts?"

"You've *got* to have a big wedding," Bailey insisted, her face falling. "I could help you plan it."

Mortician winced.

He and Bailey had gotten married in Las Vegas. Although Bailey had never once complained, as a child, Roxy knew her baby had had dreams of a huge wedding.

"This important to Bailey, Roxanne," Mortician said.

"Ummhmmm." Roxy gave him an under-eyed look. "I know what the fuck else is important, too, but I don't see you bending over backwards to give my baby the big wedding she's always wanted."

Mortician scowled. "Your ass just had to go there, huh?"

"Sure the fuck did. Keep your nose out my goddamn house and take care of your own."

"Mama! Lucas!" Bailey cried, then grabbed Mortician's hand and kissed the back of it. "I wouldn't change our wedding for anything. I'm perfectly happy with our Las Vegas marriage."

"Roxanne telling the truth, Bailey?" Mortician asked sullenly, giving Roxy the side eye. "You always wanted a big wedding?"

"What the fuck you mean am I telling the truth, boy?" Roxy snapped. "Why the fuck would I lie about that?"

"Okay, people, this is getting out of hand," Bailey said through tight lips. "As a little girl, I dreamed of a huge wedding, Lucas. But I was a child, so—"

"So you got every fucking right to want to see that dream come true," Mortician cut in.

"Even if we do eventually have a "big"—" Bailey used air quotations — "wedding, we won't do it now. This is Momma's time to shine and she should do so with a fairytale wedding, the kind *she's* always dreamed of."

"The kind I've already had," Roxy reminded Bailey. She could've kept her fucking mouth shut with the way every motherfucker ignored her.

A thoughtful looked crossed Mortician's features before he smirked at Roxy. "Tell you what, pretty girl, how about we have a double wedding? Then, all your dreams would come true. You'd have your fairytale marriage and your momma would get hers just like *you* want her to have."

Bailey's eyes lit up, while Roxy threw Mortician a look that called him several types of motherfuckers.

"Are you willing to do that, Momma?" Bailey asked, awed.

"For you, baby, sure," Roxy responded, thinking of ways to seek vengeance on Mortician's head.

A huge grin curved Bailey's mouth and she gave Mortician a look of adoration.

Seeing her daughter's happiness, Roxy supposed she'd let the motherfucker off for his scheming that suddenly had her locked into a big wedding.

Behind them Kendall stood, looking so lovely in her couture gown, on the fringes of the women she both loved and hated. Though she'd come with her husband, Johnnie, Kendall also looked completely and utterly alone, unsure of where she fit in. Johnnie wasn't around. He'd brought Kendall and abandoned her.

For the time being, Roxy would let her be. Either all her sins would sink into the girl's head and she'd learn from them. Or she wouldn't.

"Roxanne," Knox called, pulling her into his arms and wrapping her in his embrace. "What do you say we get out of here and celebrate our engagement?"

Grinning at his sexy smile, Roxy met his gaze and placed her arms around his neck. She kissed his lips. "I think that's a wonderful idea, sugar," she murmured, ignoring the catcalls, hoots, whistles, and hollers.

Knox dropped the mic and grabbed her hand. Roxy's pussy throbbed, imagining all the things Knox would do with his hands, lips, tongue, and cock.

Val stepped in front of them and folded his arms as Mortician placed his hands on Knox's shoulders. "Nah, son," her son-in-law said with a shake of his head. "No hanky-panky 'til you make a honest woman out of my momma-in-law."

"*What?*" Roxy screeched, dropping Knox's hand and rushing around him to glare at Mortician. "Get the fuck out the way, motherfucker," she snarled. "You are fucking with my fucking."

Mortician glowered at her. "I didn't hear that."

"You sure the fuck did," Roxy snapped.

"Roxanne, sweetheart, let me handle this," Knox implored, tugging her behind him.

"Val, get the fuck out of their way," Zoann, his wife, ordered. "Or else."

"No, Puff," Val braved. "All us fucked you bitches before we married. We doing right by Roxy."

Zoann and Bailey bristled, glanced at each other, then turned their attention to Val.

"Shut the fuck up, fool," Mortician grouched. "That's not getting them on our side."

"What's going on here?" Johnnie asked, strolling into the madness.

"Besides Val about to get his face bashed in and his balls cut?" Zoann asked sweetly.

Johnnie smiled. "Yes, besides that."

"Knox just proposed to Roxanne, Johnnie," Mortician explained. "Now, they want to go and uh..." He rocked on his heels and scratched the side of his head. "Celebrate..."

"We want to fuck," Roxy called.

"Love, please," Knox inserted, throwing her a meaningful look over his shoulder. "I can handle this." He faced the guys again. "Gentleman, I appreciate your concern for Roxanne's virtue."

"I don't have no fucking virtue," Roxy huffed.

"Roxanne!" Knox implored.

"Fine, Knox, handle it. Just know what the fuck you're doing. These boys will have us apart before you blink your fucking eye."

"Never, my love," Knox reassured her. "Mortician, Val, thank you for being concerned about her, er, reputation."

"I don't have—" Roxy began, pausing when Knox shushed her. She'd let him get away with that shit this time, seeing as how she was overcome with engagement bliss.

"Roxanne is a grown woman. My beautiful fiancé. We've lived together for months now. Therefore, we will continue to reside in the same residence until our nuptials. Tell them, Johnnie."

Johnnie glancing over his shoulder and looking at Kendall surprised Roxy. If he hoped to find answers from Kendall, he was met with disappointment. Her expression was unreadable as everyone else looked between Knox, Roxy, and Mortician in amused attention.

"I actually agree with Mortician and Val," Johnnie said to Knox, after seeing he'd get no help from Kendall. "You need to move to the clubhouse until after the ceremony."

"*Move to the clubhouse?*" Knox echoed on a gasp. "If Roxanne and I were to live apart, which we aren't, I'd go to my parents' mansion or rent a hotel room. Not move to that clubhouse."

Roxy winced at the sadity sound of Knox's statement, while Mortician, Val, Johnnie, and the girls stiffened.

"You heard me," Knox went on, joyful at thinking he had the upper hand, not realizing he'd just turned most of the guests against him since they were connected to the club in one way or another. "Furthermore, if you *force* the issue, Roxanne and I will go to a private island and elope. Not only won't you be invited, but the big wedding that *Bailey* wants will be ou—" His voice trailed off as his words caught up to his brain when Bailey's face crumpled and Mortician growled.

"Hold the fuck on." Roxy stomped in front of Knox and whirled to face him. "Us living separately until our big day is one thing I'd stand with you on. But not inviting my family? *Threatening* my Bailey?"

"Is the quickest way to get you fucked up." The violence brimming in Mortician's voice matched the hostility on his face.

"Bailey, I'm sorry," Knox started. "I didn't mean that..." He looked at Roxy. "Sweetheart..."

Though Knox had pissed her off, he'd also dug a very deep hole for himself. A lot of the bikers already saw him as uppity and having a chip on his shoulder. Now, their impression would be underscored. Basically, forcing Roxy's hand.

She wasn't sure if she or her pussy was more disappointed.

She glared at Knox. "I think you living at the clubhouse will be time well-spent," she told him. "We'll be living under separate roofs but we'll still be near each other."

"No! No!" Knox protested. "Absolutely not."

"Guess what, son?" Mortician grinned without warmth. "You don't have a choice."

"Or what? I won't marry Roxanne?" He narrowed his eyes at her. "You won't marry me?"

"Of course I'll marry you," she told him, frustrated. "Maybe, just not as soon as we intend to now. You can't threaten Bailey and then think things will be honky-dory just like that."

"Bailey's a grown woman. If she wanted a big wedding, she should've opened her mouth and told Mortician. This is about *you*, not *her*. It'll be *our* wedding day, Roxanne. Not theirs. I want a grand wedding with the focus on *us*."

"Listen, Knox. I don't mind sharing the spotlight." At Knox's scowl, Roxy planted her hands on her hips. "There's nothing wrong with a double wedding, and don't tell me how the fuck to deal with my baby. Bailey wants a big wedding. This is a way for all of us to be satisfied."

"No!" Knox managed. "I'm putting my foot down. Bailey and Mortician can get married some other time. This will be your day."

"I'm about to raise my foot up and stick it the fuck up your ass," Roxy yelled, losing her temper. "If it's *my* day, I should be able to spend it *my* way!"

"Mama, no!" Bailey rushed to her and hugged her. "Knox is right. I've had my day. Your wedding is about you and Knox." Her voice caught and she cleared her throat. "Don't argue over this."

Kendall stepped closer, bit down on her lip. Looked at Roxy. Then Johnnie. And back to Roxy again.

"Say your piece, sugar," Roxy encouraged.

"Knox doesn't want Bailey to have her wedding with you because he knows a lot more of the bikers will be in attendance." Sending him a sugary smile, Kendall shrugged. "In his mind, how would it look with all those bad bikers mixing with his privileged family?"

"That isn't true!" Knox protested. "And frankly, I'm fucking insulted that you're even commenting on this. Who asked you?"

"She's my wife," Johnnie said. "She can comment on what the fuck she wants to."

Fuck, this was getting out of hand. If they couldn't get through the engagement without arguing, how would they ever make it to the altar?

No, she was making too much out of this. Quarreling amongst them was nothing new. It was how they showed affection. She really had nothing to worry about. As long as Bailey was happy, Mortician was happy. Outlaw's sanity had returned now that Meggie was back and safe. Meggie was dealing with the aftermath of her kidnapping like a trooper. Johnnie was finally getting a grip on his reality with Kendall and learning how to handle her. Kendall was working to overcome all her demons. Everyone else was living their best lives.

She had nothing to worry about, except the here and now.

Deciding to take control, Roxy placed two fingers between her lips and whistled. Immediately, the room fell silent. "Enough!" she said.

"Enough like hell," Knox said. "Stand with me on these issues—Kendall *and your* wedding—or I'll move out myself until our big day."

Roxy narrowed her eyes. "You fucking threatening me now?"

"What?" Knox widened his amber gaze. "Of course not, Roxanne! I'm just saying—"

"Fuck all," Roxy finished.

"I've had it!" Knox shouted. "You're either my fiancé, Bailey's mother, or Kendall's crutch."

"I'm all three," Roxy said. "And if you don't understand that, kiss my fucking ass."

Knox scowled at her, then turned and stalked toward the door.

Roxy watched him go, angry in her own right. She'd been married three times before and had four baby daddies. The one man she should've married—KP—she hadn't. She'd be damned if she'd make another mistake.

She glanced at her engagement ring. They'd be nothing but happy, Knox said, because of how happy his great-great grandparents had been.

She sighed. The disagreements were just par for the course, she reminded herself. Nothing to concern herself over.

Yet, she knew. She *felt* shit going sideways. Already Knox had some atoning to do, or she'd give him his ring back and tell him to shove it up his fucking ass.

Maybe, it was bad ju-ju swirling in the air because of superstitions turning into reality. Or, *maybe,* Knox was just a spoiled motherfucker, who had no clue about how to share the spotlight with anyone else.

Only time would tell the story. Hopefully, it would be a classic romance instead of a chilling nightmare.

CHAPTER TWO

Knox

Leaning his head back, Knox rested against his desk chair, still unable to find a comfortable position. He couldn't believe how his engagement to Roxanne had turned out last night. Of course, he should've known better than to propose at one of *their* functions. It should've been a private matter or at a function at his parents' house.

Those assholes would ruin a fucking funeral.

Instead of stopping him, Roxanne had allowed him to leave. He thought she'd at least apologize. But no. She'd let him leave!

Yanking his limp tie from around his neck, Knox threw it on his desk and growled, the sharp pain of her betrayal sending tears to his eyes. He loved her so much. How could she reject him? She'd torn his heart out.

Kendall's words came to mind. That bitch! He hated that she wasn't far off the mark. Better *her* to say it, though, than him.

The sensor on the entry door chimed, indicating someone had come in. Hopefully, it was only his business partner, Cameron Baptiste.

Knox closed his eyes. He didn't feel like talking. Cameron would back away if he thought Knox was asleep. Anyone else would, too. He didn't care about customers. Or clients. Or bad guys.

He wanted to curl into a ball and die. Roxanne had allowed him to leave. She'd made a mockery of their engagement, consenting to a big wedding because of Bailey, not because she wanted to celebrate their love in lavish style.

"Get the fuck up, motherfucker."

At the sound of Outlaw's voice, Knox tensed. He didn't feel like seeing the man gloat. Outlaw had never liked Knox. As a matter of fact, he'd beaten him to a pulp on two separate occasions.

"I know you a-fuckin-wake, Knox. Your fuckin' fists clenched the fuck up when you heard my ass."

The asshole wouldn't leave until Knox dealt with him. This morning, Knox was in a dangerous mood, so Outlaw had best back off.

Knox opened his eyes, straightened in his chair, and glared at the club president, who stood feet away with his arms folded and an annoying smirk on his face. "Get out."

Outlaw lifted a brow. "I know your ass in pain, assfuck, but I ain't know you in so much pain you wanna make me fuck you up."

"You can try," Knox sneered. "In my current state, I do believe *you'll* be the one fucked up."

Snickering, Outlaw drew his nine before Knox blinked. "Ain't talkin' 'bout with fists. Ima just shoot the fuck outta you."

The barbaric asshole would do it, too. He stared at Knox without flinching or blinking or doing anything that would lead Knox to believe he wasn't a psychopath. Outlaw was just the type of bad guy Knox had thrived on bringing down when he was in law enforcement.

Refusing to be intimidated, Knox narrowed his eyes. "I..." *Dare you to* died on his lips. Outlaw wasn't a man to taunt. Knox amended his statement. "I still have friends on the force. My death won't go unnoticed."

"My opinion different. Can't say you fucked up if they ain't got evidence. You might be *missin'* but no motherfucker gonna prove you fuckin' *dead*. So you want me to shoot the fuck outta you or you gonna listen to me?"

"Do I have a goddamn choice?"

Outlaw shrugged. "Do you?"

"You know the answer to that."

For a moment longer, Outlaw stared at Knox, before shoving his gun away, still within hand's reach. "Before I say what the fuck I need your ass to do, Ima talk to you 'bout Roxanne."

"You know, *Christopher*, I'm not interested in what you have to say about Roxanne. Instead of interfering, why don't you make up your mind how to talk. Sometimes, you're proper and other times you sound like a goddamn idiot. Your son talks better than you but even he vacillates between correct English and backward trash."

Something flickered in Outlaw's features—hurt? shame?—before he stiffened. Rage darkened his eyes and he stormed forward, yanking Knox up by the collar and punching him in the mouth. That should've been the end of it, but Outlaw smashed his fist in Knox's face—once, twice, and again—before releasing him and pummeling his gut a few times, until Knox slipped to the ground, coughing and sputtering.

"You say what the fuck you wanna *about* my fuckin' ass, talk *about* CJ or my Megan, and you die. The *only* fuckin' reason Ima give you another chance is cuz of Roxanne. Hear me, motherfucker?"

"Y-yes," Knox answered, his physical pain matching the emotional turmoil he'd been in for the last few hours.

"Now, get the fuck up and listen to what the fuck I gotta say."

A tear slid down Knox's cheek. Instead of complying, he coughed again and curled into a ball. Until Outlaw stopped next to him, his steel toed boots too close to Knox's head for comfort. With determination, he grabbed the arm of the chair. He slid it against the wall to better brace it, then dragged himself up and plopped down on the brown leather seat. He laid his head on his desk and shuddered, blood dripping from his mouth and nose. His eyes and skull hurt. Maybe, they were broken. Maybe, Outlaw had blinded him.

Maybe, Knox would die. He couldn't imagine surviving with this much pain.

"Roxanne love you," Outlaw started.

Knox refused to dignify that with a response. Her actions suggested otherwise.

"I know you fuckin' love her."

Still, he wouldn't answer. Once Outlaw left, he might call his friends on the force anyway, and have him arrested for assault and battery.

"This what you need to do, motherfucker."

Knox wouldn't take advice from a violent criminal like Outlaw. Instead, he diverted his attention. "Did you hear what Kendall said about me? Don't you think that's how *she* feels?"

Outlaw's smile was thin. "Right go where right belong. The shit she said apply to her fucking ass, too. But she wasn't wrong 'bout *you.*"

He wouldn't allow Outlaw to turn this back to him, so Knox could slip up again and get another ass beating. Besides, he was curious about something. "Since you rewarded her with so much, a few weeks ago, why didn't you get her a car, too?"

"Re-fuckin-ward that bitch? What the fuck you mean?"

"A house. An office. Her law practice. An allowance. Visitation. Entry to the club."

Instead of shame, Outlaw shrugged. "In case you ain't figure shit out, I got a fuckin' reason for every-fuckin-thing I do."

Knox processed that, then decided to point something out. "You know what I think your main problem is with your speech? You're lazy. You know how to talk to sound like you have a brain. It's just easier not to."

"Just cuz I said you can talk 'bout my ass, don't mean you gotta be fuckin' stupid e-fuckin-nuff to keep doin' it."

"Your speech annoys me."

"Tell me the last time my ass gave a fuck 'bout *what* up-fuckin-set you?"

"I'm dropping the subject," Knox grouched. "Tell me the method to the madness that led you to become Kendall's Santa Claus."

"Kendall Santa Claus?" Outlaw scoffed. "Ima let that big ass insult slide, motherfucker, and Ima tell you as soon as I finish up 'bout Roxy."

"Stay out of my relationship with her."

Outlaw smirked. "To my ass, it seem like some-fuckin-body need to inter-fuckin-fere cuz you don't know what the fuck you doin'."

"I take umbrage to that."

"Don't give a good fuck."

Life presented some inalienable truths. The right to free speech. The right to be your own person. And the fact that Outlaw always seemed to *be* right. Such was the case this time. Knox could say he was so angry and embarrassed he'd never forgive Roxanne. He could tell himself he didn't need any man's advice and, if he did, it would be that of Cameron, his best friend.

All lies. Outlaw studied people. He was a connoisseur in that respect. With those he considered family, he made knowing *them*—their whereabouts, weaknesses, and wants—his priority.

Knox nodded. "What do you suggest?"

"Move outta her house. Megan and Bailey gettin' a room ready for your ass at the club."

"I'm not living at that club when I can go to my parents' house."

"Ain't no skin off my fuckin' ass. You do that shit, it'll just lead Roxanne to think that you ain't compatible to her. Be-fuckin-sides, seein' you gonna make her miss you since she love your preppy ass."

Outlaw had a point. Knox sighed. "Fine. I'll move my things to the club."

"No, leave your things right the fuck where they at. In her house. Get *some* shit, a few pieces, and leave the rest there. Just reassure her you love the fuck outta her. Then, your things gonna be there with her and she gonna miss you more. Then, Mort will back off cuz Bailey gonna see how miserable her Ma is. She gonna talk to Roxanne *and* Mort, then you can move the fuck back in with Roxanne and it ain't gonna be no problem for no-fuckin-body."

"Fine. Done. Anything else?"

"Romance her, fuckhead. Girls like that, too. Oh, and tell her Bailey and Mort welcome to have their wedding with yours."

"Even if I don't want it?" Knox pressed. "This should be about Roxanne. No one else. I'm not paying a huge amount of money for Roxanne to share her day."

"Listen up, assfuck, ain't no-fuckin-body asked your ass to pay for Roxanne wedding. She belong to *us*, so *we* gonna pay."

Knox opened his mouth to disagree, but Outlaw raised his hand and changed the subject.

"Now, 'bout Kendall."

"Now, 'bout Kendall."

CHAPTER THREE

CHRISTOPHER

"Megan!"

For the longest time, Christopher had searched the house and grounds of the property Kendall sent him to—the one where Megan might be kept. He'd searched almost everywhere. Val, Mortician, Johnnie, and Digger had searched almost everywhere, too.

Now, they'd reached the edge of the property line. Though the house was dilapidated and the wooden porch was rotted, the land was huge. Acres of outbuildings, rusting cars, old motorcycles, and overgrown weeds. But this...this was something new. A door that opened onto an underground structure.

"Megan," Christopher yelled again, close to losing his mind. She'd been taken days ago. He couldn't sleep. He couldn't eat.

He couldn't function.

When he opened the door, the sunlight beamed into the darkness below, revealing stone steps. Without hesitation, Christopher rushed into the abyss. He couldn't see into the corners. He only saw ahead of him, the long shadows cast by the sunlight gleaming from above.

Grabbing his cellphone, he turned on the flashlight. He aimed it to the right of him, but found nothing. Then, he turned left.

There she was. Still. Lifeless. Curled up, in rivers of blood...

Christopher bolted upright and his eyes flew open. Air escaped him in bursts of breaths and his heart pounded hard enough to serve as a drum in a rock band. Sweat poured down his face, dripped down the center of his chest.

Megan was there, safe, in their bed, next to him. Sleeping peacefully. Looking like an angel bathed in the soft lamplight that she insisted on having at night.

Not wanting to disturb her, he shoved the covers aside and swung his legs over the side of the bed. He hung his head and covered his face, resting his elbows on his knees.

He hated that motherfucking dream. Each time he had it, he found Megan the same way. *Dead.*

Now, tonight, blood. A shiver passed through him.

He couldn't go through this for the rest of his fucking life. He'd been fine. Marching the fuck on. Helping Megan to cope with *her* nightmares. Making sure she wouldn't return to cutting herself.

Then...then...Megan decided to go grocery shopping alone. She'd told him she wouldn't let fear rule her life and she was determined to not allow her kidnapping to frighten her from the things she enjoyed doing alone.

Fine. What the fuck ever. He'd had her tailed, with express instructions to not let Megan know.

Did the motherfuckers *obey* him?

FUCK NO!

That led to ass beatings for them and a two-day pussy lockout for him. Megan said he was taking away her way of dealing with the trauma she'd suffered during her kidnapping.

Fuck. Fine. Lesson fucking learned.

Once he was admitted back into the Promised Land, he decided to watch over her himself. *That,* however, fucked with church. He hadn't realized how much his girl rolled out until he'd had to cancel the weekly club meetings, including the most important end of month one where all the reports were read and discussed. He could always push church back to the evenings, but *that* would inter-fucking-fere with his family time.

Still, his woman left him no choice but to give in to her wishes. Megan had grown so much during their marriage and she attributed that to the room he gave her to spread her wings. She admired and respected him for that, so he decided to back off. Maybe, life could return to normal for them.

So far, it hadn't for her. And for him? The goddamn nightmares commenced. They were relentless, pussifying him more than Megan already had. Now, he had some old dogs on her detail, whether she liked it or not. They'd sooner cut off their fucking cocks, then let anything happen to her.

She moved, and he peeped over his shoulder in time to see her sit up and turn on the lamp on her side of the bed. The motherfucker she kept on at night was across the fucking room. It would've been harder than a motherfucker for him to sleep with a light shining in his fucking face from either side of the bed. But did it really fucking matter? As long as she was happy.

He rested his elbows on his knees again and scrubbed a hand over his face.

"Another nightmare?" she asked.

"Yeah, baby. This time, you was in a pool of blood. Still deader than fuck. Just surrounded by rivers of red."

More movement behind him. Moments later, she skimmed her fingers over his bare back. Chills rose up on his skin, her touch the balm he needed to soothe all his hurts.

"Roxy thinks what I'm doing is a good idea," she told him.

Christopher grunted. His visit to Knox in the early morning hours after the Big Argument had happened almost twenty-four hours ago. As far as he knew, Roxanne and Knox hadn't made up.

"What kind of message would I send to CJ if I cowered inside *or* if every time I left the grounds, I needed to be surrounded by security."

"The motherfuckin' message you wanna stay a-fuckin-live," Christopher snapped, tired and cranky. Mortician had been in a fucked-up mood because Bailey had been crying most of the day. Val was upset because Zoann was angry over his interference. Roxanne looked as if she'd been weeping with her eyes all red and shit. Johnnie went from joking to annoyed to boo-hooey. And Christopher was determined to get fucking rid of Kendall once and for fucking all. He needed cooperation *some-fucking-where* in his life. Why not his wife? What the fuck was wrong with his girl? "It would fuckin' show you thinkin' about your fuckin' safety, Megan."

"No, it would show I'm allowing maniacs to dictate how I live. How to be your wife. The kids' mom. Imagine the worry you'd feel if I didn't want to go anywhere because of fear?"

Truth. How-fucking-ever, his worry didn't lessen with things as they were. Maybe, he *would* be more concerned if she cowered at the thought of going places. Right now, though, he preferred if she stayed home. How could he get her to cooperate?

He wanted her alive. Safe. Unharmed. No matter the cost.

He released a frustrated growl. "Fuck, Megan, you fuckin' listened to my ass and stayed the fuck home when you was filled with my kids." He shoved aside the thought taunting him.

The one that kept showing itself and then running away like a scared motherfucker.

Dick snip.

Dick snip flip.

Dick pain.

Balls swollen.

No fucking. For days.

Megan kissed his jaw, rubbing her soft cheek against the bristles on his face. Her sweet scent invaded his nostrils and his cock jumped. She rose up behind him and put her arms around his neck, resting her chin on his shoulder. Her golden hair tickled the places on his body that it touched.

She was warm. Vital. Alive.

And, fuck, he wanted to keep it that fucking way.

"Christopher," she whispered, her breath fanning his ear. "I was pregnant. I know how much you worry about me because of my risks. I also didn't want to do anything to put our babies at risk. Besides, if

I'm pregnant and get into some type of trouble with club enemies, I can't do much to try and defend myself."

What the fuck was she talking about? "Your lil' fuckin' ass wasn't pregnant this time and you was taken," he grouched.

"CJ was with me," she reminded him, her gentleness soothing his turmoil.

"Why the fuck you gotta be such a stubborn lil motherfucker, huh, Megan?"

Instead of answering, she leaned forward and kissed his jaw again.

"I'm sooo sorry, Christopher," she crooned, not sorry at all. She tickled the hair at his nape with a soft caress. "Maybe, I can find a way to make it up to you?"

Her words stiffened his cock. She slid around him, trailing the silk of her hair behind her. Pausing, she kissed his stomach, then continued onto her knees. Her beautiful blue eyes met his and she grabbed his throbbing dick.

"I love you, Christopher," she murmured, wrapping her lips around his cock and holding his gaze.

He grabbed handfuls of her hair. "I love you, too, baby."

His cock filled her mouth so she didn't respond. She always sucked him off after his nightmares. If there was any benefit from the bad dreams, Megan blowing him was it. To-fucking-night, though, she was also trying to distract him from his need to have her escorted wherever she went.

Little bitch.

She'd won this fucking battle. But *he'd* win the goddamn war and he'd do it however the fuck he had to.

In the meantime, he laid back on the bed and lost himself in the warmth of Megan's mouth sucking him off.

CHAPTER FOUR

Knox

Spine straight, Knox walked into the clubhouse, later that evening, meeting every gaze that landed on him. Which was virtually everyone in the crowded place. And almost all of them had witnessed the big blowup between him and Roxanne.

Not to mention his face looked like a bruised and bloated cow stomach with the reminders of the beating Outlaw gave him yesterday.

"Nobody want you here, Knox," a voice sneered.

Himself included.

If he didn't love Roxanne so much—if he wasn't looking forward to making her his wife—he would've left. He was a Harrington; he didn't have to suffer such indignities.

Except he did. Because he adored Roxanne and would be lost without her. He had every confidence that she wouldn't allow Mortician's shenanigans to last too long. Just enough to appease his oversized ego.

Knox didn't know most of these people. Didn't care to know

anyone here. But they were all dangerous, so he must not underestimate them. They'd jump on any weakness.

"Talk to Outlaw," Knox responded with cool authority. "*He* said I'm welcomed here. Megan has prepared a room for me."

"*I'm* saying you're welcomed here, too," Johnnie called from somewhere behind him.

Despite how annoyed he was with Johnnie, Knox almost sagged in relief at hearing a friendly voice. Looks filled with resentment followed him as he made his way to the table he always sat at with Roxanne.

He stopped himself from taking a seat, as he usually would. Was he even allowed? She hadn't called him since he'd last seen her, which Knox resented. She owed him an apology. Didn't she?

"Sit," Johnnie encouraged, setting an expensive bottle of scotch, along with two plastic cups, on the table.

Plastic cups for an expensive scotch. The travesty.

Scowling, Knox sat and watched as Johnnie poured each of them scotch in a plastic cup. Here he thought Johnnie had class. This was the first time Knox observed how uncouth Johnnie could be. Was it due to Kendall's absence?

"Who got to you?" Johnnie asked, taking his own seat.

Knox sipped his alcohol. "Outlaw."

"He has a special spot for Roxanne. He'll never admit it but he sees her as a mother figure. Not only to the guys, but to him, too."

Knox grunted. "Wasn't over Roxanne. It was because of CJ."

"Cardinal rule, Knox. Don't talk about CJ and don't talk about Megan."

The words almost mirrored Outlaw's. That didn't stop Knox's scowl. "Might I remind you Kendall almost *punched* CJ. What did Outlaw do? Gave her a house and license to practice law. Bygones were bygones."

On the surface, anyway. If Knox's most recent meeting with Outlaw had shown him anything, it was that Outlaw didn't forget and he didn't forgive.

"It seems bygones are bygones, Knox. But he let Kendall off too easily." Johnnie emptied his cup and poured another drink for himself. "If Kendall would just fucking behave...It might be too late, though. I think her days are numbered." A bleak sigh escaped him. "What do I do? She almost got me killed. Almost got Megan killed. I'm so fucking tired of her bullshit."

"You're leaving her to her fate?" Knox asked in surprise.

"Of course not, fuckhead. Did you hear anything I just said? I'm keeping my eyes and ears open. Listen for any special assignments one of the probates might have that the rest of us don't know about."

Meaning he was listening for an order that Outlaw gave to have Kendall killed.

Guilt hit Knox. He should tell Johnnie the truth. Kendall's life *was* in danger, but not from an outsider. By her own hand. After Outlaw saw her marriage destroyed and her sanity completely gone. He couldn't say anything, however. Not only would he betray client confidentiality—*Outlaw* no less—he'd lose his chance to finally rid himself and Roxanne of Kendall. The woman had been a thorn in his side from the time they met.

Knox emptied his glass, grabbed the bottle and filled his cup to the brim. Roxanne hadn't called him. She hadn't stopped him from leaving, either. She wanted her damn way. She wanted him to give in and to show him he couldn't tell her what to do. If he didn't stand his ground, she'd soon try to rule him like Callie had tried to.

Roxanne wouldn't compromise on Kendall. She wouldn't compromise on her involvement in the club. And she wouldn't compromise on not having Bailey and Mortician renew their vows during *their* wedding.

As her fiancé, he had a say in the ceremony and in her life. The sooner she realized that, the better.

He glanced around the club. Potter, now a full member, stood behind the bar, big and intimidating and tattooed. Knox kind of liked him, though. He had sense.

"I want to help Kendall, protect her, keep her alive," Johnnie continued. "I just don't know if I want to continue to be married to her."

"Does she know that?"

"Not yet. Whatever happens to our relationship, I've decided I'm not holding anything back any longer. Kendall has to accept *me*."

"You need to accept her," Knox reminded him, almost unable to believe he sounded as if he was defending that witch. Still... "You want her to be Megan."

"That isn't true," Johnnie protested, weakly, to Knox's ears.

"It's always interesting to watch you interact with Megan. There's a rapport there between you two. Outlaw sees it, too, but he accepts it because he knows her eyes aren't big enough to see him. She adores the man. Kendall can't accept it, because you're always throwing Megan in her face."

Johnnie didn't respond, so Knox pressed on.

"After all these years, Megan should be a non-issue. Yet, you're still dealing with it. Did you ever truly love Kendall? Were you in love with her, ever? How many times have you been asked that? By how many people? Open your eyes, man. You say you've been patient with Kendall. I say you've been reticent. You can't put the energy in because you really don't give a fuck. Oh, you've put on a good show, but you've never gotten over Megan Caldwell. You either have graveyard love for her, a sick fascination, or a deathly obsession with her. As long as Megan is in your way, in your life, not only won't you have a future with Kendall, but no one else, either."

~

JOHNNIE

It took effort, but Johnnie restrained himself from pulling out his blade and shoving it into Knox's throat. He held off for Kendall. She was looking forward to Roxanne's wedding and being a part of their group again. For a ceremony, a bride *and* groom were needed.

If he slit Knox's throat, one part of that equation would be morbidly absent.

Knox had overstepped his boundaries, though. How dare the motherfucker tell him he'd never loved Kendall! That he hadn't given a fuck about her, so he'd allowed her to barrel through his life—every-one's—unchecked.

Johnnie loved Kendall. He missed her like crazy. His children missed her. No, Kendall wasn't perfect. She had problems and issues, but she was beautiful, classy, and sexy. She gave Johnnie's life meaning.

Yet, he was so fucking tired of her drama. She stayed busy. And by busy he meant into shit she shouldn't have stuck her nose into. She stayed on Christopher's bad side. She couldn't decide if she loved or hated Megan.

But *no one*, Knox included, had the right to dismiss Kendall as if she were expendable.

"Fucker," Johnnie snarled, so angry his voice was a growl, "if you ever tell me I've never loved Kendall, I will fucking gut you."

Knox's eyes widened.

"Furthermore, don't try and give me fucking advice when your own relationship is so fucked up. When I go to my room here in the club-house at night, I know Kendall is my wife. Roxanne is in no way, shape or form legally bound to you."

"Hold on, Johnnie. I haven't heard a word you said past you having a room at the clubhouse. That means you sleep *here*? What about your house? Your kids?"

"My kids sleep at Megan's house. And Christopher's," he added quickly, when Knox lifted a brow. "Megan and Christopher offered me a guest room, so I could be with my children, but I can't see their happy family and know that mine is close to collapsing."

Besides, Kendall had decorated their house. Everywhere Johnnie looked reminded him of her.

"You specifically brought your children to Megan," Knox said with disapproval, either brushing off Johnnie's death warning or just plain ignoring it. "Oh, and Outlaw," he added with infuriating sarcasm.

"Knox—"

"Knock it off. Can't you see how fucked up that is? You could've brought them to Bailey or Zoann or Fee or Bunny. Even Roxanne. Those kids think she's their grandmother. They would've loved being with her."

"One of the things Kendall has to recognize and accept is how much I admire Megan. She's my friend. I'm not giving our friendship up. But I'm tired of discussing my wife. Why don't we talk about the state of your relationship with the woman you haven't gotten down the aisle yet?"

"There's nothing to talk about. I'm giving in and sleeping here at the club house."

"That should win you points with the woman."

Knox lifted a brow. "The woman has a name, asshole."

"She also has a nose that she sticks in my goddamn business too fucking much. She thinks she knows what's best for Kendall—"

"She knows better than you do," Knox growled. "Kendall acts like a spoiled goddamn child and you're the idiot who agrees with everything she says. For whatever damn reason."

Johnnie stiffened. "Really, fuckhead? If I agreed with everything, she'd still be here, so that line is tired. Find a new one."

Glowering at him, Knox finished off his drink then poured himself another one. Before Kendall and while they'd been together, Johnnie would never have thought to drink such an expensive alcohol out of plastic. Now, it was an unimportant quirk, developed to flip off his wife's dictates. Scotch was scotch and did the job it was meant to do, even if he drank it straight from the bottle.

"Okay, I'll put the reticence argument to bed," Knox conceded. "How about this one? You two shouldn't be together. You're toxic. You don't like Roxanne interceding on Kendall's behalf, on *your* behalf? Then fuck you. You're a shitty excuse for a husband with the way you handle the Megan situation, but, at heart, Kendall is a mean-spirited witch who means you, Roxanne, her children, Megan, *no one*, any good."

"Watch it, Knox. You're treading on dangerous territory. I'm a moment away from taking you to the meatshack and draining you of blood in slow degrees."

"Stop acting like Outlaw. All the barbarian does is threaten to kill people. Me, especially. I'm your friend, Johnnie. You and I have bonded almost from the moment we met. And you know that. You also know what I've said is true."

"Not about Kendall, it isn't," Johnnie warned. "If you don't have anything good to say about her, keep your fucking mouth shut. We *are* friends, Knox. But you cross the line when you degrade Kendall. Believe me or not. I will torture you and then kill you if you keep it up. The agony won't last as long since we're friends."

"Gee, how fucking thoughtful of you," Knox spat. "I have a stipulation of my own: Check your resentment for Roxanne."

Johnnie smirked. The fucker had balls. "Or what? You'll beat my ass or something?"

"Yes," Knox said tightly. "Roxanne's *mine*. She means well and that's all that matters. Stop downing her or else."

Johnnie hooted with laughter. "Or else," he echoed, banging on the table.

"I've gotten into a few fist fights in my life. I served on the force for a number of years," Knox reminded him.

"Child's play," Johnnie dismissed with a wave of his hand. "I'll stomp you to the fucking ground if you lay your hands on me, so find another way to protect Roxanne."

Knox gave him a nasty grin. "I'll tell Mortician."

Johnnie's humor fled. Mortician wouldn't win in a battle against him again. Not like he had when Kendall had drugged Johnnie. Still, it would be one hell of a fight. One that Johnnie didn't care to engage in. "Let's just drop the goddamn subject."

"Yeah, I thought so."

"I'll ignore that," Johnnie gritted, thinking of Kendall and how lovely she'd looked last night at the ball. He'd kept his distance from her. If he hadn't, he would've spent the night at her house. They didn't need sex. They needed tolerance and acceptance. Understanding.

"I have to save Kendall from whatever." Johnnie scrubbed a hand over his face. "Christopher let her off too easy, Knox. She was almost responsible for Megan's death. She was the reason he shot me. And, worst of all, she almost hit CJ. *Punched* him."

"In the face," Knox supplied, as if the mere knowledge wasn't bad enough.

"In the face," Johnnie echoed bleakly.

"If you feel as if Outlaw has something dire planned, talk to him. He's direct. He'll tell you if he plans to kill her or have her killed."

The words echoed in Johnnie's brain, in his heart, and a chill passed through him. That was it. More than likely, Christopher would personally kill Kendall.

"Do you know she arranged a gun deal after Christopher had turned it down?"

The bleakness Johnnie felt at the admission made him ignore Knox's shock.

"It ended up being a set-up," Johnnie went on, trusting Knox to keep this confidence. "She stowed away on the plane carrying the arms and didn't listen when I told her to stay in her rented room. She, along with Val and Christopher, were kidnapped."

"Fuck," Knox gasped.

Johnnie commiserated with Knox's disbelief. "Christopher suspended me from the club. Kendall only wanted to be accepted and thought this would do it. The deal was supposed to be very lucrative. *Too* lucrative."

"I'm so sorry that she got you into so many problems." Knox sipped his drink, a question gathering in his eyes. He opened his mouth, then snapped it shut.

"What? Ask me whatever's on your mind."

"Do you..." Knox's voice trailed off, then he sighed. "Did she not understand club dynamics?"

"Kendall's a very smart woman." Johnnie knew that hadn't been Knox's original question, but he didn't pursue it. He had more important matters to concern himself with. Remembering that fateful holiday season, where Kendall's interference had cost so much, sent waves of panic through him.

Christopher had so many reasons to kill Kendall.

"What happened to the guns?"

Johnnie shrugged. "Who the hell knows. It was a huge loss." He heaved in a sigh. "If only she'd been successful."

"Do you think Outlaw wouldn't hate her as much?"

"He'll never like Kendall, but I do believe *she* would've felt worthy. She wouldn't have continued to insert herself where she didn't belong. It also would've made the club a lot of money. Other members would've cut her more slack."

"Does the club run guns often?"

Knox seemed not to care about Kendall's precarious position. Johnnie might've taken offense, if not for the genuine interest in the man's voice.

"We did more when Big Joe ran our outfit. Once Megan came into the picture—"

"It was too dangerous?"

"It required too much time away. Payoffs to keep law enforcement from hassling us. Help from support clubs. Of course, everything depended on the amount of merchandise we ran." Johnnie finished his Scotch and poured himself another measure. "I think Big Joe had us in more of the gray area."

"Neither strictly legal nor illicit."

Johnnie grinned. "The cop in you is showing."

Knox shrugged. "Vice wasn't my thing, but I am familiar with laws." He copied Johnnie by finishing his whisky and refilling his cup. "Has running arms been very lucrative for the club?"

"It has been." Johnnie remembered Kendall's interference again. "With the exception of the last shipment. I would give anything to make that up. Now that Kendall and I have separated, who knows?"

"You'd go behind Outlaw's back and cut your own deal?"

"Are you insane, man? I would find a deal and bring it to him."

"Ah."

A loud whistle screeched through the air, interrupting their conversation. Realizing Knox wasn't a club member, so he'd said to much already, Johnnie was grateful for the distraction.

"Spoke to Outlaw," Potter announced, then pointed at Knox. "I quote, '*Knox Harrington movin' to the fuckin' clubhouse. Re-fuckin-spect him or deal with my fuckin' ass*'. End of quote."

Johnnie scowled at Knox's grin. "Diplomatic immunity, huh, Knox? How does it feel to be so special?"

As noise returned to the main room, Potter headed to the table and laid a set of keys down in front of him.

"Val's old room where you'll be sleeping," Potter declared, then walked off.

Knox frowned, then glanced at Johnnie. "You think Megan and

Bailey did a good job cleaning the room?" he asked with real worry. "How many gallons of bleach would it take to sterilize the room and make it safe for human habitation?"

Johnnie grinned. "Gallons, motherfucker. Gallons."

Knox covered his face and groaned.

CHAPTER FIVE

EMILY

As if the years fell away, Emily Riser watched as Kendall Miller glided toward the table she sat at. Emily couldn't have been more shocked when she'd received a call from the redhead. They'd never been friends. Emily had never wanted to be Kendall's friend, but she hadn't been able to resist accepting the dinner invitation to see what the stupid, overgrown cow wanted.

"Emily?" Kendall greeted tentatively as she stopped at the table.

Emily pasted a smile on her face. "Kendall, darling, it's positively lovely to see you," she lied, standing and air kissing each of Kendall's cheeks.

They slid into their respective booths and grinned at each other. Emily hated Kendall's expressive brown eyes and flaming red hair. She hated the creamy skin, fine features, and long legs that every boy in school had found so fascinating. Kendall had gone from being a bullied outcast to a whore for any man she met. Yet, here she was, in spite of everything, still smiling, still gorgeous.

Still her...?

"I heard about your mother." Compassion oozed from Emily's voice. "You have my deepest sympathy."

Kendall nodded. "Thank you."

Was that a tentative note in the redhead's voice? Did Emily, by any chance, still intimidate her? Maybe, she remained that insecure little girl who Emily had shut out.

"Oh, I'm so glad to see you! You've grown from an ugly duckling to a gorgeous swan, Ms. Miller."

"Not Miller. *Donovan*," Kendall stated with surprising coolness. "I've been married for a number of years. I have three children." She smiled. "Poor you, still haven't found Mr. Right. Oh, Em!"

Bitch!

Emily cleared her throat, surprised at Kendall's comeback. "I...well, yes, I have a magnificent life, darling," she lied. "I wouldn't want a husband and kids tying me down." That was true, but she was stuck in a menial job, with no hope of getting her life back on track. She'd had a terrible cocaine addiction and lost everything, even her family, because of it.

"Who is the lucky guy?"

"John Donovan. Vice-president of the Death Dwellers Motorcycle Club and CEO of Wellchris Enterprises, the parent company of the Wellchris Medical Labs."

Hadn't she read something about Wellchris in the newspaper a few months ago? And hadn't she seen news stories, good and bad, about the Death Dwellers? She'd Google both later. Right now, she acted duly impressed.

"Wow! You moved up in the world. What a lucky woman. Congratulations."

"You're too kind," Kendall responded with a genuine smile that Emily intended to eat up and spit out.

Kendall

To save her marriage, Kendall had decided she needed to face all her fears and dislikes. Her greatest of both was Meggie. Partly because Johnnie was such an idiot, but mostly because of the woman sitting across from her.

Emily was slightly taller than Meggie. Shocking, Kendall knew; Mortician didn't call her Smurfette without cause.

Kendall wrinkled her nose, cataloging how much bustier and curvier she was than Meggie. Emily's face, though...her face was almost the spitting image of Meggie. Yet, Meggie's blue eyes were kinder, warmer. Her skin smoother, creamier, silkier than both Kendall's and Emily's, which was galling, but whatever. The words Meggie spoke, she meant. She didn't patronize anyone in the hopes of walking over them.

As if.

Kendall had called Emily with an open heart and an open mind. She'd wanted bygones to be bygones. She wanted her demons put to rest. In order to do that, she needed to confront her nemesis once more. To see that Emily was nothing special, after all. She'd been easy to find. A couple of calls to mutual school acquaintances with whom Kendall had seen from time-to-time over the years, and she'd gotten Emily's phone number.

It had been a long twenty-four hours. First, the big Valentine's Day party, then Knox's proposal, then the argument—Knox was the biggest asshole on earth, even bigger than Emily.

Kendall didn't have the time or the inclination to allow Emily to think she'd still suffer her bullshit.

Kendall drummed her fingers on the table. "Emily, darling, it's been so good to see you. I've had a long day, so I don't find the need to draw this out. When I was a young girl, I only ever wanted to be your friend. You taunted and ridiculed me. For years, I suffered image problems because of *you*. But I look at you now and see absolutely fucking nothing. Just a cunt who was jealous of me and my beauty..." Maybe, that was stretching it, since Emily was so gorgeous in her own right, but Kendall wouldn't back down., even as the other woman's face reddened and her mouth fell open.

"You're the dirt beneath my feet, cow," Emily spat, recovering fast.

"And you're the fucking dirt that I *walk on*, bitch," Kendall shot back. "I came here with good intentions, but fuck that. Fuck you. Fuck off." Grabbing her purse, she glared at Emily, slid out of her booth, and stalked away.

Two hours later, Kendall leaned against her headboard, sniffling. She pulled another tissue from the box and dabbed at her eyes and nose. She was watching *Two Women*, an old movie starring Sophia Loren. Her character had been close to her daughter until tragedy struck and changed them for the rest of their lives.

Just like all the different tragedies she and Johnnie had shared, most of which *she* caused.

Unable to watch anymore of the movie, Kendall flicked off the TV. Sad movies served as a catharsis lately. That, along with a different medicine, extensive therapy, and self-help books was easing Kendall's way.

The combination of these things had inspired her to confront her arch-nemesis, Emily. *Bitch!*

Kendall should've slapped the fuck out of her. Emily deserved it, but she'd missed her chance so she'd let it go. Emily was out of her life for good now, therefore she'd lay that ghost to rest.

She had more important things to think about. Such as, she was actually a practicing attorney again! At first, she'd been so shocked that Outlaw relented, she'd meekly—and graciously—accepted all that he'd offered.

Then, she'd thought about it and realized the barbarian had probably been so overcome with guilt over shooting Johnnie, he was using her to atone for all of his sins.

If it got her practicing law again, so be it. Everyone thought she'd enjoy her life so much as a lawyer that she'd decide she didn't want to be married. But she loved Johnnie and she loved her kids. She just needed to work on being a mother and a wife, and figure out how to process her love. If she still had her family—her friend, Meggie—her life would be perfect.

Well, if she could survive *without* medication, her life would be perfect. She hated depending on pills to shape her personality. She lost the real her in dosages and side effects. Was she the calm woman who the medicine brought out? Or the hell-on-wheels she was known to be?

She liked her edginess. She liked not knowing what her next adventure would be. And she loved making everyone prove to her that they'd love and accept her *no matter what she did*. Just as they'd all promised.

Johnnie's everlasting patience and unconditional love had given her the courage to contact Emily. Yes, therapy and medicine had aided the decision. But it was thoughts of Johnnie who sealed it. It was his strength that had boosted her own. Without him, she felt so lost.

However...and it was a big however...being Johnnie's wife meant having to deal with a few unsavory people, including that brat, CJ. Outlaw and Meggie had to know how out of hand he was. CJ needed a firm hand and manners beat into him. That thought didn't make her unmotherly. It made her a disciplinarian. Period.

Marie, Kendall's mother, had taken that approach and Kendall was the woman she was today because of Marie's discipline.

Until she got her husband and children back, though, she wouldn't concern herself with CJ Caldwell. He was little more than a speck of dirt in her pristine life.

She had to tow the line. *Behave*. She wanted to be in her home, in her bed with her husband, so she'd do everything in her power to better herself and get her family back.

CHAPTER SIX

Megan

Stuffing her change away and then dropping the wallet into her purse, Meggie pushed the grocery cart out of the safety of the store and rolled it into the shadows. She'd parked as close as possible to the entrance, so she didn't have far to walk, but she had to make herself move every time she went through this routine.

This morning, she had the same nausea to deal with that had come upon her last night at their family dinner at Bunny and Digger's house. It could've been something she ate, but Meggie knew her terror contributed to her upset stomach.

The guards Christopher wanted her to have was the easiest solution. She thought of the four, older men. Well, they were *kind of* the easiest solution. Even without experiencing their rude grumpiness from time-to-time, she didn't want to go back to the way things had been before her kidnapping.

She liked the point in her life that she'd gotten to. Having alone time. She'd liked the trust Christopher had placed in her and her ability to look out for herself.

As long as she was at ease, he was at ease. He could effectively be Outlaw *and* Christopher. One of her jobs as his wife was to make sure nothing interfered with his life to upend the balance he'd created. He led two separate lives because of her, so she was determined to do her part and stand by his side in whatever way he needed her.

Her life was full but hectic. Besides her home healthcare business she had with Zoann, she had her husband to care for and their five children. CJ was the equivalent of four kids. He was so lively and inquisitive—some would say bratty. But he was her first child, whom she'd given birth to months before her nineteenth birthday. Essentially, they'd grown up together. He'd turned into an active little boy with a will as strong as his daddy's and she'd come into her own as a wife, a mother, and a woman.

Then, of course, there was the club. She still cooked for the members at least twice a week. She didn't serve them as much as she once had. Sometimes, she even cooked meals in her own kitchen and had one of the brothers pick it up and bring it to the club. But the Death Dwellers were her family, too. She made it a point to go to the clubhouse once a week, to mingle with the old ladies and the brothers, too. Although she wasn't supposed to interfere, there were times when she had to put in a word or two—drop a hint or two—to Christopher on one of the guys' behalf.

Then, there was Diesel, preparing for graduation and scouting colleges. He'd very likely win a football scholarship. However, he had his heart set on joining the club. The only way Christopher would allow it was if he got some type of degree. At times, Diesel had struggled in school and with his parents' abandonment. He'd needed attention but a different type from her younger kids.

She couldn't forget their ever-growing family, and their weekly get-togethers. Now, she also had Johnnie and Kendall's children in residence. She really didn't mind it. Rory spent more time with CJ than any of his other cousins, so having him, his sister, and brother stay with them while their parents worked on themselves was a logical choice.

Given everything, Meggie relished alone time to slow her pace.

Without her escorts, though, she was terrified of being taken again. Usually, she cowered in the shadows for twenty or thirty minutes until she worked up the courage to get to her car. It wasn't normal. She knew that. Yet, she'd deal with it and overcome her fear in time. She had to. For her sake and Christopher's sake.

He couldn't be distracted from club business. Enemies popped up from everywhere and she couldn't have him preoccupied by having every little move she made reported to him.

Anxiety was getting the best of him anyway. Worse, he was exhausting himself with his nightmares. Admitting any trauma would affect him doubly.

Now, Meggie needed to harden herself more so for Roxy and Bailey, and their upcoming wedding ceremony. She didn't want the drama in her household to affect their special day. She'd do whatever needed doing to ease her husband's fears and to keep the peace amongst everyone on Roxy and Bailey's behalf.

The sound of Harley pipes reached her and she shrank back, tightening her grip on the cart. Bile rose to her throat.

Usually, she spent her time in the shadows talking herself into going to her car. Today, her worry for her husband distracted her. Either way, she never really paid attention to the people around her. She thought it was better that way. If she saw anyone who reminded her of the men who'd taken her, fear would paralyze her.

The noise grew louder and the bike drew closer. Meggie's stomach heaved but no vomit came up.

Her kidnapping ordeal had begun with the innocent sound of motorcycles.

Drawing in deep drafts of air, she told herself one day she'd feel normal again. She'd feel confident to take her kids out again. To her relief, Christopher had yet to note that she didn't go anywhere alone with their kids anymore.

CJ had been in the car when she'd been taken. She'd been so frightened they'd harm him.

A hand touched her shoulder and she jumped. Her heart accelerated. Her stomach lurched.

"It's me, baby," Christopher said. "I was callin' your name but your mind was wanderin'."

She released a nervous chuckle. "I'm fine," she claimed in a high voice, feeling anything *but* fine. "I was just going to the car."

He stared at her, then glanced at her car. Folding his arms, he met her gaze, and she flushed at his knowing look.

"So, um, I'll see you at home."

Sighing, Christopher pulled her into his arms before she could guide the cart away, and kissed the top of her head. "Why you so fuckin' stubborn?"

She buried her face against the leather of his cut, then shook her head. "I'm not," she insisted in a muffled voice. She stood on her tiptoes and wrapped her arms around his neck, clinging to him. He was warm and there, a towering, muscular wall of protection that she adored.

"I have to do this," she whispered, wondering why she still felt so sick. "We have to do this." Instead of keeping her reasons to herself, she explained them to Christopher.

"You can have me-fuckin-time in the bathroom while you takin' a shit. I don't come in then. Pissing, yeah."

She wrinkled her nose. "I'm still doing something, Christopher."

"Well, fuck, baby, ain't you doin' something when you shoppin'? Just change the shoppin' to shittin', then we all happy."

"It isn't the same," she insisted, suddenly feeling more than a little selfish.

"You say you ain't wantin' your fear to affect my ass. I'm still fuckin' worried, so stop soundin' fuckin' ignorant. You out here, alone, scared like a motherfucker, and I'm supposed to fuckin' *concentrate?*"

"I shouldn't have told you," she said on a groan. "Some things are better left unspoken."

"Since fuckin' when?"

She shrugged.

"You ain't even takin' our lil' motherfuckers nowhere by yourself."

She gave him a sullen stare, and he grinned. He had one of the most beautiful smiles in the world. Seeing it always left her weak in the knees. His grinned deepened and he winked at her. He knew her so well.

Tipping her chin up, he stared into her eyes, his green gaze filled with concern.

"I have to do this," she whispered. "You trusted me to look after myself."

"Megan, you got my heart, my soul, my trust. You got my every-fuckin-thing," he said gruffly. "But there some things you need my ass to hold you up for you to get through. This one of them. It ain't meanin' you weak. It just mean you human. You was kept in a fuckin' hole, naked and starvin', so—"

"You were taken twice," she reminded him. "Both times, I thought I'd lost you."

"Baby, the only thing get my ass and make me cry like a pussy is bein' buried the fuck alive. If I ain't had to rescue you when Snake did that shit to me, I'da just been fucked. But you, *you*, gave me the fuckin' will to get the fuck outta there. You give me strength."

"And you give me wings to fly, Christopher, so let me fly this time."

He grabbed her face between his hands and leaned down to kiss her. "Megan, baby, you one stubborn lil' motherfucker. Why the fuck can't you just do this shit *my* way?"

"Because showing myself, showing *you*, that I can stand on my own two feet, is important to me."

"Your safety important to me. I ain't only worried about you bein' taken a-fuckin-gain. My ass worry that you gonna start cuttin' a-fuckin-gain." His look turned pained. "Tell me you ain't thought about that shit once or fuckin' twice?"

"Maybe," she mumbled. "But not all the time. The idea comes and go, especially after my nightmares."

"So eatin' your pussy after you have them ain't keepin' you relaxed?"

"Is my sucking your cock after *your* nightmares keeping *you* relaxed?" she sniffed.

He scowled at her. "You got my ass, baby," he admitted grudgingly. "Maybe this gonna help. The only fuckin' thing I ain't trustin' you with is Kendall. You for-fuckin-give that bitch every-fuckin-thing she do. So since I think you stupid and fucked outta your head about her, I ain't trustin' you to handle her ass right. Look what the fuck you made me do, when I wanted to ball her fuckin' hands to fists, cleave them motherfuckers in two, them chop the pieces the fuck off."

"Forgiven and forgotten," she lied. "Why are we still on this subject? She came to the ball. CJ interacted with her. There wasn't a problem."

"Cuz Knox told my ass I was Kendall fuckin' Santa. Chafed my fuckin' nuts. I ain't gonna forget."

Meggie wouldn't, either. Every time Christopher brought up Kendall's run-in with CJ a few weeks ago, Meggie adopted placid serenity. Once again, if Christopher knew how hearing about Kendall almost punching CJ infuriated Meggie, he'd kill Kendall.

As it was, Meggie had the distinctly uneasy feeling, her husband was planning dire retribution. He wouldn't tell her because he wanted vengeance. As usual, she'd tell him to overlook Kendall's actions for Johnnie.

Meggie understood that the excuse was old. It also gave Kendall license to do whatever she wanted.

Meggie only hoped Christopher wasn't planning her death and then making it look like an accident. He'd said no, when she asked him weeks ago, then changed the subject. A big, old red flag that he was indeed planning something.

Meggie had already vowed to herself if Kendall even looked at CJ wrong, she'd be sorry.

"You ready to fuckin' go?"

She nodded, then a thought occurred to her. "What…are you going in the store?"

"No, baby," Christopher answered irritably. "I fuckin' came here for you."

He knew her location because he tracked her via her telephone, her car, and her wallet.

"I'm heading home."

"I'ma be right the fuck behind you, baby."

"Everything is going to be fine." As she spoke, she realized her nausea had lessened.

Christopher's smile didn't reach his eyes as he nodded. She knew he was thinking of a way to satisfy them both.

The coming months promised to be busy. Christopher would want to fix her issues to make everything easier for her.

Hopefully, whatever method he came up with wouldn't be needed, and she'd conquer her fear on her own.

CHAPTER SEVEN

Roxy

"**I** didn't raise no scary bitch, Roxanne!"

Roxy winced as her mother yelled those words through the phone. It had been several days since the argument with Knox. She knew he was staying at the club because Mortician had come to pick up some clothes for him. Knox was a stubborn motherfucker, determined to have things his way.

Roxy, though, was just as stubborn. He wouldn't make her change her mind about having a double wedding with Bailey. He could pout, stomp, and kick. She wasn't entertaining any of it. It was too fucking selfish on his part to want to shut her daughter out.

But she missed Knox so much. In the evenings and on weekends, they did everything together. They loved each other's company. They loved each other's bodies.

She glanced at the ring on her finger. Cherished antique or cursed motherfucker?

The ring meant a lot to Knox, prioritizing its specialness over her than stupid fucking superstitions.

Yet, how the fuck had their relationship suddenly become so contentious? She should've been calling her mother to bring her up to speed on wedding plans for a ceremony that, in Roxy's mind, was six months away. Such a short period was cutting it close to plan the type of wedding Bailey dreamed of and Knox required. She and the girls should've started discussing food and alcohol and bachelorette parties and music and flowers and...*everything*.

Instead of going to shops with Bailey and the other women, Roxy wrote down ideas to be decided upon later. This morning, she'd almost given in and called Knox. But she feared that meant she'd be conceding to his wishes, so, instead, she'd called her mother, Pearllene.

Her response was to fuss and cuss, and accuse Roxy of allowing fear to rule her.

"I'm not afraid." Roxy gritted the lie. Truth be told, she didn't want another marriage to fail. "I just don't want any man thinking he can run my life."

The only man who hadn't tried to turn her into something she wasn't had been K-P. He'd accepted her for her.

"No, you don't want to face the fact that you got a man that love you," her momma challenged. "He love you for you. Just like Kaleb Paul did. Just because you failed at three marriages already don't mean you're not destined to find true love, baby. If he don't want Bailey to have a wedding with you, so be it. It's that motherfucker's wedding, too. He got a right to say what he do and don't want."

Her lower lip trembling, Roxy swallowed. "I didn't want a big wedding. I only agreed for Bailey's sake."

"You must really love Knox," Pearllene said, not addressing Roxy's comments. "It's not like you to be such a pathetic, sniveling coward."

She sniffled.

"Is that tears I hear?" Pearllene asked in outrage.

"Maybe," Roxy answered, her cheeks flaming at her mother's tone.

"Lawd, Jesus, girl, you're gonna send me to my grave. If I die, you're gonna be all alone. Your daughters got their own lives, even Bailey. And Duke, that little motherfucker, been hating on you for months."

Another arrow of pain twisted inside Roxy. Her youngest child, her baby boy, despised her. He thought she was ignorant, uncouth, and unworthy. She wondered if Knox saw her as unworthy, too. He hated her cussing and he despised her purple Navigator.

"I can drop dead in the next minute. Then, what are you gonna do?"

"Mama, you been about to drop dead for over thirty years. Would you stop already?"

"My fucking mouth. My fucking right to say whatever the fuck I want to. Besides, *one* of these days I'm really gonna kick up daisies. Nobody meant to live forever."

"I know," Roxy responded on a sigh. "It's just that...oh, Mama, what would I do without you?"

"The same thing you doing with me, girl. *Live your life.* I didn't raise a bitch that just crumple and give up because of a little setback. Whenever I die, know that I lived a nice, full life. I loved you with all my heart. And I didn't have no regrets. When I breathe my last, I just pray to Jesus, Hamish is pumping my chooney real good."

"Mama, I'm not going to listen to you talk about sex with your boyfriend. That's just too damn much information."

"When did you become such a prude, Roxanne?" Pearllene asked with disapproval. "I get sex tips from Alexia and Carissa all the time."

Her daughters were giving their grandmother *sex tips?* She decided she didn't want to know.

Pearllene's hearty laughter boomed through the phone. "You love Knox," she said after a moment.

"I do."

"Then you don't need no double wedding. I'm so surprised at Bailey. It's unlike her to be so selfish."

Roxy stiffened. She didn't want to get into an argument with Pearllene, but casting aspersions on Bailey crossed a line. "She isn't selfish, Mama. I think it would tighten our bond further if we shared the experience of planning our wedding together. Besides, it was Mortician's idea."

"Oh. I see. Then, why don't you *ask* Knox, instead of just making that decision for him. It's his fucking day, too," she said for the thousandth time. "Even Mortician knows that!"

"*Ask* him?" Roxy protested, ignoring the last part. Mortician knew a lot. He just didn't give a fuck about things he didn't agree with. Whoever went against what Bailey wanted would always be on the losing end. Therefore, Mortician wanting Bailey happy should also appease Knox, since he wanted a huge fucking wedding, too. Apparently, her mother didn't see it that way. "Why the fuck should I *ask* that motherfucker a fucking thing?"

"A man's gonna be a man. You couldn't even enjoy your new engagement before you telling the man you sharing your day. He wanted to feel like he wears the pants in the family and take control of the situation."

"That's exactly my point! He wants to control me. Mortician has nothing to do with that!"

"Where the fuck is your brain, child? That man knows you the last person he can control. But a man like to look at his woman and know three things: *He's* her provider, the most important thing in the world to her, and that he lay down some good pipe in the chooney."

"That's old school shit," Roxy snapped.

"No wonder your marriages didn't last. Maybe, the provider part old school, but it's relevant. I tell you, chile, you can't handle a man for shit, if you don't know that."

"That isn't true!" Roxy countered, crushed at those words. "I know how to handle men. But, maybe, Knox feels like Duke does. I mean he hates my ride and my language and—"

"Knox love you for the strong bitch that you are," Pearllene interrupted. "Maybe, that iron will of yours intimidate him a little. Put that together with the way he feel about Outlaw and you got a recipe for a hurt ego over that Navigator. And, fuck, Roxanne, your fucking ass cuss worse than a fucking sailor, so I understand what the fuck the man mean. You give advice to all those little girls in that club. You need to learn how to apply it to your own damn life."

"I apply it all the time."

"Roxanne, baby, listen to me. You smart and beautiful and lively, but you so fragile when it comes to men. You been trodding along just fine, hoping Knox popped the question, and dreading it when he did. Don't fuck this up. Talk to him. Tell him your stubbornness not about nothing more than nerves before he call the engagement off. You want that?"

"No, of course not. I haven't talked to Knox in three days. He's being as stubborn as I am."

"His shit still there," Pearllene reminded her. "He gotta come home some time. Call him and ask him to come now so you can talk."

"Roxanne?"

Knox's voice floated to her and she snapped her head in his direction. A gasp escaped her. His eyes were black, his nose bandaged, and his lip split. What happened to him? Oh fuck!

Mortician. He'd been upset because Bailey wouldn't get to have her big wedding, so he'd gone and taken out his frustrations on Knox.

"Mama, I have to go. Knox is here."

"Let me give you a suggestion. Me and Hamish use bacon grease to make his dick go in easier. But he love the taste and aroma of bacon pussy—"

"I'm not listening to this. Goodbye, Mama!"

"Remember, bacon pussy..."

Those words rang in Roxy's ears as she disconnected the call and stood from the chair in the living room. All anybody had to do was talk to her mama to figure out why Roxy was the way she was.

Knox shoved his hands into the pockets of his pants and rocked on his heels. Besides him having his face looking as if it was on the wrong side of a battering ram, redness rimmed his amber eyes. Stubble shadowed his strong jaw. His blond hair was disheveled.

He was still one of the most beautiful men she'd ever seen.

"What happened to you?"

He shrugged.

"Mortician got to you, didn't he?"

Knox lifted a brow. "*Mortician?*" he sneered. "No, baby, it wasn't your son-in-law. It was the thug. Outlaw."

"I'm going to talk to him. He shouldn't have hit you over what happened between us."

"Don't bother," he said coldly. "It wasn't on behalf of *you*. It was because I called him out on his ignorance."

She fisted her hands on her hips. "What the fuck does that mean?"

"It means Outlaw is a goddamn brute."

"No, it means you press your luck with those boys too damn much."

They looked at each other for a moment and grinned.

"Roxanne, sweetheart, I'm so sorry for my assholery. Of course, we can have a double wedding. I don't know what I was thinking."

"Knox, I'm sorry for being so fucking insistent. We'd just gotten engaged and I should've respected that." She rocked on her heels. "Or at least a-a-asked you." She almost choked on her words, but her momma gave good advice.

He stared at her and then burst out laughing. "My God, where did that come from. Are you sure you're not going to go into fits for making that statement?"

Picking up a small pillow from the sofa, she threw it at him. He ducked and laughed more.

"Shut up," she ordered, her own laughter bubbling up.

He walked to her and pulled her into his arms before claiming her mouth in a deep kiss.

"Where'd you ever get the damn idea you needed to ask me anything?" he asked between kisses.

She wrapped her arms around his neck. "From Mama. She said it's your day, too, and I was wrong not to..." she cleared her throat... "*Ask* you."

He tasted her lips again. "I thought Pearllene knew you better than that."

"Mama doesn't think I know how to handle men," Roxy confessed. "She was just advising me so I wouldn't fuck up our relationship."

He rubbed his nose against hers. "You know how to handle me just fine. As a matter of fact, I think I need a little refresher on how well you *handle* me."

She giggled, feeling giddy and happy and content. "I'm all up for that," she murmured, grinding against him.

"Uh uh," a voice interrupted, scaring the fuck out of Roxy. She jumped out of Knox's embrace.

Mortician stomped forward and grabbed Knox's arm.

"Boy, what the fuck you think you doing?" Roxy shouted, as Knox struggled to yank himself away from Mortician's grip.

"Getting him," Mortician answered, jerking Knox to indicate him. "He keeping his cock to himself until he put a ring on it."

"No fucking way!" Roxy shouted. "This shit is fucking ridiculous. I don't know where the fuck you got this in your goddamn head."

"This shit not up for negotiating, Roxanne," he said, his ire turning to uncharacteristic sullenness. "He might get too used to the milk and run out to pasture before he walk you down the aisle. Don't you know nothing, man? Suppose Knox decide to string you along, get pussy, never set a date, and just jet?"

Knox glared at Mortician.

"Knox would never do that," Roxy protested. He was too much of an upstanding man to even dream of such bullshit.

"You never know," Mortician insisted. "Maybe, he intend to have the longest fucking engagement in history."

"You're an asshole," Knox gritted before Roxy had the chance to do so.

"I been called worse, son. No pussy 'til you walk her down the aisle."

Mortician's words almost touched Roxy. *Almost.* "No pussy for him, mean no dick for me."

"He lucky, Roxanne. I wouldn't want to have to chop it off."

Knox opened his mouth to speak but Roxy shouted, "I'd fucking kill you if you harmed his cock."

"I'm not worried about that," Mortician said in dismissal. "Me, Prez, John Boy, Val, and Digger, all decided he living at the club until you married. You're going to be a wife now, not just a momma, momma-in-law, and grandmomma. You can't live in no momma-in-law quarters no more. We got to have talks with him about if he want to build on club grounds or what. Basically, we going to be too busy getting him up to what we think you deserve. He has to live at the club."

Mortician was absolutely serious.

"Sugar, Knox is all the man I need. He's everything I've ever wanted."

"We got to toughen him up a little bit."

"He's fine just the way he is!" Roxy yelled.

"Helloooo, I am right here," Knox inserted.

"Okay, if you going to be that stubborn, Roxanne," Mortician started, still ignoring Knox, "we really don't give a fuck about toughening him up. He's going to treat you with respect. That mean no fucking until he make it legal."

"Fine," Roxy said, going along with it for now. After a couple of days, they'd tire of babysitting Knox and her, and they'd be free to fuck and do whatever they pleased. If the guys wanted to express some misplaced code of honor, she'd let them live in ignorant bliss. "I just need to say a couple of things to Knox."

Mortician nodded, but remained where he was, holding onto her man.

"That means leave for a minute," she snapped.

"I'm going right over there." He pointed a short distance away, near the entrance of the room.

"I'll be there later tonight," she whispered to Knox, once Mortician stepped away.

Knox grinned. "I admire them for wanting to protect you so fiercely.

"It is kind of sweet," Roxy admitted, "if it wasn't so fucking annoying."

"Time up," Mortician called.

"Later," Roxy mouthed again as Mortician yanked Knox toward the door.

Where there was a will, there was a way. Roxy just had to show those boys that, until they tired of their game and forgot all about protecting her non-existent virtue.

CHAPTER EIGHT

Knox

"Let go of me!" Knox shouted, yanking himself out of Mortician's grasp, halfway along the trail back to the club. Roxanne might've decided to go along with this insanity on the surface, but Knox wasn't amused.

"I know you not happy, Knox, but you just have to deal with it, since *you* the motherfucker that first came up with a long engagement."

"I was just annoyed. I didn't mean that. If I had, I never would've proposed."

"Oh, yeah, why the fuck *did* your fucking ass pop the fucking question?"

"I love Roxanne, jackass. Why else would I propose?"

Mortician stopped so fast, Knox ran into him. The club's enforcer turned, looking very...*enforcerish*.

Knox stepped back.

"First, son, I'm not a jackass. Feel me? Don't call me that again."

"Digger, Outlaw, Val, and Johnnie call you worse!" Knox reminded him, annoyed he didn't have such freedom.

"You not one of us, Knox."

"You don't say? That's quite the newsflash for me."

"You here, you *alive*, because of Roxanne. But you'd prefer not to be around us."

"Can you blame me?" He wouldn't bother to deny it. "You people are violent animals. When Roxanne's around you, her dignity slips fifty notches. I've tried to fit in, but I will never agree with your free-wheeling philosophy and criminal tendencies."

"And that attitude, right there, is why you don't get to call me a jackass. That's why I believe you might decide to walk away from Roxanne when it gets close to the wedding. If you miss her, you'll know how to cherish her. See her as a sweet woman to be protected and romanced; not a biker bitch to use and discard. I don't trust your uppity ass. So no fucking. You're giving her flowers and romance and respect, but no dick." Mortician shoved a finger in Knox's chest. "She love you but Bailey say her momma scared because she had so many failed relationships. Roxanne think marriage ruin relationships, but then, she told Bailey, she ruined what she had with K-P and she don't want to do that with you."

The words stunned Knox into silence. Roxanne afraid? That seemed incomprehensible. She was the bravest, most fearless woman he'd ever met. He'd admired her courage, her wit, her beauty. *Her*. "She neither wants nor needs my protection, and I'll thank you to stop trying to turn my fiancée into a simpering mass of nerves. That's not Roxanne. By the way, if I didn't want her, I wouldn't have asked her to marry me. And, in case you've forgotten, marriage doesn't mean anything. I can still walk away from her."

"You got a lot more to lose if you leave *after* the wedding."

"Nothing but my dignity if it comes to that. I'm having Roxanne sign a prenuptial agreement." He hadn't considered that before, although he knew his parents would expect it of him, to protect the Harrington interests. Listening to Mortician, however, and seeing a future filled with interference led to Knox's conclusion that a prenup was needed. He'd stick it out with Roxanne as long as possible.

When he had enough of the violent barbarians she insisted on cavorting with, he'd walk away. "A prenup is a requirement in my circles."

"You signing one for her?"

"What does she have that I'd want?" The moment the words left his mouth, Knox regretted them.

Mortician's growl didn't help.

Backing away, Knox raised his hands in surrender. "That came out wrong. I meant she doesn't have any assets to protect like I do."

Mortician grabbed Knox by the collar and lifted him off his feet, without much effort. "You not ruining her wedding, her happiness, with no mention of a prenup. Understand?"

Knox tightened his jaw. It wasn't any of Mortician's business. Besides, it was because of *him* Knox felt the need for the legal document.

"Do. You. Understand?" Mortician snarled, shaking Knox like a rag doll with each succinct word he spoke.

"Do *you* understand?" Knox finally shouted. "I guess you don't know what it means to have so much at stake, but I have a lot to lose if this marriage fails."

"You shouldn't open your fucking mouth about things you don't fucking know. Especially about me."

Mortician set Knox on his feet and thrust his face forward. They were almost nose-to-nose, but the biker was several inches taller than Knox and the fulminating looks and threatening posture worked.

"Would you have a house without insurance?" Knox asked in even tones. "It doesn't mean your house will be destroyed. It just means it is protected in the event something does happen. That's the only reason I intend to ask her to sign a prenup."

"Whatever your goddamn reason, it's bullshit." He shook his head and released a humorless laugh. "I don't have to worry, Knox. Lay that shit down to Roxanne and you *won't* have a wedding."

"I doubt that. She loves me. Unlike you, she'll understand my reasoning."

"Want to make a fucking bet?"

Knox brushed off the sleeves of his jacket. "No, I don't. Everything you've said is a crock of shit. Roxanne never told me she was afraid of our relationship failing. Besides, she's tougher than that."

"Tough on the outside, soft on the inside," Mortician corrected. "And she didn't have to tell *you*. Why would she, motherfucker? That's what women got other women for. If Bailey say her momma scared, then she scared. *Think*. You ever know Roxanne to get ass-hurt over whatever silly argument happened at the ball and hold a grudge *three* fucking days?"

Refusing to admit how much sense Mortician made, Knox gave him a sour look. He'd address this with Roxanne. He wouldn't stand here, in the cold, talking to a man who had no perception of what was at stake and no real understanding of Roxanne. He changed the subject. "If you and Bailey still want to renew your vows and make it a double ceremony, you're welcomed to do so."

He puffed out his chest, silently showing Mortician who was in control of this situation.

A muscle ticked in Mortician's jaw. Instead of commenting, he stared at Knox for one long, intimidating moment.

Knox scowled. "Do you still want a double ceremony or not?"

"I'll talk to Bailey," he said grudgingly, then relented and sighed. "I lost my momma when I was a kid. I never got to see her happy, Knox. My father was a motherfucker who made her cry all the time. That's not happening with Roxanne. I don't give a fuck what *you* or *she* says. You not living under her roof and you not sleeping with her until you marry her. *Without a fucking prenup*. After the wedding, if you fuck up and divorce, she'll be a rich woman and I'll have no choice but to de-cock you, shove it in your mouth, then cut your fucking head off."

"What is wrong with you people? Johnnie threatened me with the meatshack and draining my blood. Now, you're threatening me with castration and decapitation."

Mortician grinned. "Don't fuck with John Boy. He like torture. He'll use a few steel straws to puncture you with and talk to you as you bleed out."

"Johnnie? College-educated, suit-wearing, *Johnnie*? You're a liar."

"Appearances deceiving, Knox," Mortician said with a glare. "*Don't get on Johnnie bad side. No bullshitting.*"

"I'll remember that." Knox didn't believe for a minute that Johnnie enjoyed torture and murder. Maybe, at first, he'd thought so. But since he'd gotten to know Johnnie more, the man had never shown anything but a light-hearted, classy side. Even when he was in his cut. "It's time for me to stop bullshitting with you, Mortician. I'm not adhering to your stupid no-sex, no living-together rule, and neither is Roxanne. She wants to appease you, but she makes up her own mind. I'm going to be with Roxanne before the wedding. We're grownups. We don't need your permission to do anything. Who the hell do you people think you are? Outlaw with his dictator complex, giving *my* woman a goddamn tacky, purple, Navigator. It reeks of classlessness...Now, this? Fuck you. Roxanne's visiting me tonight and there's nothing you can do about it."

The cold look Mortician gave Knox chilled him, but if he allowed himself to be intimidated, he'd never have a chance with them. Until now, he and Mortician had been on good terms.

"What are you going to do about that?" he taunted. "Neither me nor Roxanne will allow you to use your need for a *momma* to carry out this ridiculous bullshit. It's pathetic to think you can substitute Roxanne for a dead woman who didn't have the sense to leave her husband and make a good life for herself."

Mortician's punch to Knox's Outlaw-abused jaw would've knocked him to the ground, if the enforcer hadn't grabbed his hair and land a few more punches on various places of Knox's body. Just as he released him, he landed a blow to Knox's stomach.

Moaning and choking, Knox rolled on the ground.

Mortician crouched next to him. "Don't talk about my dead momma. In my eyes, the woman next to a saint and you defile her with your fucked-up words. Roxanne like a substitute momma to me, to *all* us. More than that, she Bailey momma and they adore each other. You fucking lucky I liked you enough to let you be her boyfriend, instead of disappearing your fucking ass by running you through a goddamn wood chipper. Deep in your heart, you don't think she worthy of you, because of us. You think you doing her a favor by marrying her."

"I-I don't," Knox gasped. "I swear. I-I love her. I swear," he said, close to tears from the pain.

"Roxanne a good woman, Knox. Bailey close to her momma. *She* scared, too. Know why? She think you going to take Roxanne and move her away, just to get her away from us. I'll fucking kill you if you hurt Bailey like that. That's part of my reason for doing this, but mostly, it's because of Roxanne. If you don't accept *us*, really fucking accept us, you'll never truly accept her. You staying at the fucking clubhouse. We going to teach you about who we really are. You keeping your cock to yourself. You going to show Roxanne you can't live without *her*, not sex, not her cooking. *Her,* motherfucker."

Despite his pain, Knox raised his head and glared at Mortician. *He* was his soon-to-be son-in-law? The man with the 'all-mothers-are-chaste-and-in-need-of-protection' complex?

Standing, Mortician loomed over Knox, muscles bulging, eyes angry...Motorcycle boots near Knox's head.

Into the tense silence, Knox's cell phone rang. He forced himself to a sitting position, moaning and grunting and cursing Mortician to high hell, and grabbed his phone out of his pocket. He scowled at the familiar number.

"Yes, Outlaw?" he answered, irritated.

"Johnnie at the club, talkin' about a meetin' Kendall had with Emily Riser."

"Is the name Emily Riser supposed to mean something to me?"

"Yeah! She the bitch got psycho cunt hatin' on Megan."

Jesus Christ! These people!

Knox rubbed his hurting forehead. "What about her?" he asked, as if Outlaw's explanation made a difference.

"She in Portland. Contact her and set up a meetin' where her and Johnnie meet some kinda way. If she look so much like Megan, then that should fuckin' nudge him another fuckin' step away from Kendall."

Although he liked the sound of Kendall being one step closer to being gone for good, Knox couldn't believe Outlaw's audacity. "That plan is pretty fucked up. You're basically owning the fact that Johnnie wants Megan and using that to come between him and Kendall."

"Yeah," Outlaw said without remorse. "So? One way or a-fucking-nother, Ima make sure Kendall have her day of reckonin'. Now, do what the fuck I told you to do and shut the fuck up."

The call disconnected.

Cursing in frustration, Knox got to his feet. His body hurt, but he'd survive. Seeing Mortician standing a short distance away, Knox limped to him, just as the enforcer was ending a call.

"Shit covered," Mortician announced.

"What do you mean?"

"Guards going to be posted at night by Roxanne and in front of your door at the club. She try and sneak by you or vice versa, she'll be stopped and you'll be detained, then I'll be called to deal with the situation."

Mortician smirked at him, then turned on his heel and started off, whistling a merry little tune.

The entire way back to the club Knox wished a painful death upon Mortician's head.

CHAPTER NINE

Roxy

With Kendall away, Johnnie declined to take his turn to host a family dinner, so it was moved to Roxy's house, three days later. With all of the big bikers in her small, open space, it looked over-crowded. Bunny, Bailey, and Roxy sat on the sofa, eating their meal of stewed chicken, boiled rice, and steamed carrots. Johnnie sat in one wing chair while Zoann sat in another. Outlaw was stretched out on his side in the middle of the floor, eating casually, as Meggie leaned against him, also eating. Digger sat at the bar, already on his second plate, while Knox stood behind it. He'd refused to eat, claiming he wasn't hungry. Mortician sat on the floor, on the side of the sofa, near Bailey. Val lounged against the wall, eating with contentment. He'd already put it out there that he wanted some of Roxy's pecan pie and hoped she'd made one or two.

She had, but she kept that information to herself. Like a big child, he'd put his food aside and go straight for the sweets.

She leaned back, contented. It had been a very productive day. The only blight—the thing that pissed her off the most—was having last night's plans to visit Knox thwarted.

Mortician, the motherfucker, was too suspicious for his own good. How the fuck did he know to post guards? She'd argued. When that didn't work, she'd brought her ass back inside, deciding she needed a firm plan to outsmart her misguided son-in-law.

The door opened, and Diesel walked in, carrying a handful of empty paper plates. He was in the garage with the kids, where there was TV, video games, central heat, and all types of toys.

Diesel was a sweet kid, with sad gray eyes, and black hair. He'd filled out since Outlaw had rescued him from the streets. They'd miss him when he left for college, *if* he left. He might choose some place nearby. He'd told Roxy he didn't want to leave Outlaw and Meggie, fearing they'd get used to him not being there and decide he was no longer a part of the family.

Roxy knew that wouldn't happen, but he just had to see for himself.

He loped to the trash can, threw out his load, then went to the refrigerator, and pulled out two packs of juice boxes. With a grin, he headed back out and closed the door behind him.

Knox poured a Scotch for himself, then held up the glass. "Anyone care for a drink?"

What a mighty fine man he was, with eyes that reminded Roxy of sparkling amber, a chiseled jaw, slim waist, and a fine ass that was quite squeezable as they made love.

He sipped from his glass, his gaze never leaving hers, lit with promises and innuendoes.

Licking her lips, Roxy patted her hair. Tonight, she didn't wear a wig. At their family dinners, she usually went without. Still, her hair had grown even longer, which she was so happy about, considering one of the side effects of Tamoxifen was hair loss.

"Drinks, anyone?" Knox asked again, after another heated look at her.

Johnnie lifted his glass of Scotch. "We still have what we were given before we started eating."

"All right." Knox sipped, then cleared his throat. "Everyone, may I have your attention?"

The low conversations going on amongst everyone stopped as the group quieted.

"Thank you."

Knox was so proper and polite. She loved that about him. She loved how they made their differences work. Sometimes, though, doubts crept into her. Roxy would shove them away and remind herself that Knox loved her, so much so he hadn't even asked her for a prenup.

He probably knew that would be a deal breaker.

"Roxanne and Bailey have set a date for the dual ceremonies," Knox announced. "August of this year. On the sixth."

Digger licked his fingers. "That's months away."

"Glad to know you can fucking count," Mortician joked around a mouthful of food.

In response, Digger opened his mouth to reveal the half-chewed contents.

"Nasty motherfucker," Roxy complained. "Do that shit again and your ass is barred from eating in my house."

"Aww, Roxanne, I didn't mean no harm," Digger complained.

"Not to *her*," Mortician pointed out. "You wanted to turn my fucking stomach so I wouldn't eat the rest of the week."

"More for my ass, then," Digger retorted.

"That's where the fuck all that food goin'," Outlaw said with a snicker. "Straight to your fuckin' big ass."

"Bruh, that's fucking cold," Digger said, pointing a chicken bone in Outlaw's direction.

"Excuse me!" Knox inserted, his smile thin. "As much as I'm enjoying this banter, we want to settle a few things about the wedding."

"Yeah, Digger. That mean shut the fuck up," Mortician ordered.

Digger started to say something, but Roxy stood and clapped her hands as a teacher would, to restore order. "Enough, boys!" she called. "Show some manners."

Digger gave her an under-eyed look. "What that mean?"

"Nothing you would know about, since you never had any class," Val put in with a snigger.

If she didn't forge on, shit would get out of hand, so before anybody else made a comment, Roxy looked at Outlaw.

"Mortician is going to be a groom that day, Outlaw," she started, suddenly nervous. She was having a big wedding where she needed to be given away. At her age. Maybe, asking to be escorted down the aisle was just too fucking much. She could walk her own ass up to the altar. Only Bailey needed to be given away. Ignoring her silly disappointment, she waved her hand and sat back down between Bailey and Bunny. "Don't worry about it, sugar. It was just a stupid idea I had."

"It isn't stupid, Mama!" Bailey cried, turning to Outlaw. "Mama wants you to give her away."

Instead of answering, Outlaw glared at Roxy. She kept a smile pasted on her face, but his reaction poured even more embarrassment into her. She'd grin and bear his words since she was the one who'd started this.

"I gotta put a fuckin' monkey suit on to give your fuckin' ass the fuck away, Roxanne?"

She sagged in relief and expelled a breath. This was only a discussion and she was nervous. How would she be on her wedding day?

Meggie elbowed Outlaw. "You have to wear whatever the bridal party wears, Christopher."

"I ain't accepted yet, Megan. Not 'til my question answered."

"It's going to be a formal wedding," Bailey acknowledged, "so, yes, a tuxedo will be required."

Outlaw glowered between Roxy and Bailey.

"Sugar, it's fine," Roxy said with a laugh, hoping she hid her disappointment. "I don't need a motherfucker walking me down the aisle. Johnnie, since Bailey asked on my behalf, I'll ask on hers. Will you walk her down the aisle?"

"Roxanne, babe, how fuckin' important it be that I walk your fuckin' ass down the aisle?" Outlaw asked before Johnnie responded.

"She said not to worry about it," Knox said coolly. "You've made your feelings known, so we're moving on."

"I ain't talkin' to you, motherfucker," Outlaw snapped, "so shut the fuck up 'til I do." He looked at Roxy again. "You really wanna be walked down the aisle, yeah?"

She gave Outlaw a smile that she hoped covered up all the emotions running through her but decided to answer honestly. "I do, sugar."

He huffed out a breath. "Fuck, fine," he grouched. "If the shit that important to your fuckin' ass, I'll walk you down the fuckin' aisle."

"Thank you, sugar." Roxy decided not to say anything else. Knox didn't look pleased. Before this sudden turn spiraled into an argument, she let it go.

Bailey grabbed Roxy's hand and squeezed. Smiling, Roxy nodded to her daughter, telling her without words, that she was fine.

Satisfied, Bailey looked at Johnnie. "Will you give me away?"

"What about me?" Digger called. "I'm not bride-giveaway material. Or Val?"

"Don't put me in that shit, Digger," Val warned. "I'm not interested in playing that role."

"Well, I am," Digger responded.

"You my best man, fool," Mortician told him.

Digger grinned. "I can handle that."

"May I answer Bailey now?" Johnnie asked, glancing around the room. His plastic surgery had left very little evidence that Outlaw had shot him in the cheek. "I would love to give you away, sweetheart."

"Thank you, Johnnie," Bailey said. "I really appreciate it."

"Since we like fathers of the fuckin' brides, that mean we gotta pay, right?" Outlaw asked.

Johnnie shrugged. "I guess so. This will give us a lot of practice for when Matilda and Rebel are married."

"Rebel ain't gettin' married. At least 'til she about forty," Outlaw announced.

Meggie rolled her eyes. Obviously, they'd had the discussion before. They talked about everything…unlike Johnnie and Kendall.

That reminded Roxy.

"I'm putting this shit on blast right now," she said. "Kendall will be part of the ceremony."

No one said anything, but Outlaw's face darkened.

Looking for support, Roxy glanced at Meggie. The girl was sharp because she gave Roxy the slightest nod.

"I think it's a wonderful idea to include her," Meggie threw out. "She's still Johnnie's wife. Still a part of the family."

When no one responded to Meggie, Zoann looked between Roxy and Bailey. "What are the wedding colors?"

"We still deciding on the colors," Roxy said.

Bailey nodded. "I want gold and white."

"I look too washed out in gold, sugar," Roxy protested. "That's why I want scarlet and white."

"Why not both?" Bunny asked. "It could be a very elegant, very regal wedding with the right shades of silver and gold."

That was an idea. The bridesmaids could alternate in each color in the lineup, as long as the dress styles were the same or similar. It could work.

"We're talking to Father Wilkins soon," Bailey said, almost unable to contain her excitement. "We want the ceremony at the church."

"Fuck me. Not only do I gotta wear a fuckin' monkey suit, I gotta deal with that lil' fat motherfucker?" Outlaw asked in outrage. "What the fuck I ever do to you and your Ma, Bailey? Why you puttin' me through that fuckin' torture?"

"If there are too many pitfalls for you to handle, we'd understand if you backed out," Knox said casually.

Roxy frowned at Knox.

"A-fuckin-gain, Knox, I ain't fuckin' talkin' to you," Outlaw gritted.

Knox glared at Outlaw, so Roxy decided to intervene.

"Girls, we all need to meet," she said. "Come up with menus. Set a budget. Look at dress styles."

"It's your wedding, sweetheart," Knox said. "You and Bailey don't need their input for your big day."

"Yes, we do," Roxy answered. "Me and Bailey already talked about it. It's going to be a big ceremony. We need help."

"Hire a wedding planner," he said flatly.

"We don't want a wedding planner, Knox." Bailey gave Roxy an uneasy look. "We want a planning committee with the family."

"Yeah, Knox," Roxy said in warning. She didn't like that it sounded as if he was looking for ways to shut everybody out. "A wedding planner would be a waste of time."

"We also need to plan a bachelorette party," Zoann chuckled.

"Oh, yeah," Bailey agreed happily. "Meggie has to plan it."

Roxy had heard all about the bachelorette party Meggie had planned for Bunny. Strippers and stripper poles and alcohol. Oh, yeah, Meggie could definitely plan the party.

"I'll be happy to," Meggie said with a smile.

"That mean you and Mortician get to have a bachelor party, Knox," Val declared.

"Sounds like a plan to me." Digger grabbed his beer bottle and swigged from it, then pounded on his chest and belched. "Don't worry, ladies, we not having too many strippers."

"Neither will we," Meggie retorted, earning a scowl from Outlaw.

"We not havin' no fuckin' naked bitches at the bachelor party, Megan, so you ain't havin' no naked motherfuckers at Roxy party."

Meggie gave her husband a serene smile.

In six months, all this planning would become a reality. There'd be parties and rehearsals and joy. Roxy's thoughts slammed to a halt. There'd also be the club and business and whatever came up. Bloodshed and biker wars...

Roxy wanted to curtail an unforeseen event that would ruin the big day. "I have one final request."

Outlaw twisted his fingers through Meggie's hair. "What's that?" he asked, not looking in Roxy's direction.

They couldn't completely stop club business. "The two weeks before the wedding, there's no...no..." How could she put it?

"Fuckin' ups?" Outlaw supplied.

"You mean fuck-ups," Johnnie corrected.

"Nope. I mean *fuckin' ups*. She ain't wantin' bloodshed durin' that time, assfuck."

"Is that what you mean?" Johnnie demanded.

Roxy nodded.

"You got it, babe," Outlaw said. "What the fuck ever need seein' to, Ima make sure to have wrapped the fuck up by then."

"Thank you," Roxy said with a relieved smile.

"Oh, and don't fuckin' worry about a budget. Me and Johnnie meant what we said. Whatever the fuck you and Bailey want, we gonna get."

"No way!" Knox protested. "Roxy's my woman. I'll pay for her. Let Mortician pay for Bailey's portion if he can afford it."

"How you going to speak out of my fucking pocket, son?" Mortician snapped.

Digger hooted with laughter. "Knox, don't you know this motherfucker so tight, he got spiderwebs wrapped around his money?"

"I'm not tight with Bailey!" Mortician countered.

"No, Lucas is very generous with me," Bailey agreed.

"Yeah, fool. My woman got her own bank account and everything."

"I did the same thing for Bunny," Digger told him. "And I didn't almost lose her cuz I didn't want to cough up bet money."

"Shut up, Digger," Bailey ordered, sitting up and grabbing Mortician's shoulder. "Don't annoy my husband for your amusement."

Mortician threw Digger the evil eye. "He an asshole like that, pretty girl."

"All this shit started because Outlaw and Johnnie offered to pay," Roxy began. "There's no need. I can pay for the ceremony my own damn self."

Knox lifted his brow. "Is that so?"

Fuck. Her momma told her men liked being the protector and the provider. Shit, Roxy knew that, but Knox had been spoiling for an argument with the guys all evening. He had a burr in his dick, that he refused to ignore.

"Our wedding will be a society wedding," Knox said. "Mother will invite all her friends and their families. My father will invite his business associates and their families. It's going to take deep pockets to host the grand wedding I want us to have, Roxanne."

She didn't like the censure in Knox's voice. More to the point, she didn't like how his cool words made her feel so inadequate.

Roxy shifted in her seat, swallowed, exchanged a glance with Bailey. "I don't want a grand wedding, Knox. Big, yes, but with my own special touch. A day we all can enjoy."

"Since you insist on having a planning committee with family, I want my mother included," Knox supplied.

Roxy and Knox's mother had come a long way, since that first disastrous meeting, so she didn't see a problem with that. "Of course. I'd love to have her help."

"Her help means expenses you can't even dream of. Deep pockets. Harrington money."

The room at large looked in her direction, as if they were at a tennis match, and waited for her serve.

"I can pay for my own fucking wedding," Roxy insisted.

"How?" Knox pressed. "I'm not trying to embarrass you. I just want you to know that my money is your money, and you're free to start using it, even before we're married. You don't have to take whatever you've saved up from your years of working to pay for something I can easily afford."

"Excuse me?" Roxy huffed.

"Knox, you need to sit the fuck in a corner and keep a finger shoved in your fuckin' piehole," Outlaw snapped, getting to his feet.

Meggie hopped to hers and dusted off her backside, smiling with unease and grabbing Outlaw's bicep.

Mortician stood, too.

"Lucas?" Bailey squeaked. "Knox didn't mean anything."

Yes, the motherfucker did, but if Roxy said that, Knox just might die. It was a tossup who'd take him out first. Outlaw or Mortician.

"Roxanne got her own fucking money," Mortician stated flatly. "Know why, motherfucker? Because I got more money than I know what the fuck to do with."

"Illegally obtained," Knox cut in.

"I got," Mortician continued as if Knox hadn't spoken, "so Roxanne got. Don't think you lifting a broke ass bitch out of the mire of a fucking biker club."

"I didn't mean that!" Knox declared, an angry flush suffusing his face. "You people look for reasons to fight."

Oh, Lawd Jesus. Knox said *you people*, as if he thought himself better than them.

"Us fuckin' people?" Outlaw echoed.

"Goddamn it! Why is everything I say the wrong thing around here?" Knox fumed. "I meant nothing by any of what I said. All I wanted to do was reassure Roxanne. That's it."

"Mort, it ain't his fault he a stupid motherfucker that don't know how the fuck to reassure nobody. Cuz, Knox, motherfucker, your reassurance full of fuckin' shade and insult."

"*Shade?*" Knox repeated in confusion.

"Sly comments," Meggie supplied. "Giving an insult without coming right out and insulting someone."

Knox gave Roxy an imploring look. "Roxanne, baby, I wasn't trying to insult you. I swear."

"Leave him be, Outlaw, Mortician," Roxy said, glaring at Knox. "He's going to learn how to reassure me about his money."

"Don't give a fuck," Outlaw announced. "*Ima* give your ass the fuck away, so *Ima* foot the bill and I ain't givin' a good fuck what bitch on the plannin' committee. Deal with it, Knox. Choke on it. *Die* over it. Your fuckin' choice. Me and Johnnie payin'. Case fuckin' closed."

"Fine with me," Mortician said. "My bank account like the sound of that."

"Cuz you still a stingy motherfucker," Outlaw said.

"Yep, and proud of my stingy motherfuckery," Mortician quipped.

The boys all laughed, breaking the tension. Roxy smiled, her heart filled with joy, hope, and dreams of her future with Knox.

CHAPTER TEN

Knox

"I'm tired, sugar," Roxanne announced around a yawn, giving Knox a friendly pat on the knee.

Somehow, he'd managed to insert himself next to her after settling into his usual pattern of acting as co-host for the dinner. He missed the cozy little place, just big enough for him and Roxanne to create a love nest. She'd allowed him to personalize the place to his tastes, too, so it wasn't exclusively hers.

The pastel colors she'd had when he'd moved in had been changed to neutral tones. The feminine décor in her bedroom had been switched to a genderless theme.

They both had family photos out as well as pictures of their integrated families. Roxanne with Knox and his son. Knox with Roxanne and her daughters. Duke was a little asshole who refused to deal with his mother, so he wasn't included in the display. There were photos of family gatherings and birthdays and special events.

Yet, Knox had never felt lonelier or more abandoned. He missed her so much, but the exile Mortician imposed on him didn't seem to phase her one damn bit.

Knox had never been one for PDA, but he just couldn't seem to keep his hands to himself. He'd stroked her hair, caressed her neck, wrapped an arm around her.

She'd sat next to him, as if his touch meant nothing to her, only now responding—with a goddamn pat like he was a fucking dog.

For over a week, he'd suffered through their separation. Not that time apart mattered to her.

"Stay as long as you need to," Roxanne continued as she stood. "Bailey, lock up once everyone leaves. I'm going to turn in for the night."

"Momma, are you okay?"

"Fine, baby," Roxanne said with reassurance. She gazed at Knox.

He swore he saw longing and need. And love.

"Just tired," she said on a sigh.

"Are you too tired to talk to me about an issue I'm having?" Zoann asked in a small voice.

Val frowned. "Puff, what the fuck going on?" he asked gruffly. "You sick or something? Why the fuck you talking like that?"

"Because Roxy's tired and I don't want to tax her," Zoann answered. "She has a lot on her plate."

"I'm fine," Roxanne said, her strong, sure voice leaving no doubt to the truth of her words. "Come on upstairs with me."

Bailey gave the smallest nods to Megan. If Knox hadn't been staring at each woman, feeling as clueless as the bikers looked, he might have missed it.

"Mortician," Megan started. "I made a new drink for you to try. I completely forgot about it and left it at home. Would you like to come to the house and try a bit?"

"Meggie girl, what—"

"Lucas, I would hate for Meggie's hard work to go unappreciated," Bailey said quickly. "Why don't you go and try the drink?"

"Can I try it too?" Digger asked. "Or it's just for Mort?"

"No, silly," Megan said with a beaming smile. "I've actually made a special snack for you."

Outlaw folded his arms and smirked at Megan, who quickly averted her eyes.

"Val, Johnnie, come and try the new drink and snack, too," she said after a moment. "Let's leave Roxy to talk to Zoann, so she can get the rest she needs."

Her words seemed to amuse Outlaw all the more. Flushing, she threw him the evil eye and he winked at her.

"Harrington, since all these motherfuckers comin' the fuck over, bring your ass, too," Outlaw ordered, grinning at Megan and ignoring Knox even though the invitation was for him.

Megan glared at Outlaw, then sniffed. "Knox isn't invited," she said on a sullen mumble.

"I want the motherfucker there, baby," Outlaw said firmly.

"If Meggie don't want Knox there, Outlaw, you can't force the child to welcome him," Roxanne stated, not in the least offended that Megan had just snubbed him. She nodded to Knox. "Why don't you go back to the clubhouse, sugar? I'll give you a call in a bit."

He wouldn't make a scene in public, so he conceded with all the graciousness of a Harrington. "Of course, sweetheart."

Pretending her attitude didn't hurt, Knox departed the house and left Roxanne in the care of Bailey and Zoann. She didn't try to stop him or kiss him or even *acknowledge* him.

That cut. Each night apart from her was like a knife wound. His bed, his heart—fuck!—his *soul* felt empty without her. Yet, she was being Biker Mom, instead of his love.

He didn't say much during the walk along the path. Outlaw led the way, holding Megan's hand, and whispering to her. Every now and then, she laughed. Digger kept an arm around Bunny's neck as the two of them chatted with Mortician, while Val and Johnnie walked side-by-side, in low conversation.

Knox walked alone. He wasn't sure how much more of this he'd take. His first marriage had broken down because of a lack of communication. He and his ex-wife had gotten to a point where all they did was go out of their way to hurt one another. It had been a shock to Knox. Everything in life had always come so easily to him. But marriage had been work. It had been compromising and adjusting to someone else's needs and ideas.

When they reached the gate to Outlaw and Megan's place, the biker punched in the code. Still holding Megan's hand, he stepped aside and allowed everyone to enter.

Knox hovered back, waiting to hear that they'd changed their minds. That he'd be allowed to come in with them. That he was one of them, the way Roxanne always insisted.

But, no. Outlaw slammed the gate closed.

"Johnnie?" Knox called. "Come to the club and have a drink with me."

"Fuck no," Outlaw growled. "Fuck off. Good fuckin' night, Knox."

Knox waited a moment to hear Johnnie's protest, but none came.

"Assholes," he growled under his breath, stuffed his hands into his pockets and started off toward the club. He refused to ponder the events of the last half hour. If he did, he'd get his personal effects, go to his car, and walk away for good. That was the last thing he wanted, so he concentrated on getting to the clubhouse.

At the entrance, it surprised him to see Cash McCall lounging outside, smoking a cigarette. Cash, Stretch, and Ophelia stayed mostly to themselves. Knox speculated it was because of their unconventional relationship the three had, with neither being married to Ophelia, but to each other. She was just their girlfriend and mother of their children.

"Cash," Knox rumbled, not in the mood to talk to him. He was one of them and had never been particularly nice to Knox.

Cash blew out a ring of smoke and turned to Knox. "Come with me, Harrington."

His hand on the door handle, Knox glared at Cash. "Fuck off."

Cash's soft laughter chilled Knox. He reminded himself this man had been a sniper in the military and was now the club's explosives technician.

"You can fucking walk or I can fucking do it my way. Your choice."

"My God, you people are all maniacs! Even you, McCall. What happened to your goddamn upbringing?"

"Not that it is any of your fucking concern, but my father

happened. He couldn't keep his cock in his pants. Now, are you coming or...?"

"Fine!" Knox snapped. "I don't feel like getting bruised and battered again."

"Does that mean you've learned your lesson and will stop challenging Outlaw?"

"Someone needs to challenge him," Knox complained, and thought of a tall, muscled brown skinned man with dreadlocks. "And Mortician, for that matter."

Instead of answering, Cash started toward a bike a couple of spots down from where they stood.

Knox stomped behind Cash as the biker mounted and started his Harley. "Hop on."

"Where?"

Cash grinned. "Bitch seat. Tonight, you're my bitch."

He wanted to go to his shitty room and lick his wounds, but the sooner he got this over with, the better. Cursing under his breath, Knox slid on the small second seat and rested his feet on the footrests for each side. He didn't have biker gear, so it worried him how his Italian loafers and expensive trousers would fair.

"I hope I don't regret this," he said to himself, since the idling Harley pipes were loud and obnoxious.

Without warning, Cash started off. At the gate, he stopped to use his preprogrammed card to exit. Outlaw once explained that if motherfuckers somehow got on the property without the proper credentials, they wouldn't be as lucky leaving since authorization was needed to exit too.

That just proved how fucking stupid Outlaw was. If someone took the trouble of sneaking onto club grounds, they'd probably have an escape route all planned out.

A block away from the dead-end street, at the stop sign, Cash paused his Harley. No vehicles came in either direction on this main thoroughfare, so it annoyed Knox that Cash remained at the intersection for five minutes before finally taking off by turning right at Mach 1.

Knox's boiling anger didn't allow him to be afraid at Cash's high rate of speed. Had he still been on the police force, this was exactly the asshole that Knox would've ticketed. He was endangering himself and any hapless soul who might've been out.

Knox had only worn a suit jacket, so the cold night cut into him. When Cash turned off from the main street onto a back road, noticeable if one knew where to look and covered by canopies of trees, the darkness swallowed them up and the temperature plummeted by another few degrees.

Although it galled Knox to admit it, Cash handled the bike with expert ease, not deterred by the bumpiness in some places, or the pitch black, or the howls and cries of night roamers. The zig-zagging and twists and turns confused Knox so much that, by the time they reached a gate similar to the one at the club's entrance, he was thoroughly lost.

Once again, Cash halted longer than Knox liked. He was sure wolves and bears and *creatures* roamed this forest. Not to mention animals of the human variety. Why had he ever agreed to go with Cash? What the fuck had he been thinking?

He'd been lost in his hurt and anger, but this would stop. Either Roxanne stood up to Mortician or Knox would. They were grown! Mortician couldn't keep watch over them. He couldn't keep them separated.

Unless this was Roxanne's idea and she was hiding behind the excuse of Mortician's stupidity. In turn, it led to Knox's stupidity. He could be in the clubhouse room he'd been exiled to. But, no. He was *here*. Wherever that happened to be.

The gate slid open and Cash started off again. They rode along for five or ten minutes more—time was becoming harder to define— before Cash pulled alongside a stream. Once he parked and they were both on their feet, Cash nodded to the darkness ahead.

"Walk."

"Fuck you. I demand you take me back to the club."

"As much as I'd like to oblige you, I can't. Meggie asked for my assistance." Cash nodded again. "Walk, motherfucker, and don't stop until I tell you to."

"Megan?" Knox asked in outrage. "What the fuck does she want? Fuck her."

Cash sighed. "In the interest of time, I won't take issue with your language. However, *in the interest of time*, get the fuck to walking. Knocking you the fuck out and dragging you there would defeat the entire fucking purpose and I'd much prefer to be home with Stretch, Fee, and our kids."

"Fine, McCall. As long as you know I intend to chew Megan a new asshole for her treatment of me."

"I'll be sure to count your graves, so I'll have enough markers for each piece of you."

Knox glared at Cash.

"Walk," the man said, giving no indication he'd seen Knox's look.

Of course he hadn't. Knox couldn't see his own hand in the pitch-black surroundings.

Arguing served no purpose with none of these assholes. Even if he had protested, Cash would make light of or ignore Knox's words altogether. Aware of Cash close behind him, Knox started off. With each step he took, he damned Megan Caldwell to everlasting hell. The soggy ground ruined his shoes and trousers. Expensive clothing wasted on stupidity.

"If this is some rite of passage, fuck all of you. I'm in excellent shape. I'm not going to fail at your dumb fucking games."

"Don't expect you to," Cash responded. "Don't give a fuck if you did."

Knox scowled into the darkness, but said nothing more. A chill set into him. The cold air chapped his face, hands, and neck. They wanted to exploit his weaknesses, so he kept his misery to himself.

Those animal sounds, though...Christ. Haunting and frightening, the noises echoed all around them.

After an eternity, reflections from outside lamps cast shadows upon the club grounds. As they drew closer to the entrance, the light grew brighter, allowing Knox to see the back façade of Johnnie and Kendall's house in all its pale stucco splendor.

Knox halted.

"Asshole!" Cash complained, crashing into Knox at his unexpected pause.

"What are we doing here?" Knox demanded, suspicious.

"To bring you to your execution," Cash retorted with unnecessary sarcasm.

"I'm shaking in my loafers," Knox sneered.

Unless it was true...?

According to Johnnie, the cave had been used in the past to hide guns, drugs, and money. Megan had even given birth in it. It wouldn't be a stretch that they'd use it to sacrifice a poor innocent soul.

"That's not fucking funny."

Smirking, Cash pulled out his cell phone, typed a message, then pressed send. He waited a minute before the ding came.

Realization dawned. "You've been texting someone?"

"Stretch," Cash said on a grunt. A moment later, he was pressing something against Knox's chest. "You have one fucking hour. Probably less than that because this shit took longer than expected."

Knox ignored whatever Cash was trying to hand him. "One hour for what?"

"You're a stupid motherfucker, you know that?" Cash snapped in disgust. "It hasn't dawned on you why all of this subterfuge is necessary?"

"Because Megan doesn't want Outlaw to know she's meeting me?"

"Jesus Christ." Cash snorted. "Take this fucking money and walk until you get to Roxanne's. The guards Mort has stationed there are waiting for you. Give them five hundred a piece."

"Roxanne?" Knox echoed with cringe-worthy stupidity. He grabbed the money out of reflex.

Cash shoved him. "Go."

The investigator in him wanted to ask more questions, but, instead, he listened to Cash and continued on toward Mortician's property line, where Roxanne's mother-in-law quarters were located. Once he cleared Johnnie's land, it took another couple of minutes before he came upon the first of Mortician's guards. The man stopped him immediately.

"Knox, you got something for me?"

"Yes," Knox answered as the man held up a flashlight and shined it in Knox's face. He raised the wad of cash, seeing a bundle of hundreds. Knox counted off five and held them out.

The guard grunted, then whistled and stepped aside. Knox went through this routine two additional times until he came to the last guard who stood watch on Roxanne's door.

"If Mort find out, we in a lotta trouble, Knox," the man said. "But Roxy cook us good meals and Meggie always got her door open to our old ladies. When Roxy tell you to go, don't ask no questions. Just go." He held out his hand. "My money please?"

Please? He didn't know these men understood the definition of that word. Knox held the last bit of cash out to him. After taking the money, the guard stepped aside, allowing him entrance to Roxanne's place.

~

CHRISTOPHER

"I can't believe I only discovered this recipe," Megan said to Mort as she poured him another glass of starbursts melted in vanilla vodka.

"Don't drink all that, Mort," Val complained, holding out his glass for Megan to pour him more.

"Meggie, all this garlic going to make my ass sing all night," Digger called, adding more deep-fried jalapenos stuffed with cream cheese, shrimp and garlic, onto his plate. "My ass will really be singing, too. Trumpeting. Farts for fucking days. I could probably compose an entire symphony piece."

Bunny wrinkled her nose, but smiled at her nasty ass husband.

"I got to get up early tomorrow," Digger went on. He stuffed food into his mouth until all the jalapenos were gone, then pushed his empty plate aside and stood. "I think we need to start home. Ready, babe?"

After exchanging a panicked look with Megan, Bunny smiled at Digger. "Er, babe, I'm going check on the kids."

Digger frowned. "But—"

"I'll be back soon," Bunny interrupted.

"Damn, girl," Digger said as Bunny hurried the fuck away, "your ass just got back from checking the little motherfuckers. Blame Meggie if my farts nauseate you."

Bunny's laughter trailed behind her but she didn't stop. Frowning, Digger sat back down.

"Wait until you try my next snack, Digger." Megan smiled at Mort. "I have another drink for you to try as well, Mortician."

"Meggie, thanks, girl, but I need to get going." Mort stood. "Something not right. Bailey didn't even come here. She hasn't called or anything."

Megan opened her mouth to speak, then closed it.

Her panic and disappointment nearly killed Christopher, so he decided to step in. She was such a fucking novice at scheming.

"We need to fuckin' talk business, Mort. All you motherfuckers meet me in my cave."

"Tonight, Outlaw?" Val said with disappointment.

"Ain't I just fuckin' say that?" Christopher snapped. "Yo, John Boy, see to it these motherfuckers stay fuckin' put 'til after I talk to Megan."

Johnnie nodded. Once the guys cleared out, Christopher leaned against the island and grabbed the almost empty bottle of vanilla vodka and starbursts, swirling the contents.

He stared at Megan. She glowered. He grinned and winked at her.

"Only fuckin' reason I ain't cluein' Mort the fuck in is cuz I'm so fuckin' proud of you. You learnin' so fuckin' good."

Megan pursed her pretty lips. "What are you talking about?"

"You plannin' a sneak fuckin' attack with Roxanne and the rest of the girls."

Megan drew her brows together.

"Ain't no use fuckin' denyin' it, baby. Some fuckin' kinda way you helpin' Roxanne get Harrington to her."

She flushed, but didn't answer.

Draining the bottle, he set it down and walked around to her side of the island, drawing her into his arms. He kissed the top of her head and she melted against him.

"Lemme see, since mosta the motherfuckers here, except Cash and Stretch, my guess is them motherfuckers helpin'."

Silence.

"My guess is Roxanne ain't knew of the plan 'til some fuckin' time tonight cuz she wouldna volunteered her fuckin' place, yeah?"

She nodded.

Nosing her golden hair, he threaded his fingers through the silken strands, then took her face between his hands and kissed her lips.

"First, baby? When you fuckin' schemin' you gotta take all type of shit into account. Second, Knox the wrong motherfucker to try to help the fuck out. He ain't gonna fuckin' appreciate it *and* he gonna lose valuable fuckin' time bein' a fuckin' dumb ass. My bet instead of fuckin' askin' what the fuck goin' on, he gonna be objectionin' cuz he think he better than us."

"I know Mortician has his reasons, Christopher, but Roxy misses Knox."

He kissed her again. Her lips were just too fucking inviting to resist. "I'm sure she do, but, baby, she probably feel Mort right in some ways. Other-fuckin-wise, she woulda been tellin' him to fuck himself."

"Perhaps," Megan said quietly. "Especially after Knox said all that about money. We almost changed our minds and called the whole thing off."

Instead of answering, he bent and covered her mouth with his. She opened so sweetly for him, meeting his tongue with her own and standing on her tiptoes. Lifting her into his arms, he set her on the counter. She wrapped her legs around his waist and she deepened the kiss.

"I wanna fuck you," he rasped, his hard cock threatening to burst his zipper.

"I want you to fuck me," she breathed.

He laughed against her mouth, then forced himself to pull his lips away. "The idea for Roxanne to get some dick, baby. You gettin' mine in a lil while."

She stretched and thrust her tits out, tempting him with her hard nipples. "I want to ride you tonight."

"After I fuck you hard, Megan," he told her on a groan. "Right now, baby, I gotta go keep these motherfuckers here." He licked the shell of her ear and she rewarded him with a little tremble.

"A couple of hours," she said on a moan. "Enough time to get Knox to Roxy and then get him back to the club."

He thumbed her nipples, kissed her once more, then stepped away from her. "Okay, baby."

She licked her swollen lips. Passion darkened her blue eyes and flushed her face. "I'm going to make sandwiches."

"Don't fuckin' bother, baby. Re-fuckin-lax 'til I get the fuck upstairs. Ima talk to these motherfuckers."

"Okay," she said, trusting him to handle everything.

Hopping off the counter, she sashayed to the refrigerator. The swing of her hips made Christopher's dick hurt he wanted inside of her so bad.

She hit a panel on the door and pulled up an automated grocery list, one she'd programmed into her new state-of-the-art appliance, and he forced himself to focus on this moment.

For some fucking reason, Megan had decided she wanted to redo a few rooms in the house.

"How your new shit workin'?"

Her face lit up. "OMG, I can't wait to show you all the refrigerator panel does with just the touch of a few buttons."

Christopher smiled at her.

She rushed to him, grabbed his neck, and pulled him to her, so she could kiss him again. "The bigger range top and built-in ovens allow me to cook so much more at once," she said after she broke away. "And then the dishwasher...do you know it has a separate drawer for utensils? It's no longer just a little basket. The convection microwave is fabulous, too! I started thinking that, with all the new appliances, I really should remodel the rest of the kitchen. New cabinets, sink, flooring, and paint. What do you think?"

"Aintcha doin' it ass backwards. If you wanted to redo the whole fuckin' kitchen, you shoulda waited to buy the appliances."

Her look thoughtful, she nodded. "You're right. Besides, this is our hub and it would be out of commission for at least a week."

Disappointment shone in her eyes.

"I was thinkin', maybe, we need to take the kids to see Mickey fuckin' Mouse, since CJ love that lil rat so much."

"Mickey's a mouse. You know? Mickey *Mouse*."

"Still a fuckin' rodent."

"Mice are cute. Rats aren't. Can you imagine Robert Rat instead of Mickey Mouse? Rats carry all types of diseases. Mice are kept as pets."

"Scientists fuck rats the fuck up all the fuckin' time for experiments. Without them motherfuckers, ain't no tellin' where we'd be in the medical field. And motherfuckers keep rats as pets. None of this shit the point. We get a fuckin' family vacation together. While we gone, motherfuckers come in and redo the kitchen. Problem fuckin' solved about it not bein' usable for us."

"Omigod, really?" she squealed, the adoration that made him fucking fly dropping into her gaze.

"Yeah, baby, really."

"Deal," she agreed. The announcement added a spark to her already energetic self.

He started to turn away.

"Christopher?" she called, stopping him.

"Yeah, baby?"

"I love you so much. You are my everything."

"I love you, too, Megan," he responded. "You my reason for livin', baby."

She gave him her look of love—the one that said everything. *Meant* everything and told him all he needed to know.

Smiling softly, she blew him a kiss, then walked away, leaving Christopher alone and thankful that she belonged to him.

CHAPTER ELEVEN

Knox

The house smelled of cinnamon, vanilla, and apples, spicy and warm just like Roxanne. No evidence of their earlier dinner party remained. The chill that had invaded him on the harrowing journey heated immediately. Soft lamplight bathed the living room. The sound of smooth jazz flowed down the staircase, where, at the bottom, red rose petals left a trail that went up. Smiling, Knox followed the petals, noting the small candles situated on every other step. As he reached the landing, the sound of the music grew louder.

Even before he stepped into the room he shared with Roxanne, he had removed his jacket. He threw it on the empty bed, started unbuttoning his shirt, and glanced in the direction of the bathroom. From beyond the door, gentle splashes, the evocative scent of her bubble bath, captivated him.

He heard the water, smelled her bubble bath. Shirtless, he went to the bathroom and halted in the doorway, mesmerized as she raised her leg and stroked from her knee up to her thigh. Suds dripped from her beautiful skin.

She smiled at him, lowered her leg. Tendrils escaped her pinned-up hair and plastered to her neck and forehead.

His gaze dropped to her brown nipples and he licked his lips.

"Are you going to join me, Knox?"

Join her. Yes. It wasn't often they bathed together. Knox found it extremely uncomfortable in the standard-sized bathtub, but he wouldn't deny her, especially since he was so grimy and sweaty.

Fixating his gaze on her, he stripped. The hungry stare she gave his hard cock pulled a smile from him. Proud of his mighty package, he strolled forward.

"Scoot up," he instructed.

She did, slow and methodical, her every move temptation. Sin. Need. From the sensuous glide and small moan that suggested she'd teased her clit, to her searing look, and the way she cocked her head to the side to reveal the tenderness of her damp neck.

Knox slid in behind her and she leaned back, settling her soft body against his. She ignored the water sloshing on the floor, so he did too, and instead, wrapped his arms around her. She stroked his knee, and he forgot the discomfort he had because he was unable to extend his legs completely.

"I've missed you," he told her.

"I've missed you too, Knox."

He skimmed his hand along her breast, then tweaked her nipple. Some feeling had returned since her mastectomy and breast reconstruction. But he didn't linger.

"You went through a lot of trouble," he told her, caressing her belly as he slid his hand lower.

"I just found out about it tonight," she admitted.

He fingered the top of her mound, before finding her clit.

"Knox," she whispered, her little cry setting his entire body on fire.

"What do you mean you just found out about it tonight?" he demanded, between raining kisses on her sweet neck.

She shivered. "They were not sure they'd have anyone to help pull this off."

He inserted two fingers into her, intoxicated and surprised by her dewiness, and continued to thumb her clit. She jerked up. He wanted to know what she meant, but more than anything he wanted to make her come. Forgetting the conversation for now, he roared to his feet, stooped and lifted her into his arms, then sloshed to the bedroom and laid her on the bed.

She laughed, a full, throaty sound that elicited a chuckle from him. Masculine satisfaction filled him. He positioned her knees on her chest, exposing her pussy to him. Keeping a tight hold on her ankles, he speared his tongue inside of her, darting in and out of her, encouraged by her moans.

Intoxicated by her scent and her taste, he licked her seam, found her clit, and released her ankles with reluctance. Using his fingers to open her delicate pussy lips, he laved back and forth. Her groans grew louder. Gripping his hair, she grinded against his mouth. He hastened the speed of his tongue, increasing the pressure against her clit.

"Let's come together, baby," she breathed, as if that was the last thing she wanted to do.

He blew on her clit, stole another lick. "No—"

But she was already scooting up, moving to the side to make room for him. He laid next to her and pulled her into his arms, thrusting his tongue into her mouth, sweeping against hers.

"Knox," she whispered.

He tangled his fingers through her hair. "I'm here, Roxanne. I love you. I'm so glad to have you as mine. To feel you in my arms again."

"I love you too, Knox. I can't wait until I'm your wife."

She kissed him sweetly, this private, vulnerable side of her in direct contrast to the tough woman she presented to the world. Not that she wasn't a firecracker when they were alone. In bed, though, where their souls were laid bare and their bodies exposed, she opened herself to him and gave to him. The intimacy he found in her arms extended beyond the physical.

He met her gaze and her light brown depths consumed him, threatened to overwhelm him. She offered him a little cat's smile, the kind that drove him insane.

Kissing him again, she sat up and straddled his thighs, bent and began planting kisses on his chest. She twirled her tongue around his nipple, trailed her lips to his heart, his side, his hip. His nerve endings blazed, set his blood on fire. Overcome with sensation, he shivered.

Her mouth teased his manscape, semi-circled around his cock and licked his balls. She fisted his dick head, stroked along the length, and gently suckled his nut sac.

Finally, she slurped his cock into her warm mouth. He released a strangled groan. As she sucked his dick, she wrapped her hand around the inches that couldn't fit into her mouth and squeezed, massaged, jerked.

Suddenly, her mouth and hand left him. Climbing on top of him, she took him inside of her, inch-by-inch, shivering, meowling, and frustrating him. Unable to bear any more, he grabbed her luscious ass and thrusted up, burying himself to the hilt.

As much as he wanted to turn her onto her back and drive into her, he didn't. He let her ride him and set the pace, loving the sight of her bouncing breasts and the sheer ecstasy on her face.

When she lost all reason, all sense, screamed his name, he embraced her, then flipped them over, still connected to her. Usually, he'd kiss her, absorb her cries. Tonight, though, he pounded into her, reveled in the sound of her voice.

One last time, he pumped into her, and cum gushed out, taking his breath and making his head spin. For long moments afterwards, they lay silent. She stroked along the valley of his spine. Goosebumps rose on his flesh and he trembled.

After a moment, she drew in a shuddering breath.

He turned onto his back. The sheets, wet from their bathwater, felt cold and uncomfortable underneath his hot skin. He grinned. "The bed has to be changed."

"Hmm," she said drowsily. "And the floor mopped."

Drawing her into his arms, he kissed her forehead. "Why don't you go downstairs, while I tidy things up?"

Her lashes fluttered and her eyes popped open. "Fuck! What time is it? How long have you been here?"

Leaning over, he flipped on the lamp, to better see her. The light that had been flooding into the room from the bathroom was adequate but not good enough.

"Does it matter?" He sat up and swung his legs over the side of the bed. "This ridiculous edict Mortician has in place has to end."

She sighed, then sat next to him and snuggled close. Tempering his annoyance, Knox wrapped an arm around her.

"The boy is only looking out for me, Knox," she told him. "Let him do this. Cooperate to show that you understand the club dynamics. The *group* dynamics."

"I don't give a fuck about the club dynamics, Roxanne," he snapped. "I'm not one of them and hope to never be. I don't have a tattoo. I don't ride a bike. I'm not ignorant!"

She jerked away from him and jumped to her feet. Hands on hips, she turned and glared at him. It didn't seem to matter to her that she was nude. Her breasts were round and firm, thanks to her surgery. Her waist curved in, then flared out into hips and ass that was all the current rage. He reached for her, but she knocked his hand away.

"That's so unworthy of you. Those boys aren't ignorant. Besides, what the fuck is wrong with a tattoo? Or a motorcycle? I happen to like those things too."

He narrowed his eyes at her. "Really? That means you intend to get inked and ride the wind?"

"No, Knox. Would it bother you if I did?"

He didn't want to answer that, not even silently, afraid of what he'd say. Instead, he changed the subject and went back to the topic they'd been discussing before they made love. "What do you mean you didn't know about this until tonight? This should've been your idea," he grouched.

"Don't think I don't know what the fuck you're doing, mother-fucker. By not responding to me and pulling a dirty, lowdown trick of changing the subject, you've actually answered me loud and clear. In the interest of time, I'm going to let that sneaky shit slide, Knox. To answer your question, this was my baby's idea. She went to Meggie and together, they got the others involved. They didn't want me to get my hopes up that we could thwart Mortician and Outlaw so we could spend time together. Once they decided it was doable, they told me. That's when I stood up and said how tired I was."

He stormed to his feet. "Right, and it took your daughter and Megan Caldwell to arrange this? You're the one going along with Mortician and you didn't have the courtesy to want to see me."

She raised a finger, then pointed it at him. "Look, motherfucker, I don't remember you coming up with one motherfucking scheme for us to get together." With each word, her finger wiggled and twisted, punctuating her anger. "Don't stand there and play the fucking victim. You already set yourself above almost every motherfucker in this motherfucker, except maybe Johnnie because you think he's on your level. I'm trying to get the boys to accept you. Instead of bitching and complaining and accusing *me* of not thinking about your ass, you should be taking this time to get to really know Mortician and the others. You should be thanking him for wanting to protect me."

"You're a grown fucking woman, Roxanne," he bit out. "What do you need protection from? Certainly not me!"

She made a face at him.

"You're fucking kidding me? I deserve your trust and devotion!"

"You have it, Knox." She heaved in a breath. "I want to get this right, though. I want to be with you until my dying day. But I don't have the best track record with marriage. You and me, we come from two different worlds in so many ways, sugar. For months, we've lived in our own little isolated paradise, not allowing much outside influence to touch us. You're everything to me. Our marriage is important to me. Still, there's something there. Something between us, and I know it's the way you feel about my family."

"The only family you have here is Bailey, Roxanne."

Her look turned disapproving. "I also have grandbabies, in case you've forgotten," she said with so much hostility Knox took a step back. "And Mortician is my son-in-law. Kendall is like a daughter to me. Outlaw—"

"Don't bring Kendall into this." The same guilt he'd felt since he started working with Outlaw to get rid of that redheaded bitch surfaced in him.

"Kendall is my family, too," Roxanne said patiently, like he didn't have a smidgeon of sense. "Outlaw is like a son to me."

"A son who gave you a fucking *purple* truck. A very high-end one at that. His criminal behavior allowed him to buy that. Besides, he's almost as old as you. Brother material. *Lover* material, but definitely not qualified to be your son."

She growled. Actually growled! "You're working on my last ever loving, motherfucking nerve," she spat, her eyes hardening. "Let me put it to you this way, I see them all as my family. I expect you to at least *try* to fit in with them. Didn't you tell me to put your mother on my wedding committee? Why can't you just go along with Mortician for now?"

"Because I don't appreciate his interference. Furthermore, I don't fucking like to think you're consenting to this because of *something between us*. What does that even mean? You think I'm not going to go through with the marriage?"

"This just feels too good to be true, Knox. A dream. A fairytale." She shrugged. "I don't want to lose you. Think about how much more special our wedding will be if we haven't been living together and—"

He stiffened. "If that's the case, why did I move in with you?"

"I never expected you to propose to me," she admitted softly.

When he'd moved in with her, he hadn't intended to propose to her. He loved her and wanted to spend the rest of his life with her. Marriage, though, meant legalities. And he had so much at stake if their union was to crumble. Still, he'd become increasingly annoyed at how the bikers gazed at her and interacted with her. They were always respectful—she gave them no choice—still Knox knew lust when he saw it. Roxanne was his, and he wanted the world to know it.

Of course, the pressure Mortician had put on him also precipitated the matter, but that wasn't important.

"We can think of our little rendezvous as adventures," she went on, twisting her engagement ring and giving it a quick glance.

"What?" he asked suspiciously, not liking the look he'd glimpsed.

"What do you mean *what*?"

"You don't like the ring? It's a Harrington heirloom."

"The ring is beautiful."

"But...?" He heard the word in her tone.

"It's just silly old superstition. There's a very defined culet on the ring."

It was rare that he didn't know the meaning of a word, but this was one of those times. "What the hell is a culet?"

She slid the ring off her finger and his stomach sank. It was the worst feeling in the world. As long as she wore it, she was his.

"Put that back on."

She smiled at him and came closer, then turned the ring over and pointed to the spot under her diamond. "Do you see that little point? It's a culet. They are hallmarks of this type of antique cushion ring. It's an heirloom," she acknowledged. "Most of the rings in the late 1800s, early 1900s had this, whereas the majority of modern rings don't have this sharp point."

Her explanation lost him. "And?"

"Well, there's a superstition that says evil spirits can enter through the culet and put a curse on the wearer."

His mouth dropped open. "You can't be serious."

She nodded. "There's another one that says if the engagement ring is secondhand then however the previous owner's marriage went, so it would go for the current owner."

"Are you fucking kidding me?" He shook his head in disbelief. "You can't believe that nonsense. You're the most pragmatic woman I've ever met. This isn't you talking."

By the look on her face, he knew she *did* buy into that ridiculousness. He blew out an annoyed breathed, torn between frustration and his need to reassure her.

"My great-great grandparents, my great-grandparents, my grandparents, my *parents* had and have very happy unions, thank you very much."

She shoved the ring back onto her finger. "But *you* didn't. As far as I know, your ex-wife is the last owner of it."

"Callie wanted her own ring. She didn't value the Harrington history. Before I met you, I intended to pass it on to Grant."

"Of course, you'll be able to give it to your son when he's old enough to marry. It should stay in your family where it belongs. I'm honored to wear it. My feelings just go back to the fear that my dream of being your wife will turn into a nightmare."

Before he responded, her cellphone started ringing. He knew from the tone it was Bailey calling. Like the rest of them, Roxanne had special tones for everyone.

"I guess time's up for us," she sighed.

"Hey, sugar," she answered. The keen disappointment, so clear on her face, appeased Knox. Pausing, she listened then laughed and went silent again, nodding although her daughter couldn't see her. Roxanne was so expressive. "Okay, I'll send him down," she said after another moment.

Huffing out an annoyed breath, Knox stomped to the closet and found a pair of jeans and a thermal shirt. Instead of ruining another pair of shoes, he grabbed old running shoes. After snatching a pair of socks from the drawer, he pulled on his jeans than sat on the edge of the bed.

"You're kilting it, hmmm?" she asked as he pulled the first sock on.

"Kilting it?" He glanced over his shoulder and took his fill of her still-nude body. The incision on her stomach went from hip-to-hip. He tried not to focus on it too much, tried not to imagine the pain she must've been in when she'd had the surgery to remove fat from her stomach to reconstruct her breasts after her mastectomy. She was so brave. Such a fighter.

"What do you mean by kilting it?" he asked, realizing his mind had strayed.

"No underwear."

He finished putting on his socks and running shoes, and stood. "Ah," he responded. "Didn't see the need, sweetheart. I'm just returning to the club and going to my lonely bed. You know the one? It's missing my beautiful queen."

She smiled at him and stepped into his arms. "You have a silver tongue, sir."

He brushed his lips across hers. "I'd say it was golden."

"I'd have to agree with you." Wrapping her arms around his neck, she welcomed his kiss. "You have to leave," she said breathlessly a few moments later.

He nodded and sighed. Going to where his trousers lay ruined in one of the bathroom floor puddles, he got his wallet and stuffed it in the back pocket of his jeans.

"I wish you'd consent to allow me to hire a maid for you."

"I don't need a maid, Knox," she said firmly.

"When we're married and move into our own house, you will. It'll be too big for you to keep up by yourself."

"What do I need a mansion for? I've already lived in one and I didn't enjoy it after a while."

That's right. Duke's father was "wealthy". Knox bet he couldn't touch the Harrington wealth.

"Besides, I was hoping we could live here."

He looked around the room in an exaggerated manner. "You're joking, right?"

"Not *here* in this place. *Here* on the grounds."

"Oh. Well, I have no problem with that."

She beamed a smile.

"It's the least I can do for you. You didn't push me to buy an expensive engagement ring, just because I can afford it. You don't hassle me for money. Or to go shopping. You're a truly independent woman, earning her way in life by helping her daughter out."

Her smile slipped away. "We've been through this before. You have access to my bank accounts—"

"You have access to mine, too," he cut in. "It doesn't matter, baby. Most of the money from your divorce settlements are tied up in retirement accounts. The property you own in New Orleans just brings you several thousand dollars a month. Let's be real, your money can't compare to mine. It would be easy to assume my money was what attracted you to me."

"Fuck you," she snarled. "Take your fucking money and shove it the fuck up your dick. It doesn't matter if my fucking money compares to yours. It's my fucking money and is enough to sustain me. Stop being such an uppity, dumb motherfucker, Knox. Money don't make a man. What's in your heart and soul does. Right now? Plain fucking bullshit is in both places."

"If my money makes you so uncomfortable, you have the problem, not me. The things you want me to have? A tattoo and a bike? That will never happen, unless I'm fucking desperate. Arrogant I may be, but desperate? Never!"

"What the fuck does a fucking tattoo and motorcycle have to do with the fact that you need to shove your fucking money up your goddamn ass?"

"You said you like tattoos and bikes. I don't have either of those, but at least I have money. You'll live in luxury."

"I don't give a fuck if you ever get a tattoo. I know a bike is out of the question because you'd have to learn to ride and that's not your thing. When I want to go for a spin, Mort, Digger, or even Outlaw will be happy to take me."

Any of the other bikers she knew would, too. Knox really, really didn't like that, but he'd put his foot in his mouth enough, so he stayed quiet. And he'd definitely not bring up the prenuptial agreement at this particular time.

"Lawd, you think having money is the fucking end all, be all. Well, it's not. You're just a man," she said flatly. "A man who can work my last fucking nerve, but one I love with all my heart. I don't give a fuck if you have money, a tattoo, or a motorcycle. As long as you have a fucking J-O-B, I'm good."

"I don't have a job," he corrected, wondering why she spelled it out. "I have a career."

"What the fuck ever it is, you've made your own way in the world. You don't sit around all day, doing nothing."

He nodded, then went to her and pulled her back into his arms. "We never argue. Why are we doing so now especially over trivialities?"

"Frustration," she answered, hugging his waist and resting her head on his shoulder.

"Roxanne—"

Footsteps pounding up the staircase interrupted him. Immediately, he pushed Roxanne behind him and faced the open door.

"I have no wish to see your naked ass, Harrington," Cash called, "but if you don't fucking get the fuck out of here in the next minute or two, all our sneaking will be for nothing. Meggie texted me and said the guys already said they're leaving in half an hour. That means, there's a greater chance Outlaw or Johnnie or Mort will see Stretch's momentary scrambling of the outside feeds. In which case, you're fucked and so am I."

"He's coming, Cash," Roxanne called.

"I really wish I was," Knox told her.

She laughed and thumped his back. "Dirty dog."

He turned and kissed her again. "Sweet kitten."

"Uh, dead dog and crying kitten if you don't move your ass," Cash retorted as if he was part of the conversation.

"Stop being such a nosy motherfucker, Cash," Roxanne told him.

"I'm sorry for being such a jerk, sweetheart," Knox said. "Forgive me."

She caressed his lips. "Always, sugar."

Forcing himself to pull away from her, Knox stopped at the door, awed all over again by her nudity and her beauty. He blew her a kiss and the smile she gave him lit her entire face.

Suddenly, he was yanked by the back of his shirt and dragged away.

"McCall," he growled. "I wasn't fucking finished."

"Yes, the fuck you were," Cash insisted, hauling him down the stairs so fast Knox nearly lost his balance.

Outside, they trekked the same way Knox had come earlier, passing the same four guards, who turned their backs and pretended they hadn't seen them. Cash set a grueling pace to his bike. When they finally reached it, Knox didn't ask questions. He took the bitch seat with the same urgency Cash jumped on.

Even if Knox had been inclined to complain about the brambles and branches they hadn't gone through the first time, he doubted Cash would've heard. If he did, then he wouldn't have cared. Besides, he'd spent time with Roxanne, had her in his arms, so that was worth all the scratches, nicks, and bumps he received on the wild ride.

When they reached the main road, Cash turned his bike on a dime, so sharp Knox knew they'd crash. They didn't, making it to the dead-end street where the club was located, in one piece. Cash halted in the middle of the deserted road, not speaking, allowing his bike to idle. A few minutes later, he started off again. At the gate, it slid open almost as soon as they reached it.

Cash rode to his spot and killed the ignition. "Come on," he instructed as they dismounted.

"Where are we going now?"

"To fucking fantasy world," Cash said, rushing ahead. "Where does it look like we're going?"

"The club."

"Give that motherfucker a silver dollar."

Cash paused long enough to glare at Knox. Opening the club door, he allowed Knox to precede him inside. Though after two in the morning, a few bikers remained in the club. Heavy breathing drew Knox's attention to the pool tables. One of the brothers was fucking a girl. She was completely naked, not caring that the man had merely pulled his cock out through his fly since his pants were still up.

Knox walked on. At the bar, another girl was on her knees sucking Potter's dick. He'd never been in the club at this hour without Roxanne and the rest of them. The hypersexual atmosphere disgusted him.

"Knox," Johnnie called over the fuck-sounds, and laughter, and Harley pipes rumbling from outside.

Keeping his eyes forward, Knox went to Johnnie's table where Cash had sat.

Johnnie poured a glass of Scotch for Knox and kicked out the chair for him to sit. "I think it's nice that you spent a little time getting to know Cash, Stretch, and Fee."

Knox looked over his shoulder and nodded toward the indiscriminate sex happening. "This doesn't bother you?"

Johnnie and Cash exchanged confused glances.

"Do you see something that should?" Johnnie asked. "Is a girl being mistreated?"

"They're engaged in public sex. Doesn't that count?"

"Are any of them being forced?" Johnnie persisted.

Knox looked behind him again, then turned to Johnnie and shook his head. "No."

"Then what they're doing is none of our business," Johnnie decided.

Knox searched Cash's face and then refocused on Johnnie. He'd heard about the wild parties, the orgies, the Bobs, those special women who'd gotten their names because of dick-sucking skills. He'd probably even glimpsed this behavior before, once or twice. It was different now. He *lived* on the premises.

"I'm going to my room," he said and walked away.

In the privacy of his room, he leaned against the door. Only for Roxanne would he live in a place like this, surrounded by seamy thugs and illicit activities. Once he was undressed and in bed, though, he decided he'd allow this to go on for another week or so. He missed Roxanne and wanted to be with her.

As he closed his eyes, he didn't think of her. Cash had given him a cover story about spending the evening at his house. He'd have to thank the man the next time he saw him.

CHAPTER TWELVE

Megan

Darkness surrounded Meggie. Underneath her, cold concrete froze her naked body. She twisted, the chains imprisoning her clanking with her movements. Her determination to live, survive, seeped away like sand through an hourglass. She shivered, losing the hope she'd tried to maintain. Her strength deserted her, even as she fought the darkness threatening to claim her. Her children needed her.

Her husband needed her.

She wanted to live. Raise CJ, Rebel, Rule, Ryder, and Ransom to adulthood. Grow old with Christopher.

A deep chill spread through her, stealing her breath. She gasped. The beat of her heart sped up, then slowed down. A sob escaped her as she gave into the inevitable. She drew in one last breath, but death robbed her midway. The frantic pounding of her pulse rose in her ears, then all went silent.

Even as her brain shut down, deprived of much needed oxygen, Meggie resisted. She didn't want to die.

Someone was screaming...

"Megan, baby, wake the fuck up. You dreamin'."

"Christopher," Meggie sobbed. "I want to live. Please don't let me die."

"Shhhh. I'm here, Megan. I got you."

Her husband's scent surrounded her. Spice. Man. A hint of smoke and vestiges of alcohol.

Safety.

Shuddering, Meggie opened her eyes. Christopher's arms wrapped her up. One of his hands cradled the back of her head. Tears streaming down her face, she clung to her husband and wept, angry, afraid, and ashamed. Nightmares plagued her like demons. Once in the midst of one, it gripped Meggie in its dark clutches.

"Wanna talk about it?" Christopher asked.

His subdued tone made her cry harder. "You shouldn't have disturbed your sleep, Christopher."

"Baby, you was screamin' like a motherfucker. Woulda had to be fuckin' grounded for my ass *not* to wake the fuck up."

"I'm sorry. I didn't mean to wake you."

He released her, lifted himself up and braced on his forearm to look at her. His look tender, he thumbed away tears from her cheeks. "If you ain't sleepin', I ain't sleepin'. That shit simple, so don't fuckin' apologize. We in this shit together."

She nodded, grateful to be alive, thankful for the beautiful man who was her husband.

"Neither of us motherfuckers ain't understandin' that you fine. You alive. I just keep dreamin' I get to you too fuckin' late and you keep fuckin' dreamin' almost the same shit."

"I don't understand what's going on. Things have happened to me before."

"Yeah, baby. I guess you just fuckin' outta practice. Shit been goin' fuckin' good, so ain't no motherfuckers been tryna fuck you up."

"I'm out of practice to be harmed?" she asked, to be sure she'd heard him right.

"Fuck, yeah. My ass outta practice for havin' you fucked up."

"That sounds a little—"

"Fuckin' psycho?"

She giggled. "I wasn't going to say that."

He grinned at her. "Ain't nothin' but a thing, baby." Rolling onto her, he nuzzled her nose with his own. "We gonna get through this, Megan," he promised on a rough whisper. "It ain't a good three fuckin' months since we fuckin' found you. Ain't no wonder that we both trauma-fuckin-tized."

"We'd reached such a happy place."

"Life what the fuck we make it. We gonna make it a happy fuckin' place again. We just gotta fuckin' work through you bein' snatched the fuck up in broad fuckin' daylight when we wasn't at war with nobody. That shit right there e-fuckin-nuff to fuck with any-fuckin-body."

Her lips trembled.

"Don't cry," he said, low and sexy, brushing his mouth over hers. "I ain't able to pro-fuckin-tect you from what the fuck goin' on in your fuckin' head, in your fuckin' dreams, but I gotcha back in every-fuckin-thing else."

"I'm so angry with Mystic. And-and afraid." She thumbed his mouth. "And-and ashamed that I'm so affected."

"I shot the fuck outta that motherfucker and my ass still fuckin' furious with Mystic. I wish I coulda brought him the fuck back to fuckin' life and killed him five, ten more fuckin' times. I ain't even able to chop the motherfucker the fuck up cuz of your fuckin' ball."

Caressing his jaw, she gave him a gentle smile. "It's okay. You saved me."

"No, it ain't okay. Motherfucker hurt my fuckin' soul when he snatched you. And, yeah, my ass scared like a motherfucker something else gonna happen to you. More than fuckin' that, Megan, I'm shame, too. You trust me to protect you. You trust me to protect our boy."

"Stop that," she ordered. "You're being too hard on yourself. You—"

He put a finger over her lips. "Ain't sayin' that for you to comfort my ass. You had the motherfuckin' nightmare, not me. I just wanna let you know that my ass angry, afraid, and ashamed, too, and that shit pissin' me the fuck off so fuckin' much."

"We're quite the pair."

"Yeah. Mr. and Mrs. Fuckin' Pussified Motherfuckers."

They met each other's gazes and broke into laughter.

Christopher stole another kiss. "Megan, baby," he croaked. "You my fuckin' world. You the air that keep my breathin'. You my fuckin' everything and I ain't ever gonna get tired of sayin' that to you. If I..." His voice trailed off and he swallowed. "If you woulda been...*gone*..." He paused. "I told my-fuckin-self you woulda fuckin' know how fuckin' much I love you cuz I tell you all the fuckin' time."

"If I would've been, er, *gone*, when you found me, I would've departed having no regrets about my life with you, except that it ended too soon. It is an honor and a privilege to be your wife and the mother of your children. I would've left knowing I am well-loved and knowing I let you know how much I adore you."

They fell silent, staring at one another, drinking in their closeness, their love, and their friendship.

Ever so slowly, Meggie opened her legs, offering her husband a cradle between her thighs.

He turned onto his back, grabbed her hand, and tugged her toward him. "Fuck my mouth."

Her nipples hardened at Christopher's command. Removing her nightgown, she climbed onto him and settled her pussy onto his mouth, the stubble on his face abrading the skin on her inner thighs.

The warm pad of his tongue lapped her inner lips, circling her clit, and thrusting into her opening. She moaned, riding his lips, her juices hot and flowing. Her legs trembled. He worked her pussy with his tongue, lips, and mouth, tasting her, sucking her, and licking her.

"I'm coming," she screamed, out of her mind with ecstasy, unable to contain her loud, breathy moans or the trembles in her body.

His tongue still buried in her, he wrapped an arm around her waist and flipped her onto her back. Meggie stretched her legs open, arching her back and pushing against his face.

"Your pussy delicious," he told her in a thick voice that threatened to make her come again. "Ima keep your cunt in my mouth and devour it."

"Christopher," she groaned, squeezing her nipples almost to the point of pain. "Get my pussy off."

He raised her legs, resting her knees on her shoulders before burying his face against her and sucking her opening, his nose teasing her clit.

"The smell of your pussy the best scent in the world," he growled, sniffing her seam and inhaling like a man lacking oxygen. Using his fingers, he opened her pussy lips, and met her gaze. "Ima lick your cunt til you come. Look at my fuckin' tongue eatin' your pussy up."

She nodded, frantic, lifting her hips to offer her hungry clit to him.

He swirled his tongue around her bud, gentle touches that hinted at what he intended. He abraded her mound by rubbing his hair-roughened cheek against the delicate skin. He tongued her, gently at first, until he finally gave her what he always did. A relentless assault on her clit that made Meggie wild in her movements, her words, and her screams. She exploded over his tongue and he slurped her cream in wet laps. Lost in her orgasm, her body floated to another plateau where nothing but pleasure resided. A place where her flesh burned and her nerve endings crackled.

"You so fuckin' wet." He released her legs and braced himself above her. His green eyes were dark and hooded, smoldering with desire. Sinking into her, he closed his eyes and groaned, withdrawing and then slamming into her again.

"You feel so good," Meggie gasped. "I love having your cock inside of me."

He pumped into her harder, faster. "My cock yours, baby. Put it in you wherever you want."

She loved the power he gave her, while still remaining so firmly of control. He swiveled his hips, grinding against her swollen clit. Clinging to him, Meggie arched, exposing the column of her throat to his probing lips. He rained kisses up, paused to nip her chin, then claimed her mouth, thrusting his tongue between her lips. She tasted the remnants of her orgasm, met his deep thrusts. When he withdrew, she lifted, rotating against him.

"Fuck, Megan. Fuck," he repeated. "I'm about to flood your cunt with my cum."

"Give it to me," she demanded, jerking against him, tremors starting in her center and spreading throughout her body. "I want every last drop," she got out, trembling.

"Look at me," he ordered.

Powerless to deny him anything he wanted, Meggie met his gaze. Passion flushed his face; his labored breathing fanned across her skin. His dazed expression gave way to a curled lip. His body stiffened and his cock jerked inside of her before warmth flooded her insides. She wrapped her arms and legs around him, holding and caressing him through his most vulnerable moment, their souls and hearts laid bare.

He rolled onto his back and pulled her into the crook of his arm, then kissed the top of her head. "Sleep, Megan," he whispered. "I got you. Always and forever."

"I love you," she whispered drowsily, snuggling close to him.

As she drifted off, his words, "I love you more," reached her, and she smiled, thankful, once more, that the Fates had put Christopher in her path.

CHAPTER THIRTEEN

Kendall

"What was your childhood like?"

Dr. Briscow posed her question as she had the others, with calm detachment. She was an older woman, who wore horn-rimmed glasses and a severe bun that pulled at the skin of her temples. Despite her no-nonsense attitude, similar to all Kendall's previous psychiatrists, Dr. Briscow seemed different. Interested. As if what Kendall had to say really mattered.

"To get to the root of your problem, we have to dig deep, Kendall."

Nodding, Kendall rung her hands together. "When my father died, my entire world changed." In low tones, she explained how her mother had lost her mind—literally—and ended up in an insane asylum. Her father had adored her, but she'd figured out early that her mother didn't want her or like her. She'd sought her mother's approval for years, even after her little sister, Caroline, had been born. "When Caro hanged herself, Mother preferred to die, too. She shot herself in the head, sitting a few feet away from me."

The image of the blood streaming from Marie's head replayed in

Kendall's head. She sniffled. After typing a moment, Dr. Briscow handed Kendall a box of tissues.

Dabbing at her eyes, Kendall twist her wedding ring. It—*Johnnie*—was the reason she'd sought a new psychiatrist. She was so afraid, she'd lose her husband, whom she truly loved. She just couldn't seem to stop herself from ruining her life.

"My childhood was lonely," she finished. "Deprived of love. My mother was a very strict disciplinarian, though she withheld her affection."

Dr. Briscow continued typing her notes. "Do you withhold affection from your children?"

Kendall opened her mouth to answer with a definitive *NO!* She couldn't get the word out, though, recalling Rory's little face during the times she'd forced him to sit at the table to finish his meals. That practice had ended because of Johnnie. She'd barred Rory from wearing jeans and demanded he call her and Johnnie by their first names. As if she wanted to disassociate herself from being a parent. She didn't allow any of her children in certain rooms in her house, but it had been her first born, Rory, who had gotten the brunt of her...her *mistreatment*.

"Yes," she answered, shame ringing in her voice. "I-I thought I was raising Rory to be..."

"To be?" Dr. Briscow pushed when Kendall couldn't find the words to continue.

"*Not to be*," Kendall corrected. "Not to be a biker. Not to be like his cousin, CJ, or his uncle, Christopher. I wanted my son—all three of my children—to be better. But it came out as resentment and hostility toward Rory."

"I see." Dr. Briscow tapped on her keyboard. "Have you ever beat your children?"

"I've disciplined Rory when he was bad. I've spanked him."

"And your other children."

"Matilda is a little girl and JJ is too young."

"You've never abused your children or any minor in your care."

Kendall thought of CJ, but quickly pushed the incident with him out of her mind. He hadn't been in her care. Besides, what he needed went beyond disciplining. That boy was out of hand.

"You have to be honest with me about everything," Dr. Briscow chided, as if she knew Kendall withheld information. "You're wasting my time and your own if you don't be completely open with me." She gave Kendall a knowing look.

Shifting in her seat, Kendall nodded. "I understand, Dr. Briscow."

The woman waited a moment longer, but Kendall refused to budge. "I promise I will never lie to you, doctor," she swore. "I want help. I want my life back. My husband. My family."

"I understand," Dr. Briscow said. "I will get to the bottom of your problems. As long as I have your cooperation and honesty, you have my promise."

"Thank you," Kendall responded, determined to pretend she'd never hated a little boy through no fault of his own at first. It was simply due to who his father happened to be. Now, she couldn't stand his lack of manners and his determination to emulate everything Outlaw did.

This wasn't about Outlaw and CJ, though. This was about Johnnie, Rory, Matilda, and JJ, and how meaningless her life felt without them.

Roxy

"My lady."

Roxy smiled at Knox's words as he held open the back door of Bailey's Escalade. This morning, as she'd cleaned up from breakfast, a bouquet of long-stemmed red roses had arrived. A gift from Knox with a dinner invitation on the enclosed card.

For the entire day, she'd went over in her mind how she'd style her hair; if she wanted dramatic makeup or sexpot; whether she'd wear panties or not. In essence, she'd floated on a cloud. She hadn't been momma of four with a son who hated her or glam-ma or club mother.

She hadn't been divorcee or cancer survivor or *anything* but Knox's lady. His fiancée. She'd reveled in that wonderful feeling.

Until thoughts of how Mortician would fuck with her date intruded. A way to beat her son-in-law at his own game inspired her to call Knox.

"Invite Mort and Bailey to join us," she'd suggested.

As expected, Knox had resisted, capitulating when she explained her reasoning.

"Tonight's church. If we fuck with *his* schedule enough, maybe the motherfucker will stop fucking with our fucking."

"I'll handle this, Roxanne. Knowing that man, he'll decline the invitation then tell us we can't go either like we're fucking five-year-olds. I will invite him, but when he declines, I intend to inform him we're going with or without him."

Roxy had grinned. "You do that, sugar. Call me back."

An hour had passed before she heard from Knox again.

"It's all set," he'd said, grim. "We're going on a double date."

Although she knew there was a story there, Roxy decided not to press Knox for an explanation.

Now, as they started off, with Mortician in the driver's seat, Bailey next to him up front, and Roxy cozied up to Knox on the second row, she chuckled when he nuzzled her neck.

"Do you want to make out, sweetheart?" he breathed against her ear.

"Fuck yeah, but not here."

"Knox, son, you too close," Mortician called. "I didn't skip church to watch you pushing all up on Roxanne."

"Lucas, they can't do anything in front of us," Bailey said with exasperation. "They're just snuggling."

"How about I pull this motherfucker over and *we* snuggle, too?"

"How about I knock you the fuck out and leave you on the side of the fucking road, Mortician?" Roxy growled.

Mortician met Roxy's eyes in the rearview mirror. "I didn't have to consent to this date, man."

"Yes, you did," Bailey said on a sniff. "You're taking this way too serious, Lucas. I appreciate how much you want to protect Momma, but this is really getting out of hand."

"It's not," Mortician insisted. "Just trust me, pretty girl."

"I get that you don't like Knox," Bailey went on, not as irritated as before, "but Momma loves him. They're going to marry. This is just ridiculous. You weren't even going to *allow* them to go on a date, for crying out loud."

"Don't remind me, Bailey," Mortician snapped. "Motherfucker had no business calling you."

"You think not?" Knox finally put in. "If I would've left it up to you, you would've given me all kinds of bullshit. I took a page from the playbook all of you use when you want something from Outlaw and call Megan first."

"I resent that shit," Mortician said. "That should work on Outlaw not me."

Roxy cocked her head to the side, biting her lip to keep from dissolving into laughter at how deftly her man had outsmarted Mortician. "You called Bailey, Knox?"

Grinning, Knox winked at her, then nodded.

"Woohoo," she chortled, leaning forward and tapping Mortician on the shoulder.

"What?" he growled.

"Burn, motherfucker, *burn*."

"Shut up."

Roxy thumped the back of his head. "Don't tell me to shut up, boy. You lost your fucking mind talking to me like that? I'll fuck you up."

"Fuck, Roxanne. I'm sorry. I didn't mean to disrespect you, but my pride stinging."

"Oh Lucas," Bailey clucked. "Knox just wants to enjoy time with his lady."

"I don't give a fuck. Roxanne our family. She important to us. As head of the family, I have to protect her from stupid motherfuckers."

"I resent that," Knox spat.

"Hold on, Knox," Bailey said, twisting around to offer a brief smile. "Lucas, is there something...there's a reason you're acting like this, isn't there? What has Knox done?"

"You're supposed to be on my side, Bailey," Knox fumed. "Suddenly you're switching loyalties and turning against me? How can you be so traitorous?"

"Wait a goddamn minute, Knox—" Roxy started.

"Knox, motherfucker, you talk to my woman like you got some goddamn sense or I'm cutting your fucking tongue out of your fucking mouth," Mortician interrupted. The chill in his voice dropped the temperature in the SUV by degrees. "Bailey didn't do this for you. She did it for her momma and don't fucking forget that."

"Fuck off, Mortician," Knox retorted. "I'm sick to death of all you barbarians. Outlaw threatens me. Johnnie. Now you. And it usually has to do with Megan, Kendall, or Bailey. Your women are capable of defending themselves."

"They more than capable," Mortician agreed, "but why do they have to do it, when they got *us* to do it for them?"

"All right, everybody," Bailey inserted, "this isn't the way to start our date. Let's just drop it."

Deciding to take her daughter's advice, Roxy settled back into her seat, refusing to explore the merit of Bailey's question.

~

Knox

"Mr. Harrington, a pleasure to see you, sir."

Knox nodded to the maitre'd at J's, the restaurant his mother owned. "Thank you, Geoff. I've reserved the Tea Room."

"Very good, sir. Ms. Doucette," Geoff greeted with a smile. "I'd like to offer my congratulations on your engagement to Mr. Harrington."

Roxy grinned. "Thank you, sugar," she said, her friendliness always on display. It didn't matter if she spoke to a prince or a pauper, she was always herself. "This is my daughter, Bailey, and her husband, Mortician." She indicated each of them with a nod.

Geoff took in Bailey, beautiful and elegant as usual, in a little black dress. The maitre'd focused on Mortician, glanced at him from head to heel, then stared at the patches on the front of his cut. "You're acquainted with Mr. Outlaw, sir?"

"That's my prez," Mortician answered without shame.

Geoff nodded. "Please send my regards to him and his lovely wife."

It still blew Knox's mind that Outlaw and Megan were regulars at this elegant restaurant.

"If you'll follow me, your private room is ready," Geoff announced.

"Of course." Knox placed his hand at the small of Roxanne's back and started forward. Along the way, several acquaintances stopped their little party to greet and congratulate him and Roxanne on their engagement.

Although he wanted to pretend Mortician wasn't one of his guests, Roxanne always included him when she introduced Bailey.

Her pride in her daughter came through in her every word. As put together as Bailey was, Knox didn't think she had anything on Roxanne. His fiancée redefined the word gorgeous and gave it her own special flare. *Her* little black dress had cutouts on each side that showed her beautiful skin. She wore heels so high that Knox didn't understand how she walked in them. "Red bottoms" she'd called them.

"What?"

"Louboutins," she'd replied.

Those, he knew. They were designer shoes. *Very expensive* designer shoes. He'd had enough manners not to ask how she afforded them without asking him for money. She wore cubic zirconia earrings, necklace, and bracelet. The only authentic diamond—his engagement ring —outshone the other jewelry.

"Your mother has a beautiful restaurant, Knox," Bailey said.

Mortician held her chair out, surprising Knox. The biker was the only one of their foursome who looked out of place with his thuggish clothes and diamond earrings.

"Thank you, Bailey," Knox responded, holding Roxanne's chair out, too. The already-short hem of her dress rode up her thigh a couple inches more. It took effort but he restrained his need to touch her.

Once she settled in her seat, Mortician settled next to Bailey. It almost seemed as if he knew one of the marks of a gentleman was waiting to sit until after all ladies were comfortable. Adjusting the lapels of his jacket, Knox scoffed at the idea, sitting between Roxanne and Bailey. He slid Roxanne's chair closer to him and draped an arm around her.

"Please bring the champagne and caviar out," Knox instructed.

"Yes, Mr. Harrington," Geoff said and hastened to do his bidding.

"We aren't getting menus?" Roxanne asked.

"No, sweetheart." They would've gotten menus if they had been alone, but Knox didn't want to hold up the evening while Mortician tried to navigate the menu. "I called ahead and planned what we'd dine on."

"You thought of everything to make me feel special." Roxy leaned in and brushed her lips over his. "You're a wonderful man, Knox. So romantic. I'm so lucky to have you." Another quick kiss. "I love you so much."

He caressed her cheek and smiled at her. "I love you, too, Roxanne."

"Roxanne, don't tell me you turning into one of *those* women," Mortician said with disapproval. "So blinded by dick, you don't know when a motherfucker being a motherfucker."

Knox glared at Mortician. He'd managed to avert suspicion away from Mortician's motives by putting Bailey on the defensive. These bikers were so predictable, Knox knew what Mortician's reaction would be. The man wouldn't let go of his hostility over a few words Knox had said in anger. Mortician had to be as stupid as Outlaw, if he believed Knox had proposed to Roxanne for any other reason but love.

Mortician threw Roxanne an accusing look. "You always been so tough. Why you got to act like a starry-eyed bitch over him?"

Bailey elbowed Mortician. "Stop it, Lucas. All Knox wants to do is make Momma happy."

"Yeah, Mortician," Roxanne added. "All damn day, Knox has been doing romantic gestures. He sent me beautiful roses. Why would I think Knox is up to no good because he planned our menu?"

"You know why, Roxanne. The motherfucker think he better than us. He planned it because he didn't think I'd know how the fuck to act."

"Oh, please," Knox scoffed, refusing to admit that Mortician was correct. "I don't have time for those silly games."

Mortician scowled at him.

"Can you two please get the fuck alone?" Roxanne bit out. "If your ass wouldn't be a fucking Pussy Patrol, Mortician, you wouldn't be such a grouchy motherfucker."

"Excuse me, Mr. Harrington?"

Knox looked toward the sound of the voice and saw several staff members standing in their private room, carrying trays of appetizers, plates, glasses, and a silver wine bucket with the champagne. Wondering how much these young people heard, Knox pasted a smile on his face.

"Come on," he instructed. "Foie gras," he announced when a waitress placed the first silver tray on the table. "Jamon Iberico. Iberian ham produced in Spain and Portugal." He sidled a smug glance at Mortician. "We'll eat it with toasted baguettes, garlic, tomatoes, and olive oil." He pointed to the last dish. "Caviar tartlet. A Beluga hybrid with crème fraiche."

Leaning back in his seat, Mortician folded his arms, a muscle ticking in his jaw.

"Knox—" Roxanne started with disapproval.

"One moment, my love," he interrupted a waiter handed him a champagne glass filled with a taste of the Armand de Brignac. "Very good. You may pour a glass for each of us." He gave Mortician a polite smile. "We have beer if you'd prefer."

"Knox," Bailey chided.

"It's okay, pretty girl. We not going to be at the fucking restaurant all night."

"Knox, stop being an uppity motherfucker," Roxanne demanded, not caring that employees were in their midst. "I'm sick of your bullshit. Don't fuck up everything you've done for me today by ruining our date."

"Thank you," Knox responded as he accepted his glass of champagne and sipped to get control of his temper.

When the workers all cleared out, Knox and Mortician drank their champagne in silence. Roxanne and Bailey kept up small talk between swallows from their glasses and tastes of the food. Somehow, Mortician inserted himself into the conversation by commenting on whatever the women discussed. After draining his glass and pouring himself another one, Knox decided to join in.

"I don't know, man," Mortician was saying. "I'm with Outlaw. He don't want Meggie girl with a tattoo. I don't want you with one, Bailey. Your skin so gorgeous on its own."

"Not even a tramp stamp?" she asked, blinking her eyelids in an exaggerated manner.

Mortician grinned, then leaned over and kissed her. "Maybe, you can convince me of that."

"What would you think if I got a tramp stamp?" Roxanne asked.

"Even if I knew what the hell that is, which I don't, why would you want anything associated with the word tramp?"

Roxanne's saucy smile made Knox laugh. "Me talking about being a tramp benefits you."

He gave Bailey an uncomfortable look, but the girl's attention was on her husband and whatever he was whispering to her.

Knox gave Roxanne a wolfish smile. "I'm listening, sweetheart.

"Why we never went on a double date before?" Mortician's timing with that question was so precise, Knox swore he did it on purpose. "We family. We should've been getting to know each other on a one-on-one basis months ago."

"Yeah," Bailey said in agreement. "Outlaw, Meggie, Johnnie, and Kendall used to have a double date once a month like Lucas and me, and Digger and Bunny."

"An oversight on our part, sugar," Roxanne answered. "We're going to make up for that."

"We go out with Cam and Jordan a couple of times a month, love," Knox reminded her. "I have to share you then and also at the weekly family dinners. I don't think I could bare to cut into our couple's time with anymore double dates."

"Of course you can, Knox. We won't bring Mortician and Bailey home with us. We'll still get to fuck."

Mortician frowned at Roxanne.

"Please, dearest heart. Don't discuss intercourse in front of your daughter."

Roxanne and Bailey looked at each other, then broke out into peals of laughter. It was so happy, so contagious, that Knox couldn't help but join in. Even Mortician chuckled.

"Since we all here, why don't we talk about wedding plans," he suggested.

Knox shook his head. "This isn't a night for those discussions," he disagreed. "This is a night for me to honor my fiancée."

It *had* been a night to discuss the pre-nuptial agreement. He'd chosen today specifically because he knew about church, which Mortician never missed. After Roxanne told him to contact the biker and convinced Knox it would keep down bullshit that might ruin their date, he'd decided to get Bailey on board first.

For the next couple of hours, Knox decided to give Mortician a chance to show he was more than a killer and a biker. More often than not, he found he enjoyed Mortician's witticisms. Other than his prolific use of the word *fuck*, the enforcer showed he at least knew his ABCs and the fundamentals of Civics and American History.

At the end of the night, when Roxanne excused herself to go to the ladies' room and Mortician left to smoke, Knox found himself alone with Bailey.

She picked up her second glass of champagne and sipped.

Knox drummed his fingers on the table, then glanced at his watch before adjusting his tie. "You aren't much of a drinker," he said after five minutes and he was still alone with Roxanne's daughter. "We've gone through four bottles and you've only had a glass from the first and last."

Setting her glass aside, Bailey pursed her lips and stared at him, drawing her brows together. Obviously, she wished to impart something to him.

"Yes?" he inquired politely.

"Lucas told me," she announced.

Knox lifted his brow. "About?"

"What you said about having the longest engagement in history. Asking my mother to sign a prenup."

"He had no right to open his fucking mouth."

"He had *every* right," Bailey argued with coolness. "You can't act so high-and-mighty to Lucas, Outlaw, and the others, and not expect repercussions. I've defended you! Helped to arrange a night for you and Momma. I should've known Lucas had reasons for his actions. How dare you? Don't hurt my mother. Don't insult her by asking her to sign this document."

"Or what?" Knox sneered, offended that she thought to chastise him. "You'll tell Roxanne? I didn't mean what I said, Bailey. You, of all people, should realize that. Out of the two of you, *you* have the brain."

Bailey drew herself up. "My husband was a double major. He earned a math and music degree."

Knox laughed. "If you say so."

"I'm not going to argue with you over this. My mother is vulnerable to you. She loves you, so don't be a jerk to her. Don't ruin her wedding with bullshit."

"I can't believe you're telling me not to ruin *our* wedding, when *you* already have. You had no fucking business allowing your husband to run roughshod over the situation and force you to be in our wedding. How dare me? How dare *you*? Being a spoiled brat and ruining my wedding to your mother."

Her eyes watered and her nose reddened. Knox thought she might cry. Instead, she narrowed her eyes. "Fuck you," she hissed, shocking the hell out of him.

He'd never heard Bailey cuss.

"Right back at you, babe," he responded.

"You about ready, pretty girl?" Mortician asked, walking back in a moment later. He paused and looked between her and Knox. "What the fuck he said to you, Bailey?"

Bailey got to her feet. "Nothing, Lucas. Where's Momma?"

Mortician stared at her a moment longer, then glowered at Knox. "She saw Cam and Jordan at a table. I told her I'd come in here to round the two of you up."

"Let me run and say 'hi' to them," Bailey said, rushing away before her husband could respond either way.

Mortician watched her leave, then turned to Knox and lit another cigarette.

"Smoking isn't allowed in this building."

"Knox, let me tell you something, son. I know my woman. You said something to upset her."

"I'm not getting into this with you."

"You know what, motherfucker? I don't have to do a fucking thing. Why waste a fucking bullet on you? All I got to do is tell Roxanne you hurt Bailey and you'll be looking for your fucking nut sac in the garbage disposal."

"Don't ruin this evening," Knox said, not dignifying the gruesome scenario with a response. He wouldn't even bring up his irritation that Mortician had told Bailey about the engagement conversation. "Don't tell Roxanne anything."

Mortician smirked at Knox, blew smoke in his face and walked away.

For the duration of the ride home, Knox expected Mortician or Bailey to tell Roxanne about the confrontation. But neither of them said nothing.

At the clubhouse, Mortician parked the Escalade, near the door, and got out.

"Bye, sugar. I really enjoyed myself," Roxanne whispered, laying her palm against his cheek.

Knox hugged her. "Me, too. I'll see you—"

Without warning, Mortician jerked Knox out of the SUV. It was so sudden that he nearly went sprawling.

"Asshole," Knox growled, jerking away from Mortician.

"Mortician, boy, what the fuck is your problem?" Roxanne yelled.

"Nothing. Your date over."

"I'm tired," Bailey announced.

"I'll be right back, pretty girl," Mortician promised, then pointed to the door. "Get to stepping."

Roxanne started out. "I'm coming. You acting like a damn fool again."

"I need to talk to you, Momma."

"Fine, Bailey," Roxanne said without a moment's hesitation. She blew out a frustrated breath but said, "I'll call you later, Knox," then slammed the door shut.

Mortician held the door open. Knox stalked into the clubhouse, surprised to find only two bikers at the bar, talking to Potter. Knox nodded to them, then continued on, aware of Mortician hot on his heels.

At the door to his temporary room, Knox used his key to unlock the knob.

"We not telling Roxanne nothing. Bailey still haven't told me. But Knox, motherfucker, you walking on thin ice. Don't fuck with Bailey. That will get you killed quicker than you fucking with Roxanne."

"Mortician—"

A mighty shove by the enforcer interrupted Knox's words and sent him stumbling into the room. Unable to regain his balance, he went sprawling on the floor. He lifted his head in time to see Mortician's glare before he slammed the door so hard, it shook and reverberated through the room.

He'd suffer this indignity if it meant Roxanne never discovered Knox's run-in with her Bailey.

CHAPTER FOURTEEN

Sipping a coke, Emily wondered if she'd recognize the President of the Death Dwellers. When the PI, Knox Harrington, had visited her during her shift at McDonald's, he'd claimed he needed her to come to his office because a long-lost relative had left her an inheritance.

NOT! Her family had *dis*inherited her. No way would any of them, from the oldest to the youngest, ever leave her anything. Wouldn't happen.

Knox Harrington had finally confessed he was there on the orders of Outlaw, Death Dwellers MC president. Apparently, the biker had a job for her to do that involved a lot of money.

Whatever the assignment was, she didn't want to hear about it from the PI. She wanted it straight from the outlaw's mouth. She giggled at her play on words, continually amazed at what a Brainiac she was.

Outlaw.

What a big, bad name. But was he a big, bad biker?

She'd sent a message to Outlaw through Knox: either he met with her or she wasn't interested no matter the amount of money involved. Simply put, she smelled a rat. It was just too coincidental that Kendall Miller had sought her out, had a husband affiliated with the Death Dwellers, and now the president of that same club needed Emily for a job.

She hadn't been able to make it to the library to Google the club president, so she really didn't know how he looked. She'd already eaten up her usage on her phone plan, too. And she couldn't ask any of her coworkers for help since none of the bitches there liked her, so she refused to associate with any of them. They were terribly jealous of her blonde beauty.

At one time, she would've laughed in their faces. Now, she worked alongside the low-class. People who needed the shitty job to survive.

People like...*herself.*

That reality hit her once again as she sat in a burger joint waiting for...

A tall, muscular man, wearing a leather vest, jeans, and motorcycle boots, strolled toward her...

Him...? Outlaw?

Every woman, every *man*, turned his way. He stopped at her table, widened his green eyes, and stared. Thick black lashes ringed his eyes in a beautiful display of masculine perfection and gave them a burning intensity. His temples had gray in them, but his black hair and tanned skin enhanced his stunning appearance.

"Fuck me," he breathed. "You look just fuckin' like her."

She found her voice. "Like who?"

"My wife," he responded, much to Emily's disappointment. She *tried* to stay away from married men. She didn't always succeed, since the male species found her so irresistible, but she gave herself credit for her valiant efforts.

He slid in the booth across from her. Fluttering her lashes at the biker enthralled him with so little effort, she almost laughed. He continued to stare, seeming speechless.

She offered him a saucy wink, wondering how close he was to his wife. "Are you happily married?" she asked.

He held up his big, left hand and wiggled his ring finger, indicating his simple gold band. "This repre-fuckin-sent the most important fuckin' thing in my life."

Licking her lips, she nodded, not believing him in the least and liking the way his gaze followed her mouth. Met her eyes. Looked at her mouth again, then glanced at her breasts.

She decided to follow his lead. With one look from his gorgeous eyes, one command from his sexy lips, he could get her to do anything he wanted.

Finally, he glanced away and stared into the distance.

"Big Joe, Big Joe, Big Joe," he chanted on an annoyed mumble. "What the fuck you did?"

"Excuse me?"

Outlaw looked at her again. "You look just like her."

Back to this. "Your wife?" She stopped short of rolling her eyes. Men always needed a reason to justify their cheating.

He nodded. "You just shocked the fuck outta me. Made me wonder about some shit." He shrugged. "I can now fuckin' under-fuckin-stand why psycho cunt go so fuckin' crazy over my girl."

Maybe...maybe, he was insane. He wasn't making sense.

He scrubbed a hand over his face, then met her gaze again. "I ain't got much time, babe, and I just fuckin' used half the motherfucker oglin' you," he stated in a voice laced with just the right amount of roughness. "I'm off the grid right now and motherfuckers gonna be lookin' for me, so lemme get straight to the fuckin' point."

She smiled, breathless and overheated, unable to contain her anticipation of feeling him inside of her.

"We got a common fuckin' enemy," he said flatly.

She frowned, confused.

"Kendall," he clarified.

She straightened. "Kendall Mill...Donovan?"

"Psycho cunt."

She laughed. "Psycho who?"

"Psycho cunt," he repeated with a disarming grin.

Oh my God, he was gorgeous. Emily's panties melted.

"Yeah, uh, yes. Kendall." Her words were breathless. "Psycho cunt. I've never liked her."

He cocked his head to the side. "Any particular fuckin' reason why?"

"Does it matter?" she shot back. "If she's your enemy, you wouldn't care why I disliked her."

"Answer the fuckin' question," he demanded.

At his tone, she instantly obeyed. "I just never liked her, Outlaw. She was poor with no daddy and a nut for a mom. She always wanted attention. *My* attention." Remembering Kendall as a child shot jealousy through Emily. "All the boys liked that stupid cow and she was too fat and oblivious to see it. All she worried about was being accepted, *by me*. By anyone." She tossed her hair over her shoulder. "She gave me the power. I just wielded it."

"You ain't ever thought bein' nice to her woulda been better? She was a fuckin' kid, only needin' a motherfucker to understand her."

Emily bit back her retort, arranging the dynamics of the club in her head. He was the president. Kendall's husband was the vice-president. They possibly had a close relationship, so...so Outlaw wanted her to do a job for him. Yet, he was still a little outraged on Kendall's behalf.

Not quite enemies then.

Her guard went up, but for completely different reasons than from the earlier one. If he was *for* Kendall, he was *against* Emily. That wouldn't do. She refused to allow that redheaded bitch one more victory. Closing her eyes, she squeezed tears out. "I'm so sorry to have mistreated her all those years ago." She sniffled and rubbed her cheek, giving him an imploring look. "I know I need to make it up to her."

"First of fuckin' all, I ain't givin' a fuck about your tears. They fake as fuck any-fuckin-way. Five fuckin' minutes ago, you said you ain't ever liked her ass. Now, you sittin' there spoutin' bullshit about wantin' to make up your fucked-up behavior up to her?"

She blinked, then widened her eyes. Not many people read her so well. "Your crankiness will not get you your way," she sniffed, dropping her theatrics. "As a matter of fact, I might be so turned off by it that I refuse to help you."

"That's on your fuckin' ass if you ain't wantin' to help me. Usin' you would be easier, but I got a fuckin' Plan B, C, D, E, and into in-fuckin-finity."

Oh my God! This man. He intrigued her so much, she couldn't refuse him.

"Fine, Outlaw. Fine. I don't regret what I did to Kendall. In my eyes, she'll always be a pathetic, overgrown pig, who grew up to be little more than a slut."

"A whore in designer clothes," Outlaw agreed.

"Yes!" Emily said with a clap of her hands, happy at his putdown.

"That might be, Emily, but Kendall ain't wantin' for nothin'. She get on my last fuckin' nerve. And I wanna fuckin' kill her and box small pieces of her body the fuck up, but you ain't got room to fuckin' talk. She a strong bitch, pulled herself up to be a lawyer. She selfish as a motherfucker. Only think about her fuckin' self. Jealous of my woman. Stole Johnnie balls. Wanna fuck me..."

Who could blame Kendall? Emily wanted to fuck him, too.

"Do you hate her or admire her?" she demanded.

"I hate that fuckin' bitch with every fuckin' thing in me, but I ain't tryna get rid of her fuckin' ass only to end up with a worse fuckin' bitch. Ten times as hypocritical, judgmental, and who like to cause fuckin' trouble. Johnnie and Kendall separated. I want her fuckin' gone for good."

Emily's ears perked at the news. "Kendall didn't tell me that. She told me she was married."

"She is."

"Like they were together. Better?"

"They ain't. *How-fuckin-ever*, Johnnie gonna end up takin' that bitch back. He always fuckin' do. But Kendall hate my wife and obsessed with your fuckin' ass."

Those words brightened Emily's perspective. This just got better and better. "Is that so?"

"Yeah, babe, so I wanna hire you to get Johnnie away from Kendall and drive her in-fuckin-sane. All part of my plan to get her the fuck outta his life, *our* lives, for fuckin' good."

That sounded ominous. She was all in. "For good? How?"

"Don't fuckin' worry about that. Just do your fuckin' job and shit gonna fuckin' fall into place."

"If you intend to kill her, I can do it for you. I'll be happy to." At one time, Emily had loved indulging in the death sites on the dark web. Corpses fascinated her. She wanted to wield that power of life and death over someone. "I don't need some ugly biker named Johnnie. You and me can work together."

He smirked at her. "You think Johnnie a ugly motherfucker? You think Kendall woulda took him if he was?"

"Most bikers are big hairy brutes. You're the exception and I think Kendall was so desperate to marry, she would take any man who offered."

Without answering, Outlaw pulled a cell phone from his pocket. A moment later, he held the device in front of her. A close-up of a golden-haired man with golden skin and silver eyes stared at her. He was magnificent!

"Johnnie."

"Johnnie," Emily breathed, unable to drag her gaze away, until realization dawned. "Kendall's husband?"

"He got a college degree," Outlaw said on a nod. "He a real preppy motherfucker. Bitches love this motherfucker." He pulled the phone back and stared at her. "He good and bad all rolled into one."

"And you want me to seduce him away from Kendall?"

"No. Seduce ain't the right word. Have a fuckin' relationship with him that Kendall know about."

"He has a roaming eye," Emily decided with satisfaction. Something must've been wrong with him if he'd married Kendall.

"Johnnie been wantin' to fuck my woman for fuckin' years," Outlaw announced, a cold glint dropping into his green gaze.

"I thought Kendall wanted to fuck you."

"She do. And her man wanna fuck my girl. That ain't hard to understand."

"It sounds like a soap opera."

"What the fuck ever," Outlaw said in dismissal.

"You know you really need to learn to deal with women. You're rather overbearing."

"Ain't here to fuckin' impress you, Emily."

Oh, God. When he said her name...

"You got one-up already to take Johnnie from Kendall."

"Because I look like your wife who Johnnie wants to fuck?"

"Ain't I just said that, babe?" he asked with impatience but stopped to stare at her again, his gaze touching every plane and angle of her face.

She glowed under his look. "Will I just fuck him or do I get you, too?"

~

CHRISTOPHER

Only half-listening, Christopher blinked at Emily's comment, his brain still trying to process why the fuck this bitch looked so much like his Megan. He kept staring at her, wondering who the fuck Big Joe stuck his cock in. Christopher also wanted to study the woman that had driven Kendall crazy and made her hate Megan to the point of *psychopathness*. The more he looked at her, the clearer Emily and Megan's differences became.

Across from him sat a very fucking pretty woman. But Megan was drop-dead, heart-stoppingly, dick-hardeningly gorgeous.

"You're staring again," she murmured. Her voice had moments of sweetness, but it was more nasally than Megan's. Irritating as fuck. He just...fuck, Megan had a nephew she didn't know about. Could she have a sister, too?

What was the fucking odds that years before psycho cunt crossed paths with Megan, she'd been on the fringes of their lives because Emily belonged to Big Joe? Then, to end up, at the club...

"How much are you paying?"

Her question snapped his gaze away from her face. "Johnnie'll fuck you cuz you look like Megan, but to keep his interest e-fuckin-nuff where he want a relationship with you, you gotta dress a certain way. Business-like, at first. That remind me. Get some fuckin' business cards."

"What should I list as my profession?"

"You decide." Christopher went back to what she needed to do to win Johnnie over. "You gotta act a certain way around John Boy. High class but a whore on the downlow."

Her expression didn't change.

"You got the type of clothes Johnnie like?"

She swallowed. Guilt crossed her face. Instead of admitting she probably didn't have those types of clothes, she nodded.

"As for the pay, 5Gs a month 'til you accomplish what the fuck I want." Kendall's suicide, but she didn't need to know that shit.

"Meaning this job will last about six months?"

Christopher shook his head. "Nope. Got a fuckin' event comin' up and I need all this shit over with in the next four or five months."

That would give motherfuckers enough time to grieve for Kendall without ruining Roxanne and Bailey ceremonies. He couldn't imagine nobody grieving for Kendall for more than a month.

Lowering her lashes, Emily affected a pout and then faked a giggle. "Please let it be six months."

"No." Two weeks had sped by since Knox's proposal, and Christopher hadn't put the Kendall Die Plan into action yet. He couldn't start the campaign late *and* fucking end it late, too. "Five months."

She pursed her lips. "It'll be our secret," she whispered. "The extra month will help me."

"It gotta stay our secret. Me, you, and Knox. And, babe, if Johnnie ain't so solidly on your side in five fuckin' months that he tell Kendall about you, he ain't ever gonna be. You got *five fuckin' months*."

"Fine," she said with a sad sigh. "What happens if he falls for me and wants to keep me?"

Christopher shrugged. "You might fall for his ass and want to stay with the motherfucker."

Her look hardened. "That'll never happen, Outlaw. I guarantee. My heart is closed to love here and forever more."

Unease slid into Christopher. He wanted Kendall gone so fucking bad, but Johnnie *could* fall for Emily because of her resemblance to Megan. He'd never known Johnnie to be that fucking shallow, though. On the other fucking hand, Christopher barely knew his brother anymore. But what happened if Johnnie fell for Emily and she walked away?

Johnnie could get any bitch he wanted—except Megan—yet Emily was fucking different. This bitch wanted to kill motherfuckers. No matter how much she tried to play the role of a helpless woman, Christopher saw through her. Fuck, maybe, he needed to leave well enough the fuck alone.

Besides, Megan would be so fucking pissed if she ever found out that he'd met a bitch behind her back *AND* because he intended to use said bitch to drive Kendall to her grave. The Kendall bit *could* be classified as club business. That was a fucking stretch. She was Johnnie's woman. Christopher would be unable to excuse meeting Emily without telling Megan. Sometimes, it was a simple, '*Ima be meetin' this chick today on club business, Megan.*'

But fuck...he didn't want no shit thwarting his plan. All Megan would have to do was nod—and he'd open his fucking mouth, thus allowing Kendall to get away with her latest bullshit.

She *had* to pay for what she'd almost done to CJ and especially for getting Megan kidnapped. Because of her miserable ass, their lives were forever changed.

And, fuck yeah, he hated on Johnnie a little, for always backing his bitch up, no matter what the fuck she did.

Emily would be the best possible revenge. Christopher was almost insane with rage and Megan didn't want him killing Kendall.

She'd never said anything about guiding Kendall to suicide.

He wanted Kendall fucking gone. Period. He wanted her body buried in some remote place on earth with her grave salted over to keep the evil bitch and all the demons invading her from rising up again.

Emily reached across the table, grabbed his hand, and slid her finger down his palm.

Christopher snatched his hand away. "My hands. My cock. My *heart* belong to Megan. Ain't puttin' up with you fuckin' with her. And tryna fuck me fuckin' with her. Shit like that get you killed.

Narrowing her eyes, she stiffened. "You've been sending me these signals for an hour now."

"I been starin' at your fuckin' ass in shock cuz of how much you look like Megan."

"If Johnnie can pretend I'm her, can't you?"

"You *ain't* her. Megan special. One of a fuckin' kind, and I love the fuck outta her. Ain't a bitch alive can change that or take me from her. I don't give a fuck if you was her twin."

She scowled. Her blue eyes were darker, duller, than Megan's. Everything about his girl sparkled. Her eyes, her face. Her soul. Emily, on the other hand...he ignored the warning bells going off in his head.

She was a fucking means to an end. He'd do any-fucking-thing to get back at Kendall.

Emily tapped her finger against her cheek. "I take it you wouldn't want Johnnie—or Megan—to know about your role in my relationship with him?"

Christopher snapped his brows together. Setting his arms on the table, he leaned forward. "I ain't one to fuck over," he warned in a deadly voice. Bitch either believe him. Or fucking not. "I fuckin' had it up to my fuckin' eyes with schemin' psycho fuckin' bitches. You on *my* dime, you do shit *my* fuckin' way. Take my fuckin' money and fuck over me, I'm shootin' the fuck outta you. *Especially where Megan concerned.* Under-fuckin-stand?"

Swallowing, she nodded quickly.

He got to his feet and pulled a wad of cash from his cut, tossing it on the table in front of her. "Knox gonna be in touch to give you fuckin' instructions. That money for a new wardrobe to impress John Boy. And, Emily, don't *ever* fuckin' try to play me a-fuckin-gain like you did when I mentioned fuckin' clothes."

She blinked. "I didn't—"

Christopher held up his hand. "Yes, the fuck your ass did. I saw your fuckin' look when I told your ass to wear a certain fuckin' type of clothes."

Again, guilt crossed her face.

Glaring at her, Christopher walked away. Maybe, he should call this shit off. His fucking gut told him that Emily was a worse fucking bitch than Kendall ever was. At least with psycho, he knew what the fuck he was getting.

Besides, if, by some fucking twist of fucking fate, a relationship between Emily and Johnnie really did grow, just what the fuck would he say to Megan? By then, it wouldn't be a fucking secret who Emily was.

He weighed his options. Weighed his plans. Early on, he'd need to introduce Megan to Emily...But the planning for Roxy and Bailey's ceremony would keep all the girls busy and distracted.

Emily could be eased in as Johnnie's new old lady, and not a motherfucker would fucking know how the fuck Christopher manipulated shit.

Fuck it. He wouldn't second guess himself. The plan was already in motion. Shit would be fine. As long as Emily kept to the script, not a fucking thing could go wrong.

CHAPTER FIFTEEN

Roxy

"Are you sure you're fine with the colors?" Roxy asked, looking closely at Bailey as they sat in a private room in an exclusive little boutique Mortician had found for them. Knox and Mortician, along with Grant, were on the other side of the building, where grooms-to-be shopped for their wedding apparel. "I know you wanted gold and white."

"Scarlet and white are lovely colors, Momma," Bailey said with reassurance.

"Black tuxes for the men?" she pressed, feeling as if Bailey was hiding something from her. "With red tie and cummerbund or red vests?"

"Tie and cummerbund," Bailey answered. "Now that I think on it, I prefer the scarlet instead of the gold. I think it'll look better on the men."

"Is there anything you need, Ms. Doucette? Mrs. Banks?" The proprietress interrupted.

The overabundance of fawning irked Roxy. "We're buying shit from you, okay?" she snapped. "Stop coming in to kiss my fucking ass to get business."

The woman blinked, but nodded.

"Er, Mrs. Whittlestone, my mother is under a lot of stress," Bailey said with her usual diplomacy. "We were just about to call you." She opened her sketch book, comprised of exclusive offerings. "I'm really thinking of this one. Should I go with it or not?"

Mrs. Whittlestone's eyes widened. "Oh. Oh! Y-yes, of course, my dear. Y-yes. Anything...anything you want." Both awe and gratitude resounded in her words.

"Look, lady." Roxy felt like a bitch for snapping at the older woman. "I didn't mean to go off on you. You coming in here every ten minutes worked my last fucking nerve. That's all. But I'm so glad Mortician brought us here."

Gracious, the woman smiled. "I will get out of your hair. If you need me, just holler."

"Won't have to," Roxy mumbled as the lady left them alone again. "I'm sure your fucking ass will be right outside the door."

"Momma!" Bailey said around a giggle. "You nearly shocked the shoes off the poor woman."

Roxy sighed. "I know. I need to watch what I say."

Bailey gave her an odd look, then turned back to the sketchbook, casually flipping through. "I've been thinking," she said after a moment.

"About what, child?" Roxy lingered on a page in a LookBook that contained a bridesmaid dress. It was black, made of tulle and lace. She was sure it would look as fabulous in scarlet.

"How I've hijacked your wedding."

The statement came out with nonchalance, but Roxy knew Bailey. Her daughter was lowkey and avoided drama if at all possible. "What do you mean, Bailey?"

Bailey closed the sketchbook. "Knox proposed to you. When he did, it was for you and him to get married. Not share the spotlight with another couple. Lucas kind of railroaded you into allowing us to join in."

Tenderness at Bailey's thoughtfulness welled inside of Roxy and she pulled her daughter into her embrace. "Oh, baby. Don't think that! I'm happy and proud that you will be walking down the aisle the same day as me in a dream wedding."

Bailey kissed Roxy's cheek, then pulled away and grabbed Roxy's hand. "You deserve every happiness." She stroked her mother's hair. "This is your time to shine. You said you didn't want a big wedding, but you were like a giddy little girl on the way here."

"And you were muted all the way here," Roxy said gently, returning Bailey's gesture and stroking her hair. Currently, it was bone straight, but the rich highlights accentuated Bailey's beautiful face.

Roxy had always been proud of Bailey. She was the one who gave her the least trouble. The one who reasoned things out. And the one who accepted her, warts and all.

"I was wondering what was wrong." She pulled her daughter back into her embrace and Bailey laid her head on Roxy's shoulder. "Why *you* weren't excited. Your dream has always been to have a huge church wedding. You're getting it, sugar."

Bailey nodded. "Knox was so angry, though." Pulling away again, she sat up and bowed her head. "It's just...I wish..." Her voice trailed off and she sighed. "The day will still be perfect. Johnnie will be perfect to walk me down the aisle. Nevermind."

Grabbing another sketchbook, Bailey started flipping through the pages so fast Roxy knew she wasn't seeing a fucking thing. She placed her hand over Bailey's.

"K-P is with you," she said softly. "He sees and he approves. He might not be here to walk you down the aisle, but he's here to watch over you and keep you safe."

Tears glistened in Bailey's eyes; Roxy swallowed, choking up, too.

"I miss him," Bailey confessed. "And I...that doesn't mean I don't like Knox—"

"Stop it!" Roxy demanded. "This has nothing to do with Knox. K-P was your daddy, not Knox. And a good daddy he was. He loved the ground you walked on. He was a good man and I mourned his loss,

Bailey. I understand that a perfect wedding needs the bride's daddy to give her away. If that is the reason you don't want to have a double wedding, I'll respect that. Even though your daddy would say go ahead with it."

"It's not all about Daddy. Mostly, it's about you. I feel like a usurper."

Suspicion rose in Roxy. "Knox talked to you?"

"No, Momma," Bailey said with a grin, swiping at a stray tear. "But I understand his point."

"I love that man something fierce, Bailey. Your daddy was my first love and there will always be a spot in my heart for him. I'm thankful to have found Knox to have a second chance at love."

"You've been married four times."

"Three," Roxy sniffed. "And?"

"Didn't you love them?"

"You haven't realized what a romantic your momma is, girl?"

Bailey smiled. "Where do you think I get my romanticism from, woman?"

"My marriages didn't last because, deep down, I knew going in, I didn't really want to be married to those motherfuckers. I wanted...I was searching for what I lost with K-P."

"Knox couldn't be less like Daddy. They are complete opposites."

"I wasn't searching for a clone of K-P, Bailey. I just wanted...I don't really know what the fuck I wanted. Maybe, the perfect man, and discovering these other motherfuckers' imperfections served as a good excuse to walk away. Always measuring them against K-P."

The confession rankled her. It was really the first time she'd admitted that to anyone—even herself. She sighed.

"As I had started to say, I would be content marrying Knox on a little raft in the middle of the Pacific with just me, him, and Father Wilkins. I don't need a big wedding. It's not about the production. It's about the love between two people. Knox wants a big wedding, but he would've given in to me and had a small ceremony. No, this big to-do is for you. *Was* for you," she amended. "I can't believe how much I am enjoying putting plans together and getting a custom-made dress."

"You've had a big wedding before."

"Yes, to Creighton." She clenched her jaw, determined to move on from thoughts of her son's father. She was sure Creighton had bad-mouthed her to Duke and played a very active role in turning her boy against her. She shoved thoughts of both Creighton and Duke aside. "I want *us* to enjoy the planning and the celebration, sugar."

"Have you talked to Duke?"

Roxy opened her LookBook again. "I'm not good enough for him to talk to," she said breezily.

"Oh, Momma! I want to go to New Orleans and take my turn whipping his ass. Carissa broke his nose and he was still talking bullshit about you, so Alexia called an ambulance. They were arriving just as she knocked him unconscious. Along with a few police cars and—"

Alarm raced through Roxy. "What the fuck do you mean? Why am I just finding out this shit?"

"Because Duke deserved it. Grandma took her housekeys from him. Creighton was urging Duke to press charges. Grandma said she would take care of it, and she did."

"Well, knock me over and call me a motherfucker. None of you thought to tell me about any of this?"

"No, Momma. Duke is taking away your self-confidence and your self-esteem. He's making you...I don't know. He's making you not be you and I want to fuck him up! He's a little asshole."

"*Bailey*!" Roxy said, impressed at her daughter's heated language but shocked. Not to say Bailey didn't cuss. It usually wasn't so vengeful.

"You know he is, Momma," Bailey fumed.

"He's being influenced by his father."

"I don't buy that. He's not a child anymore. He's eighteen. He knows what he's doing. Stop making excuses for him. He's horrible."

"He's my child—"

Bailey glared at her. "Get off that song! He's disrespecting you, abusing you, insulting you. If he was saying all these things to Grandma, would you make excuses for him?"

"Of course not, Bailey," Roxy said in exasperation.

"Then why do it now when it is directed at you?"

"Think about it!" Roxy jumped to her feet and placed her hands on her hips. "He's my child. Somewhere along the way I did something terribly wrong for him to be able to fix his mouth to say those things to me. We didn't go to church as much as we should have. I was always in school. Always switching majors." She swallowed, her vulnerability rising in her all over again. She tried not to think of Duke. His feelings towards her tore her in two. "It was my job to teach him respect and loyalty."

"You taught it to him and he learned it well. He's just using his lessons on Creighton."

"Can we not talk about this?" Roxy returned to her seat. "Let's focus on the reason we're here, sugar."

A few moments of silence went by before a question occurred to Roxy.

"What makes you think I'm acting any differently?"

Bailey cocked her head to the side, then nodded to Roxy's left hand. "That ring for one. I know it's an heirloom but it is...not you. The Roxanne I know would've told Knox the truth."

"This is a small matter, Bailey, and this ring is important to Knox."

"Not as important as you are to him," she insisted.

"It's fine," Roxanne said stubbornly.

"Okay, if you say so. *That's* fine, but what about what Lucas is doing? Forcing Knox and you to live separately. Why aren't you saying go fuck yourself?"

From her tone, Roxy got the sense that Bailey now agreed with Mortician. "I've asked myself the same thing," she admitted, then shrugged. "The truth is it feels good to have someone take care of me and think about my well-being."

Sitting back in the slipper chair covered in ivory satin and tied at the back with a big bow, Bailey folded her arms. "I'm sure that's true, Momma. You take care of everyone. But this isn't you. You're stronger than that."

"Maybe, I'm scared," Roxy confessed. "No matter the reason I married before they didn't work out and I...Knox is nine years younger than me and refined. Classy. What am I?"

Bailey gasped, then narrowed her green-gray eyes. "I'm sending Lucas to kill Duke. He's gotten into your head and is ruining you."

"Leave Duke alone," Roxy ordered. "It's not only our differences...

Or, maybe, it is…I'm afraid this is a dream and I'll wake up and he'll be gone. Besides, I want Knox to be accepted by the boys. If he listens to Lucas, this will go a long way in them accepting him."

"Please don't let Duke do this to you. The problem is his. Not yours. You're perfect just as you are."

Roxy forced a smile. "Kind of hard to believe that when one of your own kids thinks you nothing but garbage." It was meant to be breezy. Yet even she heard the dismal hurt. "Let's plan our lovely weddings, sugar. I promise I will give myself a good talking to."

"Yeah, okay, Momma," Bailey said grouchily. "I still want to punch Duke."

"I understand, baby." Roxy opened to the black bridesmaid gown she'd seen a bit ago. "Get Mrs. Whittlestone so we can have our measurements taken and talk numbers."

Bailey nodded and got to her feet, opening the door and leaving Roxy alone. Watching as her daughter left, she felt a deep gratitude for the woman Bailey had become.

"I know you're so proud of our little girl, K-P," Roxy whispered, smiling, then turning her attention back to the gowns when Bailey followed Mrs. Whittlestone in to get on with the planning.

~

Knox

Knox stared at the tattoos staining Mortician's back, chest, and arms, as the tailor took the biker's measurements. He stood in their private room in only a pair of black boxer briefs, not caring that he was nearly naked in front of other people. That was bad enough. But he'd had to de-weaponize himself, removing guns strapped underneath his clothes and on various parts of his body. The four weapons sat in a neat pile on a bench, right next to his clothes.

"That grim reaper tat is cool, Mort," Grant gushed. "I want one when I grow up."

Mortician smiled at Grant, holding his arms out as Mr. Whittlestone spread out a tape measurer. He was standing on a stepstool to reach Mortician's arms and shoulders.

"Are you getting a tat, Dad?" Grant asked.

"No," Knox answered with irritation. The very idea! "And neither are you. Ever. You're not a biker."

"I want to be!" Grant complained. "CJ said he's going to be a big biker like 'Law—"

"Outlaw," Knox gritted.

"CJ said I can call his dad 'Law."

"CJ is four years old, Grant! You do not do what that little boy tells you to do. If anything, you should be trying to impress your good manners on him." Christ! What was he saying? "On second thought, don't. Just leave him alone."

"Mr. Harrington, have you reconsidered allowing me to take your measurements?"

"No." Why bother with measurements when he didn't know what Roxanne—*Bailey*—had chosen? Besides… "I have my own haberdasher. The same one my father uses." He smirked at Mortician. "In North America, a haberdasher is a dealer in men's clothing."

Instead of answering, Mortician began strapping up again.

"Can I get measured here?" Grant asked hopefully. "Mr. Hocking is too mean."

"He is no-nonsense and firm," Knox stated. "And, no, you will get measured with me and your grandfather."

Grant's face fell.

Whistling, Mortician pulled on his jeans, then grabbed his T-shirt.

"Tell him, Mort," Grant said.

Heat rose up Knox's neck and into his face.

"Can't, little dude." Mortician said and put on his socks, then began pulling on his boots. "Knox your old man. I'm not."

"Will that be all, Mortician?" Mr. Whittlestone asked.

"Yeah. Whenever Bailey tell me if I'm wearing a vest or cummerbund, I'll call you so you can order it. She might be telling your woman, though, so just get whatever she says I'm supposed to wear."

"Wait a damn minute," Knox said, outraged. "You're just allowing *Bailey* to choose what you want to wear?"

"It's her fucking wedding, Knox," Mortician said flatly. "I don't give a fuck if I walk down the fucking aisle in my drawers."

Grant giggled.

"That isn't what civilized people do, son," Knox said.

Mortician shrugged into his cut. "Civilized motherfuckers sure got a lot of fucking rules. Glad my ass so uncivilized."

"Refinement only comes from years of gentle living and good manners," Knox retorted.

"Wealth, you mean," Mortician told him.

"Those weren't *my* words," he said smugly. "But, yes, wealth."

Mortician sat next to Grant on the sofa, lit a cigarette, then grinned at Knox. "What is it like to you to be rich?"

Knox drew himself up. "It isn't easy to explain to someone like you." He glanced at Grant. "Besides, I made my own way in the world. I didn't want my father's money to give me an easy ride."

"Pure bullshit. Whether you wanted it or not, you got it. You never had to worry about a poor man's problems."

"The families we were born into isn't my fault," Knox pointed out.

Eyeing him, Mortician blew smoke sideways. "True," he agreed. "Still, you made your own way after having the luxury of deciding to do so. If you'd wanted to, you could've been nothing but a trust fund brat."

"Never! My father wouldn't allow me to slack. If I hadn't followed my own career path, I would've had to work in the company."

Another puff in, then out. "You're your father's heir. Shouldn't you want to learn the business? Unless he has someone else in mind."

"You don't understand the workings of trust funds and inheritances." Knox shook his head. "I don't have time to explain the intricacies to you."

Mortician's amused grin rankled Knox. "Didn't you investigate us before you ever came to the club?"

Knox would never admit he hadn't investigated all the members. "And?"

"Bet you a thousand dollars you didn't investigate me."

"That is gambling, and I don't gamble in front of my son."

"Do you piss in front of him?" Yawning, Mortician leaned back and placed his hands behind his head, not displacing his manbun. "Fuck, man. What the fuck do you do in front of him? He know you got a cock like him?"

"Cover your ears, son," Knox said in alarm.

His face red with laughter, Grant stuck an index finger in each ear. Knox knew the rascal could still hear, but he'd followed his instructions so that was good enough. "Around Grant, we have penises."

"*You* might have a penis," Mortician said. "*I* got a cock."

Delight lit Grant's eyes, confirming Knox's suspicions that he could hear.

"I don't understand you people," he confessed.

"*Us people* don't give a fuck, son. I don't understand you. You say you want the privilege of being under Roxanne roof until the wedding, yet you acting like a stupid motherfucker and not getting your measurements taken. Not because a tux hasn't been decided on, but because you one uppity motherfucker. Any shop we frequent not good enough for you."

Embarrassment coursed through Knox, and he turned to Mr. Whittlestone. "I apologize for my friend's vulgar behavior. I know better than to discuss such things in front of proprietors. My choice to not do business with you is nothing personal."

Mortician snorted. "It's very fucking personal. The Whittlestones own this place. Despairing *it* casts aspersions on *them*."

"Can I unstop my ears, Dad?" Grant called.

Knox rubbed his temples. He'd had his son sticking fingers in his ears for five minutes to deal with a moron. It had been an exercise in futility, anyway. Mortician was beyond educating and Grant had heard everything. "Sure, son."

"If I consent to do business with the Whittlestones, it'll make you think you're in charge," Knox spat to Mortician, taking up the conversation where they'd left off.

"In case you didn't realize, I *am* in charge."

"The hell you are. I might not be able to get around your living arrangement rule—*yet*," he added with supreme smugness. "But that's the only other thing you're getting over on me with. You've already muscled your way into my wedding to Roxanne." He shrugged. "I understand. You want a big wedding and I can pay for it legitimately."

Mortician cocked his head to the side, a muscle ticking in his jaw. "Bailey being here your first saving grace. Grant your second," he said coldly. He nodded to Mr. Whittlestone. "Him and his woman your third. Don't need to fuck up their shop with your blood, brains, and bone." He got to his feet. "As I said, you don't know shit about me. If you had really investigated me..."

His voice trailed off, so Knox seized the opportunity to continue. "What would I have found? A rap sheet a mile long? Records of foster homes? Some sob story that explains why you turned into a criminal who marks up his body and carries more guns than a cop? Tell me what would I have found? I didn't need to investigate you. I wanted Outlaw. Once he fell, the rest of you would, too. You don't know what power is. You have it through force. I have it through *money*. Legitimate business that is the hallmark of the Harrington family. I am my father's sole heir. Being around all of you has made me realize what it means to have true wealth. True power. And I revel in it. I thank God that I was born with the world at my feet, not in a gutter that turned me into trash."

Grant's eyes widened, and Knox realized the vitriol he was throwing Mortician's way. Fury tightened the enforcer's features, darkened his eyes. He looked ready to kill Knox.

Instead, he nudged Grant's shoulder. "Tell your old man not to be so uptight and nervous. He might not lose his temper."

Grant gave Knox an uncomfortable look, then turned back to Mortician. "You're not mad? Dad doesn't mean what he says. He gets like that when he's stressed."

"I'm pissed like a motherfucker, Grant," Mortician said. "But I'll let it go, *this time*, if you promise me two things."

"Okay, Mort."

"First, teach your old man to be more down-to-earth. His current attitude has a high chance of getting his teeth pried out, one-by-one, with a butcher knife."

Mortician glared at Knox. Still angry, Knox glowered right back.

"Next, have your phone out to take pictures of the moment Roxanne finds out Knox didn't get measured. I want to preserve that shit for prosperity." He held out his hand. "Deal, little dude?"

"Deal, Mort," Grant said happily, shaking the hand Mortician offered him to seal the deal and ignoring Knox when he sat down heavily in the closest chair.

Mortician was right. Roxanne was going to be furious. It would play right in her fears and superstitions. He swallowed.

"Grant, I think you might be right. Why don't you let Mr. Whittlestone measure you?"

"Oh boy! Really? I'll be able to dress with CJ and the others."

Knox nodded.

Shaking his head, Mortician looked at Mr. Whittlestone, who'd been standing silently by. "I'll be back in a few days with my brothers for their fittings. By then, we'll definitely know what the fuck we wearing."

"Thank you." The old man smiled. "You don't know what this means to us."

Mortician shrugged. "Boy and his woman slayed in their wedding shit. He referred me."

"Danicka is our daughter," Mr. Whittlestone announced.

"Who?" Knox asked.

"That's Boy's old lady, Dad," Grant informed him. "He's the president of the Night Fliers. One of Outlaw's support clubs."

"Who told you this?" Knox demanded.

"Nobody—"

"No one," Knox corrected.

"I went with Mort and Bailey one time when they had to stop in."

"You took my kid on club business?"

"I took your kid on personal business at a club house," Mortician stated without humor.

"Danicka found the man of her dreams in Boy," Mr. Whittlestone inserted.

Mortician smiled and held out his hand to the old man, who shook it eagerly. "We think he a good dude, too."

Knox had a very good idea who was included in the *we* Mortician referred to. The guys at the club, mostly especially Outlaw.

At this very moment, the man was having lunch with Emily Riser. That not only threatened to ruin Knox's wedding day but his entire relationship with Roxanne. He prayed they'd pull this off, get rid of Kendall and continue on with their lives as if the woman had never existed.

CHAPTER SIXTEEN

CHRISTOPHER

"MegAnn say we going to see Mickey Mouse," CJ admitted, leading Christopher into through the pencil-shaped, staggered fence, painted in primary colors. "I want to see that lil' fuckin' rat."

Christopher hid a grin, but he knew he couldn't let his boy's language slide. "Son, it ain't...*it's not* lil' fuckin' rat. It's *little fuck-ING* rat. Hear, boy?"

"Yeah...*yes,* 'Law. I hear."

"Motherfuckers think you ain't got no fuckin' sense when you talk the fuckin' way my ass do."

CJ stopped and looked up at Christopher. "You got sense!"

"Yeah, I got..." He blew out a frustrated breath. "I fuckin' mean *I have* sense. You do, too, boy. Don't let no motherfucker ever tell you no different."

"'Kay, 'Law."

"You gonna get a good education. Be a doctor or some shit."

"No, I not. I gonna be a biker. *Prez*. Like you."

Christopher crouched down and smiled. "Listen up, boy, you be what-the-fuck-ever you wanna be. I ain't ever gonna stop lovin' you and bein' proud you mine. You wanna be a biker, a wizard, a lawyer, a fuckin' badge, a goddamn *genie*, Ima be right the fuck in your corner."

CJ gave his exaggerated nod.

"My ass just askin' you try to talk better than me. You ain't got to say *I not* and *I gonna*."

"Ransom, him talk like that, and MegAnn clap for that bitch-ass baby, 'Law. I still Mommie's baby when I say it, too."

"A bitch-ass baby a bitch-ass baby, CJ. If you callin' Ransom that cuz he a lil' kid, then you one as-fuckin-well."

"Nah-uh!" CJ declared. "*I* MegAnn's potato. *Him* just a lil' motherfucker. That's what you call them, 'Law."

"I call *your* lil' ass that, too, boy," Christopher reminded him.

CJ scrunched his face up in a scowl so similar to Christopher's, he stopped short of puffing his chest out in pride. "I not no bitch-ass baby *or* lil' motherfucker. I MegAnn potato. Case-fuckin-closed, 'Law."

"I ain't gonna stop callin' you no lil' motherfucker cuz that's my special fuckin' name for you lil' motherfuckers. But we can both fuckin' agree you Megan potato." He held out his hand. "Shake on it?"

Nodding, CJ placed his chubby little hand in Christopher's and shook.

"Can we keep going to the treehouse?"

Christopher stood. "Ain't that's why we out here?"

"Uh-huh." Starting forward again, CJ resumed his conversation. "When we goin' to see that lil' rat."

"Mickey a mouse."

"I know," CJ said in exasperation. "MegAnn told me. *You* call him a rat."

"Okay, son," Christopher said on a sigh. "You got my ass."

"Motherfucker still a rodent, huh, 'Law?"

"Yeah, boy, motherfucker is."

"MegAnn was telling Aunt Bunny that you said that and she

couldn't stop laughing. Her say *I just love Christopher so much, but I had to point out that Mickey is a mouse so he wouldn't call him a little fucking rat in front of the kids*. That's what her say, 'Law."

Before Christopher responded, his burner phone beeped—the one whose number he'd given the Riser chick—so he took it out of his cut, discovering a message from Emily. He clicked it open and saw her in a dress that managed to reveal her curves while still being high-class. She worked fast. He'd left her at the diner just about three hours ago.

CJ grabbed his arm, tugging on it to see the cell phone. "What MegAnn say?"

Evading CJ's grasp, Christopher shoved the phone back into his cut. "This not your ma."

At another beep, CJ gave him a curious look, but Christopher decided not to even bother with the phone.

By the time, the sixth notification came through, he knew he had to respond. "Give me a few fuckin' minutes. This business. I gotta answer."

"I going on the swing."

"I ain't gonna be long," Christopher promised, not protesting his son's announcement because the swing was just up ahead, within a few feet of where they stood.

"You got to push me, 'Law."

"Okay," he responded, distracted, opening each of Emily's texts to see her in a new outfit, including a negligee that revealed more than it covered.

You the fuck out your mind texting my ass?

He couldn't believe this bitch was sending him these types of photos. He gave her money to purchase outfits. He had never asked to see the motherfuckers on her. If Megan had been home this evening, they would've been in each other's company and there was no fucking way Christopher could've explained this shit.

Of course, he wished she was fucking home. She wouldn't be out on a playdate with the old lady of one of his support club presidents and their kids. Alone. Without fucking escort. She would've been here and safe. For some fucking reason, she thought the drastic fucking action of taking their little motherfuckers with them would help her through her trauma. CJ hadn't wanted to go—and neither had Christopher—so him and his boy stayed home for a playdate of their own.

The phone beeped again.

I want to make sure they meet with your approval.

Her text response came within a few minutes, as if she expected his immediate response. It annoyed the fuck out of him that he'd fallen right the fuck into her trap.

Ain't gotta meet with my fucking approval, Emily. It gotta be what the fuck Johnnie like.

You hired me to do a certain job and gave me the money to buy these clothes.

Yeah, well, he couldn't fucking dispute that.

You're my boss, Outlaw.

As your fucking boss, I'm telling you don't hit me up on my goddamn phone like you got a fucking right. If my woman had been with me, I wouldna been able to explain this shit.

You either want me to steal Johnnie away from Kendall or you want to spare your wife's feelings.

Sparing Megan's feelings meant allowing Kendall to live.

"LAW!" CJ yelled, impatience clear in his tone.

Christopher glanced at his boy, who sat on the swing, his dangling legs not long enough to touch the ground. He suddenly felt lower than a motherfucker, dealing with this Emily bitch behind Megan's back. No reason he'd give would be sufficient enough to appease her sense of betrayal if she ever discovered this.

I'm a very good listener. Why don't you come to my house and let me model the clothes for you in person, while I lend you my ear.

Fuck you. Fuck no. Fuck off. My woman my best fucking friend. Don't need you for a motherfucking thing.

Really? You need me to help you with Kendall.

Do I? Ain't lied when I told your ass I got another fucking plan.

He didn't at the moment, but she didn't need to know that. He'd motherfucking come up with one, though. Or, maybe, he did.

Your fucking ass acting just like Kendall, trying to get dick from me.

Me like Kendall? Never!

Prove it to me. Act like you got some goddamn sense in your fucking head and understand I ain't fucking over my woman. You ain't sent me fucking pictures for my approval. You sent me those motherfuckers for my cock. Don't give a fuck how the fuck you look. Don't give a fuck what the fuck you is or ain't wearing. You ain't my Megan, so you ain't even a blip on my fucking radar. What the fuck don't you two bitches understand about that? I. LOVE. MY. FUCKING. WOMAN.

Goddamn it, but he was sick of having to tell bitches that. Couldn't they fucking respect the bounds of matrimony? It wasn't only Kendall and Emily, either. Random bitches who came to the club; bitches he met when he had to go on runs; bitches he ran across when he was fucking out and about.

Am I really acting like Kendall?

You acting worse than her. YOU the one that supposed to have sense.

From now on, I will respect your marriage vows and make sure you do, too.

Christopher sighed.

Babe, what the fuck you not understanding? It's up to my ass to respect my fucking marriage vows. Nothing in this world more important to Megan, except my vows to her. If you fuck with that, I'm killing you.

He supposed it was time to get a new burner. He couldn't threaten a bitch and have it traced back to him. Now, he'd had to think of a fucking reason to tell Megan he was getting a new throwaway number. It was as if it was his legitimate number. Still, Megan would ask questions.

I will behave. I promise.

He fucking doubted that, but what the fuck was he supposed to do? It was Kendall who had found this bitch, then told Johnnie, who opened his big fucking mouth and gave Christopher the idea. If she was still that fucking stuck on what the fuck Emily Riser did to her that she had to go searching for her, then Kendall would come unhinged if his plan worked. She was vulnerable to Emily.

"DAD!"

CJ's yell startled Christopher.

"I been calling you," his boy said, a frown creasing his brow. "Why you using your phone so much for not MegAnn?"

Fuuuuucccccckkkkk. CJ would run and tell Megan if Christopher didn't do something.

Shoving the phone away, he walked to where his son stood by the swing. CJ tipped his head back to glare at Christopher. In return, Christopher folded his arms.

"This business, boy. Business you ain't able to tell your Ma about." He hated Kendall a little more for the position he found himself in. He'd told his son to never hide anything from Megan. He sighed, then got down on one knee, settled his hands on his son's shoulders and looked him in the eye. "I know you ain't understandin' why I'm askin' you to hide somethin' from your Ma when my ass been tellin' you your entire fuckin' life to never lie to her. But this...this...your Ma wouldn't like it."

CJ studied him. "Law get in trouble with MegAnn?"

To say the fucking least. Christopher nodded. "This...just keep your fuckin' mouth shut. You ain't able to ever fuckin' tell her I was on the fuckin' phone to-fuckin-day."

"Can we play video games longer in the treehouse?"

"Wait a fuckin' minute. You fuckin' bribin' my fuckin' ass, tellin' me if we play video games for fuckin' longer you keepin' your mouth shut?"

"Uh-huh."

"What the fuck?" Christopher growled. "You ain't even six yet and you gettin' the drop on me?"

Not answering, CJ blinked at him.

"Fuck, fine." He dropped his hands from his son's shoulders, then glowered at him. "But if you end up tellin' your Ma anyway, Ima spank you *and* take your fuckin' video games away for a goddamn week."

Water filled CJ's eyes and his lower lip trembled. "Law mean."

No, what *Law* was, was fucked. "I ain't bein' mean, son. You ain't blackmailin' a motherfucker then goin' back on your goddamn word. That shit get you fucked up *quick*. And if you ain't grounded for it, then you beat the fuck up and put in a body cast, then motherfuckers ain't ever trustin' you a-fuckin-gain."

"'Kay."

Standing, Christopher dusted off his jeans, while CJ grabbed his hand and guided him to the extravagant fucking treehouse Megan had built for the children. It was split level—a mini mansion twenty-five feet from the forest floor and sitting amidst huge trees. He was glad he'd thought to have a delineated property line. Instead of open woods that would invade Val and Bitsy's land, Christopher had fenced in acreage for each house. And, luckily, said acreage had huge fucking trees to hold huge fucking treehouses with a spiral staircase that CJ was currently bouncing up. Not wanting to frighten his boy from just being a little kid, he stayed close behind. If the little motherfucker fell back, Christopher would catch him.

CJ ran to the door and opened it. "Want to play hide and seek, 'Law?" he asked, stepping in and skidding to a halt. He gasped as Christopher walked in and froze. "Dee! What you doing to Lyndsey?"

What was he doing to Lyndsey? *What the fuck was he doing to Lyndsey?* The question pounded through Christopher's head as he took in the scene.

He was fucking her that's what the fuck he was doing.

"CJ, go away," Diesel ordered, then moved away from his girlfriend, allowing her swollen pussy to be shown to the world. "Uncle Chris!"

It dawned on Christopher to grab CJ and cover his eyes, while, he, too, turned the fuck around.

"I hope the fuck you on birth control, Lyndsey, cuz from what the fuck I saw Diesel ain't covered his cock."

"Condoms are annoying," Diesel said.

"Your fuckin' cock fallin' the fuck off gonna be annoyin' too."

"Mr. Caldwell, please don't tell my parents," Lyndsey said.

Christopher rolled his eyes. "Is your pussy covered, cuz I sure the fuck ain't interested in seein' it again?"

She sniffled. "Y-yes, sir."

"'Law, it smell funny in here and it's hot."

"It smell like musky dick and fucked pussy."

A sob escaped Lyndsey. Christopher drew in a deep breath. He was failing this fucking test, but Diesel had shocked the fuck out of him. Yeah, he knew the motherfucker was fucking. He just didn't fucking know the motherfucker was fucking in something that a kid could walk in on at any time. He probably needed to be more...more *gentle*, especially toward Lyndsey.

"Go upstairs, CJ," Christopher instructed. "Ima be up in a few fuckin' minutes."

"The video game down here."

"I know, son. Just go the fuck upstairs. I gotta talk to Diesel and Lyndsey."

"Cuz her 'gina was out?"

Jesus fucking Christ. What the fuck was he supposed to say to that? And he knew just where the fuck CJ got *gina* from. "Yeah, boy, and it shouldna been out in here."

"Why was it out and what was Dee doin' to it?"

Gritting his teeth, Christopher thought quick. "We gonna talk later, CJ. Go up-fuckin-stairs."

"'Kay."

CJ's motorcycle boots pounded on the wooden stairs, then stopped near the top. Crouching slightly, Christopher saw the top of the boots, resting on a stair. His boy had sat his little ass down to eavesdrop.

He turned. Lyndsey sat on the edge of the couch. The same place Diesel had been fucking her on. The only difference was she was dressed and tears were streaming down her face.

"I guess it's time for a lecture," Diesel said with resentment.

"What the fuck you think my ass gonna say?"

Diesel shrugged. "How I shouldn't have brought her to CJ's treehouse and how this belongs to him."

"This not just for him." He was the one who used it most, however.

"Okay, it belongs to your children."

The underlying anger was clear in his voice, but Christopher heard vulnerability, too, the kind that came upon a motherfucker when he felt as if he didn't have nobody else in the entire fucking world.

Taking his time to light a smoke and take a few puffs, he offered one to Diesel.

"You're allowed to smoke?" Lyndsey asked in awe.

Standing taller and nodding, Diesel grabbed one from Christopher's pack and lit it.

"This treehouse belong to *the* children," Christopher started. "Meanin' lil' kids. Motherfuckers who ain't got the fuckin' right to see you in some bitch and have they innocence stolen the fuck away."

"You've said it belongs to your kids, Uncle Chris."

Christopher drew on his cigarette again, then released the smoke. "My fuckin' ass lied about that?"

Diesel glowered at him.

"Look, motherfucker, Ima wipe that fuckin' look off your face. You in this treehouse, fuckin' your *sixteen-year-old* girlfriend, throwin' fuckin' digs at my ass, and tellin' me I gotta watch what the fuck I say cuz your fuckin' ass on your goddamn shoulders. Lemme ex-fuckin-plain somethin' to you, Diesel. *You* one of my kids, but I fuckin' thought you was fuckin' smart e-fuckin-nuff to know I see you as a fuckin' man and give your ass that fuckin' respect. Ain't nothin' like findin' your own footin' and knowin' you got a motherfucker there to guide you when you need him, not cuz he wanna make you do what the fuck *he* think best. You almost eighteen-years-old. Megan still think you ain't knowin' what a pussy smell like; ain't knowin' how it feel to be *in* a pussy or get your cock sucked. Left up to her, you'd be sittin' the fuck around in the fuckin' playroom with the fuckin' kids cuz that what she see you as. Her kid. From here on fuckin' out, if you want me to say *the kids* to include you, Ima treatcha like a fuckin' kid. As a matter of fuckin' fact, Ima let Megan set your curfew, pack your fuckin' lunch, deny you cigarettes and alcohol and Aunt Mary. And Ima *tell* Megan you and Lyndsey been fuckin'." He glared at Lyndsey. "*She* gonna call your fuckin' parents."

Diesel hung his head.

"Lyndsey, you still a kid. Don't let no motherfucker get in your pussy, fill you with a kid, and ruin your fuckin' life. You got time for fuckin'."

"I love Diesel, Mr. Caldwell."

Lifting his head, Diesel frowned.

"Be a kid while the fuck you can," Christopher told her, wanting to knock the fuck out of Diesel and his wayward cock. "Bein' a grown-up hard as fuck."

She wasn't convinced.

"You ain't able to come over un-fuckin-less we home. You ain't able to go in Diesel room or anywhere, unless CJ with you."

"Uncle Chris, that's not fair. He'll tell on me."

"Shut the fuck up. You about to graduate and you goin' away to college and—"

"You said you'd changed your mind about going away?" Lyndsey interrupted, her face crumpling as she looked at Diesel.

Diesel shifted. "I just haven't told Uncle Chris, yet," he mumbled.

Christopher snorted. He had to teach his fucking girl not to fall for a motherfucker's bullshit, especially a good looking assfuck like Diesel that had girls falling at his fucking feet.

"Lyndsey, get the fuck outta here," Christopher ordered, stepping aside since he still stood in the doorway.

"I picked her up," Diesel announced.

"Go wait in the fuckin' family room. Ima take you fuckin' home my-fuckin-self."

"Why can't I take her?"

"Cuz that's exactly what the fuck you'll do. *Take her,* and not just to her fuckin' house."

"'Law, I tired waitin'," CJ called.

"I know, boy. We got a new fuckin' plan, though. We gotta bring Lyndsey home."

"Then we coming back to play video games?"

"Yeah, boy."

"'Kay."

Christopher looked at Diesel. "Where the cock covers I gave you?"

Diesel shrugged again, his go-to gesture to show his insolence. "Somewhere."

"You ain't got a motherfuckin' dime to take care of a fuckin' kid."

"You fucked at my age."

"I did," Christopher agreed. "But I was also earnin' my fuckin' money. I was usin' condoms, too."

"I want to earn money, but you won't let me become a probate."

"Not now."

"If I'm your son, you should be happy I want to follow in your footsteps."

"If I'm your old man, you should be fuckin' happy I want you to have better than my fuckin' ass," Christopher countered. "Ain't tellin' you no different than Ima tell CJ or any of my fuckin' sons or nephews."

Diesel fell silent, then glanced away. "You're really telling Aunt Meggie?"

"Diesel, look, boy. It's fuckin' okay to be fuckin' angry," Christopher responded, unsure if he would tell her or not. "Pissed the fuck off at the world. You been through a lot. Both your Ma and your old man ducked out on you and left you homeless. My ass would be madder than a motherfucker, too. But we ain't leavin' you. You for me and Megan. You *ours*. You ain't goin' through this shit alone, no matter what the fuck I call this fuckin' treehouse."

A tear slid down Diesel's cheek. "You might decide to throw me away."

"So you tryna throw our asses away first, huh?"

Another tear. A third shrug. A sniffle.

"I ain't tellin' Megan, but I was fuckin' serious about how you interactin' with Lyndsey. You ain't wantin' nothin' but to fuck her. Mean-fuckin-while, she lookin' at you like you a fuckin' god."

"She's so pretty."

"She is," Christopher agreed. "She also a good fuckin' girl that think you her fuckin' soulmate."

Diesel groaned. "Girls are so stupid."

"No, girls smart. Us motherfuckers the ones that's stupid. We see a pretty bitch and we just see our fuckin' cocks in them. We ain't carin' that they got feelins and shit cuz the motherfucker between our legs ain't carin'."

"Are you going to tell Lyndsey?"

"About you just wantin' to fuck her?"

"Yes."

"Nope. It's up to your ass to do the right fuckin' thing. All the fuck I can do is guide you to the right fuckin' path. Whether you take the motherfucker up to you."

His main phone dinged. When he pulled it out, he saw a text from Megan.

The kids are enjoying themselves. We're going to stay at Gypsy's a little while longer. I love you.

This fucking evening just got better and fucking better. He might have to bribe his boy with cash because, after he dropped Lyndsey off, he was heading over to Derby and Gypsy's place, so his woman would have an escort home. He might not be able to do anything about some of this bullshit, but it was becoming more and more obvious drastic actions called for drastic fucking measures.

CHAPTER SEVENTEEN

One week later...

Knox

Although he'd watched Kendall leave her house, ten minutes ago, Knox still carefully opened her entrance door, using Outlaw's spare keys. The ones Kendall knew nothing about.

The alarm beeped, so Knox set his suitcase of equipment down and hurried to where Kendall's security system was located. It deactivated without a hitch.

Knox grimaced, unimpressed by Outlaw's high-handedness, but wanting Kendall gone more so. It also didn't help that Mortician babysat him, night after night, giving him or Roxanne no chance to see each other alone again.

He thought a similar scheme would've taken place after this week's family dinner. It had been at Zoann and Val's house, which, in Knox's mind, made logistics for a secret rendezvous so much easier. But, no. Not a damn thing!

Roxanne had just offered sultry smiles and stole teasing kisses after Bailey momentarily distracted her stupid husband and Roxanne asked for Knox's help with Harley and Lou. Except they'd gone nowhere near the children. She'd led him to an alcove in the log cabin styled house and kissed him senseless. Until Mortician found them and yanked Knox away from Roxanne as if they were horny teenagers instead of sex-starved adults.

It still irked Knox that Roxanne had allowed Mortician's actions to pass without complaint.

Frustration had become Knox's daily companion. He missed Roxanne so much. He missed sleeping next to her. He missed her scent. Her laughter. He couldn't believe *she* hadn't rebelled, but, no, she seemed perfectly happy with the arrangement as it was.

He wasn't. He wanted his sweet Roxanne, who gave his life meaning, made him laugh and see things from a different perspective.

Not only was Mortician shutting him out of Roxanne's house and company in private, but Outlaw had been on his ass to wire Kendall's house for observation. Knox should've known the maniac had little understanding about logistics. He couldn't very well storm the house and do what needed doing while the redhead was home. Besides, he'd needed to prepare for the job. He'd needed to purchase the equipment.

Tired of the constant belligerence from Outlaw, Knox had finally *suggested* to Roxanne that she and Bailey needed to set up the first wedding committee meeting with all the women. That would get Kendall out of the house. Besides, he wanted to order his wedding attire as Mortician and Grant had. After avoiding Roxanne's wrath *and* winning brownie points by pushing for the wedding planning, she took his suggestion and scheduled the meeting for today. That had given him three days to acquire the tools he'd use to rig Kendall's house. Knox spent hours upon hours making sure he had everything he'd need.

This needed to be a one-and-done. He didn't relish breaking and entering even with a secret key.

Except it was Kendall, who deserved every retribution Outlaw planned. Except Kendall was one of Roxanne's babies.

Was he really as hypocritical as Outlaw? The man smiled in everyone's face while planning Kendall's destruction. Her *death*. Just because he wouldn't pull the trigger, if Kendall killed herself, he'd still be responsible.

One more example of how little logic Outlaw had. It was obvious the biker thought he couldn't be accused of her demise.

Stupidity was Outlaw's problem. Knox had a job to do.

First, he'd get a feel for the place, and then he'd get to work. Luckily for him, knowing how the women liked each other's company, leaving Knox with hours to do his job. Besides, his mother had begged him to have the meeting moved to her house. Something Knox was glad to do. He hadn't relished his gentle mother going to a biker club. She was a well-respected society matron and a premier restaurateur, unused to such rough surroundings.

And in her capable hands, she'd see to it that Roxanne and the others were entertained for hours.

~

Kendall

"I know Joan Harrington," Charlotte Redding said with dismay as Kendall almost missed the turn that led to the entrance door of the Harrington estate. "I was so happy to hear that her dear boy is marrying. I must admit I was shocked to hear *who* the bride is."

Kendall gave Charlotte the side-eye.

"Thank you for letting me be on the planning committee," Charlotte continued, ignoring Kendall's disapproval.

"Only if Roxy agrees," Kendall reminded her friend and mentor. "I shouldn't have listened to you. I should've asked her before I allow you to crash the meeting."

"That woman needs all the guidance she can get to have the type of wedding a Harrington deserves."

"Come on, Charlotte," Kendall chided. "Don't be like...like Knox. He pretended to accept our lifestyle just to get Roxy, then reverted back to being an asshole. It was all just a façade."

Look who's talking. Regret and guilt hit Kendall hard as the thought drummed through her head.

Charlotte lifted her chin and drew herself up. "What do you mean *our lifestyle*? It is *their* lifestyle. You're not one of them. Don't ever debase yourself in my presence in such a way."

"But I am one of them," Kendall protested, her sadness almost overwhelming. "If only they'll have me."

"Bah!" Charlotte waved a hand, the gesture as dismissive as the tone of her voice.

"Charlotte! Stop this. If it wasn't for Roxy, Knox's uncle would've killed you."

"I know the woman saved my life when Avalon took a dark turn. For that, I'm grateful to her. However, her deed didn't change her overall character. She was trash before she saved me and she's still trash. She's classless. I just cannot abide her."

"Give her a chance. Please. For me. I invited you without her knowledge. Please behave as you taught me to do. With calm decorum."

"As you know, I was wrong in regards to *them*. You, especially, should understand that they make you sink to their level. Those people don't allow you to keep your decorum. You have never been able to accept those barbaric bikers, even though, for the time being, you are married to one of them."

"I hope it's longer than for the time being," Kendall retorted. "You apologized to Roxy," she added, turning the subject away from her marriage and back to Charlotte's behavior. "I thought your words to her were sincere, Charlotte. I've never known you to fib."

Charlotte gasped. "Fib? You accuse me of being a fibber? That is such a harsh word, dear."

Kendall bit her lip. "I'm so sorry."

"I will have you know I was quite sincere when I said sorry to that woman. I was overwhelmed with emotions, thankful to be alive. These people try your patience. Test your resolve. Make you rethink if it is a good idea to socialize outside of your class. Think of Knox! *He* apologized to them also after they beat the tar out of him. *He* said he'd changed and accepted them, too. They are the ones who never change. They are the reason good folk like you and me and Knox Harrington go back on their word. We realize our efforts are useless. They are all morons. I see that clearly now. And I also clearly see Roxanne as a baseborn, ignorant, loudmouth piece of trash."

Kendall gasped. "I won't stop being her friend because of how you feel, Charlotte. Just as I won't stop being yours." Not that Roxy had ever, or would ever, demand such a thing of her. "Please don't ruin this afternoon."

"Just as that woman is the same, so am I. Thanks to them! I abhor the lot of them. My status hasn't changed much since Brooks has gotten back into Outlaw's good graces. Brooks is lucky that I love him. He still has me living like a pauper, while that Roxanne-woman is about to marry into one of the richest families in the country. It's an appalling, ironic travesty."

Kendall was getting nowhere with Charlotte, so she remained silent, advice offered to her by Dr. Briscow. Every statement didn't require a response. Every topic up for debate didn't have to turn into a battle. Kendall lived her life at war because her emotions and thoughts were always in turmoil. Wanting her family back was top priority, so Kendall would try her best to heed the psychiatrist's suggestions.

A few minutes later, Kendall drove up to the Harrington mansion and stopped behind two cars already parked. She got out of her car and started toward the door, smiling at Roxy's purple Navigator and scowling at Zoann's Jeep Cherokee.

Charlotte was right on Kendall's heels as they paused at the front entrance. Before they rang the bell, the door swung open and a butler in uniform stood there.

"Mrs. Donovan," he greeted. "Mrs. Harrington and the others are awaiting your arrival."

"Traffic held me up," Kendall answered smoothly, when in fact, it was the detour to Charlotte's house. She really hadn't wanted Charlotte to tag along, but the poor woman had lost most of her society friends, and her family had drifted apart because she'd gotten on the wrong side of Outlaw. Kendall felt somehow responsible since the stand Charlotte had taken against Outlaw had been on Kendall's behalf. She stepped aside so Charlotte could enter. "This is Mrs. Redding."

The butler nodded, not betraying his thoughts about the extra, uninvited guest. "Very good, ma'am." Once he shut the door, he walked past Kendall and Charlotte. "Follow me," he instructed politely.

As she walked behind the butler, Kendall noted the crystal chandeliers, silk wallpaper, marble floors, and fine artwork in the corridors. The Harrington house was magnificent, suggesting not just wealth, but *wealth*. A bank account that would last for generations.

The butler opened a pair of double doors. "Mrs. Harrington, Mrs. Donovan and Mrs. Redding have arrived," he announced.

"Mrs. *Who?*" Roxy asked sharply, unseen but quite loudly heard. "No, you didn't, Kendall."

A throat cleared. "Please, show them in, Merrick," a voice as cultured as Charlotte's said.

The servant stepped aside, and Kendall entered an airy room with traditional décor in tones of cream and white, with a French antique Aubusson rug in the center. She'd looked at something similar for one of the rooms in her house, but ultimately decided against it. In retrospect, it was because Johnnie wouldn't have liked it even if he'd accepted on her behalf.

"Joan, darling," Charlotte greeted, walking forward with the dignity of a queen.

Joan Harrington stood. "So good to see you," she told Charlotte as they air-kissed each other's cheeks.

Roxy threw Kendall a dark look.

"I'm sorry," Kendall mouthed.

"Kendall, Charlotte, we have orange juice, coffee, pear spritzes, and cranberry-champagne cocktail." Joan indicated the elegant setup of tables near the huge bank of windows. "I thought buffet style would work best for the meeting."

"What would you like, Charlotte?" Kendall asked nervously, withering under Roxy's burning anger. "I'll get it."

"The pear spritz," Charlotte responded, seeming to stand taller in surroundings she felt she should be in. "Thank you, dear." She headed to one of the Bergere chairs, while Joan seated herself in the other one.

"Meggie, Zoann, Bunny, Bailey," Kendall greeted, since they only seemed to want to stare at her. "Roxy."

"Hi Kendall," Meggie greeted with a smile.

Kendall couldn't place the tone in the girl's voice. It almost sounded *cool*, but that wasn't Meggie's style, so Kendall dismissed it and headed to the table containing the drinks. She picked up the pear spritz and the cranberry-champagne cocktail, admiring the crisp, white tablecloths on the two tables. One held drinks and the other held fine china plates, cloth napkins, silverware, and trays of food.

Kendall brought Charlotte her drink, then sipped her own, assessing the room. Charlotte and Joan sat on one side in designer clothes with legs demurely crossed.

Meggie wore brown suede pants and a cream-colored cashmere sweater. Kendall had actually been with Meggie the day she'd purchased the outfit. She actually looked decent. Zoann wore scrubs—of all the tacky things. Bunny and Bailey wore jeans, while Roxy had on a stylish jumpsuit, drop earrings, and heels. Roxy dressed like she deserved to be a Harrington. Looking at each side of the room, where women who were worlds apart sat on separate sides, Kendall's uncertainty surprised her.

Charlotte's designer clothes might've been from a resale shop, but they were still name brand and added to her inherent elegance. On the other hand, Meggie's outfit had been extremely expensive, but she was still low-class.

Roxy, Meggie, and Bailey sat on the sofa. Two extra chairs had been brought in for Bunny and Zoann—and placed on that side of the room. If Kendall sat on Joan's side, she would have more space. Besides, that setup would form a nice circle.

Joan had drawn a dividing line between her and Roxy. Kendall was almost certain the chair Charlotte sat in had been meant for herself.

The door opened and the butler who'd led them to the room carried a chair. His silent, efficient movements impressed Kendall as he sat the spare chair next to Charlotte.

"The seat Charlotte took was going to be yours," Joan confirmed to Kendall.

She offered Joan a gracious smile. Though she didn't want to offend

Charlotte or Joan, hurting Roxy was out of the question. Whether the other women spoke to her or not, they'd agreed to let Kendall plan the weddings with them. They could have just as easily told Roxy it was either her or them.

Kendall sat her glass on the coffee table, then dragged her chair midway between each side, hoping everyone understood.

"Well, then," Joan started with a little laugh, not giving away her feelings on Kendall's actions. "First, I'd like to congratulate my soon-to-be daughter-in-law on her recent engagement." She lifted her glass, waited until the other women did the same with theirs, then took a sip.

"Thank you, Joan," Roxy responded politely. "Although this is a surprise, considering you had almost three fucking weeks to congratulate me."

Kendall shifted in her seat, needing to gulp a glass of scotch, instead of a weak champagne cocktail.

"Oh, Roxy, darling, forgive me. I've been so busy and Knox took me completely by surprise when he told me and his father he'd proposed to you."

"How many days did you stay in bed upon hearing the news?" Charlotte asked sweetly. She offered Roxy a false smile. "Knox is her only child and, yet again, she's losing him to the vagaries of his heart."

"In a fucking minute—" Roxy started.

"May I say something?" Kendall interrupted. She didn't want Roxy to burn her bridges with Joan. No matter what, the woman was that asshole's mother—Roxy's soon-to-be mother-in-law.

"Yeah, *bye*," Roxy snapped, "and take this bitch with you. *She* wasn't invited, Kendall. What the fuck is wrong with you, bringing a bitch that hates me to plan one of the most special days of my and Bailey's lives?"

"That's what I wanted to say," Kendall said quietly. "But first I want to thank you." She met each of their gazes—Roxy, Meggie, Zoann, Bailey, and Bunny—hoping she conveyed her gratitude. "You didn't have to include me, yet you did."

"As long as you're Johnnie's wife, you're part of the family," Zoann told her, without warmth, her look and her tone telling Kendall she hoped that situation would change soon.

Kendall lowered her lashes. "But I haven't been invited to the family dinners in weeks."

"You know when they are held," Bunny replied with a shrug. "It was up to you to attend or not."

Meggie sighed, and glided her fingers through her golden hair. "Kendall, please come to dinner tomorrow night. It'll be at my house, and I'd love to have you."

Staring at Meggie, Kendall saw the strong resemblance to Emily. Wasn't it written somewhere that there were seven people in the world who mirrored each other's looks?

Meggie did look like Emily, which had tortured Kendall for years. But the girl wasn't Emily. Most importantly, she had a completely different personality, a completely different outlook. She wasn't vile and evil like Emily. Then, Meggie's build was smaller. Her hair was lighter. Emily was a honey blonde and her eyes were a darker blue than Meggie's.

In Kendall's mind, though, Emily and Meggie had been the same. Kendall had ruined everything because she'd set Emily—and therefore Meggie—as the ideal.

Emily never would've extended a dinner invitation to Kendall, under the circumstances.

"Thank you. I'd love to attend," she answered.

"Well, I hope everyone brought their appetites," Joan said into the silence. "Tempers are always cooler on a full stomach. Let's eat, then we can get into the wedding discussion."

Knox

Kendall's house was beautifully-appointed, just the type of home she'd appreciate, with the airs she liked to put on.

Bitter anger rushed through Knox. Outlaw had bullshitted him with a story about this house being one of the club's safe houses. Specifically, his family's.

Riiigggghhhttt, and Knox was the King of England. Artwork, elaborate lighting, and Persian rugs, wasn't for Megan Caldwell. Even if it was, it certainly wouldn't withstand the bratty onslaught of Outlaw's Baby Thug, CJ.

No, this house had been purchased with Outlaw's diabolical plan for Kendall in mind.

Walking around, Knox scoped out places to install his various cameras. He also had listening devices for rooms he couldn't install cameras. Outlaw had given him blueprints of the house, so he knew where each room was, but he needed to get a bird's eye view for installation purposes.

The master bedroom had light gray walls and white trimming. The bed—with white sheets and white comforter—was neatly made. A pair of burgundy alligator pumps stood in the spot between the wall and the nightstand. A silk robe lay on the back of an overstuffed chair.

It surprised Knox to see photos of Johnnie, Rory, Matilda, and JJ on the dresser.

A camera in the bedroom meant complete lack of privacy, but Outlaw insisted on it. He wanted to know if Kendall was cheating on Johnnie. Not that he had any reason to believe that. It was just another excuse he used for his spying.

Once again, Knox didn't like it, but he wanted to be rid of Kendall bad enough to follow through on the orders.

It was easiest to install a light-bulb camera in this room. He'd have a panoramic view, motion detector that alerted him to movement, night vision, and microphone. Unlike in the other rooms, once the subject or subjects laid in bed, he'd get a clear view of a face.

It was easy enough to switch bulbs in the spherical light fixture. He set the old light bulb on the dresser, reminding himself to take it with him, then headed to the master bath. There, he found two wet towels on the floor, makeup and perfume scattered on the vanity. The door leading to the closet stretched wide open, inviting Knox to take a peek.

Her clothes were neatly arranged by dresses, skirts, pants, and tops, further separated by color. A wall of shoes faced him, while belts and purses took up a small section.

Would Outlaw want a camera in here...No. Kendall might walk in undressed. Her bedroom was bad enough. No camera in the bathroom or closet.

Since he needed to get started downstairs, Knox grabbed the old light bulb and returned to the first floor, heading for the kitchen.

He needed a visual of faces. With a panoramic lightbulb recording from above, he'd only see the top of heads, so Knox decided the microwave was the best place for the kitchen camera.

Though Stretch was recovering from his final surgery, he'd still coached Knox on quick and efficient installation. Stretch hadn't asked why he needed the knowledge, and Knox hadn't volunteered. If he didn't know, it was up to Outlaw to tell him. Besides, Stretch had already hacked into her alarm system and created a master passcode for Outlaw's benefit.

Once Knox installed the microwave's new start button, the rest of the job should go smoothly.

CHAPTER EIGHTEEN

Roxy

"Which hor d'oeuvres did you enjoy?" Joan Harrington asked Roxy with expectation.

She'd had poppy seed and Parmesan cheese straws, tomato tartare stuffed in mushrooms, steak tartare in cherry tomatoes, smoked trout chevrons with dilled crème fraiche, pecan stuffed dates wrapped in prosciutto, grape leaves stuffed with shrimp cannel, goose rillettes with French baguettes, pink meringue kisses, white chocolate lavender hearts, and mini kiwi tartlets with whipped cream and candied lilacs.

The entire time they'd eaten, no one said much. Every now and then, Joan would break in with the name of the next food they were tasting—as if the fucking place cards weren't enough.

"My favorite was actually the steak tartare in the cherry tomatoes," Roxy answered, undecided as to whether Joan Harrington was happy about Knox's proposal or not.

If Roxy had to guess, she'd say *not*. After the first disastrous meeting with Knox's parents, they'd made her feel welcome whenever she saw them. Roxy understood that a marriage was permanent, something Knox couldn't easily walk away from and she believed that made all the difference in the world to his parents.

"I will put them on the menu," Roxy went on. She looked at the girls. "What do you think?"

"I liked the rillettes," Bailey said. "I'm going to add that to the menu as well."

"Darlings," Joan began, "I didn't have these dishes made to add to *your* menu. We are taste-testing so we can come up with *the* menu."

"And *the* menu is what *we* decide," Roxy stated.

Joan tittered. "You're precious. We want to keep the food elegant and simple. You're not only *dating* Knox. You are about to marry into the Harrington family. A very philanthropic family with excellent social standing."

"Roxy is a very good cook, Joan," Kendall offered. "She probably has the menu all figured out in her head."

"We don't want an oyster boat, red beans and rice, gumbo, and fried alligator," Joan said with a saccharin smile. "That's fine for New Orleans, but not for Portland."

"Don't waste your breath, Joan," Charlotte had the nerve to chortle. "She's one of *them*. A biker woman."

"That's uncalled for," Kendall said quickly.

Roxy threw Kendall another glare. What made her think bringing Charlotte's ass to their meeting was a good idea, Roxy didn't know. She and Charlotte had *never* gotten along. The few hours of commiseration they'd shared when they'd been taken by Knox's crazy uncle was long since gone.

However, Roxy felt a little off-balance. All the girls did, she suspected, with the exception of Kendall probably. They were in a high-society mansion of a high-society snob. Even for a goddamn taste-testing, the atmosphere lacked the down-home, easy-going vibe they all liked.

Kendall was the only one who hated those situations.

Kendall...and Knox.

Roxy couldn't forget some of Knox's words from the dinner on the night they'd made love. She knew he hadn't meant to be condescending, yet he had been. No wonder Mortician was so relentless in his quest to have them live separately until after the wedding.

The dick and pussy policing annoyed Roxy. Although it didn't. Not really.

She frowned. Her thoughts made absolutely no fucking sense. Either she was pissed with Mortician's interference or she was happy. She couldn't have it both fucking ways.

Could she?

She hated to fail, and she'd done so three times. Three marriages. Three divorces. Four men. Four baby daddies. The bane of her existence were her relationships. She couldn't get them right. Even K-P, who'd loved her so much and whom she'd loved just as much had worked better as close friends, rather than lovers.

Besides, Knox's cockamamie story about why he wouldn't allow Mr. Whittlestone to fit him for his tux, still rankled. He'd gotten away with it *then* because she'd been a googly-eyed bitch, thinking with her pussy.

She absolutely loved Knox to eat her out. He'd given her some bullshit excuse about a fucking bridal party—what the fuck that had to do with *his* ass getting fitted, she didn't know—then he'd licked his lips, his eyelids heavy. The motherfucker knew he was so fucking sexy, Roxy could barely stand it. Seeing his tongue reminded her of his pussy-eating skills. Which, in turn, made her all plaint and agreeable.

A bitch was dick-whipped...tongue-whipped. But he laid good dick; she enjoyed his company; and she loved him. What the fuck was she supposed to do when he hadn't wanted to do business with the Whittlestones?

However, suppose she discovered, *after the ceremony*, that it was the same with her and Knox? Maybe, she went along with Mortician's ridiculousness so she had a buffer between her and Knox to see things clearer.

Already it was working. Wasn't it? She and Knox needed to have a heart-to-heart about several issues. He needed to open up and tell her how he really saw her. If he looked down on the bikers, what did he think of her? Was she truly good enough for him? To *him*. Not to herself.

Right? Riiiggghhhtttt.

She'd never lacked confidence in herself. Until she did.

Logan Donovan's voice crept into her head. He'd been a singular motherfucker. As a matter-of-fact, deeming him a motherfucker was too good. The word to describe him hadn't been invented.

How she hated him! If only she could find one of the pieces they'd left of him to flush it down the toilet. That he could still get into her head after all these years galled the fuck out of her.

He was a narrow-minded, pig-brained, miserable racist. Further, the place he told her she'd *never* have in the club, in K-P's life, was now hers.

She'd also married into New Orleans Black High Society, as cutthroat as any fucking place on earth. After a year, she'd been so unhappy with Duke's father, Creighton.

She glanced around. House managers and butlers and maids and cooks and chauffeurs filled the Harrington mansion. When Roxy had arrived with the girls, one of the staff members had led them to Mrs. Harrington's personal drawing room.

The handful of times she'd come here, she tried not to roam the halls to gawk. Somewhere, in the huge place, there was a ballroom and a banquet hall, along with a bunch of other rooms that Roxy felt were completely unnecessary.

Knox was heir to this.

When she'd walked into Joan's drawing room, her almost mother-in-law had stood, wearing an olive-green wrap dress and square-heeled, pointy-toed pumps that reeked of...of... Roxy wasn't sure.

It had just overwhelmed her. Now, Joan mocked her New Orleans roots. Roxy didn't want a war with Knox's mother, but if she didn't stop the woman in her tracks, the wedding would turn into *Joan's* ceremony, not Roxy or Bailey's.

"No, Mrs. Harrington, you're wrong. New Orleans food is delicious," Bailey was saying, bringing Roxy back to the conversation.

Mrs. Harrington, huh? Try Mrs. Bitch.

They were supposed to have this meeting at Bailey's place. Then Knox had called last night and begged Roxy to allow his mother to host this first meeting.

Joan wanted to be on her own turf. All the better for fucking condescension.

Grabbing her purse, Roxy got a pen and small notepad, then turned a level gaze to Joan. "If I want a pirogue filled with dirt and live crawfish, that's my fucking business. I didn't have to include you at all, Joan."

"Knox wanted me included," Joan returned. "He wouldn't have been happy had you not."

He probably wouldn't have, but it went back to him wanting a society wedding, since they were having a big ceremony, with all the bells and whistles that went with it.

Roxy would've been happy going to Las Vegas and letting Elvis marry them.

"You're right," Roxy conceded. "He wouldn't have. That doesn't mean he wants you to plan it. Me and Bailey are in charge, not you."

"I'm only trying to help," Joan told her. "Besides, I need to be in on the planning so I can tell you the flowers I'm ordering to decorate the ballroom and banquet hall—"

"I'm not having the ceremony or the reception here," Roxy interrupted.

"Of course you are," Joan said, as if that had been a foregone conclusion. "It is a Harrington tradition. Knox had his first wedding here, too."

Roxy scowled. "Then I know I'm not having anything here."

"Maybe, you can have the rehearsal dinner here," Kendall suggested.

"That sounds like a good idea, Mama," Bailey said. "We would love that, Joan."

Joan sidled a glance from Roxy to Bailey. "There seems to be some type of miscommunication here."

"On your part," Roxy said, not unkindly. She came up with a quick solution. "Could you plan the rehearsal dinner? Food, decorations, everything?" That would also keep Joan away from the wedding committee meetings.

Roxy expected to have a lot of laughs with the girls, instead of all this silence and tension.

She held her left hand out. The diamond on the ring winked at her. *Are you to blame for all this bullshit, motherfucker? All the doubts and panic and issues thrown our way?*

Joan cleared her throat and glared at the Harrington ring, not hiding her displeasure. "That's a priceless Harrington heirloom. I trust you know what to do with it."

"I sure do," Roxanne retorted. "I know how to shove it up your fucking—"

"Mama!" Bailey yelled as Joan narrowed her eyes. "Mrs. Harrington is just, um, er..."

Go ahead and make an excuse for this sadity bitch, sugar.

Bailey glanced at Meggie.

"Joan is just expressing the importance of the ring to the family," Meggie said after a moment's hesitation.

"I know how to speak for myself, girl," Joan spat at Meggie.

"I hope you know how to protect yourself," Zoann flared. "Because I'm ready to shove that ring up your ass and my fist down your throat."

"Savages!" Charlotte hissed. "The lot of you." She smiled at Kendall. "Except you, dear."

Kendall shifted uncomfortably, but kept her mouth shut, which the girl should've done before she invited Charlotte.

"Joan, this isn't going as planned, but imagine how happy Knox will be to hear Roxy wants you to plan the rehearsal dinner," Kendall gushed. "He loves Roxy so much and knowing his mother and his fiancé are getting along will make him *so* happy."

Joan scowled at Kendall, who didn't blink or back down.

"Fine," Joan huffed, glaring at Roxy. "I'll do the rehearsal dinner only if Charlotte and Kendall help me. Do you have a problem with that, Roxanne?"

Kendall's face fell.

"You can have Charlotte, but Kendall stays on *my* committee," Roxy replied.

"Why don't we let Kendall choose," Charlotte suggested.

"I'm flattered to have this tug of war over me," Kendall started with a smile. "Charlotte, I want to be with Roxy and the other ladies."

"You're right, dear. They do need all the help they can get," Charlotte said.

"I've already talked to Reverend Mackey," Joan cut in.

"For?" Roxy asked, contemplating dragging Charlotte from her chair and punching her in the mouth.

"The service, of course," Joan said. "What do you think?"

"We're not having Reverend Mackey," Roxy said with a shake of her head. "We're going to have Father Wilkins officiate."

"Oh, my goodness," Charlotte said faintly. "Are you kidding me? Kendall tell me she's not serious."

"Who is Father Wilkins?" Joan asked.

"A despicable crook who pretends to be a priest," Charlotte said, then shivered delicately.

"He's the man who's marrying me and Knox," Roxy said.

"Yeah, and renewing the vows between Lucas and me," Bailey added.

"Father Wilkins heads up all of our religious events." Besides a greeting and her invitation to Kendall, Meggie hadn't said much, so Roxy was glad to have her input. "It's a tradition that started when I married Christopher."

Charlotte wrinkled her nose.

"We'll see who Knox prefers," Joan said.

"Knox prefers whoever the fuck *I* want," Roxy snapped. She stood, tired of the drama. "I think it's time to go. We have some difference of opinions that can lead to a nasty argument. Knox loves you, so I'd really prefer not to have a falling out with you."

"How considerate." Venom laced Joan's words.

Meggie, Bailey, Zoann, Bunny, and Kendall stood.

"Kendall, dear, please stay. I can have a tete-a-tete with Charlotte."

"I really need to get going, Joan. I'm sure you and Charlotte can catch up with each other some other time."

"Charlotte, you can stay. I'll see that you get home."

Charlotte hung her head. "The place I live in is horrible. Nothing like where I once resided. I'm ashamed for you to see it."

"My dear, don't tax yourself," Joan said. "I am not one to judge."

Bitch, please.

Deciding she'd had enough, Roxy bid Joan and Charlotte farewell, then led the other girls out of the room, where a butler stood, waiting at the door.

"It's a good thing we didn't bring in the magazines," Meggie chirped. "We would've carried them in for nothing."

"We can still find a bridal shop to stop in. Perhaps, even make an appointment for a later date," Bailey said, pressing the unlock button on her key fob. She turned to Kendall. "I'm not sure where we're going, but you're welcomed to follow us."

Kendall shook her head. "No, but thank you. I need to get home."

Roxy went to her and hugged her. "Hang in there, sugar," she said.

"I'm trying," Kendall whispered, for her ears alone. "But it's hard. I feel like the outsider."

"Come to dinner tomorrow night. You'll see you're still just as much part of the family as ever," Roxy said.

Kendall nodded. "I will. Right now, I think I'll go home and relax in a bubble bath."

"Do that," Roxy said.

They all left together, although, once they reached the main road, Bailey turned Roxy's Escalade, followed by Zoann in her Jeep, in the opposite direction from Kendall's Navigator.

Tomorrow night would be just like old times. Meanwhile, Roxy intended to find a way to talk to Knox in private.

They had a lot to discuss and some very dirty fucking to engage in. Roxy couldn't wait.

Knox

In the living room, Knox found the shelf of knick-knacks Outlaw had told him about, and added another one to the mix, one with a camera in the eye. Time was racing by. In the blink of an eye, over two hours had passed.

He needed to get everything else finished. He didn't think the meeting would be over for a few hours, but he didn't want to chance Kendall returning home early and finding him in her house.

In Kendall's elegant little office, where her degrees graced the wall, she had more family photos on a shelf behind her desk.

Knox almost believed she missed her family. But not Kendall. She had no motherly genes. Nor the genes that made her a good wife and friend.

As he started to open one of the desk drawers, he remembered Outlaw had asked Knox to find Kendall's medications, note the date they'd been filled, the quantity of each bottle, and the amount of pills left.

Too bad he didn't have time for such an inconsequential task. Outlaw would just have to deal with it and find another way to invade even more of her privacy.

Knox scowled. He hated Kendall but the cop in him despised Outlaw's criminal behavior. A problem to solve another day.

Brushing aside his annoyance, Knox yanked open the top desk drawer, finding nothing.

Slamming the drawer shut, he went to the fake plant on the file cabinet and attached the tiny camera on the stem. Satisfied at his progress, he left that room behind and went to the den. A huge TV hung on the wall.

Knox pulled up one of Stretch's programs, punched in the code the man had given him, then logged into his surveillance system.

There he stood, in the middle of Kendall's den, playing on the phone while being watched by the Smart TV Stretch had hacked into.

Satisfied, he went back to his suitcase, picked up his checklist, and scratched off another room. He still had the kids' rooms and the patio to do, along with the foyer. Unfortunately, there were not many places to hide a camera in the foyer, so he wired a tiny microphone along the baseboard near the front door.

At his suitcase once again, he decided to bring it upstairs with him, since he also needed to do the hallway. That would be a lot to lug in his arms.

Just as he zipped up his suitcase, grabbed the handle and stood to head to the second floor, the front door opened.

Fuck!

Not having time to explore his options, he rushed behind the den door, attempting to angle his body and the suitcase to hide. Through the crack, he watched as Kendall sailed into the room.

Knox tensed.

She stopped in the middle of the floor and turned in a circle.

Quickly, Knox diverted his gaze away. He didn't want Kendall to notice his eye staring at her.

"Something's not right," Kendall said in confusion. "What's not right...*Shit*! Hello? Whose here? Johnnie?"

She drew in a deep, quivering breath. Knox could almost feel her rising panic. Her footsteps drew steadily closer to the door he stood behind.

Suddenly, she stopped again, pulling out her cell phone.

Knox held his breath, worried that she'd hear him. He was afraid to move, afraid to do anything that would give him away. He prayed his cell phone didn't ring.

Any minute he expected exposure. He waited. His heart pounded. Sweat slid down his temples.

If she discovered him, Outlaw would be furious that Knox had failed to do the job he'd been paid to do. Johnnie might be angry on Kendall's behalf. Even if he wasn't, Roxanne would be.

"Johnnie?" Kendall whispered, still standing near the door.

"Yes, Kendall?" His voice rang through the speakerphone.

"Are you here? I got home and my alarm was off. I turned it on before I left. I know I did."

"Are you sure? And, no, I'm not in your house. Where are you?"

"In the den."

"Why?" he snapped. "If you think someone's in there, get the fuck out."

"You're right," she said, her footsteps pounding out of the room. "I would've called 911 but..."

As the door opened, Kendall's voice faded away.

Closing his eyes, Knox leaned against the wall and drew in a deep breath. He had to calm down.

But, fuck, he needed to get out. Kendall might be outside. At a neighbor's. In her car...Goddamn it! Why hadn't the women socialized as he'd expected?

He had to take a chance on leaving. One thing he couldn't do was be here when Johnnie arrived.

Holding onto the suitcase, Knox hurried to the door. Before he opened it, he looked out of the window on each side. Saw nothing.

His heart banged against his chest.

He held his breath. Opened the door painfully slow, just wide enough for him to slip into the afternoon cloudiness.

He didn't see Kendall, but her Navigator sat in the driveway. She was around.

Knox stepped forward, swallowing hard, his breathing accelerated.

He made it off her property. Around the corner wasn't far away.

One step. Two steps. Three steps...he walked with purpose, head down, one hand gripping the suitcase and the other hand stuffed in his pocket.

Had he closed the front door? Fuck. He didn't think so.

Too late now. He refused to go back just for that. Finding the door open would confirm to Kendall that someone had been in her house. Knox only hoped Johnnie didn't do a sweep of the premises...

Knox reached his car. Opening the trunk, he threw the suitcase in, then ran to the driver's side and slid in. A moment later, he sped off.

Damn, that had been close! He still wasn't free and clear. There was a high chance Kendall had seen him as he left from wherever she'd hidden herself.

CHAPTER NINETEEN

Megan

Trying not to panic, Meggie disconnected a fifth call she'd placed to Christopher, all of which had gone straight to voicemail. She hadn't heard from him since right after breakfast when he kissed her goodbye. Nothing unusual about that.

He'd seemed relaxed, at ease, without a care in the world. As a matter of fact, he hadn't had a nightmare in three days. So why wouldn't he answer any of her call? She understood one or two, but *five*?

Panicked, nausea swirled through her. For a second, she felt so light-headed she thought she might faint.

"I have a question," Bunny said, unaware of how Meggie felt.

She and Bunny sat in the second row of Roxy's Escalade, heading to an unknown wedding shop, while Bailey once again drove and Roxy sat in the front seat.

Meggie was so glad to be gone from Joan Harrington's house! She'd prefer being out in the open and going from shop to shop over spending another minute with that judgmental woman and Charlotte Redding. The two looked down on all of them and—

The sound of Roxy digging through her purse reached Meggie.

"What is it, Bunny?" Roxy asked in a distracted tone.

"Last night, Mark began talking about Mortician's chaperoning," Bunny confessed. "Of Roxy and Knox," she clarified.

Roxy peeped in the mirror on the visor and met Bunny's gaze. "And?"

"He seems to think we are all going to band together and arrange a secret rendezvous between you and Knox." Bunny sighed. "For a minute, I thought he'd found out about the secret meeting we arranged between you and Knox. When I realized he hadn't, I still felt guilty and I told him even if we did, Bailey would never go along with it. She's like Switzerland in this situation. Neutral. That started the whole 'no-room for neutrality' conversation. Mark said Bailey's allegiance should be to her husband, first and foremost. The conversation still bothers me, especially in light of what we did. I want to know, when you *have* to choose a side between your mother and your husband should you just ignore what might be best for your mother, even if her side is right?"

Roxy drew her brows together, still observing in the visor mirror. "Somewhere in the bible it says *a man shall cleave unto his wife*. I don't know exactly where. Last time I read the Good Book all I remember is this one begetting with that one, and that one begetting with this one. They did a lot of begetting in those days."

"Mama, move closer to the door. When lightning strikes you, I don't want to be in the line of fire," Bailey grumped.

Roxy laughed. "Don't worry, sugar. If I haven't been struck by lightning yet, I think we're safe."

"Does it say anywhere that a wife should cleave unto her husband?" Bailey asked, staring at the road ahead as she deftly moved through traffic.

"Not that I recall," Roxy answered. "There is something about how a wife shouldn't separate from her husband. If she does, she has to remain unmarried the rest of her life or reconcile with her man."

"I wish I knew the bible like you," Bunny said wistfully.

"Chile, please," Roxy responded. "I know bits and pieces. Most of what I remember is just brought out for situations like these. Not because I'm religious. I quote the bible to make a point, so what good does it do me to know scripture if I don't really apply it to my every day life?" She shrugged, her question rhetorical. "Don't do me one damn bit of good. This is a conversation for another day. Besides, religion and politics... remember the rules. Those topics shouldn't be discussed in polite society."

The four of them gazed at each and roared with laughter.

"We're so fucking far from polite, 'til the shit not even funny," Roxy hooted.

Even Meggie felt brief peace at the light moment. Covertly, she speed-dialed Christopher's number again. Once again—straight to voicemail.

"Let me answer," Bailey piped up as Meggie refocused on the conversation, pretending, for the moment, she wasn't almost crazy with worry.

Christopher was the club president. He had many, many enemies, and he'd already been kidnapped once. Twice, if she counted the time Snake had gotten him.

Meggie drew in a shaky breath and swallowed.

"So you would always side with Mortician?" Bunny asked.

Lost in her thoughts, Meggie missed whatever Bailey said.

"Yes," Bailey told Bunny.

"I disagree, baby," Roxy said. "You helped me and Knox because you know, in this situation, you husband is being totally unreasonable. Knox has given him no reason for Mortician to lay down the law like he has and not allow us to live together."

Meggie cringed. Yes, he had given Mortician a reason. Christopher had told Meggie all about the conversation the guys had, where Knox said he could always propose to Roxy, eff her, and then leave if they cornered him into proposing. Knox had a way of talking out-of-hand, especially when he was annoyed. Meggie felt those words came from one of those times. But the guys didn't want to take the chance that he'd follow through on his threat. His proposal had taken them all by surprise. A few weeks before, he'd sworn to the guys he had no intentions of proposing. They were beyond suspicious of him.

More recently, Bailey had called her, Bunny, Zoann, and Fee on a conference call and told them all about Knox's behavior at the dinner. The man was being a complete moron. But they had to protect Roxy at all costs. They believed Knox loved her. He was just an idiot and used to having things his way. But there would be no more help from any of them to arrange secret hook-ups between him and Roxy.

"It's all about Girl Power," Roxy inserted.

Even glummer, Meggie leaned her elbow against the arm rest on the door and cradled her head in her palm.

"Especially now," Roxy went on. "We should totally plan another secret rendezvous between me and Knox. Mortician is being so goddamn unreasonable."

Deciding she'd let Bailey handle that, Meggie speed dialed Christopher's number yet again, just in case she'd caught him between calls. Same thing, though. Straight to voicemail.

"Are you okay, Meggie?" Bunny asked. "You've been awfully quiet.

"I haven't heard from Christopher since early this morning. The last time I talked to him was when he was walking out of the door to head to the club. This isn't like him at all."

Roxy twisted in her front passenger seat to look back at Meggie. She hadn't felt like driving, so Bailey had offered to do so before anyone else could. "Don't worry, sugar. I'm sure he's fine. Something must've come up."

"But what? He would've let me know if he had to go on a run. Or *anywhere*."

"Lucas isn't with him," Bailey said with assurance. "We've been texting back and forth, and he said he was taking care of club business. A lost shipment or something."

"Mark is in one of the warehouses, overseeing the packaging of merchandise," Bunny added.

Speed dialing his number again, Meggie's heart sank when she got the same result. "He has to be okay."

"Nothing happened to him, baby," Roxy said with the utmost confidence.

Meggie nodded. "Things happen so fast. One minute you're driving along and the next minute you're being surrounded by motorcycles and taken."

"Aww, Meggie," Roxy clucked. "I know you're traumatized but Outlaw knows how to take care of himself. If he was really worried about something going down, he'd have us surrounded by guards."

"He wants me to have guards," Meggie confessed, "but I told him I need to be the way I once was. Running errands on my own. What kind of message would I send to CJ? How would Christopher ever get anything done if he got a report on every move I made?"

Roxy snorted. "To CJ, it would seem as if his momma wanted to stay alive. To Outlaw, he'd focus *more*. Imagine how he must feel, all alone, knowing you're out there where anything can happen? I'm surprised at how selfish you're being."

"Maybe not selfish," Bailey amended quickly. "Just too overwhelmed to realize your life is different now. As Outlaw's wife, you always have a target on your back."

"Unless you wear a disguise," Bunny suggested. "But then you'd have to drive different cars and change up your looks every so often. It isn't worth it. I'm with Outlaw on this one."

"We all are," Roxy said sharply. "But it's not up to us."

"When I'd run errands on my own, I used it as me-time," Meggie confessed.

"You had a lot of fucking me-time when you were chained up," Roxy retorted. "I'd say you don't need more for awhile."

She hadn't always had that much time to herself. At one time, it had been when she soaked in the bathtub and that had been fine to rejuvenate herself. She was sure it would be fine again. She was just adding to Christopher's worries with her stubbornness and refusal to see his point of view.

Roxy was right. What had gotten into her? Didn't that mean Mystic would've won, though? Christopher was strong and brave, and he needed her to be the same.

"I'll talk to him," she said. "Just as soon as I hear from him."

"I'm tired, Bailey," Roxy said around a yawn. "Why don't we head back to the club?"

"Okay, Mama."

Meggie didn't say anything. She just hoped by the time they got back to Hortensia, Christopher would've turned up.

CHAPTER TWENTY

CHRISTOPHER

C hristopher grimaced as he slid into the passenger seat of Bailey's Escalade. The anesthesia was wearing off, leaving his balls with a pain that extended down his cock.

"Prez, you good?" Mort asked after he slammed the passenger side door and got into the driver's seat. He'd commandeered Bailey's SUV to serve as Christopher's chauffeur.

"No, motherfucker," he growled. "I ain't. And I gotta get my ass to-fuckin-gether before I see my girl."

He'd been gone since early this morning. Between the surgery and the recovery time, he hadn't spoken to her since that time, either.

Drawing in a deep breath, Mort started the ignition. "Meggie girl gonna know something wrong, Outlaw. You walking like you got sausages stuck up your ass. You stepping like you about to break out in a scene from the Nutcracker. You ever saw that ballet? The most boring shit ever. I went to sleep and Bailey didn't disturb me neither.

The best sleep I ever had in a public place. Drool was running down my chin and shit. That should've taught Bailey not to bring me to a boring ass ballet. I guess she didn't learn her lesson. We going to see something else in a couple of weeks. About the time it'll take you to get back to yourself. I have to hear the shit you telling Meggie for her to believe your cute little walk not related to your cock."

"Whatever, motherfucker," Christopher grumbled, Mortician's voice echoing through his head like a menace in a dark tunnel. His pain was grouching him out. He pushed the seat into a reclining position and closed his eyes. "Shut the fuck up, so I can get some fuckin' rest."

"Guess I better leave you alone."

One of Christopher's eyes popped open. "I guess the fuck you better. Talk to me when my cock ain't feelin' like it got weights attached to that motherfucker that's dragging it on the fucking ground."

Mort backed out of the space and went to the parking lot exit. "Damn, prez. Now, normally, I don't comment on another motherfucker dick, but I can't let this shit slide. Prez, bruh, I saw your cock in all states. Fuck, more than I want to see the motherfucker and I don't give a fuck how you might want to dispute me, your shit not big enough that weights'll make him drag the ground."

"Shut the fuck up, Mortician," Christopher snapped, glaring at his friend and folding his arms. "I ain't gettin' into no dick-sizin' conversation with you. Wasn't even re-fuckin-ferring to the size of my big cock. The motherfucker *hurt*. It hurt so bad, it got the crack of my ass burnin'."

Finally easing into the traffic, Mort shook his head. "I hope your ball reversal worth it."

"I ain't have the motherfuckers switched, assfuck."

"Okay, your sac reversal."

"It's a fuckin' dick snip flip, so shut the fuck up and let me fuckin' sleep."

Christopher didn't sleep, though. He thought of Megan. She was with him all the time—in his heart and his head. Except when he had to fuck a motherfucker up. He wouldn't mar her goodness with that gruesomeness, even in his mind. She was his sweet angel and he'd do whatever the fuck he needed to do to keep his woman safe, including going through a dick snip flip. He hadn't told her or asked her feelings about the situation. Megan loved little motherfuckers, so she wouldn't have a problem with Christopher wanting her pregnant again.

How-fuckin-ever, he'd made such a fucking commotion about getting the dick snip in the first place. She'd been disappointed but already pregnant. Since then, they hadn't discussed it.

Her current unreasonableness left him no choice but the low-motherfucker-move that currently had him and his cock in such misery. He'd feel her out before he told her what he'd done. Would she be his sweet angel or hell bitch again? Based on prior interactions, she'd welcome another pregnancy. She'd worked hard, though, to get her body back after all the babies. She hadn't had much weight to lose. It was more of toning herself up. She was proud of the rewards her efforts achieved.

Christopher couldn't help but wonder if her firmer body meant something deeper? Or was she doing it because she'd been resigned to the fact that she wouldn't ever get pregnant again?

She knew how much he worried about her when she was knocked up. She stuck close to home and, if she did go out, she allowed the bikers Christopher assigned to her to go with her.

Of fucking course, he couldn't keep her knocked up. It was too fucking easy for him and Megan to make babies. At the rate they'd been going, they'd end up with enough kids to start their own country.

Right now, though, he needed her either under guard, with him, or at home. Just until...until *what*? He sure as fuck would never forget she'd been stolen from him. Maybe, during her next pregnancy, it would register with her that he only wanted her safe. All the mother-fuckers assigned to her detail loved it. She was young, gorgeous, and upbeat. *She* was the one who thought fuckheads were bored. *They* didn't. Assfucks fought to be on her detail. Some of them, like Johnnie and Val, would *never* get that privilege.

Christopher's foresight helped them to keep their dicks attached to their bodies and their heads on their shoulders.

"Fuck," Mort grumbled.

Christopher opened his eyes. Bumper-to-bumper traffic, heavier than usual, greeted him. He sighed. Whatever was causing this snarl on the 205, it would take them hours to get home, when all he wanted to do was get past Megan and get in bed.

Tension rose in him. The longer he took to face his wife, the more nervous he'd become. He'd never get any shut eye in his current state, so he pulled his seat up.

"If I ain't been so scared of losin' Megan she woulda been pushin' another kid out soon."

Mort drummed his fingers on the steering wheel. "You saying you don't fear she'll die in childbirth anymore?"

"Yeah, Mort, Ima always be fuckin' scared of that shit," Christopher said quietly. "But I'm more scared a motherfucker takin' her from me, and Megan ain't listenin'. She ain't wantin' another detail cuz she so happy bein' free to do her own shit. It's fuckin' killin' me she fuckin' agreed to a fuckin' detail for my fuckin' sake. How unhappy she gonna be with that? She like me-fuckin-time. She bein' a stubborn lil motherfucker. Un-fuckin-reasonable as a motherfucker. I gotta do something to keep her home."

"We got her back."

"She was fuckin' *dyin'* in that fuckin' hole, Mortician. If we wouldna found her when we did, I woulda…" He would've climbed down the stairs that led to the underground room, and found her corpse, just like in his nightmares. "I just come too close to losin' her too many times. Megan my sun and my moon. I ain't know what else to do but torturin' my cock."

His balls felt as if they'd swelled to twice their normal size. He needed ice dumped on his dick. He needed to lay down in their bedroom, without a stitch of clothes, legs open, to cool his nuts.

"Prez, I think you a little delirious talking about suns and moons, but I feel what you're saying. You and Meggie share a love for the ages, brother. It's a special connection."

Christopher's eyes drooped closed before he opened them again. "She my heart and soul," he whispered. "If I ever lose her, I lose me. My sanity. My life. I love Megan from the top of her head to the bottom of her feet. I just love her, Mort. She gotta be safe. Ain't nothin' happened to her in her other pregnancies, so I think my way the right way."

"You know her, Outlaw. If you think this will keep her inside, then you right."

Two hours later, Mortician shook Christopher awake as he pulled up in front of Christopher's house, the place Megan made a home.

"Let me help you to the door."

"Fuck no," Christopher barked. "Cameras every-fuckin-where. If Megan see you helpin' me, she gonna know shit ain't right."

"You been snoring for ninety fucking minutes. You sure you can make it?"

In response, Christopher opened the door and got out of the Escalade. Pain streaked through him, and he moaned.

"Prez?"

"Bye, Mort!"

Mortician snickered, then drove off. For laughing at his pain, Christopher intended to fuck Mort up. Later, though. Right now, he wanted to crawl to his gate but he forced himself to walk and punch in the code.

By the time he reached the back porch, sweat was popping from him and tears slid down his eyes.

He took slow, measured steps through the mudroom and into the kitchen. He thanked whatever motherfucker was watching over him that Megan wasn't in the room and dropped onto the nearest stool. Grunting, he braced his elbows on the counter and grabbed paper napkins to wipe his sweat and tears, then bowed his head.

"Hey, you."

Her sweet voice floated to him, a moment before she laid her hand on his arm.

"Hey, baby," he responded, turning his face to her and stealing a kiss.

She thumbed his lips. "I've been so worried about you," she whispered in a trembling tone. "I haven't heard from you in hours."

He was in too much cock pain to feel fucking guilty. "I had some fuckin' shit to deal with off the radar." It wasn't exactly a lie.

Stepping back, she eyed him, suspicion replacing her concern.

"I ain't fuck no motherfucker up, Megan," he said.

Relief brightened her eyes and she nodded. "Okay, I have your dinner plate all wrapped up. Let me warm it for you." She headed to the stove.

He sighed. The last thing he wanted was food. "I ain't hungry, baby."

"You ate already?"

"Something like that," he answered, then quickly changed the subject. He rarely ever ate any place but home if she wasn't with him. "Where the kids, baby?" The house was very fucking quiet, the biggest clue him and Megan was alone.

"CJ, Rory, Lou and Ryan are with Fee, Cash, and Stretch. Rebel is at Bailey's with Matilda and Harley, and the rest of the kids are at Bunny and Digger's house.

She leaned against the counter, across from him. "We have the house to ourselves," she announced with a saucy little wink.

His dick twitched.

Motherfucker was *un-fucking-believable*. For several hours, he'd given Christopher signs that he was wrecked. *Ruined.* All Megan had to do was hint at giving him her pussy and it was trying to stand up.

After the trauma his cock had suffered, how was that even possible?

He couldn't think of a motherfucking thing to say. He certainly couldn't say, yeah, come the fuck on, hop in my lap and ride my cock.

At his silence, she gave him a curious look. "Are you sure you're okay? You're flushed and a little warm."

"Just hot, baby. Central heat doin' its job."

She narrowed her eyes at him. "Heat isn't on."

Fuck, of course the motherfucker wasn't. He couldn't be that fucking lucky.

"You don't look well," she insisted.

He wasn't feeling fucking well, either. But he needed to call Knox and see if he'd gotten all the surveillance equipment put up in Kendall's house.

He supposed he'd have to build another safe house for Megan and his kids. The one Kendall was living in would be sold as soon as he got rid of her. Too many motherfuckers knew of its existence. He had to have a place for his family if the club's grounds were ever compromised.

He also needed to call Emily and make sure she was ready to kick shit off.

Seeing as how he was keeping so much else from her, he supposed he should tell her about the surgery.

Maybe, if Megan agreed with him about how to take revenge on Kendall, he'd clue her in...*No.* She had too much of a soft heart. She wouldn't want Kendall gaslighted.

Christopher sighed and squeezed the bridge of his nose. "I gotta talk to you, Megan."

Immediately, she snapped to attention and slid into the seat next to him. "What's going on?"

"I was thinkin' about how much I like you filled with my kid. I kinda miss seein' you so round and full of me." He shrugged. "I been regrettin' my dick snip."

Shock crossed her features and she shifted in her seat. "I, um, I don't know what to say." She cleared her throat, then bit her lip.

Warning bells went off in his head. "Tell me what the fuck you thinkin'."

"When you first decided to get your vasectomy, I was crushed. Then, I ended up being pregnant and...and...I came to terms with the fact that Ransom would be the last baby I'd give birth to. I—I started exercising and...and...you know I'm in really good shape now." She pursed her lips. "I don't want to be pregnant again."

A feather could've knocked his ass the fuck over at her announcement.

"We have five children."

"We woulda had fifty of them lil motherfuckers if I ain't got my snip."

She stood from her seat and stepped closer to him. "I love you," she whispered. "I'm going to be fine. You can't keep me barefoot and pregnant for me to stay safe."

He scowled. He could never get one over on her. "What the fuck you mean, Megan?"

"I mean, Christopher, you think I'll remain at home if I'm pregnant. As long as I'm home, I won't be in danger of kidnap."

"What if I say I wanna do a dick snip flip?"

She pulled away and stared at him, a frown creasing her brow. "A vasectomy reversal?" she squeaked.

"Yeah."

"I'd get on birth control."

Frustration filled him, and he huffed out a breath. "Then wherever the fuck you go, you gotta have a detail. Case fuckin' closed."

She shook her head. "When I was rotting away in the place Mystic had me, I told myself I'd never decline security again. But then he wins. He's making me live my life in fear. I like not having the guys dog my steps. Every place I go, they are right on my heels. It can be overwhelming, especially when I have to buy feminine stuff."

Christopher squinted at her. "What the fuck that mean? They ain't lettin' you buy your pussy plugs by yourself?"

"No. And if they see someone on the outs with the club, they insist on *paying* for my stuff, including my tampons. I don't like that."

He didn't either. If *he* wasn't buying them for her, no other motherfucker should. He'd have to take care of that and make sure that never happened a-fucking-gain. That fuckeduppedness had made Megan dig her heels in about not having escorts. Rage bubbled inside of him.

"Suppose I get the snip, you get on birth con-fuckin-trol, and we see what the fuck happen?" he pressed.

"No. I don't want you going through that pain again."

Too motherfucking, goddamn late. He forced a smile. "It ain't nothin' but a thing, Megan."

"I'm worried that if you get a reversal, the birth control will fail and I'll get pregnant anyway. I would die for our children, but five kids are...it's a lot sometimes. I don't feel as if I give you enough time because I'm distracted by our sons and daughter. Then, I worry you'll complain about how much money I spend on them."

"Megan, I get in your pussy at least two times a fuckin day. We have dinner together and we tuck the kids in together. You make a point to spend time with me every fuckin' night in the den and we talk and laugh and shit. Ain't no way in fuckin' hell you ignore me."

She studied his face before her eyes brightened and she nodded.

He took her in his arms again and kissed the top of her head. "You love lil babies."

"I do," she agreed, laying her head against his chest. He threaded his fingers through her hair. "But having too many kids would also limit the time I have with each of them."

"Megan..."

She stole a kiss from him. "Didn't the doctor mention something about a failure rate? If, for any reason, your vasectomy fails and I end up pregnant, I'd be happy and I'd love that baby as I do each of our other kids. Let's not actively try to get me pregnant, though."

"Ima talk to the new motherfuckers on your detail. Tell them to give you space but still keep a eye on you. Ain't no fuckin' reason motherfuckers should be buyin' your tampons. Why the fuck you didn't tell me that was the problem?"

"I didn't want you to shoot anyone."

And motherfuckers *woulda* got shot.

He grunted, arranging the confession in his head that he'd had the procedure already. Words fucking failed him. Of-fucking-course, she'd discover it on her own when it came time to fuck.

To curtail that, maybe, he needed to purposely piss her off...?

They were above such bullshit. Weren't they? Their relationship worked so well because they talked to each other. Although, usually, they were on the same fucking page. He didn't know what to do now. This was so important.

She came to him and stood between his thighs. He winced at how the slight movement sent pain tearing through him.

She lifted a brow. Before she had a chance to speak, he bent and kissed her.

"I love you, baby," he said.

She placed her arms around his neck. "I know," she murmured. "And I love you. So much. I just want to be the wife you deserve."

Shaking his head, he took her face between his hands. "Baby, don't start with this fuckin' bullshit a-fuckin-gain."

"Oh, Christopher," she whispered. "I don't want you to worry about me and I'm so sorry for being difficult and selfish and..." She stepped back and wiped at the sudden tears slipping down her cheeks. "I don't know what to do…I *didn't* know what to do. I talked to Roxy today and she thinks I should have the guards. Now, hearing you tell me you'd get a vasectomy reversal…omigod, Christopher!" She sniffled. "I'm so sorry to have put you through such worry. There's no way I'd have you go through that pain when the solution is so simple. I mean I'm scared anyway. No matter how I try, I can't get over that fear. And…and I did feel safer with the detail. I was so wrong. Can you ever forgive me? I'll have my detail again," she announced and launched herself into his arms, burying her face against his chest.

Meanwhile, his cock ached, his balls throbbed, and his stomach heaved.

And his Megan, his pain-in-the-ass little motherfucker, decided to get her detail back because he fucking *offered* to have his dick snip flip.

Well, fuck.

CHAPTER TWENTY-ONE

JOHNNIE

When Johnnie arrived at Kendall's house, he found the front door ajar. That alone concerned him. Even at their house on club grounds, she never left her door open.

Frowning, his heart speeding in worry and agitation, Johnnie drew his Glock and stepped inside. "Kendall!"

No answer.

"Kendall!" he called again, his insides spasming at all the different scenarios running through his head. He tightened his finger on the trigger, prepared to fire.

God...if something happened to her...Shit!

"*Kendall!*" His voice shook with urgency.

But...nothing. No sound. No movement. No eerie feel of someone else's presence.

Rushing from room-to-room on the first floor, he found it clear, so he returned to the entry hall, turned in a circle, then glanced up the winding staircase.

"Who the fuck is in this fucking house?" he yelled in frustration, aiming his Glock. "Show yourself and pay with your fucking life."

Nothing, just as before.

He pounded up the stairs, deciding he'd employ Christopher's tactics—shoot and bury the motherfucker. No need for torture. Just an easy dispatching of the fuckhead who'd terrorized his wife.

Johnnie searched the bedrooms, the bathrooms, the closets—any place someone might hide. Still...nothing. No one. Not even a sign anyone else, besides Kendall, had been here, other than that open door.

Did that mean whoever had been in the house got away after Kendall left? Perhaps, in her quest to leave, she'd forgotten to close the door. Overcome with fear for her safety and unease at the entire story, Johnnie paused on the second floor landing.

Holstering his gun, he rubbed the back of his neck as another thought invaded him. Kendall had sworn someone was there; she didn't have the best track record for honesty, however. She *could* have lied to get him there. Yet the fear Johnnie had heard in her voice had been real. She'd left her alarm on and it was off when she returned.

"*FUCK!*" Johnnie roared, as he drew yet another conclusion, this one more harrowing than the others.

Christopher had been in the house. Possibly, he'd hidden himself to ambush and kill Kendall.

"Johnnie?"

Her shaky voice traveled to him from the first floor. She must've been nearby and saw his Navigator in her driveway.

"I'm here, Kendall," he said on a bleak sigh and made his way downstairs.

She stood in the center of the entry hall, wearing the barest makeup, her hair piled high on her head. She'd never needed much. Without makeup, she was still a perfect beauty. Her lacy pencil skirt and black blouse hugged her curves, made her look elegant, profes-sional, and gorgeous.

Fear—real, true, and genuine—shone in her lovely brown eyes.

Not wanting to alarm her, Johnnie decided to keep what he

suspected happened to himself. Telling her that Christopher was hunting her served no purpose.

"It's all clear, sweetheart," he said gently, his mind racing.

The situation cornered him and left his hands tied. Unless he packed his bags and took Kendall and their kids away. Christopher wouldn't leave Megan to follow Johnnie and Kendall to wherever. Nor would he send another club member to do his bidding in this instance. Not only was it too personal, but the club supposedly didn't kill women.

Supposedly being the key word. Kendall had committed the cardinal sin and fucked with Megan. Johnnie doubted Christopher would be as outraged over CJ—if not for Megan's kidnapping.

"J-Johnnie?" Kendall whispered. "What is it? What are you thinking about?"

"Club business," he blurted, an automatic response he'd learned to give her when he didn't want to share his thoughts.

She nodded, started forward, and then stopped, waiting for his encouragement.

Yet he couldn't give it to her. As badly as he wanted to. As much as he *needed* to. If only he could take her in his arms and love her. Feel her warmth and vitality, and know that she was alive.

He couldn't make that move or encourage her to do so for the same reason he wasn't rushing her to pack up so they could escape tonight. He hadn't figured out if he could continue on in their marriage. He didn't want to lead her on and he didn't want to take advantage of her.

Lifting her chin at his rejection, she wrapped her arms around her waist. "I don't know who could've been in here. Or, maybe, it was my imagination?" she asked with hope.

"I don't think it was merely your imagination," he told her, deciding on a partial truth. He took his Glock in hand, put the safety on, then held it out to her. "Keep it near you at all times."

Nodding, she grabbed the gun from him, then met and held his gaze. "I won't hesitate to shoot, Johnnie."

"I know."

"Then you're giving me permission to shoot him?"

He lifted a brow. "Shoot who?"

"Don't be asinine," she sniffed. "Outlaw. We both know it was him who was in this house."

Johnnie winced and started to speak.

"Don't," she interrupted. "You don't want to kill him but you'd see no problem if someone else did."

"That isn't true!" he snapped. "This is part of the problem, Kendall. You believe the things I do are for completely different reasons than what I actually intend them to be. I don't want Christopher dead, by your hand or my own. I do want *you* safe."

"Safe?" she asked in disbelief, then held up the gun. "Safe? If it *is* Outlaw who broke into here and does so again, what then? If I point a weapon at him, either I have to fire, or die myself."

Scowling, Johnnie snatched the Glock from her and shoved it away. "Do you have to make a fucking argument out of everything? I always have your best interest in mind with *all* that I do."

"I doubt that," she spat. "Shooting Outlaw is a moot point anyway. I'm no longer in possession of the gun."

He huffed out a breath. "Don't ignore the fucking issue. Address the subject. I want to hear what you have to say."

She shook her head, stubborn as usual. "I'm moving on from the conversation," she said, tossing her hair over her shoulder. "How was your day?" she asked, folding her arms as if daring him to challenge her change of subject.

He wanted to clear the air between them, have the conversation that laid everything on the line. But he knew it wouldn't be tonight. As usual, she wanted her way and was digging her heels in. Fuck, but she was childish and annoying.

He drew in a deep breath to calm himself, deciding to find something positive in the conversation. Besides, if he wanted to be completely honest, her question pleased him. She seldom asked about his day. "It was long," he admitted.

"Meggie invited me to the family dinner tomorrow," she told him, not commenting on his answer, as if it didn't matter to her and had only served her own selfish purposes. "If you don't want me there, I'll stay home."

"I have no problem with you being there, sweetheart," he said gruffly, hating her uncertainty. That same primitive feeling of possession and the need to protect her returned. He wanted to take her in his arms and shield her, kiss her from head-to-toe and lose himself in the ecstasy of her body. But they needed more than a physical relationship. They needed openness and honesty. They needed trustworthiness. "Even if I did, Megan invited you. It isn't my house. All I ask is that you leave CJ alone."

A guilty look crossed her face. "What do you mean?"

"You don't like that child."

She wrinkled her nose. "I'm sure I won't see him, Johnnie. He'll be too busy playing with the other kids. Besides, I'll have a chance to spend more time with Rory, Matilda, and JJ."

"Right. Focus on our children. Don't concern yourself with what CJ does."

She nodded, then shifted and clasped her hands together. "I haven't eaten," she said. "Have you? I have leftover black bean salad. Enough for both of us."

"Sounds delicious," Johnnie said, meaning it. "I'm starving, so your offer is quite welcome."

She glanced at him through her lashes. "I'd like to offer you something else."

His cock perked at the thought of taking Kendall, but his brain rebelled. "Let's stick to dinner and drinks tonight."

"Of course," she said coolly, then brushed past him.

"Kendall," he said, following behind her.

Stopping, she stiffened her shoulders, but didn't turn. "Yes?"

"I want to have dinner with you. Enjoy your company, but I'm not dealing with your damn attitude. Either get over the fact I'm not fucking you tonight, or I leave."

Though she remained silent, with her back still to him, she seemed to wilt. Her shoulders slumped and her head bowed. A subdued Kendall was a new concept.

"Our food will be on the table in ten minutes." She walked away.

Sighing in frustration, Johnnie followed behind her. In the kitchen, she was pulling a glass bowl out of the refrigerator.

"No protest to my words? I expected at least a discussion. Instead, you want to keep me guessing at your thoughts?"

Setting the bowl on the counter, she faced him. "What do you want me to say, Johnnie? No, what do you *want* from me? If I respond, I'm a problem. If I don't respond, I'm a problem. Basically, in your eyes, I'm just a problem."

"No, you're not. When you're acting like you have some goddamn sense, you're a dream come true. Otherwise, you're a fucking demon."

"I have issues!"

"So fucking what?" Johnnie snarled. He'd tried to help her with her emotional problems, but she never cooperated. Or, if she started out following advice and doctors' orders, she stopped. Kendall's mind closed when it came to her mental health. "We all have issues," he reminded her, hoping to appeal to the side of her looking to identify with others. "We don't destroy all of our relationships because of them."

Tears rushed to her eyes and she held her hands out. "I have a new diagnosis," she rushed out, her gaze pleading. "New medication."

He almost took her in his arms and asked for an explanation. He forced himself not to. She'd just seize upon his softening to manipulate him. "For once, Kendall, I don't care." This new, hard-nosed approach might give her incentive to cooperate. She loved to do the opposite of whatever he asked of her. The thought angered him, and he glared at her. "A new diagnosis? New medication? What the fuck does that mean if you get tired of your plan of recovery? Not a fucking thing. You start out with hope—*I* start out with hope and dreams and plans for our future—then you fucking self-destruct. A man can only live with so many disappointments about how his marriage is going. Only so much hope. When you lose hope, *faith*, you have nothing."

She sucked in a breath.

"For so long, I cared about you, your mental health, getting you well, but you rewarded me with more bullshit. You have a new diagnosis? Good for you. Take your meds; don't take them. That's on you. My children are safe from your moods. My life is more peaceful." The truth of those words stunned him. He'd always felt so broken and guilty when they separated. This time, he didn't. "I don't have to tiptoe through my fucking life to keep you happy. Rory is at ease."

Her mouth opened and closed, before she finally found words. "You don't love me anymore," she stated in a broken whisper.

"I love you, Kendall. I always will. I just don't know if I'm *in* love with you any longer. I don't know if I want to stay married to you." He didn't need her in his life as he once had.

She released a pitiful sob. "Is there someone else?"

"No."

"Are you looking?"

"As long as you're my wife, I won't break our vows," he swore.

"Suppose someone comes along, someone who isn't *psycho-cunt Kendall*."

"You're not a cunt."

She gasped, swiping her cheeks to remove the tracks of her tears. "But I'm psycho?"

"You're something," he retorted.

"As if you're perfect," she sneered, then closed her eyes. When she reopened them and stared at him, there was no derision in her gaze, no anger on her face, only an openness Johnnie was determined to ignore. "I'm fighting, Johnnie," she said with quiet dignity. "For myself and my children. I'm fighting for you and our marriage. I don't want to lose you."

Regret enveloped him and he gave her a sad smile. "You already have."

CHAPTER TWENTY-TWO

Knox

Sitting on the edge of the bed in the club room he didn't want to be in, Knox watched as Johnnie imparted his flat words to Kendall before turning on his heel and sauntering away. Because of all of the cameras, Knox tracked Johnnie's progress to the front door. The man looked as if he didn't have a care in the world. He looked at peace.

Meanwhile, Kendall slid to the floor in near hysterical sobs. She sat, angled between cabinets, rocking herself, before she finally curled up on the floor and cried. After ten minutes of watching this, Knox sighed and exited the program. He almost felt sorry for her.

Almost.

The other part of him, the *biggest* part, felt vindicated. He got a certain sick satisfaction at watching her fall apart. She deserved every heartache.

However, Knox cursed himself for forgetting to close the front door. Just as he'd gotten back to the club, he'd gotten an alert of activity in Kendall's house. He'd opened the needed app on his tablet and saw Johnnie searching. Knox knew, without a doubt, it was because he had indeed forgotten to shut the door.

Putting the tablet's screen to sleep, Knox had called himself a dumb asshole all the way back to the bedroom he occupied, ignoring everyone, just as they ignored him. He'd called Roxanne, but received her voicemail, then he'd waited, expecting her to call and tell him what a fabulous time she'd had with his mother.

He'd gotten nothing. After ten minutes, he'd decided to check on Kendall, wondering if Johnnie had left.

Now, he set his tablet aside, once again waiting. This time for Outlaw's call. He'd been expecting to hear from him for hours. Frankly, it shocked him that the man had left Knox to his own devices for the entire day.

Another ten minutes slid by in slow, tortuous minutes. He never realized how important the space and freedom to move around was to him, until he'd lost it with the forced exile at the club.

He could always move in with his parents. That, however, would put him too far away from Roxanne. He wanted to be as close to her as possible, since he couldn't live with her because of Mortician's hypocritical mandate.

Knox and Johnnie were the only two with both logic and education out of that whole group of men.

Reaching for his cell phone where it lay next to him on the bed, Knox intended to try Roxanne again. Before he dialed her number, the phone started buzzing, indicating an incoming call.

Mother popped up on the screen, and Knox smiled.

"Hello, Mother," he answered, excited to hear about the wedding plans.

"Knox, dear, I simply must talk to you as soon as possible."

An inkling of unease spread through Knox at her anxious tone. "Why?"

"Roxanne, of course," his mother answered irritably. "What else? The woman isn't fit to be a Harrington. She says she won't hold the ceremony here at the estate. She has her own minister chosen, some little priest that Charlotte Redding says is a greedy creature. She only wanted *two* of the items...no, she wanted *one* and Bailey wanted another of the menu items that Chef painstakingly prepared. She used the f-word in my house! She insulted Charlotte. She is just not the woman for you."

"Let's not get into this again," Knox started calmly. "We've put all of these differences behind us. You and Dad accepted Roxanne—"

"As your girlfriend," she screeched. "Not as your future wife! Girlfriends are expendable. Wives aren't as easy to get rid of. She's classless, clueless, and cash-hungry."

"That's enough!" Knox barked. Roxanne didn't fit any of those labels. That his mother returned to her original feelings annoyed him. "You're snobbish, elitist and judgmental, so you're even."

His mother gasped. "*You* asked me to be on her stupid committee."

"And you agreed! You even wanted it moved to the estate. Something you begged me to do."

"To have control," she snarled with vicious spite. "She doesn't deserve the honor of having you in her life. What woman has a *committee* of friends to plan her wedding, rather than a wedding planner? A job well-paid is a job well-done. Your marriage should be of singular focus. What is she doing? Sharing the ceremony and allowing her already-married daughter to renew her vows! She's clueless about what it means to be a Harrington."

Knox winced at hearing his mother voice the attitude he'd taken in the beginning. No wonder Roxanne had been so furious. Having them thrown back at him shamed and insulted him.

"Bailey had every right to be included in the double ceremony, Mother. As long as I'm happy with Roxanne's vision of being a Harrington you have nothing to say about it," he stormed. "She's going to be *my* wife, not yours."

"The twain shall never meet, Knox," his mother said briskly. "You are wealthy and cultured. She isn't. Before she breaks your heart, she's going to humiliate you. Charlotte—"

Charlotte Redding. His mother's statement from moments before about Charlotte being at the meeting sunk into Knox. "What was Charlotte doing there?" he asked, tuning out whatever else she'd said. No way would Roxanne want her there.

"Kendall Donovan invited her."

He heard the smile in her voice.

"I knew this was going to be a trial, so I made sure to use my personal drawing room. I wanted to show the clear line between us by sitting on one side in my Bergere chair and having *them* sit amongst each other."

Knox's mouth fell open. *Fuuuuccckkkk.* "Mother, tell me you didn't really do that?" He hated his begging tone, but if his mother...More than likely, Roxanne was livid.

"I most certainly did. How else could I make my disapproval clear? I congratulated that horrible woman on your engagement and she had the unmitigated gall to call me out *and* use the f-word again. I'm completely within my rights not to have called her right after the engagement."

"Mother, listen to me. Whether you like it or not, Roxanne *will* be my wife. I love her and she loves me. You either accept her or lose me." He thought of Outlaw. "Case closed."

"Knox, you didn't even do the engagement in the proper manner. You should've had an engagement party and invited our friends and family. Society columnists. Your second engagement should've been a showstopping moment amongst the elite of the elite. And, if that makes me an elitist, so be it. I'm proud of it. You once were, too. You even did the politically correct thing and followed Cameron into a career. You never needed to do that. You're a wealthy man. Something you enjoyed lording over others."

Except Cam. The errant thought flitted through Knox's mind as he came to a conclusion about himself. "I've changed. I've grown," he amended.

"Because of Roxanne."

He wouldn't deny his mother's putrid statement. "Because of Roxanne," he echoed with finality. "I'm a grown man. Capable of making my own damn decisions and judging for myself who I want to spend the rest of my life with."

"Ha!" his mother snorted. "Do you hear yourself? You don't even like her friends. You gave them a chance. You were considerate enough to apologize. Yet, they didn't deserve it."

He supposed he'd always be a cop at heart. His apology had come back to haunt him during a situation with Cam's then-friend-now-wife. Jordan had been Megan's OB first, then Roxanne's friend, and then Cam's everything. A former relationship had put her life on the line. When all the bad guys were captured, Knox wanted them taken into custody. Outlaw's opinion that they needed to be executed on the spot had prevailed. Knox had realized once a criminal, always a criminal. The bikers would never place the same value on life that he did. "They can be hard to swallow."

"Exactly! You think about them the way I do about Roxanne. You've *told* me so many times before. She's just like them. How can you expect me to believe you want her, when you can't stand to have her friends around you? In spite of your feelings towards them, you suffer through vulgar family get-togethers every week for her. The least she can do is respect my house!"

Knox sighed. "I'm sorry if I gave you the wrong impression, but Roxanne's friends are *my* friends," he lied. "If you insult them, you insult me. Now, you owe my fiancé an apology."

"*What?* No, absolutely not. Thankfully, Kendall suggested I plan the rehearsal dinner. Roxanne, however, is in charge of the wedding plans with her ridiculous committee. I shudder to think how that'll turn out."

"It will turn out beautiful," Knox snapped. "Roxanne has excellent taste. Besides, it's *her* wedding. If she wants to decorate in purple, green, and gold, and have a second line, that's up to her."

Silence, then: "What's a second line?"

Something his mother would never participate in. He couldn't see her following a band, the *first line*, and being part of the crowd of participants collectively known as the second line. "Never mind. I should've just taken her away to Vegas like she wanted. I wouldn't have to have such bullshit going on all around me."

A knock sounded on his door. Knox silently thanked whatever providence had sent an interruption to his mother's nonsense. "Some-one's at the door. I have to go."

"Don't be angry," she ordered. "You know this marriage won't last. Why else would you ask her to sign a pre-nup?"

Damn his father!

"Knox?"

The sound of Roxanne's voice startled him. He'd been waiting to hear it all day.

"I have to go, Mother."

"You have no chemistry..."

Those were the last words he heard before he disconnected the call and rushed to the door, throwing it open and pulling her into his arms. She tasted so sweet and smelled so good.

She placed her arms around his neck and returned his kiss with the same vigor that he gave it. The feel of her left him breathless and giddy. It—

Without warning, she was jerked out of his embrace. It was so sudden both Knox and Roxanne stumbled.

"Boy, you lost your damn mind?" Roxanne yelled to Mortician, who stood in the hallway holding Roxanne's arm and glaring at Knox.

Before Mortician answered, she elbowed him in the gut. The man didn't flinch.

"Let me go!" she demanded.

"Let her go, Mortician," Knox warned.

"Or what?" Mortician asked in bored tones.

"Or I'm beating your ass," Roxanne snapped. "I'll give you a beat-down so ferocious, you'll wonder what the fuck happened to you. I'll fuck you up so bad, it'll be days before Bailey knows it's really you."

"I'm not that easy to bring down, Roxanne," Mortician said flatly.

Roxanne jerked herself out of Mortician's hold. "I was just greeting my man before I talked to him, motherfucker."

Knox pulled her behind him and straightened to his full height, staring at Mortician with cool authority. "I resent your interference and it ends now."

Mortician looked him up and down, then back up again before laughing in his face. "*Not*. Your bitch of a momma insulted Meggie, Bunny, Zoann, Roxanne, and most of fucking all, *Bailey*."

Knox flushed in anger, his blood boiling with the need to call the enforcer out.

"Enough, Mortician. You will *not* disrespect my mother by calling her out of her name. You will keep your nose out of my relationship with Roxanne." Glaring at him, Knox hoped his expression conveyed his rage. "You can't get away with your dictatorial attitude. I take it from Outlaw because I like living, but I don't have to take a goddamn thing from you."

"Knox, Mortician, stop this," Roxanne demanded, trying to scoot around Knox, but was unable to because he'd boxed her in. She stood between him and the corner of a wall.

"If I don't stand up for my momma-in-law, who the fuck else going to do it? I'm the only goddamn man in her family, so it's my fucking job to protect her."

"Mortician!" Roxanne said in exasperation. "This is the 21st Century. I can take care of my own damn self."

"*After* you walk down the aisle," Mortician insisted. "He real close to his momma, Roxanne. What if she put a bug in his ear about *not* marrying you and he end up listening to her?"

"Knox wouldn't do that," Roxanne said with a certainty that filled Knox with pride. "He loves me and I love him. He proved it by asking me to marry him without even mentioning a prenup like most wealthy men would have. He knows I'm his ride or die chick."

Folding his arms, Mortician smirked at Knox, who stood unable to move at Roxanne's words. Did she really expect him to marry her with no legal protection in place?

"Some things not as they seem, Roxanne," Mortician said quietly. "His momma insulted the whole fucking bunch of you, with the exception of Kendall. That type of shit go deep. Knox not just changing overnight. No matter what the fuck he say. Your ass might be dickmitized but *I'm* sure the fuck not."

"Move, Knox," Roxanne ordered, shoving his shoulder.

Sighing, Knox stepped aside and allowed her space to look at each of them, first left, and then right. Her light brown eyes lingered on Knox.

He saw her tenderness, her trust, and her love. In her eyes, on her face, he saw that Roxanne truly did believe in the fairytale. That marriages lasted. They survived any and everything, even despite her previous failures.

"Mortician, sugar," she started, breaking her intense gaze with

Knox to look at her son-in-law. "What you're doing is so old-fashioned and chivalrous. You're trying to protect my honor and I will appreciate that to my dying day. But this is my choice to make and I want Knox beside me, in our bed."

Mortician squeezed the bridge of his nose. "I might be a fucking hypocrite for keeping you from him, but there's too much shit going on. Who knows what disagreement you'll have before the wedding? He might want something that you don't and decide to breakup with you if he don't get it." His face remained blank, not giving away the truth, gotten from Knox himself, behind those words. "Same with you."

"There's nothing that Knox would ask that he knows I wouldn't be willing to give him," Roxanne insisted, which not only annoyed Knox but sent guilt through him.

Mortician shoved his hands into the pockets of his jeans. Knox waited for the interfering asshole to tell Roxanne about the prenup.

"You from two different worlds, Roxanne," Mortician said instead, sounding weary. "You from our world and he's from the other. One percenters, on different ends of the spectrum. We, *this side of the one percent,* accept you for who you are. His doesn't."

Roxanne studied Mortician a moment. "If you have something to tell me, spit it out. I'm not reading between the lines, Mortician."

He shrugged. "I'm saying exactly what I need to say. If there's more, it's up to Knox to talk."

She glanced at Knox. "Is there more?"

"No." The lie fell from his mouth in a rush. Her emotions were running high. He didn't want to risk her wrath by bringing up the prenup.

Mortician glared at him, but since Roxanne's head was turned, she didn't see the flare of anger.

Knox refused to budge. When he got her to sign the legal document, he intended to take her to dinner and discuss his reasoning. He wasn't just going to spring it on her in front of a man who didn't know how to mind his own business.

"I'm ready to leave, Roxanne," Mortician announced.

"Good for you, boy," she retorted. "I'm not."

"We can do this easily," Mortician started, "or I can knock Knox the fuck out and then carry you out. Your choice."

Knox narrowed his eyes. "I'm sick of the threats around here."

"You need another punch or something? You already on my bad fucking side. Don't fucking push it."

"Get over him wanting me with him," Roxanne said, misunderstanding Mortician's meaning.

"And, you right, Knox. I'm *not* Outlaw. But I *will* kill you. As a matter of fact, I've lost fucking count of how many motherfuckers I fucked up. *Enforcer.* Remember? When I go to enforce club law, if death warranted, that's what the fuck you get."

"This is getting the fuck out of hand," Roxanne shouted, planting her hands on her hips. "Knox is on the No-Kill list."

"What the fuck does that mean?" Knox blurted, appalled. "There's a No-Kill list?"

"Yeah, sugar," she said matter-of-factly, frowning in his direction. "It's a short list and mainly for Outlaw. Meggie made him put Kendall, Val and Johnnie on it."

"Roxanne, I don't want your heart broken," Mortician said. "That's it. Once he put the ring on your finger, your relationship yours to handle. I swear I won't interfere."

Lifting her chin, she folded her arms. "I'll agree as long as you put him on the No-Kill list."

"The list belong to Prez," Mortician reminded her. "Talk to him."

"So everyone is fine that that psychopath has a No-Kill list like we're a bunch of animals?" Knox demanded.

"We the only ones that know," Mortician informed him.

"Yeah, just Outlaw's inner circle," Roxanne added.

Knox glared at her. "What? I'm not part of his group where this is concerned? You didn't think this was information I needed to know?"

"I thought I mentioned it to you, sugar," Roxanne said, waving her hand as if having a *No-Kill* list wasn't a big deal. "If I didn't, it was just an oversight." She leaned in to give him a kiss. He wrapped her in his arms, reveling in her nearness and the feel of her so close to him.

Mortician allowed the kiss to go on, until Roxanne pulled back, and thumbed Knox's lips.

"You got my lipstick on you," she said with a grin.

"I don't mind, sweetheart," he said gruffly. "It marks your territory. Allows everyone to see I'm taken."

"Damn straight," she said, a little breathless. She backed out of Knox's embrace and looked at Mortician.

The disgusted look on the man's face almost made Knox laugh.

"I need to talk to Knox."

Mortician opened his mouth to speak, but Roxanne raised her hand.

"Five minutes."

"Fine," Mortician conceded. "I'll be in the hallway. Leave the door open."

Rolling her eyes, Roxanne sniffed and stomped into the room Knox slept in. The enforcer's interference hadn't allowed Knox a chance to invite Roxanne in.

"I could knock him out and have my wicked way with you," Knox offered.

Roxanne laughed, a musical sound that lit his soul. "Don't bother. The boy'll come to and be madder than a motherfucker. Besides, he's just looking out for me."

Knox nodded. "I admire his determination and resolve." As the words fell from his mouth, he realized he spoke the truth. Mortician took his duties as head of the family seriously.

She stepped closer to him and placed her arms around his neck. "I lied, sugar. I don't have anything to discuss with you. I just wanted to get in here so we can make out."

Chuckling, Knox wrapped his arms around her. "I've been dying to hear how the meeting with my mother went," he said, interested to know her side. "From what Mortician said, it didn't go well."

"It's all good, Knox," she said with an enigmatic look on her face. "Joan is just worried about you. She doesn't want you to make the wrong choice. Mortician is just fired up because of the way Bailey must've explained the situation to him."

Knox settled his hands on Roxanne's ass, and he patted one of her round cheeks. "If Bailey thought it was that bad, then my mother must've have been acting without any decorum."

Roxanne plastered a smile on her face. "Don't worry, Knox. Joan and me are going to work things out. As a matter of fact, she's planning the entire rehearsal dinner. No interference from me."

"And no interference from her as you and Bailey plan the ceremonies."

"My man has a big brain that he knows how to use," Roxanne said, brushing her lips over his.

Knox nipped her chin. "That's not the only big thing that I have that I know how to use."

"We just have to find a way for you to use it again," she whispered.

"You could tell him to go and fuck himself."

"Maybe, I like what he's doing," she confessed. "I think a small part of me is a little overwhelmed, knowing I'm marrying a *Harrington*. As I keep saying, I don't want to wake up and find this is a dream. Or, worse, have you decided that you really don't want to spend your life with me."

"Hey, hey." He took her face between his hands, hating the hint of sadness. "Don't ever think I doubt my feelings for you. I'll be at your side through thick and thin."

"I believe that you will. It's just a little overwhelming sometimes. I wonder how your friends and family will mix with mine."

Not good or not at all, but Knox kept that to himself.

"I want our wedding day to be perfect."

"It will be," he said with certainty. "Whatever you want, however you want it, is yours. I'll never, ever leave you."

The sadness on her face tore at Knox.

"Johnnie said something similar to Kendall." Moving his arms away from her, Roxanne stepped back. "But she called me, Knox. I could barely understand her, she was crying so much. She's heartbroken because she thinks her marriage is over. I don't know how to comfort her."

"Whatever is going on, she brought on herself," Knox reminded her, knowing full well what happened. He'd watched it in real time. "I know you love her, but, you have to admit Kendall is a handful. You can't fault Johnnie for getting tired of her bullshit."

"Kendall is as important to me as the rest of the girls. I want to fix this for her."

"You can't. Only she can. If Johnnie is still available to her."

"Johnnie has a lot to do with how she is. He said shit to her, did shit, that made her act out. Between him and her illness, the child didn't have a chance. Outlaw forces deference to Meggie. Kendall got into shit because she wanted to show her husband, Outlaw, and the club, that she was as good or better than that little girl."

"None of those women are little girls," Knox pointed out.

"I know. Not even my Bailey. I'm just so angry with Johnnie for the way he hurt Kendall. I want to deball that bitch."

"Er, Johnnie, right?"

"Yes. That's the bitch I'm talking about. Kendall's been hurt enough in her life. I have no use for motherfuckers who hurt her just because she exists."

"Then you must have a use for everyone since their retaliation is justified. She's done something to almost all the people at the club."

"With the exception of you and me."

Knox begged to differ. She'd pretended she was on his side during his investigation of Outlaw, then had secretly recorded Knox admitting to wanting to take the club down. After she'd played Knox, she'd threatened to expose him to Johnnie and Outlaw. He'd hated her ever since.

She sighed and covered her face. "This is such a clusterfuck, Knox. On the one hand you're right, but on the other hand, I feel so sorry for her."

"She's a big girl, sweetheart. She can fend for herself."

"Kendall is fragile and vulnerable."

"Time way up," Mortician called from the hallway.

"Kendall has made her bed, so she has to lie in it," Knox replied to Roxanne, ignoring Mortician.

"I know you don't care for her because of how she protected Johnnie, but she was only doing what any good woman would do for her man. You need to get over that incident, because Kendall is very important to me."

Knox didn't comment, since there wasn't much to say. The argument could go round and round all night, and neither of them would change their minds.

"I'm going to call you in a little while," Roxanne said, stealing another kiss, then walking into the hallway and closing the door behind her.

She called it a clusterfuck. Times ten.

Roxanne thought he wouldn't ask her to sign a prenup, while he was still determined to do so. Meanwhile, Kendall was falling apart and Roxanne wanted to comfort and protect her, while Knox intended to do everything in his power to see the woman gone forever.

Dead.

Shit! It just proved how worthless Outlaw's ridiculous No-Kill list really was.

Knox hated the precarious position he found himself in, one in which nothing good could come out of his dilemma.

CHAPTER TWENTY-THREE

Roxy

Taking care with her appearance, Roxy dressed in a hot pink, ruched wrap, body-con dress that she paired with black thigh-high boots. She kept her hair simple, her jewelry non-existent, and her make-up pared down to lipstick.

She opened her front door, slow and careful, not wanting to make the smallest sound. The cold air hit her, but she ignored it. Hopefully, Knox would warm her up soon enough. Morning fog hung low and swirled through the trees, giving it a scary-movie-evil-psychopath aura. The same scenery that said *you will be fucked up* also hid her from the guards Mortician had posted. Motherfucker didn't know that Roxy had caught on he allowed the guards to grab shut-eye in the garage during the hours they thought she was asleep.

Wrapping her arms around herself, Roxy hurried along the path, cursing herself for not taking a coat. It was the second week in March, so she figured she'd be fine. Her dress had three-quarter sleeves but the material was thin, and underneath her pussy was out.

If Mortician ruined her plan, she'd kill him. Focusing on the reward instead of the cold, Roxy rushed along the pathway, happy that she didn't run into any of the guys. It was just slightly earlier than her normal time she went to the club, but sometimes she'd find Val or Digger, even Outlaw, already heading out.

This morning, all was quiet and clear. Leaving the fog behind also allowed her to enjoy the peacefulness. She finally cleared the pathway, reaching the edge of the parking lot. A couple of minutes more and she made it to the door. Inside, she found the main room dark, but the warmth quite welcoming. Instead of flipping on the lights, then heading to kitchen as usual, she darted to the hallway and turned left, colliding with a hard, male body.

"You made it," Knox whispered, wrapping her in his arms.

It was dark so she could barely see him, but she felt his muscles and his warmth, smelled the scent of the soap he used, and pressed against his rock-hard cock.

"I...you're really here." He threaded his fingers through her hair.

"Did you fucking doubt me?" she asked with a grin.

Knox didn't respond, and instead, covered her mouth with his.

"You're so fucking delicious," he said between kisses.

"Some parts more than others."

"Come on, sweetheart. Let's go to my room."

That was safer and more logical, but Roxy had something else in mind, something she'd always wanted to do. "No, Knox. We don't have time for that. Besides, we couldn't hear if Mortician came in."

"What--?"

"Follow me." The words were rhetorical because she took his hand into hers and pulled him into the main room. "I've always wanted to fuck in the clubhouse."

"You have?" He sounded confused.

"Yeah, sugar. I never have. It just seems so freeing."

She stopped at one of the stools in front of the bar.

"This is so public."

Jumping up on the stool, she spread her thighs. "Neither me nor my pussy cares." She grabbed his hand and pressed it against her mound.

"Fuck, you're actually wet."

She snapped her brows together. "Don't sound like me having a juicy pussy is the eighth goddamn wonder of the world."

Thumbing her clit, he slipped two fingers inside of her. She groaned.

"Never, sweetheart," he whispered, running his tongue along the shell of her ear, igniting her senses. Goosebumps rose on her skin. "I know you have some lubrication. But...you just...we just—"

"Need help," she finished for him, throwing her neck back. "But the last time and this time my pussy has been suffering a cock drought." She didn't know why her pussy suddenly decided to moisten and refused to get into a discussion about this. She sucked his neck. "Who gives a fuck, Knox? Just fuck me. Me and your dick wondering why we're still talking."

He chuckled. "Whatever my lady commands, I'm obliged to do."

Assisting him in pulling his cock through the slit in his pajama bottoms—the only thing he wore—Roxy slid to the edge of the stool. He slid into her and she moaned, her body jerking at the contact of his hot cock filling her. As he pulled out, then pushed back into her, his dick brushed against her pussy walls. She leaned back, resting against the bar, then grabbed Knox's shoulders and urged him forward. He withdrew his cock and she thrust her pussy up, meeting each move that he made.

"I love you," he told her.

"I love you, too, baby," she breathed. "I miss you so much."

"I miss you more."

Abandoning words, they crashed their lips together, their bodies slapping together in raw, animal pleasure. It was hard, fast, out in the open, and Roxy loved every moment of it. The sheer intensity of Knox powering in and out of her. His grunts and heavy breathing mingling with her sighs and moans.

He inserted his hand between them and found her clit again, massaging and caressing it, until Roxy started to shake. As her orgasm overtook her, Knox stiffened and growled, coming with her.

"Are you okay?" he asked, a few minutes later.

She nodded. "More than okay."

Slowly, he withdrew from her. They gasped, their bodies still in overdrive.

Knox stepped back and Roxy stretched, sated and relaxed. A moment later, the overhead lights flickered on.

Knox sauntered back to her. "Where are your panties?"

"At home," she responded, hopping from the stool and wobbling slightly.

"Hey!" Knox clutched her shoulders and steadied her. "Are you okay?"

"A little boneless," she murmured. "Otherwise, I'm wonderful."

Grabbing her chin, he pulled her forward and kissed her again.

"I need to go and clean-up, then start breakfast."

"Come to my room. Get one of my Tee-shirts and some sweatpants to wear."

"If I go, we'll only end up fucking again."

"I'll stay out here."

"I do need to change," she agreed. "I didn't think this through, sugar. I'll have a cum-and-pussy-juice stain on the back of my fucking dress."

He wrinkled his nose.

"It's true!"

"Yes, but do you have to say it?"

"Why the fuck shouldn't I? We're grown. This shouldn't be a topic of conversation off-limits."

Nodding, he smiled at her. "You're right, sweetheart. I just...I'm still not used to being so open about things like this."

"I understand."

"Go, before one of those assholes come in here and I'll have to beat the shit out of them."

She loved his confidence, but she didn't want to test his theory, so she hurried through cleaning herself up and finding clothes to wear. She only had her thigh high boots, but who the fuck cared? She'd once come in slippers. Wearing boots with sweats was her damn business.

Not knowing what to do with the dress, she shoved it under Knox's pillow. It would be a good reminder of their hot fucking.

Back in the main room, she found Knox talking to Cash.

"Breakfast isn't ready yet, Cash," she said.

He nodded, then sidled a glare at Knox. "Didn't come for breakfast, Roxanne. Had some business to discuss with Knox." With that, he turned on his heel and stomped away.

"What was that all about?" she asked, once he'd left the building.

Sighing, Knox waved away the question. "Nothing to worry about."

She gave him a long, assessing look, but his look of dismissal didn't change, so Roxy decided to let the subject go.

"I'm going to change," he said, kissing her again.

"You do that, sexy motherfucker."

He winked at her, then swatted her ass. "I love you in my clothes. Fuck, I love you any way I can get you."

"Go on, man," she said with a chuckle, "before I throw you down on the floor and have my wicked way with you."

His laughter floated behind him as he headed to the hallway and disappeared.

Joy flowing through her, Roxy headed through the double doors to start her morning duty, pausing in the smaller kitchen, which had come to be known as Meggie's kitchen. She'd used it to cook Outlaw meals and to store her Milky Way candy. Those days were gone, though, as the child had a beautiful kitchen, the size of this one and the one for the clubhouse combined. The love she and Outlaw shared was special, rare, and inspiring.

For the first time in many years, Roxy felt as if she'd found the man of her dreams. Or her soulmate? Could she actually have two? K-P had been her first everything—lover, baby daddy, man she wanted to spend her life with. She might not be able to give Knox children but he was her lover and the man she wanted to spend whatever remaining years she had left to her life.

Smiling like a giggly girl, Roxy started forward, pausing again when she heard the swinging doors creak. She thought it was Knox, so she turned—and came face-to-face with Mortician.

She scowled at him.

Holding out her cell phone, he looked her up-and-down. "You here real early this morning, Roxanne."

She marched to him and snatched the phone out of his hands. "It's too fucking early for your bullshit, motherfucker." And she was too fucking happy for his overprotective attitude to put doubts in her head.

"Where Knox?"

"Sleeping, I guess. How the fuck should I know?" Concerned he might see the lie in her face, Roxy raised her phone, unlocked the screen and saw that she had two missed calls with a '504' area code. Someone from New Orleans tried to contact her. The number was unfamiliar but the early time alarmed her.

"You wearing Knox clothes?"

She wouldn't panic until she had reason to; therefore, she wouldn't mention her concern to Mortician. He'd want to take over and the motherfucker was giving her enough problems.

"You got sweats and a Tee-shirt on with Tamara Mellon boots."

"How the fuck you know the boot's designer?"

"First of all, it's my job to know shit. That way, when I confront motherfuckers, the evidence irrefutable and they know why the fuck they dying. Second, Bailey showed me the goddamn boots before she ordered them for your ass. I know the motherfuckers cost a grand, so why the fuck you wearing Knox workout clothes with expensive boots? As a matter of fact, that motherfucker wouldn't be caught in *those* motherfuckers. He just got them to pretend he regular."

"Mortician, what the fuck is going on? Did Knox do something that I don't know about that's making you act like a fucking uptight, hypocritical asshole? I know you and Bailey slept together before you married her. She even slept here at the clubhouse, so I'm asking you right now be straight with me or back the fuck off. Knox is a good man and he's not going to leave me high-and-dry."

A muscle ticked in Mortician's jaw. He met her gaze and she lifted her brow.

"I deserve to know if Knox did something that's making you act like this."

"Motherfucker didn't do nothing," Mortician growled.

"Then—"

He shoved his hands in his pockets. "This just important to me, Roxanne. I don't...think about how Joan acted. Suppose she get in his head or something? What if she convince him that you need to sign a prenup?"

"Knox wouldn't ask me to do that. I'm not after his shit and I don't intend for us to divorce."

"Anything can happen," Mortician insisted. "I'm surprised you not thinking of this shit yourself. How would you feel if he came to you and said he's momma convinced him he shouldn't marry you? Or he shouldn't marry you without the goddamn prenup?"

Roxy cocked her head to the side. "Has Knox mentioned a prenup to you?" she asked in a thin voice, torn between anger and despair. "Because if he did, tell me, and I'll confront him. The way you going about protecting me is all fucked up."

Mortician glanced away. "I just don't trust Knox, Roxanne. Can you just humor me with this? I'm doing this to protect you."

"Whether me and Knox are living together or apart, if we break-up, it'll still devastate me. What the fuck is wrong with you, thinking our living arrangements will make a difference?"

"At least, this way, you'll be used to not having him *living* with you."

"Mortician—"

"Look, Roxanne," he said in frustration, looking at her again, "I couldn't protect my momma from Sharper bullshit. Knox not a motherfucker like that. He know better than to cheat on you. But my momma *died* when she came face-to-face with Sharper ways. She couldn't deny he was a piece of shit. I don't trust Knox. He an uppity motherfucker and he think he better than me and Prez and Digger and Val. He think he better than Meggie. He can't stand Red."

"Knox don't have a problem with Kendall."

Mortician released a harsh breath. "You Bailey momma, *my* momma-in-law. You so important to us, man. Just...just *please* keep shit the way it is now."

"Baby, I appreciate you and admire the man you are. You're a good son-in-law, a wonderful husband and a loving father. I'm so glad Bailey found you. You take care of her and your children, and that's all I can ask. Given that, I am going to leave shit just as it is. Suppose I decided not to, then what? We'd be at a stalemate."

"No. Then I kill the motherfucker."

"How the fuck you say you want to protect me, then in the next breath say you'll kill the motherfucker I love? And for what? Bullshit!"

"It's not bullshit. *I'm* the head of the family, so it's my job to protect you. If a motherfucker disobey, he can't live. Every motherfucker around'll think I'm a fucking bitch."

"As a bitch, I take offense to the insinuation that I can't take care of my goddamn self because I got a pussy. Being older than you, shouldn't my ass be the head? The matriarch?"

"We forward thinking, Roxanne. We don't have a choice 'cause of Meggie girl. But even Prez draw a fucking line and takeover when he want to."

"He always give Meggie a reason. You haven't told me one thing that makes me think I can't handle shit on my own. Other than this is important to you."

He lifted a brow. "That's not enough for you?"

"Fuck you, motherfucker," she yelled, at wit's end. "I'm agreeing to this bullshit because it's important to you. No other reason, since you like a son to me." The fact that he'd kill Knox might have something to do with it, too. "I believe you're under the misguided assumption that you're protecting me because you think he's some kind of mama's boy that will listen to Joan."

"He's also uppity and think he's better than us."

"He's a work-in-progress," she countered.

"He's a pain-in-the-ass."

"Whatever, boy." She should tell him she'd rendezvoused with Knox this morning, but then the motherfucker would figure out she'd caught on to the guards' schedules. Setting her phone on the butcher block table, she turned toward the huge refrigerator. "Either help me start breakfast or get the fuck out of my face."

"Yeah, fine, Roxanne. Later."

Cursing under her breath, Roxanne yanked open the stainless-steel refrigerator door and grabbed the unopened bacon, two packages of sausage, and two cartons of eggs. As she sat the food down, her phone started ringing. Picking it up, she saw that it was the same unknown number that had already called her twice.

Concern raced through her. What had happened? Was it her momma or one of her daughters? Or, maybe, something was wrong with Duke. That made more sense with the unrecognizable number.

Sighing, she heaved in a deep breath and answered. "Hello?"

"Roxy?" a man responded. The owner of the voice floated of the fringes of her memory.

"Who is this?" she demanded, because try as she might to identify the caller, he remained unknown. His chipper tone alerted her that everything was fine.

"Joyner," he answered. "Amfinger. Joyner Amfinger."

Creighton's motherfucker of a friend. "What do you want, asshole?" she hissed.

"Tsk, tsk. I could be calling you about Duke. I am his godfather."

"You're not. You wouldn't fucking bother to pick up the goddamn phone to tell me anything about my son."

"Still the same classy woman Creighton married. I can't see why my friend ever thought he could turn trash into a trophy."

"I'm not listening to your bullshit," she snapped, hating how Joyner's words arrowed straight through her. Her baby boy, her Duke, felt the same way. "Fuck off, motherfucker."

"Don't hang up," Joyner commanded. "We wouldn't want that man you're about to marry to accidentally get a phone call."

"I don't have anything to hide. Call Knox all the fuck you want to."

He chuckled. "I might do that. I had an offer for you, but you're being difficult."

"Bye, Joyner."

"Creighton's willing to send you fifty thousand dollars if you get out of Duke's life. Give up all claims to him. Agree to a new birth certificate. Duke is dating good people now and he doesn't want garbage floating to the surface that will humiliate him."

"Joyner, the only reason I didn't hang up on your ass was because you brought up calling Knox. I know the fucking games you motherfuckers play."

"We're adults. We don't have time for games."

"Good, because I'm telling you to fuck off. There's no fucking way I'm allowing Creighton's crooked ass to falsify a birth certificate and give my son a new momma."

"It wasn't Creighton's idea. It was Duke's."

Tears rushing to her eyes, Roxy pressed down on her lips to hold in her sob. She stiffened her shoulders and swiped at a tear. "Tell him, fuck no. I gave birth to him and I'm not hiding that or allowing him to."

"So high and mighty since you've gotten with that young, rich boy. What are you going to say when Knox Harrington throws you ass over for a woman his age, who has more class and more education? Your own son despises you. You can't really believe a sought-after bachelor from one of the country's wealthiest families wants you for more than anything but a good fuck? That's about all you're good for."

"Joyner, don't fucking call my number anymore. If you do, you might just fucking disappear." Before he responded, she disconnected the call, her happiness crashing and burning.

"Look who I brought for you," Mortician said.

Rushing back to the refrigerator to get her bearings, Roxy made herself focus. She grabbed butter and milk, drew herself up, closed the door, and turned, pasting a smile on her face.

Knox met her eyes and his grin faded. "What's wrong, sweetheart?"

Mortician narrowed his eyes. "You been crying!"

She set the milk and the butter next to the other items. "I'm just feeling a little overwhelmed," she said in truth.

"What this motherfucker did?" Mortician demanded.

"Oh, I like that," Knox snapped. "I was the one who noticed something was wrong with her. If I was the cause for her distress, do you think I would've called attention to it?"

"Maybe," Mortician retorted. "You kind of a stupid motherfucker. Think your balls bigger than they actually are."

"The size of my testes are just fine," Knox told him.

Roxy and Mortician frowned at him, but the bickering allowed her to reassemble her thoughts and shove aside the call from Joyner Amfinger. He was, and always would be, a fucking asshole.

Knox

"Thank you, Tottingham," Knox said, accepting a glass of rare whisky from the owner of Tottingham's Haberdashery.

"Harold has given me your measurements. We will set to work on the tuxedoes immediately," Tottingham said. He was about Knox's age and had inherited the shop from his late father. "When can we expect the others in the wedding party, sir?"

Knox sipped his drink. "They are being fitted elsewhere. Only my father and I will utilize your skills."

His father walked into the private room, followed by the shop's general manager, Harold Rubens. He was an older man with a bald spot in the middle of his head. His white hair gave him a distinguished look.

"Speak of the devil," Knox said with a smile as his father sat in the chair across from him. "Would you like a drink, Dad?"

"Of course, son."

"Mr. Harrington, Mr. Knox informs me that there will be no others for fittings," Tottingham said, handing his father a glass."

An unhappy look crossed his father's face. "That's correct."

"Not even the young sir?"

"Not even Grant," Knox confirmed.

"Tottie, can you give me a moment with my son?"

"Of course, Mr. Harrington, sir. Come, Harold."

The two men offered slights bows, then walked out of the room and closed the door.

"Son, I'm not one to interfere in your private life. It's your business, but I must admit to concern."

Although Knox would prefer if his father kept his opinion to himself, he respected the man too much not to give him the courtesy of hearing him out. "I understand, Dad."

His father took a deep swallow of whisky. "Look around you, Knox. What do you see?"

Doing as his father asked, Knox noted the wooden floors offset by top-of-the-line area rugs. Walls divided by chair rails donned silk wall-paper and white-painted wood. A crystal chandelier hung from the ceiling. On the opposite side of the room, a round table stood, surrounded by four chairs, and stacked with design books. The lone case in the room held samples of ties and other accessories men needed. All of it screamed money and status. *Class*.

"I see the world I was born into." For as long as Knox remembered, he'd come to Tottingham's. As he'd gotten older, he'd spread his wings and went to stores with Cam, where ready-wear items were available. But the majority of Knox's clothes were tailored just for him.

"What will Tottie and Harold think of Roxanne if and when they ever meet her?"

Knox drained his glass. "I don't care what they think of her, Dad. I love her and that's all that matters."

"She was fine as your girlfriend—"

"Enough!" Knox interrupted. "Either you accept her as my wife or you lose me as your son. There's no negotiations."

"You'd risk your mother and me disinheriting you for a woman who's past her prime and can't birth you more children?"

"Have you ever heard of adoption?" Knox snapped. "And, yes, I don't need your goddamn money if it means following your every dictate. Take it and burn it." He set his glass on the small table next to him and got to his feet. "If this is the only reason you agreed to accompany me to our first fitting, you could've stayed home."

He hated to admit it, but the fitting at the Whittlestones had been much more enjoyable. The atmosphere had been relaxed and not so pretentious. In spite of the disagreeability of Mortician, Knox had had a much better time. As a matter of fact, he couldn't imagine Grant enjoying the sternness of Tottingham and Harold.

Knox almost—*almost*—regretted his refusal of purchasing his tuxedo from the same place as the bikers.

"Tell me now. Is this a threat? Do you intend to disown me?"

"No," his dad said after a tense moment. "You're my only son, my only child, and I want what's best for you."

"Roxanne is best for me. She makes me happy. She gives my life meaning."

"She's abnormally common."

Despite himself, Knox laughed. *"Abnormally* common? Really, Dad?"

His father smiled. "You know what I mean."

Knox nodded, though he felt as if he betrayed Roxanne by agreeing. But she did have a very foul mouth. Not to mention a certain Navigator that remained stuck in Knox's craw. He *could* just talk to her, but she could be so stubborn. He was afraid any conversation about either of those topics would dissolve into an argument. His words got ahead of him sometimes. By the time his brain caught up, he would've spewed his resentment and she'd never forgive him.

However, after the hot sex this morning, his mood had lifted—until Cash had come storming in and reminded Knox about the cameras.

"You know the ones, motherfucker? They aren't turned off unless we decide not to record. Which is rare. Your saving fucking grace was that it was fucking dark. The footage has been erased. If Mortician had gotten to it, Digger would be cleaning your fucking guts up."

"It wasn't my idea," Knox had fumed.

"Don't give a fuck. It's up to you to convince her to go to your fucking room. It's your fucking job to protect her."

"I forgot about the fucking cameras." He hadn't known they were on at all times.

"Next time, remember them."

At that point, Roxanne had walked in, her body defining his Tee-shirt and sweats, her skin glowing and her eyes heavy-lidded. She'd been floating on the same cloud as him since he'd gotten her pre-dawn call where she told him she intended to do a booty call. Or, as she said it, a dick call.

He laughed.

"Son?"

His father's voice reminded him he wasn't alone. "Yeah, Dad?"

"Care to share the joke?"

"Private matter between Roxanne and I."

"I understand." He fell silent, then heaved a breath. "At least tell me she's signing a prenup?"

"Of course she is, Dad."

"She's already agreed?"

The relief in his father's voice got to Knox. He didn't want his parents to worry that he'd allow any woman, even Roxanne, to swoop in and bankrupt the Harringtons. He nodded. "Of course."

Smiling, his father clapped him on the back. "Good, good. You're not my boy for nothing."

Swallowing, Knox decided he needed to secure Roxanne's agreement, and signature, soon, so they could move past this pesky detail and focus solely on their wedding plans.

And, of course, outsmarting Mortician.

CHAPTER TWENTY-FOUR

Kendall

BPD – Borderline Personality Disorder, characterized by an inability to maintain personal relationships, uncontrollable anger, fear of abandonment, impulsiveness, and poor self-image, among other things.

Usually, it was ignored for more common diagnoses, such as major depressive disorder, anxiety disorder, eating disorders, PTSD, and bipolar disorder. *AND* BPD usually co-existed with one of the other mental illnesses. As was the case for Kendall, who, according to Dr. Briscow, suffered not only BPD, but depression and anxiety, too. When she'd left Johnnie for those six months before Rory's birth, her then-psychiatrist said she was borderline schizophrenic. He'd never once mentioned BPD, but it made so much sense now.

Kendall had had so many different diagnoses, she didn't know which one was accurate, and so latched on to any new one in an effort to help herself when she became too extreme. Yes, she hated the medicine. And, yes, it changed her. But Johnnie and her children were more important to her. This time, she'd really try to follow her recovery plan. She'd intended to explain all of that to Johnnie, last night, but he hadn't wanted to hear. He hadn't been interested. She'd wanted to tell him about her new form of therapy, DBT, or dialectical behavior therapy. There was even a course for family members to take to better be able to cope with their loved ones' BPD.

Another fact Johnnie hadn't allowed her to explain.

Yesterday, when he'd left her, he'd ripped her heart out and torn her to pieces. Somehow, she'd spent most of the day working with Charlotte on plans for the law offices. But true contentment escaped Kendall. The unease she'd felt all day didn't make sense. Or, maybe, it did. When Johnnie walked out, her entire world tilted.

Swallowing, Kendall hesitated as she stepped onto the pathway that started just beyond the club grounds and led to their homes. The house she'd shared with Johnnie stood at the very end of the path, right near the cave and stream that served as a beautiful backdrop.

Had she truly lost her home and her family?

No! No! She wouldn't still be on the wedding committee if she had. As long as she was a part of Roxy and Bailey's ceremony, she had a fighting chance to win Johnnie's love again.

She turned back toward the clubhouse, uncertainty and fear coursing through her. Maybe she shouldn't have come to the dinner tonight. It was meant for family. Absolutely no one saw her as such. Especially not her beloved Johnnie.

A harsh draft of air hit her and she burrowed into her Moncler flower-padded jacket. Her black Brooks Brothers Shearling fur gloves kept her hands warm. But nothing, *absolutely nothing*, warmed the chill inside of her.

Darkness had set in, but lights along the pathway penetrated the eerie blackness created by the trees surrounding her.

She took a step toward the clubhouse, then stopped. Meggie had invited her. And Roxy would be there. Kendall was sure they'd discuss more of the ceremony...if Roxy hadn't decided she'd walked away from Knox since the apple didn't fall far from the tree. Didn't Roxy see how alike Knox and his mother were?

Scowling, Kendall turned again, this time back in the direction of the houses. If no one else wanted her there, Meggie and Roxy did. Still, when she reached the gate to Meggie's house, she hesitated.

The last thing she'd ever expected was fear of rejection from anyone at the club. Her family. Her friends.

Meggie had invited her, Kendall reminded herself for the thousandth time. Besides, she could go in and not make herself immediately known. She could listen...maybe overhear...*something*, anything. Anticipation to see her...disgust that she had been invited...Meggie confessing she'd only invited Kendall out of politeness.

Clearing her throat, Kendall punched in the code, and smiled when she heard the buzz, click and release that allowed her entry. Her journey to the front door felt a little unnerving. All the times she'd walked this same path with Johnnie and their children haunted her.

Despite her worry about how tonight would go, she still scowled at the moat surrounding the house, as if it sat on a little island of its own. Just one more precaution Outlaw had put in place to keep Meggie safe.

At the front door, she stopped again. Pulled off her gloves, hating her uncertainty. She was afraid of her reception, not unlike the feeling she got whenever she'd come across Emily in school...Fuck Emily! That wicked bitch was a closed chapter in her life.

She had more pressing concerns. Such as... If the other guys saw Johnnie giving her the cold shoulder, would they follow suit, too?

She licked her lips. Thought about turning and leaving. But what else did she have to do? Her children were on the other side of that door. Her husband. Her friends.

Her family. Everything she wanted and everything worth fighting for.

Steeling her spine, she shoved her gloves inside her pocket, twisted the door knob and walked into the house.

As she quietly closed the door, the inside warmth enveloped her. The familiarity of her surroundings comforted her. How many days had she come here to visit Meggie? Or to confront her? Or try to guide her in the right direction and out of her husband's shadow?

Or to work at her desk as the attorney for Meggie and Zoann's healthcare company? She, herself, owned such a minute share, she didn't consider it a true vested interest.

Kendall had spent as much time in this house as she had at her own. And she'd always been welcomed. Despite everything. She'd always gotten a much warmer reception than she gave when Meggie visited her.

The entrance hall Kendall stood in had a very traditional look. There were the corners where Meggie placed her fiberglass Pilgrims and Christmas scenes during the holidays. Just beyond the wide archway was another central hall that led to various rooms in the huge house. Beyond that was the massive staircase that led to the second and third floors.

With no one there to greet her, Kendall was glad she'd left her Balenciaga tote bag in her Navigator in the club parking lot. There was a private access road to the houses, but she couldn't bring herself to use it.

Footsteps grabbed her attention and Kendall darted into the nearest corner. She didn't want to be seen. She wanted to hear…that she was missed. Or hated. Or loved.

The sounds of a little boy and a grown man playing the-monster-will-catch-you brought a nostalgic smile to Kendall's lips. She knew it was Johnnie because he liked to play the game with Rory and Matilda. But the child's laughter didn't sound like Rory's. It was loud and boisterous and joyous, whereas her son always hesitated to smile, as if innate happiness didn't come easily to him.

Because of her?

"Uncle Johnnie, you're funny," CJ said around giggles. "Ro funny, too."

"You know why?" Johnnie asked in a mock-growl. "Because you have a very funny mom and Rory has a funny aunt. Now, I'm going to get you!"

A funny mom. A funny aunt. *Meggie.* All at once, Kendall's anger rushed back, layering her insecurities with destructive force. She covered her mouth to hold in her sobbing roar, sick to her stomach.

"Stop tickling me, Uncle Johnnie," CJ yelled, laughing hysterically.

"I'm the tickle monster," Johnnie responded.

"Tickle me, Dad!" Rory shouted, sounding truly happy and full of life. Much more so than when she'd been involved in his life on a day-to-day basis.

"Megan let you dress yourself again, son?" Johnnie asked.

Kendall's nostrils flared, another arrow piercing her heart.

"Aunt Meggie said I'm a big boy and I can wear what I want to."

"Your Aunt Megan is not only funny but nice."

Johnnie's words poured fuel on Kendall's bubbling emotions. Had they seen her coming? Thcy must have! Cameras were all around the place and at the gate.

Because, Jesus, what were the odds that she would immediately hear this conversation?

Her progress felt as if it imploded, collapsed from the inside and left her the same empty shell she had been.

"Mommie said she's going to punch you if you tell Ro that her funnier than Aunt Kenda," CJ explained. "Aunt Kenda his mommie and MegAnn mine."

Getting control of herself again, Kendall dropped her hands to her sides, irritated. Why couldn't the little asshole say Kendall?

"When's Mommie coming home, Dad?" Rory asked. "I miss her."

Kendall pressed a hand against her belly at the sound of her son's sadness.

"Aunt Kenda a big giant bitch, Ro," CJ said. "Why you miss her?"

"Nuh-uh, fuckhead! Take that back," Rory cried.

Kendall scowled at Rory's foul language, waiting for Johnnie to correct him. Of course, he didn't.

"My mommie is gorgeous." Rory continued his defense of her, and she smiled. "Dad says it all the time."

"Don't push me," CJ grunted, just before Rory shouted and the sound of little boys scuffling reached her. "Ima make you bleed, fuck-your-mother!"

"Stop this minute, boys!" Johnnie commanded.

"What the fuck goin' on in here?"

Instant silence at Outlaw's question. Kendall rolled her eyes.

"Uncle Chris, CJ call me a fuck-your-mother and said my mommie is a big giant bitch. And he pushed me."

"It's motherfucker, boy," Outlaw corrected as CJ shouted, "Ro pushed me first!"

"I already told your lil' fuckin' ass stop sayin' that about that bitch," Outlaw growled, ignoring CJ's whiny explanation.

"That's very fucking adult of you," Johnnie said sarcastically. "CJ, do *not* call your Aunt Kendall out of her name. You're a child and you're showing supreme disrespect. If I hear it again, I'll spank you myself."

"Lay a fuckin' hand on my fuckin' kid and I'll fuck you up *my-fuckin-self*."

"Then tell him he's wrong, Christopher," Johnnie snarled.

"You ain't tellin' me how to raise my fuckin' kid."

"What is going on in here?" The question came again, this time by Meggie. "We can hear the four of you in the den."

"Ain't nothin', baby," Outlaw answered casually. "Just boy talk."

"CJ?" Meggie said firmly, for once not simpering to her fuckhead husband.

"Ro and John-John mad because I called Aunt Kenda a big giant bitch. 'Law say that bitch my aunt and—"

"*Enough!*" Meggie shouted. "Time out, young man. *Now!*"

"What the fuck that's gonna do, baby?" Outlaw asked in confusion. "The lil' motherfucker do the same thing. Time out a waste of fuckin' time."

"Come on, CJ," Meggie ordered, still ignoring Outlaw. "You have a time out for five minutes."

Sudden sniffles punctuated the air.

"Aunt Meggie, I'm thirsty," Rory said. "Can I have some juice?"

"It's may I," Johnnie corrected.

"Ask your dad," Meggie responded.

"I defer to you, Megan," Johnnie said. "You're such a good mother. I trust you know what's best."

Meggie sighed. "Let's get you some juice, Rory."

"Thank you, Aunt..."

Her son's voice faded away. Kendall shook, and thought about showing herself, then decided against it. She wanted to hear more. Wanted to hear how Johnnie was brainwashing Rory to put Meggie on the same pedestal he did.

"I'm tired of your son disrespecting, Kendall."

"Don't give a fuck. Cuz you know what the fuck my ass tired of? You actin' like Megan *your* lil' motherfuckers' ma, then you comin' here thinkin' you *my* lil' motherfuckers' old man. Ima spank CJ lil' ass for sayin' what he did about Kendall, but how I get to that fuckin' point my business, not yours. Cuz the way my ass see it, you ain't no better than your bitch. *She* got a fuckin' reason for bein' a cunt to Rory, Matilda, and JJ. She psycho. *You* supposed to have all your goddamn sense, so why the fuck your kids stayin' with me and my woman?"

WHAT?

Her kids were living with Meggie and Outlaw? Johnnie never told her that!

"Because it is too hard to look at them, without thinking of Kendall. I miss her so much, but I...she is so hard to handle. She is always getting me into trouble. Or herself."

"Cuz she a busy bitch," Outlaw told him. "And I wanna knock you the fuck out, cuz you always make *my* fuckin' ass defend that cunt, when I hate the fuck outta her. All the fuck I'm hearin' is she, she, she...What the fuck about your motherfuckin' ass? You got faults comin' out the ass, Johnnie. That bitch get into all type of shit, but I gotta give her ass fuckin' credit for at least *tryna* change once in a fuckin while. If she ain't hatin' on Megan so much and doin' shit to irritate the fuck outta me and just basically fuckin' breathin', I might actually like that bitch. She fuckin' tough. She ain't easily a-fuckin-fraid. She got a fuckin' brain. She pretty. She been through a lot and she still fuckin' standin'. She shit for a ma, but even that coulda been different if your ass ain't such a assfuck to her."

"Am I in the Twilight Zone?" Johnnie asked, sounding as awed as Kendall felt at Outlaw's words. "You're defending *Kendall?*"

"Johnnie, I want that bitch gone, *dead,* for so many different fuckin' reasons, I ain't got time to list them all. But I fuckin' *hate* you givin' Megan the responsibility for your fuckin' children."

Kendall did, too. She almost broke down in sobs to know that someone thought she was worthy. That was all she'd ever wanted. Maybe, just a few weeks ago, she would've been feeling vindicated that it was *Outlaw* who defended her. Now, it only left her sad and hopeful that Johnnie would eventually come to see her as Outlaw did.

"What's wrong with Megan looking after my kids? CJ—*all* of your children—are happy and well-adjusted. CJ is like you because Megan allowed him to be your son. She allowed you two to bond. Kendall hates the biker in me, so she did her best to turn Rory into who she thought he should be. He's quiet and reserved, and it's all Kendall's fault."

Outlaw snorted. "Keep believin' that, motherfucker."

Johnnie said nothing.

"I thought your bitch was comin' up the walk."

"Do you see her here? It wasn't her. It must've been someone else."

"Matilda still a lil' kid. Kendall the *only* red-headed grown bitch that got the code to the gate. Unless that bitch dead and I saw her fuckin' ghost."

"She's not here, Christopher."

"What the fuck ever, motherfucker," Outlaw grunted, before the sound of his bootfalls carried him away.

A moment passed, then: "You can come out, Kendall," Johnnie called. "Wherever you're hiding."

Kendall stalked into view. Johnnie stood there, tall and imposing, and gorgeous in gray trousers and white dress shirt. His sleeves were rolled up, partially revealing his biceps.

"Did you get what you wanted?"

She blinked at Johnnie's question. "You knew I was here."

He shrugged. "Of course. I saw you at the gate and watched you walk to the door. "You play so many fucking games, I decided to beat you at this one. Doing what you love to do. Listen for a snippet to justify bad behavior. I gave you what you wanted, sweetheart."

At Johnnie's pettiness, Kendall was torn between rage and despair. For now, the feelings buried all dreams of reconciling with her husband. She'd always known Johnnie wanted Rory to be another CJ...a mini Outlaw...but the extent in which he blamed her for Rory's woes shocked her.

Glaring at him, she got straight to the point. "Is it any wonder why

I despise that little bastard? You think CJ is as perfect as Meggie. Because he's her son."

"Enough, Kendall," he warned, walking closer. "Don't start this tonight."

"He called me names and you couldn't even defend me!"

"I did! I said I was going to spank him. You heard Christopher. What did you expect me to do?"

"Why am I fighting for you, *for us*, if I can never live up to your ideal? Not only do you want me to be Megan, but you want Rory to be CJ," she spat. "Why can't you appreciate us for who we are?"

"Let's not discuss this here."

"The kids aren't even staying with you. They're *here*. Where your perfect ideal of a woman lives."

"Goddamn it, don't start this bullshit!"

Was that all he could say? Of course it was! What other defense did he have?

"I want a divorce," Kendall blurted around a sob.

Johnnie tightened his jaw. "That's a decision we must reach mutually."

"No, it isn't. It's *my* decision to make. I want a divorce and I want full custody of the children."

"Fuck you. Fuck no."

Kendall stared at Johnnie, hating him and Outlaw and Meggie and CJ. Hating them for making her feel inferior. Hating them for acting *superior*. Even Meggie, with all her kindness, behaved with some condescension toward Kendall.

"File for divorce," Johnnie went on, "but you're *not* getting my children."

"I gave birth to them!"

"When has that ever mattered to you?"

"Fuck you."

He stepped closer to her, his gaze ice-cold. "Don't you wish you could? It was *you* who came back in search of my cock after I fucked you the night we met."

"That was the biggest mistake of my life," she snarled. "I wish I had never fallen in love with you."

"You never loved me. You loved the security. You loved being around Christopher."

"I'm not going to stand here and try to convince you of my feelings or lack thereof. If you believe I never loved you, and loved being around Outlaw, then you're a brainless motherfucker."

"Leave, Kendall," he ordered.

"Fuck you," she threw at him again. "You didn't invite me. Meggie did. Besides, I have a thing or two to tell CJ."

"I wouldn't fuck with that child if I were you. Then again, you never listened to me, so go ahead and risk your life. I'm done."

Giving her one last hard look, Johnnie turned on his heel and stormed in the direction he'd come, while Kendall remained inside the hallway.

Her head pounded and she felt as fragile as delicate glass. She had to leave. She couldn't stay there tonight. Johnnie would make her life miserable.

A sob escaped her.

Would he take her seriously and start divorce proceedings? She just didn't know what to do. She felt so backed into a corner.

She *should* leave. But could she? She wanted to see her children. She needed to give her regards to Meggie and Roxy. She craved their kindness. Roxy might even hug her.

Kendall lost track of time as she debated what to do, but the sound of running snapped her to the present.

"Go get more candy, Ro," CJ whispered, sounding as if he was chewing. "MegAnn not going to see. Meet me here."

"Okay, CJ."

Like a little lamb, her sweet Rory did CJ's thieving business.

CJ stood a short distance away, in a corner of the main hall, digging in his pocket, and pulling out chocolates. As he unwrapped the candy and stuffed it into his mouth, he threw the foil on the floor.

"CJ!" she called, barreling forward, so angry she could hardly contain herself.

CJ looked up as she reached him and grabbed him by his shirt, yanking him forward, up and off his feet. His green eyes widened.

"Aunt Kenda!" he squeaked in a shaky voice.

She shook him. "You little motherfucker. It's *Kendall*." She shook him again. "*Kendall!*"

"What's going on in here?"

Knox Harrington's voice interrupted Kendall's rage. Breathing deeply, she sat CJ on his feet. The little boy stared at her, shocked into silence, fear gleaming from his face.

"I asked you a question, Kendall," Knox said with authority.

CJ ran off, so Kendall turned and faced Roxy's fiancée.

"What are you doing here, fuckhead?" Kendall asked coolly. "After the way your mother treated Roxy, *us*, I would think she would've kicked you to the curb."

"If I were you, I'd worry about myself and keep your goddamn nose out of my business. I'm as much family as you are."

"Yeah, but you're more of an asshole," she retorted, then smirked at him. She refused to show how much his jab about worrying about herself bothered her. She'd get in a few of her own. Everyone thought she was crazy and stupid, but she saw things. She read people. That's what made her such a good attorney. "It doesn't matter who invited you," she said. "I'll bet Outlaw doesn't know you don't particularly like him and you're just using him to stick around for Roxy...? Or is there a motive to your method? Do just enough to stay alive, if beaten to a pulp on a regular basis."

His eyes narrowed and he stiffened. As if she gave a fuck. She smiled without humor.

"Oh, you hide your feelings, bastard," she went on, then shrugged. "For Roxy. To save your own miserable fucking life! But you're a fucking coward. At least, I'm honest about how I feel about him."

"Including the fact that you want to fuck him so bad, your pussy gets wet every time you're near him."

She wouldn't dignify that with a response, so she returned back to the original subject. "This is Roxy's wedding, not Joan's."

"Stay out of our business," Knox ordered.

"Roxy *is* my business," Kendall said, undeterred. "She had a tough time in her past relationships. Everyone wanted her to change. Be someone she isn't. To say it like she would, she's the *realest* person you'll ever know. Your mother will make her miserable. Before she does, get Joan in line."

"I don't need advice from a woman who can't hold onto her husband."

"I don't give a fuck what *you* need, prick," Kendall snarled. "This is for Roxy's sake. Stop being a fuck dick-douche and tell Joan to butt out."

"That's my mother! You will not disparage her. Nor will you interfere. If I want my mother involved, that's up to me. Roxanne can't put up with my mother, yet I tolerate that classless fucking *purple* Navigator that *Outlaw* bought her?"

What? Where was this coming from? The asshole's complaint caught Kendall completely off-guard. She recovered fast. "That Navigator is *her*. It's colorful, loud, and fun."

"It's *purple*," he reiterated. "And another man gave it to her. *Outlaw*."

"Oh shut up, cry baby. Is your lack of self-worth an indication of a lack of...*prowess?*" She ignored the dark look he threw at her. "Or maybe it's an indication that you lack brain cells? Because, as I see it, you'd realize what a jewel Roxy is and not give a fuck about what she drives."

"I just brought that up to make a point," Knox snapped.

"Really? It must be on your mind—"

"It isn't," he gritted. "I haven't...look, Kendall, let's lay our cards on the line. I've already put my mother in her place, but I don't like you."

"Join the fucking club, asshole," she said blithely. "As if I give a fuck who likes me. *Roxy* likes me and that's all that matters."

"If I were you, lady, I'd watch your fucking step. I don't want you in our wedding. I don't want you around. Let's see who wins this round. *You* have the enemies. *I* don't." He brushed past her, and left her standing alone in the hallway.

CHAPTER TWENTY-FIVE

Knox

Drawing in a breath and fuming at the confrontation he'd had with Kendall, Knox followed the sound of the laughter and headed to the den. Through the crowd, he zeroed in on Roxanne, who stood and stretched, turning this way and that, torturing Knox without mercy.

She wore a pair of black jeans that made her ass so fucking fabulous, Knox almost went to her, dropped to his knees and kissed it. Her skin was as smooth and as sweet as liquid caramel. And her voice, her laughter...there was nothing Knox loved better than hearing those sounds. Seeing her joy. She was an innately happy, optimistic woman, and brought sunshine to whoever she befriended. She'd certainly put a spark in his life.

"Ladies," Knox greeted, nodding to the women, as Roxanne turned and grinned, her light brown eyes lit with mischief, telling him, without words, that her little display was solely for his benefit.

Shaking his head and laughing, Knox winked at her, sharing in the glow of this morning's secret sex fest.

Her face lit up and she waved at him, then blew him a kiss. She leaned over and whispered to her best friend, Dr. Jordan Baptiste, while Cam stood at the bar with the rest of the guys. It was a full house tonight. Bunny, Bailey, Ophelia, Zoann, and Roxanne sat around Megan Caldwell, as they held a conversation in low tones, ignoring the boisterousness of their men at the bar, blissfully unaware of Kendall's presence. Hopefully, she'd decided to leave.

Shoving his annoyance toward Kendall aside, Knox headed toward Outlaw.

"'Law!" CJ yelled, just as Knox reached the man. Baby Thug didn't seem the worse for wear from his run-in with Kendall. "I wanna ride your cycle like you let me do before."

A frown crossed Outlaw's face and he glanced in Megan's direction. Her brows snapped together.

"Not to-fuckin-night, boy," Outlaw responded. "We ain't ate yet."

"The way Meggie girl glaring at you, you not eating no time soon," Mortician observed with a snicker.

"The lil' motherfucker just don't know how to shut the fuck up. I think he do that shit on purpose."

"Nuh-uh, 'Law," CJ said with a grin, then looked up at Johnnie. "I want to play monster again, Uncle Johnnie."

Johnnie held up his drink. "Later. For now, play with the other kids. Where's Rory, anyway?"

"Him stealing candy for me." CJ dug in his pocket and came up with a chocolate. "I sent him, but him didn't come back yet. Maybe, he saw his ma."

Digger, Val, Cash, Stretch, and Mortician sniggered. Cam turned away and sipped his drink. While Outlaw stared at the Baby Thug, Knox felt a spark of anger towards both the biker and his son.

"Fuck me, boy. I ain't even knowin' where my ass need to start," Outlaw said on a sigh.

"Try with the stealing?" Johnnie suggested, not at all happy.

Knox wouldn't be either if his kid was involved in criminal activity at the behest of someone else.

"Wait a fuckin' minute, CJ." Outlaw sat his bottle of rum on the bar and gave his full attention to his son. "My fuckin' ass heard your ma say you ain't able to have candy 'til after dinner. You fuckin' asked her when she let your lil' ass outta time-fuckin-out for callin' psycho cunt a big giant bitch."

CJ's lower lip trembled at his father's harshness and his face crumpled.

"Not only aintcha listenin' to her, you gettin' another fuckin' man to do *your* fuckin' dirty work. Don't lie to your ma and don't send no motherfucker on a job you ain't willin' to fuckin' do."

CJ's face brightened, and he held up the chocolate that had been wrapped but now was partially squeezed out by the child's fisting it. "But, 'Law, I stoled already. When Mommie let me up."

The idiots who'd been laughing before howled again.

"You ain't supposed to fuckin' steal and you ain't supposed to fuckin' lie. A thief as miserable a motherfucker as a fuckin' liar. Motherfuckers ain't able to trust neither, and if you got nothin' fuckin' else you gotta be a man of your word, boy."

"I'm is," CJ protested, his brief moment of happiness disintegrating at his father's stern lecture.

"What about your ma?" Outlaw continued, surprising Knox with his correct pronunciation of *about*. "You ain't listen to her." He swatted CJ's butt. "That's for your fuckin' thievery." Another swat. "That's for tryna bitch your ma out. You always respect your ma. *Al-fucking-ways*," he roared, ignoring CJ's tears. "If she tell you to fuckin' do somethin' or don't fuckin' do somethin', follow what the fuck she say. Hear me, boy?"

"Yes, 'Law," CJ sobbed.

From Knox's point-of-view, the taps on the brat's ass hadn't been enough. Outlaw should've given CJ a real spanking. Therefore, Baby Thug's screaming wails were unnecessary.

"Come here, potato," Megan called from the other side of the room.

"MegAnn," CJ sobbed, running to her and throwing himself into her open arms. She pulled him onto her lap as he cried against her neck.

"Rory and CJ aren't men," Johnnie snapped, glaring at Outlaw, as CJ's tears quieted. "They're little boys."

"No fuckin' shit," Outlaw said. "They gonna be men one fuckin' day, Johnnie."

"They're children," Johnnie said flatly. "So let them be children."

"Uncle Johnnie," CJ called in a pitiful voice. "Monster."

"Later," Johnnie responded.

"'Kay," he said hoarsely, sliding from Megan's lap. "I going by Diesel." Still sniffling with such force his shoulders shook, he walked from the room.

Knox supposed Outlaw's adopted son was somewhere watching over the brood of kids as he usually did.

Shaking his head, Johnnie walked behind the bar. "What are you drinking, Knox?"

There was a definite strain on the man's face. He looked sad and angry and on the verge of exploding. If Knox couldn't sneak Roxanne away later, maybe he'd ask Johnnie to join him for a drink.

In the meantime... "I'll take a Scotch neat."

"I see your ass almost all healed from the whipping Outlaw gave you, Knox. What your ass did this time for Outlaw to fuck you up like you was? You was to'e up from the flo' up," Digger told him. The sergeant-at-arms sipped from his bottle of beer.

"I resent that." The bruises from Outlaw and Mortician's punches were practically non-existent now. Still, he didn't think either man had gone and broadcast the fact that they'd beat him. Scowling, he accepted the glass of Scotch that Johnnie held out to him. "How do you know it was Outlaw? I could've fought someone else and won."

"Not," Val put in. "You don't go places to fight."

"I'm always in dangerous places. I'm a PI," Knox reminded them, ignoring the lift of Cam's eyebrow, his business partner, that called bullshit on the claim.

Cash grinned and elbowed his husband, Stretch. "Barely. I can do better investigating than you."

"Fuck, CJ can do better than Knox," Digger added.

"All right. Give the poor man some slack," Johnnie demanded. "He's under a lot of pressure right now. Something I can identify with."

"You and Kendall going to work things out, John Boy," Mortician said with reassurance.

Everyone glanced at Outlaw, but he said nothing to Johnnie and instead looked at Knox. "Still enjoyin' bein' en-fuckin-gaged, Knox?"

"Yes. It's wonderful," Knox replied. "How did it feel when you were engaged?"

"Ain't never was engaged. Ask John Boy. He know."

"*He* would," Knox retorted.

"You share Val disease, Knox," Mortician told him with a smirk.

Knox sipped his Scotch, then looked at Mortician. "Which is?"

"The fucking masochistic need for Outlaw to beat your ass every couple months," Mortician said, grinning at the laughter of Digger, Val, Cash, and Stretch.

"You're funny," Knox gritted.

"Fucking hilarious," Mortician agreed. "Just so you know, me and Bailey was never engaged either."

"I see," Knox said with irritation. "That's why you're encroaching on my wedding to her mother."

"*Encroaching?*" Mortician echoed. He started to say something else, then huffed out a breath. "Knox, I don't want Bailey and Roxy wedding to have a cloud hanging over it. If we have issues and problems all through the planning, it might make for a shitty wedding day. Let's keep shit friendly."

"Since when have you become so fucking superstitious?" Johnnie asked.

"Since all this bullshit started. You and Kendall not together. Never thought I'd see that day. Then, Knox bitch-ass momma and Charlotte-fucking-Redding started with their bullshit. Personal bullshit sometimes more vicious than club war." He nodded in the direction of the women. "They waiting for Red to get here, so they can start looking through that stack of wedding magazines. And, fuck...I just got a bad feeling about tonight, man."

"Bailey and Roxanne gonna get it to-fuckin-gether, Mort," Outlaw promised. "They already got the motherfuckers walkin' them down the aisle. Shit gonna fall into place. I fuckin' swear. Anytime Val got his fuckin' ass shot off and I fucked up my old man on me and Megan second weddin' day, and shit still went on, ain't nothin' so bad that it'll stop the upcomin' ceremonies."

Instead of responding, Mortician drank more vodka.

Knox decided to take matters in hand and confront Mortician, so he could move back in with Roxanne. He'd done it once. This time, he'd prevail.

"Mortician, I'm moving out of the club." When Knox had gotten back to his room at the clubhouse, he'd found Roxanne's dress, stuffed under his pillow, her scent clinging to it. Memories of the morning flooded back and made his cock so painfully hard that Knox had jerked off, his cum exploding from him and raining on his hands and stomach —as well as her dress.

That infamous blue dress had nothing on the cum stains on Roxanne's hot pink one.

"I'm returning to Roxanne's place," Knox finished.

Amusement curved the enforcer's lips. "When this death-inviting event happening?"

"Enough," Knox gritted. "This is bullshit, and you know it."

"No," Mortician insisted. "What the fuck is bullshit is all the fucking threats you made when we told you to marry Roxanne."

"Maybe, it's your own damn guilt," Knox bit out. "You know the pressure you put on me was unfair. I have every right to lash out."

"You not a goddamn child," Mortician fired back. "I once lashed out at Bailey and she left my fucking ass. Taught me a goddamn lesson. Channel anger into something positive or risk ruining your fucking life."

"It's my fucking mistake to make," Knox said.

"Why the fuck you asked Roxanne to marry you now?" Val questioned.

It surprised Knox that it had taken this long for another one of them to stick their nose in the conversation. It was nobody else's business, but the bikers excelled at interfering in each other's business.

"What the fuck is wrong with you people?" Knox demanded. "First, you weren't satisfied because I hadn't asked Roxanne to marry me. Now, you're questioning why I proposed to her."

Mortician pinned Knox with an unhappy look. "The question fair,

Knox. You asked her because you love her or because of our conversation?"

Knox didn't even have to think about the answer. "We've been through this already, but I'll repeat it. I love her. It's as simple as that."

"Then why the prenup?" Digger demanded. "It's like you expecting your marriage to fail."

"Anything can happen."

"You right, Knox," Mortician agreed. "When she tell you to go fuck yourself, then what?"

"Then I call off the wedding."

"And your ass wonder why the fuck I don't want you cohabitating with her until after the wedding. It just seem like you looking for a reason to break it off."

"That isn't true. I don't trust the vagaries of love. Sue me."

"You can't even shop for your tux with us."

"As the groom, it's my prerogative to purchase my attire wherever I choose."

Mortician shrugged. "That's on you. That view just not helping me change my mind."

"I wasn't asking your permission to move back in with her. I'm doing it no matter what you say. I love Roxanne and I want to be with her. I *will* be with her."

"I would hate to make you disappear, Knox," Mortician said with a straight face.

"I'm not a criminal on the fringes of society. If I go missing, it will be noted."

"I hate to disappoint you, but we don't give a fuck who you are. If you need to go missing, you disappear."

Knox couldn't refute Mortician. Charlotte Redding's son-in-law had been missing for months. He was gone without a trace, last seen at the clubhouse. No one could prove the Death Dwellers were responsible for the young lawyer's death.

Deciding to drop the subject for tonight, Knox was determined to win this war. He was also pretty certain that he and Roxanne would have another secret rendezvous. If she shared his feelings, this morning's taste hadn't been enough.

Silence fell around them, leaving Knox stewing in resentment, but anticipating being in Roxanne's arms again.

"You know what I've just realized?" Johnnie suddenly asked the group, looking into each of their faces as a broad smile curved his lips. "Megan hasn't spoken directly to Christopher once tonight. Could it be that Mr. and Mrs. Happily-Ever-After are arguing?"

"Damn, son," Mortician said with a shake of his head. "You don't have to sound so gleeful."

Outlaw looked in his wife's direction. Megan must've felt her husband's gaze on her because she turned, the long strands of hair escaping her messy bun wiggling with her movements. Not only did she seem angry, but hurt, too.

"I ain't gonna talk to Megan for at least another five fuckin' days," Outlaw confided in a low voice.

"I beg your pardon?" Johnnie glared at Outlaw. "Is that why she's looking so wretched? Because of *you*?"

"Back the fuck off, Johnnie," Outlaw snapped. "This between me, my cock, and my woman. Megan ain't gonna get kidnapped *ever* a-fuckin-gain. I almost lost my fuckin' mind."

"And we almost lost our fucking noses," Digger quipped.

Outlaw hadn't even had it in him to shower.

"Ha fuckin' ha ha," Outlaw grumbled. "Laugh all the fuck you wanna. This shit serious. Megan gotta sleep with a fuckin' light on. She scream in the middle of the fuckin' night. What them motherfuckers did fuckin' harmed her a lot."

"We still don't get where you're going with this," Cam put in.

"I got a dick snip flip," he confessed, still in a tone that suggested secrecy. Or betrayal. "Ima get Megan pregnant again. Fuckin' problem is she ain't wantin' no more lil' motherfuckers and I ain't told her about my plans 'til after I had the procedure that she still ain't knowin' about. I gotta see...I don't know what Ima do."

"What do you mean by that?" Johnnie asked in suspicion.

"Tell her and hope she change her mind, or pull a lower-motherfucker-move, don't tell her and hope she end up filled with my kid."

"You wouldn't," Johnnie managed, anger lighting his eyes. "You can't take away her choice. It's her body, Christopher, and her body isn't your fucking receptacle."

"Yo, Johnnie, back the fuck off," Outlaw ordered. Even his soft voice was filled with menace. "This between me and Megan."

"Prez," Mortician started, "you saying you created an argument between you and Meggie girl so she don't know your cock injured, in case you decide against telling her?"

Outlaw nodded.

"You're such a barbaric asshole," Johnnie barked, taking Outlaw's cue and keeping his voice quiet.

Outlaw put his bottle down and grabbed Johnnie by the collar. Much like he'd done to Knox days ago.

"Look, motherfucker——"

"Don't 'look' me, Christopher," Johnnie spat. "I'm telling Megan what you're doing."

A chill dropped into the air. "If you do, Ima cut your fuckin' tongue outcha fuckin' head and watch you bleed to fuckin' death," Outlaw snarled.

Johnnie yanked himself away, but fell silent. Perhaps, thinking about the day Outlaw had shoved a gun in his mouth and pulled the trigger…?

"Why do you want to cut Johnnie's tongue out?" Megan called.

"So he ain't usin' it no more, Megan," Outlaw answered in frustration. "What the fuck you think for?"

She glowered at him, but turned her attention back to the women.

Outlaw bowed his head. "Fuck, but Megan breakin' my fuckin' heart." He drank more rum, then rubbed the back of his neck. "She wanted to talk to my ass this mornin', but I had to turn her away, and that's why she look so fuckin' hurt. Fuck, Ima have to make this up to her."

"Start by telling her the truth."

"Fuck, I might just gotta do that, Cash."

Knox hid a smile. He'd love to be a fly on the wall for that conversation.

CHAPTER TWENTY-SIX

Megan

Sighing, Meggie tried to follow the conversation of the other women, but it was so hard. All she thought about was Christopher and the arguments they'd had. She couldn't understand what was wrong with him.

Did he really want another baby so badly that her response to his question about a vasectomy reversal upset him to the point of resentment that she'd turned him down?

They didn't handle disagreements through anger. They talked openly and honestly. They didn't push each other away.

"Why is Christopher walking so weird?" Fee asked, frowning as she watched her brother hobble next to Johnnie behind the bar.

"I don't know," Meggie said glumly. "He's been in a horrible mood for since last night, yelling at me for no apparent reason. I tried to be understanding. I thought maybe something happened at the club…" Voice trailing off, she gasped. "Do you think he's been shot?"

Despite promising to ignore him, Meggie couldn't help but glance at her husband. He was leaning nonchalantly against the bar, engaged in conversation, his smile making her breathless.

As if he felt her gaze on him, he looked at her. And frowned.

"What burr is up his dickhole?" Zoann asked, narrowing her eyes at Christopher.

"I don't know," Meggie admitted. "Yesterday morning was the last time we made love."

It was no secret that she and Christopher had a very active love life.

"Dr. Will, I need to come in and talk to you," Meggie said.

"Are you pregnant again?" Bailey asked.

"No, but Christopher wants me to be," Meggie answered.

"Wasn't he the one who said he didn't want more babies?" Roxy asked.

Meggie nodded. "We had a very long talk last night, then I left him in the kitchen. He never said goodnight to the kids or anything. By the time I got to our room, he'd locked himself in the bathroom. He never does that."

"I wonder what's wrong with him," Bunny said. "That isn't Outlaw's style."

"Maybe, there is something going on at the club," Zoann suggested. "I'll ask Val and see what I find out."

"Thank you," Meggie responded. "Let me know."

"Maybe, if you talked to him, Meggie," Dr. Will suggested. "Mr. Caldwell can be gruff but he stops everything for you."

"I tried to talk to him this morning. He was so…so *different*. He wasn't *my* Christopher at all. I got to a point where I had enough, and we argued all over again. As far as I'm concerned our fight was baseless."

She'd busied herself with preparing the food for their get-together and was sure Christopher would've calmed down by the time he returned from the club. He hadn't.

But, he had been limping. He hadn't given her a chance to ask him what had happened. Things had spiraled out of control. Now, though, his behavior was thawing slightly.

"Hello, everybody," Kendall greeted.

The room fell silent. As a whole, everyone glanced in Kendall's direction. Looking uncharacteristically nervous, she shifted her weight and wrung her hands together.

"Hi, sugar," Roxy said with a smile.

Relief removed some of Kendall's uncertainty. "Hi, Roxy."

Meggie stood. "Come and join us, Kendall. We've been waiting for you. Roxy and Bailey want us to pick out the kids' wedding clothes." She indicated the two stacks of magazines, where an iPad sat on top. "We're even going to visit websites."

"You waited for me?" Kendall asked, sounding unsure and out-of-sorts.

"Of course, Kendall,' Bailey responded, not unkindly. "You're part of the planning committee."

As she walked forward and completely ignored the men, Kendall's face brightened.

"I'm so glad you made it," Meggie continued.

Kendall searched for a seat. However, the only available place was a spot next to Zoann on the loveseat. Pursing her lips, Kendall smiled, then decided to stand behind Roxy's chair.

"I'm not going to bite you," Zoann said sharply.

Instead of replying, Kendall shrugged.

"Lawd Jesus, give me strength," Roxy said, getting to her feet, and walking to the loveseat. She plopped next to Zoann. "Now, sit, child."

"Yes, please," Meggie said, sad at how uncomfortable and awkward this was for everyone. "Let me take your jacket."

Shrugging out of it, Kendall held it out to Meggie. "It's going to be in the usual place," she said, heading to the mudroom and hanging it on one of the hooks.

When she returned, the room had fallen silent. The men seemed lost in their own thoughts and the women were twirling their hair, picking at their clothes, or playing on their phones.

Girding her resolve, Meggie reseated herself, trying to think of something to say. The problem was Kendall. No one wanted to share even a little secret in front of her because they didn't trust what she'd do with the information. Too many times before she'd burned them.

"Rory misses you," Meggie started, then regretted the words. She didn't want the drama of Kendall discovering her children were living under Meggie's roof.

She hadn't been able to tell Johnnie no, because he'd seemed so distraught, in no condition to care for his kids.

"I miss Rory, too," Kendall said in a soft voice. "All my children. I worry they'll forget about me."

"I thought Johnnie brought them over to visit you?" Fee asked in surprise.

"He does," Kendall confirmed. "But it isn't the same as living with them and watching their daily milestones."

"Just hold on, baby," Roxy encouraged. "You're going to get through this."

Kendall blinked away the tears glistening in her eyes.

"Er, Kendall, would you like to be my matron-of-honor?" Bailey asked.

"Really?" Kendall whispered.

Bailey nodded.

"I'd love to. Thank you for asking."

Silence fell again.

After an eternity, Kendall cleared her throat and smiled at Roxy. "I can't believe your hair came back like normal hair."

Zoann rolled her eyes. "Oh my God, you're beyond fucking ignorant. I just remembered why I didn't talk to you."

"Your hair is so long now. So pretty," Kendall went on, ignoring Zoann. "*Normal.*"

Roxy scowled at Kendall. "What the fuck you mean, sugar? Normal? My hair was always fucking normal."

Kendall frowned. "How so? I mean..." She gulped at Roxy's glare. "Um, you know, um...your hair was really considered normal hair?"

Shaking her head, Roxy laughed. If she let the matter drop, Meggie hoped Zoann would, too.

"Johnnie?" Kendall called, drawing his attention in her direction.

She pointed to Roxy's long curls. "Isn't it gorgeous? Even prettier than it was when it first started growing back."

Johnnie winced and offered Roxy a sheepish smile.

"Please, boy," Roxy said with a snort, perceptive as always. "Nothing Kendall thinks, says, or does, embarrasses, offends, or shocks me. You're the one always caught off-guard."

"I asked her not to repeat that to you," Johnnie confessed. "I tried to explain that your hair is normal. It's just a different texture." He gazed at Roxy's hair. "Or had been until the cancer took it and it re-grew."

"I know about hair, Johnnie," Kendall huffed. "Fine, limp, brittle... See? I know about hair."

"Wrong," Knox snapped. "I'll thank you to stop insulting Roxanne with your ignorance. There's fine, medium, and coarse hair."

If Johnnie and Kendall couldn't find common ground for many things, they found it when someone insulted her. At Knox's sharp words, they both stiffened.

Roxanne gazed at Knox. "Don't sweat it, sugar," she said to him. "If we can't discuss something as simple as the differences in hair texture without flinging insults, then we can't discuss shit. This is nothing to get ass hurt over."

"How does Johnnie know this difference but Kendall, a woman like you, doesn't?" Knox demanded, sounding as grumpy as Christopher had been acting.

Roxanne cleared her throat. "Johnnie has spent years around Mortician," she explained. "These boys like brothers, so, of course, he'd know about hair texture."

"I've also dated a Black girl and slept with more than a few."

A murderous scowl spread across Kendall's features at Johnnie's casual information. Meggie felt like strangling him. It seemed as if he *wanted* to get a rise out of Kendall.

"Check your bullshit, Kendall," Roxanne warned, seeing Kendall's reaction. "The boy had a dick before he met you. Just like you had a pussy, and used it, before you met *him*."

Kendall poked out her lower lip. "I don't flaunt my affairs in his face." She turned to Johnnie. "I don't flaunt my affairs in your face."

"Not your past ones," Johnnie reminded her. "But every chance you get, you remind me you want to sleep with Christopher."

Kendall glowered at Knox, then focused on Roxanne and sniffled. "Do you see how Johnnie treats me? As if I mean nothing to him. Johnnie hates me."

"I don't hate you, Kendall," Johnnie told her. "I'm just sick of you."

Huffing, Kendall got to her feet, then started for the door. "Excuse me for a moment."

The thought to go after Kendall and talk to her crossed Meggie's mind, but to say what? More than likely, Kendall didn't even want Meggie's interference.

She looked at Christopher. He didn't smile or move, so she started for the door that led to the kitchen. "I'm going to start heating the food," she said morosely.

"We can all help," Zoann put in, following behind Megan.

Once they reached the kitchen, Meggie headed to the oven and turned it on. She loved to serve fresh-baked rolls and favored frozen ones that had to sit out for hours and rise. Setting the oven to four hundred degrees, she could almost taste the buttery goodness in her mouth.

Fee pulled the bowl of salad out of the refrigerator and handed it to Zoann, who put it on the counter. They repeated the process with a bowl of fresh fruit.

"I'm going to start warming everything in the microwave," Roxy said.

"Sounds like a plan to me," Bunny responded, carrying Meggie's favorite set of dishes from the pantry.

"Stop!" CJ cried in a teary voice. "You hurtin' me, Aunt Kenda."

"Ouch!" Kendall yelled. "You little motherfucker, I'm beating your ass again for kicking me."

"*Mommie!*" CJ yelled, alarming and angering Meggie, propelling her in the direction of the sounds. "'Law! Aunt Kenda got me."

"Fuck!" Roxy said, running behind Meggie. "What the fuck is wrong with that girl?"

It took only a few moments for them to reach the main hallway, but Christopher, Knox, and the other men already stood there.

Johnnie grabbed Kendall's arm and whispered to her, pointing to CJ.

"Come here, boy." Christopher threw a death glare in Kendall's direction. Wincing, he stooped down when CJ reached him and took their son into his arms.

Meggie wondered at her husband's fleeting look of pain, but let it go as she watched CJ hug Christopher.

"What happened, boy?" he asked gruffly.

What happened? Kendall happened, as always. The woman terrorized everybody, but Meggie would be damned if she allowed her to frighten CJ.

"Then what the fuck happen, son?" Christopher asked, and Meggie regretted missing CJ's first response.

"Does it really matter?" she asked, a dull ache in her chest.

"Aunt Kenda mean," CJ sniffled, answering Christopher despite Meggie's question. "She treat me like at the ball, when MegAnn was there. And you. A whole lotta peoples."

"What the fuck happen now, CJ?" Christopher asked.

"Her grabbed my arm and shook me, then her hit my booty and legs so hard, 'Law. Real hard. Her say she was going to beat me again cuz I won't say Aunt Kend-All. I call her Aunt Kenda."

Kendall squinted at CJ. "He's lying," she said without flinching.

Meggie bristled. Kendall looked perfect and put-together, not a hair out of place, her make-up flawless. Her surface beauty hid so much ugliness. *Too much.*

Too much for Meggie to keep ignoring. Someone had to stop her.

"You and Johnnie got a bad fucking habit of wanting to hit other people's kids, Red," Mortician told her.

"I don't want to hit him. I *didn't* hit him," Kendall insisted. "I told you he's lying."

"Nuh-uh, Aunt Kenda!" CJ cried, tears wetting his reddened little face.

"My boy ain't a liar."

Folding her arms, Kendall lifted her chin. "Even if it was true, which it *isn't*, there's not a lot you could do to me."

A buzzing started in Meggie's head at Kendall's boast. The past few days had been so difficult for Meggie. She was worried about Christopher, heartsore over their arguments, and upset with herself for denying Christopher's want of another baby. She'd pushed all that aside to make Kendall feel as welcome as possible, so she wouldn't feel so alone. Being isolated from everyone had never helped Kendall in the least.

But Meggie was on the verge of exploding, leaping on Kendall and pummeling her into the ground.

She'd defended Kendall to Christopher time after time. Had even talked Christopher into giving Kendall the house that was meant for their protection should the need ever arise. After overlooking the rumors of Kendall almost punching CJ, she came into Meggie's *house* and actually *hit* her son?

"You would never hit me," Kendall boasted.

No, *Christopher* couldn't hit her. "Leave, Kendall."

"And," Kendall went on, ignoring Meggie, "because of Johnnie, you wouldn't kill me, either."

"I could shake the fuck out of you," Christopher snapped. "Dangle your motherfuckin' ass from a fifty-story building and accidently let you go."

"As if," Kendall bit out. "CJ is a stupid little nothing, Outlaw. Just like you." She turned angry eyes to Meggie. "Your son's a goddamn liar."

"Kendall!" Roxy shouted in anger, while everyone else seemed shocked into speechlessness, even Zoann. "Get the fuck out of here, girl."

Instead of following Roxy's order, Kendall stared at Johnnie, with accusation and anger. Even hate.

"My son isn't stupid and he isn't a liar." Meggie marched to where Kendall and Johnnie stood. "I'm telling you once more. It's time for you to go. I was going to talk to you about the incident from a few weeks ago. The supposed punch you almost gave to CJ. I defended you, but..." She huffed in a breath. "Oh, never mind. Just leave before I do something I regret."

"Ha! Another shallow Caldwell with empty fucking threats."

Kendall let out a nasty laugh. "I fucking dare you to raise your hand to me. That'll be the last fucking thing you do for a while."

"Touch Megan and that'll be the last motherfuckin' time you ever fuckin' breathe, cunt," Christopher snarled.

"Back the fuck off my wife, Christopher," Johnnie warned.

"Fuck him, my love," Kendall called. "This is between Meggie and I. Unlike her, I fight my own fucking battles."

Meggie swallowed. Balled her fist. Swallowed again. "I gave you the benefit of the doubt, but no one abuses my kids," she said, very near to lashing out and really hurting Kendall. "*No one* hurts my children and then has the gall to believe I won't retaliate on their behalf."

"Fuck you," Kendall yelled. "You're a pissy, wimpy, drooling asslicker. CJ is a stupid, no-talking cum-shoot. He's a—"

Meggie's punch to Kendall's face stopped her words cold. After that first hit, all restraint deserted Meggie. Years of pent-up hurt and anger sent her on the offensive. Mostly, she battered Kendall's face for her abuse towards Meggie's precious CJ. It enraged her that Kendall had gotten away with it so often, the fact that *Meggie* had believed her, defended her. Another punch made Kendall teeter on her heels.

Somehow, Kendall regained her balance, and shoved Meggie into the table, containing family photos. It crashed to its side, sending frames in all directions.

"Mommie!" CJ cried as Meggie went sprawling. "Don't hurt my mommie, Aunt Kenda!"

"Get back, boy," Christopher instructed. "Don't interrupt your ma. Hit that bitch again, baby," he called.

The shouts around Meggie began to blend together. She didn't know, if, like Christopher, they were encouraging her, or doing the opposite and trying to talk both Meggie and Kendall down.

Tangling her legs around Kendall's, Meggie wrestled her to the floor and sprung. When Meggie freed Kendall, she started to move. Just not quick enough.

"Megan, fuck, stop this!" Johnnie demanded, reaching for her, but, she sidestepped him, and shoved Kendall. Her crash into the wall stunned her and she sat, panting.

Turning her anger on Johnnie, Meggie looked at him in disgust.

"Fuck you!" she spat, balling her hand. The bone her fist connected with crunched under the forceful hit. Blood sprayed everywhere and he reeled back.

"*FUCK!*" Johnnie roared, holding his nose, and rushing away.

Without warning, Kendall grabbed Meggie's hair and yanked her around. "You punched my husband, you little cunt?" she snarled. "Of course you did. You think all the men belong to you, but *especially* Johnnie and Outlaw. Everyone talks about me wanting to sleep with Outlaw. What about you? You keep my husband twisted around your little finger, like a dick in a glass case, that says *break in case of an emergency*. Well, fuck you! He's mine."

"*Bitch!*" Meggie yelled, throwing a good punch to Kendall's eye. "I don't want Johnnie. This isn't about our husbands, anyway. It's about my child. Do *not* fuck with my son. Christopher can't hit you, but *I* can fuck you up."

Roxy attempted to rush forward, but Mortician blocked her. "Meggie, Kendall, stop this!" she cried, unable to spring into action.

Meggie and Kendall circled each other like angry lionesses defending their territory.

Out of patience, Meggie threw a jab, connecting with Kendall's jaw.

"That's my fucking woman," Christopher boasted with gleeful pride.

"Stop this, you two!" Zoann ordered.

"Meggie, please, she isn't worth it," Bunny called.

"We're all family," Fee cried. "Don't do this. Neither of you can ever take this back."

Meggie ignored the pleas, while Kendall shoved Meggie. She stumbled back. Growling, she sprung on Kendall, grabbing handfuls of red hair and yanking. Screaming, Kendall jerked away, leaving some of her hair in Meggie's hand.

"Stop this, this fucking minute!" Johnnie's high-pitched command deterred neither of them. "Kendall, *enough*! Megan, back the fuck up!"

"Uh, bro," Digger called. "No motherfucker taking your ass serious when you around here sounding like a castrated hog."

"Fuck off," Johnnie squealed as Kendall connected with Meggie's eye, the conversation distracting her.

"Concentrate, Megan," Christopher said in exasperation.

"Prez, we letting Meggie girl and Red fuck each other up?" Mortician asked.

"No, we aren't!" Johnnie answered, stepping toward Meggie and Kendall.

"Make one motherfuckin' step and Ima shoot the fuck outta you," Christopher warned, pulling his 9mm and aiming at Johnnie's head. "Your bitch need to be brought down a peg or two. I ain't able to do shit about her shenanigans, but my Megan can."

"Outlaw, baby, this isn't the answer," Roxy said, frantic. "Stop this."

"You crazy little cunt," Kendall spat, barreling forward.

"I'll show you a crazy little cunt." Meggie stood her ground and landed a fist in Kendall's mouth, then shoved her with all her might.

Kendall careened into Johnnie and toppled both of them.

Breathing hard, Meggie held her stomach, where she'd taken a lot of blows, and limped forward. Before she made it out of Kendall's reach, she grabbed Meggie's leg and pulled her down.

Another surge of adrenalin, and the instinct to survive, protect, *win*, made Meggie hop to her feet.

Kendall started to stand.

Taking *ass kicking* for real, Meggie kicked Kendall right in hers. If her ass had been bare, Meggie's toes probably would've gotten caught in Kendall's butt crack. That's how accurate it was.

Still, it didn't deter Kendall. She crawled to her feet. Remembering the pro fights she'd watched with Christopher, Meggie got into a fighter's position, so sick of Kendall's meanness she just wanted to erase it.

"Mommie, please stop!"

At CJ's sob, Christopher walked into the middle of the fight, pushing Kendall aside and grabbing Meggie.

"Motherfucker!" Kendall screamed because Christopher pushed her harder than necessary and she sprawled onto the floor again.

Meggie struggled against Christopher's hold. "Let me go, Christopher!" she demanded. "I'm going to kill her."

"Come on, cunt," Kendall taunted from the floor. She positioned herself to lunge "Try it! I fucking dare you."

Meggie broke free of Christopher's grasp, and punched Kendall on the side of the head. Suddenly, Digger grabbed Kendall as Christopher grabbed Meggie again.

"If you ever set foot on club grounds again, I'm going to beat your miserable ass with a bat," Meggie snarled, burning with rage and disappointment and a deep hurt. "How dare you think you can treat CJ any kind of way? Call him horrible names. What do you do to your own kids? You're such a poor excuse for a human being. My God, you're lower than low."

"You can't bar me from the club, bitch," Kendall retorted. "Only a member can."

"The hell I can't, cow," Meggie shot back. "If Christopher wants in *there ever* again, he'll see to it you're never on the grounds again."

"Now wait a fuckin' minute, Megan," Christopher growled. "Shit gettin' the fuck out of hand. This bitch pissin' you off so much, she messin' with the business of my cock."

Meggie elbowed Christopher in the gut. "You've already messed with the business of your cock," she fumed, thinking of how he'd been treating her most of last night and all day today.

"You're such a manipulative little bitch," Kendall shouted, drawing Meggie's attention again. "I've known all along you hated me."

"I didn't before, whiner. Now, I do. Don't fuck with my man and don't fuck with my children." Meggie didn't know where those words were coming from. She didn't use bad language. But, maybe, they were dredged from the same place as her need to pummel Kendall into the ground. "Tonight, you fucked with both, bitch."

"Megan, stop with the cussin'," Christopher ordered. "That ain't you and I don't like it."

"Yes, little cock servant, do what your master tells you," Kendall taunted before Meggie could respond to Christopher.

At Kendall's words, Meggie struggled to free herself. Digger lost his hold on Kendall and she rushed to Meggie. Before Christopher had a chance to tighten his hold or protect her, Meggie escaped him, met Kendall in the middle of their ring, and punched her so hard, she knocked her out.

"Kendall!" Johnnie yelled, rushing forward so she wouldn't hit her head on the floor. He kneeled down and cradled her head. Bloody pieces of Kleenex hung from each of his nostrils. Gently, he laid her head on the floor, stood, and glared at Meggie. "Megan, I should shake the fuck out of you."

"Johnnie, I already shot the fuck outta you once," Christopher reminded him. "You shake my woman, I might accidentally throw your cunt on concrete and break every fuckin' bone in her body."

Stomping to Johnnie, Meggie shoved him. She was done. Past done. "Kendall is never allowed near my children again. She's not allowed on the grounds. She's not allowed to *blink* at CJ. She's a horrible, evil bitch."

"Because of CJ?" Johnnie gasped, his swelling nose squeaking. "She's an adult and your child disrespects her all the fucking time."

"Oh, shut up, asshole," Megan commanded. "Kendall can walk all over you for the rest of your miserable life, but she better not *ever*, *never*, *ever* mess with my children or my husband ever again. Am I clear?"

A few heartbeats went by, then his eyes widened. He turned sheet-white, shell-shocked by Meggie's vehemence.

His anger deflated. "You're clear, sweetheart."

Drawing in a deep breath, Meggie knelt in front of CJ and hugged him tightly. "I'm *sooo* sorry, potato," she whispered. "And I'm sorry I upset you tonight, but Aunt Kendall needed to be dealt with for what she did to you."

"Okay," CJ said in a tired, watery voice.

"What's wrong with you people?" Johnnie demanded. "Not one of you stopped this fight."

"Shut the fuck up, Johnnie," Zoann ordered. "It's past time Meggie gave you *and* Kendall a beat down."

Johnnie touched his nose and winced. "I think she broke my fucking nose."

Getting to her feet, Meggie picked CJ up and limped out of the crowd. "I should break your head. Kendall is this bad because you allowed it, Johnnie."

"I resent that." Johnnie tried to scowl. "Kendall's a grown woman. I'm not responsible for her behavior."

All at once, the fight left Meggie, replaced by a deep weariness.

Nothing was going as it should. This should have been an enjoyable family gathering, focused on Roxy and Bailey's ceremonies. Once CJ had cried out, Meggie hadn't even considered the wedding. Kendall had made her so livid, she'd forgotten everything.

Their family. The children. Their friends. Thank God most of them were upstairs!

Meggie had forgotten Kendall's illness and her own dignity.

Her eyes watered.

"Ahh, baby, now come on," Christopher started. "You gonna ruin all my happiness if you start to cry."

CJ lifted his head from her shoulder and frowned at the tears glistening in her eyes. "It's okay, Mommie," he whispered, his chubby little fingers sweeping across her cheeks.

Christopher wrapped her in his arms, trapping CJ between them. "Motherfuckers gettin' out of hand and that shit just not gonna fuckin' fly, especially if it got my sweet Megan cussin' and beatin' a bitch to the ground."

Johnnie helped Kendall into a sitting position as she regained consciousness.

"You're nothing but Outlaw's cocksucking whore," Kendall slurred, barely able to speak through a bleeding split lip.

"The child isn't even looking at you, Kendall, so shut up," Roxy ordered.

"Shut up?" she cried. "How could you? You didn't try to defend me."

"You have something against poor little CJ. I didn't want you girls to get into a fucking fist-fight, but you needed your ass beat," Roxy told her. "I should have punched the fuck out of you when you balled your fists up."

Roxy's words made Meggie cry harder.

"It's okay, baby," Christopher whispered.

"No, it isn't." Meggie stepped out of his embrace and set CJ on his feet. She looked at her son's precious face. He resembled Christopher so much. No matter how much he tried to emulate his father, CJ was just a little boy. And Kendall tried to hurt him. *Had,* in fact, hit him tonight.

Meggie wouldn't forget Kendall's actions any time soon.

"Stay here while I collect our children from upstairs in the play-room, sweetheart," Johnnie said to Kendall.

"No! Meggie's going to face me like a woman so we can finish what we started." She stood, swaying on her feet.

"Kendall, I don't want to hear your voice anymore," Megan said in dismissal. "Get out of my house."

"I should sue you for assault and battery," Kendall said.

"And I should kill your fuckin' ass for bitchery and misery," Christopher shot back.

"Fuck you, asshole," Kendall retorted, then focused on Meggie again. "You can't bar me from club grounds."

"She can't," Christopher said. "But my ass can." He walked around Meggie and CJ, went to Kendall and glared at her. "From this fuckin' moment to fuckin' infinity, don't fuckin' ever set foot on club grounds a-fuckin-gain. That mean all your permissions gonna be revoked. You can't get passed the mechanical fuckin' gate. You can't attend club functions. You can't socialize with club members."

"Oh, please. Johnnie's a club member. Are you saying I can't socialize with him?"

Christopher offered her a nasty grin. "You always the smartest fuckin' bitch in the house, aintcha? You fuckin' figure that shit out." Ignoring Kendall's gasp, he made a three hundred sixty degree turn, meeting each person's gaze as he did. "Dinner cancelled. All you moth-erfuckers get the fuck outta my fuckin' house."

Without another word, he grabbed Meggie's hand on one side of him and CJ's on the other, and started limping out of the room, leaving everyone in stunned silence.

CHAPTER TWENTY-SEVEN

CHRISTOPHER

"Hold on, Prez," Digger called. "You can't put us out before we eat. Think about all the food in the kitchen."

Christopher paused. "Fine, eat," he relented. "Then get the fuck out."

A few years ago, every one of those motherfuckers would've been fucked up. Shot in the fucking head. Now, though...He hadn't even been able to kill Johnnie when he should have.

Clearly, he had to find punishments that would be acceptable to both his principles and his pride. Threats didn't work with family because a conscience wouldn't allow you to fuck up assfucks you cared about.

He concentrated on keeping a straight face as he walked, refusing to give in to the pain he felt. Since he wasn't walking with the care he had been, his cock was in agony. He wanted to undo the dick undoing. It was making his life so fucking miserable.

As he guided Megan and CJ up the staircase, he met Johnnie, Rory, Matilda, and JJ, whom Johnnie carried, making their way down.

He paused, allowing Christopher to pass. Neither of them said a word.

"Hey, Ro," CJ said quietly.

"Hey, CJ," Rory responded on a whisper, like the boys knew their parents were feuding and it would affect them, too.

"Rory can stay if he wanna and you let him," Christopher called over his shoulder.

"Can I, Dad?" Rory's little voice sounded hopeful.

"Of course, son," Johnnie responded. "Come with me to tell Mom goodnight."

"I don't want to," Rory responded tearfully. "I don't like Mommie. She's mean."

"He overheard some of what happened before he ran upstairs and hid." Johnnie sighed. "Fine, Rory. Go upstairs with CJ, Aunt Megan, and Uncle Chris."

A moment later, Rory joined them, and Christopher continued on to the third floor. Megan had turned a room on the second floor into a huge playroom for the kids for when they hosted family night. Diesel was in charge of keeping a watch on them. Lyndsey hadn't been over again since the treehouse incident.

Christopher had dropped her off at her house, told Diesel he had faith in his honesty, and dropped the fucking subject. No use harping on the shit. Either the motherfucker would listen or he wouldn't.

Although CJ enjoyed playing with his cousins and Diesel made sure they didn't get too out-of-hand, Christopher felt the rambunctious little motherfuckers would be too much for CJ tonight.

Christopher stopped in front of CJ's room, released his hand, and then opened the door. His boy stood on his tiptoes to flip on the overhead light.

"Ima be back in a few minutes. Lemme take care of your Ma."

"'Kay," CJ answered. "I tired, 'Law. Ima lay down 'til you come back."

"Okay, boy," Christopher agreed.

"I tired, too, 'Law," Rory echoed.

Now wasn't the time to remind Rory he didn't have to emulate CJ, who, in turn, was mimicking Christopher. He didn't want assfucks like Knox and Kendall teasing his boy for the words he used. But correct...*ish* speech was a lesson for another day.

Once his son and nephew gave him and Megan hugs, Christopher brought his wife to their bedroom and led her to their bed.

He pointed to the edge. "Sit."

Obediently, she followed his directions. Focusing on what his woman needed, he put one foot in front of the other and headed to the bathroom to find peroxide, cotton balls, and antibiotic ointment for her cuts. He also took a washcloth and ran cold water over it, for her black eye.

"Place this on your eye," he told her when he returned to their bedroom and handed her the wet cloth.

Without question, she did as she was told.

Sighing, Christopher took her free hand and examined the cuts on her knuckles. Pouring peroxide onto several cotton balls, he dabbed her injuries.

"Ow!" she moaned. "That hurt."

"I know, baby," he said gruffly. "When you give a motherfucker a beat down, your hands get as fucked the fuck up as their face. Punch a motherfucker in the mouth, you graze fuckin' sharp ass teeth. Hit a assfuck in the nose, you hit fuckin' cartilage. Shit ain't as hard as bone, but, dependin' on the velocity of your fuckin' fists, you still injure yourself."

"You sound like an expert on fist fights," she said with a small smile.

"I had my fuckin' fair share," he admitted, leaning forward to kiss the top of her head. He drew in a deep breath and focused on tending to her injuries, not on her scent, her nearness. "You okay, Megan?" he finally asked.

"No. Yes. I don't know." Her lower lip trembled, then she sucked in a breath, and anger transformed her features. "I cannot believe Kendall." She shook her head. "No, I can't believe me. I gave her the benefit of the doubt so many times, Christopher. I sided with her over you. I'll never forgive Kendall. *Never*. I don't ever want to see her again."

On the last word, her voice broke.

"We are...we were family," she sobbed. "How could she do this to us? To CJ? To *Johnnie*?"

"Cuz she a conscienceless cunt, baby. She don't see people. She see steppin' stones." Abandoning his triage, he sat next to her, put an arm around her shoulder, and hugged her close. "This a valuable lesson, Megan. I been tellin' you to leave that bitch the fuck alone, but you wasn't ready. I shoulda backed the fuck off and trusted you was gonna get to a fuckin' point where you had e-fuckin-nuff. It's just that you hurt now and I don't never want you in pain."

"You can't protect me from everything. Life is a learning experience. That's the only way we grow and become better."

Christopher nodded and dragged her onto his lap, resting his chin on the crown of her head. He grunted and covered the jolt of cock-and-ball pain with a forced smile. "What the fuck you mean when you told me I already fuckin' messed with the business of my cock?"

Did she know what he'd done?

"We were...are...were, um, there's an argument going on between us. I didn't think we'd make love tonight. That's what I meant. Why what did you think I meant? What else is going on?"

He'd sworn to Megan that he'd never lie to her. He could always *not* tell her something, but, for the most part, if she asked him a direct question, he'd answer her honestly. There were some exceptions to this rule, as in Traveler and Dinah's deaths, but that was about it.

As proud and as gleeful as he was that Megan had fucked up Kendall, he knew, too, a certain innocence had been lost within her. She might become less trusting.

Less forgiving.

He also had the sin of meeting Emily without Megan's knowledge to live with. Kendall was on her No-Kill list. He'd promised he wouldn't kill her. He'd also sworn never to hide any meetings he had with other women. Fuck, but he was batting a fucking thousand.

In comparison, his procedure seemed inconsequential.

"I got my dick snip flipped," he confessed.

She was quiet for a moment. "You got the vasectomy reversal?"

"Yeah, Megan. Yesterday. I ain't sure I was gonna tell you, so I let our disagreements get the fuck outta hand."

The washcloth slipped down as her hand went slack and mutiny gathered in her one punched-up blue eye; the other motherfucker was red from her crying. "You would've just let me end up pregnant and think your vasectomy failed?" she asked, appalled.

"Not at fuckin' first," he said quickly. "Then you threw me a fuckin' curve when you told my ass you ain't want no more lil' motherfuckers."

She heaved in a breath, then cocked her head to the side, her anger leaving her. "Do you really want us to have another baby that bad?"

He picked up on the hopeful note in her tone.

"Do it matter?" he asked cautiously. "Ain't you said you ain't want no more babies cuz you were in shape and shit?"

"That's what I'd been trying to talk to you about this morning, when you got up and walked away," she said in a hurt tone.

"I ain't able to fuck you for two fuckin' weeks, but I fuckin' figured in five or six days, my cock and balls woulda looked normal a-fuckin-gain, so we coulda made up."

"You only want to control my movements, or do you truly want us to have a bigger family?"

They definitely didn't need more children. *But* she probably wouldn't like that answer *and* he'd do *whatever* to protect her. If that meant manipulating the situation, so be it.

Tipping her chin up, he brushed his lips over hers, ignoring the dried blood.

"You love lil babies, Megan. I ain't ever shoulda took that away from you, baby."

Her unfucked eye lit up, while the blackened motherfucker swelled a little more. "I thought long and hard about this, last night. When you brought up another pregnancy, you shocked me. Then, I realized how happy I was at the thought of carrying another baby by you. How many more do you want?"

What the fuck did she mean? One more wouldn't be enough?

He cleared his throat. "How many more you want?"

"Three," she said breathlessly.

What the motherfuck? "You want *eight* fuckin' kids?"

She nodded. "Then I'll get back on birth control."

He'd cross that bridge when he came to it. Right now, he had to get their sixth kid in her. Until then, Christopher wouldn't rest easy. At least, though, they were on the right fucking road and on the same fucking page.

Now that he had Megan's consent, it was of the ut-fucking-most importance to stay on track for Roxanne and Bailey's fucking ceremony.

Well, fuck. Did that fucking mean he'd have to hold off on his plans for psycho cunt?

Ex-fuckin-scuse me. Beat-the-fuck-up psycho cunt.

No. Fuck no. Just fucking NO! The quicker he got rid of that bitch the better. Delaying shit would derail the plans; going forward with his plans would ensure smooth sailing right to the fucking altar and Wilcunt.

Megan hugged him, recapturing his attention. "I love you so much."

He wrapped his arms around her and nosed her hair. "I love you, too, Megan. More than my own fuckin' life."

If she wanted three more babies, he'd just have to find a fucking way to make their house bigger. As long as his woman was happy and safe, he'd be fine.

CHAPTER TWENTY-EIGHT

Knox

Early the next morning, Knox banged on the front door of Mortician and Bailey's house, purposely bypassing the bell. He wanted to break down the fucking door. The asshat had guards on the path that led to Roxy's little house. Knox spent the entire night seething. At Mortician's dictates. At the return of Roxanne's indifference and his own disappointment when he'd realized there wasn't an assignation planned. His combined emotions made sleep impossible, though Mortician's orders riled him the most. Well, it would stop *today!* If Megan Caldwell finally grew a spine and stood up to Kendall, then Knox could surely do the same with Mortician, Outlaw, and whichever other imbecile gave him guff.

Throwing the door open, Mortician glared at Knox, not inviting him into the warmth of the house.

"It's six o'clock in the fucking morning, Knox. What the fuck do you want?"

"I want my woman," Knox stated with cool firmness. "And I intend to take her. You aren't stopping me, so call your goons off."

Mortician stepped outside, closing the door to just a small gap. In his bare feet, he only wore jeans, but he seemed unaffected by the cold.

"Make me, motherfucker," he said, so close to Knox's face that their noses almost touched.

Holding firm, Knox stiffened his shoulders. "This is ridiculous. You're treating Roxanne as if she's a little virgin from the 1950s. Well, she's far from it, and you're not keeping me away from her a moment longer."

Mortician's eyes flared in surprise and Knox puffed out his chest. Mortician was going to back off and give in to the inevitable.

"Okay, have it your way," Mortician conceded. "On one condition."

Knox rolled his eyes. Did Mortician really think to outsmart him again? For curiosity's sake, Knox would go along with this silly game. "Name it and it's yours, if it'll bring this ridiculous moratorium to an end."

"I'll escort you to Roxanne, *this fucking minute*, and let you move back in, if you confess to the bullshit about proposing to her, fucking her, and then walking away because you really don't want to marry her."

Knox's mouth fell open and he released a pathetic squeak. "What good would that do? Besides, I didn't say those exact words."

"You said something to that effect, motherfucker. You also said she showed her ignorance by driving the purple Navigator that was a present from another motherfucker."

Mortician really felt as if he was protecting Roxanne because he didn't trust Knox's intentions. If it wasn't so goddamn interfering, it might be a little endearing that a big, bad motorcycle man protected his wife's mother so fiercely. "I didn't mean what I said, Mortician! How many fucking times do I have to repeat myself so you'll under-stand the meaning of my words? You people pissed me the fuck off. How did you expect me to respond?"

"By acting like you had a little fucking respect for your head being in one piece. 'Cause, you know, I almost blew it the fuck off."

"I didn't mean—"

Mortician raised his hand and indicated silence. "You meant *every* word, Knox. Know how I know? *You* the motherfucker that said your parents wouldn't be happy if you married Roxy. Look how your momma treating her? And we all know how much you hate her purple car. The fact that Outlaw gave it to her make it that much more unbearable. So, yeah, Knox, you meant all of what you said."

Knox lifted his hands in supplication. "I swear...*I swear*," he started in desperation, "I didn't. I love her so much. I can't wait to marry her. There's no way I can tell her what I said."

"You know that shit won't go over well with her."

"And so do you. You want to sabotage our relationship."

"No. I want you to be fair and honest with her. I want her to know you man enough to own up to your shittiness. I want you to apologize to her for even thinking that disrespectful bullshit."

"There's nothing for me to apologize to her for. You're being ridiculous." A thought popped into his head. "I'll pay you. What do you want? A million dollars? Two? Three? I'll go as high as five."

"Just what the fuck you paying me for? To let you move back in with her or to shut the fuck up about your bitch-ass words?"

"I don't know." Knox thrust a hand through his hair. "Either. Both."

"First off? You don't know shit about me. I don't need your fucking money. Second, even if I did, no money in the world enough for me to turn away from protecting Roxanne. I value her well-being over some bitch-ass blood money."

"A little gung-ho, aren't you?" Knox sneered, losing his patience. "What man in your position wouldn't want *five million dollars*? Whether it's for silence or cooperation, the point is moot. It's still *five million dollars.*"

"Can't miss your money if I never had it. But, in case you don't realize it, I don't need your goddamn money. I got my own."

At that statement, Knox laughed. "A pittance compared to what I'm offering, I'm sure."

Mortician threw him a nasty grin. "As much as I want to break every bone in your face, the way you itching for me to do, I'm not. Go back to the club, Knox. I don't trust you anymore than you trust me.

Therefore, you and her still being chaperoned." He backed into his house. "See you at the club."

Before Knox had a chance to respond, Mortician slammed the door in his face.

Knox slammed his hand against the door. "You're an asshole!" he yelled.

If Mortician heard, he gave no indication because Knox received no answer.

Kicking the door one last time, Knox growled, turned on his heel, and stormed back toward the club. For now, he was thwarted, but he was determined to find a way back into Roxanne's arms before the wedding.

Before, this chaperoning had been an annoying nuisance. Now, it was a matter of pride and principle.

Roxy

"Psst."

The loud sound stopped Knox in his tracks, just as Roxy hoped. It was still dark outside, but the lights interspersed amongst the trees assisted her in tracking his progress.

She glanced over her shoulder, to make sure she was still alone. Mortician had all kinds of fucking tricks up his sleeve.

Knox stood within a beam of artificial light. It glinted off his blond hair and revealed his frustration in the tight lines on his handsome face. He hadn't spotted her yet, so he turned and started to storm away again.

"Knox," she called. "Wait! It's me."

"Roxanne?" he whispered in disbelief, swallowed up by the darkness.

"Let's get off the pathway," she suggested, rubbing her arms at the chill in the air. She wore a snuggly fleece bed jacket that offered some warmth, but her silk pajamas weren't much of a barrier, especially her legs.

"I refuse to hide like I'm a damn boy," he told her, still at a distance. He hadn't come any closer. "I'm sick of this. I don't want to sneak around anymore, like we had to do yesterday."

Roxy sighed. Motherfuckers and their egos. Getting pussy-blocked was damn annoying, but, after she stewed over Mortician's explanation, she found it funny and a little endearing that he was going through all this trouble to protect her.

"We can get another quick forest fuck," she suggested.

"No."

The one word came out terse and final. Counting to ten, Roxy told herself to stay calm. Knox had every right to be so put out.

"Why don't we go to the club house and get a cup of coffee?" she asked as sweet as can be. "I can meet you there. I'll throw some clothes on and start breakfast early."

He released an irritated sigh. "Are you sure Mortician will allow you to—"

"I understand you're frustrated," she broke in. "But it's kind of funny, too. The boy is going through so much trouble..." Her voice trailed off and the little voice in her head that made her confront Mortician yesterday and insisted there was a method to his madness rose up. The one thing Mort wasn't was a fucking hypocrite. As distasteful as the thought was, both he and Roxy knew he'd fucked Bailey before they were married, then acted like a pure 'D' fool afterwards. A grade-A ass...A...Roxy's train of thought slipped away.

She hated how much she forgot. Her oncologist insisted she'd had very strong chemotherapy, and was still taking another type of strong chemotherapy, so side effects were to be expected.

"Roxanne, why did you stop me if you have nothing to say that I want to hear?"

"Knox—"

"You promised me you'd find a way for us to be together. Yet, you find Mortician's bullshit *endearing*."

Her hackles rose at how he sneered the word. "I did find a way for us to be together yesterday."

Knox ignored her. "Why the fuck are you allowing his high-handedness?"

"I told you—" she started.

"Excuse me, but I don't believe you. You're the first person to tell someone to fuck off. You've done it to me. You've done it to my mother. Everyone, except Outlaw and Mortician. What gives, Roxanne?"

Roxy sighed. "I miss you as much as you miss me, sugar. But protecting me is important to him, Knox. He's a good man. Let's just go along with him to put him at ease."

After hearing from Joyner, she knew it also went back to how many times she'd been married—and divorced. It stemmed from Duke's words—how he saw her. Each day a new fear rose up; a new concern that marrying Knox wasn't the best idea. She couldn't get over her fear that she would ruin a good thing if she married Knox.

His uppityness didn't help. Roxy had only to look at Kendall, and how unhappy she stayed because she could never find her place in the club. Thought herself *above* everyone.

Knox was the same way. And his mother was the worst bitch in the world, which really didn't help matters.

"Maybe, I want to see how well you fit in at the club. Those boys are my family. I don't want you to decide you've made a mistake *after* our vows, Knox."

He released a bitter laugh. "I told you that wouldn't happen when you first mentioned this to me. Obviously, you don't believe me. You think that little of me?"

"Of course not," she protested. "I love you very much. That's just the point. Think about Kendall. The child is so unhappy because she doesn't think she's on the same level as Meggie and any of the other women."

"She isn't," Knox told her. "However, I resent the comparison."

Revealing herself to Knox had been a mistake. She hadn't been able to sleep, so she'd decided to go stand on her landing for a little fresh air.

She'd been relishing the serenity of damp earth smells, barren trees, and cold air and missing Knox with everything in her. Since he'd moved to the club, she hadn't slept well. Surrounded by quietness, she'd heard the banging on Mortician and Bailey's front door. Two guards, who'd not so long returned to duty, after sleeping in the garage, rushed from their posts around her quarters. They weren't alarmed, so Roxy's suspicions had roused. She'd casually invited them in for coffee since it had already been brewing, then told them she needed to talk to Bailey.

Getting away, she'd quickly run to find Knox. She didn't expect to find an argument.

"Roxanne, if all you're going to do is stand there and stare at me, I will take my leave. I have nothing more to say to you, until you tell me what I want to hear."

"What about what I want to hear, Knox?" she snapped, frustrated by his attitude, He took offense at everything the boys did.

"And what might that be?" he sneered. "Maybe, how I'm fed up with Mortician's interference? Or, maybe, that I'm sick of hearing you tell me why you have to keep a *purple* fucking Navigator? It has ignorant trash written all over it. Just like Outlaw is."

"Wait a goddamn minute, Knox. Don't bring Outlaw into this when he's not here to defend himself. As for Mortician, what the fuck did *you* say or do to make him even think of this stupid shit?"

Knox reddened, the flush creeping from his neck and into his face spreading like a poison ivy rash.

"Confess now, motherfucker, or forever hold your peace," she demanded.

He huffed out a breath. "Fine. I didn't want to propose to you! They forced me to do it. Why pay for something that I was getting for free? I regret asking for your hand, given your allegiance to them and not to me."

Roxanne listened to Knox's bitter words and let them sink in. He must've been some kind of a motherfucker in his refusal to marry her if Mortician had gone through the trouble of making sure they lived apart until after the wedding. "What kind of a motherfucker let another motherfucker force them to do shit they don't want to do?"

she snarled. "Cuz, motherfucker, if your fucking ass didn't want to marry me, all you had to do was say so. Instead, you propose to me out of what? Fear? Pity? Just why the fuck did your ass propose, Knox?"

"Oh, so I'm Knox again and not motherfucker, huh?"

"Answer the goddamn question!" she ordered. "As far as I'm fucking concerned you can be Santa Claus."

"Yeah, exactly," Knox shot back. "That's what I am to you. Santa Claus. You saw me and you saw money. You saw a younger man you wanted to lead around by his dick and force your degenerate friends on, thinking I'd just jump to your wishes. I'm sure it comes as a surprise to you, Cougar, that this cub has a brain of his own. I fucking resent having to follow another man's wishes and that's all I've been doing for weeks where you're concerned. Well, it stops now. Either you're doing this my way or I'm out. You can live the rest of your life in wretched loneliness, without me or my money."

As Knox's tirade ended, Roxy saw light beginning to filter through the trees. That meant, if she saw him, he saw her. Her devastation. Her humiliation.

Her tears.

Try as she might, she couldn't withstand the onslaught of Knox's venom. What little self-worth she had after Duke had finished with her, the man in front of her, the man she loved so completely, destroyed what was left.

He narrowed his eyes. "My way," he started, "includes you signing a prenup. Another issue Mortician had, as if it is any of his business. He wouldn't know what to do with wealth. He'd squander it on you and Bailey."

Roxy blinked and swiped at the tears sliding down her face. She'd lick her wounds later. At the moment, she had to put a motherfucker in his place.

"First of fucking all, fuck you. I wouldn't fucking marry you if my goddamn life depended on it. Second, it's nobody's fault but your dumb ass that you didn't have the fucking nuts to tell Mortician you wouldn't marry me."

"How could I when that psychopath was there, threatening my life in tandem with the rest of those criminals?" He stepped closer to her.

"It was a fucking conspiracy. You knew I'd never marry you as long as you stooped low enough to drive the car Outlaw gifted to you, so you got to them and had them threaten me, *bully* me, into marrying you."

"Back the fuck off me, Knox," she told him, refusing to budge. He'd invaded *her* space.

He stood taller. "And what's going to happen if I don't?" he sneered. "You're going to call one of your guard dogs? Hmmm? Or what? Cry louder since your silent tears aren't working? Get down on your knees and beg me to move?"

"The day I beg you, motherfucker, is the day Satan rises from hell and shoves his pitchfork up your fucking dick. I don't have to call one motherfucker to protect me because I'm perfectly capable of protecting myself." She threw him a look, then yanked the engagement ring he'd given to her off her finger. "As to all that other shit you *think* you know, I'm not bothering to educate you. I have a good fifty years of living left and I don't intend to spend it schooling you on shit you know nothing of. Besides, it would be a waste of my breath like your goddamn brain is a waste of your head space." She held the ring out to him. It took everything in her not to release a heartbroken sob. "Take it, Knox." Her voice wobbled, so she paused and cleared her throat. "I don't want to marry you. As a matter of fact, I never want to lay eyes on your uppity ass again."

He stared at her as if he'd never seen her. Suddenly, his beautiful amber eyes widened and the color dropped from his face.

"Roxanne," he started, holding his hands up. "I didn't mean—"

"Stop, Knox. Just stop. You meant every fucking word you said, otherwise you wouldn't have said it."

"No," he protested, shaking his head. "No. I'm just…I'm just…I love you. I miss you."

"Either you're a fucking fool or you think I am," Roxy spat, dropping her hand since Knox refused to take the ring. "I get enough of that bullshit from Duke. I don't need it from you, too."

"I've never called you ignorant."

"A fucking oversight on your part, since you implied it by talking about my ride. You *did* call me a gold-digging, lonely, criminally-minded, old bitch."

"Roxanne—"

"Shut the fuck up, Knox. I'm not interested in hearing anything you have to say ever again. Even if you hadn't called me those names—"

"I didn't call you anything of the kind."

She glared at him and huffed out a breath. "Excuse me. Even if you hadn't *implied* those things about me, I wouldn't marry you because I would never sign a fucking prenup. So anyway it goes, take your fucking ring and shove it."

Instead of holding it out to him again, she shoved it in his shirt pocket, turned on her heel, and marched away.

"Roxanne, wait!" Knox called. "Please. I'm begging you."

Flipping him off, she walked on, and vowed to forget the day she'd ever met Knox Harrington.

CHAPTER TWENTY-NINE

CHRISTOPHER

itter cold threatened to swallow him up and freeze his body just as his heart had frozen. Blackness surrounded him, except for one, pristine white glimmer. The shine gleamed through the darkness of the black décor—walls, floors, seat covers, even clothing.

It struck Christopher then. Other people were there, sitting in the pews, faces grief-stricken and silent. He saw them in monotone vignettes, as if the edges of the scene refused to fully crystallize.

As if the reality of the situation was too unbearable.

Nothing made sense. Not the vicious temperature that seemed only to touch him. Wasn't his boy in black shorts, sandals, and a summer T-shirt? Didn't Rebel have on a summer dress?

Didn't Meg...Christopher squinted. Where was she? He didn't see her anywhere. Everyone else was there, but not his Megan. Frantic, he glanced all around. He wanted to move, wanted to run through the aisles, go from pew-to-

pew, until he found her. She must be playing hide-and-seek with one of their kids.

His legs wouldn't work. His attention kept straying to that white glimmer. Now, when he looked at it again, a bloody handprint marred the perfection.

"Megan!" he yelled. "Megan, baby, where you at?"

His voice sounded horrible, a combination of hoarseness, fear, and anguish.

"Law, I want MegAnn," CJ said around sniffles.

"Megan!" he called again, spying Mortician. "Mort, where she at? Where my woman?"

"Prez, fuck," Mort murmured, his tone filled with the same pity so clear in his eyes.

Panic filled Christopher. "MEGAN!" he boomed, wild desperation creeping into him. He raised his hands. Blood coated them, dripped from his fingertips, ran down his arms. "No, no, no! Megan, baby, please?" he begged. "Come to me, please. I need you. You my everything. Where you at?"

"Her there, 'Law," CJ cried, pointing to the white sheen that became horrifyingly clear.

A coffin. Megan was in a coffin?

He shook his head in denial. Finally—finally—his legs allowed him to move. He didn't feel so heavy and rooted to his spot. His hands trembled, but he had to show his boy that their MegAnn wasn't in a casket. She was somewhere in the church, alive and well and vibrant. And loving him as no one else ever had or ever would.

He lifted the lid. No! No! No! No!

She was there. Still. Lifeless. Pale. Dressed entirely in white, like a little princess from one of the original Grimm's Fairytales.

Forever young.

"Megan!" he cried, falling to his knees. "Megan, baby, wake-up."

Through his tears, he saw a big, blond man, position himself in front of Megan. He glared at Christopher.

"My baby girl is with me now. You lost her. You failed her. Mystic took her from you. How could you let that happen? You never deserved her."

Big Joe's vision morphed into Mystic's, the president of the Imperials. The one who'd taken Megan and hid her from Christopher, until it was too late. When Christopher finally found her, she was dead, her mouth frozen open as if she'd tried to gasp for breath but hadn't been able to receive the life-giving oxygen she'd needed.

Mystic grinned at him. "Wasn't me, Caldwell. You did this to her. You!"

With a furious growl, Christopher lunged at him, but Mystic disappeared. Instead, Christopher landed right next to Megan's coffin. His bloody handprints laid against each of her cheeks, and marched down her white dress, ending at the bump in her belly.

Not only was Megan lost to him...Mystic had been right. Christopher *was the reason she was dead.*

Megan had been pregnant.

Christopher screamed.

"Law, stop!"

"Christopher, you're fine. I'm fine."

Her soothing little voice hit him in the center of his chest and he trembled.

"No, baby," he sobbed, screaming again because he didn't know what else to do. "You gone. I lost you."

Small hands touched his shoulder and shook him. "Law, wake up, please!"

"No! She gone..."

"MegAnn, right here, 'Law!"

Christopher resisted CJ's impatient voice, still screaming, still seeing Megan in the coffin, pregnant, bloody, and snuffed from him. Sudden weight settled onto his chest, threatening to squeeze the life from him.

Her soft mouth brushed his cheek. "I'm here," she swore. "Just open your eyes. You'll see."

"Wake up, 'Law," CJ demanded. "Stop being a bitch-ass baby."

"Do *not* cuss, potato," Megan chastised.

Bitch-ass baby. Potato. A mother's loving sternness.

None of that would be in such a horrific scene as the one he'd been...Cautiously, Christopher opened one eye. CJ sat on his chest, staring down into his face. He scrunched his nose as Christopher opened his other eye.

"You all sweaty, 'Law." CJ glanced to the side of him. "He gotta take a shower, MegAnn. Tell him."

The scent of cherry blossoms filled Christopher's brain. *Megan.*

Just as suddenly as it had descended, the weight lifted as Megan removed their boy from Christopher's chest.

CJ squealed. "Put me down, Mommie!" he said around giggles. "I'm a big boy."

Megan kissed Christopher's cheek again. "We'll wait for you downstairs," she said softly.

She knew him so well. She knew when to wrap him in her pussy to comfort him and when to leave him alone so he could collect himself.

She waited until he sat up before she offered him another gentle smile, still holding their raucous boy in her arms.

"I love you," she told him.

Christopher rubbed the back of his neck. "I love you, too, baby," he mumbled.

"You okay, 'Law?" His boy stopped squirming against his Ma long enough to ask him.

"Yeah, boy."

They both smiled at him, as the full weight of that dream hit him and he scowled.

Setting CJ on his feet and grabbing his hand, Megan blew Christopher a kiss, then guided their boy out the door.

Alone, Christopher growled and jumped to his feet. His cock twitched with a slight pain, but he ignored it. This shit was absolutely un-fucking-acceptable. He'd gone the fuck ahead and had a dick-snip-flip, thinking he had the solution to his nightmares, when the mother-fuckers decided to fuck with him even more and lead him to believe the cause of Megan's death was pregnancy.

He had lost his goddamn, motherfucking mind.

Pacing, he thought of the nightmare he'd just had, and shivered.

What if it had been real? What if Christopher hadn't found her in time after Mystic had taken her?

What if the pregnancy part was an omen?

He had to get control of himself. He was more fucking traumatized than Megan. What the fuck was fucking wrong with him? No matter what the fuck he did, his girl's kidnapping haunted him. And he yelled. And cried. And screamed. And trembled.

His boy had done right to call him a bitch-ass-fucking-baby. He was a baby-ass-fucking-bitch.

Disgusted with himself, he kicked at one of Megan's stilettos. It was white.

It fucking figured. Snarling like a rabid dog, he picked up the unkicked motherfucker, then went to the kicked motherfucker and got that one too, before slamming both into the waste basket.

Every piece of white clothing Megan owned, he'd fucking burn to fucking smithereens. No, he'd blow those motherfuckers the fuck up. He never wanted to see her in white again.

White walls in the house had to fucking go. White décor. Bedding. Plates...but most especially those white fucking clothes.

He stomped to her closet, found a fucking white leather dress, and grabbed it with all the fury in him. Without thinking this through, he took it to the bathroom, and threw it into the tub. Once he found rubbing alcohol, he poured it on the leather, lit a match he'd also brought with him, and threw it onto the dress.

Flames overtook it almost immediately, and he grinned, wishing pieces of Mystic was in the conflagration. His fucking hands for taking Megan. His fucking brain for thinking of the plot in the first fucking place.

"Boy, what the fuck are you doing?" Roxanne's voice broke through his madness. "Turn that fucking water on before you burn down this goddamn house. Fuck! I'll be right back."

Obediently, he did as instructed. Roxanne returned before she was even missed, holding a fire extinguisher and quickly doing the work that the water seemed to be failing at—containing the flames.

He looked at her. Somewhere, in the back of his mind, he saw her swollen red eyes, her pain...but before it fully registered, she gave him a gentle smile.

"Oh, sugar. Your woman is fine. Nobody is taking her away from you."

She held out her arms.

Christopher hesitated. He looked at Megan's ruined dress. The motherfucker had been new. Now, it was fucking burnt pieces and smoking embers. She was going to have his fucking ass.

At least she was alive to do so.

Sucking in a breath, he looked at the ceiling, and couldn't stop the tears sliding down his face. He hated himself for being a weak bitch, and he hated Megan for making him a weak bitch.

But he loved her so fucking much.

"Roxanne, Megan can't never leave me," he said in a broken whisper, blinking. "But one day we gotta leave each other. We all gotta die. All I want is for me to be fuckin' first. I can't fuckin' make it without her." He drew in a sob. "And I fucking hate her for it."

"Come here, baby," Roxanne responded.

His nostrils flared, but he gave into the temptation of the comfort she offered and stepped into her arms, leaning down to rest his head on her shoulder. She tightened them around him, and he relished her motherly embrace. His mother had hugged him in such a manner on rare occasions, and he'd missed this since her death.

"I'm a grown-ass motherfucker, Roxanne, actin' like a weak-ass bitch."

Roxanne sniffled. "No, baby, you acting like a human motherfucker."

She sounded so very sad. Suddenly, the devastation that he'd noticed in her face fully registered and he stiffened. An image of Knox fucking Harrington rose in his head, giving him something else to focus on.

Maybe, even, a motherfucker to make bleed.

~

Roxy

Roxy had arrived at the house, just as Meggie was complaining about something burning. She was going to head upstairs and investigate since everything downstairs seemed to be fine. But CJ wouldn't let her out of his sight, so Roxy told Meggie to stay downstairs while she investigated.

This being a Saturday, all the Caldwell kids and Rory were there, so Roxy wasn't sure if they all would've followed Meggie.

Roxy had come to talk to Outlaw. After running away from Knox a couple of hours ago, and going to her quarters to cry her eyes out, she'd realized she had to do one last thing on his behalf. She didn't want the boys to kill him. Motherfucker that he was, he really didn't deserve to die. Maybe, have his ass beat. By her. But even that wasn't worth it. She was just too hurt to muster up the strength to kick his cock in.

As she'd rushed upstairs, Meggie had yelled to her, "Christopher had another nightmare."

"Okay, sugar, I got this. Just take care of the kids."

The fact that she was needed refocused her attention away from her and Knox's breakup. And she arrived not a moment too soon. The flames had fascinated Outlaw so much that he hadn't even recognized they were beginning to creep up the sides of the bathtub.

She'd taken care of that fire. Now, she had to take care of the emotional one. Duke might not want her, but these boys here needed mothering, too. Outlaw cried silent, bitter tears. Here, in this moment, she believed he did hate Meggie just as much as he loved her.

Roxy knew those conflicting emotions. At the moment, she was in the same predicament. She hated Knox for being a motherfucker. But she loved him, too. That's why she wanted to save his life. She had broken up with him, but it was his words that brought her to that action.

Suddenly, Outlaw stiffened. Straightened. And stared down at her.

"What the fuck that motherfucker done?" he demanded as if a light had gone off in his head.

Stepping back, she turned away from him. "Knox didn't do anything," she lied, damning her voice for breaking. "I did it to him. I broke it off." Tears threatened again. "I realized I don't want to marry no motherfucker ever again."

Silence greeted that firm-ish statement, then he barreled to her and narrowed his eyes. "You ain't wantin' to marry Knox fuckin' Harrington?"

She forced herself to meet his eyes. "Nope."

He contemplated her, and Roxy squirmed under the intensity of that cold, green gaze. "You a fuckin' liar. I'm dialing Mort, tellin' him to bring the fuckin' chainsaw, so we can split Harrington down the fuckin' middle and kill him."

"What the fuck kind of statement is that? You cut Knox down the middle with a chainsaw, the motherfucker will be deader than fucking dead already. You won't have anything to kill, Outlaw."

"I'll still have pieces to rip apart."

She frowned at him, unable to believe that this chillingly murderous man now before her was the same heartbroken husband she'd walked in on. That was the beauty of Outlaw. Of Mort. Johnnie. Digger. Val. They lived in a world of violence that the love for their women tempered. They could be killers one moment, and family men the next. More important, they were as significant to her as their wives.

Why couldn't Knox see that?

"Why you standin' up there cryin'?" Outlaw demanded.

Angrily, she swiped at her tears. "We don't belong together," she said, not believing it while having no choice but to find a way to accept it. "Please, leave Knox alone. He doesn't deserve your wrath or Mort's."

When the boy scratched his bare chest, she realized he stood only in pajama bottoms. He glanced at Meggie's ruined dress, then back at Roxanne, and shifted his weight.

In that moment, he reminded her of CJ, and she couldn't help but feel a little more tenderness toward him. Outlaw must've missed his mother something fierce, and Roxanne was more than happy to step into the role as a surrogate. She needed to pull herself together, though. He considered her as much of a family member as Mort did, and they'd protect her with berserk fierceness.

She drew in a deep breath. "Just let him be. Our breakup was my decision."

"What about Bailey wantin' to remarry Mort the same day you and Knox got hitched?"

Fuck. She'd forgotten about that. Goddamnit! "I'm going to talk to

Bailey." She forced lightness into her tone. "I need you to talk to Mortician. We can convince them to still go ahead with their vow renewal."

The silence stretched, before Outlaw nodded. "Ima do that shit for your ass, *after* I talk to fuckin' Knox."

She struggled to keep the panic out of her face. Even though she didn't want to, she'd have to call Knox and tell him to let the story stand as she'd told it—that she'd broken off the engagement because she'd decided another marriage wasn't for her.

Otherwise...she didn't want to consider the otherwise.

"Get the fuck outta here, so I can take a fuckin' piss, Roxanne."

Hurrying away and closing the bathroom door behind her, Roxy gave in to the tears that had been threatening to fall for the past few minutes.

CHAPTER THIRTY

Knox

Had he fucked up so bad that he'd lost Roxanne?

Did his dislike of the club president, the *club*, trump his love for his woman?

Of course not!

He stared at the ring that sat on his desk. According to her, she was no longer his woman. She never wanted to see him again.

He should never have gone over to Mortician's house this morning. Or, at least, so early. He'd challenged Mortician and...and ruined his relationship with the woman he loved as much as life itself. Worse, he'd spewed pure venom at her, when he'd meant none of it.

How could he make her forgive him? How could he express how absolutely sorry he was? Even as he was yelling at her, his words—along with regret—began to sink in. They'd been unworthy of him, her, and their relationship. Yet, they'd kept coming, as if he had no control. His heart had told him to stop. His anger, pride and frustration egged him on. He'd only thought of her lame reasons for placating

Mortician. His ego suffered that she hadn't missed him enough to arrange another secret meeting. Either at the clubhouse or at her quarters. Fuck, his self-respect smarted *because* their meetings had to be in secret.

All her words, *reasons*, had seemed like excuses. That she'd said the same thing time and again should've alerted him that this really was an issue for her. He should've looked for ways to put her at ease. Damn it, he should've *listened* to her and just went along with Mortician.

His phone indicated an incoming text message. Listlessly, he picked it up. Roxanne. Calling him a motherfucker as only she could? If he wasn't so desperate to stay connected to her, he would've ignored the text. It would kill him to read how much she hated him. Seeing a text message from her felt like a lifeline, no matter what she wrote, so he opened it.

For your own safety, tell everyone I ended our engagement.

She had, though, so why would he lie about it?

You did, he responded. The words nauseated him, made him dizzy. Another piece of his heart shattered.

So I did. Just don't tell them why. You will die.

Oh. Right. Mortician would kill him for all the things he'd said to Roxanne. More than that...*Outlaw*.

In some mystifying way, he respected Outlaw's...*intelligence...?...instinct...?...suspicious nature...?* What about the man drew him to accept cases and even take his advice? He sounded so ignorant and acted so belligerent.

Maybe, it just came down to plain, old envy. Outlaw said what he wanted, *did what he wanted*, wherever and whenever. Women found the brute overwhelmingly gorgeous and sexy. Knox wasn't pulling this from his ass, either. He'd overhead conversations during parties at the club. Whether they feared him or were fascinated by him, women wanted to fuck him. Because of his intense green eyes...his silky black hair...his height...his muscles...blah, bla-blah, blah, blah.

Roxanne was a woman. Had she ever seen him as more than just a friend? More than just an *adopted* son?

The man every woman wanted had bought *Knox's* lady a custom-made Navigator.

Added to that insult was the fact that his upbringing forbade him the same freedom of expression that Outlaw was known for.

Sighing, Knox glanced at the wall clock in his office. He'd been here for an hour and hadn't gotten one thing done. Thoughts of Roxanne consumed him. He'd fucked up so bad.

Roxanne was a proud, no-nonsense woman and he'd hurt her to the depth of her soul. He'd mocked her. Bullied her. Berated her.

His phone lay silent. He hoped for her forgiveness, yet he couldn't fathom the words he, himself, had spoken. To humiliate and crush. He should be killed. Closing his eyes, he willed another message to come through from her. But, nothing. Unable to stand the thought she'd shut him out, he decided to take a risk. She'd taught him how to be more open and to show his feelings. Grabbing his phone, he started typing words poured from his heart.

I'm so, so sorry, Roxanne. Please forgive me. Give me another chance. I'll do anything you ask of me to prove how much I love you. Please. I'm begging you.

Just when he thought she wouldn't respond, her reply came.

Forgiven.

The one word instilled such hope in him that he released a laugh-sob.

Then you'll take my ring back? I love you.

Another long stretch before she answered.

No. We're through. We don't belong together, Knox. We're too different. You want a prenup. I don't. You hate my family. I don't. You're rich. I'm just a gold digger.

Knox winced. He'd been a sonofabitch. He hated himself as he never had before. He'd do anything to rewind the clock and take the words back. Impossible, he knew. Once said, the spoken word could never be recalled.

Please, he typed.

I can't.

He shuddered at the simple words.

I'm so sorry, Roxanne.

Me, too, Knox.

Her words were poignant. He'd bet she cried as she texted them. He wanted to hold her and comfort her. As he should have when he saw her tears earlier. Instead, he'd sneered at them. He needed an ass-kicking. The type that Outlaw had given him so many months ago. Knox had been hospitalized as a result and needed plastic surgery. Confession would be his penance.

Maybe, I should tell Mortician and Outlaw myself, all the god-awful things I said to you. I'll take whatever they dish out.

DEATH!

That warning came immediately.

They will kill you. Gruesomely. Don't do anything you wouldn't survive to regret.

He almost regretted being born, at that particular moment.

I'll think about it and discuss it with you when I see you this evening.

Another immediate response.

Let me know what time you intend to pick up your things from the clubhouse, so I can be long gone.

No. He wouldn't do that. He couldn't give in without a fight, so he stared at his phone, as if he could find the answers to his misery. One thing was certain, if he didn't respond, he knew she wouldn't. She considered herself done with him.

The ringing of the office phone startled him and he jumped, on edge and out-of-sorts. He thought of ignoring it and allowing the answering service to take the call, but he needed something to distract him. On what would've been the fifth and final ring, he snatched up the received. "Harrington."

"Mr. Harrington."

This better not be a telemarketer. "Yes?"

"This is Joyner Amfinger. I was calling because I have a small case I'd like to hire you for."

Losing Roxanne crowded out most of Knox's other memories, so it took him a moment to place the name.

"I asked you to provide me with a new identity," Amfinger reminded Knox just as the thought popped into his head.

"Did I hear you say a small case?" Knox couldn't keep the incredulity from his voice. He'd said the same thing the last time. Just what did the man consider a big case?

"To me."

"I'm still not interested," Knox said with irritation.

"Good, because I'm calling in regards to another matter."

Knox didn't want any other cases right now. Outside of the Kendall job, he needed to use every other working moment winning Roxanne back. If today wasn't the day for Johnnie to cross paths with Emily Riser, Knox wouldn't have even come to work.

"Just hear me out," Amfinger said into the silence.

Knox didn't know why he wasted his time, listening to whatever scheme Amfinger needed help with this time. The jackass was lucky Knox had merely declined him, and not called the police. A man didn't decide to change identities if he wasn't into some serious crimes.

"Give me ten minutes."

"Five," Knox conceded.

"I have light arms to get rid of," Amfinger announced.

It took a moment for the man's meaning to dawn on Knox. "Guns?" he gasped.

"Machine guns. Light and sub," Amfinger clarified.

Knox straightened in his seat. "Are you out of your fucking mind?" he shouted. "Where the fuck did you get my number and why do you think I'm willing to break the law?"

"Gun-running isn't illegal, as long as it is done through the proper channels."

"You'd be an arms dealer," Knox sneered. "You wouldn't make a fucking cold call to a stranger and ask for help."

"You're a private investigator. I'm sure you know a lot of people. You can't tell me all your cases are on the up-and-up."

"I can't tell you anything about other cases."

Amfinger sighed. "I heard you were affiliated with an MC."

"That doesn't mean I have illegal dealings," Knox snapped. "Who gave this information to you?"

"It isn't important."

"You're goddamn right. I really don't give a fuck. You could be a cop, a federal agent, using me as a pawn to get to a club you *heard* I was affiliated with."

Amfinger fell silent, then sighed again. "I'm an old friend of your Uncle Avalon. He told me about you."

"I don't ever want to hear that bastard's name again." Knox tightened his grip on the receiver. Amfinger knowing Avalon was worse than any other scenario Knox could've imagined. "Avalon is no uncle of mine." He'd kidnapped Roxanne and Charlotte, and intended to kill both of them. Avalon had even injured his own brother—Knox's father—in his quest to bring down the Death Dwellers to hide his own double-dealing with the club.

"What Avalon did was pathetic," Amfinger agreed. "But please don't penalize me for his actions."

"Amfinger—"

"As part of the deal, I have two crates of Kalashnikovs. I would be willing to include them as a bonus. A sign of good faith."

Knox scrubbed a hand over his face. AK-47s—Kalashnikovs—were so numerous that many dealers didn't bother with them. Prices varied wildly. On the dark web, they were sold for nearly three grand a piece. In some countries, where they were locally made, one rifle mist go for under two hundred dollars. The dealers who ran or traded them usually used them as Amfinger proposed—loss leaders. Guns to give away to build a relationship.

"Mr. Harrington, I understand you originally went to investigate the club to see them behind bars."

"Avalon couldn't keep his fucking mouth shut."

"If not for your uncle, you wouldn't be engaged to a member's mother-in-law."

Knox frowned. "Roxanne and I recently got engaged, so Avalon wouldn't have known that."

"You're a Harrington. The announcement was in society columns everywhere."

Knox huffed out a breath. "Okay, fine. What's your point?"

"If you want to get in good with the club, imagine what bringing this deal to them would do for your standing."

Would it also show Roxanne how sorry he was for being so critical of her, the club, and the members? Everything and everyone important to her, he'd complained about.

"Give me your phone number, Amfinger," Knox ordered. He needed to think on this.

"You'll help me out?"

"I didn't say that." Knox chose his words with care. If this was some type of setup, they couldn't get him on anything because he hadn't agreed to work with him. Most important, money hadn't exchanged hands.

After Amfinger gave Knox his number, the call ended.

"Knock, knock," Cam greeted, pushing open Knox's ajarred door and walking into the office.

Deciding not to involve Cam in this—one way or the other, Knox ripped the paper with Amfinger's number from the notepad and stuffed it into his shirt pocket.

Cam set his briefcase on one of the chairs in front of Knox's desk, glancing at his phone. The wide smile told Knox Cam had gotten a message from his wife. Knox sighed. The simple gold band on his ring finger lowered Knox's spirits even further. Lost in whatever Jordan had sent to him, he barely glanced at Knox.

"Did you review footage of Kendall?" Cam asked in that same distracted manner.

Knox shook his head. "No," he mumbled.

Cam looked at Knox. He touched Roxanne's ring, then spun it, drawing Cam's gaze. His eyes widened.

Self-recriminations tore through Knox and he bowed his head. "I haven't even thought about Kendall Donovan," he admitted with a sigh.

"What happened, Wafer?" he asked, using the nickname he'd given Knox years ago. "Roxanne..." Cam's voice trailed off and he studied the ring again.

"Yeah," Knox answered, not sure what the question was and not caring.

Roxanne broke it off with him? Yeah.

He'd been a motherfucker? Yeah.

She didn't intend to forgive him? Yeah.

He was so fucked if Mortician or Outlaw found out what Knox had done but he didn't care? Yeah.

"I-I was so horrible to her. For no reason."

Unbuttoning his suit jacket, Cam sat in the other chair in front of Knox's desk. "In your head, there's a reason, Wafer, and his name is Outlaw. Get over the man," he warned. "The cop in you can't get over the criminal in him. You can't understand why a beautiful woman like Roxanne considers them her family. Your feelings are affecting your life and risking your relationship. You love Roxanne. Besides, Outlaw isn't so bad."

"I was hot under the collar from an argument I'd had with Mortician," he confessed. "I should've kept walking when I heard her calling me. Ignoring her would've pissed her off, but she...she would've forgiven me. No, wait. She says she forgives me now but she's done with me." Once again remembering the names he'd called her, he cringed.

Disgust dropped into Cam's face. He wished the man would act on his anger and deck him.

"You don't have to say it. I should be ashamed of myself. I know she's not used to wealth—*legal wealth*—but she wasn't after me for money."

"I should punch you in your fucking mouth for being such a stupid-ass bastard."

"Please, do. It might make me feel better. I have to find a way to win her back. Get through this day. Outlaw is implementing another phase in his plan to destroy Kendall."

For a moment, Cam's attention turned from Knox's stupidity. "The day has finally arrived."

Knox nodded, jumping on the chance to discuss the case before he broke down in sobs. "We'll see if Johnnie loves Kendall as much as he claims, or if he just wanted a woman to fill in the void left by Megan Caldwell."

"My bet is he's not going to take the bait."

"I really don't give a fuck."

"You should. It's part of the job we're doing for Outlaw."

"I understand, but...but...goddamnit...I want Johnnie to get rid of Kendall. After last night, I would think that would be a given. I just... Roxanne loves Kendall, too, and I'm happily working to annihilate her."

"Yes," Cam agreed, grave. "You're working to precipitate her death."

"Roxanne would hate me."

"According to you, she already hates you."

Instead of answering, Knox gave another nod.

Cam folded his arms. "You owe her an apology."

"I've already apologized."

"Apologize again. Kiss her ass in the middle of downtown and admit over a loudspeaker what an unintelligent fuck you were."

Knox slumped back in his chair. Cam's stare chastened Knox and made him feel so low he almost slid to the ground.

Cameron Baptiste was the brother Knox never had. He loved him as if he were his own flesh-and-blood and valued his opinion. To see Cam's unspoken disappointment because of his actions, gutted Knox.

Relaxing his position, Cam relented in his silent annihilation of Knox. "Let me school you a little, my brother," he started. "Remember some months ago, the news story about mega-preacher, Sharper Banks?"

How could he forget it? Reverend Banks had been killed in an explosion in an Atlanta hotel, across the country from where his home and huge church was located in Los Angeles. Not long after, the church had been blown up, too. Those two stories had dominated news cycles for weeks.

The man had been ultra-wealthy, having written books and enjoying a huge, devout following that donated money to him faithfully. He'd lost his wife years ago in an automobile accident.

"Sharper Banks was Mortician and Digger's father."

Knox blinked at Cam's matter-of-fact statement. "No," he managed in a strangled voice.

Cam nodded. "Yeah."

In shock, Knox stood from his seat and sat again. Heat crawled up his neck and into his face. "You're joking...No. I would've known...My god...please, tell me this isn't true."

"Feel like a big, diseased asshole yet? Because, believe me, it *is* true. And you didn't know because whenever his children were mentioned, it was reported they wanted to remain anonymous. In this day and age, that's hard to do. Unless you have the reach and the power of the Death Dwellers. Not to mention the world at your feet as two wealthy men."

"Noooooo! That can't be right. They don't even act rich," Knox ranted. "It's illogical. No. You're lying, Cameron," he decided. "No wealthy preacher's son is going to be a notorious criminal."

"Unless the preacher was one."

"How the fuck is a rich man supposed to act?"

"Not like the Hortensia Hillbillies, goddamn it!" Knox yelled.

"Jesus Christ! So acting like Uncle Avalon is excusable?"

Second time today Avalon had been brought up. "Do you know Joyner Amfinger, by any chance?" Or was it just coincidence that he'd called Knox and had been a friend of Avalon on the same day Cam spoke of his uncle?

"Who the fuck is Joyner Amfinger?"

"Never mind." Bleak, Knox looked at Cam. "Why wouldn't Mortician have told me who his father was whenever I called him poor?"

Cam lifted a brow. "Why did the man have to explain himself to you, Knox?"

He got up from his seat and stumbled to the window, wanting to throw-up. "My god," he said again. If Mortician was wealthy, then Bailey was, too. And if Bailey had money, then..."Roxanne...Roxanne... has her own money," he finished on a painful gasp.

"You don't say."

Knox spun around and faced his best friend. "Why didn't she tell me?"

"Again, why did she have to? She left it up to you to figure out. She ever asked you for anything? Exorbitant gifts? Expensive trips? Designer clothes?"

"No, of course not! Roxanne isn't..."

"She isn't that type of person, right, jackass? Even if, in fact, she was as poor as your small brain thought she was, she wouldn't ask you for a goddamn thing. I don't know what the fuck else you called her, but gold digger?" Cam snorted, and glared at him. "Why should she ever come back to your insulting ass?"

"Cam—"

"Fuck, Knox! I don't want to hear it. Instead of asking why didn't *they*, ask yourself why didn't *I. Why didn't I love her enough to shut the fuck up? Why didn't I recognize that she didn't tell me anything because she took me as I was so she expected me to do the same?*"

Knox couldn't listen to anymore. "Stop!" he shouted. "Stop. Just stop." He shoved his hands into his trouser pockets. "What do I do? How do I get her back?"

Cam threw another angry glare at him.

"Please, help me," Knox begged. "I love her."

"You don't treat anyone you love with such disregard and disrespect."

"I know, Cam," Knox said close to tears.

Cam sighed. "Give her a few days, Knox," he relented. "She's probably hurt to her core. All that woman does is talk about what a wonderful man you are to my wife."

"I feel like kicking my own ass."

"You should."

Knox sagged against the windowsill, while Cam stood.

"I didn't roll out of bed and leave my gorgeous wife on a Saturday to unfuck what you've fucked, so let's review the recordings before Outlaw and company arrives."

Having to watch Kendall Donovan wade through her myriad problems, when he had so many of his own, didn't interest Knox at all. He had no choice in the matter. Outlaw had hired him to do this job.

If Roxanne ever found out what Knox was up to, she'd have one more reason to never talk to him again.

CHAPTER THIRTY-ONE

Kendall

Kendall had spent most of yesterday reviewing plans with Charlotte for the Donovan and Redding Law Firm. She'd been happy, if not content. Something had niggled at the back of her mind, preventing her from real enjoyment. Between then and now, it seemed as if a lifetime had passed.

Raising her vintage French Louis XV hand mirror as she lay in bed, Kendall stared at her black eyes and various bruises, courtesy of Meggie, and scowled. She couldn't believe Johnnie had been the only one to intervene on her behalf. Anyone of them could've entered the fray...

A memory of Outlaw firing a round into Johnnie's cheek rose in Kendall's head. The barbarian had pulled his 9mm last night, too. Knowing he wouldn't hesitate to shoot must've stopped them all, so Kendall decided she couldn't really blame them.

However, and this was a huge revelation to her, the discontent she'd felt yesterday as she made plans with Charlotte made sense now. Outlaw had *shot* Johnnie, a relative who'd been as close as anyone to him, because of Kendall's actions. Then, he'd turned around and rewarded Kendall.

What gave?

It could be argued that he *was* grateful that Kendall had given up Meggie's location; in essence, saving her life. He'd known that when he'd shot Johnnie, though. Suddenly, he'd given Kendall, *her,* his most hated human, the go-ahead to practice law again, effective immediately.

She'd get land, a house in her name, access to money in the form of her own bank account, and a bigger percentage in Meggie and Zoann's company, if she and Johnnie stayed married.

But, after last night's fight with Meggie, and Outlaw's glee, nothing made sense to Kendall. His allowing her to practice law concerned her. He hadn't had to allow her to practice again *and,* on top of that, design the building, all at his expense.

Besides her husband and children, her degree mattered most to her. All of the other things she thought she'd wanted so she could feel equal to Meggie just wasn't important. She'd give it all up, if only Johnnie gave her another chance.

Sinking further down into the covers, she raised the hand mirror again and sniffled. Before she noted any other marks on her, her cell phone rang.

"Hi Charlotte," she said by way of answering, after seeing the woman's name and number pop up on her screen. "How are you today?" She forced cheer into her voice.

"Darling," Charlotte started. "I just heard your voice message, canceling our dinner plans. Are you all right?"

No. She was heartbroken, lonely, and afraid. "Of course I am. Why wouldn't I be?"

"You mingled with those people last night, that's why," Charlotte said in a huff.

"Yes," she whispered, then cleared her throat. "It went fine. I'm just exhausted from all the wine I drank."

"Was that uncouth woman, Roxanne, behaving herself?"

"I don't want to discuss Roxanne with you, Charlotte. Let's not talk about any of them. Why don't we have a phone meeting? I'd love to know how your search for a receptionist is coming along." Lies! All lies! She couldn't give less of a fuck.

"I have a couple of women I think will work out fine. We just have to go over the requirements you put in place," she said cryptically.

Kendall didn't like the sound of that. "I'm not changing my mind on one point. I refuse to have any young receptionists and secretaries in that office. I can't have Johnnie coming over and finding some little slut attractive."

Charlotte sniffed. "Threaten to take him to the cleaners, my dear. He'll never stray again."

She realized to get to those points, he had to want to take her back, a prospect that grew increasingly unlikely. But what if they divorced, God forbid, and he visited her at the office for some reason and saw... saw a younger woman? A blonde little goddess who reminded him of Meggie? Suppose there would be a younger employee who'd jump when Johnnie told her to?

Yes, he could meet other women anywhere, but Kendall wouldn't make it as easy as finding her in the office.

"Johnnie kicked me out," Kendall reminded Charlotte, gripping her phone tighter.

"A pure abomination," Charlotte retorted. "And it took *Outlaw* to allow you to hire Ella back."

That happened weeks ago. Ella still hadn't returned.

"Johnnie's still so furious with me. I just want my husband back. I'll behave."

"*Behave?* Do you hear yourself? You aren't a child who needs disciplining. You're a grown woman. That man...that *club* is lucky to have you."

"But I got Meggie kidnapped. To Johnnie, that's unforgivable."

"She should've been murdered and tossed into the ocean like the garbage she is. While they were at it, they could've thrown that Roxanne woman with her. Ignorant piece of trash. I can't understand what an elegant man like Knox wants with her."

"I love Roxy, Charlotte," Kendall bit out. "So do *not* talk about her in such a manner. As for Knox, he's a fucking uptight asshole. *I* don't see what *she's* doing with a prude like him."

"Knox is better suited to you, dear."

Charlotte's comment sent disbelieving horror through Kendall. "I hate that bastard. He was snooping around with the express purpose of sending the men to jail. That would've included Johnnie. I don't trust him as far as I can see him. I think he'll betray Roxy and the entire club the first chance he gets."

"As if he shouldn't. They are thugs! Killers. *Arsonists*! They burned my mansion to the ground."

"Johnnie isn't a thug. Furthermore, if my husband and his brothers can trust Knox, you have nothing to say about it."

"Well, Brooks told me Outlaw knows Knox doesn't like him. He was so suspicious that he had him investigated. When it turned up that Knox was clean, and he made Roxanne happy, Outlaw backed off."

"Well, what do you expect? Outlaw isn't stupid. If I was in his place, I would've had Knox investigated, too."

Charlotte harrumped. "Outlaw is quite suspicious of those he perceives as his enemy," she started in high tones. "Therefore, I question his generosity to you."

Kendall did as well, but she'd never admit that to Charlotte. It would just give her one more reason to denigrate the club. One more reason to make Kendall feel like a failure for not living up to Charlotte's standards after she'd been like a mother to her. "Oh, please. There's no reason to question his gifts. He considers me family. In effect that ties his hands. He *has* to do this for me. It's a requirement because I'm his brother's wife."

"My darling Kendall, you're still so trusting. Remember Emily Riser. She was unworthy of you as a child and from what you said of your recent meeting, she's unworthy of you as a woman."

"The perfect, little blue-eyed blonde," Kendall sneered, anger rising in spite of meeting with Emily and closing the door on that chapter in her life. "Meggie reminds me of her." Her distasteful tone registered in her brain, but she needed to vent. She'd confess her regression to Doctor Briscow during her next appointment. Right now, she wanted a familiar shoulder to cry on. "Emily pretended she wanted to be my friend, then humiliated me and made me bite off the head of a butterfly."

"You *trusted* her, and sincerely thought she'd accept you into her clique. You're doing the same with Outlaw."

No, she wasn't by a long shot. Outlaw had plans for her. Serious, devastating, deadly plans. The more she juxtaposed his generosity with last night's reaction to the fight, the more convinced Kendall became that she was in danger. Something else she wouldn't tell Charlotte, so she just said, "I was thirteen-years-old! I'm a grown woman now."

"Okay, dear. I'll trust your judgment but reserve the right to say *I told you so*, if Outlaw's motives aren't aboveboard."

Kendall pursed her lips. "Let's get back to the office plans, please."

The rest of the conversation consisted of Charlotte making the plans to decorate the law offices with high-end luxury décor and furnishings that would cost a lot of money. Whenever Charlotte was angry with Brooks, she got her revenge by spending as much of his money as possible...well, she *had* before Brooks fucked over Outlaw and lost everything.

Once she bid Charlotte goodbye and threw her phone aside, Kendall rested against her pillows. The silence nearly drove her insane.

The club, in the evening, was frenetic; Meggie's mansion, where Kendall had had an office, was always a beehive of activity. Her own home was quieter, a place to unwind, but Meggie, Roxy, Bailey, Fee, Mort and Johnnie contacted her throughout each day. Ella needed direction. Kendall had to make sure she kept up with the latest fashions for herself and her kids, especially Matilda, and home furnishings. Or she was out shopping. Or at some committee meeting. Or at a day spa. A stylist to color out the few gray strands she'd found in her hair.

In essence, her life had been rich and busy and filled with family and leisure. She hadn't had to worry about anything, not even her safety.

Especially not her safety.

Now, though...she shivered. She felt watched and stalked and...and unsafe.

She felt...

Her thoughts screeched to a halt.

Watched?

She was in a house Outlaw had given to her. And...and he might've *pretended* to listen to Meggie and overlook Kendall's participation in Meggie's kidnapping. Furthermore, he *said* he disciplined CJ for disrespecting Kendall. *Still*, Kendall had gone overboard in what she'd intended to do to the boy. It was a situation Outlaw wouldn't allow to pass without retaliation.

Shoving the covers aside, Kendall jumped out of bed and glanced around her room, inhaling and exhaling as if she'd run a marathon.

What should she do? What could she do?

Call Johnnie?

No, he wouldn't care. She was on her own.

Ordering herself to calm down, Kendall considered her options. If she showed any fear, Outlaw would move in for the kill soon. *Sooner.* But if she bought some time, challenged him, she could get away.

She paced, nausea churning in her. One last time she'd have to deceive her beloved Johnnie. She'd have to lull him into allowing her more freedom with Matilda. Rory and JJ she'd leave with him. Her daughter, however, was coming with her.

A sob escaped her and she covered her face. Outlaw might be watching her give into her weakness. At the thought, she straightened her shoulders, swiped a hand across her runny nose, and drew herself up.

Biting down on her lip, she tugged her silk nightie off her shoulders and allowed it to slide to the floor. She wasn't sure where the camera might be located and she really didn't care.

She wished to have her family, her friends, back. But wishes were for dreamers and children, and she was neither.

So she turned in a circle, slow, provocative, hands on hips.

"Do you have the house bugged, *Christopher*?" she sneered into the air. "Do I fascinate you that much? Take your fill of what you'll never have."

How could she have been so stupid? Why had she believed he'd forgive her enough to gift her with so much, when Johnnie was barely on speaking terms with her?

For most of her adult life, she'd survived by shielding herself from pain and hurt by doling it out. How could anyone get to her if she struck first?

She spun again, swinging her hair, tweaking her nipple before sliding her finger to her bare pussy.

"Don't you want it, *Christopher*? How does it feel knowing I'm the one woman you'll never have? My pussy belongs to Johnnie. You'll never have a taste."

She cupped her pussy, then dissolved into tears and sank to the floor. She didn't care if Outlaw *was* spying on her and saw her brokenness. She didn't care that all her behavior would earn her is more disgust and a label of being obsessed with Outlaw.

Covering her face, she cried in loud, broken sobs. Scenes from her life at the club shuffled through her memory. The first time she'd seen Johnnie and fucked him. The next time when she'd sat and had a drink with him.

The day she'd met Meggie, who'd turned into Kendall's destruction and her deliverance.

She thought of last night, and what seemed like her *last night* with her husband. She'd been in so much pain and infused with anger, cursing Meggie and Outlaw, as Johnnie ushered her to her Navigator then had gotten into his and followed her to the house.

It would've been better if he'd bade her good night and drove off.

Instead...

Kendall curled into a ball on the floor, thinking of all that had gone wrong.

She'd limped to the sofa and sat, staring at her husband. One way or the other those fucking Caldwells were trying to ruin his beautiful face. "How's your nose?"

"Broken," Johnnie answered flatly, fingering the bandage Zoann had put on it.

"That little bitch is going to pay for what she did to us."

"No!" Johnnie said in a hard voice. "Leave Megan the fuck alone. You've fucked with her one time too many."

"Are you taking up for her?" Kendall had demanded in outrage.

Heaving in a breath, he glanced away from her.

"Look at me!" she'd yelled. "I have black eyes, a split lip, bruises on my jaw. On my body."

Johnnie stomped to where Kendall sat and leaned forward. "You fucked with CJ. *Again*. What did you expect?"

"Oh, go to hell," Kendall cried in frustration, getting to her feet and moving out of Johnnie's aura. The scent of him. The strength of him. "All you ever do is defend her. For our entire marriage, I've lived in her shadow."

Johnnie rounded on her. "For our entire marriage, you've placed yourself in her shadow."

"That isn't true!" Kendall spat, stomping her foot. Even that sent jarring pain through her abused body. "You measured everything I did against what *she* did. I've tried, Johnnie, I swear I have. But it's so hard to like her, knowing how much you love her."

"I don't love her, Kendall," Johnnie had gritted. "There are many days when I despise her."

Kendall drew herself up. "Because you love her and can't have her. If she opened her legs to you tomorrow, you'd fuck her."

"Stop turning the subject away from the real issues here. Megan would never give herself to me..."

"Goddamn you!" she screamed, noting he hadn't denied he'd sleep with her if given the opportunity. All he'd admitted was what *Meggie* would never do. "Fuck you!" She'd burst into tears. "I wish she had. I wish she *would*. Maybe, then, you'd get over her."

"Really, Kendall?" he snarled. "What will it take for you to get over Christopher?"

She'd dissolved into more tears. "I love you, Johnnie," she sobbed. "I do, and I don't want him in the way that you think I do. But what does Meggie have? Tell me! She has you wrapped around her little finger and Christopher blindly obsessed. No matter what I do I can't get him to want me so she can see how it feels to have a husband who pines for another woman."

"That's such bullshit!" Johnnie barked. "You don't want to fuck Christopher because of how you think I feel about Megan. You're attracted to him."

Sniffling, she'd swiped at her tears. "How can that be when I abhor him?" she asked in real dismay. "Can't you understand that he hurt my pride when he shoved me off his lap? Don't you see if he would've slept with me all those years ago, my sister would still be alive? If...if not for Megan, you'd really love me. Not find the idea of love, of having a woman like the rest of the guys, so motivating. Because that's *it*, Johnnie. You married me to be equal to Christopher, Mortician, and Val. Not because you love me."

Johnnie released a frustrated sigh. "I love you, Kendall, but you're just so goddamn infuriating. You—"

"Stop right there," Kendall had ordered, holding up her hand. "There should be no buts. If you love me, you love me."

"Ditto, babe. I've left the club because of you. I've gotten beat up because of you. And I've gotten shot *because of you*. Now, I've gotten my goddamn nose broken because of you. All in all, I'd say I've been pretty fucking patient with all the bullshit that you've done that's endangered my life."

Kendall's shoulders drooped. "Where do we go from here?" she'd whispered.

"I don't know, Kendall. I want to be happy. I don't want to live the rest of my life, wondering if my wife is into bullshit that might get me or *her* killed. I want to have a woman who knows how to be a mother and a friend. Who knows the meaning of loyalty. That's not you."

"I know the meaning of loyalty," Kendall spat on a sob. "I'm always defending you and Roxy."

Johnnie narrowed his eyes. "What about loyalty to the club? Loyalty to the women of the club? To our kids? To Christopher's kids?"

"I'm the best mother I know how to be."

"Well, go back to school, because you're shit at it. Rory is afraid of you."

"He is not!"

"Yes, Kendall, he is. He told me so."

"I was never afraid of my mother, and she treated me the way I treat our kids. I loved my mom."

"Your mother was fucked up and she fucked you up."

"Oh, my God! Why are you being so mean to me? Why aren't you holding me and calling me gorgeous and saying we'll work this out?"

Shoving his hands into his pockets, Johnnie sighed. "Because I'm done. We're done. Tonight was the last fucking straw."

"No!" Kendall screamed, limp-running to Johnnie and throwing her arms around his neck.

He disentangled her from him and watched with dispassion as she crumbled to the floor.

"Please! Please, don't do this, Johnnie. I love you. I'm so sorry for everything."

He stared at her, then looked away, sadness drooping his features. He suddenly looked haggard and drawn. "It's too little, too late," he told her, and walked away.

"*JOHNNIE!!*" Kendall had hollered, but he hadn't answered and he hadn't looked back.

He'd walked out on her.

And their marriage.

CHAPTER THIRTY-TWO

Knox

Knox had just witnessed the dissolution of a couple, and he sat in stunned silence until Cam whistled and said, "Fuck, that was brutal."

Slowly, Knox nodded, still too shocked to speak. Johnnie adored Kendall, in ways so pathetic Knox sometimes felt sorry for him. Yet, after years of patience, he'd reached his breaking point with her.

Thinking of the argument he'd had with Roxanne, Knox shifted in his seat. He'd always looked down on Kendall for the games she played, and the things she said. Wasn't he guilty of the same thing? Maybe, his position was a little more understandable. *Still,* Roxanne had overlooked Knox's underhanded reasons for originally courting her, and given him a real chance.

She'd trusted him enough to believe he wouldn't go after her family.

Yes, Outlaw was so ignorant and stupid he could only form a sentence if it had the word 'fuck' included two or three times. And, yes, the entire club engaged in criminal activity. They were important to her, though. Besides, *she* wasn't involved in felonious activity, so...

"Knox?" Cam called.

Frowning, Knox focused on his friend and business partner.

"Are you okay?"

He scrubbed a hand over his face. "I could've overlooked Mortician's games on Roxanne's behalf," he said miserably. "I just...Damn it! I didn't know he was wealthy. I just took him to be a violent offender, like the rest of them."

Cam snorted. "Really, jackass? Mortician's wealth changes the way you see him? Newsflash, brother: he *is* a violent offender. They all are, but they are also loyal to those who show them the same respect. Besides, your fucking uncle kidnapped Roxanne and intended to kill her. Not to mention the fact that he was embezzling money. That's criminal too, Knox."

"I know," Knox whispered.

"We're here to do a job," Cam reminded him. "I want to salvage some of my Saturday to spend with my family."

"You're right," Knox agreed on a swallow.

Cam nodded toward the now-black screen. They hadn't switched back to the live feed.

"Knox," Cam started, giving him a level look. "Are you sure you want to participate in this? Kendall Donovan..." His voice trailed off and he shook his head. "It won't take long to drive her to suicide. She's so broken already."

Knox snapped his eyebrows together. "Are you taking up for that woman?"

"Roxanne loves her. If you are a party to her demise, that might affect your relationship a bit."

Not only a bit. Another part of him, the side that allowed him to take the case, disagreed. "If Kendall is out of the picture, the whole club will breathe easier."

"I don't know her well enough to agree or disagree. However, you can just tell Outlaw to handle her death on his own."

"That's impossible," Knox snapped on a scowl. "First of all, Megan Caldwell would never agree with his decision to murder Kendall.

Second, Outlaw would also have to kill Johnnie in order to save his own life. Johnnie wouldn't allow his wife's death to go unavenged." Especially given the sordid history of the four. Sudden anger infused him. "Kendall deserves to suffer for all her sins. She needs to be so fucking haunted that she can't live with herself. I'd gladly supply the gun, the rope, or the poison."

"Give her a break. She has severe mental problems. She's lost her family and her friends. Her marriage is over—"

"Couldn't have happened to a nicer person," Knox sneered, not feeling a bit of empathy toward the redhead.

The chime on the entrance door sounded. Glancing at his watch, Knox saw that it was five minutes to eleven.

"Hello," Emily Riser called from the small reception area just outside of the conference room. Her voice still had edges of culture in it, but, according to what he'd discovered about her, the roughness in it had been born of cigarettes, hard liquor and cocaine.

"She's here." In spite of Knox's intense dislike of Kendall, unease slid into him.

Cam nodded, and looked toward the conference room door. It was ajar, allowing no one to see in or out. He seemed as rooted to his chair as Knox. They both knew they were about to set a chain of events into motion that would have far-reaching—and possibly—deadly consequences.

The same hesitation Knox felt showed in Cam's face.

"Fuck, man. Jordan and Roxanne are best friends," he said, the look he turned to Knox grave. "If she knows of my involvement should anything happen to Kendall, and Roxanne is hurt, even emotionally, that'll be my ass."

"Cam, I swear, this is the right thing to do. Before she curled up on that floor, and we switched to last night's recording, she stripped, apparently so paranoid that she feels as if she's being watched. Instead of cowering, she showed her pussy. Who does that?" Knox growled in frustration. He wanted bleach for his brain. "As if anyone but Johnnie is interested in seeing her naked ass."

"Knox—"

"Hello?" Emily repeated with a touch of impatience.

"I'll be right there," Knox responded as both he and Cam stood from their seats.

In the waiting room, the gorgeous blonde stood in black trousers and a blue silk blouse that enhanced the color of her eyes.

He stepped aside to reveal Cam. "This is my partner, Cameron Baptiste."

Emily nodded. "Good morning."

Cam cleared his throat. "Hello. Welcome to our office."

She glanced around. "Are they here yet?"

Before either of them responded, the door opened and Johnnie walked in, wearing his cut, a white T-shirt, a pair of faded jeans, and his motorcycle boots. His hair was windblown and the bandages on his nose gave him a bad boy vibe.

"Christopher asked me to drop this off to you." Johnnie took out an envelope from inside the pocket of his cut and held it out to Knox. He barely noticed Emily as Knox accepted what Johnnie handed to him, then started to turn.

Knox sidled a glance at Emily.

"Er, don't leave on my account, sir," she said in a sweet tone that surprised Knox. She hadn't been the nicest person the day they'd met. "I have a lot of time on my hand, if you need to speak to Mr. Harrington a moment."

Johnnie stopped and looked in her direction. He went still, not moving a muscle. Not uttering a sound. He merely stared, before his breath caught, and his mouth fell open.

"Jesus," he mumbled, blinking.

Emily lowered her lashes. "I didn't mean to catch you off-guard."

Slowly, he shook his head, taking in every detail of her face, squinting at her upswept hair. He closed his eyes. "Fuck."

"Are you okay, Mister..." Emily pressed.

Johnnie drew in a deep breath. "Excuse me, sweetheart." He grinned, and Knox wasn't sure if it was forced or not. "Where are my manners? I shouldn't burn the ears of a lady with my foul language."

Emily smiled. "I've been known to burn a few ears a time or two," she admitted. She held out her hand. "I'm Emily."

For the longest moment, Johnnie stared at her hand, before

accepting it. When he wrapped his hand around hers, he frowned and released it, as if his skin had been burned.

"Your hands have callouses," he blurted.

In other words, they weren't soft like Megan's.

Emily's lips tightened before she covered her displeasure with a smile. "I'm a working woman who still doesn't know your name."

"Johnnie," he told her.

He sounded, and looked, as if he'd gone into a state of shock. Once again not moving, he stared at Emily.

Those blue eyes gave Johnnie a slow perusal. "You're a biker?" she asked into the silence, and Knox had to give her credit for her effort to draw Johnnie out.

"I am," Johnnie admitted with pride. "Vice president of my club."

"That's so interesting. I've always wanted to ride with someone on a motorcycle. I couldn't convince my ex-husband to purchase one. He loved base jumping, but said bikes were too dangerous." She rolled her eyes. "Go figure."

Silence.

"Johnnie, er, maybe, one day you can take Emily for a spin," Cam suggested, investing himself into Outlaw's scheme with that idea.

Johnnie hesitated again.

Emily smiled and opened her designer handbag.

Knox noted her manicured nails, a far cry from the first time they'd met. She'd heeded Outlaw's words and made herself more desirable to Johnnie from head to toe.

She held a business card out to Johnnie. "If you ever decide to invite me for a ride, give me a call."

At first, Knox thought Johnnie wouldn't take the card, but then he looked at Emily's face again, a sense of wonder crossing his features. He grabbed the card from her as if he'd change his mind and stuffed it into the pocket of his cut.

Spying the clock on the wall, she frowned. "Goodness, is that the time?"

"Yes," Knox responded. "It's 11:20."

"I'm so sorry," she cooed, offering Knox a hesitant smile. "Can we reschedule? I really have to get going."

Sudden suspicion dropped into Johnnie's face. "I thought your schedule was free?"

"Wanting my itinerary so soon?" she asked with amusing sass.

Johnnie narrowed his eyes. "This doesn't make any fucking sense," he said in a tone that suggested he spoke more to himself than to any of them. He studied Emily again. "Why are you here?" he asked, doubt and desperation framing the words. "You look like...this can't be a coincidence. Christopher just happens to send me to drop something off to Knox and you're here."

"Christopher?" Emily asked in confusion.

"Did he hire you because you look like her?"

"Like who?" Emily responded, blinking.

Knox knew the words didn't muddle her in the least. The second time they'd met to set this up, she'd told him all about how Outlaw compared her to his wife.

"Megan," Johnnie bit out.

"Look, bud, I don't know who the hell these people are," she said with just enough outrage to be believable. "Maybe, you shouldn't take me for a ride. You sound like a lunatic."

Johnnie drew in a deep breath again. "Did Kendall hire you?"

Emily rolled her eyes. "Who is *that*?"

"My wife," Johnnie growled. "The woman who thinks I should sleep with Megan to get her out of my system."

"Golly, gee," Emily spat. "First you rant about a Megan and Christopher, now you're spouting off about a Candy."

"Kendall," Johnnie corrected. "Her name's Kendall."

"In answer to your question—no, your wife didn't hire me." She smiled at Cam.

"It was nice meeting you." She threw Johnnie a dirty look, nodded at Knox, then stormed out of the office.

"Emily's almost a carbon copy of Megan Caldwell." Knox decided to jumpstart the conversation, since Johnnie made no move to speak.

Johnnie swallowed. "Yes." His shoulders drooped. "One of them hired her, Knox. Was it Christopher or Kendall?"

"I'm sorry, Johnnie." Knox met Johnnie's eyes. "It was neither. I've just met her today when she came in for an appointment she made over the phone. It was a cold call, out of the blue. I'd never heard of her in my life."

Cam huffed out a breath. "Knox, I'm done here. I need to salvage what's left of today."

Glaring at him, Cam strolled to the door and left Knox to dig his grave without backup. That wouldn't stop him. He had Outlaw's job to do, and his own agenda to fulfill.

Johnnie sat in one of the waiting room chairs.

"Fuck, Knox."

"You and Kendall are separated," he pointed out. "If you don't have plans to reconcile with her, you need to move on with your life."

Wildness crept into his eyes. "With Emily?"

"She's the next best thing to Megan."

Johnnie leaned his head against the wall and stared at the ceiling. "That wouldn't be fair to her."

"Who? Megan or Emily?

"Emily," Johnnie answered.

Knox nodded, thoughtful. Hadn't they had a similar conversation, a few days ago, in the clubhouse? It was worth repeating, though, especially as a means to an end. "How many times have you compared Kendall to Megan?"

"It doesn't matter anymore." Johnnie turned his head and stared into space. "My marriage is over."

Knox sat in a chair across from Johnnie. "You sure about that?"

His jaw tightened, but he remained silent. If Johnnie filed for divorce and then got with Emily, it wouldn't have the same impact on Kendall. She would already be in the midst of permanently losing Johnnie. But if she had even a smidgeon of hope that her marriage could be saved, then the devastation would be all the greater. All the sweeter.

"My marriage is over," Johnnie insisted after long moments of silence.

"You don't love Kendall anymore?"

Johnnie snapped his attention to Knox. "I will always love her—"

"I thought that was Megan you'd always love."

Johnnie tipped his head back again. "I loved Megan," he said tiredly. "With my whole being. I still love her, but I'm not in love with her. I don't feel about her the way I once did. No one believes me."

"That's because you don't act like it. Of all the women in the club, you're constantly telling Kendall you've went to Megan for advice. Fuck, why not go to Roxanne? Why Megan? For that matter, why not Outlaw? Or Mortician? *Me?*"

"Christopher is always ready and willing to give advice to me. All the guys are."

"I would think I'd be the one you'd seek out, more than anyone else, since you and I have the most in common. For instance, we're both educated."

Johnnie stiffened, then raised his head and offered Knox a cold glower. "Comments like that will get you fucked up, motherfucker."

Knox was merely trying to show Johnnie he identified with him.

"Don't insult me by believing I think I'm above Christopher. I'll—"

"Don't you?" Knox interrupted, cocking his head to the side. "That's why you're so fucking stuck on Megan. You think you're better than him, yet he got her anyway."

Instead of responding, Johnnie stretched out his legs, lit a cigarette, and then pulled out a K-Bar from inside his cut. It was one of the most awesome knives Knox had ever seen, with its silver handle and skull tip.

Dragging on his cigarette, then releasing smoke, Johnnie held it between his fingers and raised the knife up with his other hand. "This blade is special. Unused. Nearly new," he started, offering Knox the grin of a mad man. "Paid a grand for it. The E.W.Stone Knife." He turned it first one way and then the other. Inhaled smoke then exhaled, never once taking his chilling silver eyes off Knox's face. "Do you want your blood to be the first to stain it?"

Knox raised a hand.

"I think you must," Johnnie went on. "You're speaking lies. I don't consider myself above Christopher."

How had things spiraled so far out of control so quickly?

"We're friends, Johnnie," Knox reminded him.

"Then, as your friend, I'll give you this warning. Back the fuck off.

I'm on edge, and that's not a very good place for me to be. My marriage is over," he said for the third time.

It hit Knox that Johnnie repeatedly expressed those words because he was trying to convince himself as much as anyone else.

"I don't need you to spout your bullshit about believing I think I'm better than Christopher. Or that I still love Megan."

Not responding, Knox decided it was in his best interest to steer the conversation back to Emily. He wouldn't search for a way to ease into the topic. With Johnnie out of patience, Knox was out of time.

"Give Emily a call," he pressed. "You and Kendall are separated, so maybe, you need another woman to fill your bed."

"Kendall and I are separated but not divorced."

"True, but seeing someone else might help you to decide, once and for all, if you *do* want to divorce Kendall."

"What if Kendall finds out? What then? Knowing Kendall, she'll find another man to fuck just to spite me."

Johnnie flicked the ashes off his forgotten cigarette onto the floor. But Knox stayed silent, since Johnnie still held the K-Bar.

"If Kendall sleeps with another motherfucker while we're still married, I'll cut his cock off and watch him bleed to death." He squeezed the cigarette out. "On that principle, I refuse to sleep with another woman."

"That's commendable. So don't sleep with Emily. Just spend the time getting to know her."

"Don't you think my life is complicated enough? How would Kendall feel if I brought this woman around?"

"She doesn't have to know," Knox pressed. He deserved a bonus for the pressure he was putting on Johnnie. "Kendall's barred from the club and the grounds. If you and Emily hit it off, and you ended up in a relationship..." His voice trailed off and he shrugged. "You deserve happiness."

"Yes. As do my children." He glanced at the door, then got to his feet. "Maybe, I'll send her a text and invite her for a drink at the club."

Knox stood as well. "Do that," he said, clapping him on the back.

Shoving his knife into a special pocket he had made into his cuts,

Johnnie seemed as if he would talk again. Instead, he took his leave without another word.

Sinking down into his seat, Knox released his breath. He hadn't known he'd been holding it until that moment. That was to be expected with the intensity of the meeting that had just taken place.

Heading to his office, Knox grabbed his phone and went to the keypad, preparing to call Roxanne as he normally did during the course of the day. He froze.

He couldn't call her because she no longer wanted to talk to him.

Instead of calling her, he went to the stored photos and pulled up her pictures. He touched the screen, wishing he'd feel her skin beneath his fingertips, praying he'd hear the sound of her voice, but knowing he wouldn't. Until she forgave him.

He was determined to make that happen.

CHAPTER THIRTY-THREE

JOHNNIE

Leaning against the headboard on the bed in his old room at the clubhouse, Johnnie tipped his bottle of whisky back and drank. Thoughts of Kendall ran through his head. She had such luxuriant red hair and a gorgeous face, with brown eyes that always held a touch of sadness. No matter what he said to her or did for her, she'd never escaped that lost little girl buried inside of her.

Two nights ago, at the family dinner, she'd tipped him over the edge. He hadn't been able to control her. As usual. She'd fucked with CJ one time too many. It hadn't been Christopher's retribution Kendall had to face but Megan's. Johnnie had never seen her more furious. He was so used to defending Kendall, he'd automatically jumped into his role as her protector. For his efforts, Megan had broken his goddamn nose.

Johnnie had followed Kendall home, their kids in his car, to make sure she got home safe. She'd come to his Navigator, face bloodied, bruised, and streaked with tears, so he'd gotten out, left his sleeping children, and escorted her inside. He couldn't remember if they'd closed the entrance door to Kendall's house or not. He'd just been absorbed with *her*. Her theatrics. Her drama. Her self-pity.

Glowering at the ceiling, Johnnie drank more whisky, recalling Knox questioning Johnnie's real feelings for Kendall. It was unfortunate, but Johnnie had loved Kendall with everything in him. He didn't know what he felt for her anymore. Love? Hate? Pity?

Nothing?

He missed her. He missed having their family unit, but she didn't know how to treat children. Kendall didn't know how to treat *anyone*, especially those who loved and needed her.

He was sick to fucking death of her bullshit. If only she behaved... no! Fuck that. If onlys were done. Over with. He'd thought the same thing on so many different occasions. Made excuses for her. *Believed her*.

The blind trust he put in Kendall time and again made Johnnie wonder if he needed his own fucking head checked. Yet, he'd believed in her, given her the benefit of the doubt too many times to count because he trusted her words.

Goddamn her!

Fuck her!

He drank again and sighed, then picked up the book he'd purchased today. It gave insight into Behavioral Personality Disorder. It listed the characteristics of BPD and explored options.

It read like a checklist for Kendall's behavior.

Explosive anger? Check

Fear of abandonment? Check

Out of touch with reality; extreme mood swings; and unstable relationships? Check, check, and check.

Uncertain self-image, suspiciousness?

Impulsiveness?

Self-destructive behavior?

It was *yes, check, fuck yeah*, to all of the above. If she truly had been diagnosed with the disorder, then what? He wouldn't take her word for it. She'd burned him too many times before. Still. *Then what?* If she didn't take her mental health seriously, how could he? The 'why' was easy. He'd do it for their children. They deserved a loving mother. But he'd do it for Kendall. She deserved peace and happiness.

Sitting up, he set the almost-empty whisky bottle on the nightstand. Emily Riser's business card caught his attention. She didn't list her profession, but her phone number was big and bold.

She was a beautiful woman, resembling Megan at first glance. Then, with more clarity, he'd seen hardness in her eyes. Blue but cold as ice.

Johnnie rubbed the back of his neck. Maybe, he wanted to see that. Because she wasn't Kendall. Or Megan. Maybe, he should give her a chance. See how he felt talking to another woman, outside of business, who wasn't a family member or his wife. He rarely spoke to the club girls anymore. Kendall didn't like him to.

He sighed again, then picked up his cell phone and the business card, dialing Emily's number.

"Hello?"

Her voice was clear and authoritative.

"Hi, Emily. This is Johnnie. The biker."

"Oh, heyyyy," she greeted, sounding genuinely happy that he'd called her.

He smiled. "What are you up to?"

"Er, reading some reports," she said around a small cough.

"Really? What type? What business are you in?"

Papers shuffled in the background. "Oh, mercy me! I'm not going to spend our time discussing business. How boring is that?"

Johnnie chuckled. "You're right, sweetheart."

"Are you calling to offer me a ride?"

The question oozed with insinuation. He thought about responding in kind, then changed his mind. "Not now."

"Oh, poo. You didn't even ask what type of ride I wanted."

He'd always been so playful, even when he was just shooting the shit with a woman and had no intentions of fucking her. Since meeting Kendall, he'd changed so much. The more he tried to make her happy, the worst she got. "I can think of several kind to offer," he responded. "Which type do you want?"

She laughed, a carefree sound that represented no ill will, no tears, no acidic words.

Johnnie stretched out on the bed and decided to enjoy this woman's conversation.

CHAPTER THIRTY-FOUR

Megan

The wind blowing threw her hair, Meggie clung to Christopher as he took a curve. Exhilaration shot through her and she tilted her head back, feeling the warmth of the sunshine and the cool breeze. The fumes from the exhaust pipe, the scent of leather and oil, of Christopher, hit her nostrils, and she breathed in deep.

Turning off the main road, Christopher rode to one of two secret entrances to the club's property. It was right at the edge, where the stream that ran by the cave, was clear and shallow.

When Christopher told her they didn't need helmets, she'd known where they were going. It surprised her that he'd gone the long way, but she didn't complain. Handling a bike was second nature to him. Besides, he'd never do anything to put her in danger. If he thought it was safe to go helmetless, then it was.

He'd surprised her this evening by asking her to go for a spin.

Although they didn't go for rides as often as they once did, they still stole those special moments together. Something about his look and his words grabbed her attention.

Last week, he'd burned her dress. She'd been angry until she listened to his reasons. The next morning, she'd stored all her white clothes in the attic. That afternoon, he'd returned them to her closet. When she'd found them back in place, she'd pressed her hand over her heart and laughed through her tears, then sought him out, finding him cleaning his guns in a secured room, specially designed with the kids in mind.

She'd hugged him. "Everything will be fine, Christopher. You'll see."

He'd given her a half-smile and a kiss, then went back to taking care of his weapons.

Now, as he coasted to a halt, planted his feet on the ground for balance, and allowed the bike to idle, Meggie laid her head on his shoulder, breathing in the leather of his cut. The feel of him, his scent, her love for him, ignited her body. They hadn't made love in weeks because he'd been healing.

She touched his side, roamed around to his washboard-hard stomach, going lower still to grip his erection through his jeans. She slid off the bike and got to her feet. Christopher looked at her, his eyes a green enigma, his face rough with five o'clock shadow. She took off her boots and socks, curled her toes at the feel of the cool earth beneath her feet.

Meeting and holding his gaze, she unfastened her leather pants, then slid them down her legs. When they pooled at her feet, she stepped out of them. Christopher lifted her by the waist and sat her in front of him. Grabbing her throat, he bent and smashed his mouth against hers, sweeping his tongue past her lips in hot demand. Her legs wrapped around his waist, Meggie twirled her tongue around his, giving him what he needed and wanted, grinding against him. He grunted, a primeval, animalistic sound that sent a rush of wetness between her legs. She thrust her fingers through his hair, consumed by his fierce possession, intoxicated by his sheer domination. This kiss wasn't gentle and mild and sweet. It was wet and wild, the kind that led to fucking and not lovemaking.

He released his hold on her, inserted his hand between their bodies and ripped her panties away.

"Turn," he ordered.

Desire spread through her body at his rough tone. Once she faced forward, she grabbed the handlebars. A moment later, she felt the smooth head of his cock teasing the entrance of her pussy. He grabbed her hips and thrust fully into her. The vibrations of the idling bike massaged her clit each time it came into contact with the fuel tank. She groaned, squeezed the throttle on the handlebar to heighten the stimulation. He pounded into her, with hard, fast strokes that made Meggie cry out over and over again. Christopher worked her pussy with ruthless skill.

Her screams of pleasure crescendoed as her orgasm hit and her body shook. Christopher pummeled her, then stiffened, pouring into her with a harsh groan.

Suddenly, the silence surrounded her and the vibrations of the bike stopped. Christopher had cut the engine. She remained still, catching her breath, allowing her body and mind to reconnect.

"You okay, baby?"

She nodded. "Perfect."

"You ready to head back?"

Her eyes popped open and she sat up. "I brought snacks for us. Let's commune with nature and talk a bit."

She got off the bike and grabbed her pants, pulling them on, taking care because of her sensitive clit. By the time she put her socks and boots back on, Christopher had found the blanket, beer, Coke, and sandwiches she'd packed in the saddle bag. Together, they arranged the blanket underneath a tree. Meggie sat and leaned against the trunk, smiling as Christopher laid his head in her lap.

She bent and brushed his lips with her own, brushing her fingers through his black hair. The gray entwining with the dark strands made him even sexier.

"You know what the fuck I been thinkin', Megan?" he asked after a sweet silence where they just enjoyed being in each other's presence. "Roxanne and Bailey gettin' married, but the fuckin' ceremonies the last thing on my fuckin' mind."

"I know what you mean," Meggie agreed. "I know plans are being made and nearly a month has already gone by since Knox proposed, but..." Her voice trailed off.

"A fuckin' weddin' the last thing on any motherfucker mind," Christopher finished for her. "Even the motherfuckers the weddin' for."

Meggie nodded. "What's going on? It seems like our ceremonies are always filled with drama. Remember when we were planning our church wedding?"

He looked at her. "Ain't able to forget that bullshit, baby. Cee Cee was on the fuckin' loose. You was left a dead fuckin' head. I almost got my fuckin' ass shot the fuck off."

"But we ended up married anyway. I hope things work out that way for Roxy and Bailey."

"Look at the shit this way. If the ceremony called off, I ain't gotta wear a fuckin' monkey suit."

Meggie giggled. "You're sooo bad, Christopher."

"My ass ain't knowin' how the fuck you got me to fuckin' wear a fuckin' tux more than one fuckin' time."

"I ask you really nice."

"No, you bat your pussy at me and I ain't able to fuckin' resist."

She laughed, bent and kissed his forehead. "How are you feeling?"

"My cock back to it-fuckin-self, so I'm fuckin' fine." He flattened his palm against her belly. "Motherfucker so good I probably fuckin' filled you with my kid."

Unable to stop herself, she kissed him again. "I don't want you to be disappointed if it doesn't happen soon."

He tipped his head up to her, and grinned, a combination of confident smirk and disarming charm. If she'd still been wearing panties, they would've melted off.

"What you gonna be if it take awhile for me to knock you up? Disappointed or relieved?"

"Disappointed," she said without hesitation.

"You sure about that?"

She nodded. "I swear." She sighed. "You'd had a vasectomy, Christopher, so I had to make myself content that we wouldn't have any more children unless we adopted again. A baby this time."

"When we got Diesel he was self-sufficient. Motherfucker ain't needed his ass-wiped. I ain't needed to show him how to piss. He ain't needed to be fed. If we woulda adopted a-fuckin-gain, my vote woulda been for a older kid."

"I understand, but I love the baby stage. Yet, I-I..." Her voice trailed off as she tried to arrange the words in her head. "I don't want to be nothing but a baby-making machine. I also have my figure back."

"You never lost your goddamn figure. You always perfect in my eyes."

She could never express the joy and contentment she felt because she belonged to Christopher. He kept her on a pedestal; never hid the fact that she was the most important thing in his life.

"You was just five or ten pounds heavier."

"My stomach had paunches."

"Your stomach had fuckin' proof you was a ma. Your stomach goddamn beautiful. You kept my kids safe."

"I still have the stretchmarks," she reminded him. "My belly is toned again but there's still reminders of my pregnancies."

Sitting up, Christopher settled next to her, then pulled her into his arms and settled her between his thighs. He kissed the top of her head.

"You a girl, so I guess you gonna worry about your body. Baby, as long as you *you*, I ain't givin' a fuck if you a size two or a size twenty-two. It ain't about your weight, height, or age. It's about your fuckin' outlook on life. It's about what the fuck inside of you."

Drawing her knees up, she rested against her husband. "I know, and I love you all the more for it."

"Suppose I ain't never had my dick snip? You woulda pushed out one or two more lil' motherfuckers by now. Would your belly bothered you?"

Meggie thought about that for a moment, then glanced up. He must've felt her gaze on him because he looked down. The curve of his lips, the sight of his stubble, invited her to lift-up and steal another kiss.

"Hmm," he murmured after she pulled away. "Can't keep your fuckin' hands to yourself this evenin', huh, baby?"

She climbed into his lap and bounced, giggling when his cock stirred. "I've missed having you inside of me."

He bit her chin. "I miss bein' in you."

She rolled her pussy against his growing erection. "I've missed you coming on my tongue."

"What a dirty lil' bitch," he growled, thumbing her aching nipples. "We shoulda went in the cage, then you coulda wore a skirt. I woulda just lifted the motherfucker, took my big dick out and buried it in your lil' cunt."

As he spoke, he held her and guided them to the blanket, lifting himself on his elbows and hovering over her. Bending his head, he stole long kisses, worshipping her mouth with leisure. He slid her shirt up, exposing her belly, and running his fingertips along her heated skin, leaving a trail of goosebumps. He took care in exploring her recesses with sweet, gentle touches that left Meggie gasping.

He slid down her body, parting her thighs with his shoulders, and burying his face between her legs.

Meggie arched in frustration, needing to feel the contact of his tongue without the barrier of leather. "Take off my pants," she whined.

He responded by sitting up and untying first one boot, and then the other before sliding her pants off, aided by her kicks.

He smirked at her. "You wantcha pussy ate bad, huh, baby?"

"Yes," she groaned, lifting her hips. "Please."

"Keep your ass in the air and hold your cunt lips open," he ordered.

Trembling, Meggie followed his directions. He bumped her clit with the tip of his nose before sniffing her seam, teasing her without mercy. Her juices bubbled at the anticipation to feel his tongue on her most sensitive areas. He inserted a finger inside of her.

"Lick me!" she demanded.

His laughter fanned his breath over her wet flesh, but he stopped her torture, fluttering her clit with the flat of his tongue, circling her lips and tickling her fingers because she still held herself open to him. Moving her hands away and taking his finger out of her, he drew her sensitive bud between his teeth and sucked her.

Meggie twisted and screamed, the pain morphing into pleasure, and sending her over the edge. She came with such force she thought she might faint. Instead of giving her a chance to recover, he buried himself inside of her.

"Fuck, baby, you so fuckin' wet," he breathed, masculine and satisfied. Slanting his mouth over hers, he pumped into her.

His lips and tongue tasted and smelled of her, driving Meggie insane. She writhed underneath him. When he withdrew, she lifted her hips to meet his downstroke and rolled against his cock.

"Come in my mouth."

"Fuuccckkk, Megan," he managed, increasing his tempo into her, harsh pants escaping him. "I'm about to nut." He withdrew from her, rose up, and brought his cock to her mouth.

She wrapped her lips around his hot cockhead, and sucked, before opening her mouth and exposing her tongue, allowing his seed to gush out. Drunk from his salty taste, she lapped every last drop, vaguely away of his strangled groans. She massaged his testicles, coaxing a last bit of cum from him. He shuddered, then stretched out next to her and drew her into his arms. Drowsy, she snuggled close to him.

"I shouldna tore your panties," he said into the silence, a few moments later.

Meggie's eyes popped open. "You didn't hurt me and I have more."

"It ain't that, baby." He sat up and lit a cigarette, before continuing. "I got a cock, so I ain't gonna have pussy itch," he offered around plumes of smoke.

Lifting her head, Meggie frowned. "What?"

"Leather and wet pussy equal itchy cunt."

She glared at him, then sat up, her hair falling in tangles around her. "Omigod, that's disgusting."

"Ain't givin' a fuck. That shit real. And you fuckin' know it."

"Christopher, why are we discussing *yeast infections* after making love?"

"Just worried about your pussy, Megan."

Unable to help herself, she laughed. "I appreciate that. As soon as we get home, I'll run and take a shower."

He nodded, satisfied. "Don't wait to get that stuff if you start itchin'."

"Would you shut up?" Meggie said on a sniff.

Snickering, he jammed his cigarette into the corner of his mouth, got to his feet, and straightened his clothes. Meggie thought it best to keep her own off. Just in case...

She grabbed the bag containing the sandwiches, handed Christopher his once he finished his cigarette, and sat down again, and then got her own, before opening her Coke and sipping.

She broke off a piece of her sandwich and held it up to Christopher's mouth. He grabbed the food with his lips, then offered her a bit of his sandwich. They continued this back-and-forth until both sandwiches were gone. Opening a beer, Christopher took a deep swallow.

The conversation before their lovemaking came back to her and she realized she hadn't answered him. "If you'd never gotten your vasectomy, I think I would've given the size of my belly just a passing thought. But, after the procedure, I had to satisfy myself, so I think I built up a bunch of excuses in my head."

"Megan, the last thing I ever wantcha to fuckin' do is think my ass take you for granted. You ain't a baby-makin' machine. You just the girl I love that got a fertile fuckin' cunt. I just gotta look at that motherfucker and fuckin' think about comin' and you fuckin' knocked up."

They laughed together at his words, before he sobered up again.

"I'm so fuckin' lucky that you honor me and treasure me e-fuckin-nuff to keep my babies, Megan." His tone was quiet, almost sad. "That you..." Shrugging, he glanced away, then met her gaze again. "My ass just glad you ain't sayin' you abortin' my kid cuz you tired of bein' pregnant or we got too fuckin' many. If that's what the fuck you wanna do, Ima support you. As long as you happy—"

Crawling into his lap, Meggie kissed him tenderly, then placed a finger over his lips. "Stop," she whispered. "All I've been hearing lately is *as long as I'm happy*. I'm happy because of you. My life has meaning because of *you*. You and our kids are my world, Christopher. And I go to sleep every night and wake up every morning knowing that I have your unconditional love and undying support for any and everything I do. What's gotten into you?"

"Ain't nothin' I ain't said before."

She took his face between her hands. "Hey! Stop this." She kissed him. "I know you think my kidnapping—"

He stiffened and turned his head away. "Don't fuckin' bring that up, Megan."

"It affected both of us in more ways than I can count," she admitted. "But it wasn't your fault. You always do everything in your power to keep me safe."

"Except kill fuckin' Kendall," he growled, lifting her up and setting her beside him. Sidling her a scowl, he finished his beer than opened another bottle. "I hate that fuckin' bitch. She deserve to be fuckin' dead."

Her husband hated to feel powerless. The fact that he'd been unable to prevent her from being taken—and that Kendall had been the catalyst—gnawed at him. He wanted justice. Even the fight Meggie and Kendall had had wasn't enough in Christopher's eyes. He didn't say it, but Meggie knew him. Knew he struggled with the helplessness of their nightmares and the fear that something else might befall her.

"Think of Johnnie and their children. If you kill Kendall—"

"I would do them a fuckin' favor. I want John Boy to meet another bitch."

"He's not going to as long as he's married to Kendall."

"Another fuckin' reason that bitch gotta die."

"*Christopher!*"

"What?" he grouched.

"Tell me you aren't planning to kill her. She's on the No-Kill list. You promised me she'd be safe."

A muscle throbbing in his jaw, he looked away. Alarmed, Meggie grabbed his face and turned him back to face her.

"Don't kill her." Another thought popped into her head, goaded by what he mentioned about Johnnie needing to meet someone else. "And don't interfere in their marriage. How would you feel if someone tried to break us up by introducing me to another man?"

"First of fuckin' all, a motherfucker try to intro-fuckin-duce you to another motherfucker or me to another fuckin' bitch and he or she dead."

"You've been...you know...talking about killing a lot recently."

"Maybe, cuz I ain't fucked up a motherfucker in months. *E-fuckin-specially* the bitch that need fuckin' up."

"Kendall is more to be pitied than to be scorned." A good reminder for herself, too.

"Nope. That bitch deserve nothin' but fuckin' scorn."

This was an argument she wouldn't win, especially given the recent turn Meggie's relationship with Kendall had taken. "Christopher, my breaking point with Kendall, doesn't mean you have free reign to harm her."

"Can't harm a fuckin' demon, Megan. You just exorcise that motherfucker away."

"If you kill Kendall, you'll ruin Roxy and Bailey's wedding plans."

"If that bitch die, that don't mean a fuckin' thing. Added to all the other fuckin' shit that happened on our fuckin' church weddin' day was Val gettin' shot. Did that fuckin' stop *our* fuckin' ceremony?"

Chugging his beer and lighting a cigarette, he got to his feet. "It's gonna be dark soon. Let's fuckin' roll out."

Huffing out a breath, Meggie grabbed her pants and pulled them on. "Leave Kendall alone," she ordered, shoving a foot into her sock in a jerky motion. "Leave her marriage alone. Let her and Johnnie figure things out."

"What the fuck ever."

"Promise me," she insisted.

He stared at her, then released a puff of smoke. "Yeah, Megan," he said, then glared at her, turned on his heel, and stomped to his bike, where he mounted up and started the engine.

Glowering at her stubborn husband, she finished putting her shoes and socks on, then stood. After gathering their mess and grabbing the blanket, she went to Christopher. She stuffed the trash in one of the saddlebags, folded the blanket, and put it away, too.

Once she'd climbed into her seat and he started off, Meggie deflated. It didn't escape her that Christopher hadn't actually given his word about Kendall. Therefore, whatever happened, he wouldn't have broken the promise Meggie demanded.

CHAPTER THIRTY-FIVE

CHRISTOPHER

Wearing safety glasses, Christopher walked amongst the tables in one of the club's warehouses, studying each plant carefully. Even though he'd relegated the day-to-day care of the grows to Slipper and Potter, club members handpicked by Christopher, he still felt as if the hydrogrows were his own personal pet project. At least once a week he visited to make sure the right amount of light from each lamp shone on the plants at the perfect angle. He checked the moisture, looking for any signs that a plant needed to be thrown the fuck out. The clones were thriving in the soil he'd mixed with coco and perlite. Still, he was using *soil*, which meant he had to watch for fungus, bugs, and rot.

The grow house was where he'd first made his own money. Big Joe had allowed him to experiment. The club sent out weed to sell. But Christopher hadn't liked the middleman—paying a grower to supply such a big money maker for them. He couldn't trust the ingredients either. The only thing Big Joe made him promise was he'd not give up if the venture wasn't successful the first time around.

"Fail once, try again," Boss said, a fatherly hand on Christopher's shoulder. "Don't just give up. You can do this. I have confidence in you, boy."

Boss had confidence in him that Christopher himself wasn't feeling. Still, he nodded. "What the fuck I do if I fail a second time?"

"Try a third," Boss said instantly, as if he'd expected the question.

"I ain't gonna keep tryin' somethin' that don't get no traction, Boss."

Boss dropped his hand from Christopher's shoulder and lit a cigarette, all the while studying him with those too-blue eyes. "Three times, Christopher," he said around a puff of smoke. "Try three times. If it doesn't work, then at least you would've tried your damnedest."

Since Boss was fronting the money, Christopher conceded to the man's demand. It wasn't so bad anyway. He was only asking Christopher not to be a fucking loser that gave the fuck up at the first sign of hardship. He stiffened his backbone, prepared to put his all into this project. "I ain't gonna fail, Big Joe," he swore with conviction.

Boss smiled. "I know, son. I'd trust you with my life, my money, my family. You're loyal, dedicated, and a hard worker." He puffed on his cigarette again. "Come on. Let's find some pussy to celebrate your new venture."

The memory running through Christopher's mind sent a pang of nostalgia through him. Not for random pussy. No. He couldn't imagine sinking into no other cunt but Megan's. She was everything he needed.

It was Big Joe that made him so wistful. Christopher had fathered most of the man's grandchildren—except Snake and Hopper's son, Randolph—and married Boss's baby girl. As a result, her life had been put in danger too many fucking times to count. Would Boss still feel the same way about Christopher with that type of statistic? He'd once told Christopher he wouldn't want him with Megan anyway. That was before Christopher had even known her name. It had been easy for him to brush off the comments.

Was it any wonder Boss felt as he had? Megan had gotten *kidnapped* and almost died in a fucking hole-in-the-ground.

Maybe, Boss would've killed him for his negligence. Or took Megan away from Christopher. Presumably, Boss would've still been club president, so Christopher would've had to obey or die.

Even if Boss had still been alive, Christopher knew what he would've chosen. *Death*. He loved her that much. If she ever decided to leave him, he'd step the fuck aside and let her walk away. Just as he'd told her in the forest, his goal in life was to make her happy and keep her safe. But, fuck, he wouldn't survive long without her. She held his heart and soul in the palm of her hands. Big Joe "Boss" Foy's baby girl completely owned Christopher.

Up or down, wherever Boss might be, Christopher knew he was ridiculing the fuck out of him that he was so pussified.

The ringing phone snapped Christopher out of his thoughts. It was Megan's ring, so he answered immediately. He swore his fucking toes had *just* un-fucking-curled after her cock suck this morning.

"'Law."

CJ's voice startled Christopher. Not because his boy didn't call him from time-to-time. It was just that his thoughts had been all about Megan.

He cleared his throat. "Yeah, boy?"

"Whatcha doing?"

"Workin'. Every-fuckin-thing okay?"

"Uh-huh."

CJ fell silent, and Christopher sighed.

"Ima be home as soon as I fuckin' can," he said. "Okay? Ima read to your lil' ass. Hear me?"

"Uh-huh. 'Law," CJ whispered. "MegAnn say her cooking your favorite meal. She want to surprise you. Aunt Bun say that is a good idea. And, 'Law, Mommie ask Aunt Bunny to take us for the night. MegAnn, her say that is a surprise for you, too."

Christopher scowled at the phone. Of course his boy wouldn't know the difference between telling Christopher things he really needed to know and opening his little fucking trap about surprises Megan had for him.

"Don't let your Ma know you told me, CJ," he ordered, thinking of all the ways Megan would drive him the fuck out of his mind tonight, with her pussy, hands, mouth, and ass. "Her feelins gonna be hurt."

CJ was silent a moment. "You mad at me?"

"No." He blew out an agitated breath. "I just...is your Ma there?"

"Her in her office. Mommie left her phone on the counter in the kitchen. I pretend I real tired and Aunt Bunny took me to my room. When her left I got up, though, and did a reeeaaaal quiet foot and come to the kitchen to call you to tell you what Mommie doing and cuz I miss you, 'Law."

Any reprimand Christopher might've given died on his lips at CJ's confession. His heart melted for his boy and he felt like a fucking dickhead for his irritation. "I miss you, too, boy," he said gruffly. "And don't say cuz. It's *because*."

"You say cuz," CJ pointed out.

Fuck him. He'd already started saying shit like *about* when he was home. More and more, when he was out, too, although he did enjoy annoying the fuck out of Knox. He didn't mind talking correct...*ly*...as possible, if it meant his children benefitted. Even if it was a pain in the motherfucking ass. That shit also fucking doomed him to say because instead of 'cuz'.

"CJ!" Megan's call came through the line and Christopher's ears perked.

"Bye, 'Law," CJ whispered. "Gotta go so MegAnn don't find me."

"Put—"

The line disconnected. Just like that his irritation returned. He thought about calling her but he had a lot to see to today. Somehow, distribution day had fallen on the same day as his hydrogrow check.

He'd been having a wonderful fucking time with his girl and their children the past few days. He'd taken Megan for a ride, then found a secluded spot to fuck her on the bike.

He'd taken Megan shopping for another dress to replace the one he'd burned. She'd been upset but when he told her his reasons, she'd hugged him, then stood and removed every piece of white clothing she owned. Some were her favorite pieces, too. She hadn't flinched. Christopher had given himself a good fucking talking to. He couldn't allow his girl not to wear whatever the fuck she wanted. An hour after she'd stored the motherfuckers in the attic, he'd gotten them out and returned them to her closet.

Be-fuckin-sides, since his last nightmare, he hadn't had another one. It was as if his subconscious registered the dick snip flip and knew he'd found a way to protect Megan.

Just as fucking awesome was Johnnie had finally met Emily. It was already Friday, and the motherfucker had been walking around like a fucking zombie. Emily kept Christopher updated, though, and Christopher knew Johnnie had called her twice.

Megan's face rose in his head. Guilt hit him hard. He thought again of calling her, just to hear her sweet voice and hope she never found out about Emily.

If he called Megan, he might pussy out and confess. Besides, he needed to get finished with work, so he could get home for her "surprise" that wasn't a surprise anymore.

He couldn't not communicate with her, though.

Hey, baby, he texted. *I love you and I miss the fuck outta you.*

A minute passed, then two...three...four. Nothing came through. She was probably dealing with their terror of a son.

Unbidden, he wondered what Big Joe would've thought of CJ. He was growing so fast. A part of Christopher wanted his boy to stay a kid forever. He had only Big Joe to go by as a role model for a fatherly figure. While CJ was still young, it was easy for Christopher to make up his own rules. But what about as he got older?

He could've brought his boy with him today. Other than fifty fucking questions, CJ wouldn't have been a problem. In all honesty, Christopher would've enjoyed having his boy with him. But would that be fair? He'd be introducing him to the darker side of club life without CJ being old enough to really have a choice, indoctrinating him into a world that wasn't for everybody. What type of pressure would that put on his boy? If Christopher brought CJ with him to the warehouses and to distribution days, by the time he grew up, the members would expect his son to be a mini him.

Christopher refused to have any of his children live in his shadow. They were their own people with their own personalities. And if *he* didn't expect CJ to be the next "Outlaw", another motherfucker better not think to do it.

His phone indicated an incoming message.

I love you too, he read. *CJ told me he told you about my surprise.*

Christopher re-read the line, then guffawed. The lil motherfucker *always* told on himself to his Ma.

Ima pretend I ain't knowin a fuckin thing Megan

In response, she sent three heart emojis and an emoji blowing a kiss.

Still grinning, he turned his attention back to the plants. It seemed as if Potter and Slipper were doing their job and maintaining the crop sufficiently. Slacking off meant certain death. This warehouse represented a lot of money. Especially since legalization hadn't affected his operation. First, it was geared to medicinal and recreational users.

He snickered. He wasn't either.

And the market was so glutted with "legitimate" growers that their yields were losing value.

But Christopher still had buyers along the Pacific Coast and North of the Border. He still had portions sent to the other chapters, delivered by brothers he personally chose. He had overseas buyers and buyers along the all-important I-95 Corridor, although the badges there were fucking formidable, and harder to pay-off.

Footsteps grabbed his attention and he looked in the direction of the sound.

"Jesus Christ, what the hell do you have in here?" Knox said on a pussified gasp.

Johnnie rushed behind him and offered Knox a pair of safety glasses. "I told you not to comment on what's in here, Knox."

Knox snatched the glasses and held them up. "What are these for?"

"To put the fuck on so these fuckin' lights don't fuck up your fuckin' eyes."

After answering Knox, Christopher glared at Johnnie. Or dumb fucking assfuck. "What the fuck you bring him in here for, motherfucker?"

"He's fine, Christopher." Johnnie slid his own glasses on. "He's about to be a member of the family."

"Yeah cuz space about to be made when I fuck you the fuck up," Christopher snapped. "Besides, him and Roxanne ain't back to-fuckin-gether as far as I fuckin' know."

Knox's entire fucking face drooped.

What had the motherfucker done to piss Roxanne off so fucking much that she called the engagement off? For the last six days, she'd stuck to her story, while Knox stayed close to fucking tears, watching with a begging-dog expression. When she talked to the motherfucker, Knox seemed as if he could sprout fucking wings and fly. She went out of her way to *not* say a fucking word to the motherfucker. Meanwhile, the assfuck stuck close to the club. Closer than he had before the fucking breakup.

"What other illegal operation you have going on here?" Knox asked like the stupid motherfucker he was.

Disgusted, Christopher yanked his glasses off and threw them aside, then stomped past Johnnie and Knox.

"Hold on, Knox," Johnnie complained.

Both him and Knox were hot on Christopher's heels.

Sunlight blasted his eyes when he stepped outside, releasing the door in hopes of slamming the fuck out of both motherfuckers.

"Wait, Christopher," Johnnie called. "Knox, you're not supposed to mention—"

Christopher spun on his heel, forcing Johnnie and Knox to an abrupt halt. They almost collided with him. He stared at Knox. "We ain't got one fuckin' illegal operation goin' on here, motherfucker. My ass just fucked you up a few weeks ago. Don't make me carve your fuckin' eyeballs out and use a vegetable fuckin' peeler on your goddamn tongue."

"You're a fucking savage," Knox gritted.

"And you a fuckin' assfuck, so we fuckin' even."

"Me?" Knox said, outraged. He indicated himself with a sweep of his hand. "I didn't beat myself up. More than once, I might add."

Christopher didn't have time for this shit. He needed to make sure the pills and powder were all accounted for and ready for delivery before the pickups from the support clubs in a few hours.

"Knox accepted us months ago, Christopher. He even apologized," Johnnie reminded him. "Why do you still have such an attitude with him."

"Cuz un-fuckin-like *you*, motherfucker, I know this motherfucker a motherfucker. He ain't meant that shit."

"I did mean it, Outlaw. Do not put words in my mouth."

Shoving Johnnie out the way and ignoring his indignant growl, frustrated as a motherfucker with Johnnie and his dumb fucking choices, Christopher stopped inches from Knox and narrowed his eyes. "What the fuck happen then? One fuckin' minute you makin' up and apologizin' to the club and the next fuckin' moment you puttin' yourself above us motherfuckers again."

Knox stiffened. "What are you talking about? I invited you into my home when it was Roxanne's turn to do the family dinners. I share my expensive alcohol with you. I try to expand your horizons."

"Ain't your fuckin' crib. Unless you suddenly grew a cunt, *you* livin' in the Ma-in-law quarters. You know what Ma mean right? A pussy. As far as I fuckin' know you don't have one. Ain't my fuckin' fault you act like one."

"Whatever!" Knox said in frustration. "My point is you have no reason to believe I didn't mean my apology."

"I don't just fuckin' believe it, assfuck. I know it."

"You're a mind reader now, Outlaw?"

"Nope. Just not a fuckin' stupid motherfucker." Speaking of *stupid motherfuckers*, Christopher glared at Johnnie.

"Hey!" Johnnie blared. "I resent that look."

"Maybe, you pre-fuckin-fer this: You a fuckin' stupid motherfucker. Better?"

Johnnie scowled at Christopher, but he glowered him into pussification. When Johnnie dropped his gaze, Christopher turned the same look on Knox.

"Fuck! Fine!" Knox raised his hands. "This way you handled Jordan's situation made me realize..." His voice trailed off and he shrugged.

"That I ain't leavin' no loose fuckin' ends?"

"Yeah, that," Knox agreed.

"I ain't got fuckin' time for this." Christopher turned on his heel. "You just a elitist motherfucker. Be-fuckin-sides bein' a fuckin' badge at heart. You just ain't able to come to fuckin' terms with our lifestyle."

Kind of like Kendall. Those two belonged together. But Johnnie wanted that bitch and Knox loathed her. It crossed Christopher's mind that Knox might be there to talk to him about the Kendall Mission, but before Christopher could ask if Knox needed to talk to him in private, Johnnie spoke, and stopped Christopher in his tracks.

"Knox has someone who's interested in selling light arms to us," Johnnie said.

Sure he'd misheard, Christopher frowned. "What the fuck you talkin' about, John Boy? What the fuck we know about sellin' fuckin' weapons?"

"Oh, please." Knox snorted. "Don't insult my intelligence with your bullshit."

"Can't fuckin' insult what the fuck you ain't got," Christopher snapped.

"Oh, I like that," Knox responded.

"Ain't givin' a fuck," Christopher responded.

"What we doing?" Val asked, creeping up to them, along with Mort and Digger. "Shooting the shit outside?"

"The Cosmetics together." Digger elbowed Mort. "Plastics would be fucking better for you and Knox, Johnnie, but *Mean Girls* took that."

"*Mean Girls?*" Christopher echoed. "What the fuck your bitch ass watchin' that shit for?"

Digger shrugged. "Bunny like it and watch it a lot."

"That don't mean you got to watch it," Mortician grumbled.

"Says the motherfucker who watch *Frozen* on repeat because Harley like it," Digger retorted.

"Outlaw watch *Cinderella* with Rebel," Mortician complained.

All eyes turned to Christopher and he glowered at Mort. "If I knock your fuckin' teeth out, motherfucker, you ain't gonna be able to repeat my fuckin' secrets."

"Didn't mean to let that slip, Outlaw," Mortician said in a conciliatory tone. "Anyway, we watch the shows with our fucking daughters." He pointed an accusing finger at Digger. "This motherfucker watch *Mean Girls* 'cause of his wife."

"What's *Frozen?*" Johnnie asked, clueless as usual.

"A kid movie." Val threw an exasperated look to Johnnie. "Ryan and Devon watch it. They like it. So do Rory."

"My son likes a movie for girls?" Johnnie asked with indignation.

"That shouldn't matter, Johnnie," Knox said with a frown. "As long as it is age-appropriate. When Grant visits, he plays with Harley's dolls sometimes."

"That's your son and your business. My son should be playing with cars and blocks and...and knives."

Digger leaned against Mortician and shook his head. "You showing you a Cosmetic in more than one fucking way, bruh."

"I told you to stop calling me that," Johnnie said. "Just because both Knox and I had plastic surgery to repair damage doesn't make us *plastic* or give you the right to call us a cosmetic."

"I like Cosmetic better then the Motherfuckers-Outlaw-Broke-and-or-Shot." Digger straightened and shrugged. "But I can call you that, too."

"Fuck you," Johnnie growled, balling his fists.

"Digger, I'm all out my cigarettes," Mortician said, staring at Johnnie in warning. "Give me one of yours."

Knox snorted. "Rude as ever."

Snatching the cigarette Digger held out to him, Mortician threw a foul look to Knox, then returned to staring at Johnnie.

"Back the fuck up off each other," Christopher ordered. "Leave Digger the fuck alone, Johnnie. Mort, Johnnie ain't gonna do Digger nothin'." He was out of patience because they'd strayed so far off the bombshell Johnnie and Knox had dropped before Val, Mort, and Digger walked up. "I wanna know what the fuck gave Knox the fuckin' impression we fuckin' run guns, Johnnie?"

"We were having a conversation about the guns we lost to our brothers," Johnnie answered in exasperation. "Remember them?"

Christopher stared at Johnnie as if the motherfucker had grown two heads. He couldn't fucking believe he'd heard that shit right. He couldn't forget those fucking guns or their assfuck half-brothers. He'd been kidnapped because of them. Them—and Kendall.

Those guns had been a problem from the moment the club purchased them. Christopher had run guns before and was successful, but these motherfuckers had seemed cursed. Just in the purchase, they'd lost fucking money. Since the fucked-up mission where a motherfucker named McCallister had supposedly wanted to buy them—in fucking truth, he'd been a lure to get Christopher in his half-brothers' clutches—Christopher had stayed far the fuck away from running arms.

Fuck him but he was going fucking soft. He was having nightmares like a girl. He was allowing a potentially lucrative deal to slip away like a dickhead...*Fuck*!

He scrubbed a hand over his face, tired from his lack of sleep. "Who the fuck the seller and how much he askin'?" Christopher demanded.

"Joyner Amfinger."

"Never fuckin' heard of him."

"Does that admit you make illicit deals?" Knox pressed.

Yeah, in-fuckin-deed, Christopher was getting soft. Johnnie needed to be fucked up for discussing club business with a non-member. And Knox needed to be fucking grounded for knowing the shit.

Christopher sidled a glance at Johnnie. "Johnnie, you can't keep your fuckin' mouth shut."

"Do you want the details or not?" Knox asked before Johnnie answered.

"*Not*," Christopher snarled. "Not from you, motherfucker. We go to make the fuckin' deal and you gonna have badges swarmin' my fuckin' ass."

"I would never do that!" Knox protested. "I love Roxanne. If the club goes down, she'll be affected, too."

"Your savin' grace is Roxanne love your fuckin' ass," Christopher pointed out.

"Yeah, bruh," Digger added. "The moment we discover *you* fucked up is the moment we kill you."

"Luckily, that hasn't happened. We don't have to kill you," Johnnie said.

Knox glanced at Johnnie and widened his eyes. "What do you mean *we*? I thought you were on my side."

"He on the side of the club, son," Mortician said. "That mean we might've been shooting the shit with you last night but then you fuck up today and we got to fuck you up I don't fucking believe

Roxanne a fucking but when she say she decided marriage wasn't for her."

"Even though you have tattoos and smoke weed and wear a cut, I thought you were more like me, Johnnie."

Ignoring Mortician and staying focused on Johnnie, Knox sounded devastated.

Digger and Mortician looked at each other, then roared with laughter.

"Johnnie a stone fucking killer, Knox," Val said, smiling.

While his boys laughed at Knox's expense, Christopher lit a smoke. "Forget about the fuckin' guns we lost, Knox," he said. "It's in your best fuckin' interest. Don't stick your fuckin' nose in club business when you ain't a member and never will be."

"Suppose I want to become a member?" Knox asked.

Christopher lifted a brow, momentarily stunned at Knox's answer, then he looked at Johnnie, Mort, Val, and Digger. Together, they guffawed.

"That's not that fucking funny," Knox spat after several minutes went by and they were all still laughing.

"Yeah, the fuck it is," Christopher said, wiping tears from his eyes. "You sayin' you wanna be a Dweller like me sayin' I wanna be a badge." He howled again. "That shit just ain't ever fuckin' happenin'."

"You people are so juvenile," Knox complained.

"And you got a fuckin' stick up your fuckin' cock," Christopher fired back, his humor leaving him. "As well as your fuckin' ass."

"At least let me bring an offer to him," Knox said, not responding to Christopher's words.

"No." Christopher spoke the word with a fucking finality Knox should've picked up on.

"No? Just like that? No?"

"Be happy Outlaw said no, Knox," Mortician said. "If, somehow, she telling the truth about her leaving you and you get her to take you back, you still not marrying my momma-in-law if you making shady fucking deals."

Knox's mouth dropped open. "You can't be fucking serious."

"The fuck I can't be. Roxanne met you being a straight-laced motherfucker. She not expecting you to roll to our side. Don't want her in no danger because you get in over your fucking head."

"As her son-in-law, you don't put her in danger?" Knox sneered.

"Sure the fuck don't," Mort answered with confidence. "I know what the fuck I'm doing. You don't. Sometimes, it's all about plain fucking luck. Motherfuckers still get the drop on you no matter how fucking skilled you are."

Knox stiffened. "I was a cop, trained to shoot and take down bad guys."

"Bruh, Knox," Digger said woefully. "You not helping your cause."

"So you're admitting you're bad guys?" Knox asked, scowling between them.

"How about you answer that fucking question strapped to the table in the meatshack?" Mortician snapped.

"You're getting a little big for your britches, Mortician," Knox said. "You demanded you and Bailey share a wedding with me and Roxanne. You told me I couldn't live in her house. Now, you're threatening my life. Again."

"Knox doesn't mean any of this," Johnnie inserted, looking at each of them. "In his line of work, he meets a lot of people. One was this man in question."

"Motherfucker might be a fuckin' cop or any-fuckin-thing," Christopher snarled.

"He's not," Knox said stiffly. "I swear I only want to help."

Christopher didn't trust Knox one fucking bit. "Why?"

"I want to prove to Mortician that I'd never duck out on Roxanne. I want to show all of you that I'm willing to put my freedom on the line to be with her."

"Roxanne ain't gonna want you to do that shit," Christopher pointed out.

Knox nodded. "All of you are very important to her. Let me do this, Outlaw. And when the deal is made, you'll see I'm trustworthy. Then, she'll see it, too, and take me back. I can move back in with her before our wedding. See? I take care of you all and, in return, you get the hell off my back."

"Your fuckin' ass ain't gettin' to set fuckin' terms," Christopher said.

"Besides, you don't make these types of deals overnight," Val said. "There must be something more than that involved."

Knox looked from Val to Christopher. "Joyner needs to get rid of the guns. AKs will be a loss leader. The Death Dwellers and Amfinger will do good together.

"You fuckin' talkin' what might be club fuckin' business without fuckin' permission?" Christopher asked. "With-fuckin-out bein' patched the fuck in?"

Johnnie winced. It was quick but Christopher still saw it. Fuck, Kendall was a fucking busybody but she got that shit from Johnnie's dumb ass. He opened his fucking mouth too fucking much. Worse, it was to motherfuckers who couldn't shut the fuck up and keep the shit they discovered to themselves. No, Kendall and Knox used the information Johnnie provided to try to manipulate the club into doing what the fuck *they* wanted done.

Christopher tossed his cigarette away, grabbed Johnnie by the collar and dragged him closer to Knox. "Text me this motherfucker number, Knox. *Ima* talk to him my-fuckin-self."

"You got—"

Christopher grabbed Knox and banged his head against Johnnie's, stepping back when they fell to the ground, knocked the fuck out, side-by-side like the stupid motherfuckers they were.

He looked at Val, who stuffed his hands in his pockets and began whistling some off-fucking-key tune. His gaze roamed to Digger, who raised his hands, as if he was in a fucking holdup. Mort merely sighed, not saying a word as Christopher stormed the fuck away.

CHAPTER THIRTY-SIX

Roxy

The banging on her door doubled the pressure in Roxy's head, and she forced herself into a sitting position. It seems as if she'd been living in a never-ending nightmare for the last week. After putting out the fire in Outlaw's bathroom, she'd made it to her house, shut the door, and began sobbing all over again. The ending of her relationship with Knox devastated her. His words replayed in her head, over and over again, seeming to confirm the horribleness of Duke's opinion of her.

She tried to act normal by smiling and joking, as if her heart hadn't been torn out. It was so hard, especially during her times at the clubhouse. Knox seemed to be in the main room for dinner more than he'd had in all the months they'd been together.

Standing, Roxy rubbed her eyes. Alone at night, she cried so much her lids were painful to the touch.

"Roxanne, open this fucking door," Mortician yelled, pounding on her door again.

Her quarters were her private sanctuary, the perfect place to hide until the time came for her to get back to the clubhouse to start dinner. She was uninterested in seeing anybody, especially her overprotective son-in-law. She just wanted silence. Maybe, a day or two on her own, where she didn't have to go to the clubhouse, would help her. Yet, she didn't have that luxury. Not if she wanted Knox to live.

In all honesty, she shouldn't have been looking as if she had a broken heart. If Mortician saw her now...Before she decided on the story she'd give to him for why she looked such a hot mess—she didn't need a mirror; a woman just *felt* her own wrecked appearance—the door opened.

She hadn't heard any wood splintering, so she knew he'd used the spare key. Sauntering into view, Mortician spied her and halted, narrowing his eyes. He gave her the once over, then folded his arms and glared at her.

"What the fuck wrong with your ass?"

Sliding her gaze away, Roxy shrugged. "I was really tired, so after I finished breakfast, I came home for a nap," she told him. The words sounded truthful but, to her, felt wooden. Fake. Just as her engagement to Knox had been. He hadn't wanted to marry her in the first place. He'd been backed into a corner by the boys.

"You sure you broke it off with Knox?" Mortician asked with skepticism.

Roxy nodded and turned away, heading to her kitchen. She started clearing away the dishes she'd used for herself this morning, setting them in the sink to rinse them out and place them in the dishwasher.

She did neither. Only stared at the dishes, unable to gather the motivation for such a simple task.

A hand touched her shoulder. She didn't jump, though. She knew Mortician was there.

"Why you broke it off? The real reason."

She'd been avoiding all the boys, the women too, to evade a detailed explanation. After her simple, '*I decided it wouldn't work*', they hadn't pressed her. They'd left her alone.

Unfortunately, her time was up.

She shrugged, determined to keep her cool, her pain deep. She didn't want to have this conversation, now or ever. Yet, she couldn't keep avoiding it, so she settled on a partial truth. "He wanted me to sign a prenup." She made herself laugh. "That shit isn't my style, so I told him to go fuck himself."

"He finally fucking told you about that dumb shit," Mortician grumbled.

"Yep, sugar. He finally told me." It didn't surprise Roxy that Mortician knew. She'd known he'd had his reasons for his actions.

Guiding her by the shoulder, he turned her to face him, backed up, and slouched, all the better to study her.

"You sure that's all that happened, Momma-in-law? I knew you were going to be fucking furious. But *you* broke it off, so shit shouldn't make you look so devastated or walk around like a fucking zombie."

"It was that prenuptial agreement and his admission that he didn't want to marry me in the first place. It doesn't mean I stopped loving him. I just don't want any motherfucker who has to be threatened into proposing to me."

So true. Had that been the end of it, she would've been one mad bitch. His *words*, though... His view of her...

Mortician dropped his hands and went to the coffeemaker. The pot was empty. "Sit down," he instructed. "Let me make you some coffee."

"I don't want anything, except time to myself."

Pausing, Mortician kept his back to her before heaving and turning around. "What the motherfucker did to you?"

"Nothing, baby," she lied, lowering her lashes and moving to the stool at the counter.

As she sat, he stalked over, halting across from her, on the other side of the counter. "Knox was a frustrated motherfucker, wanting to have my rules lifted. I know that contributed to the argument. My boys told me they heard y'all shouting after you fucking *sneaked* to catch up to Knox."

She scowled at him. "I'm a grown woman, Mortician. If I wanted to talk to Knox, that's my business."

Tapping his fingers on the counter, he studied her. "If you broke up with that motherfucker only because of the shit you said, you'd be cross with my fucking ass for interfering. The fact you not, proof that more shit than what you admitting to happened."

Frustration filled Roxy and she glared at Mortician. "I'm not one of your fucking marks that you interrogate before you decide on my fate."

He smiled at her, but it wasn't nice. She'd heard rumors about the club enforcer—Mortician, her son-in-law, Bailey's husband, her grandchildren's father—but she'd never witnessed his chilling countenance firsthand.

"You fucking crushed, Roxanne. It's written all over your goddamn face. *You* not a mark, but that motherfucker is. I warned him not to fuck with you. Fucking with you, fuck with Bailey, and not a motherfucker in this world fuck with my woman."

"What do you want me to say?" she shouted. "I'm not giving you the go ahead to fuck Knox up."

"I'm not asking you for permission," he shot back. "I don't like seeing you like this. Eyes all red and swollen, like you have a fucking industrial-grade pink eye that's so contagious your fucking eyes popping out of your goddamn head any second. Even your nose and lips look fucking swollen. You well fucking past a hot mess. You more like a blistering cauldron of fuckedupness."

"Boy, fuck you," Roxy growled. "In a minute, my foot is going to be a blistering cauldron straight the fuck up your goddamn ass." She jumped to her feet. "What the fuck do you want me to say? Knox and me are over. That doesn't mean I don't love the motherfucker. We just don't fucking belong together."

"*ROXANNE!*"

The earsplitting call boomed into the house. Lawd, Jesus! Was Knox fucking insane?

"*ROXANNE!*" he cried again.

Mortician rolled his eyes. "Some motherfucker been watching too much of *A Street Car Named Desire.*"

"*PLEASE COME BACK TO ME! I LOVE YOU!*"

Amusement lit Mortician's eyes.

"Not a fucking word," Roxy ordered over her shoulder, hurrying to the door. She needed to stop this disaster-in-the-gruesome-making.

Before Knox said something he shouldn't, she needed to get matters in hand.

Outside, she found Knox sitting in a chair on her porch. It was the one he always sat in whenever they enjoyed fresh air in the mornings or evenings.

His amber gaze fell on her and he drew in a shuddering breath. "Roxanne," he breathed.

"Hey, sugar."

He swigged from a bottle of scotch. His eyes lit up and he tried to stand, but dropped back into his seat.

"I'll do anything," he slurred, staring at her as Johnnie, Outlaw, Val, and Digger arrived.

Val's eyes widened as he stared at her. "Fuck, babe, what the fuck happened to you?"

"That's not how you talk to a woman, asshole," Johnnie chastised.

"What you mean, John Boy?" Digger countered. "She not a woman. She Roxanne."

"She got a pussy, motherfucker," Knox snarled, drunk off his ass. He almost sounded like one of the guys. As if he belonged in the club with the rest of them. "That makes her all woman." He slammed a fist against his chest, his attitude quite a distance from his usual walk on the uppity side of life. "*My* woman."

He looked at her again. Regret and pain shone in his eyes.

"Knox," Roxy blurted, "come inside so we can talk in private."

He shook his head and swayed where he sat.

Digger laughed. "Motherfucker full."

Outlaw and the others snickered. By now, Mortician had joined them on the porch, the only one who didn't look amused.

"You're not ignorant, Roxanne," Knox started. "Or classless. Or a gold digger."

Her insides quaking at his words, she laughed, high-pitched and loud, then rushed to him, snatching the bottle from him mid-drink. Liquor sloshed all over. "Shut the fuck up, Knox," she whispered. "If you want to walk away alive."

"No!" he yelled, blowing fumes of alcohol in her face. "I don't want to live if I don't have you." He pounded his chest again. "You're not a gold digger, my love. I've been such a stupid motherfucker."

"In a minute, you're going to be a *dead* motherfucker," she snapped under her breath, so he alone could hear her.

As if that worked.

On cue, Mortician said, *"Gold digger?* What the fuck he talking about?"

"He's just repeating what Duke said to me," she blurted, turning to face Mortician, and shielding Knox with her body.

"No, my love! It was *me*. All me. I called you so many horrible names. I don't deserve to live. I don't want to live if you won't forgive me."

The intakes of breath and heated curses alarmed her.

"I forgive you, Knox."

"NO! NO!" He pointed at her. "You listen to me, Roxanne," he slurred. "You're not a cougar who is trying to lead me around by my dick. You're not trying to force these degenerates on me. I know you don't think I'm Santa Claus."

"Knox—" she started.

An arm wrapped around her waist. She struggled against the iron-hold, winning her freedom. On her feet again, she met Outlaw's grim look.

"Time for us to take the fuck over, Roxanne," he said.

Mortician yanked Knox to his feet. Roxy rushed to his other side and grabbed his hand, tugging with all her might.

"No!" Knox cried. "Let them kill me. I don't deserve to live."

"You sure the fuck don't," Mortician answered, yanking Knox toward him.

Roxy stumbled. Outlaw's quick reflexes allowed him to steady her.

"This is personal shit, boys. This is between Knox and me. It's not your business," she added, because nothing she said seemed to matter. She rushed to Knox again as Mortician bent and started to toss Knox over his shoulder.

"Not our business?" Outlaw lifted her again, set her down, and then blocked her way. "What the fuck that mean?"

"Yeah, Rox," Digger added, "me and Mort fucked up our own old man. The club helped us get him and that was fucking personal."

"The fuck it was," Outlaw said in a hard voice. *Harder*, since he'd been sounding pretty fucking cold for the last several minutes.

"Prez, for you it wasn't," Digger responded. "For me and Mort? Yeah. If Sharper didn't come in our momma we wouldn't been born. That make it personal as a motherfucker."

Snickering at the discussion of cum and mothers, Mortician started down the steps, a limp Knox thrown over his shoulder. Roxy didn't know if he'd passed out or if Mortician had knocked him out.

"John Boy," Mortician called, the words floating over his shoulder, "stay with Roxanne, while we work on Knox in the meatshack."

"No, no, no!" Roxy cried, starting down the steps to stop this death march.

Johnnie blocked her, allowing Mortician to continue on, with Outlaw, Digger and Val behind him. Only one way she could stop them.

Later, when Knox was safe, she'd send him away. Only a drastic reversal would sway her to marry him, so this was a temporary fix to save his life.

"Stop them, Johnnie. I love Knox. We just had a misunderstanding." She heaved in air. "I still intend to marry him."

Johnnie's eyes widened. He studied her a moment, so she nodded, to reaffirm her statement.

"Fuck," he growled, and turned on his heel. "Call Meggie," he ordered, then took off running.

"This can't be right," Meggie mumbled, using the syringe to suck up pee from the cup, then squeezing drips out onto the stick. Sitting on the toilet, she put the timer on her FitBit, ignored the other pregnancy tests that told the tale, and waited.

Days ago, she'd told Doc Will that she needed to see her—the night of Meggie's fight with Kendall—but she hadn't gotten around to it. A visit was imperative now.

She kept putting off her visit to Doc Will, but she could no longer do so.

The urge to vomit had awakened her early this morning, so she'd rushed to the bathroom and gave into the nausea demon.

She hadn't been feeling well for a few days. Since the fight, she'd been dragging.

On so many levels, that confrontation had just devastated Meggie. She'd taken up for Kendall, *against her own beloved CJ,* and that witch still put her hands on her child. Even when she said she wouldn't, Meggie had given Kendall chance after chance. For every reaction Kendall had, Meggie had felt an action had precipitated it.

But Kendall would never change. She didn't take her illness serious. She didn't take her family into consideration. And she didn't look toward the future. All in all, she was so poisoned with hatred that it would take drastic actions for Kendall to change.

That realization, too, had devastated Meggie. Then the news of Roxy and Knox's break-up had taken precedence and Meggie had set her hurt over Kendall aside. On the days she hadn't felt well, she'd chalked it up to stress and worry.

This morning, after vomiting, she'd rinsed her mouth and washed her face, then stumbled back to the room and climbed into bed. Christopher was gone, and she'd been too sick and tired to inquire about his whereabouts.

A few minutes later, he'd called her and asked if she wanted breakfast in bed or if she was coming downstairs. Not wanting to worry him, she said she'd be down in a few minutes and then hung up.

As she laid in bed, trying to will the nausea away, she'd realized that this was the third time this week she'd thrown up in the morning.

For her, that meant one thing. Yet, it was impossible. Christopher had his vasectomy reversal, a month ago, and they'd resumed making love two weeks lagter.

Hysterical laughter escaped Meggie. That meant she'd gotten pregnant *before*.

It was history repeating itself, only with a flipped script. When he'd gotten the vasectomy, she'd found out she was pregnant. Now...now...*this*.

If it wasn't so...so...frustrating, it would be hilarious.

After forcing herself to dress and go downstairs, she'd put on a brave face, until Christopher went to the clubhouse. Then, she'd texted Bunny to go to the drugstore and buy pregnancy tests. Three or four different types. She'd returned with six.

And every last one of them came back positive.

She was pregnant. She loved babies and wouldn't mind having ten or twelve or...or...however many she was blessed with. On the other hand, despite all the needless trouble Christopher had gone through, another pregnancy would only stress him out more. He'd have her to worry about, as well as the baby she carried.

Her agreement to his plan had been given after much consideration. He was taking her kidnapping so hard, and all Meggie wanted to do was help him.

It didn't matter that she needed help herself. This was the closest she'd consciously come to dying. When she'd been shot in the chest, she'd been unaware the gravity of her injuries. This time, though, she'd *felt* her life draining from her and her soul slipping away.

She'd known the end was near.

A shiver went through her and her nostrils flared. She slid her gaze to the door that led to her closet. Her hands trembled and she clutched the material of her shirt. A small pocket-knife hid amongst her purses. All she had to do was get it, sink it into her flesh...and regain control.

Meggie closed her eyes. She'd fail Christopher, though. One of his greatest fears was that something would tip Meggie over the edge and send her back to self-harm.

Her kidnapping had definitely triggered her. She was doing everything possible to return to normalcy.

Trying to go out on her own had been a major fail. Still, the goal had been so important to her. How would she ever feel normal, *safe*, if she feared her own shadow?

Her fear didn't help Christopher at all. Now, she had to tell him she was pregnant. She really, really, *really* didn't think the news would ease his mind. Honestly, she didn't think he was ready for her to be pregnant. Not yet. She was sure he'd believed they'd have six or eight weeks before she dropped the news on him.

Seeing the same results on the last test, Meggie sighed. One more time, she'd sneak out, arrange her thoughts, then find a way to tell her Christopher. Her words would have to soothe her husband. Although she didn't believe he was ready for her to be pregnant yet, neither would he be pleased at the timing. Because of his unnecessary pain and suffering, he might show his displeasure to his urologist. In the meatshack.

She'd find the right...The pealing of Roxy's ringtone broke into Meggie's thoughts, and she grabbed her cellphone.

"Hey—"

"Meggie, baby, they are going to kill Knox. You have to stop them!"

"What—"

"Go now. They should be nearing the walkway in front of your house soon. I want to marry Knox. Tell them!"

"Okay, bye," Meggie breathed, hanging up the phone without a goodbye, and racing down the hall, then three flights of stairs.

"MegAnn?" CJ called in confusion.

"Not now, potato," Meggie yelled, reaching the front door and yanking it open.

"Meggie?" Bunny cried.

Meggie didn't have time to stop and explain. The little parade was reaching the walkway beyond the gates of her house just then.

Mortician, with Knox thrown over his shoulder, paused as Johnnie stepped in front of him.

"Move your ass, John Boy. You constantly stopping me just delaying the inevitable."

Sliding to a halt so fast she stumbled against the iron gate, Meggie met Christopher's gaze.

"Fuck," he growled. "Don't say a fuckin' thing, baby. This motherfucker hurt Roxanne."

"That may be, but she still intends to marry him," Meggie told him.

Mortician frowned. "No, the fuck she don't."

"She does, Mort," Meggie countered.

"I do." Roxy screeched to a halt on the curb in her purple Navigator. "You boys got this all wrong. I was going to tell all of you that Knox and me been working things out."

Meggie sent Christopher a pleading gaze and he glared at her. She had sway in this matter because it involved their family. He knew it. She knew it.

They *all* knew it.

"Fine, fuck." Mortician dropped Knox to the ground like a sack of potatoes.

Her hands flying to her mouth, Meggie squeaked.

"This motherfucker still living at the club." Mortician pointed to Knox, then rounded on Roxy. "And I fucking swear if I see one more fucking tear in your eye because of him, I'm cutting his fucking head off."

Without waiting for a response, he started to stomp away.

"Wait!" Roxy called in outrage. "You can't just leave him there."

"Motherfucker heavy." Mortician's tone indicated the blatant lie, as he marched on.

"We too fuckin' outta shape to fuckin' deal with him," Christopher announced with a snicker, winked at Meggie, then signaled the guys to head to the club.

Leaving Knox on the ground. *Alive.*

CHAPTER THIRTY-SEVEN

Roxy

Rushing to where Knox lay sprawled on the ground, Roxy checked for injuries by laying her hand on Knox's forehead and cheek, touching his chest, threading her fingers through his hair.

Meggie knelt at Knox's side. "Is anything broken?"

"I don't know," Roxy responded, relieved to feel the strong beat of his heart.

"Oh my god!" Zoann said around puffs of breath. It was obvious she'd run there, carrying a medical bag. She switched places with Meggie.

"Mama!" Bailey cried, hurrying over and throwing her arms around Roxy's shoulders. "I came as fast as I could. I was home. I can't believe I didn't hear or see anything."

Bailey and Mortician's house sat in front of Roxy's quarters, so it didn't surprise her that Bailey hadn't heard anything. Her front door faced the back of the main house, connected by a covered walkway, and bordered by the natural beauty of the forest.

Roxy nodded. "Where are Harley and Lou? You can't leave those babies alone."

"They're with Cash and Stretch," Fee commented, as she arrived on the scene.

"Yeah, and Meggie's and my kids are with Diesel," Bunny announced, walking out of the gate.

"I not," CJ announced, squeezing next to Meggie and frowning at Knox. "Why Uncle Knox sleeping on the ground?"

"He fell," Meggie answered. "Stay close to Mommie so Aunt Zoann can check him out."

All the girls gathered around Knox as Zoann listened to his heartbeat, checked him for broken bones, and felt his head. Even though Kendall had more than fucked up, Roxy missed her being there amongst the rest of the women.

Knox moaned, and Zoann assisted Roxy in lifting him to a sitting position. His head lulled back, but they caught him in time before he fell back again.

Zoann shone a small light in his eyes. "Follow the light," she instructed with a bedside manner that contradicted her general no-nonsense attitude. Completed with that test, she pressed her fingers in various spots on Knox's head. One particular spot she touched made him moan again.

"I want Roxanne," he mumbled.

"She's here, baby," Zoann soothed.

"She left me." Knox sounded pitiful. "I love her."

Unable to hear those words from Knox without being affected by them, Roxy stood. Maybe, he did love her. Just not enough.

"ROXANNE!"

"Roxy is right here, Knox," Fee said. "She hasn't gone anywhere. She merely stepped back."

"Tell her to take me back," Knox begged. "I didn't mean anything I said."

Meggie glanced in Roxy's direction. "Oh no. That's why they were taking him to the meatshack." She frowned. "But...but what did he say to you for Christopher and the rest of them to have such a reaction?"

"I called her a gold digger." Knox sounded close to tears. "I told her she just wanted my money. I told her to live the rest of her life in wretched loneliness without me or my money."

Humiliation returned, lurking just beneath the surface of Roxy's emotions since the argument. "Shut up, Knox!"

"He said those things to you?" Zoann asked, aghast.

"Yeah, baby, but—"

Zoann released Knox's head, allowing it to hit the ground.

Squat!

"Oh, shit," Bunny blurted as Knox's eyes rolled back in his head and he lost consciousness all over again.

"Oh, Mama." Bailey hugged Roxy again. "Why didn't you tell us?"

Because she hadn't known how to say the words to the girls. Knox's accusations strengthened Duke's claims about her.

No! She wouldn't address those thoughts now. There were more urgent matters at hand.

Standing, Zoann snapped her medical bag closed and dusted off her legs.

"We can't leave Knox unattended," Roxy protested.

"The fuck we can't," Zoann snapped.

"Nope, we can't," Meggie insisted. "He needs attention."

Offering Meggie the stink eye, Zoann knelt again. "He has a concussion," she grouched.

"We need to get him inside," Roxy said.

Knox. was a big man, tall and well-built, with well-defined abs that she loved touching. She couldn't see much of his toned body now because he was dressed in trousers and a button-down. That didn't matter, though. His muscles were imprinted in her mind.

"Get 'Law, MegAnn," CJ instructed. "Him can get Uncle Knox inside." He tipped his head back to see if his mother agreed.

Meggie grinned at him and ruffled his hair. "We don't want Daddy or any of your other uncles near Uncle Knox," she said.

CJ nodded, then thought for a second. "Aunt Kenda...*Kendall*," he corrected. "Aunt Ken*Dall*?"

"You know how to say her name, potato."

"I like Aunt Kenda better," CJ informed Meggie. "Aunt Zo let me call her Aunt Zo and don't get mad and try to beat me, Mommie. Why Aunt Ken*Dall* gotta be so mean?"

Meggie stared off into the distance and her chin wobbled. "She doesn't mean to be, CJ. Aunt Kendall has a lot of problems."

"Yeah," Zoann agreed as Knox moaned again. "Bitch crazy."

"A psycho cunt like 'Law say?" CJ asked.

"Christopppphhheeerrr," Meggie moaned, then gave her son a sharp stare. "Do *not* call Aunt Kendall those names. It isn't nice."

"Why, MegAnn? 'Law say those names and he nice."

"Daddy is very nice," Meggie agreed. "He's also a grown man. You aren't. You're a little boy and you have to respect adults."

"What were you going to say about Kendall, bud?" Bunny asked after a moment of silence while CJ considered Meggie's words.

"'Law say herlike a big, strong man tree." He ignored their collective gasps. "Don't that mean Aunt Ken*Dall* coulda pick up Uncle Knox and bring him inside?"

"No, of course not!" Meggie said in annoyance. "Kendall is as delicate as the rest of the women."

CJ grinned at her. "Mommie beat that bitch ass!" he said with glee. "'Law say that. Him talk about it a lot."

"Let's see to Uncle Knox," Meggie ordered on a sniff. "Later, you, me and Daddy are sitting down and talking."

"Mama, what happened?" Bailey asked as CJ turned to Meggie, buried his face against her stomach and sniffled. "When you called, the only thing I got from you was that Lucas was going to kill Knox."

"I want to be dead," Knox whined. "If I can't have Roxanne, I don't want to live. Outlaw is an ignorant idiot and I fucking hate that you drive around in that ugly purple Navigator, but I don't care. If you want a stupid asshole in our family, I don't care."

"Shut up, mudna fucka!" CJ yelled, struggling to get out of Meggie's hold. "'Law *not* stupid. 'Law smart!" He strained, grunting in his efforts. "Let me go, Mommie! Ima make this mudna fucka bleed."

"Oh, shut up, Baby Thug," Knox slurred. "You're lucky Roxanne loves you, or I'd take a belt to your little ass."

"You think?" Meggie glared at the back of Knox's head. "You touch my son and I'll take a belt to *you*."

"Somebody needs to get control of that fucking kid and it isn't you, Blondie."

"Knox, that's enough!" Roxy demanded. "You can't want my fucking ass if you're still being an insulting motherfucker."

"Roxanne?" Knox breathed, attempting to stand. Between the alcohol and the hits, he fell flat on his ass each time he tried to get to his feet. "I love you. Please forgive me. I didn't mean anything I said. I'm just so frustrated and that's the way I handle it."

He wasn't sober or coherent enough for an in-depth conversation, but she needed to get through to him, so he'd stay out of the meatshack.

Roxy knelt in front of him and took his hand. Though he looked haggard and drawn, in her eyes, he was still beautiful. She brought his hand to her face and rubbed her cheek against his palm, her eyes filling with tears again. "Knox," she whispered, gliding her fingers through his silky hair. "I didn't question why you proposed to me. I just thought it was because you loved me. That's what I wanted to believe. I saw no problem with Mortician separating us until after the wedding because..." Her voice trailed off. They'd had this conversation too many times.

He got to his knees. If she hadn't grabbed him and wrapped her arms around his waist, he would've toppled over again.

"The truth is you never wanted to marry me." Her voice caught.

"Oh, Mama," Bailey said again.

Knox pulled Roxy closer. "Roxanne, please believe me. *Please*. I do want to marry you. *Please*. Take my ring back."

The ring. Right. She'd felt it was bad luck from the moment he'd put it on her finger.

"Please. I'll give you my fortune. I'll do anything you ask of me."

"Knox, there are some things you just don't recover from," she told him. "And the things you said to me...*Hurt*."

Knox bowed down and wrapped his arms around her thighs. "Please, baby. Please. Forgive me. I tried to drink the horrible words away. I tried to drink away the memory of you giving me my ring back.

I tried to drink away my loneliness. I don't even know how I got home. I might've walked. But I don't care!" He tightened his hold on her. "Please!"

"Knox, *stop*! You're embarrassing yourself."

"I embarrassed you. I deserve to have the same happen to me."

Roxy tugged at his shoulder. "What happens when you get frustrated again? I'm not going to live my life listening to your putdowns and insults because you're fucking frustrated. I'm not going to live my life wondering if you married me because you really loved me or because you were afraid to die."

Getting to his knees again, he took her face between his hands. "You don't want us to end. I can see it. I know you've been crying. I know how you look after Duke hurts you."

Roxy yanked her face away and guided him to a sitting position and then stood. "You also know what he says to crush my soul. It was unworthy of you to imply the same things. He sees me as garbage, and so do you."

Knox laid on the ground. "That isn't true. I see you as a beautiful, smart, witty, strong woman. Just tell me what I have to do?"

"Nothing," she reiterated. "What can you do? We have nothing in common, even though I tried to believe otherwise. These boys are all tatted up. They wear leather. They ride Harleys. They—"

"*They* have nothing to do with *us*, Roxanne," he interrupted, sounding so pathetic Roxy almost felt sorry for him.

"They do, sugar," she said sadly. "*They* are the main problem you have with *me*. You put yourself above them. They are my family. *Kendall* is my family. You think I don't know how much you dislike her? *Outlaw* is like a son to me. *Mortician* protects me just the way he protects my baby girl. It might not strictly be for my ass, but that doesn't matter. He still watches out for me. I'm part of this club, this world, and you don't want to be."

A burst of male laughter and amused voices carried on the wind. Roxy went on alert. The Fearsome Five were returning. To finish Knox off?

"Do you have the ring with you?" she demanded.

"In my pocket," he told her. "I'll keep it with me until the day you put it back on your finger."

"That day is today," she rushed out, as Mortician, Outlaw, Johnnie, Digger and Val appeared on the pathway, carrying bottles of alcohol and talking amongst themselves as if they hadn't been planning a gruesome murder. She patted Knox's shirt pocket.

"It's in my left trouser pocket," he told her.

She leaned over him, shoved her hand in and retrieved the diamond engagement ring.

Knox groaned. "You feel so good leaning against my cock. I need to fuck you so bad."

His dick jumped and she moved away, refusing to acknowledge any desire. She jammed the ring back on her finger just as the guys reached them.

"You awake, motherfucker," Mortician chortled.

"Lucas, what are you doing?" Bailey demanded.

Mortician hesitated. "What you mean, pretty girl?"

Bailey placed her hands on her hips. "You were going to *kill* Knox. That's what I mean."

Later, Roxy would explore why her crushing heartache had lifted the moment she slid the ring back on her finger. For now, her sense was returning and she realized the boys needed to be dealt with.

"What the fuck were you five thinking?" she demanded, glaring between Mortician and Outlaw. Those two motherfuckers were the ringleaders. "You always fucking talk about family, well, Knox is fucking family, motherfuckers. You don't fucking kill family! That would devastate me."

"If you ain't with the motherfucker, then the motherfucker ain't family," Outlaw imparted. "Especially if you ain't with him cuz he fuckin' hurt you in any-fuckin-way."

"Better you bastards hurt me, than him, right, Outlaw?" she demanded.

"Roxanne," Mortician huffed, "we fuck him up, you just got to go through one, big hurt. We let him live and you might have to go through the shit over and over again."

The logic of that statement, and her understanding of it, was frightening. To them, he'd broken her heart, then apologized and she took him back. Perhaps, to hurt her again.

"Look, baby, I appreciate you wanting to save me a lifetime of heartache and just get it over with in one, fell swoop. While that might seem good to you, it isn't to me. I would blame myself for the rest of my life if you killed him."

"Wouldn't be your fucking fault, Roxanne," Digger said. "It would be his fucking fault for being such a uppity-impressed-with-himself motherfucker."

Roxy held her left hand up and wiggled her ring finger. "This makes him our family, boys."

"*That* do." Mortician acknowledged the ring with a nod. "But you wasn't fucking wearing it earlier."

"He pissed me off." The dismissive words helped her nonchalance sound believable. She slid the ring off and held up her hand again. "He's still our family. That means he has immunity from your death squad."

"That don't mean shit," Val put in.

"Val, if I were you, I'd shut the fuck up and stay the fuck out of this," Zoann warned.

Bailey folded her arms as Val scowled but backed away. "Lucas, if you hurt Knox, you hurt Mama. In turn, that hurts me. Back off of Knox."

"That's my woman," Knox slurred, drawing unneeded attention.

Clenching his jaw, Mortician balled his hands into fists at his side, but glanced away and nodded at his wife. "Fuck, fine, Bailey. Motherfucker get to live as long as he family."

"Come fuckin' on, Megan." Outlaw swigged from the bottle. "Say what the fuck you gotta say, baby."

Meggie and CJ exchanged glances. Roxy knew Meggie wouldn't repeat Knox's words to Outlaw, but CJ? He loved to spill the beans.

"Baby?" Outlaw cocked his head to the side. "You ain't a pissed lil' motherfucker at my ass?"

Meggie gazed at Roxy, then smiled at Outlaw. "Christopher, Knox is part of Roxy's family and Roxy is *our* family. As long as she wants him to stay alive, he stays alive." She glared at the back of Knox's head.

"And, no, I'm not angry at you." Without another word, she grabbed CJ's hand and walked away.

Outlaw contemplated Meggie as she opened the gate and guided CJ onto their property.

"Our fuckin' hands tied." Outlaw stared at the vintage engagement ring Roxy still held in her hand. The one that seemed to have let all the evil into her relationship. Damn, she really wasn't a superstitious bitch, but this was some complete bullshit. Until she put the motherfucker on her finger, she and Knox had had a wonderful relationship.

The *moment* he'd slid this fucking thing on, chaos had entered their lives. This. Was. *BULLSHIT!*

She almost wanted to throw it away...oh, hell no. Maybe, melt the motherfucker down? No, that was some black magic alchemy shit. She could sell it or return it to Knox's father. By right, it really wasn't hers anymore.

"Havin' second fuckin' thoughts?"

She gritted her teeth at Outlaw's question and slid the ring back on. Bad luck or not, she had to wear the ring for the time being.

Once the situation settled, she'd give it back to Knox.

"Roxanne, whether Knox fuckin' Harrington live or die now completely in your fuckin' hands."

Outlaw swept Knox with a cold look, then followed the path Meggie had taken, soon disappearing from view, unconcerned with the weight of responsibility his words held.

CHAPTER THIRTY-EIGHT

Knox

His head pounding as if Thor's hammer beat upon his skull, the scent of Roxanne's perfume surrounding him, Knox flopped onto his back and groaned. His stomach churned like an angry sea. As a matter of fact, his entire body hurt, as if he'd been slammed against concrete countless times.

He groaned again. What happened to him? The last vague memory he had was leaving the office and stopping at a bar. But...

He lifted his head. The room spun, so he rectified his mistake and laid it back onto the pillow.

But as he'd started to say...he was in his room at the club.

How had he gotten there? Certainly, he hadn't driven in his condition. Had he?

Had he called Roxanne and she'd acted as his sober driver? No matter how much she hated him, she didn't want harm to befall him. She'd kept a friendly pretense for days on his behalf.

Roxanne.

When he'd tried to sit up, he hadn't noticed her, but he *smelled* her. Notes of flowers with an undertone of citrus.

"Roxanne," he called, her presence surrounding him. He received no answer. His imagination played tricks on him again.

Sighing, he patted his pocket, unsurprised to find himself still fully clothed. Feeling nothing in the left pocket, he frowned. Before full panic set in, he repeated his pat-down on his right side. Nothing!

Jesus! Roxanne's ring!

Attempting to sit up again, he gave into the god of hangovers and plopped backwards.

"Oh, Jesus. God," he begged, turning onto his side. "Forgive me. I swear I'll never drink again. Or...or...Just fucking kill me now." What had he drank?

Before he could try to remember, his door slammed opened. The noise sent tears to his eyes and vomit twisting in his stomach, like a strange brew waiting to gush out.

"'Law!" CJ yelled. "Uncle Mudna Fucka awake."

"Get out," Knox tried to demand, afraid to raise his voice above a whisper. He didn't even care that the kid had cussed him.

CJ banged on the door. Or kicked it. Or threw his miserable little body against it as a special form of torture.

"Him up," CJ said. "Him groaned. I been sitting outside his door just like you told me, 'Law."

Outlaw walked into Knox's line of vision and smirked.

"Outlaw, please—" Knox began feebly.

"Boy, Uncle Motherfucker ain't wake e-fuckin-nuff. Come jump on his fuckin' stomach like you do to wake my ass up."

"'Kay, 'Law," CJ said without hesitation.

"Please," Knox mumbled.

Neither of them heard. Or they pretended not to hear. CJ climbed onto Knox's bed then bounced onto Knox's stomach.

Once...twice...Knox could hold back no longer. He twisted toward the floor, vaguely hearing CJ yell in fear, and released all the vomit created since the beginning of time.

"You done good, boy," Outlaw said. "Go fuckin' wait for my ass at the fuckin' table."

"'Kay, 'Law," CJ squealed, apparently just fine.

Finished with throwing up and thanking the heavens that his guts remained inside of him, Knox sprawled out on the bed, flat on his back. "Godddd," he begged. "Where are you? Is this the reason for my miserable existence? Please strike alcohol out of existence. Turn it into a pillar of salt. Let a whale swallow it. Throw it into the lion's den..."

"Knox, shut the fuck up. The fuck you askin' for that shit? Daniel got the fuck out the lion's den and the whale spit Jonah the fuck up. About the only one outta the three ain't survive was Lot wife. Ain't comin' the fuck back from just crumblin' the fuck up."

"Have I gone to another dimension?" That would explain the devastating hangover and also how in the hell Outlaw knew about biblical characters. "I didn't think you knew how to spell church. Yet here you are shocking me with your knowledge of...your knowledge."

The door slammed shut, and Knox moaned, Thor's hammer knocking the fuck out of him again. He had begun to feel better, after he'd thrown up.

Daddy Thug and Baby Thug were gone now, so he could rest and... A chair scraped across the floor. There was rustling. The sound of a lighter flicking. An exhalation of breath.

"What do you want?" Knox demanded, remembering he'd lost Roxanne's engagement ring and annoyed that Outlaw lingered. "Why are you here?"

"My ass here cuz I fuckin' wanna be."

"The scent of vomit should run you away." If Knox focused on it, he'd vomit again. What kind of irresponsible jerk was he?

"I ain't a weak, bitch-ass motherfucker, motherfucker. Seein' a motherfucker hurl or smellin' it after, ain't ever bother me."

Knox grunted.

"My ass also not a fuckin' *stupid* motherfucker."

"I reserve the right to withhold my opinion."

"And my ass reserve the fuckin' right to shoot the fuck outta you."

"Would you get to the point so I can die in peace?"

"A night of fuckin' drinkin' ain't gonna kill you. If your ass had alcoholic poisonin', we probably woulda seen some fuckin' signs by now."

"Okay. Leave me alone so I can pray to die and be put out of my misery."

"All you gotta do is ask my fuckin'ass to fuck you up."

"What do you want, Outlaw?" Knox demanded.

"You helpin' me get Kendall outta Johnnie life. The gun deal you brought to me seem to be fuckin' on the up-and-fuckin-up. But you fuck over Roxanne, and you fuckin' forfeit your fuckin' life. I ain't needin' your ass no more for Amfinger and I just gotta deal with Kendall longer 'til I find some-fuckin-body else to do what the fuck I need did if I gotta fuck you up."

"She broke up with me." At some point, Roxanne had text him. A month ago...?...A week?...Today...yesterday...*when...?* She'd told him to say she ended the engagement.

"In-fuckin-deed," Outlaw agreed. "It's the fuckin' *reason* she broke up with your fuckin' ass."

"What are you talking about?" Knox hedged, his brain betraying him for once. A reasonable explanation escaped him.

"I wantcha to sober your fuckin' ass up and get the fuck gone. Your ass don't fuckin' belong round us. Go to your fuckin' family e-fuckin-state. You ain't fuckin' welcome here no more."

The words hit Knox like bricks. "No!" He struggled to sit up and swayed when he did so. The room spun and bile churned in his gut. He didn't care. He had to make Outlaw understand. The situation was too important for Knox to give into his drunken ailments. He met the club president's unyielding gaze. "This is where I belong, Outlaw. I love her. This is my home because it is hers." Why hadn't he realized that before he'd blown up?

"Fuckin' fine time for your ass to figure that shit out, assfuck," Outlaw grumbled, as if he'd read Knox's mind.

"Tell me what to do," he begged.

"Tell me what you done," Outlaw countered.

Knox looked away, his voice, his *words* to her, echoing in his head. He couldn't bring himself to repeat them. Not only because Outlaw would execute him, but because they shamed him so much.

"You almost fuckin' died to-fuckin-day. About three, four hours ago. You fuckin' went to Roxanne, drunker than a motherfucker, while

Mort was there." Outlaw dragged on his cigarette. "Your woman saved your fuckin' ass."

"She's not my—"

"If I was you, I'd shut the fuck up, cuz accordin' to her, you and her just had a fuckin' argument. She even took her fuckin' ring back and wearin' it a-fuckin-gain."

"Oh, thank God." Knox sagged in relief. The ring was safe. More important, she was his again.

Throwing the cigarette onto the concrete floor, Outlaw stomped it beneath his motorcycle boot. "Ain't no time for fuckin' rejoicin', fuckhead. You want her the fuck back, you gotta lotta fuckin' work to do."

"You just said—"

"Knox, how you got to be a fuckin' badge? You one motherfucker that miss the fuck outta clues."

"I take umbrage to that!"

"Re-fuckin-mind me when I told your ass I fuckin' gave a fuck what the fuck you ain't likin'? You a stupid, clueless motherfucker. Case fuckin' closed. Bet your docket went with the most un-fuckin-solved cases. Whatever fuckin' unit you was in."

"That isn't true!"

"What-the-fuck ever. Any-fuckin-way, lemme say this shit a-fuckin-gain: *Your ass almost fuckin' died to-fuckin-day*."

"I heard you the first time."

"You musta ain't. Other-fuckin-wise, you woulda fuckin' realized *that* mighta had some-fuckin-thing to do with Roxanne puttin' your ring back on her finger."

"I don't—"

"Under-fuckin-stand," Outlaw interrupted, and folded his arms. "You look clueless like a motherfucker, so you ain't gotta waste your fuckin' alcoholic breath sayin' you don't know what the fuck I mean."

Knox squinted at Outlaw.

"In case you ain't realize? Your ring on her finger? Give you fuckin' immunity. *That* fuckin' ring make you *our* fuckin' family, and we ain't killin' family fuckin' members un-fuckin-less Megan fucked with."

As was the case with Kendall, who'd been removed from Outlaw's No-Kill list.

"So lemme spell this shit out for your fuckin' ass. As long as you 'round us, Roxanne gonna have that fuckin' ring on. From the little I fuckin' got, your ass don't fuckin' deserve to fuckin' still be breathin'." He shrugged. "But she fuckin' love you, and you ain't fuckin' hesi-fuckin-tate when you say you belong where she at. You probably love her ass, too."

"Take the probably out of it."

"Knox, lemme clue you the fuck in. A-fuckin-gain. I was comin' to make peace with your ass. Mostly ig-fuckin-norin' your lil' jabs and shit. But let's just put it the fuck out there: we ain't likin' each other."

"That's not true!"

Dropping his folded arms, Outlaw leaned forward. "Ain't respectin' a motherfucker who not man e-fuckin-nuff to live in his own fuckin' truth."

"What do you want me to say? Roxanne sees you as one of her sons. If I don't like you or Mortician or any of you, my relationship with her is doomed."

"You ain't got a fuckin' relationship with her," Outlaw snapped.

"You just said..."

Outlaw's look of disgust offended Knox. "Listen up, motherfucker," Outlaw bit out, standing. "If you fuckin' feel that way, then your ass better fuckin' find a way to reconcile how the fuck you feel about us."

"I see you're not disputing my assumptions."

"Mortician her son-in-law, Harrington. Bailey love the mother-fucker. When you call his ass a piece of garbage, then, in essence, you callin' Bailey the same. By extension, you pinnin' that title on Roxanne, too."

"I don't mean too," Knox said with sincere regret. "I just...to me you're criminals. I don't deal with your type of people."

"Oh, yeah, cuz you ain't got a motherfuckin' uncle named Avalon, who was embezzlin' from my fuckin' club *and* tried to kill Roxanne. You fuckin' disowned his ass, like *your* fuckin' kind do, so him and his bullshit tucked away in some fuckin' coffin."

If it hadn't been for Avalon he never would've met Roxanne.

"Roxanne fuckin' love you," Outlaw said as he headed for the door.

"Whether or fuckin' not she truly fuckin' forgive you in your fuckin' hands, motherfucker."

"Outlaw, wait." Knox stopped the man just before he opened the door. "I need your help." He do anything to win Roxanne back. "Tell me what to do. How can I get her to forgive me?"

"Come off your high fuckin' horses and respect who the fuck she is, where the fuck she came from, and how im-fuckin-portant this club is to her."

"I do...I understand." Desperation crept into him. "Everything you said. I love her."

"Love ain't e-fuckin-nuff, Knox," Outlaw informed him. "It's up to your fuckin' ass to figure what the fuck else required. I can fuckin' coach you all-fuckin-day, but if you ain't really fuckin' understandin' then the shit gonna fall apart any-fuckin-way."

Turning, Outlaw walked out the room, slamming the door behind him.

The sound reverberated through Knox's head. Falling back against the pillows, he moaned, but, for the first time since he'd been such a stupid jackass, he felt something other than despair.

Hope.

CHAPTER THIRTY-NINE

Megan

"How's Mr. Mortician?" Viola, Dr. Will's long-time nurse, asked. The older woman had always been kind and helpful to Meggie, and she really appreciated her.

"He's fine," Meggie answered. "Doing his usual."

Viola nodded. "That's good. And Mr. Outlaw?"

"He's better now." Meggie explained about his vasectomy reversal.

"I always knew you two would end up with another one. That man loves to see you with his baby inside of you."

"He does," Meggie said, smiling with tenderness.

It was the morning after Knox's near-murder. Christopher was busy at the club on conference calls with Riley, the club's PI, discussing a run he and Mortician would leave for tomorrow.

Meggie had left her guards behind. She didn't need their opinions and nasty comments.

The door opened and Dr. Will walked in. Ever since Meggie had known Jordan Will, she'd had braids. Today was no different. Her eyes were sparkling as brightly as her wedding set.

"Hi Meggie," Dr. Will greeted, setting her tablet on the counter. "How are you feeling?"

"Pregnant," Meggie said on a sigh.

"That's because you are." Dr. Will smiled. "Your test came back positive."

"Are you sure?" Meggie persisted. "I peed in a cup here and on sticks at home. My pee might be wrong."

Dr. Will studied Meggie. "Would you like to come to my office so we can talk?"

"No." Tears rushed to Meggie's eyes. "I want you to tell me that I'm not pregnant. We *just* started having sex again after his procedure."

Dr. Will and Viola exchanged shocked looks.

"I haven't been with another man," she said.

"Then—"

"That means I got pregnant *before* the procedure," she interrupted the doctor. "Meaning Christopher went through unnecessary pain and paid needless money. Meaning, uh..." Her voice trailed off and she sniffled.

"Oh! Right. Mr. Caldwell won't take too kindly to this," Dr. Will said, nonplussed.

Christopher had once assisted Cam to rescue Dr. Will from very violent in-laws.

"Dr. Will, shouldn't Mr. Outlaw's doctor have run tests before the procedure?" Viola asked. "I'm not a doctor, but I'm just saying."

"He should have, but I'm not sure if he did or not. I didn't know about this beforehand."

"What reason would a physician have to not do right?" Viola asked. "You could always be just a few days pregnant."

"I guess. In answer to your first question, it might have to do with the *cash* Christopher pays for his medical expenses. Since my kidnapping, he hasn't been himself," Meggie admitted. "I don't know if he would've even thought about tests prior to the procedure. He was just looking for a way to keep me safe and, apparently, the urologist was more than willing to grab the money without doing his job properly."

Viola harrumphed. "Well, if that doctor was fool enough to double-cross Mr. Outlaw, then he deserves whatever he gets."

Turning to a cabinet, Dr. Will pulled open the door. "Let's not panic and go through this step-by-step. First, we'll do a pelvic exam. Just to reassure you, I'll also send you to the lab to get a blood test. You can't get any more definitive than that."

"Okay, Dr. Will."

Offering an encouraging smile, Dr. Will headed for the door. "Change into a gown and we'll get started."

"You were kidnapped about two and a half months ago, correct?" Dr. Will asked Meggie as they both seated themselves in the physician's private office.

Memories of that underground prison went through Meggie's head, and she could only nod.

"Were you having any pregnancy symptoms before then?"

"No."

"Were you under a lot of stress?"

Other than Kendall's lies and schemes leading Johnnie to strangle Meggie, nope, not at all. "Some," she admitted.

"Have you heard of women who are far into their pregnancies, or in labor before they realize they *are* pregnant?"

"Yes."

"The medical term is cryptic pregnancy. For whatever reason, the fetus produces low levels of HCG. It could be a genetic quirk, a chromosomal disorder, or in response to maternal stress. In the latter case, and to put it simply, there's a bit of self-preservation on the baby's part. Now, that could be what's happened in your case."

"I've just started to feel pregnant." Not wanting to wait the day it would take to get results from the blood test, Meggie had requested Dr. Will perform an ultrasound. She'd confirmed Meggie's pregnancy and then suggested they talk in her office after all. A horrifying thought crossed Meggie's mind. "Is the baby okay?"

"He's perfect," Dr. Will answered.

Meggie smiled. "We might have a girl."

"Your baby is a boy," the doctor responded kindly.

Pursuing her lips and drawing her brows together, Meggie cocked her head to the side. "How, erm, the sex of a baby can't be discovered until eighteen weeks or so."

"Yes. And you're that plus a week or two."

Omigod, that urologist was so dead. "No!" Meggie protested. "That can't be right. I was still getting periods. I just started to get nauseated two or three weeks ago."

"I took the measurements during the ultrasound. He's six point three inches and weighs about ten ounces."

"But...but...No! Dr. Will, no! What about the fight I got into with Kendall? Are you saying I was pregnant then?"

"Yes. You were pregnant when you were kidnapped."

Christopher's doctor would be tortured for a very long time with that news. "This can't be happening. I've always known when I was pregnant."

Standing, Dr. Will came around the desk, stooped in front of Meggie, and took her hands into her own. "Every pregnancy is different. Don't be so hard on yourself. You've been through a lot."

"What am I going to tell Christopher?"

Dr. Will's look turned thoughtful. Releasing Meggie's hands, she stood. "You can tell him you're pregnant but the fudge the number of weeks. Your blood pressure was slightly elevated. You're stressed out today, so I'm not concerned."

"Christopher always knows when I lie."

"You can also not say anything until he notices since your belly is still relatively flat."

Meggie nodded. "I'm sure it won't hurt if I wait a few days before breaking the news to him. Maybe, he'll take it better if a little more time has passed between memories of the pain of his procedure and my announcement."

"Sounds like a plan."

It did, though Meggie felt no comfort. Sometimes, the best laid plans were the ones that went the most awry.

~

CHRISTOPHER

Spooning with his girl on the sectional in the family room, Christopher laughed at her giggles after he'd told her a raunchy joke. Diesel was in his room, waiting for his now-nightly talk with Christopher. He didn't want the motherfucker to feel unwanted or isolated, so he made it a point to go to Diesel's room to check in with him once Christopher and Megan checked on their younger children one last time.

CJ, Rule, and Rory were asleep—or in CJ's room. Knowing his oldest boy, he'd taught Rory how to fucking fake sleeping, so they could get into shit together. Only once had CJ gotten into such serious shit that Christopher had to spank him and that was when he'd decided to chop fucking onions like his Ma, then cook the mother-fuckers.

The fire extinguisher had been enough to kill the flames.

Somehow, CJ had neither burned nor cut himself.

Tonight, Rebel and Matilda were having a sleepover with Harley, and Doc Will's kid, Ava. Ransom, Ryder, and JJ were in the nursery, while Christopher and Megan...

Yeah, life was fucking good.

Thrusting his hard cock against Megan's ass, he nosed her hair then nipped her earlobe. She hooker-moved against him, her sigh mingling with his groan.

"Want me to fuck you right here?" he whispered.

She shivered. "Yes," she breathed, then released a breath. "But, first, I have to tell you something."

Because he took up most of the space, even on their sides, Megan was one fucking move away from rolling the fuck on the floor. Whenever she gripped and tugged his hand, he knew he needed to sit up and then hold onto her as she did the same.

Once they were side-by-side, she sidled a look at him, then bowed her head.

"I'm having a baby," she mumbled.

Of all the fucking things he was expecting, that sure the fuck wasn't it. "Say that shit again."

She scowled at him. "I'm pregnant."

Cocking his head to the side, he narrowed his eyes at her. "For fuckin' real, Megan?"

"Yes! Why would I lie about that?"

He could think of a few reasons. For instance, she always worried about his fucking soul. Ignoring the fact that he'd fucked up so many motherfuckers he'd lost count, she thought stopping him from continuing his fucking-up of assfucks that fucking deserved it, would save him from hell. He didn't want to burst her fucking bubble, but he'd gotten his fucking invitation from that pitch-fork motherfucker years ago.

"My cock a-fuckin-mazin', huh, baby? Motherfucker knocked you the fuck up already."

She nodded, hard and fast, enough to snap her fucking neck. Now, Christopher understood where his boy got those exaggerated head fucking movements.

"When you found out?"

"Today," she answered. "I...yeah...I went to Dr. Will. I haven't been feeling well the past several weeks and—"

"Past several fuckin' weeks?" he said, seizing on her slip.

Her eyes rounded and her face crumpled. "Uh, the past several days."

Folding his arms, he glared at her. "You about two, three weeks?"

She swallowed, rung her hands together, and averted her eyes. "Yes," she whispered.

"If a lil' motherfucker happen to fall outta your pussy in the next... eight and a half months, that just fuckin' mean you deliverin' early, huh, baby?"

"Yes."

"That mean I ain't got to go fuck up no motherfucker cuz I got fuckin' unneeded cock trauma, yeah?"

"Uh-huh."

"If this lil' motherfucker arrive a fuckin' *day* be-fuckin-fore you reach nine months, my killin' drought fuckin' over. Hear me, Megan?"

Tears rushing to her eyes, she sniffled. "I thought you'd be happy."

Vulnerability shone in her blue eyes, stealing Christopher's anger. He drew her into his arms and kissed the top of her head.

"I'm sorry, baby," he said gruffly. "I ain't meanin' to act like a mean fuckhead. Of-fuckin-course, my ass happy."

"I am, too."

"That's what the fuck important." While that was true, he didn't appreciate a motherfucker fucking over his dick when it wasn't fucking necessary.

Oh, yeah. There was also the fucking money.

She kissed his chin. "I need to check on CJ, Rule, and Rory."

Helping her off his lap, Christopher nodded. "Okay, baby. Ima go check in on Diesel, then meet you in our fuckin' room."

"Okay."

Once Megan left him alone, he glowered in the direction of the door. Now that he thought on it, he believed she'd last had her period about six or seven weeks ago, which meant one fucking thing.

Christopher was going to hack off that urologist's cock, then torture him, and fucking see to it that he was deader than dead.

Case fuckin' closed.

CHAPTER FORTY

Roxy

Two days after Knox almost ended up in the meatshack, Roxy walked into the quiet clubhouse in early dawn. Knox and Johnnie were still in their respective rooms, for which she was grateful. After Mortician assisted Knox to the clubhouse, he'd stumbled and staggered like the drunk motherfucker he was. He fell onto the bed, gave her a goofy grin, and fell asleep...passed the fuck out.

"C'mon," Mortician had ordered.

"No. He might need something." The words were for pretense. They came automatically, unbidden.

"Motherfucker dick drunk anyway," Mortician said. "He can't do nothing."

Roxy scowled. "The *motherfucker* is drunk," she countered.

Nodding, Mortician sighed and his look softened. "I'll be in the main room," he said, then left her alone with Knox.

His face was flushed from the abundance of alcohol he'd consumed. Every now and then, a snore had escaped him, and she'd grinned.

After studying him while rooted to her spot, she'd sat on the bed before curling up against him. For a few stolen moments, she'd allowed herself to remember the intimacy they'd shared. He went to oncology checkups with her and enjoyed her healthy lifestyle. Food that was good for a motherfucker, generally wasn't good *to* that motherfucker. Knox kept her spirits up when she missed some of her old favorites. When she'd stray to far away from her diet, he'd reel her back in.

In the evenings, he'd discuss cases with her, especially the crazy ones. Grinning, one in particular had come to mind. A man's wife had gotten rid of the family parrot. Knox had been hired to track the bird down and interview him. The husband was sure the parrot had witnessed the woman's infidelity and would tell all.

As it turned out, motherfucker was right on all accounts. The wife had been cheating and the bird talked his ass off. In the end, Knox had reunited the bird with the poor husband.

Roxy chuckled at the silliness of it all, wishing for those times again and knowing they were gone.

"Roxanne," Knox had mumbled. "Please forgive me. I'm so sorry."

The miserable words dug deep into her. She'd already forgiven him. She just couldn't forget because she couldn't trust Knox not to resort to the same tactics whenever they argued. He looked down on every-thing she liked, including tattoos and motorcycles. They'd never find a gray area.

Kissing the base of his neck, Roxy had gotten out of bed. She hadn't even taken her shoes off. At the door, she'd turned and taken a last look at him, then she'd found Mortician and told him she was ready to leave.

Now, her long, sleepless night had finally drifted into morning. She was dragging her ass, just as she had since she'd awakened. Not even her coffee and chicory had stimulated her tired brain. She needed to get herself together.

Members would be stopping in soon, on their way to work for coffee, breakfast, gossip, or the smorgasbord.

She had to get a move on. She flipped on the lights, righted a chair that must've been knocked over and forgotten about, then adjusted the thermostat to remove the chill from the air.

It didn't take long for her to start the coffee to brewing. Afterwards, she headed to gather what she needed for breakfast. Today's menu would be simple: scrambled eggs, sausage, and toast.

In the midst of cracking eggs and allowing the contents to fall into a big bowl, she saw Knox sprawled on the ground, heard the awful words he'd spoken to her, and felt the weight of his great-great grandmother's ring, back on her finger to save his life.

She paused and held out her hand. The center diamond sparkled and gleamed, the brilliant appearance a direct contrast to her hollow feeling.

Knox had honored her with it. If he felt as he did about her and the prenup and so many other things that had shocked her, why would he give her a Harrington family heirloom?

Drawing in a deep breath, she leaned against the butcher block table, so fucking angry with him. However, she was even more hurt, and very afraid. If she made one misstep, Mortician and Outlaw would discover the truth, and kill Knox.

Picking up another egg, she tapped it on the table, then opened it along the fissure line and allowed the contents to drop into the bowl. There was a comfort to the rhythm she adapted. Yet, her problems—her heartache—lurked just beneath the surface of the monotony.

Just as she cracked the twenty-fourth egg, her last for the morning, the door swung open and Knox stepped in.

He resembled an extra for The Walking Dead with his pale skin and green undertones, hideous gashes and bruises, red-rimmed eyes, and slow walk.

"You are wearing it," he breathed, staring at the ring.

Fuck, but he was banged up.

"I have no choice," she said, refusing to comment on his appearance.

"There is always choice, Roxanne."

She shrugged, grabbed the whisk she'd set out on the table, and started whipping the eggs together. "A fucking pity your ass didn't choose right and kept your goddamn mouth shut."

"I'm sorry," Knox told her.

She whipped faster.

"I didn't mean anything I said."

They'd been through this already. How many times would the motherfucker apologize to her?

"You're a fucking liar," she retorted. "You meant everything."

"I was frustrated."

"I don't give a fuck."

"Roxanne—"

She recoiled at the way he said her name. Any other time, she would've melted into his arms at the sexy sound. Enough of this bullshit. "You can be frustrated. The bullshit you threw at me was plain fucking mean. It showed your true colors."

He thrust his fingers through his hair, then gave her a pleading look. "I love you."

Those words from Knox still held power over her. Whenever he said it, giddiness lightened her head and sensuality invigorated her body. Now, though, she only felt gutted.

Because she still loved him—and almost admitted it—she clenched her jaw. She'd ride the storm. Her feelings for him would flicker out in due time. She just had to keep reminding herself what a motherfucker he turned into when he was angry.

"I know you still love me."

She glared at him. "What the fuck is it to you if I do, motherfucker?"

"You do," he insisted. "Otherwise, you wouldn't put on this charade to save my life. You'd let them kill me. I want to die, Roxanne. My life is meaningless without you."

She had so many responses to that, but she refused to continue this conversation. "Knox, I'm busy. I don't have time to talk to you."

"I'll do anything if you forgive me."

"You're forgiven," she stated. "Too much fucking trouble to hold a grudge. Anything else?"

He pulled her into his arms, thrusting his hard cock against her. "Remember the last time you and I were alone in the clubhouse in the early morning?"

They'd fucked each other on a barstool, one of their intimate moments that would live in her memory forever.

Without warning, he covered her lips with his own. Roxy's body responded immediately, and desire shot through her.

This motherfucker was out of his fucking mind or thought she was. Dick whipped and dumb bitch were two entirely different things.

She elbowed his stomach, then stomped his foot. "Get the fuck away from me," she snarled, hating her breathlessness and not caring that he was hopping around like a jackass.

"Go," she ordered. "Leave me alone before I fuck you up. Don't make this any harder than it has to be." She planted her hands on her hips. "We're going to let the bullshit with the boys blow over, then we're going to announce that I've decided I really don't want to marry again. You or no other motherfucker. That's it. After that, we'll go our s-separate ways."

She turned away. Her voice shouldn't have cracked on that last sentence. It just crushed her that whatever other wonderful things destiny held for her, it seemed, true love wasn't one, when that's what she'd dreamed of from a young age.

"Roxanne—" Knox started.

"Knox, Roxanne," Mortician interrupted, walking into the kitchen and holding a stack of magazines. He nodded to them, strolled to the table and sat the magazines down.

Roxy leaned over the table. Based on the spines of the thick magazines, these were wedding based. He smiled.

"I thought you could take a look to see if you like any setups. Dresses..."

Roxy narrowed her eyes. "Boy, fuck you. You know damn well we already ordered our dresses."

Surprise crossed Mortician's face. "You didn't cancel your order?"

She'd forgotten to do so. "Fuck no!" she shouted. "What the fuck am I canceling my dress for? You want me to walk down the goddamn aisle in my altogether?"

Mortician grinned. "Knox haven't chose his tux," he said, not answering her. "He might see something he like in the magazine."

"Yes, the fuck he did. Him and his daddy went to their haberdasher."

The dilapidated condition of Knox's face gave his smirk a scary edge. "Don't worry, love. I think his suggestion is a fabulous idea. I still have time to change my mind."

"I don't," she snapped. This motherfucker wanted to play games. "I have breakfast to cook, so fuck off both of you."

"I got time," Mortician told her. "Cook whatever. I got to wait for Outlaw. We got business to see to, and he meeting me here in an hour or so." His grin came again, cool and all-knowing, meant to test her honesty. Failure meant death.

Knox's death.

Bristling, Roxy threw a filthy glare at Knox, hoping he understood she was calling him a few different motherfuckers under her breath. The satisfaction in his eyes irked her.

Joke's on you, motherfucker.

She wouldn't say a goddamn thing to either motherfucker. Sometimes, silence proved the most effective.

Roxy marched to the other side of the butcher block table, snatched the top magazine and flipped through it.

"Shouldn't you be standing next to Knox to help him look for a tux?"

Roxy tightened her lips, but didn't respond to Mortician. Knox walked over to her, bent and brushed his lips across hers.

"He's right, my love. You know I value your opinion."

"More than you value your dick, huh, sugar?" Roxy returned, a smile pasted on her mouth.

Knox slinked away from her.

"Why the attitude, Momma-in-law? I don't see a problem with this little task if—"

"Kiss my motherfucking ass, boy," Roxy shouted. "You know fucking well I'm busy in the goddamn morning, yet you bring your suspicious ass around, playing these fucking games."

Mortician glowered at Knox, then met her eyes. "We got all the tools laid out. Woodchipper all ready. All we missing is a body."

Roxy drew herself up, determined not to show how much Mortician's words frightened her. "You calling me a fucking liar?"

Mortician shifted at the outrage in her tone. "No, man," he grouched. "I know better than to do that."

"You just implied it," Knox said with heavy sarcasm.

She had to let Knox's interference pass without comment. He was doing his usual—inserting his comments.

"I'm looking through this one magazine for now, Mortician." Just to appease him. Knox was on Mortician's bad side. He needed only the smallest excuse to bury him.

Mortician looked from her to Knox. "The way you and Knox acting not a way two lovebirds should communicate."

"One lovebird about to crack you in your fucking mouth, Mortician," she retorted.

He smirked at her. Scowling, Roxy refocused on the magazine and turned the pages. After a moment, she came to a wedding dress that resembled the one she'd placed the deposit on. It was floor-length with an appliques V-neck bodice, perfect for her, and the complete opposite of Bailey's, who would look like a modern-day Cinderella with the ball gown style she'd chosen.

Swallowing, she rubbed her finger across the page. With determination, she held back the tears threatening to fall. All along it had been a pipe dream. Why had she ever believed Knox really wanted to marry her, when her own son was ashamed of her?

Mortician leaned over the side of her shoulder. "You prefer that dress?"

This motherfucker wasn't going to fucking quit.

Squelching the urge to roll the magazine up and bat the piss out of him, she flipped to the next page. "I might, but I don't want Knox to see it, boy, so shut up."

"Considering the motherfucker standing on the other side of you, he saw it."

"You're working on my last goddamn nerve, Mortician." She moved away and went back to the other side of the table. "I will do this later. If you have a problem with that, kiss my ass."

"I'm just trying to help."

"No, motherfucker, you're just trying to interfere."

"He's not *trying*, Roxanne," Knox inserted. "He's succeeding."

Grabbing the bowl of raw eggs, Roxy ignored the sloshing contents. She set the bowl on an unlit burner, braced her hands on the edge of the counter and stared at nothing, feeling the aura of Knox's presence and the weight of Mortician's judgment.

Hands on her shoulders turned her. Knox guided her to the stool that she always neglected.

"Sit."

Her head was pounding, and her heart seemed to be in tiny little pieces, so she sat.

"Mortician, I need to talk to Roxanne alone for a minute," Knox said, not taking his gaze from her.

Mortician's quick retreat surprised Roxy, but she didn't comment. Her gaze honed-in on the wedding magazines she'd left behind.

"Roxanne." Knox placed his hands on her shoulders again and squeezed gently. "I'll do anything to take your pain anyway. Tell me what to do. I've never seen you like this."

"I'm human, Knox."

"You're shutting down on me completely and will never take me back."

"I don't intend to take you back ever."

He wrapped his arms around her and kissed the back of her head. "You have to. I'm lost without you."

She disentangled from his embrace and got to her feet to face him. "We're not doing this ad nauseum. You spoke your truth. I made my decision."

"Really? Outlaw told me we're still engaged. Was that a lie?"

"You know fucking well it was. It was…"

"To save my life," he finished for her. "As Outlaw implied. And, yet, if your performance around Mortician is any indication, you may as well have allowed them to kill me the day before yesterday. You're not acting like we're still engaged."

His call-out rang with truth; she had no response.

"You look exhausted," he told her.

"Why don't I get you and me cups of coffee. You sit while I finish breakfast for those brutes."

Annoyance burst through her and she leveled him with an unhappy look.

"Fine," he bit out. "The *brothers*. Better?"

"Slightly," she agreed, leaning against the butcher block table so she wouldn't guide Knox to the stool and tend to his injuries. "Thank you but no. They need edible food."

"I've watched you cook many, many times, sweetheart. I can do this. Just give me a chance to prove it to you."

Pride told her to say no. However, it would be false pride, and would only get her burned fucking food. She was in no state-of-mind to cook right now.

"You can keep me company, while I work. You don't have to say anything to me. At least it'll keep up the illusion that all is well between us."

Unable to stop her smile, Roxy shook her head. "You're going to manipulate the fuck out of this situation, aren't you?"

"All's fair in love and war," he quipped, then cocked his head to the side. "I do love you. Let me prove it to you. That's all I ask. Just give me one more chance. If I fuck it up this time, then we can go our separate ways."

"Knox, you just don't snap back from all the vicious things you said to me." She glanced down at the ring, touched it.

Seeing where her attention was, Knox covered her hand with his own. "Don't give me an answer now," he begged. "Just give me another chance."

She opened her mouth to speak. Before words formed, he stole a quick kiss from her.

"I would wink at you if I could."

"They fucked you up pretty bad," she agreed, refusing to touch him.

"They are savages."

"Stop, Knox. Just stop. Out of one side of your mouth, you ask me to give you a chance. Out of the other side, you still insult my family."

"Family doesn't keep you warm at night. I do."

She nodded. "This family doesn't ridicule me, either. They accept me for who I am. It's no either/or with them. I can have *you* and them. But you think they are beneath you. Nothing but tattooed lowlifes."

"Just because they have tattoos don't make them lowlifes. Admittedly, tattoos are part of their criminal first impressions."

Roxy huffed out a breath. "Having a tattoo doesn't automatically make you a criminal. If you had one that wouldn't mean you were crim—"

"First, I'd never get a fucking tattoo. That would make me as bad as they are."

"That's the gist of it right there," Roxy said, her sadness stealing all her energy. "Not having a tattoo is just one of the ways you place yourself above them. It's also one of the most outstanding examples of how different we are."

He stared at her a moment, before he lifted his brows, as if a light just went off. "So if I get a tattoo, I'll prove to you that I accept you?"

"Knox," she whispered, finally giving into the urge to touch him by laying her hand against his cheek. He leaned into her. "I would never ask you to mark your skin if that's not what *you* wanted. This is not... we're never going to see eye-to-eye." Weary, she dropped her hand, walked to the stool and sat. "Give me a few days and I'll find a way for us to go our separate ways without dire consequences for you." Drawing this pretense out would only make it harder when she said goodbye. "If you really are going to cook for the club brothers, I suggest you get started."

"As you wish, my love," he told her with a sneaky grin.

Knox believed he'd win her back. She'd just have to show him how wrong he was.

CHAPTER FORTY-ONE

Knox

Arrows of pain, from Knox's head to his toes, shot through him, yet Roxanne's softening gave him the shot of adrenaline he needed to ignore his agony. She watched him with longing. The one or two times she'd laughed had soothed his self-recriminations. Her agreement that he cook propelled him to action.

He knew her so well. She intended to make a firm stance and block him out of her life, her heart, and her body, but he wouldn't allow that to happen.

"Be right back, sweetheart," he told her, in high spirits, as he picked up the platter of hash browns he'd prepared and headed to the main room. The place was moderately filled, in contrast to the emptiness he'd found just an hour ago, when he'd made his way to the kitchen to talk to Roxanne.

"You the new Kitchen Bitch now?" one of the bikers yelled as Knox sat the potatoes next to the platter of ham on the long table, near the bar, where the food always went.

"Fuck no," Mortician growled, glowering in Knox's direction.

"Only one Kitchen Bitch," Mortician continued. "*K-P.* Don't ever fucking make the mistake of trying to replace him, Foley."

"Just shitting around, Mort," Foley responded on a grunt. "Don't gotta be so touchy."

"He's right." Knox reached the officers' table, where Mortician sat and pulled out a chair. "May I?"

Mortician scowled, but nodded.

"I owe you an apology," Knox started on a sigh after he sat. "All these months, I thought you were like them. But you aren't. You have money."

"All these months, I thought you had a fucking brain, but you don't," Mortician shot back. "You just proved that by your fucking words, son."

"I'm giving you credit."

"No, you giving me bullshit. Exactly what the fuck your brain is made of. You think because I got money, I'm like *you* instead of 'them'," he said, using air quotations. "Money don't mean shit in *our* differences. You and me will never be alike. You think money put you above every other motherfucker around. I think money helps you to have one less worry in a world filled with fucking worries."

At a loss and backed into a corner by his own words, Knox thrust a hand through his hair. A groan of pain escaped him.

"Go away, Knox," Mortician ordered. "I don't have time for a motherfucker that play games with a woman's heart. Either you in it just to fuck or you in it to win *her*, whoever the fuck she might be. You don't get a girl with prenups and conditions and insults. I also got other fucking things to do than watching my momma-in-law suffer because you a dumb motherfucker. All this shit do is piss me the fuck off."

"Mortician—" Knox wanted to ask advice on how to win Roxanne back. With the man's current mood, though, he'd put his life at risk. It didn't matter that Mortician seemed to know Knox and Roxy hadn't reconciled. He was looking for any excuse to tear Knox to pieces.

"My ass must be losin' my fuckin' touch." Outlaw's voice drew Knox out of his reverie. "You walkin' around too fuckin' quick."

Refusing to comment, Knox folded his arms while Outlaw and Mortician sniggered.

"Ready to rock and fuckin' roll, Mort?"

Mortician stood. "Yeah, Prez."

As the two men turned to leave, Knox slouched in the chair. He really couldn't win with them. They took his bonding attempts with antipathy. The few times he'd offered advice, he'd been ignored.

He thought he'd found a common ground with Mortician, whom he would've preferred to have in his corner. The one thing that should've bonded them—their wealthy backgrounds—seemed not to matter.

A hand landed on his shoulder and Knox glanced behind him. Meeting Outlaw's gaze, Knox stiffened, then straightened as Mortician reseated himself.

"Everything okay here?" Roxanne asked before anyone spoke.

Having her near reminded Knox that she was worth every injury he had. He wanted to pull her into his arms and...Just like that, an idea hit him, as if lightning struck from Providence. He grabbed her wrist and pulled her onto his lap, but she didn't protest. Just as he suspected. Her entire body stiffened, though. He didn't care. She smelled so good and felt even better. He placed a kiss behind her ear and a small tremor went through her.

"Everything's fine now that you're here, sweetheart," he said gruffly, meaning it.

He shifted underneath her, his hardening dick sweet, sweet agony. "I want you so bad," he breathed against her ear. "Please, give me one more chance."

She elbowed him again, then jumped to her feet. Moving out of his reach, she faced him, hands on hips.

"Roxanne, babe, can you bring me some more eggs," another biker whose name Knox never bothered to learn, called.

She drew in a deep breath, then leveled Knox with one last glower. "Sure, Peaches," she responded and hurried away.

His heart sinking, Knox watched as she went to the buffet table, grabbed a paper plate and hefted a mountain of eggs onto the styrofoam, then brought it to the table where Peaches sat with another big brute of a man. Knox's location afforded him full view of her delicious ass.

"Ima meetcha outside, Mort," Outlaw announced and walked away as Roxanne started a conversation with the two bikers.

For a moment, Mortician stared at Knox, then he rolled his eyes and grabbed a chair. He turned the back toward the table and straddled it.

"She love your dumb ass," he grumbled. "So if you want her back, you need to straighten the fuck up."

Knox processed those words, then started. "We're still—"

"Please, motherfucker," Mortician interrupted. "Don't insult my fucking intelligence. Why you think me and Prez came back in here?"

"To kill me?"

"Can't do that as long as Roxanne think to protect you, motherfucker."

"Tell me what to do," he whispered, all pretense gone. "I love her. Please. I'll do anything."

Mortician offered him a last glower before sighing and relaxing his shoulders. "Whatever you do to win her back got to be from the heart, Knox. I can give you fucking advice for days, but if the shit not real, it's going to fall apart anyway."

"I love her," Knox repeated, just as he heard Roxanne's joyous laughter rose above every other sound in the room. Inspiration struck again. "Suppose I become one of you?"

"A roughneck?" Mortician asked with an amused grin.

"Is that what club members are called?"

Mortician laughed. "No, fool. It's up to you to find out what the fuck that is. So you want to become a Dweller?" he finished with skepticism.

He didn't ride a bike. He didn't have tattoos. He didn't...*No!* Roxanne loved these people. "Yes," he said with certainty.

"As initiation, you have to bury a motherfucker who a club enemy."

Did Kendall count? Probably not. Knox knew better than to ask the question.

"You willing to do that?" Mortician pressed. "Kill someone?"

Was he? Did winning Roxanne back mean setting aside his principles and values? Would she really expect that of him?

"You not," Mortician went on.

"I don't kill in cold blood. I don't think Roxanne would expect that of me."

"It wouldn't be in cold blood," Mortician argued. "It would be because of a crime against the club. Motherfuckers in the game know the rules."

"You live by the sword, you die by the sword."

"Something like that," Mortician agreed.

"Couldn't I do something else as initiation? The prospective arms deal...what ever came of that, by the way?"

"Initiation set, Knox. We not changing it to fit your sensibilities. And that deal with the guns? Forget your involvement. Prez giving you your cut if the deal go through."

"It was a viable contact?" Knox asked, satisfied. Surely, that would gain him some points.

"I'm not telling you nothing about it. One thing you got to know is collateral damage fuck things up when you least expect it."

"I don't...how would innocent people die? This is just a simple gun deal."

"Nothing ever simple in our world," Mortician countered. "Roxanne your collateral damage if you involved in the club or any deals. Not only her, but your parents. Grant. Even your ex-wife."

Startled at the revelation, Knox widened his eyes.

"All you got to do is fuck up or trust the wrong motherfucker or get on some motherfucker bad side, be it friend or foe. You willing to risk everybody you ever been close to? Not only for knowledge about those guns, but to get into the club."

"It doesn't have to be that way," Knox insisted. "It's about loyalty and trustworthiness. I know the meaning of brotherhood. I practiced it—"

"On the wrong fucking side," Mortician snapped.

"Mortician, please—"

"Do you even know how to fucking ride?"

"Cam does," Knox answered quickly. "He can teach me. I can

purchase a bike today and...and...and, another way I can be like you is to get a tattoo. I can get a skull on the back of my hand."

Sighing, Mortician stood. "I'm willing to teach you to ride, Knox. But don't get no perfunctory-ass, condescending goddamn ink that would be just the right size for CJ. You want to get tatted, do it fucking right or don't do it at all."

"Okay."

"Think about that long and hard," Mortician said, standing. "If you want ink, we'll take you to Bunny brother. As for the riding, your lessons start soon. One last thing, Knox. You can't let your fucking guard down in a place filled with fucking cameras. Feel me?"

Knox snapped his brows together, thinking of the conversation he'd had with Roxanne earlier. Instead of speaking and having a trembling voice betray his sudden fear, he nodded.

Mortician smirked. "See you around."

A few minutes after Mortician left, Roxanne headed back toward the kitchen, without even a glance in his direction.

He might lose a few battles because of his own tactical mistakes, but he intended to win the war and make Roxanne his again, now and forevermore. And he'd do it without any collateral damage involved.

CHAPTER FORTY-TWO

Megan

Killing the ignition, Meggie got out of her car, then leaned against the door to wait for her escorts. The four guys rode up a moment later, parked their Harleys and dismounted. Pete, Krag, Webster, and Talbot had all been around during her father's time—and before.

Not that they acted as if they'd known Big Joe or had any loyalty to Christopher. The early start to their day seemed to make them ornerier than usual. She'd had to go to the bank to take Kendall's name off as a signatory, on the home healthcare business account. Now, they'd arrived at the mall, where stores were just opening.

Krag frowned at her, then circled her Mini Cooper. She only took her Navigator out when she had two or more of her children with her.

Removing the toothpick from the corner of his mouth, Krag pointed it at her. "Outlaw needta teach ya how to fucking park,

Meggie." He toothpick-pointed to her front wheel. "You shoulda fucking straightened it, instead of parking like a fucking woman."

"I *am* a woman, Krag," she said with a smile.

He scowled at her. "No shit," he growled. "That's why we here, wasting our day for woman shit. Cuz you got a pussy." He used the toothpick as floss and removed something from between his teeth, then studied it before sniffing it, flicking it away, and shoving the disgusting little stick back into his mouth.

Meggie's stomach turned. Pregnancy kept her queasy or vomiting in the best of times. She couldn't take much more of Krag's tooth-picking habit before she threw up.

Talbot studied her from head-to-toe. His grizzled gray beard didn't match the silky beauty of the salt-and-pepper hair that reached down to his waist. He narrowed his eyes.

"Don't even mention grooming me, girl," he warned. "I didn't go for that shit when you first said it. Not going for it now."

Meggie looked at her toes. Somehow, these four brothers that she only knew from serving them at the club, had ended up on her detail. Mortician, Cash, Stretch or Digger had stopped being assigned to her long ago. Johnnie never had been, while Val...well, Val was Val. They'd laid the past to rest, so...so she'd leave it at that.

Unfortunately, Pete, Krag, Webster, and Talbot were the primary reasons she'd been so happy to have Christopher slack up on her details. Beyond gruff, they jumped sheer cantankerousness.

Biting her lip, she shifted, and wrapped her arms around her waist. She could always tell Christopher...only, she *couldn't*. He'd kill them, which left her stuck.

A loud crack punctuated the air, and she jumped. At the guys' laughter, she realized one of them had clapped their hands.

Webster belched. The sharpness of his reddish-brown hair indicated a dye job and in no way matched the intense wrinkles in his face. "I got a broad to fuck, Megan. So get to fucking moving. We not those young bucks sniffing behind your cunt and dying to be in your fucking company."

"You wish your cock still worked, Webster," Pete said around guffaws.

"It do!" Webster protested. "That Viagra shit been working wonders for my dick. I got a fucking hard-on and can fuck a young bitch for fucking hours."

"You mean you fuck your fucking hand for hours," Krag teased with a grin.

"Fuck off," Webster snapped, flipping Krag off.

Meggie sighed. "Guys, I know you don't want to guard me. Why don't you tell Christopher?"

The four of them stared at her as if she'd turned into Medusa.

"Always said you was too much of a stupid little cunt to be Joe's girl and Snake's sister," Krag said in disgust. "Now, you Outlaw's bitch. Never been worthy of him and never will be."

Tears rushed to Meggie's eyes and she glanced away. She just wasn't feeling good this morning. The baby was making up for the lost time he'd hidden himself and letting Meggie know, in no uncertain terms, that he was inside of her.

"Don't start that fucking whining, Megan," Webster warned.

"I thought we were all friends," Meggie said on a sniffle. "Why do you treat me this way during my errands?"

"We not a fucking bitch sitter," Krag said flatly. "And we don't appreciate Outlaw giving us this duty to watch you fucking shop or hang out with other bitches or all your little fucking cum squirts—"

Swiping at her tears, Meggie stiffened and glared at Krag. "Do *not* refer to my children that way."

He stepped closer to her. "Or what?"

"Or I'll tell Christopher." She met his gaze, unsure how effective she was being when her eyes were so watery. "Back off, Krag. You implied you had to be on my detail because Christopher either expected it of you or you couldn't decline him because he's your president. If you're going to treat me this way, you *should've* turned him down. Your attitude will get you killed anyway."

"Krag, brother, back off." Pete grabbed Krag's arm to pull him back. "She's right. We need to sit down and talk to Outlaw and tell him this job not for us. We never had a problem with Meggie before. We shouldn't take out our frustrations toward Prez on her."

"Me and Krag been here since Outlaw was a boy," Webster complained. "He should've knowed we not cut out for bitch detail."

"He put you on bitch detail because he trusted you," Meggie snapped. "*Because* he's known you for so long."

"So this a position of honor?" Talbot asked with a lift of his brow.

Meggie nodded.

"The fuck it is," Talbot countered, squashing Meggie's hope that they'd realize how much trust Christopher placed in them. "You fucking saying he was honoring us by trusting us to guard you? That's a crock of shit. In our fucking view, he *dis*honored us."

Hearing the disgust in their voices, Meggie went on alert, but decided not to say too much. They might hurt her. The fact that they'd die, too, didn't seem to matter to them.

Their dislike of her was almost more emotional duress than she could handle.

She rubbed her temples. She loved babies and children. But something didn't feel quite right inside of her body. Somehow, the unwell feeling seemed more than her usual intense morning sickness.

She'd suffered placental abruption during her second pregnancy and lost Patrick because of it. Then, she'd had so many other successful pregnancies. That she'd known about within just a few weeks of conceiving.

Yet...Meggie shook herself.

The feeling was just a holdover from her kidnapping. So much could change so fast.

"You know one thing I hate about your generation, Meggie?" Krag asked.

"Nope," she responded, her patience too thin to surfer the attitudes of resentful men. "And *you* know what, Krag, I really don't care."

"I'm telling you anyway."

"I figured you would," she retorted, glaring at him.

Pete's laughter surprised her. "See? Told you assholes that's why Outlaw crazy about this bitch. She got just the right amount of sweetness and sass. Just when you think you cowering her, she come back with a punch."

Lighting a cigarette, Webster grunted, then blew the smoke toward her. He stood at her side, so it wasn't a direct hit, but it still made her cough.

Krag patted her cheek, harder than necessary, then smiled. "Mad mugging me, Meggie?"

"If that's what you see, then that's what I'm doing. And if you put your hands on me again, not only am I *telling* Christopher, but I'm *calling* him right now." She shoved her hand in the back pocket of her jeans and pulled out her cell phone, waving it in front of him. "I'm giving you one last warning—*back off.*"

Krag tweaked her nose and she knocked his hand away.

"As I was saying, girl, I don't like your generation because you're a bunch of self-entitled pussies, where women don't know their fucking place. We don't have nothing in common with you and you don't have nothing in common with us." Krag looked her up and down. "Got a kid older than you. Never watched over her the way Outlaw want me to watch over you. She a tough bitch. You not." He backed away and glowered between her and Pete. "No matter what this motherfucker say."

"Yeah, Meggie, you got to give us fucking credit," Talbot started. "The first one or two times Outlaw gave you to us to watch we didn't mind that much. The motherfucker keep doing it, though. And all you fucking do is talk and talk. You don't know how to shut the fuck up."

"I was trying to make friends with you. *Real* friends, not just acquaintances who I chatter with now and then. Even less than that now, since I don't serve meals anymore. If we're going to spend so much time together, then we should have conversation."

"That's what you not getting, girl!" Krag shouted. "We conversate with a bitch if we want to fuck her or if she related to us. We can't fuck you and you not related to us, so your jabbering work the fuck on our nerves."

"Duly noted."

The next time Krag, Webster, Talbot, and Pete were assigned to her, she'd find a way to ditch them and run her errands alone. She was more than certain they'd agree to *pretend* to go with her, since they hated the job so much.

She'd cross that bridge when she got to it. Today, she just wanted to get back to her house, curl up, and cry.

~

JOHNNIE

Folding his arms, Johnnie leaned against the wall in the bathroom area, waiting for Megan to walk out. When she stumbled out, red-faced and miserable looking, he straightened.

"Megan, baby, what's the matter?"

She stilled, then scowled at him. "Go away," she ordered.

"No." He touched his still-bandaged nose. "I need to talk to you."

Her gaze touched on all angles of his face, before she met his eyes. "The guys are going to tell Christopher."

He smiled at her. "Worried for my safety?"

Clutching her stomach, Megan walked to the chair and sat. "What do we have to discuss, anyway?" she grouched, not answering his question. At least not verbally.

To Johnnie, her silence spoke volumes.

"I sent them away," he admitted.

It surprised him that his announcement didn't anger her. Everyone knew who was on her detail, so it had just been a matter of calling Krag, asking their location, and meeting them here at the department store.

He noted that his announcement didn't anger her.

Unless Johnnie was mistaken, relief crossed Megan's face and she sighed, her tension seeming to float away. He narrowed his eyes, opened his mouth to speak—

"They are still going to tell him," she interrupted.

"I paid them two hundred fifty bucks a piece to get lost." He shrugged. "They talk, they die. I'll kill them for taking my money and not doing as I told them. Christopher will kill them because they left you."

She nodded. "Right."

"Are you done shopping?"

"Yes," she said, glancing away, revealing her lie. But he wouldn't press her.

Later, he'd talk to Krag and company. They were motherfuckers on a good day, so Johnnie wasn't sure how they ended up as her guards. Yes, they'd seemed genuinely disappointed that they'd have to hand off such an easy job to Johnnie. Maybe, that was it. Meggie got along with everyone. Being Big Joe's daughter and Outlaw's wife went a long way in winning Krag, Talbot, Webster and Pete over.

They were good allies, but horrible enemies, and meaner than fucking snakes. If anyone fucked with Megan, the four older men would gleefully serve as executioners.

"Can we go somewhere to talk?" he asked, deciding to leave the subject of who guarded Megan to Christopher.

Before she spoke, he saw the denial to his request in her blue eyes.

"Please? I need...this is about Kendall. I know you don't give a fuck about her anymore but..." He heaved in a breath and held up his hand, wiggling the finger where his wedding band still sat. "I've met someone else. She looks so much like you that I feel like a pervert for even thinking of taking her out, although we've talked several times on the telephone."

Emily seemed so interesting. Almost too good to be true. She was educated, kind, funny, and witty.

"Can we go to the creek?" he pressed. "It's private. I'll stop and buy a few snacks and some wine."

"I'm going to tell Christopher I'm with you and where we're at." She flushed and glanced away. "Go ahead and accuse me of not being able to keep anything from my husband."

"I've said so many horrible things to you, Megan," he told her, wishing she'd look at him again. No eyes on God's green earth were as blue as hers. Yet he no longer felt the wistfulness he once had in her company. "He's your husband and you have every right to share with him. I was just a jealous, petty jerk."

Finally, she looked at him. "You've admitted as much before. It hasn't changed anything. You still border between love and hate for me *and* Kendall, and cross the line so many times, *your* head spins, so I can only imagine what it does to your wife."

"I told Kendall we're over." The words came easy; the thought did not. Following through would be hell.

She studied him a moment, then stood. "Let's meet at the creek in an hour."

At that moment, he realized she'd travel alone, but instead of stopping her departure, he decided to hurry to the nearest supermarket, and purchase items for their impromptu picnic.

Arriving at the creek, he found her already sitting under a tree, looking out over the water.

"Memories?"

Her hand flew to her stomach. "You startled me."

He sat beside her, setting the grocery bag next to him. "Sorry, sweetheart."

Her gaze returned to the water. "It seems like another lifetime when I was homeless and living out here."

"It does for me, too. Life seemed simpler, then."

She sidled a glance at him. "Your life," she said softly. "Mine was hell."

Because of Thomas Nicholls, her fuckhead stepfather.

"Do you ever think about death, Johnnie?"

The question, so far off-topic, came out of the blue, and sent his guard up.

"Specifically, *dying*," she amended.

"At times."

"I got my happily-ever-after when I was eighteen. My soul mate. My beautiful children. Did I experience all this so early because I'm going to die young? One day, my luck will run out."

"No, sweetheart." If that day ever came, life would be unbearable. "You're the club's good luck charm."

"So you've said before."

"The club was in shambles. Christopher was a wreck. I was drifting. Mort wanted vengeance. Digger didn't know his place. Val was pining away for Zoann. Stretch was hiding in the closet. Cash was on the fringes of life. Club members didn't know if they wanted Christopher to lead or Snake or someone else. You fixed that. You made it right."

She hung her head. "Then, maybe, if that's truly the case, that's my destiny fulfilled. I disagree with you, by the way. None of you needed me to do anything. You would've worked things out."

"Would we have?" he countered. "We were looking to Christopher, who was devastated over Big Joe's death and the fact that he killed him. He was broken. We were all broken."

She drew her knees up and rested her cheek there.

"What's going on, Megs?"

Her smile grew wistful. "Megs?" she whispered. "It's been years since you've called me that."

"That was my special name for you. You were my friend. Maybe, I saw you—*see* you—as my best friend. I know I'm not in love with you anymore."

"You need to tell Kendall. *Show* her. As for me being your best friend, that isn't true."

He leaned against the trunk of the tree. "It is." He'd given this a lot of thought since meeting Emily. "I love Christopher. I admire him. All the guys, but you've always done for me what Roxanne does for everyone else. You listen to me. You counsel me. You advise me."

"That may be so, but you don't take my advice. Otherwise, you and Kendall would still be together."

"And you defend both me and my wife," he continued, as though she hadn't spoken. "Even now, when neither of us deserve it. You're my best friend, Megan."

"Christopher is mine," she said without hesitation.

"I know. I wish Kendall was that to me."

"That works both ways. You just admitted I'm your best friend. A fact you never hid. How do you think that made Kendall feel?"

"She's so—"

Lifting her head, Megan raised her hand. "Stop right there. She was so *whatever* for as long as you've known her. That's who you fell in love with. You never gave her a break or a real chance."

"Do you think I'm responsible for her current state?" From time to time that thought plagued him. Sometimes, it kept him awake at night.

"The short answer? Yes. The long answer is complicated. She lost her father at an early age. From what I understand, he was the only one to show her real, true love. Her mother mocked her and preferred suicide over staying alive for Kendall. Spoon kept her prisoner and abused her. Cut off her hair. Made her lose your first child. Charlotte is an evil witch, but she was the first woman to show Kendall any maternal care before Roxy. *You* valued me over her. Christopher despises her. Then there were those girls from her middle and high school days. Emily Riser or whatever, who looked just like me, so, of course I triggered her at every turn. And Logan..."

Megan's voice faded into white noise. The creek became just a black hole, while his surroundings dimmed and his head pounded.

Emily.

Johnnie wondered how he'd "accidentally" ran into a woman who was almost Megan's spitting image. Suddenly, he knew.

How dare Christopher!

How fucking *dare* he? It was one thing for Johnnie to divorce Kendall and find another woman. But it became a different beast when Christopher played such a heavy hand in it.

"Johnnie?"

Megan's voice reached through his blazing anger.

"Are you okay?"

"What do you know about Emily?"

Megan shrugged. "Not much. Just that she was Kendall's nemesis in high school and that has had a major effect on her entire life."

"Suppose I told you I'd met her? That she was the Emily I'm thinking of taking out?"

Her brows lifted. "Wow, that's quite a coinci..." Her voice trailed off and her eyes widened. She groaned. "I'm going to talk to him."

"Why?" he snarled. "Do you know what my dating that bitch would do to Kendall? What kind of a low-down motherfucker is Christopher? That would drive Kendall over the edge! Is he fucking crazy?"

"Do *not* rage on my husband because you're a jackass," she spat. "What is wrong with *him*? What is wrong with *you*? He obviously knows you well enough to know that all you had to do was glance at someone who looks like me and nothing else would matter! Not Kendall. Not your marriage. Not *anything*, moron."

"Fuck you, Megan."

Megan jumped to her feet. Before she kicked him in the face, Johnnie stood, too.

"Go to hell," she blazed. "You know what's pathetic? Kendall would tell you to sleep with her to get me out of your system! How crazy is that? Yet, you two, impossible as it may seem, love each other. My husband isn't crazy. *You* are and you've driven Kendall mad."

Furious, he kicked the bag containing their food and drinks. "I should shake the fuck out of you for telling me that bullshit."

"It's true," she said, not backing down. "Back away from Christopher. He shot you once. He'll kill you the next time. Do I want to see that happen? No. But I *do* want you to stop blaming him, me, and even Kendall for *your* actions. Yes, Kendall has a mental illness but *you* made her so much worse. You didn't give her the respect she deserved as your wife. You taunted her with me. What did you think that would do? Make her into the woman you thought you wanted? A housewife? An old lady? A stay-at-home mom? Kendall. Is. Not. Any. Of. Those. Things," she gritted, punctuating each word by pounding her fist into her hand. "Grow up, Johnnie. Just grow up. Don't be angry with Christopher because you saw Emily and had some type of...of mega-erection or something."

"Drop this goddamn subject, or else," he warned, stomping back the laughter he felt at Megan's description. Mega-erection? Where the fuck would she get that from?

"My God, I am so sick of you. Maybe, Christopher's motives are a little suspect, but he seems to know you better than you know yourself."

"How would you feel if I brought Emily to the club, seeing that she looks just like you?"

"Shouldn't you be worried about how Kendall will feel if she found out that you brought her arch-enemy around?"

"They're grown women. I'm sure they've left that in the past."

"If you came here seeking my approval to go out with Emily, I don't know what to tell you."

All the fight left him and he sagged, exhausted from the emotional turmoil. "Kendall is driving me insane. She had no right to touch CJ.

Or to fight you. Or any of the shit she's done, Megan. I want to be happy."

"*She* wants to be happy. You both deserve it."

"I love her."

"That isn't enough. You have to respect her. Protect her. Confide in her. Make her first in your life. Kendall needs a strong man. Someone she can lean on. Someone to hold her up during her dark days. Someone to set her straight. You can be that man. You *are* that man. When I first met you, the only thing that distinguished you from Christopher, was your lightheartedness. You're both beautiful. You're both dangerous. And you're both charming and loyal. I chose him because I fell in love with him not long after I met him. Not because you were less. Not because you were lacking. I chose him because he had my heart and soul."

For so many years, he'd wondered exactly *why* she'd chosen Christopher over him. He'd asked her on several occasions, but the answers must not have registered. Today, though, her words touched something in him.

"Do you think there's a chance for Kendall and me to reconcile?"

"I can't answer that. All I know is the past few weeks have been so rough on relationships. You and Kendall seem to have irreconcilable differences and now Knox and Roxy..." She paused and looked away. "It's just been hard," she mumbled.

He recalled her earlier morbidity. "It seems so. With you thinking about death. Where did that come from?"

"I've been thinking about another baby," she confessed. Another glance at the ground alerted him to her second lie of the day. "I want to have it. For some reason, I'm scared something is going to happen to me this time." She looked at her watch. "I have to get home to start dinner, Johnnie." As she walked away, she paused and hesitated, before turning to him and standing on her tiptoes.

He bent and she kissed his cheek. "You have hard decisions to make, but I have every faith in you that you will choose the correct path. You're a strong, honorable man and we all love you."

She gave him a last smile, then continued on her way, not realizing, with her words, a burden lifted from Johnnie's shoulders.

CHAPTER FORTY-THREE

Slouching back on her torn leather couch, Emily sipped her morning coffee as she took in her favorite program on the new, big screen TV she'd purchased with some of the money Outlaw had given her. Shopping for, and dressing in, the type of designer clothes she'd once worn had been a balm to her soul.

Now her expensive wardrobe brightened up her rundown apartment, located in a dangerous part of town that saw its fair share of crime. Sometimes, she worried about some asshole breaking in and stealing her high-end stuff before she used everything. So far, she'd only gotten to dress up in her new duds one time, since they'd been purchased, the day she met Johnnie. Though they talked every day, he still hadn't asked her out.

She frowned at the screen, not liking the turn in the program's plot.

"No!" she yelled. One of her favorite characters was almost taken out by an invading alien. She straightened and growled in frustration at a particularly ignorant decision. "How fucking stupid!"

At a critical moment of a character's decision, her thin door vibrated with a loud knock. Resentful at the interruption, she cut her eyes away from the TV. Fifteen seconds hadn't passed before the knock came again.

"What?" she screeched. "*What?*" If it was Miller coming for a dick suck, she'd give him one or two bites to the nuts.

Jumping up from the sofa as the show cut to a commercial, Emily stomped to the door and threw it open. And froze.

"What are you—"

Johnnie brushed passed her before she got the words out.

She almost threw an army of profanities at him, until she remembered Knox Harrington and Outlaw's instructions. Johnnie needed a "demure" woman to get him away from Kendall. Breathing in deep and cursing to herself, she just managed not to slam the door shut.

Pasting a smile on her face, she turned to him. "What brings you to my place?" she asked his back, since he stood in her living room/bedroom, facing away from her. His rockers stared at her. The grim reaper in the center of his cut, scythe dripping blood, chilled her.

She shoved aside her reservations, tossed her hair, and marched to her prey. She touched his bicep, tense and taut beneath her fingertips.

"Hey," she said softly, part of the old Emily—the rich girl she had once been—surfacing. "Would you like a refreshment?"

He shifted and glared down at her. The cold edge to his silver eyes made them seem pale and frozen. Dropping her hand, Emily stepped back.

A twisted grin gathered at his mouth. "Aren't you curious about how I got your address?" he purred.

He seemed a little...*off*. Off his rocker. Off kilter. Off *something* that Emily neither liked nor trusted. Grabbing her remote and flicking her TV off, she threw it aside and started away, her intentions to put the sofa between them.

He was quick, though. In an instant, he grabbed her shoulder and pressed a gun between her eyes.

"You're her," he snarled.

"Her who?" she squeaked, shocked and afraid. He seemed ready to pull the trigger.

"*Emily*," he gritted. "Riser. The cunt who tortured Kendall."

Her nostrils flared. It crossed her mind to deny the accusation, but he cocked the trigger, scaring her into silence.

"Chris..." His voice trailed off and he thought a moment. "*Outlaw* hired you, yes?"

She should confess all. However, if she managed to survive, she didn't want Outlaw's wrath. *He* was the one who'd given her the money. Money turned men into murderers.

"No, Johnnie."

Dropping her arm, he grabbed her throat and squeezed, shaking her. His other hand remained steady as he kept the barrel of the gun between her eyes. "You're a fucking liar, you little cunt. Where do you think I got your fucking address from?"

The suffocating pressure on her throat made her grab his wrists. "Please," she gasped out. "Please, don't kill me."

"Then answer me," he snarled.

For the first time in years, she truly feared losing her life at the hands of this cold, furious killer. Whatever else he might be, she knew he wouldn't hesitate to kill her. All because of Kendall.

God, how Emily hated her. Kendall *had* told the truth. Johnnie loved that bitch.

Tears rushed to her eyes, not all of them fake. "Please, I can explain," she said in a tremulous whisper. She sniffled, hoping to snap him into remembering that Emily resembled another woman he loved or wanted to fuck.

He stared into her eyes, looked at every angle of her face, her hair, her lips. She licked them, determined to keep his attention on the side of her he liked. She needed to meet Megan Caldwell to better affect her mannerisms, to always have the upper hand with Johnnie.

The pressure at her throat lightened. "Johnnie," she whispered.

He gazed upon her as if he was seeing her for the first time, then shoved her away. Her knees hit the edge of the sofa and she fell onto the seat.

"Start talking," he ordered.

"I-I don't know Outlaw," she lied, her thoughts tripping into each other to give answers that would appease Johnnie *and* Outlaw, and most importantly, keep herself alive. "I-I-I..." Her voice trailed off. His question hit her full force. "Knox H-Harrington must've given you my address," she stammered.

He thrust his fingers through his golden hair, jerking on the ends. The barrel of his gun pointed at the ceiling. As long as he held it, she was in danger.

"You're a fucking liar," he roared. "This is just too fucking coincidental. How the fuck do I run into the cunt that tortured my wife during her teenage years?"

Tears slid down Emily's cheeks and she raised her hands.

Unmoved, he pointed the gun at her. "Fuck you. I'm sending you to hell and feeding *you* to the fucking butterflies—"

Her door slammed open and Johnnie turned, firing. Emily screamed as Outlaw danced out of the way, drawing and cocking his own weapon so fast, her head spun.

"*Fuck,* now, Prez, John Boy, put your fucking pieces down," a black man with long dreads said in a calm voice. His brown eyes took in the scene as his gaze landed on her. "Fuck! Who your daddy? Big Joe?"

"Mort, shut the fuck up," Outlaw ordered as Johnnie yelled, "Harrington! That motherfucker!"

Outlaw bared his teeth. "Knox ain't no motherfucker in this fuckin' instance, motherfucker. Now putcha motherfuckin' gun down be-fuckin-fore you piss me the fuck off."

"I can fucking kill you," Johnnie snapped.

"You pissin' me the fuck off, John Boy," Outlaw said.

If the eyes were the mirror to a man's soul, then Outlaw's were those of as cold a killer as Johnnie.

"Why, Christopher? Why did you get Emily? Where did you find her?" Johnnie asked evenly, still holding his gun. "Don't bother to fucking deny it. You being here gave you away."

"Gave *what* the fuck away?" Outlaw asked with an icy smile, as if he hadn't been caught in his own lie. "Knox fuckin' Harrington called my fuckin' ass and say you about to kill a fuckin' bitch who fucked with Kendall *years a-fuckin-go*. He was fuckin' worried you was gonna do somethin' stupid and ain't know who the fuck else to call. Now, what the fuck *you* talkin' about, assfuck?"

Johnnie's hand shook and he swallowed. "You hate Kendall."

"What the fuck new about that?" Outlaw answered, not flinching.

He pocketed his 9mm, walking to Johnnie and ignoring the gun pointed at his head. He yanked the weapon out of Johnnie's hand and slammed it against his chest.

Johnnie sat heavily on the sofa and stared straight ahead. "Kendall..." He drew in a heavy sigh. "No wonder she hates...*hated*... Megan. Emily looks...She's the woman who was Kendall's arch nemesis in school."

Outlaw's inscrutable expression gave Emily an insight into his ruthlessness. He gave no indication he knew her.

"John Boy," the man called Mortician said, stepping next to Outlaw. "Prez not a sneaky bitch like that, brother. If he wanted you to meet this Emily chick"—a brief nod in her direction to acknowledge her —"then he would've introduced you himself."

"I know." Johnnie hung his head. "But, fuck, Mort!" He shifted and looked between the two men. "Christopher, is Kendall really off the hook? I'm..." He drew in a deep breath. "I'm so scared for her life."

"Cuz you know that cunt need buryin', motherfucker."

"I might be divorcing her, but she's still the mother of my children. I don't want her dead. I want her better."

Outlaw folded his arms. "Then what, huh, assfuck? You takin' her back? You lettin' her be with another motherfucker? Think about this shit while you at it." He pointed to Emily. "What the fuck this bitch fuckin' mean to my fuckin' ass to get revenge on your bitch?"

Uncertainty slid across Johnnie's face and he stared at Emily. She wondered if he saw her at all through that chilling light in his eyes. "Emily looks like Megan. That would be the ultimate revenge on Kendall. If I end up with Megan's lookalike and her biggest tormenter. Kendall isn't mentally strong enough for that."

"That bitch Frankenstein. She strong enough for any-fuckin-thing."

Emily chewed her lower lip to stifle her laughter.

"And...and Megan," Johnnie went on in a voice so weary Emily almost felt sorry for him. "She doesn't want any harm to come to

Kendall. You couldn't deploy your same tactics to seek revenge on my wife because of *your* woman."

"I love the fuck outta Megan, Johnnie. Ain't doin' shit to piss her the fuck off and have the lil' motherfucker disa-fuckin-pointed in my ass. She my fuckin' world."

Mortician sidled a frown in Outlaw's direction as Johnnie met Outlaw's gaze. They stared at one another, until Johnnie conceded and looked away.

"That doesn't exactly sound like a denial," he said tightly.

"Ain't givin' a good motherfuck what the fuck it sound like to you."

"Swear to me that my meeting Emily was purely by chance," Johnnie demanded, turning to study him.

Outlaw snickered. "Ain't swearin' shit to you, motherfucker. You either believin' me or you fuckin' ain't."

"Kendall got Megan kidnapped," Johnnie said with distinct despair. "Megan almost died while Kendall withheld the information. Megan says it's over and done with. You almost lost your goddamn mind, Christopher. I know you. *I know you.* There's no fucking way you're letting that go. Kendall's still alive. You *rewarded* her with all kinds of shit. Trapping her in your snare. Luring her into your web." He stood. "If something happens to her by her own hand, you won't have killed her, but you'd still be responsible for her death because of your schemes." He shook his head. "Don't do this to her. Whatever it is. If it isn't Emily, then it's something. *Please.* Don't hurt Kendall. Let me send her away."

Instead of answering, Outlaw folded his arms.

"Think about how devastated you'd be if something ever happened to Megan, whether she was at your side or far away," Johnnie went on. "I love Kendall. I just can't live with her anymore. I can't take her schemes and her bullshit. I...don't hurt her," he said again. "If you need to seek revenge, kill me instead. Take my life in place of hers."

"A quarter of that bitch worth ten of you, motherfucker," Outlaw barked.

"Not to me," Johnnie shot back.

Outlaw met Johnnie's gaze. For a moment, Emily thought he was going to confess all.

"You want the fuckin' truth?" Outlaw said in a lethal tone. "I hate that cunt. She still a-fuckin-live cuz of Megan. All the fuck I wanna do is shoot the fuck outta her for so many fuckin' reasons. I want that bitch gone. Dead. Wiped the fuck off the face of the fuckin' earth. Shot from a fuckin' cannon into fuckin' space so she can fuckin' turn into fuckin' dust. I ain't able to do that cuz of my girl. Every-fuckin-thing Kendall got cuz of Megan. My life, Megan life, my boy life, *your* fuckin' life, your lil motherfuckers' lives, ain't ever mattered to Kendall. You think I give a good motherfuck what happen to fuckin' Kendall when you start fuckin' other bitches a-fuckin-gain?"

Johnnie looked at Mortician. "Talk to him."

"What the fuck you want me to say, John Boy? I fucking talk to Red 'til my balls fucking blue. She don't fucking listen and that just piss Prez the fuck off."

"You're her friend," Johnnie reminded him.

"I love Red, but she the busiest bitch around," Mortician said in frustration. He rubbed his eyes then focused on Outlaw. "Prez, Johnnie love Red. Reconsider whatever psycho stalker Wildman revenge you plan for her. We know you planning something. We all do. It might not be this." He pointed at Emily. "*Her*, but it's something. Just don't kill her."

"Christopher." Hope rang in Johnnie's voice after Mortician's speech. "I swear if she ever endangers your family again, I'll kill her myself."

Outlaw snorted. "That'll be the fuckin' day you fuckin' grow your balls back. Since that bitch chewed them the fuck off and swallowed them motherfuckers, never to be fuckin' seen a-fuckin-again, you ain't ever goin' to fuckin' kill her."

"Damn, Prez."

"Jesus, Christopher."

Outlaw smiled again and stared at Emily. "Ain't layin' a finger on Kendall," he announced, never taking his gaze off her. "If that cunt end up buried ain't gonna be cuz I fuckin' killed her."

He smirked at Emily and Johnnie, then turned on his heel. "Come on, Mort. Let's fuckin' ride."

Mortician shook his head, then glanced at Johnnie, pulling on his riding gloves. "Kendall so fucked," he sighed, and walked out, leaving Emily alone with Johnnie.

He faced her and they stared at each other. He had vulnerability written all over him. *This* Johnnie she could handle.

"I'm so sorry to have hurt Kendall," she lied, hoping Kendall never found a reason to tell Johnnie about their last run-in. Of course, Emily could always set up another lunch date and bury the hatchet. Right in her back. "Please, forgive me. Don't let what happened when we were children get in the way of our attraction."

"There's no attraction to you," he growled.

Sure, asshole.

If he didn't want to fuck her, why else would he still be there?

"From what I gather, I remind you of some woman."

"It's bad enough you fucked over Kendall. Don't bring Megan into this."

"You need someone to listen to you, Johnnie. Hear *you*. It sounds as if you haven't had that for a very long time." She patted the spot next to her. "I'm a very good listener. Let's order pizza and drink a few beers while we get to know each other."

He considered her for a moment, then closed his eyes.

"No strings attached," she interjected, determined to sway the battle he waged in her favor. His eyes popped open.

"Fuck you. *No!*" He glared at her, then stalked out, slamming the door behind him.

His dismissal infuriated Emily, but her hands were tied for now. All wasn't lost. For a moment he'd considered her offer, then changed his mind. After his smarmy begging on behalf of Kendall, Emily supposed his mind remained on that bitch.

CHAPTER FORTY-FOUR

CHRISTOPHER

Leaning against his bike, Christopher handed the binoculars to Mortician, lit a cigarette, sucked on it, then released the smoke. Sunbursts broke through the March sky, where layers of reds, oranges, and pinks painted dusk with an artist's palette.

He sniggered at the pussified analogy, dragged on his cigarette again, then puffed out, hoping life was getting back to normal. Megan was pregnant again. Kendall would soon be dead. And the club had a very profitable gun-running deal on the horizon with Knox's contact if things continued to go smoothly.

"Amfinger not doing a lot, Outlaw," Mortician informed him as if he'd heard Christopher's thoughts. "We saw the guns at the warehouse last night. They just like he promised. All the motherfucker doing at this shitty motel is leaving and coming back with food. If you taking the deal, this look legit."

Christopher ignored Mort's grouchiness. The motherfucker wanted to be with Bailey, who was fucking devastated over Roxanne. Last night, right after Christopher shared the news that he was going to be a father again, Mort told him that Bailey had just found out she was pregnant, too. Christopher knew that shit made girls emotional.

Joyner Amfinger *did* seem on the up-and-fucking-up. Riley did a detailed background check on the motherfucker. Amfinger came up for arms dealing, which was to be expected. That's what the mother-fucker had contacted Knox for. Joyner had had legitimate contracts, the kind sanctioned by governments, so Christopher didn't understand why the motherfucker had contacted *Knox* to sell weapons to the club.

Shit just didn't feel right. And, yet...the motherfucker was coming up as being who the fuck he said he was. He also had a warehouse full of merchandise. So what the fuck was the problem? Why was Christopher questioning his instinct when he rarely had before?

He didn't have to question his fucking uncertainty. It all went the fuck back to Megan. *His* fucking decisions could mean *her* life. He'd always known that shit but...Disgust hit him. What the fuck was wrong with him?

Scowling, he snatched the binoculars from Mort's hands. The man Christopher identified as Joyner leaned on the railing, his mannerisms relaxed. The Joyner motherfucker reminded Christopher of Johnny Bravo, with hair sticking straight the fuck up and tight clothes.

"We riding out today or we staying another day, Prez?"

"Ain't sure yet. I think we seein' what the fuck we need to see." He sucked on his cigarette again. "I ain't wantin' to be gone too fuckin' much longer."

"Meggie girl okay?" Mort flicked his cigarette into the gulley close to them. He nodded toward the landing that lead to Joyner's motel room.

Christopher dragged and released smoke again. "She still got rough nights," he responded. "Me, too. Mystic, the motherfucker, did more fuckin' harm than he fuckin' know."

"Snake took her and you. She didn't seem no worse for wear."

"I wasn't neither. Even though that motherfucker buried me the fuck alive. We both different now, Mort."

"We *all* different, Prez."

Christopher nodded. "Before I knew Megan was alive, I really didn't give a fuck what the fuck Snake did. I'd lost Ma. Bitsy, Fee, and the rest of my sisters, hated me." He didn't like to bring up his other three sisters. Thoughts of them reminded him they'd been killed. They were gone. Focusing on them wouldn't bring them back, so he shrugged, and got back to their conversation. "When they dug me the fuck up and I heard Megan, I had something to fight for."

A cool breeze fluttered the low-hanging branches of the trees they lounged under. They were across the highway from the run-down motel that was surrounded by a shabby gas station, a greasy burger joint, a ramshackle bar, rutted roads and deep gullies.

It surprised him to feel so out-of-place, when at one time he would've fit in like a skintight glove. Not because he was a biker, but because of how he'd seen himself. His biker life had introduced him to worlds beyond his imagination. Society had it so wrong about the one percenters, but fuck them. That was their problem, not his.

He knew no other life but this one. Since Megan had come into his life, though, he enjoyed more comforts, and didn't rough it as much. In times like this, when he went on runs and out-of-town business without his girl, he still did. Inadvertently, he'd gotten used to having a home and a family.

For some reason, the realization made him think of Johnnie. He'd pleaded for Kendall's life with a desperation that haunted Christopher. Under other circumstances, Johnnie's state would've moved Christopher and made him back off. If not for Johnnie's sake, then thoughts of Megan's wrath, or disappointment in him, would've calmed his rage.

Nothing helped. Not thoughts of Johnnie's devastation if something happened to Kendall. And, not, the idea of losing the most important thing in his life. Deep down, he hoped Megan would give him a pass. Even when she'd demanded his promise in the forest, he'd skirted around it. She hadn't pressed him or thrown in his face that he'd already sworn not to hurt Kendall because Megan had insisted he put psycho cunt on the No-Kill list.

Megan had to understand his reasons. But he was doing something he never did...fuck...*rarely* did...lying to her. About Emily and about all the "rewards" he'd given Kendall for confessing she might know Megan's location.

He wanted to, at least, tell Megan about Emily, so she didn't get falsi-fuckin-fied information. Inevitably, that would lead to him telling Megan his plans for Kendall. She might be so fucking disgusted by him and fed the fuck up that she left.

Still, he just went full the fuck speed ahead, as if he'd have no consequences. Just as his grandfather would've done. He hated Kendall so fucking much. Yet, if he destroyed what he had with his Megan, that cunt would fucking win any-fucking-way. What the fuck should he do? What the fuck could he do?

Shooting Johnnie hadn't stopped Kendall. She'd still fucked with CJ. And Megan. Christopher believed only Kendall's own death would stop her.

Or, maybe, he could have her locked the fuck away in another fucking psycho camp. Just have her snatched the fuck up, held in a cage with a key that, un-fucking-fortunately, was somehow lost. Thrown from a fucking cliff, into the ocean. Dropped in a fucking Louisiana swamp, where an alligator could swallow it.

The image of dropping *Kendall* in either of those places rose in Christopher's head, giving him a greater sense of satisfaction than doing the same to a fucking key. A missing key was easy to rectify. A dead bitch could never be brought back to life to harm Megan or CJ or Johnnie or Rory, ever again.

Still, Kendall was fucking family. Until Johnnie divorced her. If Knox was fucking off-limits with a phony fucking engagement, then Kendall being married to Johnnie had the same benefit. Unless he was turning into his grandfather. Logan Donovan had killed his own fucking son, a motherfucker he'd supposedly loved. Yeah, Christopher had fucked up his old man, but he'd never considered CeeCee his family.

It would've made more sense if Logan had killed Christopher. He'd been his grandfather's most hated object. The motherfucker had never seen people. Just objects, family or not. To play with. To use.

To destroy.

Christopher was doing to Kendall, and by extension Johnnie, what Logan had done to him.

"Mort." Christopher flicked away his cigarette. "You think my ass turnin' to Logan?"

"Lowman?" Mortician's eyes widened. "What the fuck make you think that shit, Outlaw? Not even Satan could turn into that motherfucker."

"I don't fuckin' know, Mort," he said. "Ain't I fuckin' around with Johnnie life? I just been fuckin' thinkin'. Know how I fuckin' know this some Logan-type bullshit? Cuz of the fuckin' shame my ass feelin'. In my fuckin' head, even my Megan would fuckin' change her opinion of my ass." He rubbed his eyes, tired.

He hadn't gotten much rest last night, missing Megan and worried that Johnnie would go on a fucking killing spree.

Christopher and Mort had still been in Hortensia, buying shit to take on the road with them, gassing their bikes, and mapping out the best routes, when Knox called in a panic because Johnnie had demanded Emily's address and was headed to her house.

Christopher had already had a lot on his mind because he'd told Megan he had a run to make. He hadn't mentioned that it involved guns since that had gotten *his* ass scooped up the last time he fucked with weapons. Until he figured out what he intended to do, he didn't want to unnecessarily worry her. He'd had one long conversation with Joyner. One particular fucking thing had set off alarms in Christopher. When Amfinger said he'd been born in New Orleans.

Christopher had found it odd, since Roxanne was from New Orleans, too. Of course, a lot of motherfuckers lived there and had been born in the city. But with her boy acting like he didn't like his bones in one piece, Christopher had wondered if Amfinger needed to become Aintfinger.

Riley had checked out Duke and Creighton, his father. No connection had been made between the three of them, so, maybe, it was just coincidence, and he'd grown into a paranoid motherfucker. He'd think on this shit later. Right now, Johnnie's begging for Kendall's life still fucked with him.

"Ain't I makin' the choice for Johnnie? A motherfucker do that shit to me, and I woulda killed them. Yet, look at my fuckin' ass."

"Prez, honest...?" Mort looked into the distance, then heaved in a sigh and met his gaze. "The shit you doing not your style. You don't do fucking sneak attacks. If you want a motherfucker dead, you killing them and letting every motherfucker around know what the fuck you did."

Christopher scrubbed a hand over his face. "This shit different. This family. Megan ain't wantin' me to kill Johnnie or Kendall."

"That's why the motherfucker alive today," Mortician guessed. "When you shot him a few months ago, I know you re-angled your piece at the last minute because of Meggie girl. But, fuck, what you doing getting this Emily chick involved with Johnnie?"

"Trying to get Kendall so fuckin' traumatized that she can't take livin' no fuckin' more and go fuck herself the fuck up."

Mort winced. "In other words, *you* not killing her."

"Not fuckin' directly."

"No, but, dead is dead, Outlaw. Whether you kill Kendall yourself or drive her to do it, she'll still be gone."

"And the fuckin' world be a better place without her," Christopher snapped, feeling as psycho as psycho cunt. No wonder Johnnie was so fucked up. That's what that bitch did to motherfuckers with her Franken-fucking-stein ass.

Memories of his son with members of a Dweller support club because CJ had been abandoned by the same motherfuckers who'd taken Megan hadn't left him yet. Inevitable, he thought of *Megan*, and the way he'd found her close to death. In some fucking shape or form, Kendall had been responsible for each of those events.

"Just off the top of my goddamn head, I can fuckin' name sixteen fuckin' crimes that bitch did, Mort."

"*Sixteen,* Prez?"

"She got Johnnie shot." He used his finger to tick off each crime she'd committed. "She drugged the motherfucker. She got my ass, Val, and her-fuckin-self stolen after inter-fuckin-fering in club business. She stowed away on the goddamn plane I was on to go and fix her fuckin' bullshit. She threatened to open her big fuckin' mouth and tell Megan the truth about what happened to Traveler and Dinah. She got into a fuckin' fight with Bitsy. She came to the club, on Logan orders, to get dick from me to fuck up my marriage."

"Prez, you about to run out of fucking fingers."

Christopher flipped Mort off, then ditched the current finger count and started off. "She keep flirtin' with my goddamn ass. The first time she met Megan that bitch told my girl she was the cunt that grinded her pussy on me. She paid Daphne to fuck with me to make Megan think I was cheatin'. She got that stupid bitch fucked up cuz I told Daphne to stop fuckin' with Megan. Did she fuckin' listen? Nope. Kendall made her believe other-fuckin-wise. Let's fuckin' forget Daphne a minute. Kendall blackmailed Fee. She a lyin' bitch when she told motherfuckers she knocked up. And what about her lil' mother-fuckers? The way that bitch treat Rory is fucked up and you fuckin' know it."

Mortician squeezed the bridge of his nose. "Damn, Red make it hard to plead for her life, huh?"

"Very fuckin' hard. What the fuck can you fuckin' say?"

"Red tried to get Bailey to divorce me, Outlaw. She was just looking out for Bailey, though." Mortician raised his hands before Christopher blasted him. "Hold on. Kendall selfish, but some of the shit she do is for the right reasons. She just go about them the wrong way."

"That's your fuckin' friend, Mort, so you gonna take up for her."

"I don't have nothing to say about the way she treat her kids and CJ," Mort confessed.

"A bitch fuckin' willin' to beat a kid like he a grown fuckin' man is a bitch that don't deserve to fuckin' breathe. Case fuckin' closed. Kendall need to die. *I* want to kill her. Put the gun to her head, meet her eyes with mine, and blow her the fuck away."

"I understand, Prez. Any other motherfucker and she would've been grounded a long time ago."

"Exactly, Mort. Cuz in our fuckin' world, a motherfucker fuck up, he die. Ain't no middle-fuckin'-ground. Kendall fuck up over and over a-fuckin-gain."

"That's just it, Prez. This the gray area we never have had to worry about, but now we talking about family. No matter how you feel about it, Red related."

Christopher clenched his jaw. Hearing Mort speak the words he'd been thinking, annoyed the fuck out of him.

"Whether you like it or not, Outlaw, it's true," Mort insisted. "You not handling things as you normally would, *per se*. Your means of reaching the end result is different, but Kendall still going to end up deader than a motherfucker."

"Sharper was your fuckin' old man. Johnnie was Logan favorite. You two motherfuckers still fucked up *those* two motherfuckers. Ain't no gray area there."

"What do you want me to say, Prez?" Mortician asked, a thread of frustration dropping into his tone.

"Not a motherfuckin' thing," Christopher snapped.

What was there to say? Either that bitch would live or fucking die. By telling Mort the truth, yesterday, after leaving Emily, Christopher knew he was having second thoughts.

Mort used the binoculars to look across the way. "Joyner gone, Prez."

"Let's wait a few fuckin' minutes to see if the motherfucker come back." He didn't know if he'd gone in the room or left altogether.

"Peep this, Outlaw," Mortician started after a moment. "Say Kendall fuck herself up after shit play out as you have them planned. What then? You can't fucking tell me you're going to be comfortable ever again. A part of you will always fear Meggie going to find out what really happened to Kendall."

"Unless you fucking tell her..." A vision of Knox rose in his head, and Christopher's voice trailed off.

"You planning on killing Knox, too?" Mort asked, correctly guessing where Christopher's thoughts landed. "You don't have to worry about me, Outlaw. I'll keep your secrets, even if I don't agree with them, and guard you with my last breath, as my president and friend. Don't get me wrong. I hope you don't do nothing that will get me fucked up on your behalf. I happen to like living."

"In other words, no matter what the fuck I do, that bitch win," he snarled, anger at the corner he found himself in, rising to the top. "If I fuckin' grab that bitch by the throat, shove my gun in her mouth, look her in the eyes, and pull the trigger, she win cuz I gotta waste my fuckin' brain cells thinkin' of her as she die. If I fuckin' drive her to fuck herself up, Ima fuckin' worry the rest of my fuckin' days about Megan findin' out. On fuckin' top of that, I gotta either fuck up Knox or cut his fuckin' tongue out, yeah?"

"I didn't say nothing about cutting the dude's tongue out, Prez," Mortician chided.

Christopher shrugged. "Either his fuckin' brains would have to go or his fuckin' tongue."

"Tongue would be fine. I'm sure Knox would agree."

"The most galling fucking development," Christopher continued, ignoring Mortician as he came to the obvious conclusion, "would be lettin' that fuckin' bitch live."

"You could also demand Johnnie choose. Tell him he either have to divorce Kendall or leave the club. The way you doing it now, you choosing for him anyway by putting Emily in his path and the way you have shit going down with Kendall."

"Whatcha think of that Emily bitch?" Christopher asked, changing the subject.

"I don't know her, other than seeing her ass for ten fucking minutes. What do you think of her?"

"You think she for Big Joe?"

"Wouldn't that be fucking ironic?" Mort grumbled, then nodded. "A part of me do. If she is for Boss, bitch might be a fucking psychopath like Snake or an angel like Meggie."

Christopher would bet psycho-fuckin-path. "Something about this bitch warnin' me that she bad news. I ain't able to put my fuckin' finger on it."

"She a psycho then," Mort decided.

Christopher shrugged. "And she not for Big Joe, by the way. Had Riley check into it. Got a picture of her old man. When you put that bitch next to that motherfucker, they look alike."

"That shit would've been too coincidental," Mort responded. "Prez, why you got Knox working on this Johnnie triangle shit? You using Riley for everything else."

"Knox don't like Kendall."

"I know. So you thought that would make it easier?"

"Knox don't like my fuckin' ass neither. He think he so fuckin' different from us, but especially me. It ain't dawned on that mother-fucker, that he not much different, after-fucking-all."

"I told you he want to learn how to ride. And he want a tat. I know you don't believe him, but I got it all setup with Gabe for later today."

"I don't believe him, Mort," Christopher agreed. "If he serious, I ain't got a problem helpin' the motherfucker, but if he doin' it just to impress Roxanne and ain't really into it, I ain't involvin' my-fuckin-self."

"Prez—"

"No, Mort. Think about how he act with psycho cunt. He pretend he ain't got a problem with her in front of Roxanne, but we know that ain't the case. Knox want Kendall gone. The one time that bitch did something fuckin' right and he hate her fuckin' guts for it. He bein' a cutthroat motherfucker, workin' for me, to get things his fuckin' way. He ain't givin' a fuck how Roxanne feel about Kendall and he ain't givin' a fuck that he consider Johnnie his friend. I fuckin' thought I'd help him see how fuckin' much like us he is be-fuckin-fore the weddin'. If that shit even happen now."

Mort blew out a breath. "On the real, Outlaw? What the fuck going on? Shit just seems so off-kilter. We been near the border of Northern Cali for two fucking days. Watching Amfinger not a life or death situation, meaning you don't *have* to be away from your woman. And, usually, when you don't *have* to be away from Meggie, you not. Now you away from your girl and you got me away from mine. This not like you."

"I needed time to think," he admitted. "Megan don't fuckin' know about Emily." A fucking timebomb waiting to fuck him in the ass if he didn't tell her. "Megan don't know about..." He shook his head, unable to finish. *Kendall*, he added silently.

Even now, after she whipped that bitch's ass over CJ, Christopher would bet his cock and balls that Megan wouldn't be happy with all of his plans.

Mort put a hand on his shoulder. "Prez, you can't let your need for vengeance destroy what the fuck you and Meggie got. Kendall not worth it. And I don't fucking mean that as aspersions against Red."

"That should be a aspersion against that cunt."

"Prez..."

"No, fuck, Mort, while you tellin' my ass to go easy on that bitch, you forgettin' what she was gonna do to my boy. *Two* separate fuckin' occasions. You just givin' that cunt a pass."

"I'm not," Mortician insisted, slightly offended. "Kendall got issues, though."

"Yeah, bein' alive," Christopher snapped. "That's her biggest motherfuckin' issue."

"At least admit she have a mental problem."

"Okay, Mort. Ima admit to that shit. In her mind, she think she better than every-fuckin-body. Mental problem identi-fuckin-fied."

"You letting your anger blind you."

"That shit allowin' me to see quite fuckin' clearly. If I had a fuckin' crystal ball, that motherfucker would be fuckin' red with Kendall blood. That's how fuckin' clear knowin' she gotta die is to me."

"Outlaw, if Meggie girl find out, what's going to happen then?"

Christopher turned away from Mort, went to his bike, opened his saddlebag, and pulled out a pint of rum. He uncapped it and finished half the bottle. "I ain't gonna have Megan if Kendall stay in the fuckin' picture. Sooner or later, that cunt gonna do something that really get my girl fuckin' killed. Then what?" He finished the bottle off, then used it to point at his friend. "Ima tell you then what. My fuckin' life over. I gotta get rid of Kendall, Mort. She ruinin' my life, Megan life, Johnnie life, fuck, her kids' lives. She miserable and makin' every-fuckin-body else fuckin' miserable."

"She one of us, Prez. Just like motherfucking Knox. Just like Roxanne. And Bailey. And Meggie. Kendall one of us. She belong to Johnnie."

Christopher's life would be so much easier if Kendall was gone, but what would her death do to Johnnie? Especially if Christopher backed her into a suicide. Johnnie might not ever forgive himself.

Mort's phone dinged and he grabbed it from his pocket. "Look," he said a moment later, holding the device up. "Bailey made reservations for our second honeymoon at this resort."

"When Knox first proposed to Roxanne, I told my-fuckin-self that we was gonna keep shit on the right track and just focus on the fuckin' weddin'. Yet..." His voice trailed off and he shook his head. "Yet—"

"Planning a fucking wedding, or two, is so far off the goddamn radar, we probably won't ever get it back on track, huh, Prez?" Mort's expression dropped, and matched the plaintive note in his voice.

Instead of backing off from his plans for Kendall, he'd speed things up. The quicker this was fucking handled, the quicker life would get back to fucking normal.

Using Emily was the right choice. No fucking way would Johnnie be cursed with bad e-fuckin-nuff luck to get two lunatic bitches in a row.

Emily couldn't ever be as bad as Kendall.

Never.

"Let's ride, Mort," Christopher said, pretending the dark feeling chasing him wasn't warning him to back off.

Pretending the winds of blood and death weren't moving in, and threatening not only the wedding, but their lives, too.

CHAPTER FORTY-FIVE

Knox

"Val!"

The happy greeting came from Gabe as Knox and Val walked into the tattoo shop Gabe owned. If Knox remembered, Gabe was Bunny's brother. There were so many branches of family and friends that Knox couldn't keep them all straight. One segment of their vast tree might break in one place, then pick up with the same father, sister or aunt, in another. Sometimes, he felt as if the entire town of Hortensia were connected to Outlaw in some way.

"What brings you in here?" Gabe asked, hands on hips, a walking pincushion with pierced brows, lips and nose. Big rings pulled his earlobes down in a grotesque display. "Hey, Knox," he finally decided to greet.

Surprised that Gabe knew him, Knox nodded. "Gabe."

They'd only run into each other at club functions three or four times, and talked even less than that.

As Val and Gabe caught up on happenings in their lives, Knox looked at the tattoo drawings lining the walls. Some were simple Celtic designs and black ink; others were intricate and colorful. It was a really nice shop, with a receptionist station that they stood around. In the middle of the room, half-walls surrounded an area containing a specialized chair, a sink, and utility cabinets. Amidst an arrangement of red leather couches, benches, and matching club chairs stood black lacquer tables, one overflowing with magazines.

"The reports aren't ready yet."

Gabe's words grabbed Knox's attention.

"I can do a quick printing of this month's spreadsheet, Val."

"You and Stretch do your usual," Val responded. "We not here about the shops. This about Knox."

"Shops?" Knox echoed.

Val nodded.

Gabe grinned. "The club owns part of my tattoo shop. We opened a second location in downtown Portland six months ago."

Surprised, Knox glanced between the two of them. "I didn't know that."

"You not required to know that," Val imparted.

"I'm part of the family," Knox insisted.

"But not part of the club," Val answered as though he spoke to a two-year-old. "Not a member," he added before Knox thought of a reply. He turned to Gabe. "Knox want ink."

Gabe studied Knox from head-to-toe, then burst into laughter. "You?" he said around howls. "You're not a tattoo-type man, Knox."

Knox narrowed his eyes. He had never been laughed at as much until he met Outlaw and crew. However, they didn't "pick" only on him. They teased each other mercilessly, too. "I didn't know you needed to be *type* to have a tattoo."

Val And Gabe exchanged glances; both seemed ready to explode with mirth.

"You know what we mean, Knox," Val chided. "You downed us partly *because* we inked."

Instead of denying the statement—which would be a blatant lie—Knox glanced away.

"It's like this," Val continued. "We don't give a fuck if you tatted or not. As long as you respect us, *accept* us, you fine in our book. If you want a tattoo just to get in good with us, we can leave right now."

"It isn't for any of you. It's for Roxanne."

Val's eyes widened. "She asked you to get inked?"

"No, of course not!" Knox huffed out. "But...but..."

Knox feared he'd really lost her because, for the past two days, since the morning he'd found her preparing for breakfast, Ophelia had come to the club for cooking duties. Roxanne was determined to shut Knox out.

Change for him didn't come easy. He'd been so quick to blame Callie for the end of their marriage, accusing her of tearing down his self-esteem, when he'd been as much to blame, if not more. It took his nastiness to Roxanne to realize his transgressions. Since his divorce, he'd still been living under the delusion that he'd changed. That he'd been the injured party.

That life was black and white. Nothing more. Nothing less.

"Ever wonder who yanked a potato up from the earth and decided that might be a good thing to fucking eat?"

At Val's stupid question, Knox blinked. He was waging one of the most important battles of his life—regaining Roxanne's heart, her trust—and... "Excuse me?" he asked, Gabe's snicker annoying him a little more.

Val shrugged. "Or who saw mushrooms and grabbed a few to munch on? How many motherfuckers pushed up their dicks after croaking from eating poisonous mushrooms before the non-lethal motherfuckers were found? I mean, who the fuck looked at that shit sprouting from the ground and decided it was a good-ass idea to pick them up to fucking chomp? Mushrooms sure don't look tasty, even after they cooked."

"Are you fucking kidding me?" Knox asked in outrage.

Amusement lit Val's face. "Am I, Knox? You think I got fucking time to *really* think about that shit? It might cross my mind some-times." He cocked his head to the side. "Why you think Mort called and asked me to bring you to Gabe? He could've given you directions or let you choose your own shop."

"As if," Knox said tiredly.

First, Mortician had called him and told him to meet Val at the club in and hour. Five minutes after that call ended, Val texted Knox to see if he was on the way. They acted as if he didn't have a fucking job. Because Mortician was willing to help him, however, Knox had made an exception and left the office for the day. "Frankly, I don't give a damn why he asked you to accompany me, Val. I'm just ready to be put under so I can get the tattoo."

"Put under what?" Gabe asked in confusion.

"You're the tattoo man—"

"Artist," Gabe corrected.

"Okay," Knox barked. "Whatever."

Gabe's jaw clenched.

Knox sighed. "I'm sorry," he said, meaning it. "This is all new to me. I...at least give me points for trying."

"Trying don't cut it," Val told him, his voice torn between disgust and sympathy. "This not a preschool where you get 'A' for effort. This is real life. Brotherhood. Loyalty. Accepting us for who we are, like we accept you."

Knox opened his mouth to dispute that, but Val raised his hand to halt his words.

"I know what you about to say. That we never accepted you. There's a reason for that. You infiltrated the club with the intention to bring us down. Even after you got with Roxanne, you decided we didn't make the cut. We not respecting a motherfucker who don't respect us."

Val's gruff words chastened Knox.

"Fair enough." Drawing in a deep breath, he looked at Gabe. "I would like the same general anesthesia that's used on people who get full body tattoos. Cam has a couple on his arms. I was with him for one, so I know the job was too small for him to be put under, so—"

"Uh, Knox, there's no anesthesia to get a tattoo." Gabe stared at Knox with uncertainty. "You know that, huh, man? You're just bullshitting me."

Knox prided himself on knowing a lot about most things and a little about everything. Growing up, he'd had a very comprehensive education, so he was loathe to admit he was lost when it came to tattoos. "Of course I'm not joking. A big tattoo must be quite painful. There are needles involved. A lot of them."

Val lifted a brow. "You scared of needles?"

"Of course not!" Knox lied. In truth, he was fucking *terrified* of them.

"Come on, motherfucker." Val turned on his heel and headed for the hallway that ran alongside the receptionist's station. "Follow me."

Knox looked at Gabe.

"I'll be there in a bit," Gabe promised. "I need to lock the shop up."

"It's the middle of the day," Knox said. "You can't close for business."

"Knox! Motherfucker," Val said in exasperation. "Gabe know what he doing. Stay the fuck out of it."

Without another word, Knox followed Val to the end of the hallway. They'd passed two rooms, doors opened, interior darkened. Val walked into the last room and flicked on the light as Knox stepped in. Wooden floors, painted black, gleamed like polished ebony underneath the glare of the bright light. The white paint would've given the room a sterile feel if not for the tattoo designs lining the upper perimeters of the four walls. A specialized chair, similar to the one at the station in the front, sat in the center of the room, a rolling stool next to it. Built-in drawers and cabinets framed a sink, while a red leather loveseat stood beneath three wall hooks.

Val nodded to the chair. "Sit," he instructed as he went to one of the cabinets and opened it.

As Knox sat, Val pulled out a fifth of rum, then he dug into the inside pocket of his cut and pulled out a lighter and a joint. Once he opened the alcohol and took a swig from it, he held the bottle out.

Knox eyed it with suspicion. "What do you want me to do with that?"

"Drink," Val said with patience.

He'd seen the guys do this countless times. He'd shared bottles with Cam before—other friends whom he trusted.

The thought crossed his mind and he winced. He didn't have to be told that he didn't trust any of the Death Dwellers. In turn, they didn't trust him. But Roxanne trusted them. She trusted him...Well, she *had* trusted him.

Instead of overthinking, he grabbed the bottle from Val and drank long and deep from it. Tears rushed to his eyes, and he coughed and sputtered, then handed the bottle back to Val. The rum burned as it slid down Knox's throat. Certainly not the smooth stuff he was accustomed to. It warmed him, sent the room twirling for a second.

After taking another pull, Val sat the bottle down, then began flicking the lighter in an effort to light the weed.

Successful, Val inhaled, held, and released, several times. "Take a hit," he told Knox, holding the joint out.

Alcohol was one thing; marijuana another. One was legal; the other was...*complicated.*

"This Outlaw own special herb. Cfc. Case Fuckin' Closed. An Indica strain. Mort came up with Big Roscoe—Br. The name, anyway. Outlaw was the one who grew the plants. Br a sativa."

"Outlaw came up with his own marijuana?" Knox asked with skepticism. "Never heard anyone mention that. Neither about Mort's."

"See a reason they got to say anything? That's not something you advertise. Besides, Outlaw been doing this for so long, he able to sell clones of his original plants. He even grow from clones. It's not a big deal to him."

Knox eyed the weed. "Everything he does is a big deal."

"According to you." Val took another hit from the joint, grabbed the rum, then dropped onto the loveseat. "Outlaw do what he have to, to be the best fucking prez around."

The strong scent of the "herb" swirled through Knox's head. Leaning his head against the chair, he closed his eyes. "Of course you're not biased at all."

"Not a fucking bit."

Folding his arms, Knox opened one eye. "Bullshit. He's indoctrinated all of you into believing he's the best thing since toasted bread."

The tip of the special cigarette sent a little spiral of smoke up, so Knox closed his eye. "You know what I wish a motherfucker came up with?"

Knox adjusted his position. "Do I have to know?"

Val sniggered. "Sure the fuck do."

"Then what?"

"Selling a loaf of toast."

Knox's eyes flew open. "That's called bread, asshole. Buy the bread and make the toast."

"Sometimes, a man hungry. After his wife suck his cock for a half hour and that motherfucker raw and red and all out of cum, a motherfucker need to eat. Usually, I'm too tired for much. A piece of toast or two. It's just so much fucking effort to get the raw bread out—"

"My God, man! Bread is not raw when you buy it. It's already baked."

"It's raw until you toast it, Knox," Val insisted.

"I'm not having this conversation with you."

"Don't give a fuck. It's what the fuck I want to talk about."

Knox growled. "Fine. Talk about bread that's raw until it's toasted. Not *dough* that turns into bread once it's baked. Talk away. I'm all ears."

Grinning, Val took a couple more leisurely hits, before pinching the end of the joint to extinguish it. "You already learning."

"What are you talking about? I don't need to learn anything."

"That's not true. Nobody know everything. There's always room to learn."

"Point for you. Yet I'm missing exactly what *I* need to learn in this situation."

"How to stop being such a superior motherfucker. How to respect another motherfucker right to say whatever the fuck he want to, however the fuck he want to. It don't make you better and me less. It just make us different." Val swigged from the rum. "Mortician could've waited 'til he was back in town for this, so he could come with you. He sent me with you, though, because he didn't want your newfound awareness of his wealth to affect how you interacted with him. Now that you know he got money, you wouldn't have been looking down on him. Mort wouldn't have liked that, Knox. Around here, we all equal. From me to Mort to Cash...to *you*."

Knox scowled, affronted as a thought occurred to him. "He sent you to teach me what he thinks I need to know?"

Val eyed him with disapproval. "There you go, acting like a stupid motherfucker again. Our hands tied because of Roxanne. Outlaw want to fuck you up because you...you know...*you*. Mort not happy with you because of his momma-in-law. Digger might fucking ground you because Mort his big brother. Me? I don't give a good fuck."

"Yet you were going to help them kill me?"

"Need to stay in practice. We haven't killed nobody in months."

"Jesus Christ," Knox breathed. "You're a barbarian, too."

Val smirked at him. "You got to have a little barbarianism in you if you joining the fold." He indicated him with a sweep of his hand. "Getting inked."

Knox simply said, "I love her."

"Funny what bitches make motherfuckers do. I had to pull a few low-motherfucker moves to get Zoann. I kept fucking up, and she got sick of my ass."

Before Val expanded on the statement, Gabe walked in, a joint of his own hanging between his fingers.

"It's illegal to smoke in public," Knox complained.

"It's illegal to smoke around the general public," Gabe corrected, using Val's lighter on his weed. "This is a public place, currently closed." He took a few hits, then passed it to Val, who happily indulged again.

"What are you thinking of getting?" Gabe went to the sink and washed his hands as thoroughly as a surgeon might. "How big and where?"

Knox had thought long and hard about this. "I want a heart with an arrow through it. Roxanne's name on one end and my name on the other end. About yea big." He used his fingers to measure about one or two inches.

Gabe nodded, gathering prep supplies. "Where? Your ring finger, maybe?"

"Ring finger?" Knox asked, incredulous. "No, nothing where there's so much bone. I was thinking my buttocks."

"Your ass?" Val said in surprise. "You want a fucking tattoo the size of a mosquito bite on your ass?"

"It's my money," Knox argued. "I can get it where I want to it."

"He's right," Gabe agreed. He looked at Knox. "You're right."

Knox gave Val an authoritative nod. In response, Val shook his head and took another swig from the rum. "Make sure you buy Roxanne a magnifying glass, motherfucker," he said into the silence as Gabe opened another cabinet door and pulled out a shelf that held a laptop and small printer.

Knox glared at Val, who only grinned.

"You have a state-of-the-art establishment."

"Yeah, Knox," Gabe said in an off-handed manner, his attention focused on the screen. "It wasn't always like this. Not until the club invested in it. Digger put up his own money to have it rebuilt from the ground up. I have fifty percent ownership, Bunny has thirty percent, and the club has the rest."

"Why does the club have any interest?" Knox asked, his tone peevish. Did Outlaw have to muscle his way into everything?

"Originally, they invested in my shop," Gabe answered as the printer spit out a piece of paper. He grabbed it. "Since it was club property, everything needed to be voted on. Outlaw knew Digger wanted Bunny to have a cut and that I wanted renovations. Again, club property so club decision." He squinted at the paper. The light reflecting on it revealed a very small object had been printed on the other side, too tiny to make out. "Outlaw had Brooks draw up papers that set up percentages that we all owned. He had me draw up plans and run reports on profit and losses. I even had to submit a proposal." He tapped a couple of keys on the laptop. "The day of the meeting arrived, and I was so nervous. I couldn't attend because I'm not a member. Digger said there was some wrangling, especially on the renovations. That was the big sticking point. Digger finally decided he'd pay for it himself. After that, it was smooth sailing. The members voted to sell me back half the interest in the shop."

"And all of this was Outlaw's plan?"

Gabe grabbed another sheet of paper from the printer. "Not the design of this building."

"No, I meant how you, Bunny, and the club shared interest."

Gabe nodded.

"Motherfucker brilliant at business," Val inserted. "I always thought if he would've been CEO of the club's labs, we would have more than just a couple locations."

"Then you might be stuck with Johnnie as prez," Gabe said with a cheeky smile.

"Fuck off," Val ordered. "John Boy just fine. Have you heard different?"

"No," Gabe said quickly, losing his grin. "Of course not, Val. I didn't mean any harm." He handed the paper to Knox. "A design of your tattoo."

Knox stared at the heart with the arrow, then squinted. Drew the image closer and still found it hard to read his and Roxanne's names. Val stood from his seat to peek over Knox's shoulder.

"Don't get none, Knox," Val said. "Put that on your ass and it'll just be a fucking blob."

Sighing, Knox handed the paper back to Gabe. "I have to," he insisted. "Roxanne's family is my family. I've disparaged tattoos and motorcycles and everything for so long. I want to show her what's important to her is important to me."

"You don't have to change to be part of our family," Val told him. "We not asking for that. *Roxanne* not asking for that. We just want you to be fucking fair. Give us the chance we always try to give you. You asked me if Mort sent me to teach you. No, he sent me to give you a chance to get to know me. Maybe, if you spend time with each of us, you can see we just motherfuckers like you. He doing this even though he want to slice you in little pieces again because, every time he call to check on shit, he hear how sad Roxanne is and that's making Bailey sad."

A knot dropping into the pit of Knox's stomach. "Roxanne is sad?"

"She love you. Mort said the whole time he was on the phone with Bailey last night, she was crying because Roxanne..." Val shrugged.

"Roxanne what?"

"I'm not talking for her," Val said with infuriating vagueness. "If you doubt she love you, seeing that ugly ass ring on her finger should convince you."

Knox stiffened. "That is a family heirloom."

"Don't give a fuck," Val retorted. "The shit ugly. Made for a late nineteenth century or early twentieth century bitch. Not a bitch on wheels like Roxanne. She deserve bling befitting *her*."

Alarm raced through Knox. Every time he thought of something that would put more distance between him and Roxanne, he panicked. "Has she complained about the ring?"

"Roxanne don't do shit like that," Val chastised.

Knox had seen the way she looked at the ring when he'd slid it on her fingers. She'd even expressed misgivings. Yet, he'd expected her to do just what she had—accept it without complaint because it was a Harrington heirloom.

No wonder she didn't want anything to do with him. Desperation crept into him. "I'm getting a tattoo," he said with determination. "Maybe, I can have the club's insignia on my back like most of you do, Val."

"I wouldn't do that, Knox. That shit'll get you killed," Val said calmly. "You don't wear club nothing unless you in the fucking club."

"Of course," Knox said.

"I love dragon art," Gabe said. "The dragon is symbolic for determination, bravery, and physical prowess." He removed his T-shirt and turned, presenting his back that had a tattoo of a huge red dragon, shooting black fire. It extended the width of his shoulders and the length of his spinal column, although his neck was clean.

Knox worked with Val and Gabe to come up with a variation of the dragon tattoo. Instead of his back, Knox decided to have it on his chest. Somehow, Val convinced him to also get a tattoo on his arm. Knox filled out and signed a consent to tattoo and waiver and release to all claims. The single form had all types of questions. Though Gabe knew him, he demanded a copy of Knox's driver's license. It was both impressive and legitimate.

Once Knox had his shirt off and was back in the chair, Val held out the same bottle of rum Knox drank from earlier.

"Put that away," Gabe said. "Liquor thins the blood, Val. He'll just bleed more."

"Bleed?" Knox echoed. "What do you mean bleed?"

"I always drank when I got my pieces," Val pointed out.

"You always drink," Gabe shot back with a chuckle.

Val flipped him off, ignoring Knox's question just as much as Gabe did.

"Why am I going to bleed?" Knox demanded, determined to get an answer.

"You're going to have a needle plunging into you seventy-five times per second," Gabe answered with concerning nonchalance, "so, of course, you're going to bleed. The droplets will be tiny and barely noticeable."

"Are you sure?"

"Yeah, Knox," Gabe answered. "Positive."

"Fine. Let's get on with it."

"I'm still thinking about a cock piercing," Val announced as Gabe began cleaning Knox's chest with rubbing alcohol. "You ready to do it yet, Gabriel?"

"I already told you I'm not touching your cock, even though I'll be wearing gloves. Let Amanda do it."

"No fucking way. Amanda not my wife, first of all. She don't get to touch my goods. Zoann would divorce me and Outlaw would kill me. Besides, even if Puff would be okay with it, my dick don't know it wouldn't be her hands. Motherfucker going to get a cockstand. That's just the way he is."

"It wouldn't tell the difference between my hands either," Gabe pointed out.

"You got big, rough hands," Val said.

"That would be gloved, like Amanda's would be," Gabe cut in.

"Don't give a fuck, Gabe. The motherfucker would still know the difference. My cock smart like that."

"At least something on your person is," Knox grumbled.

Val scowled at him. "Only Prez get to call me stupid, motherfucker," he warned, then refocused on Gabe. "I'll pay you whatever the fuck you want."

"I'm *not* doing it," Gabe said firmly.

"Then I guess I don't get a cock piercing."

"I guess you don't," Gabe replied.

During the exchange, Gabe had shaved Knox's chest, although he kept it smooth, then washed the area with green soap. Once his skin dried, Gabe sat. He lowered the tattoo chair and raised his rolling stool, then grabbed a long needle from the open drawer.

The moment the tip pressed against his skin, Knox yelped. "Don't hurt me," he begged.

"Knox, this is only—"

More pressure on his skin. Tears rushed to his eyes. "Owwww!" he howled.

Frowning, Gabe pushed away from him.

"Why the fuck did I consent to this?" Knox demanded, doing his best not to allow tears to slide down his cheeks. "If I don't have a tattoo that doesn't mean Roxanne will love me less."

"Knox—" Val's alarmed voice halted when Knox shook his head.

"No. This shit hurts!" He breathed in deeply. "I'm doing this," he reasoned more to himself than to either of the other two men. "If I can survive so many ass beatings from Outlaw and Mortician, I can survive needles that will drive into my skin seventy-five thousand times a second."

"They don't even make a needle that goes that fast," Val said with exasperation.

Knox closed his eyes and sat rigidly in the chair.

"It's *seventy-five* times a second," Gabe said. Though he sounded calm, there was a bit of astonishment in his tone, too. "Like seven and a half decades? Ten multiplied by seven, then adding a five to the answer. Seventy-five."

Blood poured down Knox's chest, warm over his skin. He didn't see it—he refused to open his eyes. But he felt it. It was sticky and wet, draining him of life. "I'm bleeding to death."

"You not bleeding at all, pussy," Val snapped.

"Of course I am!" Knox insisted, still not opening his eyes. "How many stitches do I need?"

"How the fuck you were a cop?" Val said. "You ran away from scenes with blood?"

"I don't care about anyone else's blood," Knox fumed. "It's *my* blood being spilled that concerns me."

Something long and skinny rubbed against Knox's nose and his eyes flew open. Val dangled a marker in front of him.

"What the fuck is that?" Knox demanded, not in the mood for teasing.

Val leaned in, almost nose-to-nose. "The fucking *marker* Gabe was using for the stencil."

"No, he was using a needle."

"No, I was using that marker," Gabe told him.

Blinking, Knox swallowed. "I don't like needles," he confessed.

"Oh, no shit," Val answered, tossing the marker back to Gabe and returning to his seat.

"Are you sure you want to do this?" Gabe questioned, studying Knox with concern. "If you do, you have to sit still."

He was doing this for Roxanne, he reminded himself. She was worth it. He nodded.

"Okay, this is what I'm going to do. Create the stencil for your chest piece, then do the linework. We'll schedule more sessions for the coloring and your arm. Does that sound good?"

"Yes," Knox responded, willing himself to relax once Gabe started the stenciling again. It was almost impossible, though, because all Knox imagined was that needle.

Passion led to strange decisions, though, and hopefully, this would help to win back Roxanne's love for him.

CHAPTER FORTY-SIX

Kendall

Afraid to move and sobbing, Kendall drew her knees to her chest, cowering in the corner of her bedroom.

Imagining eyes glaring at her from everywhere, watching her, following her every step. She couldn't prove it, but instinct warned her of dire danger. Roxy called her every day, but even she sounded different, withdrawn and distant.

Kendall hadn't heard from Meggie. Usually, after a day or two, she'd call offering an olive branch. And Johnnie—

Tears burst from Kendall. She wanted Johnnie. She needed him. He'd protect her. Since the evening they'd met, he'd put her first in his life. He had to rescue her now. Outlaw was coming. Kendall knew it, and it terrified her.

Earlier today, she'd picked up her business cards from the printer. The words, *Kendall Donovan, Attorney-at-Law*, shimmered in gold. But the satisfaction she thought she'd feel at finally reclaiming her career, had yet to set in.

Loneliness, fear, and emptiness squeezed out every other emotion and all of her peace-of-mind.

All the times she'd berated Meggie came to Kendall. The younger woman had a man who loved her without condition, who she loved just as much. She wasn't mean, selfish, and spiteful. She didn't step on anyone in her path to get her way.

No wonder Johnnie had loved her. No wonder he'd turned against Kendall.

She had no one. Charlotte would tell her she was better off without "those people". Once upon a time, Kendall had believed Roxy would come running. Since the fight, though, the woman Kendall wished had been her mother had changed.

Resting her head on her knees, she prayed for death. She was broken, lost. Even when she tried to do the right thing, she failed.

Tears streamed down her face. She couldn't do this anymore. Dr. Briscow had sworn, once the medicines set in, she'd start to feel better. As long as she'd had Johnnie and Meggie and Roxy and *everyone*, she'd had a reason to fight. Despite her attitude, they'd considered her family. That's all Kendall had ever wanted.

Rubbing the back of her hand against her runny nose, she decided she'd had enough. Her mother and sister had the right idea. Life was hard, not for the weak and self-pitying, and she was both.

She sobbed for all that she'd dreamed of as a child, when her father had still been alive, and all that she'd lost in the intervening years. She'd always told herself she'd be a much better mother than her own had been to her. It turned out she was worse.

Trembling and nauseated, she crawled to where she'd dropped her phone on the floor when she'd come into her room, and heard a click. Or saw a flash. Or...*something* not quite right.

Wanting to hear Johnnie's voice one, last time, she picked up her cell phone and speed dialed his number. She Face-Timed Rory, Matilda, and JJ once a day. Johnnie told her he wouldn't allow her more time with them. Her kids were getting so big, and seemed to be thriving and happy, not missing her at all.

Had she really been that horrible?

"What, Kendall?"

Sniffling at Johnnie's unfriendly greeting, Kendall gripped the phone. "Johnnie, come and get me. Please," she sobbed. "I'll behave. I'm so scared. Let me come home."

Johnnie huffed out a breath. "No."

"But—"

"You're not welcomed on club grounds anymore. No one wants you here."

"Can you come to me then?"

"No," he said after a moment. "I'm done with your fucking games. This is just another ploy of yours."

"It's not! I swear."

The line went dead.

Breaking into sobs, Kendall curled on the floor, feeling as if her entire world had crashed around her.

~

Knox

Hearing that Roxanne would be coming in today to cook, since Ophelia had a previous engagement, Knox had hung around the clubhouse. If Roxanne showed up, it would give him another opportunity to use her pretense of them still being a couple. Outlaw and Mortician had returned from wherever they'd gone to, last night, not long after Knox had gotten back from the tattoo shop.

Mortician had been cordial but hadn't inquired about Gabe's work or even if Knox had made the appointment. Outlaw had been in the clubhouse and out so quickly, Knox hadn't had a chance to say anything to him. He was in a hurry to get back to Megan.

Today, Knox's decision not to leave the clubhouse, had been in vain. Roxanne hadn't come in. In fact, it had been Megan for both breakfast and dinner. Frustrated and annoyed, Knox had gone back to his room and decided to do surveillance on Kendall. With everything going on, that task had gotten lost in the shuffle.

Most of the day had gone by without much fanfare. Then, in late evening, Knox had gotten an alert, so he'd picked up his tablet in time to see Kendall in a meltdown. It was so horrifying that he'd felt sorry for her, especially when he considered how upset Roxanne would be if she'd seen one of her babies in such a condition.

Because Megan was on premises, cooking and serving dinner, Outlaw was in his office. Grabbing his tablet, Knox rushed down the hallway and pushed into Outlaw's office, without bothering to knock.

"I think we need to back off Kendall." He shoved the tablet in front of Outlaw.

"I ain't payin' you to think."

Kendall had just gotten off the telephone with Johnnie. Knox hated to leave the live feed, fearing what she might do to herself, but he had to reason with Outlaw.

"Look at this."

Outlaw glared at him.

"Please," Knox added, tired, weary, and desperate. "Roxanne will never forgive me if she knows I'm party to Kendall's destruction. The woman is falling to pieces."

Scowling, Outlaw snatched the tablet out of Knox's hand and replayed the footage from the last half hour. Once he finished, he sat the tablet in front of him and blew out a heavy breath.

"She stumbled into a fucking corner and rocked herself back and forth." Watching as it happened in real time had upset Knox. His heart had sunk. "She looks haggard and harried. She knows she's being watched."

A muscle ticked in Outlaw's jaw.

"This is Johnnie's wife!"

"And Megan and CJ tormentor," Outlaw snapped.

"Don't you feel sorry for her?"

Outlaw glanced at the dark screen on the tablet, then raised a hard, green gaze to Knox. "No."

"How can you be so cold?"

"Call me what the fuck you want. You think I give a fuck about her state? How many times that bitch been in control and ain't gave a good fuck about who the fuck she steamrolled?"

"But—"

"Fuck Kendall, Knox. She gettin' what the fuck she deserve. She shoulda fuckin' thought what the fuck might happen to her be-fuckin-fore she got Megan kidnapped and tried to punch CJ."

"You're gaslighting her."

"I'd like to pour fuckin' gas *on* her and light a goddamn match." Outlaw glared at him. "If you want off the case, cuz of Roxanne, then fuckin' quit."

He made it sound so easy, but Knox knew better than to trust that simple statement.

"Will there be ramifications for me?" he demanded.

"Ain't givin' you the rest of your fuckin' money. Other than that shit, nope."

He released a pent-up breath, relief flowing through him. "I'll collect the surveillance equipment the next time she's out."

"The fuck you will. My money paid for that. It fuckin's stay. Just a lil' more and Kendall fuckin' herself up."

"Jesus Christ, you're heartless."

A glimmer of regret...?...hesitation...?...sadness...? passed over Outlaw's features before he schooled his face into unconcern. He shrugged.

Defeated, Knox took his tablet and returned to his room, his heart heavy.

Outlaw meant to see Kendall dead, and nothing was going to stop him.

~

JOHNNIE

Opening the door to Kendall's house, Johnnie stopped in the entry hall, frowning at the silence. When she called, he'd been at the club, debating on what to do about Emily. Since the scene in her house, she'd called and texted, begging his forgiveness, swearing her regret ran deep over her behavior towards Kendall. He was on the verge of giving in and inviting Emily out to dinner. Christopher swore he didn't have anything to do with Johnnie and Emily meeting.

While a little voice warned him that Christopher might be a lying motherfucker, Johnnie ignored it. In her tearful calls, Emily sounded sincere, too. Although her behavior had affected Kendall's outlook greatly, Emily seemed so far removed from the petty little girl she'd been. She'd pointed out everyone deserved a second chance.

That had hit him right in his gut. He'd always held to that mantra with Kendall, whom he'd given more than just two chances.

In the midst of his internal debate over Emily, Kendall had called. Johnnie had begged for her life to Christopher, but that didn't mean he wasn't fed up with her lies and manipulations. He wanted peace and happiness. He wanted a family.

He wanted a woman who loved and respected him.

While the jury was still out on whether or not Kendall had ever loved him, he sure the fuck knew she didn't respect him. Therefore, hearing her sobbing self-pity had annoyed him. He'd been determined to brush her off and let the chips fall where they may. He'd chosen to pursue Emily and leave Kendall to her misery.

A minute after he'd disconnected her call, Johnnie had hurried out to see about her, taking his Harley, since he'd get to her place faster.

Now, he'd arrived and saw no sign of her. Her Navigator was in the driveway, though that didn't guarantee she was home.

He walked through each room downstairs, frowning at the darkness, stopping here and there to turn lamps on.

She'd gotten him again. Made a fucking ass out of him. That call had probably been a test of his love and loyalty. Fury spread through him. Before he called and blasted her, he bounded up the stairs, two at a time, heading straight for her bedroom.

He saw her the moment he walked through the door. She lay in the middle of the floor, trembling.

His anger fleeing, he ran to her, dropped next to her and gathered her in his arms. He registered she was fully clothed, but her skin was red and splotchy, warm to the touch.

"Kendall, sweetheart," he whispered, threading his fingers through her sweaty hair. "Have you taken anything?"

She hiccupped, then lifted her head, staring at him. Her eyes were swollen with tears.

"Johnnie," she said, throwing her arms around his neck and sobbing against him. "He's watching me."

"*Who's* watching you?"

"Outlaw!"

"Kendall—"

"He's going to kill me, Johnnie." The words came out in a hysterical rush. "He's watching me and waiting for the perfect time." She hugged him again. "Please don't let him kill me."

Johnnie wrapped his arms around her. "Why do you think he's watching you? What makes you think he intends to kill you?"

"Because I deserve it. I've done so much. And...and I know he's watching me. Sometimes, I see flashing lights and hear beeps."

"Kendall, listen to me. Christopher doesn't have time for those types of games."

Anger flared in her red-rimmed eyes. Without warning, she slapped him so hard across the face that he reeled back. His nose hadn't completely healed, and pain reverberated through his head. Out of reflex, Johnnie shoved her away and jumped to his feet.

"First you abandon me, now you don't believe me," Kendall snarled, balling her fist and swinging again.

Expecting her to lash out again, Johnnie caught her hand. "Can you fucking blame me?" he growled, grabbing her other hand when she swung. "You're a goddamn liar."

She kicked his shin.

Beyond the point of reasoning, Johnnie yelped in pain, then dragged Kendall to the bed and threw her over his knee. "If you want to act like a spoiled fucking child, I'll treat you like one."

Shoving her skirt above her waist, he slapped against her backside. She wore thongs; his handprint showed immediately on her skin.

"You're a motherfucker!" she screamed, squirming.

He tightened his hold on her and spanked her ass again. "I don't give a fuck. You're a self-pitying, manipulative, selfish, vengeful, ungrateful bitch!" He punctuated each word with a slap, ignoring her flailing legs, yelled insults, and brutal punches to his thigh.

The scent of her desire rose up, stirring Johnnie's cock. He paused his hand, caressed her flaming backside, and released her. Unprepared, Kendall rolled to the floor.

"Asshole!" she hissed.

Johnnie stood, stepped away from her, and thrust his fingers through his hair. "What are we doing, Kendall?"

She stared at his growing erection, panting from exertion.

"You mean what are *you* doing?" she spat. "I'm waiting to come home. You're the stupid motherfucker who refuses to defend me and let us be a family again."

Growling, Johnnie started for her. Kendall scrambled to her feet and jumped onto the bed, wariness creeping into her eyes.

"Don't put the future of our marriage entirely on my shoulders. The only thing I've ever done is love you."

"Liar! You don't love me anymore." She sniffled.

"Shut the fuck up, Kendall, and dry your goddamn tears. They don't impress me." They did, or else he wouldn't have rushed over, but she was in shock from his spanking and harsh words.

"I hate you!"

He laughed coldly. "We both know that's another one of your goddamn lies. If you fucking hated me, you wouldn't have called me to come to you."

Her lower lip trembled. "You're so mean. You hate me," she accused, changing tactics.

"I don't hate you," he snapped. "I love you."

She lifted her chin, empowered by his revelation. "Then prove it. Take me back."

"Fuck off. I'm not proving a goddamn thing to you ever again. If you don't believe how I feel about you after all this time, that's your problem, not mine. The fact that I'm here right now should mean something to you."

Picking up a pillow, she threw it at him. "Why are you treating me like this? I love you so much. I miss you and our kids. I'm so afraid here. Outlaw is going to kill me."

"If you hadn't been into every fucking thing you had no business sticking your nose into, you'd have nothing to fear!" He wouldn't express his own concerns about Christopher's intentions. She seemed truly terrified. Then, again, Kendall was Kendall. She had games for days. "How can we stay married when I don't trust you? Even now, when I see your terror, I feel manipulated."

"My fear is real." She sounded so pitiful. Her brown eyes begged him for peace and comfort. Sniffling, she looked away. "You spanked me."

"You slapped me."

She fell silent, then gazed at him, lowering her lashes. "My pussy is wet."

"My cock is hard."

Satisfaction gleamed in her eyes and she licked her lips.

"I'm not fucking you."

"I-I...why not?"

"I don't trust you not to get pregnant. You and I both know you neither need nor want another child."

"It's my body, motherfucker. You can't tell me what to do with it."

"You're fucking right, Kendall, but I *can* and will keep my dick to myself."

She screamed in pure frustration. "Why are you acting like this?"

"How? Like I have some goddamn self-respect?"

"You don't love me—"

"Shut the fuck up with that bullshit. I do love you. Very much. *Too* much."

"No, please. Don't say that. I love you, too. So much, Johnnie. I know it doesn't seem like it but—"

"But you try. Correct?"

She nodded.

"Try harder."

"Help me. I can't do this alone."

He'd always tried to protect Kendall and stand at her side. But she hadn't gotten any better. As a matter-of-fact, his patience and belief in her, had made her worse. He shook his head. "I can't, sweetheart. You disregard all my efforts on your behalf. How many times have you lied to me? How many times have I forgiven you and put my trust in you again? Only to have you shit on me. I'm not perfect by any means. I've made my own mistakes. Always deferring to Megan. Demanding that you be her friend. I know I've played a role in your state-of-mind and I'm sorry. But you don't follow through on your own well-being. I can set alarms for you to take medicine and get to your appointment on time. I can go with you to your appointments and watch you take your medication, but unless you *want* to stay better, things will never change. You'll still be the same self-destructive woman you've always been."

She face-planted on the bed, loud sobs escaping her.

He wanted to turn and leave her to her tantrum but he couldn't bring himself to walk away from her while she was in such a state. He went to the bed, climbed on, and lifted her into his arms. Settling back against the headboard, he held her close.

When she quieted down, she kissed the base of his neck. Her soft lips against him awakened his need and longing. He missed her so fucking much. However, he had to break the vicious cycle they were in.

"I have to go," he told her. Those four words were some of the hardest he'd ever said.

She wilted, then moved away. Sitting on her haunches, she wrapped her arms around her waist.

"Is there someone else?"

"I don't know."

Her eyes wide, she processed that information.

"I just recently met her."

"A club girl? Have I met her?"

She knew Emily very well. If he revealed her identity, though, it would only add to Kendall's distress. Besides, he didn't know what he wanted to have anything to do with Emily. His sense of fairness told him to give her a chance. "No," he answered, leaving it at that.

"Have you slept with her?"

"No. As long as you're my wife, I'm not going to betray our vows."

She opened her mouth, started to speak, then changed her mind. "Come with me to see Dr. Briscow. My new psychiatrist. She can explain to you about BPD better than I can."

"I'll think about it," he told her, though he knew he'd attend a session with her. "Will you be all right?"

"Yes."

"We're going to figure this out," he promised. "We're going to do what needs to be done so you, me and our kids can be happy."

"What about Outlaw?"

"Don't worry about him. Christopher isn't going to do you anything."

She gave him a skeptical look. "He wants me dead."

"Give me a couple of days, sweetheart. I'm going to bring Val over to do a sweep. If there are hidden cameras, they will be found."

"Okay."

His heart broke for her. He'd never seen Kendall so muted and defeated.

"See you."

"Bye, Johnnie."

CHAPTER FORTY-SEVEN

Roxy

"**A**m I to understand that marrying Mortician once wasn't good enough?" Father Wilkins asked Bailey, lifting his brows and looking over the rim of his glasses with disapproval. "You mean to do it again?"

Bailey offered Roxy a hesitant glance. Understanding her daughter's reasons, Roxy gave a small nod, leaned over and grabbed Bailey's hand to give it a squeeze. The fact they were here to reserve the church felt like a knife to the gut.

Along with sharing the news of a new baby on the way today, Bailey had once again offered to cancel her vow renewal plans, but Roxy had insisted that was unnecessary. Besides, once Bailey announced the date, then Roxy would have to find a way to leave Knox.

Only a week had passed since he'd found her in the big kitchen, then tempted her nearly out of her mind. In that time, though, she'd made herself scarce. She'd missed a weekly dinner by inviting Jordan out to a restaurant. A couple of times Meggie had taken kitchen duty, but she was under the weather and Fee was still unavailable. To escape Knox, Roxy prepared breakfast at her house, then called up members to make the trek through the woods to get the pans of eggs, sausages, and toast. Nothing too fancy because of the long walk. She'd even refused an invitation from Outlaw for everyone to meet at the club for drinks.

From what she'd heard Knox stayed close to the club and all family events. He wanted another chance. Maybe, she needed to meet with him and talk. Point a few things out. Compromise on one or two issues herself.

"Momma?"

Roxy snapped her head in the direction of Bailey's voice.

"See, even Mrs. Doucette is tuning your decision out, Mrs. Banks. Notice what I just said? *Mrs. Banks*. A sure sign another ceremony is quite unnecessary."

"I don't remember asking you what was necessary, Father Wilkins," Bailey responded calmly.

Better her baby than herself. Glaring at the little priest, Roxy folded her arms.

"We'll pay you five thousand dollars," Bailey continued.

Father Wilkins gave a pained look. "My child, I'm quite a busy man."

"Ummmhmmm," Roxy put in.

"Ten thousand?" Bailey said with some hesitation.

The priest opened a drawer and pulled out a day planner. He settled the book on his desk. "Perhaps, I can pencil you in."

"No, the fuck you can't. Penciling can be erased. You better stamp that shit in your book. Why the fuck are you using a damn book, anyway, Father? This is the 21st Century. Shouldn't you have an iPad or some type of tablet? An official engagement calendar?"

"I'm a simple man, Mrs. Doucette," Father Wilkins answered. "Although not simple enough not to know foul language in the house of the Lord is a sacrilege." He gave Bailey a sugary smile. "What date did you have in mind?"

"August 6th, Father."

Flipping to that page, Wilkins shook his head sadly. "I might have a prior engagement that day."

His eyes gleamed and he rubbed his thumb and two fingers together, his hand so high the gesture was impossible not to see.

"Twenty thousand," Bailey said on a cough.

Wincing, he shook his head again.

"Twenty-five?"

"Perfect," he said with a bright smile, starting to pencil in.

Roxy cleared her throat, jumped to her feet, and grabbed the first pen she saw, thrusting it out to the money-hungry motherfucker. "Bribery is a fucking sin, too, motherfucker."

He snatched the pen from her. "I am the Shepard of this fine congregation, madam. My lambs see to it that I am well-taken care of."

Once he'd finished writing in his calendar, he set his pen down as Roxy plopped into her chair again.

"I require a deposit. Half."

"Will a check do?" Bailey asked.

"Am I set up to take credit cards and run checks to see if they are valid?" he fired back. "However, as good as that would be, I'm afraid I can't leave a paper trail. I take cash only, Mrs. Banks."

Bailey nodded. "I'll bring it by tomorrow afternoon. Will that work?"

"Perfectly," Father Wilkins responded and sat back in his chair. "I forgot to ask if you are bringing the ceremony to me or am I going to where it will be held?"

"We're having it in the church," Bailey said without hesitation. "I want my marriage blessed."

"You should try having the man blessed," Father Wilkins said with a superior smile.

Bailey frowned at him.

"However, that news brings on another set of issues. It is expensive to open up my church. Resources will be used. Lights. Water. I will need to pay for cleaning services. I cannot pay for these things with my looks."

"Motherfucker would be on the condemned list if we had to rely on your damn looks to pay for cleaning," Roxy grumbled.

"Shouldn't the diocese pay for those things?" Bailey asked, shaking her head at Roxy, her signal for taking over the conversation.

Father Wilkins laughed softly. "How little you know, Mrs. Banks. Of course, I should understand that, shouldn't I? If you knew things, you wouldn't have involved yourself in the club."

"You're part of the club," Bailey reminded him. "Jazzman. Remember?"

"Ahhh, yes, I do recall that. But I'm not a *full* member. Only honorary. I'm still on the periphery. As a matter of fact, all the business I once enjoyed from the club has all but ceased."

Roxy studied her nails, swallowing when she saw her engagement ring. She never removed it, in case she forgot to put it back on when the situation called for it. "Vengeance is mine says the Lord."

"Do I look like the Lord to you?" Father Wilkins said.

Roxy opened her mouth to reply, but Bailey quickly interrupted.

"You're being petty because you feel as if the club has abandoned you?" she asked.

Father Wilkins tsked. "Petty is such a harsh word."

"Motherfucker is much better," Roxy said sweetly.

The priest glowered at her. In response, she smirked.

"Would fifty be enough, Father Wilkins?" Bailey asked.

Roxy gasped and said, "I know you're not about to give this motherfucker fifty fucking thousand dollars, Bailey," as Father Wilkins nodded and replied, "I'll accept that."

Bailey got to her feet, so Roxy stood, too.

"I expect half of that also, Mrs. Banks," Father Wilkins said.

"Right," Bailey said. "I'll have it tomorrow."

"This is highway robbery," Roxy protested as they started for the door.

"One other thing, Mrs. Banks," Father Wilkins called.

When Bailey halted, so, too, did Roxy.

"I want no murders, shootings, stabbings, fights, or any other untoward happenstance taking place anywhere on the church grounds. That includes the parking lot."

"Don't blame Bailey for Outlaw shooting his daddy there," Roxy protested.

"She didn't pull the trigger, but she's part of the club. Therefore, it is *her* responsibility to keep my church gore free."

"The club is at peace," Bailey said. "There's no war going on."

"For now," Father Wilkins, "but with these men that can change in a blink."

Roxy and Bailey exchanged glances, unsettlement sinking into the pit of Roxy's stomach.

"Good day, Mrs. Banks," Father Wilkins said in dismissal.

Walking away, Roxy told herself her disquiet had no basis. As Bailey said, the club didn't have any active enemies, so there was nothing to worry over.

As much as she argued with herself, though, she couldn't shake the feeling of bad things on the way.

CHAPTER FORTY-EIGHT

Knox

"Who in your wedding party, Knox?" Digger asked, holding his arms out so Mr. Whittlestone could measure him. The noise of the little boys, including Grant, didn't seem to bother him at all.

But it added to Knox's headache. Nothing seemed to be going right. He'd had to beg Callie to send Grant to Hortensia for the weekend. Apparently, she didn't want Knox to marry Roxanne. Or anyone, for that matter. Somehow, he'd gotten through to Callie, and she'd agreed to send Grant for his fitting.

Roxanne had all but disappeared from the club. She knew him, so she'd figured out his plan to corner her every chance he could. He didn't dare go to her place. To win her back, he needed to be alive. She hadn't been around to see his tattoo outlines or even to inquire after his well-being. But he had to grin and bear it, and pretend they were fine. She was on the other side with the women and Mrs. Whittlestone. Knox couldn't imagine what Roxanne was doing or if she found this pretense as painful as he did.

He'd truly thought Outlaw and Mortician knew Knox and Roxanne hadn't made up, but it seems as if they did. It was Mortician who'd forced them to attend this travesty.

Then, there was Kendall. He never thought he'd see her brought so low. Her maid or nanny or whoever the fuck Ella was, had finally moved in. He'd also seen Johnnie promise to have Val do an electronic sweep. Rebelling against Outlaw's hard stance, Knox hadn't bothered to warn him of Johnnie's intentions. Something needed to make Outlaw back off.

Put together it made Knox's head pound.

"Dad, isn't Uncle Cam in your wedding?"

"Hmmm. Oh, uh, yeah," Knox answered, remembering Digger had also asked a question. "I thought your brother and me were sharing groomsman."

"You thought wrong," Mortician told him. "Especially since you didn't ask a motherfucker."

"Motherfucker!" Rory squealed.

Grinning, Johnnie turned and ruffled his son's hair, while Val wrestled on the floor with Ryan. Mr. Whittlestone seemed amused, if a little overwhelmed. The shop was closed to accommodate the Banks/Harrington wedding party. Or, most of it, since Knox hadn't ordered his tuxedo there.

His *useless* tuxedo. Depressed, he rested his chin in the palm of his hand, leaning his elbow on the arm of the chair.

"'Law!" CJ yelled.

"'Law," Ryder mimicked, around the green binky in his mouth.

"MegAnn say Aunt KenDall on the way," CJ blared over the noise of the guys and their sons.

All movement stopped. Knox's headache worsened. He wasn't sure what mood Kendall would be in today. Besides, they had a full house, including CJ, which might not bode well.

"Okay, boy," Outlaw called, meeting his son's gaze in the mirror. "Stay in here by me."

"I'll keep watch over him, Uncle Chris," Diesel promised.

"Val?" Johnnie said, buttoning JJ's tuxedo shirt. "I've been meaning to talk to you. Kendall thinks her house is bugged. Can you meet me there tomorrow or the next day to check for me so I can reassure her?"

Knox choked, his gaze flying to Outlaw's to see if he looked as panicked as Knox suddenly felt. If Johnnie found those cameras and listening devices, all hell would break lose. Had he missed this part of the surveillance? If he had seen it, he would've run to Outlaw with the news.

Silent, Outlaw arranged his bowtie, but the reflection staring at Knox from the mirror didn't change. The man didn't flinch or even look concerned.

"How you got your shit, Prez?" Digger demanded. "When you came in for a fitting?"

"I called my measurements the fuck in, motherfucker," Outlaw said. "I ain't wearin' the monkey suit I got married in no-fuckin-where. That belong to me and Megan. I already used the other motherfucker I got several fuckin' times, cuz some-fuckin-how, Megan get my fuckin' ass to where these goddamn tuxes all the fuckin' time."

"Mort, why I'm buying a tuxedo?" Digger asked.

"Fool, how the fuck should I know?" Mortician responded. "Your ass must need one."

"I'm perfectly happy renting, thank you very much," Digger answered. "All this fucking money for clothes I'm not wearing too often. After Bailey get the big wedding she want and Roxanne and Knox marry, who the fuck else going to expect us to wear a fucking tux?"

"All the bitches," Val answered from where he sat on the floor next to his sons as they played with miniature motorcycles, ramming them into one another, between '*vroom-vrooms*'. "You know Meggie always coming up with some kind of bullshit."

Outlaw turned and pinned Val with a stare.

"'Law!" CJ said. "Uncle Val call MegAnn a bitch."

"I didn't, CJ." Jumping to his feet, Val raised his gaze to Outlaw. "I didn't call your woman a bitch."

"You say MegAnn name and not no nother girl," CJ pointed out.

"Boy," Outlaw said with amusement, "lemme handle your Uncle Val. Okay?"

"By the way, CJ, it's no *other* girl," Johnnie corrected before CJ responded to Outlaw.

The little boy grinned, but didn't say anything.

"I ain't pointin' out what the fuck obvious, Val," Outlaw said, capturing their attention, not bothering to applaud Johnnie for promoting decent speech. "Even my fuckin' boy know what the fuck you did."

"Make the mudna fucka bleed, 'Law," CJ yelled.

"You still a blood-thirsty lil motherfucker, huh, CJ?" Digger asked, shaking his head. "Never got my ass kicked by a two-year-old before you."

"Assfuck Dig!" CJ said

"I prefer Ashfuck, lil' dude," Digger told him. "You said it cuter. Call me assfuck make you sound too much like your old man. Just with a fucking miniature voice. Shit like that give me nightmares. If you a scary lil' motherfucker now, how the fuck you going to be when you older?"

Knox couldn't hold back any longer. "He's only scary because he's Outlaw's son. Any other child would've been spanked a long time ago. Except CJ gets to say and do what he wants to with absolutely no discipline. He's going to be kicking your ass before long, Outlaw."

"Uncle Mudna Fucka, you mean," CJ stated.

Grant's eyes widened. "You call my dad Uncle Motherfucker?"

As the other men snickered, Knox stiffened and scowled at his son. "If you don't want to be punished the rest of the weekend, young man, you'll not use those words. You're a child. I expect you to act like one. This is your only warning."

Embarrassment crept onto Grant's face and he put his head done, then nodded. "Yes, sir."

"I not ever hitting 'Law, Uncle Mudna Fucka," CJ went on. "I love 'Law."

"And I love you, boy. What Uncle Motherfucker don't understand is the day you lay your fuckin' hands on me is the day I knock you the fuck out. We can argue and fuss and cuss and disa-fuckin-gree. But hittin'? Ain't happenin'. Got me?"

"Uh-huh," CJ answered, annoying Knox with the way he always nodded when he responded with those words.

"Now, Val," Outlaw started.

"Val," Johnnie interrupted. "I need you to meet me at Kendall's house one day this week to do a sweep of it. She thinks it's bugged."

He hadn't received a response the first time, so he must've thought it necessary to repeat the request. The words made Knox as uneasy this time as they had the first time.

Outlaw, on the other hand, still looked unfazed.

"Your turn, Mort," Digger said, stepping away from Mr. Whittlestone. "Whittie, you left enough room in the crotch to accommodate the size of my cock, right?"

Mortician shoved Digger out of the way, while the other men laughed like children and the little boys smiled. Except Grant, who looked at his feet. Diesel grinned like the horny teenager he was. Mr. Whittlestone smiled from his perch atop the stepping stool, unoffended, although Knox's exasperation made him snort.

One thing he could always count on with these men were dick jokes.

"It's loose here." Mortician tugged at the collar of his tuxedo shirt.

Mr. Whittlestone gathered the extra material and pinned it.

"Digger," Mortician said, between comments to the old man. "You got to give everybody a nickname? Whittie?"

"It's fine, Mortician," Mr. Whittlestone answered.

Adjusting his shirt, Mortician glanced from Knox to Johnnie. "Why Red think her crib bugged?"

"She has it in her head Christopher is watching her," Johnnie answered.

"Why the fuck my ass would do that shit?" Outlaw asked, finally reacting. "Oh, yeah, psycho cunts think that fuckin' way. I ain't got time to fuckin' watch that bitch."

Well, at least, that was the truth. Resentment filtered into Knox and he folded his arms.

"I told Kendall the same thing," Johnnie admitted.

"John Boy, I don't have the fucking time to deal with Kendall bullshit," Val said. "You know she's doing that to make you feel sorry for her."

Skepticism crossed Johnnie's face. "She seemed truly frightened."

Mortician looked at Outlaw. When the man's face remained inscrutable, the enforcer addressed Johnnie again. "Give it two or three weeks, Johnnie. If Kendall still feel that way, then I'll drag Val to her place myself."

Ignoring Mortician's words, Johnnie stared at Outlaw, his eyes glinting with a dangerous light. Then, Outlaw narrowed his, and Johnnie flushed, and looked away.

"You still not divorcing Kendall?" Val grouched.

"I don't know what I'm doing," Johnnie admitted. "I did promise her that I'd bring Val over."

"Unpromise her," Val ordered. "I'm not in the mood to do that bitch no favors."

"She's still my wife!" Johnnie bit out. "She's still family. You're required to do for her what you'd do for the others."

"I'm not required to do a fucking thing for Kendall," Val said, switching places with Mortician. "She don't like me. She don't like Zoann. And she never been nice to either of us. She don't consider me family and I return the fucking favor."

"Can you blame her for the way she feels? Zoann has always been a bitch to her."

Val glared at Johnnie. "It takes a bitch to know one, Mr. Bitch."

"Fuck you," Johnnie snapped.

"Fuck all you motherfuckers," Outlaw broke in, then knocked Val on the side of his head. "That's for callin' Megan a bitch." He hit him again. "That's for bein' too fuckin' stupid to fuckin' realize your fuckin' ass singled my woman the fuck out." Another hit.

Val clutched his head. "What was that for?"

"Lagniappe," Outlaw answered.

"That's Roxanne's word," Val complained. "You can't steal it from her."

"Prez, Val right," Mortician said. "Keep throwing licks on his head and what brains he have left will be knocked the fuck out."

"Do you all spend your entire lives insulting each other?" Knox demanded.

"That's how we show our love," Mortician said with a grin.

"Johnnie," Outlaw started, "what about this Emily-chick? How you still so torn over Kendall if you runnin' after another bitch?"

"You all up my ass and you sniffing after new pussy, motherfucker?" Val asked, outraged.

Johnnie snatched Rory closer to him and covered his ears with his hands. "I'm not! And I'll thank you not to talk about another woman in front of my son."

Outlaw's wince surprised Knox.

"Sorry, John Boy," Val said, duly chastened. "We just got carried away."

"Yeah, motherfucker," Outlaw added. "I apolo-fuckin-gize. Don't wanna upset your boy."

"I've been thinking about going nomad," Johnnie announced into the ensuing silence. "Take Kendall and our kids and move away. She wants me to come to a session with her. After that, I'll make my decision."

Shock settled into Outlaw's features, and he swallowed. "You love her that fuckin' much?"

"Yes, goddamn it, Christopher!" Johnnie roared. "What the fuck don't you understand about that? Why is it so fucking hard for you to believe that a couple other than you and Megan can share a deep, abiding love?"

"That ain't hard for me to be-fuckin-lieve with *other* fuckin' motherfuckers. You and Kendall, though? If you two motherfuckers got a deep, abidin' fuckin' love than it would be a blood-fuckin-bath if there was fuckin' hate there. You don't know the fuckin' meanin' of bein' in love and she ain't believin' she can be loved. So how the fuck that equal you leavin' the fuckin' club to make that bitch happy?"

"You tried that before," Mortician reminded Johnnie. "You was miserable."

"*Were*," Knox heard himself saying. "You *were* miserable."

Mortician glared at Knox, but didn't comment.

"I left for Kendall to be happy. This time, I'll leave for both of us to be happy."

"Think hard before you do this," Val advised. "You've been so care-free since she moved away. Almost back to your old self. Kendall don't bring out the best in you."

"Excuse me," Knox cut in. "Rory is still present. How can this conversation be any better for him than the other one that was off-limits?"

"You're right, Knox," Johnnie said. "Thank you."

"No problem," Knox responded.

He looked at Outlaw again, but the man seemed unaffected by it all, turning a blind eye to Johnnie's weary sadness.

~

Roxy

Attempting to hold herself stiff, Roxy sat on Knox's lap, later that night, wishing death on Mortician.

She'd gone through the torture of the fitting, knowing it was an exercise in futility and opening another wound in her already broken heart. She'd also been on edge, worried about how the girls would act toward Kendall and, more importantly, how she'd act toward them.

Her concern had been for nothing. Though Kendall arrived late, it had all gone smoothly. Everyone had been polite to her and she'd been on her best behavior. The fittings had turned into a party-like atmosphere where one of the girls used her phone to play music. They'd laughed and talked and danced, having nothing else to do once they were finished with their fittings. Roxy, Bailey, Harley, Bunny, Kendall, Matilda, Meggie, and Rebel had been a far cry from the eighteen men on the other side. If Jordan and her daughter had been in town, and Roxy's mother and two daughters had flown in from New Orleans, the playing field would've been a little more level, even if Cam would've also been with the men.

Roxy had kept up the pretense of happy bride-to-be, but she'd been so relieved when the day was coming to a close. As they were all heading to their cars, Mortician had announced they needed to meet at his house for dinner and to make sure all the plans were moving forward.

That had been simple enough.

Kendall had declined, although neither Outlaw nor Meggie demanded she do so. Johnnie, too, decided to cry off and returned to the club, sending his children with Meggie.

After dinner and discussion, Knox had gotten his mother on the phone to ask about the rehearsal dinner. Everything was full-speed ahead.

Except, of course, the sham of Roxy and Knox.

Eventually, Roxy had stood up to leave, tired of the pretense. At that point, Mortician, motherfucker number one, had invited everyone to watch a movie. Motherfucker number two, Knox, seized upon the opportunity. Everyone knew Mortician's home theater was notoriously small. The huge screen made it seem even more cramped.

Feeling cornered, Roxy grudgingly agreed. In the room, Mortician, Digger, Val, and Outlaw pulled their wives onto their laps. At one time, Roxy enjoyed these movie nights. Not now, when Knox felt so strong and hard underneath her. His five o-clock shadow gave him a rakish air, and the whisky he was drinking reminded her of all the times they'd kissed after a night out.

She was on his lap. It would've been so easy to fall back into his arms, and pretend their argument had never happened.

Knox's fingers played at her nape and she shivered. He leaned forward. "You know, sweetheart, if you're trying to save my life, you're not acting too convincing. You're sitting as far away from me as possible."

He was right. It surprised her that Mortician or Outlaw hadn't commented on how she leaned away.

Scooting backward, her ass brushed against his semi-hard cock. She regretted that they both wore pants.

Uh, no. She was *happy* they both wore pants. No chance of dick-to-pussy contact.

She settled her back against his chest, her muscles stretched taut.

He brushed his lips behind her ear, thrusting up, taking advantage of everyone's attention being focused on the movie.

"Can we meet later?"

The husky tone of his voice lulled her to say *yes*. She elbowed him. "Fuck you," she whispered.

"Would you?" he shot back.

"Not a goddamn chance."

"I want you, Roxanne. Can't you feel how hard my cock is for you?"

"My pussy is wet for you, Knox. I miss you, but this is the way things are and will continue to be."

"Suppose I change? Suppose I learn to ride? Get a tattoo."

For a moment, she stilled, knowing if he'd go that far to win her back, she'd be powerless to deny him the second chance he so desperately wanted. "Don't," she warned. "You'll come to regret it and resent me."

"No, sweetheart, I wouldn't. I've scheduled sessions with Gabe, Bunny's brother. I'm getting a tattoo. I love you. If I want to be a part of your world, I have to fit in."

"Don't do that," she said, her voice, her feelings, wavering. "It isn't about aesthetics. It's about attitude. It's about your perception and your refusal to understand that these boys aren't bad people. *I'm* not a bad person. Crass? Rough-around-edges? Y-yes." Her voice wavered. She stood. "I'm exhausted," she said, not lying. "This has been a long day."

"For me, too," Knox admitted, sliding to the edge of the theater-style seat. "I'm not getting a tattoo solely to impress you. I swear."

"Why are you getting it then?"

"Uh..." His voice trailed off.

When he said nothing more, Roxy sighed. "Exactly, sugar. Don't get ink, Knox. It's just a temporary fix to a much deeper problem." She started off, then decided to turn and kiss Knox's cheek.

The gesture wasn't for show. Purely selfish reasons guided her. Caressing his jaw, she turned on her heel and walked out, noting no one tried to stop her.

Surprised at the dilapidation before her, Emily looked at the ratty exterior of a biker bar in dire need of repairs. In her wildest dreams, she wouldn't have ever expected Johnnie to take her to such a rundown place. They could've stayed in her neighborhood. Just last night, she'd seen two low-level dealers get into an argument, with one shooting the other one in the head, right out in the open. That type of lawlessness abounded in areas plagued with dereliction.

Like this neighborhood.

The Johnnie Outlaw had described would offer Emily a taste of her old lifestyle. *This* Johnnie would keep her mired right where she was.

She turned to him, snuggling close. As usual, he went rigid. Undeterred, she laid her head against his chest. "I'm all dressed up," she pouted.

"And?" He wasn't stepping away from her, but he wasn't returning her affection either.

"My clothes will be wasted in a place like this."

He gave her a disapproving look. "This is one of my favorite bars."

Suspicion crept into her. "Really?" she asked, determined to get the upper hand. Perhaps, she'd just found the key. Her face falling, she cleared her throat and then made her lips tremble. "Oh," she said in a small voice. "This is a favorite for you and Kendall."

He scowled at her. "No. It's a favorite of *mine*. Kendall never liked this place."

Damn it! She'd miscalculated. Thinking fast, she pasted a bright smile on her face. "Oh my goodness!" she gushed. "You're sharing a special spot with me."

More like testing her, but she didn't think that would be good to point out.

If the exterior was so rough, what was it like inside?

Dressed as she was, she would stand out. She wore a tight red designer bandage dress with Louboutins on her feet, both gifts from Outlaw by using his money to make the purchases.

For makeup, she did a smoky eye and red lips, her dramatic look tools of seduction. Her blonde hair was styled in a slick ponytail. That way, Johnnie could see her face.

Since the scene in her apartment, he'd been quite the gentleman toward her. He hadn't tried to steal a kiss or cop a feel. She'd pretended to listen while he droned on about his life and his woes and his brats. Honestly, if she'd been offered a million dollars, she wouldn't be able to repeat a single thing he said. She just knew where to insert her 'awws', 'sorrys', and 'it'll be okays', so he'd believe she hung onto his every word.

Now, they were on a date at his favorite place. She'd managed to rope him in, a new luxurious life within reach. It had to happen.

It *would* happen.

Emily grabbed Johnnie's hand. "Shall we go in, Mr. Donovan?" she flirted, cooing the words.

He smiled, though his eyes were red-rimmed and tired. "Of course."

Pulling his hand away, he placed it at the small of Emily's back, then guided her past a row of bikes and into the establishment. The place smelled of stale smoke and spilled alcohol. It was small and crowded with tables, chairs, and an oversized bar.

"John Boy," a gravelly voice called.

Emily didn't see the owner of the voice, lost in a sea of faces and sounds.

Johnnie waved, receiving several in return.

She shimmied her hips as he led her through the maze of tables to the back of the place. She ignored the stares and hoots from horny bikers. While most women would be ashamed of this kind of attention, she loved it. She was a beautiful woman. Catcalls and stares came with the territory. Besides, the extra male attention validated her looks.

"Who greeted you when we walked in?" Emily asked as Johnnie held out her chair and allowed her to sit. "Or do you know?" she added as he sat in his own chair.

He shook his head. "It sounded like Marion, but I'm not sure."

"Interesting name for a biker."

He shrugged.

She clucked with sympathy, reached over and placed her hand against his forearm. "Have you started divorce proceedings yet?"

His muscles tensed underneath her fingertips.

"No." He sounded pathetic.

Emily slumped her shoulders and moved her hand away from his arm. "You're just stringing me along then? Once you get into my panties, you're leaving?"

"Emily, don't press me on a relationship. I'm still a married man. If you can't deal with that, then leave."

Annoyance flashed through her, but she breathed in deep and covered her aggravation with a smile. "I feel such a strong connection to you. I won't leave until you send me away." She sniffled. "You'll tear my heart to pieces but I'm a big girl. I'll deal with it."

"I don't know...do I want you because I'm lonely or because I'm truly attracted to you?"

To stop her glare, Emily bit her lip.

Anger and humiliation vied for a place within her. Johnnie still held feelings for her old rival. Not that it was a competition. Emily was above Kendall in almost every way, except looks. For the life of her, Emily couldn't understand why Johnnie still had feelings for the whore.

A frown marred his face. "What am I doing here?" he asked more to himself than to her.

She looked at him through her lashes. "Getting to know me. I'm here for you. Can we please talk over whatever is bothering you? Have a drink or two to unwind?"

He sighed but nodded his agreement.

A smile spread over her face. Men had always given her what she wanted. "Thank you."

A few more corny words, and he'd be ready to fall at her feet.

~

JOHNNIE

Johnnie stared at Emily, wondering why he'd invited her out. He was trying his damnedest to get into her and forget her past with Kendall, and give her the second chance he told himself she deserved. If Emily could bring him happiness, why not have a relationship with her?

Except she seemed like a phony. He wasn't sure why he felt as he did. Maybe...maybe, because of her looks. Or, maybe, he kept replaying the scene at Kendall's house in his head. She hadn't invited him to a session yet. On the other hand, he hadn't called her to check on her. His actions had to show her how fed up he was.

Even if Kendall stayed uppermost in his thoughts.

He and Emily were now on their third round of drinks, and Emily was gushing over something he didn't care about. She constantly touched him and leaned over to bring attention to her tits, already on prominent display. She was trying hard to seduce him.

Once upon a time, he would've jumped at the opportunity to date, or just fuck, Megan's doppelganger. Now, however, he felt no desire toward Emily *or* Megan. The only woman he truly wanted was Kendall. But between his wife's infatuation with Christopher, her jealously of

Megan, and numerous schemes, their relationship was on its last thread. If only Kendall could realize that she was the only woman he wanted.

Johnnie was so miserable without her. He would give anything for their marriage to work.

"Johnnie, are you listening?" Emily's question broke into his thoughts, a frown marring her pretty face.

"Yes, of course," he lied.

She sighed and leaned back. When she crossed her legs, his attention strayed to them. "Kiss me," she said.

Johnnie brought his gaze to hers. The depths of her blue eyes gleamed. Before he turned her down, she stood.

There was a small space between his chair and the table that she managed to insert herself into before sliding onto his lap and straddling his thighs.

She rocked against his cock. "I don't have any panties on," she whispered.

Johnnie groaned, his dick hardening.

Planting her mouth over his, she took his face between her hands and tapped the tip of her tongue against his lips. Johnnie opened and allowed her onslaught, returning her kiss, trying to drum up some emotion. He could fuck her then and there, but he was so passed easy lays. His marriage had ruined him for that. He wanted something meaningful. He wanted to matter.

But he didn't matter to Kendall. She'd drugged him and led him to choke Megan. She'd gotten him shot.

Growling, Johnnie grabbed Emily's ass and squeezed, thrusting his cock up.

"I want you to fuck me," Emily breathed against his mouth.

He stilled, her words tantamount to a bucket of ice being thrown on him. "Get up, sweetheart."

"Huh?"

He lifted her by her waist and set her on her feet, then stood. "Let's go."

She licked her lips. "I'm going to suck your cock the entire drive to my house."

It would be so easy to take relief in her mouth and pussy. Instead... he held his hand up and pointed to his wedding band. "As long as Kendall is my wife, I'm not going to sleep with you, Emily."

Her smile wavered. "Me in particular? Or any other woman?"

"Any woman," he corrected. "You're beautiful, sexy, everything I would want."

"Except there's Kendall," she said softly, sadly. "I thought you two were over."

"I don't know what we are. Until I figure that out, you and I can only be friends."

"Kendall is so lucky to have you," Emily said, her tone as wistful as her look.

"I was lucky to have her," he amended. "But...but she's formidable. I put every faith in her, so much so that I never questioned her actions or her motives time and time again. I just...*trusted* her."

Bending down, Emily placed a gentle kiss against Johnnie's mouth, then fingered his lips. "I'm here," she said sweetly. "For as long as you need me. I've grown to care about you so much. If you've friend-zoned me, then I have to accept that. But if you need a no-strings attached fuck, I'll gladly open my pussy to you."

Clenching his jaw, Johnnie glanced away.

"I hope tonight hasn't thrown our relationship off its intended track, b—"

"What do you mean its intended track?"

Her eyes widened and she laughed nervously.

"Emily?" Johnnie questioned, after minutes of silence.

"I just hoped by now our relationship would've progressed more. I'm just so disappointed," she added woefully.

"I understand," Johnnie said as he led her toward the door.

The whistles and stares she received didn't bother him in the least. That alone spoke volumes.

CHAPTER FIFTY

Knox

Walking into Haynes's Bike Shop, Knox paused. The sun shining through the store windows hit the chrome on the row of bikes and made them gleam with awe-inspiring brilliance. He couldn't believe when he walked out of this place today, he'd have a motorcycle in his life. Never in his wildest dreams had he ever thought he'd be a biker. A mere month after talking to Mortician about joining the club, Knox was well on his way. The outline of tattoos had been drawn on his chest and arm, and he'd purchased a stack of books on how to ride. He just had to find the time to read them.

"May I help you, sir?" a lanky boy asked, too young to have much knowledge about the powerful machines before him. His long ponytail reached his waist; huge gauges deformed his earlobes; the tattooed triangles and squares on his fingers must've been painful to receive. A biker in the making. Perhaps, a trainee at the shop.

Knox looked at the boy's name tag. "Uh, Chet, hi. I'm Knox Harrington. Can you please call someone familiar with the bikes?"

Chet smiled. "I'm familiar. My dad owns the shop. I've been around them since I was a baby."

"I see."

"What type of bike are you looking for? Touring, Cruiser, Sport?"

"It doesn't matter. As long as it is the best. Top of the line."

Chet scratched the peach fuzz on his chin. "What experience do you have?"

"What does that have to do with anything?" Frustrated, Knox started down the row of bikes. Some were smaller, probably built for speed, while others were huge, double-seated hogs, with all sorts of levers and switches. A low rider with shiny purple paint and chrome so brilliant Knox saw the reflection of his legs. He thought of Roxanne's Navigator. Bikes were meant to have unusual comments. Cars were not. Besides, *he* still hadn't bought the SUV for her.

Hands behind his back, he moved on, stopping at a motorcycle painted a dark gray, with just a dab of red on the black equipment where the chrome should be. It had two antennas, a second seat with a back as well as arm rests, and impressive handlebars.

"I want this one," Knox announced. "When you write up the specs, please be sure to order deluxe seatbelts."

"Seatbelts?"

"You do know what they are, don't you?" Knox demanded with impatience. "They keep you safe on the road."

"Uh...yeah," Chet said with some hesitation. "I mean, sure. Since you can handle any machine."

"Exactly." Knox pulled his wallet out of his back pocket and got his American Express Centurion. "Charge the card please."

"Let me get my dad," Chet said, accepting the card. He started to turn away, then stopped. "I'll also need your ID."

"Of course." Knox got his driver's license and handed it to Chet.

"You have a motorcycle license, don't you?"

"Do I need one to make this purchase?"

"No, sir. You need it to ride. You also need motorcycle insurance."

"Let me worry about that. You just do your job and make the sale."

Chet frowned. "Yes, sir," he mumbled, starting away again, then halting. "Outlaw!"

"Chet!" Outlaw said through a cloud of cigarette smoke. As he reached Chet, Outlaw shoved the cigarette in the corner of his mouth and clapped the boy on his back. "Where the fuck Haynes at?"

"I'll get him. I was going to run a card, so I'm heading that way."

"What the fuck you mean run a fuckin' card?" Grabbing the cigarette between his thumb and forefinger, he released the smoke, then glared at Knox. "You ain't chose a fuckin' bike, alfuckinready, assfuck."

Chet glanced over his shoulder then faced Outlaw again.

"You know him?"

Knox stiffened at the sound of the kid's voice.

Chuckling, Outlaw took a few steps backward and stopped at a freestanding ashtray and took care of the cigarette. "Knowin' I know this motherfucker un-fuckin-believable for my ass, too, Chet."

"Oh, I like that," Knox snapped. "If you feel that way, may I add I'm just as incredulous that I know you. How does that make you feel?"

Outlaw snatched the credit card from Chet and continued toward Knox. "Like I don't give a good fuck. We ain't here to discuss how the fuck the fates frowned the fuck on us and we ran the fuck 'cross each other path, so shut the fuck up." Slamming the American Express against Knox's chest, he pointed to the bike Knox chose. "You ain't buyin' this motherfucker."

"I beg to differ. I *am* buying this motherfucker. It's my money so I can buy *any motherfucker* I want."

"First of fuckin' all, my ass gettin' a bike just like this one, so ain't no fuckin' way *you* gettin' the same motherfucker. Second, you ain't knowin' how the fuck to ride, so this ain't the bike for you." He went to a smaller bike near the end of the row. "This the motherfucker you gettin'. It's lightweight and easy to fuckin' handle."

"I'm not stupid, Outlaw! I don't need a lightweight bike. I don't have to buy this one, since you've claimed exclusivity. But I want something just as high-end."

"Get something high-end and not only ain't I teachin' you to fuckin' ride, ain't no motherfucker at the club doin' it. You either get the motherfucker I say to get or you on your fuckin' own."

"There are riding courses I can attend. I don't need the club."

Outlaw shrugged. "Ain't no skin off my fuckin' nuts. But you ridin' that motherfucker back to the club."

"No, I'm not," Knox insisted. "We came in your pick-up to transport my new bike."

"Because you ain't fuckin' knowin' how to ride."

"Exactly. Although I'm sure I just have to watch you ride once to get the gist of it, how do you expect me to ride a bike I don't know how to operate?"

"You the motherfucker with the biggest fuckin' brain. You ain't listenin' to me on the type of bike you should get. You ain't needin' my cage to get your fuckin' ride back to the club."

"I thought I heard your voice, Outlaw," a tall, barrel-chested man said as he walked up and stepped between Chet and Outlaw. This man was an inch or two taller than Outlaw.

Grinning, Outlaw turned and clapped his hand with the big man's in some type of gang greeting.

"What's up, brother?" the man asked.

"Comin' to see what the fuck you got for a fuckin' noob. How shit goin'?"

"Can't complain. Next class is full. We got full bays on the other side, and sales of bikes and gear been good."

Outlaw nodded.

"Got some new gear Meggie might like—"

Knox cleared his throat. "Excuse me? I'm Knox Harrington. You are?"

The giant held his paw out. "Chet Haynes. But just call me Haynes."

"Yeah, this assfuck wanna learn to ride," Outlaw explained as if he hadn't exhibited his lack of social skills by not making introductions.

"Do you want to visit the machine shop, Outlaw?" Haynes asked, not responding to Outlaw's announcement.

"Ain't ever turnin' that down." Outlaw started forward, then stopped and beckoned Knox. "Come on, motherfucker."

Not trusting Outlaw not to leave him if he didn't follow the directive, Knox stomped behind him. In the middle of the showroom floor stood a spiral staircase that led upstairs. Oversized pictures of vintage Harleys hung on the walls over display cases filled with merchandise. In the center of the back wall, a few feet from a closed door, stood the circular checkout counter and another young man who resembled the two Chets behind it.

They walked behind the counter and headed to the door. Seeing daylight surprised Knox. Outside, across a small parking lot sat a building with four repair bays, each filled with motorcycles.

As they reached the shop, one of the mechanics revved an engine. The acrid scent of exhaust and hot metal burned Knox's throat and turned his stomach. Another mechanic looked toward Knox and the three others, and stopped, cutting a hand across his neck. Everything halted.

"Outlaw!" one of them called, as if the man was some type of living god.

Smiling, Outlaw greeted each of the four new men, then went from bike-to-bike listening to whatever the ass kissers told him. He'd point to this or that, drawing even the two Chets in. Knox hung back, not interested in hearing anyone else give Outlaw the idea that he was an all-knowing being.

"Knox!" Outlaw finally called, waving him over.

Scowling, Knox took care with his steps, not trusting what the black puddles might be. He didn't want his expensive clothes ruined. He stopped near the cult leader and his followers and squeezed his nose to close his nostrils. Damning his lack of a handkerchief, Knox ignored his watering eyes.

"What the fuck you doin'?" Outlaw demanded.

"Blocking the smells. What do you think?"

Drawing in a deep breath, Outlaw closed his eyes, pleasure clear on his face. He smirked at Knox. "Ain't nothin' like the smell of the machine shop. It soothes a man soul."

The other men nodded in agreement, annoying Knox to no end.

"This Knox Harrington," Outlaw introduced. "He marryin' Roxanne. K-P old lady."

Giant Chet smiled, but didn't look at Knox, so he missed Knox's rising anger. "How is she? She was always such a gorgeous thing. Two things that always stood out about her were that face and that foul mouth. Just my type of woman."

"She's my woman," Knox snapped, "so don't talk about her as if she's a piece of meat. Take note of that, Outlaw. She doesn't belong to K-P."

"Ignore this motherfucker. Roxanne pissed off at him, so he been tryna commit suifuckincide. Ain't obligin' him today, though."

"Very fucking funny," Knox said.

"You see my motherfuckin' ass laughin', Knox? I can shoot the fuck outta you right the fuck here. Roxanne ain't knowin' you with my ass. You grounded and she just gonna end up believin' you fuckin' ducked out."

"This is a business. You can't commit murders here."

"The fuck I can't," Outlaw said with irritation, "since majority of this motherfucker belong to the fuckin' club."

"Are you kidding me? You own the tattoo shop you sent me to. You own this bike shop that you expect me to buy from. What other place of business belongs to you that you want me to visit?"

"A fucking funeral home," Outlaw answered. "You interested in me sendin' you there for business?"

As Outlaw stared at Knox, the other men chuckled.

"I'm going back inside," Knox growled, spinning on his heel and walking back to the door that led to the showroom. He returned to the bike he'd wanted to buy.

It was big and beautiful, a real statement maker. It was the type of bike Knox deserved. The kind that would catch Roxanne's attention.

Footfalls pounded on the metal staircase in the center of the shop. Knox looked toward the sound and saw Outlaw following Giant Chet to the second floor. Wanting to know where they were going, Knox followed. Although half the size of downstairs, this floor contained racks and shelves of gear—jackets, shirts, boots, helmets, gloves, amongst other items.

"I'll be right back," Chet said as Knox walked up to the counter where Outlaw stood.

"Do you always have to threaten me?" Knox asked, not knowing what else to say.

Outlaw glowered at him. "You always gotta be a assfuck?"

"It irks me to see men and women show you adulation."

"That ain't what the fuck irk you, Knox. *My* ass irk you."

Knox flushed.

"Ain't gotta deny it. I ain't givin' a fuck first of fuckin' all. As long as Megan happy with me, my ass happy."

"Really? Do you think she'll be happy about Emily?"

Resting his elbows on the counter, Outlaw sidled a look to Knox. "Is Roxanne gonna be?"

Knox winced. "Touché."

"If you thinkin' to take me down and open your fuckin' mouth to Megan, then you ain't rememberin' your woman."

"Is it all about Megan? How would she take you down?"

"Yeah, it's all 'bout my woman. And, if she ever get pissed efuckin-nuff to walk the fuck away, I ain't gonna survive."

"Then why the fuck are you doing this?"

Sighing, Outlaw straightened. "I still got a club to run."

"This isn't club business."

"It is and it ain't. Family and business overlappin' in this fuckin' case. In the end, that bitch deserve to die as much cuz of club shit as she do for fuckin' with my boy and my Megan."

"I don't understand you."

"Ain't up to you to understand me."

"It is when you buy Roxanne exorbitant gifts."

"What fuckin' exorbitant gift I got her?"

"Her Navigator. A purple one at that."

Snapping his brows together, Outlaw stared at him, then shook his head. "I got a riddle for you."

A riddle? From Outlaw? Knox would solve it before he finished explaining the entire thing.

"I'm listening."

"Lou had five thousand dollars. Anita has one hundred dollars. Sarah had ten thousand dollars. Who had the most fuckin' money?"

Knox rolled his eyes. "That's easy. Sarah. What makes you think that's a riddle?"

Outlaw walked up to Knox, stopping inches away. "Cuz it is. Your fuckin' problem is you think you so fuckin' smart, you ain't got to listen to no other motherfucker. You so fuckin' smart that you stupid. The answer Anita cuz she *has* the money. Other two *had* it. Sometimes, you need to fuckin' stop and listen to other motherfuckers. Ain't a motherfucker alive know every fuckin' thing."

"I'm a college graduate. A retired police officer. A private investigator."

"Nobody givin' a fuck what you is," Outlaw growled. "Since you somehow all the fuckin' shit you say and got it without a fuckin' brain, lemme put a fuckin' suggestion on the table. If the fuckin' fact I bought Roxanne a ride upsettin' your ass so fuckin' much, give me my motherfuckin' money back and then you can say *you* paid for it. Problem fuckin' solved."

"Outlaw!" Giant Chet called from some back room.

"Yo?"

"I got a couple of things CJ might like. Come and see."

"What the fuck you got for Megan, motherfucker? My ass been standin' out here fifteen goddamn minutes."

Giant Chet boomed laughter. "My missus always saves things for your wife. When I run across things, I do too."

"You don't visit your own business?" Knox asked, somewhat chastened by Outlaw's riddle and explanation.

"Chet and his woman own forty percent. He a former Dweller. I trust the motherfucker. Ain't got to stay up his ass. He send quarterly reports."

"How many other businesses do you own?"

"Me, personally? Me with the club? Or me with Mort, Val, Cash, Digger, Stretch, and Johnnie?"

"You earn your money by legal means?" Knox asked in wonder.

Outlaw grinned. "Some of it."

"Outlaw!" Giant Chet called again.

"You a impatient motherfucker, motherfucker," Outlaw responded, turning away from Knox.

"Wait, Outlaw!"

"What, Knox?"

"Which bike should I buy?"

"Ain't repeatin' myself. You know what the fuck I said. Take my fuckin' advice or don't. That shit on you."

Saying nothing more, Outlaw turned and disappeared around the corner.

A little while later, Knox purchased the smaller, lightweight bike.

∼

"Wafer, are you sure about this?"

Later that evening, Cam circled Knox's new motorcycle, admiring it from the detachable windshield that Outlaw insisted Knox purchase to the red taillight. The bike's sleek lines reminded him of a racing bike. Except this one was street legal—and it was his.

Smiling, Knox rolled back his sleeves to show Cam his arm art. "What do you think of my new toos, Cookie."

"It's *tats*, Knox," Cam corrected around laughter. "Tats." He came closer to Knox, managing to drag his gaze away from the Harley. "Does she know yet?"

Disappointed that Cam didn't comment on the actual tattoos, Knox pulled down his sleeve and rebuttoned the cuff. "No. I was hoping she'd find out...someone would tell her. No one has. I'm still persona non grata, Cam."

"Suppose you do all of this and she still doesn't take you back? What then?"

What, indeed. If Roxanne didn't take him back, Knox...*no!* She *had* to give him a second chance. He couldn't imagine life without her forever. The past few weeks had been so hard on him. He'd never missed anyone as much as he missed Roxanne. Even Callie, by the time they'd separated, he'd been so tired of their constant arguments, that he'd been relieved to be away from her rather than regretful they were no longer a couple. As the mother of his son, he'd always hold her in the highest regard. Once upon a time, he had loved her. They just hadn't been meant to be together forever. "What if I end up alone, Cameron? I can't see myself with any other woman but Roxanne. What if she doesn't forgive me?"

Cam looked at Knox, his friend's assessing expression sending discomfort through him. Roxanne and Jordan talked on a daily basis. Had she shared something with Jordan, who, in turn, told Cam, and now, the man saw him in a different light?

"What?" Knox demanded. "What do you see under the microscope you've placed me?"

"That," Cam responded. "You, Knox. We've known each other most of our lives. If you spoke to me the way you talk to most people, we wouldn't have ever become friends."

"What are you talking about? I talk to everyone as I always have."

"That's the point. You talk to everyone with an air of superior condescension."

"I do not!"

"You do," Cam insisted.

Pain tore through Knox. That his best friend saw him in such a light, crushed him.

"Knox, listen to me. You're my brother from another mother. I love you as if you were my own flesh-and-blood, but let's be real for a minute. The world is yours to own. You went into law enforcement because that was your way of thinking you were giving back to society. You were a decent officer, but it was the Harrington money that moved you up the ranks. Donations. Politicking. Shit people like me don't have. We do what we have to do to get where we want to be. Instead of being grateful for the opportunity, you weaponize your status. And you're allergic to anyone not in your tax bracket."

"I'm not allergic to you," Knox cut in, cold and hostile.

Cam nodded. "No, you're not. Let me point something out to you. All the people in the club that are closest to Roxanne, you despise. Johnnie isn't that thrilled with her, yet, you consider him a friend. What does that say about your feelings for her?"

"Who Roxanne associates with has nothing to do with how I feel about her."

"Show me your friends and I'll tell you who you are."

"Fuck you. All these years, I thought you felt the same respect and admiration for me that I feel toward you. I've just been a laughing-stock to you, Cameron."

"I don't associate with people I don't like and respect. I love you,

Knox, *because* of who you are. I don't allow you to treat me the way you do everyone else. You're spoiled and entitled and you throw fucking fits when you don't get your way. I told you this when your relationship with Callie started to disintegrate. All of this—" He waved his hand to encompass the motorcycle and Knox— "don't mean a goddamn thing if you still look down on everything about the woman. Her friends. Her family. Her car. Her life. The change has to come from inside. You need to respect other people's opinions. You need to come to terms with the two different sides to Mortician, Outlaw, and even Johnnie. They're killers. They're underworld overlords. But they are also loyal family men and faithful friends. Most of all, they have street smarts. Outlaw wouldn't have gotten as far as he has without staying a step or five ahead of the law."

The door to the clubhouse opened before Knox responded. Mortician, Digger, Val, Johnnie, and Outlaw streamed outside, heading to where he stood with Cam.

Digger clapped Knox on the back and held out his hand. "Welcome to the other side!" he said, pumping Knox's hand in an exaggerated handshake. "Bruh, I think I'm going to call you Earp from now on."

"Earp?" Val asked, puffing on his cigarette, then taking a sip from the pint of rum he held. "Why not Clouseau? You know? From the Pink Panther?"

"You mean fuckin' Clue No, huh?" Outlaw snickered, drawing on a joint, then passing it to Mortician. "Howfuckinever, the motherfucker ain't part of the fuckin' club, so he don't need a new fuckin' name."

"He has a new attitude, Prez," Mortician countered, handing the weed to Digger, "so he need a new identity."

"Would you want a road name?" Johnnie asked, sipping from a bottle of whisky.

"Double-oh-fuckin-zero," Outlaw suggested, nudging Mortician, both of them laughing. "Triple Zee."

"Let me guess," Knox said with sarcasm. "Triple Zee for *zero*."

"You might have a fuckin' brain after-fuckin-all," Outlaw said, sounding truly impressed, as if he thought Knox a moron.

"I like Sherlock or Watson," Johnnie said. "Maybe, even, Magnum P.I. or Dick Tracy."

"Okay, why all the fucking cop names?" Knox demanded. "Why can't I be Bull or Horse or Gator? I even like Warbucks."

Outlaw glared at him. "I take my fuckin' words back. You still a stupid motherfucker."

"The road name reflects your personality, Knox," Cam explained.

"Then why aren't all of you named Outlaw?" Knox asked, laughing at his own wit.

Digger shoved him. "You not funny."

Knox jerked away from Digger's reach. "How can you make fun of me but I can't make fun of you?"

"Cuz you mean what the fuck you say, motherfucker," Outlaw answered.

"Really?" Knox responded. "And you don't mean it when you call me Clue No?"

"Sure the fuck do cuz you a clueless motherfucker. That fit your fuckin' personality, too."

"Give him a break, fellas," Cam said mildly. "This is all new to Wafer. You know? Wafer? As in he already has a road name?"

Nodding, Knox smiled at Cam, grateful for his friend's defense.

"You ain't gettin' a cut, so we can call you fuckbag for all I give a fuck."

"You're too kind," Knox said tightly.

"Knox, you ready for your first lesson?" Mortician asked.

Walking to his bike and waiting for Val to step out of his way, Knox nodded. "I was born ready." He felt around the seat. Not finding the seatbelt, he stooped down to look for a hidden nook. When he didn't see one, he stood and leaned over the seat to investigate the other side.

"What the fuck you doin'?" Outlaw demanded.

"Lookin' for the seatbelt. What do you think? Just because you bozos gamble with your lives, it doesn't mean I will."

"Seatbelt?" Mortician asked, his eyes wide, while Digger and Val bellowed with laughter.

Knox nodded, glaring at the two hyenas. "Did I stutter, Mortician? I was going to have a deluxe one installed on the bike I *really* wanted."

"Ain't no fuckin' seatbelt on no fuckin' bike, assfuck," Outlaw snapped.

When the words sunk into Knox's brain, he paused, took in Outlaw's aggravation and Cam's embarrassment.

"You a funny motherfucker, Knox," Digger said, wiping his eyes.

Grinning like an idiot, Val shook his head.

"Fuck off," Knox grumbled, then mounted, his feet touching the ground, his hands gripping the handlebars.

"Where your gear?" Val asked in horror, all humor gone. "You can't ride in no fucking trousers, loafers, and button down."

"Why not? I've seen others do it."

"Yeah, cuz others are stupid motherfuckers," Outlaw retorted. He walked to Knox. "My jeans? They ain't just fuckin' jeans. They ridin' jeans. It's thicker material. Protect you if you go down, although the best fuckin' protection leather. I wear full leathers when Ima be on a long fuckin' trip. I alfuckinways got my fuckin' gloves on. I wear fuckin' boots cuz you fuckin' go down, and boots bein' the fuckin' difference between bruisin' skin or breakin' bones. State law require fuckin' helmets. Ain't fuckin' goin' down cuz Ima stupid motherfucker, riskin' my fuckin' brains splatterin' all over the fuckin' road."

"Why didn't you tell me I needed gear?" Knox snapped. "And I've seen you ride out of here without a helmet, Outlaw."

"You ain't fuckin' ask what the fuck else you need. And, yeah, when I ain't goin' fuckin' far, I ride without a helmet. I even a-fuckin-llow Megan to do it. You ain't experiencin' real freedom 'til you feel the fuckin' wind blowin' the fuck in your hair. That don't make the shit right."

"So what now? I can't take one drive because I'm wearing clothes I normally wear?"

"Don't fuckin' insult us," Outlaw ordered. "Don't never let me hear you fuckin' say you *drivin'* a goddamn bike. You ridin' the motherfucker. Case fuckin' closed."

"Bruh, you rode a bike decent?" Digger asked.

"Of course. I'm a cross-country cyclist."

Grabbing Val's bottle of rum, Digger leaned on Mortician and took a sip of the alcohol. "You just got fucking Olympian skills at everything you fucking do, huh?" He belched.

Val snatched his bottle from Digger.

Mortician shoved him away. "Get the fuck off me, fool, with your nasty ass."

Laughing, Digger came up to Knox and put his hand around his shoulder. "Don't worry, Knox. I washed my fingers after I took them out Bunny pussy."

"If I was you, Harrington, I'd knock that motherfucker away from my fuckin' shoulders," Outlaw advised.

Grimacing, Knox did as suggested, smiling when the other men laughed. Digger more than anyone. He was enjoying the fuck out of himself.

"Ignore my fingers," he hooted. "If you know how to bike ride, you should have a reasonable amount of balance. Ride to the edge of the parking lot and back. Don't go too fucking fast or you going to regret not having the proper clothes on."

"I'm not going to fall," Knox said with confidence as Cam hurried forward and touched Knox's shoulder, blurting, "I think you should wait."

"No, Cam. I'm fine."

Raising his hands, Cam stepped back. "Okay. Just don't kill yourself."

"My ass fuckin' advisin' against this," Outlaw said.

"Of course you are. You think I'm a brainless idiot."

"Nope. I think you a stupid motherfucker."

Knox glared at Outlaw, then, keeping one foot planted on the ground, lifted himself up, pumped the pedal and squeezed the hand grips. The bike teetered, then tipped in the direction of the kickstand and stood still. He then repeated the steps three times, ignoring Cam's pained look, Johnnie's bowed head and Outlaw's shock, and tuning out Val, Digger, and Mortician's guffaws.

"Why won't it start?" Knox finally panted, sweat pouring down his face.

"Get the fuck off that fuckin' bike, Knox," Outlaw commanded, disgust clear in his voice.

"No! I'm taking that ride."

Clearing his throat, Cam stepped forward. "Where's your key fob?"

"In my pock..." His voice trailed off as realization dawned on Knox. "I have to start it."

"You also gotta take the goddamn stand the fuck off, assfuck."

"Won't I fall?"

"Jesus fuckin' Christ, who the fuck raised you?" Outlaw snarled.

"Knox, just *listen*," Cam said. "Think. This is a motorized bike. Can you ride a bicycle with its stand down?"

"Of course not."

"Why do you think you could ride a motorcycle if it's not out of the way?" Cam pressed.

"This isn't fully automatic? Once I start the bike and take off, it doesn't do the rest of the work for me?"

"NO!" all the guys chorused.

Scowling, Outlaw stomped forward, grabbed Knox by the collar and yanked him off the bike, shoving him out of the way. "Look the fuck at what my ass doin'."

Knox dusted himself off. After Cam's earlier conversation and the humiliation rising in him now, he decided to take Outlaw's advice.

"This ain't no goddamn competition," he chastised. "You ain't gotta show whether or not your nuts bigger than any of us motherfuckers. We here to fuckin' help you. Now, give me the fuckin' fob and *watch me*."

Passing along the fob, Knox studied Outlaw closely. He removed the stand, then planted both boots on the ground, steadying the bike with ease. After lighting a cigarette, he touched different mechanisms, then thumbed a button and the bike flared to life.

He jammed the cigarette in the corner of his mouth, gave Knox a pointed look, grabbed the grips and started forward in one smooth motion. He rode the bike to the edge of the parking lot, then sped past where they all stood and went to the other end, before taking a full spin around the place. When he finished, he glided to a stop, stared at Knox, then rose from the seat, leaving the engine idling.

Intimidated, Knox stared at the bike. Outlaw had made it look so easy and smooth. The man rode with a fluidity that impressed Knox and also told him he didn't have the qualifications to do the same.

The sound of sudden silence drew his attention.

Folding his arms, Mortician sighed. "I got a fucking joke for you."

Knox swallowed, then nodded, for the first time feeling as if he fought a losing battle. If he got on the bike, he'd fall and they'd laugh at him.

"God called Satan and told him he had some motherfuckers that just wasn't acting like they belonged in Heaven," Mortician started. "He told Satan he had to send them to Hell. Having no choice, Satan told God to send them on. So the motherfuckers get there. They immediately start acting the fuck up. After a week, Satan calls God and says, "God, I got to send these motherfuckers back. They complaining about the living conditions down here. Stirring unrest among all the other motherfuckers. God said, 'Satan, I sent them to you for a reason. They're your problem. You deal with them'. Annoyed, the devil hung up the fucking phone. The next week, Satan telephoned God again. 'Lord, you got to help me. The people you sent to me have been stealing from me. Some of my gold is missing. My coin collection gone. What am I supposed to do? Again, God said, Devil, you're in charge of them. They are your problem. Frustrated, Lucifer hung up the phone. The next week, that old pitchfork-wielding bastard had had enough. God had to take these people back now. Furious, he dialed God's number. 'Yes, Devil, what can I do for you this week'? 'God!' Satan screeched. "I'm not keeping them any longer. These motherfuckers just put out my fire."

Chuckles rose up around him. Knox didn't want to laugh, but he did at the unexpected punchline. None of them, not even Cam, seemed affected by the disrespect of it all. They found humor wherever, and whenever, they could.

"See, Knox?" Outlaw offered into the silence, smoking yet *again*. "It ain't nothin' but a thing. If you wanna learn to ride a fuckin' bike, take a deep fuckin' breath and learn. We was all scared our first time. You got unmatchable power between your thighs—and I ain't talkin' cocks cuz that shit a given. A bike, the road, un-fuckin-forgivin'. You *gotta* pay attention, but you still gotta have fuckin' fun. We ain't here to judge you. We here to fuckin' help you. How many fuckin' times I gotta tell you that?"

"Knox, son, it's like this. I see what you doing to win my momma-in-law back. I respect that. I also realize you just talk out the side of your goddamn mouth because you don't know how to back the fuck down. But Roxanne—"

"Knox!" As if speaking her name conjured her up, Roxanne ran at breakneck speed from the pathway that led to the houses. She skidded to a halt, out-of-breath.

"Roxanne, baby, what's the matter?" he asked, alarmed at her condition. He rushed to her, automatically wrapping her in his arms when she hugged him. "What's happened?"

"What are you doing?" she demanded, pushing away from him. "You're going to kill yourself! Why the fuck would you buy a bike?"

Keeping Roxanne in his arms, Knox glared at the circle of men. "Who betrayed me?" No one responded, so he turned back to Roxanne and took her face between his hands. "You weren't supposed to find out until after I learned."

"Oh, Knox. Don't do this for me. I don't want you to learn to ride a bike to impress me. It's not about that. It's about your attitude."

"Roxanne, please," he begged. "I love you so much. Please...just..." He huffed in a breath, close to tears. "I want to be able to drive—"

Outlaw growled.

"Er *ride* you around every now and then. I want to make you happy. If you just...please, just give me a chance."

She laughed through her tears. "You're such a motherfucker, Knox."

He smiled at her. "But I'm a motherfucker you love."

Not denying it, she glanced away.

"Can we just talk? Please."

She met his gaze. "Okay. We can talk. But I'm making no promises."

"Fair enough, sweetheart."

Wrapping his arm around Roxanne's waist, he smiled at the claps and whistles. Maybe, he'd learn to ride, after all, finally understanding the camaraderie and brotherhood that made these men so close.

That could be decided on later. Right now, he'd seize the chance Roxanne was giving him. All because he was willing to learn to ride a motorcycle. He couldn't wait to see what she'd do when he showed off the outlines of his tats.

CHAPTER FIFTY-ONE

Roxy

When Cam called her and then Digger texted her, Roxy knew she had to take action. Knox was on a suicide mission to learn how to ride a motorcycle. According to Cam *and* Digger, he was doing it to win her back. Knox was a lot of things, but she'd never taken him for a brainless motherfucker. He couldn't seem to understand, it was what was inside of him that mattered.

They walked back to her house in silence, although he kept his arm around her waist. Overcome with relief that he hadn't broken his head, she didn't move out of his embrace. Besides, his touch felt so good. She wanted to enjoy it while she could.

Inside, he closed and locked the door, turned and grabbed her wrists, pulling her close to him. He took possession of her mouth, consuming her, his taste and scent surrounding her. The rough, desperate kiss barely allowed her to catch her breath. She wanted to give in to him and her own need. Then, the harsh words he'd spoken to her pierced her thoughts, bursting her moment of weakness.

Yanking herself away from him, Roxy stumbled back. All the hurt and humiliation she'd felt flew away. Anger replaced it. She narrowed her eyes and balled her fists, punching his jaw before she stopped herself.

"You motherfucker," she snarled, kicking his shin. "Why the fuck did you say all those things to me? How could you fix your month to insult me the way you did?" She shoved him back and he slammed into the door. She tried to knee his dick, but he blocked her, then sidestepped her next advance. "Your fucked-up words isn't the way to solve a motherfucking thing."

Grabbing a glass from the counter, she threw it at him.

He ducked. "This is the fucking way to solve shit?" he yelled, twisting backwards and crunching over the broken glass to escape her.

"If you would just leave me the fuck alone! Let me get on with my fucking life, I wouldn't want to kick your cock into your throat."

"Um, ouch?"

She growled and took a step toward him, but he ran outside.

"What the fuck is wrong with you, Roxanne?" he said, only his fingers showing where he gripped the door, to hold it open. "This is too womanish for you. You don't throw shit."

"What the fuck do you mean too womanish? I haven't suddenly grown a fucking dick, asshole."

He raised his palm. "That came out wrong. I just meant—"

"I don't throw shit," she snapped. "I've never had occasion to throw shit at you. I want to bust your fucking head open and hug you; break your fucking face and love you."

Her voice trembled as hurt rose inside of her again. A sob escaped her. And another, until she broke down completely.

Knox peeped inside.

"Go away. I've decided there's nothing for us to discuss."

Being the stubborn motherfucker that he was, he walked back into the house and closed the door, leaning against it. The pain on his face didn't escape her.

"I'm so sorry," he said quietly. "I'll spend the rest of my life making it up to you, if you just give me another chance. I'll live at the club until the wedding. I'll do anything. Please forgive me. Please, Roxanne."

She felt her resistance crumbling. He sounded so humble and sincere. If she followed her heart, she'd let her guard down and let him back into her life. But, if she listened to her head—recalled the times she'd been let down in a relationship—she'd insist he leave and be done with it.

"You wouldn't still have my ring on your finger if you didn't feel something for me."

Sniffling, she held up her hand and glared at the ring. She pulled it off. "If your great-great grandparents had a happy fucking marriage, the motherfuckers cursed this ring for everyone else who wore it. Ever since I got this from you, our lives have been in fucking chaos."

Knox thrust his fingers through his hair. "Put it back on. Tomorrow, we'll go to the jeweler together and find one especially for you."

"I'm not signing a fucking prenup. Unless you sign one for me."

He laughed. "What do you have—"

Her narrowed gaze stopped him.

"I don't need your fucking money, Knox. Even if I didn't have property in New Orleans and a little nest egg, I want for nothing because of these boys here."

"Okay." Knox sounded chastened. "I'm sorry."

She licked her lips, studied the ring. Thought about Knox's ugly words. He was fallible, a mere man. She didn't hold grudges. It took too fucking much away from your soul, so she could let the argument go, accept his apology, and give him another chance.

Her heart started to pound. The weight she'd carried around for days lifted. For the first time in weeks, her world felt right again. Drawing in a deep breath, she slid the ring back onto her finger.

"One more chance, Knox. If you ever say anything like that to me again, we're done."

He ran to her and lifted her into his arms, swinging her around and laughing through his tears.

"I love you," he said. "I love you."

"I love you, too, Knox. As much as I tried, I couldn't stop my feelings for you."

Setting her on her feet, he bent and rained kisses on her face.

"You're not going to be sorry, Roxanne."

"I better not be," she said as he nuzzled her neck.

He lifted his head and pulled away from her. "I have to show you something, sweetheart."

She grinned. "I'm more than ready to see it."

"Not *him*," he said with a chuckle, unbuttoning his shirt. "This." He took the shirt off, revealing the black-ink outlines of a dragon that reached from shoulder-to-shoulder. On his arm were the makings of a full sleeve, although she wasn't quite sure what it would be. He held up his hand and wiggled his ring finger. "I'm going to have my wedding ring tattooed here."

"Knox, you don't have to do all of that."

He nodded. "I don't but I want to. That's the only way I can prove that I don't look down on what you like."

"What am I going to do with you? You're just too much!" she said, overcome with joy and happiness.

He winked at her. "I'm enjoying myself spending time with the men. Val asks the stupidest questions. Outlaw is...Outlaw is the most logical person I've ever met. And Mortician likes to joke. They all have different ways to put you at ease. All unique to them."

Listening to his words, Roxy knew she'd made the right decision. He was finally taking the time to get to know each of the men.

"If you want to learn to ride a motorcycle for yourself, then do it," Roxy said, "but if you are doing it to impress me, you've got to stop. I don't want you killing yourself."

He chuckled as his cell phone started to ring. "I want to learn for both of us," he told her with certainty and answered the call. "This is Knox Harrington."

It must have been from a number he didn't recognize.

The color dropped from his face and he gasped. "I'll be on the first flight on," he breathed out, then disconnected the call.

Roxy rushed to him and took his face between her hands. "What is it, Knox? What's happened?"

"It's Callie," he whispered.

"Your ex-wife?"

Knox nodded. "She's been killed."

CHAPTER FIFTY-TWO

Knox

Staring out the window in the back of the Uber, thoughts of Callie ran through Knox's head. They'd met and married young. Maybe, their marriage had been doomed from the start. Neither of them had known what the hell they were doing and, with a newborn added into the mix not long after, it was a recipe for disaster. She was spoiled and...he swallowed...so was he. They'd wanted things their way, neither of them knowing the definition of the word *compromise*. Trivial arguments that seemed so important to win had just been a reflection of their age. When his work on the force began to interfere with their marriage, Knox put her first. It hadn't worked. They still ended up divorced. She'd taken Grant across the country to Boston, her hometown.

"We're here, sugar." Roxanne's quiet voice reached through Knox's despair.

He grabbed her hand and brought it to his lips, kissing the back of it. "Thank you for coming with me."

She leaned in and gave him a tender kiss.

Opening the door, Knox slid out and then helped Roxanne to her feet. He didn't know how his former in-laws would receive him, but, for the moment, Grant was in their care. Other than the fact that Callie had been killed, Knox knew nothing else.

Clasping Roxanne's hand again, he walked up the steps and rang the doorbell. It didn't take long for the door to swing open, revealing Callie's mother.

"Audra, I'm so sorry," he said, releasing Roxanne and hugging the other woman. "What happened? How did she die?"

Audra stepped aside. "Come in." She noticed Roxanne and blinked. "I'm Audra," she said after a moment.

Roxanne held out her hand. "Roxanne."

"Come in, both of you," Audra said after she shook Roxanne's hand.

He placed his hand at the small of Roxanne's back; together, they walked in, following Audra to the living room, where a houseful of friends and relatives were gathered. He knew most of the people there and couldn't believe the circumstances under which he was seeing them. Seeing their grief seemed to increase his own, penetrating the shock he'd been living in for the past twenty-four hours.

But he couldn't give in to his feelings. He'd just won Roxanne back. How would she feel if she saw him crying over his ex-wife's death?

Roxanne squeezed his hand. "Knox," she whispered. "Why don't I go back to the hotel?"

"I want you here," he told her.

"I'm here, sugar. But you don't need me *here*. Grieve in peace, without thinking you're hurting me."

She'd wanted to stay at the hotel in the first place. Knox should've known Callie's family would be at this house.

"Dad!" Grant cried, running into the room and barreling to Knox. His son sobbed in his arms. "Mom's gone. Somebody shot her to death. It wasn't a robbery or nothing. The police said she let her killer in. They took Mom from me."

"What?" Knox gasped, feeling as if he'd been sucker-punched. His thoughts ran together, not allowing him to focus on anything.

"You've been listening, young man?" Audra said with disapproval.

"I want Mom, Grandma," Grant sobbed. "I just wanted to know where she was. When she was coming back."

Audra sighed, her eyes red-rimmed, her face haggard. "Go to your room," she said kindly. "Some of the....you're a little boy. It's best for you not to hear what the adults are discussing."

"I don't want to be in my room alone," Grant said around tears.

"I don't mean to intrude," Roxanne inserted, "but I can take Grant some—"

Before she finished, Grant had rushed to her. She didn't hesitate to wrap her arms around him and offer words of comfort.

"Can I go with Roxy, Dad?" Grant begged.

Knox started, then met Audra's gaze. Though she nodded, she sagged in despair. With Callie gone, Grant would come to live with Knox and Roxanne. He'd never cut Audra out of his son's life—she was his grandmother—but Grant living anywhere else was out of the question. He'd contact his lawyer before the day was out.

"Yes, son. You can go back to the hotel with Roxanne."

Patting Knox's back, she took Grant's hand." "Let's call an Uber," she said.

"Okay," he said, sounding hoarse and tired.

Overwhelmed by the sheer gravity of the situation, Knox waited for his former in-laws to protest. He always expected the worst so he wouldn't be surprised. No one said anything. Walking to Grant, he hugged his son, unsure of what to say or do. He stared at Roxanne, wordlessly asking for guidance.

She gave him a tender, reassuring smile.

"I'll meet you two at the hotel," he said, holding Grant close to him and then kissing his cheek.

"Take your time, Knox," Roxanne said. "We aren't going anywhere."

Knox nodded. Fifteen minutes later, he ushered them into an Uber, kissing them both goodbye. Once the car drove away, he headed inside, wishing he could be any other place but here. His ex-wife had been murdered, though, and he intended to get the justice she deserved.

Roxy

"Is Mom in heaven?" Grant asked, tears lurking in his eyes, though he valiantly held them in.

"Of course, sugar."

He picked up a French fry from his plate, then dropped it into the ketchup. "Will I see her again?"

Roxy pushed her own plate aside. She'd barely touched any of her salad and should've followed her original plan of ordering coffee for herself from room service and whatever Grant decided upon. She was familiar with Boston and she was tired from the long flight. The last twenty-four hours had been sheer hell, watching Knox scramble to get to his son, consoling him over Callie's death, and advising him to leave her behind. He needed her with him, he said. That was all Roxy needed to hear. Despite her reservations, she'd agreed to go.

"I miss her, Roxy. Who hurt her?"

Leaning forward in her dining chair, Roxy laid her hand on Grant's arm. His muscles were taut, seeming to shake with the grief he felt. "You'll always miss her, Grant, and yes, I believe you'll see her again. I don't know who hurt her, but I'm sure your dad will leave no stone unturned until he gets justice for her."

"Mom didn't want Dad to marry you. Am I mean for liking you anyway? I tried to tell Mom that you were really nice, but she wouldn't listen. That's why I was at Grandma's. Mom was mad at me because I was talking about the wedding. We thought she was pouting when she didn't answer. Do you think Mom still loved me?"

"You were the apple of Callie's eyes." Roxy had never talked to the woman personally, but whenever Grant visited, he was happy, well-adjusted, and boisterous. He spoke of the adventures he and his mom went on and of the places they visited. "You aren't mean for liking me, Grant, although you're young, so the situation is complicated. That just means your Mom still loved your Dad." She squeezed his arm, then withdrew her hand. "He's lovable like that."

"Dad didn't love Mom," Grant guessed.

Roxy kept her wince to herself. This child was too young to have to go through this torment. Whoever the fuck had killed Callie needed to be dealt with by the bikers, instead of the law. "Yes, your father loved Callie," she promised. "She was your mother, so she'd always be special to him. They just...they just couldn't live together because they didn't get along, so to keep liking one another, they separated. That way, they could be the best for themselves and as your mom and dad."

Tears slipped down Grant's cheeks. Her heart breaking for him, Roxy moved to the sofa and opened her arms. Without hesitation, he flew into them, settling on her lap and crying against her. When K-P had been killed, Bailey was already grown, and Roxy had been hundreds of miles away in New Orleans. However, she remembered the day her own father had died of cancer. As broken up as her mother had been, she'd still sang a couple of hymns to her, in an attempt to offer solace in an unimaginable time. Not knowing what else to do, Roxy rested her chin on Grant's head, and rocked him, singing the words to *Amazing Grace*. It was one of the few Christian songs she knew.

After he cried himself to sleep, Roxy laid Grant on the sofa. Exhausted herself, she decided a nap would do her good. Stretching out on the chaise lounge, she closed her eyes and allowed sleep to claim her.

"Roxanne?"

Knox's voice invaded her slumber and she stirred. Not satisfied, he shook her.

"Stop, fuck, Knox. Let me sleep."

"Let's go to the bedroom, sweetheart."

"I'm fine where I'm at."

"Grant is already settled in the guestroom. You need to be comfortable, too."

Grumbling, she forced herself to awareness and sat up. "What time is it?" she asked around a yawn, allowing Knox to pull her to her feet and lead her to her bedroom.

"After one in the morning."

"Fuck, how long have I been asleep?"

"What time did you go to sleep?"

"Fuck, I'm not sure. A couple of hours after we got back to the hotel."

In the bedroom, Roxy plopped down and laid her head on the soft pillow.

"I'm ready to crash, too," Knox said.

Rustling clothes told Roxy he was undressing.

"I'm bone-tired."

He climbed into the other side of the bed and drew her into his arms, spooning her. "Thank you, Roxanne. Thank you for being so understanding. I was no longer in love with—"

"Stop, Knox." Roxy changed positions, turning to face him. "You don't have to explain anything to me. You still communicated with her because of Grant. She's been a part of your life for many years."

"I don't want you to doubt my feelings for you. I don't want you to think I'm putting her family's feelings before yours."

"Your interactions with other women have never made me question your regard for me. *Your* words have."

"My actions never backed up my words, though."

"We can discuss this at length at a later time. Right now, I want to set you straight. This isn't about my feelings or your in-laws' feelings. It's about Grant. He needs to know who hurt his mother. I would expect no less from you. If I had a problem with it, I hope you would tell me to go fuck myself because that child is crushed. As his father, you do what you have to do."

Knox's nose reddened. His eyes looked suspiciously watery.

"Aww, sugar," Roxy whispered, drawing close to him, "I know you're hurt, too. It's okay. We're together, so I'm here for you. That means I'm all in. Grieve for her. Talk about her. Do what you need to do, Knox."

"I can't believe she's gone," he whispered. "Shot to death. The police have no leads. Who could've done this to her?"

"Dad?" Grant called.

Moving away from Knox, Roxy lifted her head and saw Grant standing in the doorway. "Come on, baby," she said, patting the space she'd created in the middle of the bed, by moving over.

"You're still dressed, Roxanne," Knox observed, scooting over and helping his son slip in between the covers.

"I'm too fucking tired to change," she explained, then lifted her hand up and stared at the engagement ring. She couldn't believe she'd once thought it was pretty. It was the ugliest motherfucker she'd ever seen. It would go to Grant for him to give to whoever he chose as his life's mate. If it was left up to Roxy, she'd throw this motherfucker in the deepest part of the ocean.

They hadn't even gotten to the make-up sex before Knox had gotten the news about Callie. Afterwards, it had been all about contacting his parents and his son, and making travel plans. Whether or not their wedding would go forward was up in the air. However, it seemed in poor taste that Knox would marry Roxy only several months after the murder of his ex-wife and son's mother. She might've been classless according to Duke, and her own behavior at times, but Roxy knew when to draw the line.

She sighed. "I'm going to tell Bailey that she and Mortician can still marry on August 6th of this year, but I'm pushing our wedding back to next year."

"What?" Knox gasped. "No, Roxanne. Absolutely not."

"We're going to marry eventually," she assured him. "We need to ride out this storm."

"As husband and wife," Knox insisted. "We're having the double wedding as planned."

"Dad smiles a lot with you," Grant said in a solemn voice. "I want you to marry him so he can be happy."

They both looked at her with expectation.

"How can I deny you two?" she said with a smile. "I suppose the double ceremony is back on."

Knox and Grant high-fived. Together, the three of them settled in, and soon fell asleep, wrapped in their cocoon of love.

Too soon, they had to face Callie's funeral and their final goodbye to her.

CHAPTER FIFTY-THREE

JOHNNIE

Johnnie had to know. He had to be sure that Christopher and Emily didn't know one another. He had to be sure that he could try to give her a chance, although he still wrestled with the role Emily had played in Kendall's life. He had no peace.

Emily bombarded him with calls and texts, while Kendall seemed to be withdrawing. It didn't matter that she was still part of the wedding party, and participated in whatever planning sessions or fittings the women had. The more he tried to ignore Kendall, the more his conscious beat up on him. Both her mother and sister had killed themselves. What if Kendall's behavior wasn't a ploy but a true cry for help?

In the midst of his confusion over her, to Johnnie, Emily served as a distraction. Not necessarily welcomed, but one he needed.

In the weeks since their date, he'd seen her six times. She'd prepared home-cooked meals for him on three separate occasions. Unlike Kendall, Emily was a great cook. She didn't mind evenings in.

She longed for children and an easier life. Most of all, she seemed completely into him.

His lack of desire toward her wasn't her fault. It was him. To counteract his tepid responses to her come-ons, he'd even stayed away from Kendall for the past few days. He hadn't brought the kids to see her or responded to any of her calls and texts. He and Emily talked at least four times a day, and texted even more.

Johnnie was tired of the internal conflict. Every time he gave the smallest consideration to fucking Emily, he recoiled. *She* was part of the reason Kendall suffered so greatly to this day. He believed he stayed away from Kendall more out of guilt than blossoming feelings for Emily.

Tonight, though, he was going to Digger and Bunny's house for their weekly dinner, and bringing Emily as his date. He wanted to see her next to Megan. He wanted to see Christopher's reaction to having the two of them in the same room. Johnnie might be fed up with Kendall, and worried sick about her, but if Christopher wanted to play fucking games with Johnnie's wife, then he'd return the favor.

"Do I look okay?" Emily asked nervously as they approached the cottage.

As brothers in the club, Johnnie, Christopher, Val, Mortician, Stretch, Digger, and Cash had much in common. Their love of riding, women, alcohol, money, and weed. As married men, the women they'd married defined their style.

Kendall was educated and loved the good life, so she'd chosen a two-story mansion for herself, Johnnie, and their kids. Zoann was no-nonsense and hardy, so her choice of an oversized log cabin for her family made sense. Bunny was down-to-earth and rather creative, fitting for the co-owner of an English-styled cottage. Ophelia went with the flow, and didn't mind the bungalow Stretch wanted and Cash insisted upon. Bailey was quiet and elegant. Though Mortician was a stingy motherfucker, he wanted to give her the best.

And, Megan, Christopher's heart and soul—the youngest of all their women—lived in a three-story fortress with a moat surrounding it.

Whether or not he and Kendall reconciled, in Johnnie's heart, he knew there'd be no place for Emily in this tight-knit group.

"I must look a fright," she said softly. "You haven't said otherwise."

Smiling, Johnnie forced himself to brush strands of her blonde hair behind her ear. "You look beautiful as usual," he told her. He bent and brushed her lips with his.

Words, *women*, came so easily to him. And, yet, the only woman who'd ever blinded him to reality was Kendall. In his bones, he felt Emily was playing him. That's why he needed to know, once and for all. He'd known and loved Christopher his entire life. Christopher had taught Johnnie so much. Especially fairness. In their world, fairness made the difference between life and death.

Emily glanced at him through her lashes. "We can always skip this part of our night."

Not answering, Johnnie winked at her, then turned and opened the door. He stepped aside so Emily could walk in ahead of him. Once inside, he closed the door. Laughter and conversation floated to him. The smell of fried chicken and other savory foods scented the air.

Grabbing Emily's hand, he headed to the family room, pausing in the doorway and forcing Emily to stop. The usual scene greeted him. The men around the bar with drinks and cigarettes. The women seated on the sofa, love seat, and chairs.

Knox stood next to Mortician, in deep conversation. After arriving from Boston with Grant, Knox had settled himself at the clubhouse, happy to go along with Mortician's rules. At first, Grant stuck to his father's side when he wasn't in school, not even wanting to visit Knox's parents. Usually, Grant returned to the clubhouse from school and went to Knox's room. On the rare days he was at work and couldn't pick Grant up himself, Knox always called to check on the kid. Gradually, Roxanne coaxed the boy out of the room in the evenings to help her cook. As the school year drew to a close, and Knox continued to learn how to ride, Grant acclimated himself to his new normal. The bikers and their sons embraced him, while the old ladies offered him the maternal love he needed.

Johnnie had overheard Roxanne explain to Grant that no one would ever take the place of his mother. For the first time, he'd understood Kendall's adoration of the woman. She might've been interfering, but she was also wise and kind-hearted. Eventually, Grant moved into the second bedroom in Roxanne's quarters.

Johnnie thought Knox would've decided to return to her place, too. Instead, he'd stayed at the clubhouse, getting to know the bikers, discussing bikes, tattoos, and alcohol, and reminding Johnnie what true love meant.

Megan walked through the door on the other side of the room, breaking into Johnnie's ruminations. She froze, narrowed her eyes, and pressed her swollen hands against her rounded belly.

He really didn't think she was so far along that she should have such a noticeable bump.

"John Boy, what the fuck you got her here with you, motherfucker?" Christopher demanded, following the direction of Megan's gaze.

Conversation screeched to a halt and everyone stared in Johnnie and Emily's direction.

"Good evening, everyone." Johnnie nodded to the room at large but kept his focus on Megan. "This is Emily. My date for the evening. We're stopping in for a drink before we go on our date."

"Your children are here," Roxanne said with disapproval. "Why bring another woman around them when you're still married to their mother?"

Megan cocked her head to the side. "Emily?" she said, ignoring Roxanne's comment. "Emily?" Megan repeated again, glancing between him and Emily before sidling a glare at Christopher.

"What the fuck, baby? Why the fuck you look at my fuckin' ass like that? I ain't told this motherfucker to bring no new bitch here."

"That's Emily," Megan snapped.

Emily stepped up. "Is there something wrong with my name?" she asked with a slight edge to her voice.

Folding her arms, Megan glowered at Christopher again, before meeting Emily's gaze. "It can't be a coincidence that your name is Emily and you look so much like me. I've heard about Emily Riser for years now and if my guess is correct, you are her."

"Wait?" Roxanne got to her feet. "You mean the bitch who gave Kendall such a rough fucking time? That Emily?"

"One and the same," Emily confirmed.

"Oh, my fucking God, asshole," Zoann spat, staring at Johnnie. "Kendall needs to grow a fucking brain, but it seems as if you need to as well."

"Johnnie, that's low," Fee said in disapproval.

Johnnie tuned all of them out. Taking Emily's hand again, he led her to where Megan stood. Anger washed over Megan's face, turned her blue eyes to ice.

She'd changed since her kidnapping, but he supposed the psychological effects of such a violation was unavoidable.

Side-by-side, he saw that Emily was slightly taller and had a fuller figure than Megan. Comparison seemed inevitable. For so many years, Emily had haunted Kendall and poisoned her interaction with Megan because of their resemblance.

Still, Emily's hair was a darker blonde, her skin paler, her eyes duller and slightly smaller. She had a bigger nose than Megan, a rounder face. More than that, though, Emily wasn't Megan. And Megan wasn't Kendall.

He no longer fantasized about making love to Megan. Now he knew, he'd never feel even an inkling of passion for Emily. Looking at Megan, Johnnie realized he could forgive her anything. She was his sister-in-law, and his friend. Emily was nothing to him. He'd never forget her years of abusing Kendall. He'd never get over his mistrust that she'd somehow been brought in specifically to fuck with Kendall. It didn't matter whether Christopher confessed or not. Or if he'd truly hired Emily.

Johnnie couldn't betray Kendall in such a manner. He loved her, and he preferred a lifetime of loneliness than to get involved with a woman who'd been so detrimental to her peace of mind.

"How did you even meet this woman?" Zoann demanded.

"Hold on," Knox called. The shock of his ex-wife's death had affected him for days.

Johnnie admired Roxanne for the way she'd given Knox room to grieve for Callie's violent death.

"You ladies are being completely unfair," Knox stated. "Kendall and this lady were little girls when all that went on. Johnnie and Kendall are separated," he said flatly. "Do you expect him to stay a monk the rest of his life?"

"No! Fuck no, Knox," Roxanne answered. "But Johnnie and Kendall aren't even *legally* separated yet. He could give her enough respect to not bring another woman around her kids and her family."

"I'm with Knox," Cash offered. "It won't matter who Johnnie brings around. There will always be an issue because she isn't Kendall."

"All Kendall ever did was stir up shit, Puff," Val said, eyeing Zoann. "Now your ass on your shoulder because Johnnie brought a new bitch around."

"Of course not, Val," Zoann chirped with a sniff. "It's *who* the bitch is."

"So much for female empowerment," Emily said with sarcasm.

Zoann lifted a brow. "I wasn't talking to you."

"No. Just talking about me," Emily shot back.

"What do you have to say for yourself, Emily?" Fee demanded. "How could you treat Kendall so cruelly?"

Johnnie registered Emily's hostility and distaste a moment before she grimaced and replaced the fleeting looks with remorse.

"I don't have to answer to any of you," Emily said. "If Johnnie has no problem with me, then none of you have anything to say. But, of course, I always did get along better with men. Women have forever been jealous of my overwhelming beauty." She sidled to Johnnie, wrapped her arms around him, and grinded her body against him.

"How long will Johnnie be okay with you?" Zoann questioned. "What will he tell his children when they find out their stepmother is the bitch who bullied their mother?"

"As if you really give a fuck, Zoann," Johnnie snapped. "You gave Kendall so much bullshit and never attempted to befriend her. Don't be a fucking hypocrite and pretend you're so concerned about her feelings now."

"Kendall is fucked up and I can't stand her fucking ass most of the time," Zoann spat, her eyes shooting daggers at him, "but, taking up with this woman is the worst fucking betrayal there could ever be, fucker. This is Kendall's sworn enemy and you're fucking her."

"I haven't touched Emily," Johnnie stated.

"Of course not," Zoann sneered. "You had to bring her and compare her to Meggie first. Right, motherfucker? You couldn't see Emily and Kendall side-by-side, so Meggie it was."

Anger flashed through Johnnie. He couldn't believe Zoann had the gall to believe Megan had anything to do with this. Didn't she know Christopher? Wasn't it clear that Johnnie meeting Emily had been orchestrated?

"You're overstepping your fucking bounds. Watch yourself, Zoann," Johnnie warned coldly.

Zoann snapped her brows together and barreled to him. "Or what? If you value your fucking dick, I'd shut the fuck up."

"I'm not Val," Johnnie returned.

"No the fuck you're not," Zoann answered. "Val is ten times the man you are. He doesn't make me live up to the standards of other women. He doesn't let me do shit that's way off the deep fucking end. We respect each other. I can tell him to stand down and he can do the same with me. You're nothing but a piece of fucking shit, making Kendall miserable because she isn't Meggie. You're the stupidest motherfucker alive. All the fuck you wanted was a woman to stand in for Meggie. You wanted what Christopher has, so you chose the first bitch that crossed your path after you lost Meggie to Christopher. You never loved Kendall. You couldn't have. If you did, you wouldn't have fostered her fucking jealousy. You wouldn't have tolerated her bad fucking behavior. Who the fuck cared what the fuck we did? It was up to you to tell her that wasn't fucking acceptable, you miserable motherfucker." She pointed to Emily. "Now, get this bitch the fuck out of here before I use her to fuck you up."

Humiliation roared through Johnnie and he gritted his teeth. He took a step toward Zoann, noting how she held her ground, dared him to come any closer, when all he wanted to do was grab her and shake the living fuck out of her.

Before he reached her, though, Val appeared at her side. "You put a finger on my woman, and we got problems, Johnnie."

"Johnnie, bruh," Digger called. "Take your bitch and get the fuck out my house. Don't fucking feel like cleaning blood splatter. We got a lot of wood in this motherfucker. Shit would be hard as fuck to clean up."

Johnnie blinked at Digger's words. "You're putting us out?"

This was spiraling completely out-of-control. No one saw what he saw. Instead of questioning the coincidence of how Johnnie had met the one woman who'd tortured Kendall, they were maligning him.

Digger shook his head in disapproval. "Did I fucking stutter. If I did, my bad. Maybe this better: Get to fucking stepping and take your bitch with you."

Johnnie looked at each of them—Cash. Stretch. Val. Digger. Mortician. Knox. Roxanne. Fee. Zoann, Bunny, and Bailey.

"You're Kendall's fucking friend, too, huh, Bailey?" Johnnie demanded, needing to lash out at someone. Besides Megan, he considered Bailey one of the sweetest girls in their group. "What do you have to say about me having Emily as my date?"

"Son, you lost your motherfucking mind coming down on Bailey like I'm some type of fucking bitch," Mortician growled.

Johnnie rounded on Mort. "Fuck you. You're Kendall's friend. What do you have to say, Mortician? You think I'm a piece of shit too?"

"I think you're a dumb motherfucker," Mortician said without flinching. "Red did some fucked up shit, but you helped her along. If you're divorcing her that's between you and her. But I wonder how the fuck you would feel if Red started dating a motherfucker you couldn't fucking stand."

Somewhere in the midst of the argument, Megan had gone to her seat. She sat, silent and sullen, throwing side-eyed violent looks at Christopher, who didn't flinch. Much to Johnnie's frustration. Still, he had his own methods.

"Are you jealous over Emily, Megan, or are you angry with Christopher because he put her in my path?"

"What the fuck you say, motherfucker?" Christopher snarled. "Why the fuck you think Megan jealous?"

"Is that the only thing you're concerned about?" Johnnie said, meeting Megan's gaze and gauging her reaction.

But her expression went maddeningly blank. "I'm not jealous, Johnnie," she said calmly. "Furthermore, I have no idea what you're talking about. How did Christopher put her in your path? More to the point, *why* would he do such a thing?"

"Don't play fucking stupid, Megan," he ordered. "To get back at Kendall."

"Really, jerk?" Megan retorted. "Even if he had put Emily in your path, which I don't think he did, she wouldn't have gotten here without *your* involvement. Again, why would my husband pull such a stunt? Kendall isn't around anymore. Besides, if you're so worried about Kendall's reaction, you wouldn't have made a move on Emily to begin with."

No one said anything in the wake of Megan's heated words. They all stared amongst one another, but Emily seemed to fixate on Megan. Unease slipped into Johnnie and he took Emily's hand in his own.

"'LAW!" CJ screeched into the silence, running into the room and skidding to a halt. He looked at Emily, gazed at her hand entwined with Johnnie's, then he turned to Megan. He focused on Emily again. "Who you?"

Emily smiled at him. "I'm Emily."

"*Miss* Emily," Megan inserted.

"*Emily*," Emily insisted. "Miss-ing and Mister-ing went out ages ago."

"When you have children, you're welcomed to tell them how to address adults," Megan said coolly. "CJ is *mine*, so you will not overstep my authority."

"Whatcha want, boy?" Christopher asked, sounding both annoyed and tired.

"Oh!" CJ said, running to his father. "Diesel humping Lyndsey in the bathroom. I watcheded him, 'Law. Just like you told me when him did that to her in my treehouse."

"*WHAT?*" Megan screeched, her face going sheet-white. Horrified, she looked between her husband and son.

CJ stayed focused on Christopher. "Him and her went to the bathroom and I 'lookted' under the gap between the door and the floor. Him bent that girl over and started doing this." He pumped his hips back and forth. "Then her say, 'ohh,' and him did this to her." He slapped a hand over his mouth. "Her dress wayyyyy up and his pants down, 'Law."

"How the fuck long you watched them fuckin', boy?" Christopher demanded.

"Omigod, Christopher," Megan gasped in outrage.

"That's what they was doin', baby."

"Diesel getting ass," Digger said with a grin. "That's a cool little motherfucker."

"No, he isn't," Megan protested.

"He certainly isn't," Bunny agreed.

"Miss Emily, why you holding Uncle Johnnie hand?" CJ asked.

"Because we're dating," Emily answered with a smile.

CJ nodded, then turned and started out of the room, yelling, "Ro! You got a new Ma."

"Let's go," Johnnie said. Without waiting for a response, he guided Emily toward the door, nervous that Rory would see him with a woman who wasn't his mom.

Neither he nor Emily spoke as they walked along the forested path that took them past Mortician, Val, and Christopher's houses. Behind Digger's house stood Johnnie's property as well as Cash and Stretch's. They'd created a nice little enclave for themselves and their women.

"That was interesting," Emily said once Johnnie had left the property. "Are they always so colorful?"

"Always," he confirmed. "It surprises me how much we look forward to the weekly dinners, considering they almost always turn into a free-for-all."

Emily chuckled. "Perhaps, that's the fun in it right there."

"Maybe," he agreed, hoping she stopped her small talk so he could think over the evening's events.

~

Every now and then, streetlights lit the inside of Johnnie's Navigator, and Emily saw his handsome profile with unerring clarity. Ever since she'd met Outlaw, her luck had changed for the better. Such as now. At that moment, the light glimmered into the car, allowing her to see how he was closing up. He gave her the merest of glances, then refocused on the road ahead, but it was enough to know if she shut up now, her fortunes would head south again and she'd be paddling her canoe in a sea of shit once more.

She pretended to put her anger aside. Pretended that she didn't hate Megan Caldwell as much as she had always despised Kendall. Whereas Kendall hadn't known the power she had over men, Megan was well aware of her influence. She had beauty and youth and the devotion of Outlaw. Still, in Emily's eyes, Megan was gorgeous but Kendall, with her natural red hair, was absolutely stunning. Because blondes had a reputation of being more fun, everyone wanted to be blonde. They came a dime a dozen. Redheads, though, were a rare breed, which made them all the more outstanding.

A country song invaded her thoughts. Johnnie had turned on his radio.

She blew out of breath, then turned the radio to the 'off' position.

"I was listening to that," he complained.

"I love Country music, too," she said, able to tell this truth. "But I'd prefer we talk."

"About?"

The last person in the world she wanted to discuss. "Kendall," she said softly. "Your wonderful family." She'd keep her hatred toward one of them to herself. Well, she didn't care for Zoann or, actually, none of those bitches that had been present. "I would've loved to have been part of such a huge, unruly bunch," she said in a small voice. She forced herself to sniffle. "You're very lucky."

The silence stretched by for such a long moment that Emily feared she'd overplayed her hand.

"My family is nosy, noisy, bossy, and more than a little opinionated," he finally said.

True, true, true, and true. "They are perfect," Emily lied. "I'm honored you brought me to meet them."

"Yeah, well—"

"As to what the girl...Joann, was it...?"

"*Zoann.*"

Of course, she'd never forget that bitch's name. "Oh, what an unusual and pretty name."

"She's my cousin," Johnnie grunted.

Emily would grunt that fact, too. Who would want to claim that bitch as family? "It's obvious she loves you very much."

Johnnie sidled a glance at Emily. "She could've kept her fucking thoughts to herself."

"I know they aren't the truth, so please don't be embarrassed on my behalf."

"I'm not," Johnnie said, surprising Emily.

After all, Zoann called him a piece of shit for a slew of crimes that mostly involved Megan Caldwell.

"I just can't believe she had the fucking gall to say that to me."

Emily lowered her lashes. "Was it true?" She applauded the meekness in her voice.

"Does it matter?"

Not really. Not for her end goal. "Of course," she said in a trembly voice. "How do you think I felt hearing you brought me there to compare me to another woman? One who isn't even your wife? Are you in love with that girl or something?"

"Who? Megan?"

Duh. Who the fuck else?

Emily nodded. "Y-yes." She sounded pathetic.

Outlaw needed to give her extra money for her performance.

"I once loved Megan with all my heart," Johnnie admitted. "But I don't anymore. It's Kendall whom I love and miss terribly. She's just so fucking frustrating, Emily. Besides, Megan, Zoann, all of them were right about you. You're the bitch who started my wife down that mental path."

If Emily had her way, she would put Kendall through much more, and throw Megan in to boot. "We were just children," she said, feigning regret. "I'm so sorry and ashamed over my actions. You have to know—"

He rolled to a stop in front of her shoddy apartment building. "I don't have to know anything," he interrupted. "Kendall and I have enough between us without adding you, or any other woman into the mix. And I don't believe you are truly regretful. Something about you screams scheming bitch." He shrugged. "Whatever the case might be, I can't see you anymore. I'm not interested in you. I'm not attracted to you."

Emily gasped, his words shocking her out of her pretense. Before she lost her temper, though, she managed to rein in her anger and burst into tears. "You can't mean that, Johnnie!"

"I do," he said.

She reached over the center console and threw her arms around his neck. "No! Johnnie, please. I've fallen in love with you. You can't…just give me a chance to prove how happy we can be together."

He disentangled her arms from around his neck and pushed her away. "Quit the fucking theatrics, Emily."

"Why are you doing this to us?" she wailed.

"There's no *us*."

"Yes, there is!"

Without responding, Johnnie got out of the car, walked to Emily's side and opened her door. "Get out of the truck, Emily," he ordered.

She hoped one of the crime lords saw Johnnie and confronted him, so she could watch the asshole beg for his life. The men who lived in her neighborhood were *real* criminals. Even the cops were afraid to traverse these streets at night.

"Get the fuck out! *Now!*"

Asshole. "But—"

"But, nothing. I might still end up divorcing Kendall, however, you're not going to be one of the reasons. Now, get the fuck out of my truck before I pick you up and put you out."

Usually her tears worked. "You'd leave me in this condition?" she got out on a big sob.

"The only woman's tears that ever held any power over me is Kendall's."

Hoping her expression was so woeful it kept him up tonight, Emily got out of the Navigator. She thought to kiss him then changed her mind. She'd go ballistic if he spurned her. His rigid stance told her he would. Better to leave that can of worms unopened.

"Good riddance," he told her.

Emily watched as he sped off, vowing to have the last laugh when all was said and done.

CHAPTER FIFTY-FOUR

CHRISTOPHER

"Megan?"

"Yes?"

Christopher considered her response an improvement from the past few hours. After Johnnie and Emily left, Megan got up and called for CJ and Diesel, looking as if she'd turned into a little Tasmanian she-devil, ready to tear them *and* Christopher up with her bare fucking teeth.

She'd ripped into Diesel for disrespecting Digger's house and "having sex" in it. Never mind the fact that the motherfucker—that was, Digger—didn't fucking see it as disrespectful. Then, she'd punished CJ for being naughty. Whatever the fuck *that* meant. His boy was only doing what the fuck Christopher had instructed him to do. As for Christopher, besides pinning him with her she-devil looks, she didn't say one fucking word to him. Not *one*. She wouldn't even fix her fucking mouth to utter a fucking sound in his direction.

Not a goddamn peep.

So, fuck, yeah, hearing her respond to him was a step in the right fucking direction.

"We been home for fuckin' hours, baby. You been hunched the fuck up in those covers, pretendin' your fuckin' ears plugged the fuck up with wax or something. Just ignorin' the fuck outta me."

"What do you want?"

Christopher sighed. It was the middle of the goddamn night, but fuck if he'd been able to sleep. He knew she'd been awake, too. Nightmares didn't plague them as much lately. Still, he kept a close watch on her, waiting for her to tell him the truth about how far along she was in her pregnancy.

Unless she was carrying five or ten little motherfuckers, he saw the size of her belly. Maybe, she thought by not confessing how far along she really was, she could save that incompetent motherfucker's life. One in two thousand dick snips failed, or some shit like that. It had to do with cock plumbing reconnecting. *Still*, that didn't matter. Shouldn't the doctor-motherfucker have known Christopher had a working dick again to save not only his fucking money but his fucking pain?

"Christopher?"

Once she told him she was either delivering another fucking tribe of kids or she was further along than she'd admitted, he'd tell *her* she didn't have to worry about the doctor. He was already fucked up and grounded. At the moment, he'd address the matter-at-hand. "First of fuckin' all, it would be quite fuckin' helpful if you fuckin' told my ass why the fuck you a pissed lil' motherfucker."

"You know why."

He had an inkling, but he didn't want to admit that. "Cuz of Diesel and CJ."

"Partly. Diesel is too young to be having sex and CJ is definitely too young to be spying on someone to tell you they are being intimate."

"Fuck, baby. Diesel got a cock. Whatcha expect him to do with the motherfucker? He gotta use it."

"To urinate," she yelled.

"What? Urinate? Ain't no fuckin' kid of mine urinatin', Megan. Urinate! A real cock don't fuckin' urinate. The motherfucker *piss*. Don't ever fuckin' put the word urinate in a sentence when you referrin' to any man in this fuckin' house."

"There's only one man in this house," she countered.

"Fuck, baby, then change man to motherfucker. Don't use urinate and penis about no motherfucker in this house."

"Omigodddd, Christopher," she groaned. "You're so insane."

He smiled at the back of her head, knowing she was softening toward him. Encouraged, he wrapped an arm around her and pulled her into the spoon position. She held herself stiffer than a mummy, but what the fuck ever.

He nosed her hair. "Don't be mad at my ass, Megan."

She stayed silent for a moment, then she sighed. "How could you hire Emily to go with Johnnie?"

And there the fuck it was. The real fucking basis for her anger. Megan had always figured shit out. While Johnnie *felt* as if meeting Emily was too much of a coincidence, Megan *knew* it.

"Do you know what that'll do to Kendall?" she whispered. "That'll devastate her. It'll kill her."

Quite the fucking point.

Megan stiffened a little more, almost fucking impossible considering how mummified she'd been before.

"That's the point, isn't it?" she asked, her voice sad and watery. "You want her so overcome that she'll kill herself."

He closed his eyes, hating the pain in her tone. Hating even more that he'd caused it. "I hate Kendall, Megan. She ain't no good. She got you took from me." He clenched his jaw. "I fuckin' hate that bitch. I'll never, ever fuckin' forgive her."

"She got me back," she argued. "You promised me you wouldn't kill her."

"If she fuck her-fuckin-self up, my ass *ain't* killin' her," he snapped.

Megan elbowed his chest as hard as she could. "You're splitting hairs. You'd be directly responsible for her death."

"Fuck, Megan, I'm so fuckin' tired of that bitch dominatin' our conversations. Most of our fuckin' arguments cuz of her. Most of me and Johnnie arguments cuz of her, too."

"Do you realize what you say to Kendall in front of Johnnie?"

"Do you fuckin' realize what that bitch *do* in front of that motherfucker?"

"Christopher—"

"No, Megan, shut the fuck up, and listen. That bitch my enemy, your enemy, and our boy enemy. Enemies dealt with. Case fuckin' closed. Ain't you dealt with her fuckin' ass when you beat that bitch black and fuckin' blue? Why? Cuz you was fed the fuck up. Why the fuck you suddenly flippin' the fuckin' script and expectin' my ass to look the other fuckin' way. Johnnie better off with-fuckin-out Kendall. Her kids better off with her ass gone."

"You think Emily is better?" Megan asked in outrage.

"Fuck, Medusa better than Kendall, Megan. Nurse Ratched. Fuck, Freddy fucking Kruger. *Any*-fuckin-body but motherfuckin' Kendall."

"Christopher, I will never trust Kendall again with my children or my confidences, but she's part of our family and she has a terrible illness. As long as she's alive, there's hope that she'll get better and do better. Dead—"

"Dead, we get fuckin' peace. That bitch ain't never gonna be better, Megan."

She let out a small sob. Megan had to know he spoke the truth. Kendall had had so many chances and he was sick to fucking death that she took so much of their energy and time discussing her or trying to un-fucking-do the bullshit she'd done.

"Please, don't kill her, Christopher. Please."

"I'm not the motherfucker that's gonna kill that bitch. She gonna kill her own ass."

"Because of you. *Your* actions. Don't do this. You're not that unfeeling to drive someone to suicide."

He released her and turned onto his back, staring up at the ceiling. This shit here was exactly the reason he hadn't wanted Megan to know what he was up to.

"I should've known you were going to find a loophole to our agreement," she said miserably.

Placing his hands behind his head, he glowered at the ceiling. Damn Johnnie for bringing Emily to the dinner. What the fuck was wrong with that motherfucker anyway? Him and Kendall wasn't even fucking divorced yet. The assfuck should've known the women would be on his stupid ass over Emily.

"Loophole, huh? Is that what the fuck you callin' it?" he grouched.

"I could also call it a betrayal," she retorted. "You promised me you wouldn't hurt Kendall. Your hatred of her is eating away at you. It's almost a sickness. You're better than this."

At the sound of her hurt and disappointment, Christopher froze.

"Suppose Johnnie hadn't brought Emily tonight? You would've gone ahead until Kendall found out."

His heart began a frantic, uneven rhythm at her desolate tone. His worst fucking fears were coming true. He'd pushed his woman too far!

Turning on his side, he pulled her into the crook of his arm and pressed his forehead against hers. "Don't hate me, Megan," he whispered, closing his eyes.

The feel of her fingers combing through his hair made him look at her. "I could never hate you," she whispered.

The tears shining in her eyes broke his heart and made him feel lower than a motherfucker.

"I'm very mad at you, but you explore and re-explore options. That's why you're such a good leader and a cunning adversary." A tear leaked from her eye and he thumbed it away. "Kendall can't come to any harm by your hand, at your command, or through your orchestrations and machinations to force *her* hand to take her life. Is that clear?"

"Yeah, baby," he said on a sigh. "What the fuck my ass suppose to do about Emily?"

"Have Riley pay her off. He had to have paid her when he found her."

"Riley ain't found her, baby. Kendall tracked Emily down. I just gave Knox the fuckin' info I overheard and he contacted her for me."

"Knox is involved too?" Megan gasped. "No! You're joking."

"Nope. This shit was top secret." He explained his reasons why to her.

"I understand your point but, if Roxy finds out, she'll never forgive Knox...I-I mean d-did he know what you intended?"

"Yeah. He can't stand Kendall neither. His reason more fucked up, though. He hatin' on her cuz she took Johnnie side over his when he came in to fuck over us."

"See what I mean? She can't win! You hate her because she's disloyal and Knox hates her because she *is* loyal."

"Nope. I hate that bitch cuz she a psycho cunt. Ain't no other reason."

"Make Knox send Emily away," Megan ordered, not responding to his comment.

"Fuck, fine, baby. The bitch gone, and I swear I ain't gonna do nothin' to fuck Kendall up."

He'd just have to go to Plan-fucking-B and force Johnnie to choose between staying in the club or divorcing Kendall. He'd make divorce sound quite beneficial to her. Then, once Johnnie was free of that bitch, she wouldn't be fucking family so Christopher could shoot the fuck out of her himself.

Satisfied, he smiled.

"What are you thinking?"

Christopher cleared his throat. "Uh, how I ain't riggin' Kendall fuckin' ride. I ain't stuffin' her in a cannon-fuckin-ball and shootin' her the fuck outta it. I ain't attachin' her to a fuckin' fishin' rod and usin' her for shark bait. I ain't droppin' her ass from a airplane over the North fuckin' Pole for polar bears to feed off her. I ain't boxin' her and sendin' her to the Nile for crocodiles to fuck her up. I ain't throwin' her in a snake pit or a lion's den or a tank of piranhas."

"Christopher!"

"Fuck, fine. I ain't lookin' for no bitch, *nothin'*, that'll make her go fuckin' psycho-er and fuck herself up. Happy?"

"You're the psycho," she grouched.

He brushed her lips over his own. "What the fuck I always say. My ass *your* psycho. You just gotta fuckin' deal with it."

"Forever and always," she whispered.

Encouraged, he tugged her into the crook of his arm. She snuggled close to him and he smiled. At the brush of her swollen belly, his good mood fled.

"How you feelin', baby?"

"Fine," she said quietly, as if she was anything but.

"You ain't been goin' to checkups every-fuckin-week like fuckin' usual? You ain't goin' to no high'risk doctor?" After she lost Patrick, Megan had to be closely monitored with each new pregnancy.

"Huh?"

She'd just forgiven him, so he managed to hold onto his temper. "You not in no danger?"

She went silent.

"When the next time you go for a fuckin' checkup?" he pressed.

She tensed. To keep her from moving away, he tightened his hold on her.

"What would you have said if I found out I was sixteen or twenty weeks pregnant?" she asked after a moment of silence.

Christopher glowered at the ceiling.

"There's such as thing as cryptic pregnancy," Megan explained. "In so many words, the baby hides himself from his mother because she's under so much stress."

Growing angrier by the minute, Christopher studied the top of her head. "Just what the fuck you tryna tell me, Megan?" he'd demanded.

She cleared her throat. "Nothing. It's just a scenario."

"Okay, baby. Then think of *my* motherfuckin' scenario. If you woulda be that fuckin' far along that would meant all that bullshit Kendall and Mystic and those motherfuckers put you through was affectin' you a-fuckin-lot. That *also* woulda meant that I put my kid in you be-fuckin-fore my dick snip flip. All my fuckin' pain and sufferin' woulda been for fuckin' nothin', so I woulda fucked that motherfucker up. Ain't no way you woulda stopped my ass neither, Megan, cuz he ain't a fuckin' family member."

"Yeah, so you've said before," Megan mumbled with misery.

"Wait a fuckin' minute. You tellin' my ass you five fuckin' months?"

She sniffled.

He should just tell her the motherfucker she was trying to protect was already fucked. The news would only upset her more. In the interest of her health and peace-of-mind, Christopher dropped the subject and decided he'd follow her lead.

He didn't want anybody stressing her out—himself included.

CHAPTER FIFTY-FIVE

EMILY

Sitting in the same restaurant she'd met Kendall at so many weeks ago, Emily waved her hand when she saw the redhead walk in and stop at the hostess stand. Kendall nodded at Emily, then spoke to the hostess and pointed to the table. A moment later, she was gliding in Emily's direction. She was confident and stunning. Though she was separated from Johnnie, she still had his devotion. And, maybe, even his love.

Emily loathed her.

Kendall slid into the opposite side of booth. "Receiving a call from you was quite the surprise. I'm on my way to a fitting for a wedding I'm in, so I left a little earlier to give you the courtesy of hearing you out."

Emily offered a thin smile. "When I heard from you, you could've knocked me over with a feather. You're the last person I ever thought would want to talk to me."

"What can I do for you today, Emily? You said you had important news for me, and you refused to tell me over the telephone."

At first, Emily's important news was going to be Outlaw's plans for Kendall. She decided against that. He was ghosting her, not answering her calls. She'd had Knox Harrington deliver a final check to her with a note that said her services were no longer needed. Between Johnnie backing away from her and Outlaw dismissing her, Emily's fury ran deep. She couldn't let their slights go unanswered. It would be easy to tell Kendall Outlaw's secret. Then, she'd go to Johnnie, and the two bikers would kill each other over the betrayal. However, if by some chance Johnnie survived, it would only bring him and Kendall back together. In essence, Kendall would still come out the winner.

That was the last thing Emily wanted to happen. She came up with a new plan. She didn't need to go after the men. Their women would serve her purposes just as well. Two, in particular.

Bowing her head, Emily pulled out her phone, opened the messages it seemed as if Johnnie sent, and handed them to Kendall.

She frowned. "I'm not interested in seeing your phone, Emily."

The cool tone and superior expression irked Emily. "These are from Johnnie."

Surprise slid across Kendall's face. "*Johnnie?*"

"Yes, hon," Emily answered with false regret. "John Donovan. Your husband. See his phone number at the top?"

Kendall gasped, stared at the phone, then snatched it. The shock transformed into anger and, finally, despair.

Stifling laughter, Emily flipped her hair, imagining Kendall reading the text that said Johnnie didn't care that Emily had been Kendall's childhood nemesis because her pussy was so good. Better than Kendall's.

Tears rushed to Kendall's eyes and her face flushed.

Maybe, Kendall had gotten to the message that said she was ten times the woman Kendall could ever hope to be.

She sniffled. "He's started divorce proceedings?"

"You didn't know?" Emily tsked. "He won't break his marriage vows and sleep with me before you can go your separate ways legally. He's such an honorable man. I'm so lucky to have found him."

Throwing the phone down, Kendall got to her feet, tears streaking her face.

Emily sipped from her glass of water and smiled at Kendall. "Seems I'm the better woman after all."

Kendall sucked in a breath, released a sob, and then fled the restaurant.

Proud of her accomplishment, Emily lifted the water in salute to herself, and laughed with delight. She was starving, so she'd order food before putting the next part of her plan in motion.

Kendall had always been so easy to manipulate. With her life in shambles, she wouldn't believe she had a reason to live. Megan Caldwell, on the other hand, would be handled differently.

Kendall would take care of herself, but Emily intended to personally deal with Outlaw's wife.

Megan

Sitting under a tree, near the creek she and Johnnie had talked by a few weeks ago, Meggie skimmed a rock across the water.

She wouldn't be able to hide from Christopher how far along she was in her pregnancy for much longer. She'd awakened this morning, looking swollen. *More* swollen than she had been the past couple of days. Between blurry vision and a severe headache, she'd wanted to stay in bed today. Then, she remembered she needed to get to the Whittlestones' shop for a fitting. Christopher was still working on a deal with a man named Amfinger. Knowing it was the stress of her deception getting to her, Meggie decided to keep how bad she felt to herself and go on about her day.

As she'd left Hortensia, she'd been overcome with dizziness and an awful pain in her back. Both had passed. Since she'd been much closer to the park than to the clubhouse, she'd headed there. After parking she'd sat in her car and realized she wouldn't be able to make it to the fitting. By then, she'd been sure, all the girls had left. She didn't want to dampen their day, so she'd sent Roxy and Bailey a text, stating she couldn't make it to the shop.

The thought to call Krag, Webster, Pete, or Talbot crossed her mind, but one was as bad as the other. They'd just fuss at her and berate her.

Sighing, Meggie rested against the tree trunk, her eyes sliding close. She was suddenly so tired. Maybe, a short nap would rejuvenate her and allow her to get home before Christopher ever realized she hadn't shown up to the fitting.

~

Kendall

Stumbling into her bathroom, Kendall set her note down on the counter, then stared at herself in the mirror. Her hair was limp and her eyes were red-rimmed. Her face looked pale and washed-out.

She looked completely broken. And she was. She couldn't do this anymore. Life was just too hard. Too heartbreaking.

Too lonely.

Roxy and Bailey had been calling her. She'd been due to meet them at the Whittlestones. Instead, after leaving Emily, Kendall had come home, ignoring her ringing telephone and the numerous texts.

On her way up the stairs, she made a monumental decision, so she'd gone to her bedroom and written a note. One day, someone would find her. By then, she probably would've decomposed beyond recognition. Roxy called her every day, but she had yet to visit.

Maybe, after a week or two of Kendall not answering, Roxy would decide it was time to see about her in person. Of course, there was Charlotte, but she wanted Kendall to be a certain way, *act* a certain way. Charlotte pressured Kendall to make decisions she didn't want to make.

533

She was all alone.

Tears streaming down her face, Kendall opened the first prescription bottle and poured the contents into her hands. Grabbing the glass she kept near her toothpaste, she filled it with water, shoved the pills into her mouth and washed them down.

She gagged, spitting a few out.

But she was determined. Johnnie and Emily as a couple was just too much for Kendall to bear. Of all the women in the world, he'd chosen the one who hated Kendall the most.

A sob escaped her. She opened the next prescription bottle. Bypassing her hand, she upended the contents into her mouth.

Heat rose around her and nausea churned in her belly. The room spun around her and she fell to her knees, her stomach heaving.

Grabbing the third bottle, Kendall's hand trembled. Somehow, she managed to swallow most of the pills. Once she swallowed the last of her pills, she grabbed her phone.

The screen and keypad were so blurry. Her heart pounded in her chest, its beat rising in her ears. She wanted to tell him how much she loved him, but knew she'd never finish the text, so she wrote one, simple word, and pressed send.

Bye

CHAPTER FIFTY-SIX

Roxy

"Baby, thank you for riding with me to Kendall's," Roxy said, making the turn-off onto the street that led to Kendall's house.

"No problem, Momma," Bailey responded.

The other girls were so fed-up with Kendall, they'd decided to head back to the clubhouse rather than roll with Roxy to see why she hadn't shown up to the fitting and why she wasn't answering her phone. Something didn't seem right to Roxy. Kendall had been very excited to be a part of the wedding. Roxy didn't believe she'd stay away if not for a drastic reason.

Of course, maybe, because Meggie hadn't sounded herself when she'd called and said she wouldn't make it to the fitting, Roxy was panicking for no reason. Hopefully, that was the case.

Roxy pulled behind Kendall's Navigator. "I won't be long," she promised.

"Take your time," Bailey answered, pulling her cell phone from her purse. "I'll call Lucas."

Smiling, Roxy got out of the car and slammed the door behind her. She walked up the steps, then rang the doorbell. Noting the attached camera, she waved.

"It's me, baby," she said just in case Kendall was looking at the monitor and wishing she had a key. The same unease that Roxy had been feeling for most of the day slid into her again.

Just as she rang the bell a second time, her phone rang. She'd already given Grant a special ring, so she knew it was him calling.

"Hey, sugar," she answered. The little boy had made a lot of strides since he'd moved to Hortensia.

"Hi, Roxy," he answered. "Can I have some ice cream? I asked Dad but he told me to call you."

Roxy hadn't wanted to push him, and she hadn't wanted to get in the way of him and Knox's time together. Father and son needed each other, now more than ever. Or so she thought. Knox was determined to put her in the role of Grant's maternal figure. As long as the boy didn't mind it, Roxy loved it, and she'd told Knox that. Grant had *one* mother. Just because Callie was gone didn't change that fact.

"Can I, Roxy?"

"Sure, sugar. But just one scoop and in a bowl. Don't add sugar with a fucking cone." she answered.

He laughed. "Yes, ma'am."

"I'm not going to be much longer, baby," she promised.

"Okay, I'll be here. Dad has a big surprise for you, too, so hurry up."

"I can't wait to see what it is," she said honestly, her mind running away with all types of possibilities.

Maybe, they'd make love? Now that Roxy and Knox had made up, not only was he sticking to learning how to ride and getting a tattoo but he was also adhering to Mortician's dictate that they live separately until the wedding. Roxy suspected it had a lot to do with the camaraderie he was finding with the guys. The riding lessons were one big party.

"Um, Roxy, what size is your ring finger?" Grant blurted.

Roxy went on alert. "A size seven. Why?"

He gasped. "Oh! Uh, no reason. Gotta go! Bye, Roxy."

Chuckling as she disconnected, Roxy wondered if that meant what she thought it did. Had Knox really replaced her engagement ring? She knew the sentimental value his great-great grandmother's ring held for the Harrington family.

"Momma, is everything okay?" Bailey called.

Roxy turned and waved to her daughter, who stood on the running board to look over the SUV.

"Kendall still hasn't answered the door," she responded.

A moment of guilt hit Roxy. If she hadn't been so wrapped up in her wedding plans, then her breakup, then wedding plans again, she would've been giving Kendall more time. She hadn't visited the girl at her new house once. Her behavior toward Kendall was a crying shame.

"Have you tried knocking?" Bailey asked as she bounded up the steps and onto the porch. She went to the door and turned the knob.

Finding it unlocked, they gained entry. Shocked, Roxy and Bailey frowned at each other.

"Wait, baby." Marching back to her Navigator, Roxy grabbed her purse and pulled out her pink gun. Maybe, Kendall hadn't been answering because she couldn't.

"Oh my God, Momma!" Bailey cried, when Roxy joined her on the porch again, gun in hand. "Put that away. Let me call Lucas."

"You call Mortician, while I find Kendall."

"Mama!"

Ignoring Bailey, Roxy went into the house. She barely saw the décor in her worry.

"Kendall?" she called, her gun cocked, loaded, and raised. "Where are you, sugar?"

No answer.

An eerie feeling rushed over Roxy at the silence.

"Kendall!"

Holding her gun with both hands to make sure her grip was good, Roxy went from room-to-room, but found no one or nothing that looked out of the ordinary.

Except something was. She felt it in her bones, in the hairs standing up on her skin, and the goosebumps traveling along her spine.

She reached the entrance hall again and stopped at the bottom of the staircase. "KENDALL!"

"Momma, Lucas is on his way," Bailey said, a touch of fear in her voice.

They looked at each other, then up the staircase. It seemed a long, lonely trek to the second floor, when it was no bigger than any other staircases Roxy had seen.

"Stay here and wait for Mortician," Roxy instructed, starting up the stairs.

Bailey's hand on her forearm halted her. "Momma, wait. It might not be safe."

"Trust me. I'm going to shoot first and ask questions later."

Before Bailey could protest any further, Roxy barreled upstairs, ready to keep her promise.

All the doors were closed, except one at the end of the hallway.

Still gripping her gun, Roxy crept forward, her sense of dread growing.

When she walked into the room, she found it was the master bedroom. Kendall's purse lay abandoned on the floor, next to her pumps. Sheets of paper and pens were scattered on her bed.

Light streamed from another opened door, drawing Roxy. The first thing her gaze landed on was a sheet of paper on the counter, next to an opened prescription bottle. Her gaze went to the floor.

For a moment, she thought she was imagining things. She was taking in everything so fast. Then, the scene registered.

Kendall on the floor, convulsing and foaming at the mouth, pills and medicine bottles all around her.

"Oh, no! No! No, no, no. Kendall, baby! No!"

Dropping to her knees, Roxy crawled to Kendall and gathered her in her arms.

"*BAILEY!*" she screamed, sobbing and shaking. "BAILEY!"

"Momma, what...?"

"Oh my god!" Bailey cried. "I'm going to call an ambulance."

"Hold on, sugar," Roxy pleaded through her tears.

Kendall had stilled. Somehow, Roxy didn't dissolve into hysterics. She didn't even remember setting her gun down. She only knew it wasn't in her hands. Holding onto Kendall, she willed her to have the strength to survive, when it seemed she hadn't had the will to live.

~

CHRISTOPHER

He would never forget Johnnie's screams, filled with horror and grief and shock. They'd drawn Christopher from his office and made him rush down the hall, through the crowd, and toward the sound, his gun out.

The entire clubhouse had been thrown into momentary chaos, with brothers drawing whatever weapons they carried.

When Christopher reached Johnnie's room, he'd found the door unlocked, so he'd gone in. It was then that Christopher realized that Johnnie had been yelling Kendall's name.

His eyes wild, he'd grabbed Christopher. "She coded," he sobbed. "They don't know if they can save her."

Shoving his nine back where he'd taken it from, Christopher tightened his hands on Johnnie's arms. The motherfucker wasn't making sense. "What the fuck you mean? *Who* the fuck coded?"

"Kendall," Johnnie managed. "Roxanne f-found her. She...they went...Kendall didn't show up...Kendall overdosed."

His sentences were all over the place.

"She coded," he repeated, through his tears, loud and broken-hearted. He started to shake.

"Johnnie, listen to me," Christopher ordered, holding his face between his hands so the motherfucker would focus. "You gotta pull yourself together."

Hearing the words falling from his own lips, Christopher pushed aside any regret he might've felt. But he knew his statement meant nothing. When Megan was ill or missing, he could never *pull himself together*.

"Ima getcha to the hospital."

"She's always been so fragile. I knew…that's why…I knew what I was doing. I-I…she's like a Dresden Doll, beautiful to look at, seemingly sturdy, but undeniably delicate."

That's what Christopher had counted on. Seeing Johnnie's heartache, though, gave him pause. Made him wish Kendall hadn't been such a psycho cunt, who despised Megan and wanted to beat up CJ. His remorse was on Johnnie's behalf. He loved the motherfucker, and hated to see him so devastated.

Christopher pulled him to the bed and shoved him onto it, then grabbed the whisky from his nightstand and handed it to him. Johnnie drank deeply, nearly finishing the bottle.

"Ima drive you to the fuckin' hospital but you gotta stay fuckin' calm. Hear me?"

Johnnie nodded.

"Lemme get my keys. Ima call Megan on the way to the fuckin' hospital."

"'Law!"

The crowd in the hallway muffled CJ's little voice. He didn't want his boy seeing Johnnie in such a condition, so he turned on his heel and walked out. The brothers separated to allow Christopher passage.

"'Law!" CJ wailed again.

For the first time, he heard the panic in his son's voice. Reaching CJ, who stood sobbing near the bar, Christopher ran to him and lifted him in his arms.

"CJ—"

"Where MegAnn?" he asked around sniffles. "Diesel not home yet from work. We was scared."

"What the fuck you mean Megan ain't home? And Diesel not there? Where Bunny? Who was home with you, Rebel, and your brothers?"

"Me," he cried.

"Son—" Christopher drew in a deep breath, then grabbed his phone and dialed Digger's number.

"I'm here, Outlaw," Digger said, walking in and carrying Rebel while holding Rule's hand. Behind him, Bunny pushed Marcus and Ransom in a double stroller. Ryder was in a sling, attached to her.

"Where Megan?" Christopher demanded, taking Rebel into his arms when Digger handed her to him. With CJ on one side and his girl on the other, he walked to his table and set them on their feet. "Where the fuck my wife? Bunny, where the fuck Megan? Why the fuck you ain't been with my kids?"

"Meggie didn't come to the fitting," Bunny answered.

All types of scenarios going through his head, Christopher sat and took Ryder into his arms when Bunny handed him over.

"We didn't know what to do, Outlaw," Bunny sniffled. "We were halfway home when Bailey called."

"I told Zoann to drop Bunny off at the McDonald's they was near," Digger explained. "Zoann went to where Roxy and Bailey was."

Before Christopher replied, the door opened and Megan walked in, pausing at the crowd of people.

"What's happened?" she breathed, her eyes widening.

Fear, relief, and guilt combined within Christopher, creating a toxic brew that needed to escape.

"Where the fuck you been?"

She walked to the table, close enough for him to see how swollen her fingers had gotten again and how puffy her face was. "I need to talk to you, Christopher."

"I ain't told Krag and the other motherfuckers to follow you cuz you was supposed to be with Bailey, Bunny, Bitsy, Roxanne and the rest of them."

She looked at her feet. "I need to talk to you," she repeated.

Under the circumstances that just wasn't good enough. She didn't even seem to know that Kendall might be fucking dead.

"What the fuck wrong with you, Megan?" Christopher yelled, furious that she'd left the premises again without an escort. But, more than that, enraged that shit was spiraling so fucking far out of control. Besides, Karma was a motherfucking bitch. With Johnnie's bitch fucking herself up because...well, fuck. Who the fuck knew why she'd over-fucking-dosed. It might not have had anything to do with Christopher's schemes.

Yet, he'd been planning Kendall's demise for weeks. He was so fucking angry and he wasn't sure why. However, if he *hadn't* been so angry, he would've thought better of addressing this in front of a captivated crowd, including their children and most of their family.

Barely aware that Bunny grabbed Ryder from him, Christopher stood from his seat, shoving the chair against the wall so forcefully it surprised him the motherfucking wood didn't splinter into bits and pieces.

CJ slid from his seat and went to his Ma, stopping in front of her, turning around and folding his arms, and glaring at Christopher. He was too fucking mad to care.

"This ain't like you at-fuckin-all," he ranted. He stalked to her, unable to get as close as he wanted to because CJ stood in his way. "Bein' so un-fuckin-concerned about your safety out of fuckin' character for you, so what the fuck goin' on?"

The smile she'd plastered on her face when he'd first posed his question, remained, frozen, as if she were an ice statue and her expression had been carved onto her face.

"Let's talk about this in your office."

"Fuck no," Christopher snarled. He pointed at her. "I told your lil' motherfuckin' ass not to go a motherfuckin' place off the premises without motherfuckers on your detail. What the fuck you did, though? Exactly what the fuck my ass told you not to do."

Megan narrowed her eyes, another warning that he needed to back the fuck off. "Christopher, shut up. We can talk about this in private." Her hand on her belly, she started to turn away from him.

CJ grabbed his Ma's hand, guiding her toward the door.

Livid because he felt so helpless, Christopher placed his hand on Megan's shoulder and yanked her back. She stumbled.

"Mommie!" CJ yelled. "Law," he said with a little boy growl.

Christopher raised a hand, stopping his son's advance. "Shut the fuck up, boy. This between me and your Ma. Unless you want me to spank your motherfuckin' ass, stand the fuck down."

CJ halted in his tracks, his eyes widening. Tears rushed to them and his lower lip trembled. He sniffled. "Law mean."

"Don't talk to CJ like that, Christopher," Megan ordered, kneeling down next to their crying boy and drawing him into her arms, comforting him as only she could. She threw Christopher the evil eye. "If you're angry with me, take it out on me, jerk."

"Angry with you? *Angry?*" He gave a nasty laugh. "My ass furious, you lil' pain-in-the-ass motherfucker. You was kid-fuckin-napped, baby. I almost lost my fuckin' mind. What the fuck don't you under-fuckin-stand 'bout that?"

She whispered to CJ, pointed to his seat at the table, then got to her feet, as their boy ran and reseated himself. She came up to Christopher and laid her head on his chest.

"I love you and I'm sorry for worrying you. I'm not ignoring your feelings." She huffed out a breath, then stood on her tiptoes as she tugged his head down.

Obediently, Christopher bent his ear next to her mouth, relishing her nearness, her scent. *Her.*

"I needed time to myself," she said quietly.

"Krag and the other motherfuckers did you something?" he asked with suspicion.

She shook her head. "They've been respectful."

"They ain't got a fuckin' choice if they wanna keep their tongues in their fuckin' mouths and their fuckin' brains in their fuckin' heads."

"They keep a distance because I'm Big Joe's daughter. Or Snake's sister. Or your wife. There's a lot of formality that makes me feel so guilty that I'm dragging them all around when they have better things to do."

Christopher straightened and glared at her. "First of fuckin' all, they ain't havin' no better shit to do than guardin' you."

Unlike her, he wasn't speaking in low tones.

"I grant only the motherfuckers I know layin' down their lives for you the fuckin' privilege of guardin' you."

"Can you lower your voice?" she asked. "That's why I wanted us to talk in private."

"Ain't lowerin' my voice, Megan. That mean, you gotta lower yours and my ass gettin' a crook in my goddamn neck keepin' it fuckin' bent."

"I have a lot to tell you. Can we go to—"

"No, we settlin' this now," he commanded. "Cuz next fuckin' time you leave on your fuckin' own, I'm lockin' you the fuck up. Some-fuckin-where." *Any-fuckin-where* as long as he knew she was safe.

She stiffened and gave him a look of death. "I have a headache and I'm very nauseated, so I'm going to let that comment go as I let your yelling at me and CJ go."

For the first time ever, Christopher ignored her ailments. His day had turned into a living hell, sending him spiraling. Within minutes of seeing Johnnie so grief-stricken, he'd discovered Megan was once again missing. Megan as a corpse, whether he was finding her dead body or seeing her in a coffin, lived on the fringes of his mind, ready to haunt his nightmares. She'd had near-death experiences before, but this last time, she'd been *kidnapped*. Stolen.

"When you went to the Torps' place and Spoon gotcha and you lost the baby, I kinda pulled the fuck away from you. It got fuckin' bad between us, but when we made up, I promised you I ain't ever fuckin' doin' that a-fuckin-gain. This motherfuckin' time, Megan, *you* doin' it to me."

"I am not!" she said, raising her voice an octave. "What kind of mother would I be if I give in to my fears and cower behind closed doors?"

He thrust his face into hers. "A motherfuckin' live one," he gritted. "Just the fuckin' way my ass wantcha to be."

She reached for him. "Christopher—"

He grabbed her and shook her. "No! Don't fuckin' *Christopher* me, Megan. Stop actin' like whatcha ain't—stupid." She'd always been goddamn hard-headed, though.

Even before her eyes darkened and her face reddened to devil color, Christopher's words caught up to him and he tensed, preparing to have a pissed lil' motherfucker on his hands.

Instead, her eyes wide, she hugged her stomach and released a torrent of vomit onto his chest.

Before Christopher reacted, Megan swayed and placed her hands on his chest to steady herself.

"Megan, baby, what's—"

"Christopher." She paused, drawing in a deep breath. "I'm losing the baby," she managed, then went limp in his arms.

~

Knox

Halting in the door of the waiting room, Knox watched as Roxanne allowed Johnnie to sob on her shoulder, her own tears sliding down her cheeks. He felt like an intruder, and interloper, given his role in the current situation.

It surprised Knox to see Zoann sitting in one of the chairs, Val next to her. Her attention stayed on Johnnie and Roxanne, and Knox figured Zoann was there more to support them, than because of any sorrow toward Kendall.

Across from Zoann and Val were Mortician and Bailey. She was leaning on her husband's chest, the devastation on her face making Knox swallow.

Because of his dislike of Kendall, he hadn't thought through the ramifications of his actions. He'd seen Outlaw's plan as a way to get Kendall out of Roxanne's life—and thus his—and forged full-steam ahead.

Knox hadn't considered how her death would affect *others*.

He stepped back, unsure if he could face any of them, and not confess.

In one fell swoop, everything had been thrown into chaos. He didn't know if Kendall was alive or dead. When Roxanne called him in hysterics, he hadn't made much sense of her words. He hadn't called her back. He'd summoned Grant and, together, they'd rushed to the club. Only to find another dire situation—Outlaw cradling Megan in his arms, CJ rushing to leave his parents' side, and paramedics rushing onto the scene.

Never in Knox's life had plans shifted so quickly. He'd gotten Roxanne a specially designed engagement ring that he was going to present to her tonight. Instead, he was at a hospital, not knowing if Kendall was alive or dead or if Megan had lost her baby.

The suddenness of his ringing phone startled him. Looking at the screen, it surprised him to see Joyner Amfinger's name and number pop up.

"Hello," Knox answered, hovering in the shadows of the grief-stricken waiting room. He doubted a gun deal would be a top priority for Outlaw right now, but felt obligated to talk to Amfinger in case there were any questions that Knox might be able to answer.

"Knox!" Amfinger said with jolting joviality.

Either Knox hadn't paid much attention before or the dire events had heightened his senses. The sound of the man's happiness annoyed Knox, though, and he realized he didn't have it in him to entertain this conversation.

"I'm sorry, Amfinger," Knox started, watching as a doctor walked into the waiting room. "I'll need to call you back tomorrow."

"I understand," the man responded. "I was just calling to express my sympathy about your wife's death."

Knox frowned. "Callie?" Her murder had made national news, so he supposed Amfinger could've heard about it through a media outlet. But she'd been dead nearly a month, so he couldn't understand the timing of the call. "She's my ex-wife."

"Right," Amfinger said with a disarming laugh. "Excuse me."

The doctor walked out of the waiting room.

Knox didn't hear anything, a cry of relief or a wail of grief. He had no indication whether Kendall had survived or not.

"I can't talk right now," Knox growled, not in the mood to be polite. "Thanks for your condolences." Such as they were.

"I need a favor from you."

"What the fuck don't you understand, asshole?" Knox snapped. "I'm busy, so fuck off."

"We have to move up the date of the transaction," Amfinger blurted. "Outlaw wants to wait until after August 6th. Your wedding date to Roxanne."

Huffing out a breath, Knox ignored his uneasiness at how familiar Amfinger seemed about the goings-on in his life. "My hands are tied with whatever agreement you've reached with Outlaw about those weapons. Talk to him."

"I'm talking to *you*. I'd like you to go to him and ask if you could deliver the funds and handle transport."

"I'm not a member of the club." Somehow, Knox found himself unable to get rid of the man. "If Outlaw isn't the man to see the deal through, then another member of the club will."

"A *contingent* of club members," Amfinger corrected. "Well that won't be necessary. It seems I was unfamiliar with the workings of a motorcycle club. I thought you would be my point of contact throughout the deal."

"You didn't make that a stipulation," Knox snapped, straightening when Johnnie walked out of the waiting room and halted at seeing him.

"Knox?" Johnnie said as if he'd never seen him before.

"I have to go," Knox declared to Amfinger.

"At least inquire if Outlaw would allow you to be his proxy. If you do that, I'll have a special surprised for you. To thank you, of course."

"Of course. I'll talk to Outlaw." Not waiting for Amfinger's response, he disconnected the call, then rushed to Johnnie and placed a hand on his shoulder. "How's Kendall?"

"Her stomach has been pumped and she's in ICU. It was a close call, but they think she will survive."

Relief hit Knox so hard he almost staggered back. Instead, he tightened his hand on Johnnie's shoulder. "Oh, thank God!"

"I thought I'd lost her." Johnnie shuddered. "I didn't know...a text message came through and I ignored it. She hasn't invited me to a session with her psychiatrist. I don't know what medicines she's taking. I didn't want to fall into her trap again." Tears rushed to his eyes. "She left a suicide note. She said she was tired of being alone and frightened. She told me she wanted me to be happy with Emily...*Emily*! How did she even find out I'd been contemplating a relationship with her? Our relationship will never be the same. It will be forever compromised by my transgression."

"Don't think of that right now," Knox told him, feeling such overwhelming guilt, *he* felt like sobbing. "She's alive. That's the most important thing."

Johnnie nodded.

"I need to go see about Roxanne."

"Yes, Knox, you do." Johnnie glanced away, then met Knox's gaze. "I'll be forever indebted to her. She...Her mother's instinct guided her to my wife. She truly loves and cares about Kendall. I'll never question her advice or get annoyed over her interference. If not for her, Kendall would be dead."

"Knox?" Roxanne called at the exact moment Charlotte's voice cried, "Where's Kendall? What have you filthy animals done to her?"

"Charlotte, please!" Brooks cried, haggard as always when he dealt with his wife.

"Get the fuck gone, Charlotte," Roxanne demanded, her eyes fierce. "We don't want your ass here."

Charlotte drew herself up. "You can't stop me. This is Portland, *Ms.* Doucette. Not Hortensia, where you people have the staff and board of Hortensia General on your payroll. *I* know board members here at Willow Bend."

Johnnie inserted himself between Charlotte and Roxanne. "Leave, Charlotte," he ordered. "The only thing you've ever done is confused Kendall. You're no good for her. I don't give a fuck who you know. Cross me and you'll forfeit your right to breathe. I'll show you a fucking filthy animal."

Her hand flying to her chest, Charlotte gasped. "Are you threatening me?"

"No," Johnnie said, his voice dripping ice. "I'm promising you. If I were you, I'd turn around, go back to your fucking house, and mind your own goddamn business."

"But I love Kendall!" Charlotte wailed.

"Charlotte, dear, come on," Brooks encouraged, clutching her shoulders and turning her away. "Johnnie is overwhelmed. Let's leave him."

"I just want to know if she'll be okay," Charlotte said in a pleading tone.

Brooks sighed and looked to Johnnie, who clamped his jaw, his look implacable.

On a sob, Charlotte turned.

"Kendall is going to survive," Roxanne cut in.

Charlotte turned toward Roxanne. "She will?" she asked with hope.

Roxanne nodded. "I can't stand your ass, but in your own fucked-up way, you do care about Kendall. Besides, she sees Brooks as a father, so even if *you* don't deserve the courtesy of knowing her prognosis, he does."

"Thank you, Roxanne!" Charlotte said.

"Fuck off," Roxanne retorted. "You don't mean that phony bullshit, so I'm not interested in hearing it."

Her lips tightening, Charlotte scowled at Roxanne, then started off. "Come, Brooks."

"Will you keep me up-to-date about Kendall?" Brooks asked.

"I'll do it," Knox said. He didn't want Roxanne disturbed with minutiae.

"Thank you, Knox," Brooks responded, then walked away, catching up to Charlotte down the hallway, in front of the bank of elevators.

"I'm going to Kendall," Johnnie announced, then walked off, leaving Knox alone with Roxanne.

"Oh, Knox," she said in a broken voice, running into his arms. "This has been one of the worst days of my life. I just knew something wasn't right," she said tearfully. "She was on a cold floor, all alone and dying."

"She survived, sweetheart. That's all that matters."

"You're right," she whispered, holding onto him with all her might. After a moment, she lifted her head and looked into his eyes. "Thank you for coming."

Knox brushed her lips with his own. "Of course, sweetheart. I wouldn't dream of you doing this without me at your side."

She smiled through her tears. "I would've thought Outlaw and Meggie would be here by now. Bunny didn't come, and Digger didn't stay. Johnnie said Digger dropped him off downstairs, then sped off." She sighed. "I know Outlaw is past done with Kendall. I guess Meggie finally had enough of her, too."

Knox knew he'd have to tell her Megan was in the midst of her own crisis, but he'd wait until her emotions settled down from the shock of Kendall's actions. For now, he'd leave the focus on Kendall, and pray Megan's condition wasn't too serious.

CHAPTER FIFTY-SEVEN

CHRISTOPHER

Pacing in the private waiting room of Hortensia General, Christopher thought he'd lose his mind. The last he saw of Megan, she'd been seizing on the gurney, while the paramedics tried to stabilize her. Digger rushing Johnnie out and the ambulance arriving for Megan had been a sea of chaos.

Brothers had been shouting, kids had been crying, sirens wailing. Megan hadn't been moving. She'd been pale and lifeless. Until she hadn't been. He'd wanted to get to her, but Cash had held him back, insisting the paramedics would take care of her.

Christopher hadn't seen Cash arrive, and he'd sworn he'd kill the motherfucker if he didn't allow him to get to Megan. Cash hadn't relented until they were wheeling her out.

Unlike when Megan had been shot, Christopher was able to sit in the passenger seat of the ambulance and accompany her to the hospital. He'd wanted to be in back with her, but had been told they needed the room to work on her.

Now, it seemed as if hours had passed. Doc Will had arrived not long after the ambulance did and said things weren't looking good. Megan needed to deliver immediately if there was any hope to save her or the baby's lives.

The words had made him reel back, as if he'd been kicked in the gut. All the planning he'd done to protect her had blown up in his face.

All the scheming to get rid of Kendall...he couldn't finish the thought. He hadn't completely converted to strict religious beliefs, but Megan and Roxanne had influenced him enough, for him to feel as if Megan's state was the result of what he'd done to Kendall.

It no longer mattered if his actions had directly led to her over-dose. For instance, if he'd told her she had to kill herself or he'd do it for her. Or if she'd one day discovered Johnnie giving a relationship with Emily any consideration and couldn't live with that. Christopher would know he was responsible for whatever happened to Kendall because his plans had led to it.

It might've been anything, though—from her separation with Johnnie to her inability to handle her life to paranoia about feeling watched. None of it mattered. If he'd wanted Kendall dealt with for Megan's kidnapping and for trying to punch CJ, Christopher should've handled the situation as he usually did in matters such as these—he should've shot the fuck out of her and been done with it.

That would've been justice. This was just drawn out torture that had given him satisfaction until he realized he'd reap what he'd sown.

Johnnie needed as many brothers by his side as possible. With Megan near death, however, Christopher wasn't there. Since many of the members preferred her over Kendall, they were with Christopher, leaving Johnnie with a very few people at his side.

Along with Roxanne and Knox, Val, Zoann, Mortician, and Bailey were at the hospital with Johnnie, in support of Kendall. Cash, Digger, Slipper and his sons, Potter, Gabe, Bowlie, Boy, Danicka, Gypsy, and Derby had come to await word of Megan. Stretch had stayed behind to serve as protection for the children with Bunny and Diesel. What Christopher found odd was the fact that Krag, Webster, Pete, and Talbot hadn't gone either place. They were Megan's bodyguards, so

Christopher thought they would've been amongst the first to arrive after the ambulance. Or, if not, gone to check on Johnnie. Even if they didn't like Kendall, *Johnnie* was still their brother.

"Mr. Caldwell?"

Doc Will's tired voice reached Christopher. Turning, he saw Cam standing next to his wife. Although Knox was with Roxanne, at the hospital Kendall had been taken to, his best friend, Cam, had come here because that's where his woman was going to be.

Christopher rushed to her. "Megan?" he demanded, not having it in him to inquire after his son.

"She's out of surgery and in recovery, but it's touch-and-go," Doc Will said quietly. "She developed pre-eclampsia, which led to a placental abruption. We had to deliver the baby. He's very, very premature, but he's alive."

He heard the pause at the end of her sentence, picked up on what she'd left off: *for now.*

"I-I can lose both of them?" he whispered, his entire world reeling.

She grabbed his hand and squeezed it. "I'm so sorry, Outlaw," she told him, the first time she'd ever called him anything other than *Mr. Caldwell.* "I wish I had better news."

"Christopher," Fee said from behind him, the grief in her voice gutting him.

He couldn't move. His muscles felt cemented. Blood roared in his ears and his heart skipped a beat, pounded in agony. He thought he might fall to his knees.

"When can we see her?" Gypsy asked. She was Derby's old lady, who had become a very good friend to Megan.

"And the baby?" Danicka added.

"Mrs. Caldwell will be brought to ICU in a couple of hours," Doc Will explained. "Baby Caldwell is in NICU. He can be viewed through the window when he's stabilized."

"How far along was she?" Gypsy inquired.

Doc Will sidled a glance to Christopher. "She was twenty-five weeks. The baby has at least a fifty-fifty chance of survival."

"And my Megan?" Christopher said on a swallow. "Her chances?"

"She's a strong young woman," Doc Will said, not offering a direct answer, and then changing the subject altogether. "A nurse will come out and guide you to the NICU as soon as possible."

"I know how to get there, Doc," Christopher answered. He looked at his boots. "This ain't the first time I gotta go see one of my kids there."

Doc Will nodded. "Does anyone have any more questions?"

A thought occurred to Christopher. "You say Megan was twenty-five weeks?"

Again, wariness entered Doc Will's eyes. Megan had probably told her about what might happen to Christopher's doctor if he found out the motherfucker fucked over him.

"He already fuckin' buried, doc," Christopher admitted.

Doc Will groaned. "I take it Meggie doesn't know?"

"No. Ain't wanted her to feel guilty."

"I understand," she answered. "And, yes, Meggie was twenty-five weeks."

"She gave our new boy a name?"

"No."

"I gotta name she might like. Axel. As soon as she wake up, Ima see what she say."

"That's a lovely name," Doc Will said with a smile. "I'm sure Meggie won't mind if you name him. In the event..." She glanced away. "A name is always good for paperwork."

In the event that Megan didn't wake up and the baby died.

Once Doc Will kissed Cam, she left, promising she'd inform him immediately of any changes.

Kendall

Opening her eyes, two things hit Kendall at once: she was alive and she was in a hospital room hooked up to an IV and monitors.

"Kendall?" Johnnie breathed.

At one time hearing his voice would've meant everything. Now, she just felt empty. Disappointed she hadn't died. The text messages he'd sent to Emily had ripped Kendall's heart out. She'd never, ever recover.

"Go away," she said, her tears starting because she felt so broken.

Johnnie had sworn he wouldn't break their vows and sleep with another woman. Not only had he lied, but he'd fucked the one woman who most hated Kendall and then he'd buoyed her confidence and told Emily she was better in bed than Kendall.

He'd sent Emily so many amazing texts, proclaiming her an exceptional mother-figure and cook. And friend. All the things Kendall never got right.

"Kendall, why would you try to take your life? Do you know what your death would've done to me?"

She wanted to hit him with a comeback, but she was just so tired. "I can't bear...you've been with Emily," she said, unable to stop her heartbroken sob. "If you hadn't known who she was, I wouldn't care. But you did. You made love to her, knowing her true identity."

Confusion slid into Johnnie's face. "I never touched Emily, other than one kiss," he admitted.

"I saw the texts. Hundreds of them. It just...I can't do this anymore, Johnnie."

"If a divorce will make you happy—"

"Not divorce! *Death!*"

"Kendall, what texts do you mean?"

"All the ones you sent." She repeated the several that stood out most in her memory. "I read them. She showed them to me."

Johnnie studied her, then dug into his cut and pulled out his phone. "When did you see her?"

"The afternoon I overdosed."

"A day and a half ago, then," he commented, holding out the phone to her.

She shrugged, listless, ignoring his phone.

"Take it and read the messages between Emily and myself," he ordered.

Not in the mood to argue, Kendall took the phone. The screen was locked, but she tested his old code, surprised to find it still worked.

Finding the conversation with Emily was easy, since Johnnie didn't send texts very often.

The texts Kendall read from Johnnie's phone between him and Emily were vastly different than the texts Kendall had read on Emily's phone. She'd been relentless in her pursuit of Johnnie, even apologizing to him for tormenting Kendall and swearing she'd grown out of such petty behavior. She'd begged to meet Rory, JJ, and Matilda. Wanted them to take their relationship farther, describing in graphic detail what she intended to do to him.

"Her messages are completely different, Johnnie."

"Did she tell you I went to her place to kill her on your behalf?"

Eyes widening, Kendall's gaze flew to his.

"When I discovered her real identity."

Kendall set the phone on the bed. "You still went with her."

"There's no excuse for that, sweetheart."

"There isn't," Kendall agreed, though his explanation soothed her hurt and turmoil.

"I kissed her once, just to see if I could ever be with her if you and I ever divorced. There was nothing there, Kendall. My heart belongs to you."

She could hold onto bitterness and grudges or she could turn over a new leaf and forge a new chapter with Johnnie and their kids.

He sat in the chair near her bed and leaned forward. "I love you. Very much. I want our marriage to work. I realize we have a long road ahead of us. We need intensive counseling. We need parenting classes. You should take time off from being an attorney to see to your mental health."

"The prospect of reclaiming my career didn't excite me as much as I thought it would," Kendall admitted. "It felt empty without you and the kids. Meggie...*Roxy*."

"It was Roxanne who found you," Johnnie said gruffly, taking her hand and kissing it. "She was so devastated."

"Roxy found me?" Kendall whispered.

"You weren't answering your phone and you didn't show up to the fitting. She said she felt as if something was wrong."

"She does love me," Kendall said in awe, crying.

"I do, too," Johnnie repeated. "Or is this it for us? Do you think we'd be better off apart?"

"I love you so much and I've been so lost without you."

"But?"

"I'm not well inside." She swiped at her tears. "And I'm not Meggie."

Johnnie got to his feet, bent and kissed her. "I don't want you to be Megan," he swore. "I've been so unworthy of you. I've wronged you in so many different ways."

"No more than I've done to you," she admitted.

Kissing her forehead again, Johnnie straightened and walked to the foot of the bed. "We both have to make changes. Real, true changes, not just words we blow out of our asses. I have made arrangements for you to be moved to an in-house mental facility." He glanced away. "And I'm also thinking about going nomad once you're released."

"Nomad? Why?"

"I wouldn't have ties to a particular chapter, but if I'm needed, I could be called upon. If I want to attend meetings, I could go wherever we happened to be that has a chapter. You don't like club life."

"I thought I didn't like club life, but I missed our family so much. The weekly get-togethers. The way you guys nitpick at each other. The closeness. Their acceptance."

"They won't accept you back into the fold easily," Johnnie warned. "You're going to have to earn their trust."

"I know."

"You also have to cut ties with Charlotte," Johnnie ordered.

Kendall frowned. "I do?"

"I can't abide that bitch. She's a terrible influence on you. Besides, she doesn't like Roxanne."

For the first time since she'd awakened, Kendall smiled. "Okay."

He met her gaze. "We have a long road to go, Kendall, but I believe in us. We can get there and be stronger for it. If you do your part, I'll do mine."

She nodded.

"I've rehired Ella to look after the kids. She's back at our house on the compound. You're still barred from the grounds, but I'm going to talk to Christopher about that. When you're released after your stay in the wellness facility, I'd like to bring you home."

"How long will I have to stay?"

"That's up to Dr. Briscow to determine, but normal stay time is about six months."

"Suppose I feel better after three?"

"You'll still stay the entire six, unless the doctor says otherwise. My guess is she won't."

The implacability in his tone matched the stubborn set of his jaw. For awhile now he'd been changing. She just had to recall the spanking he had given her to remind her of how he'd gotten control of the situation and didn't intend to let go.

CHAPTER FIFTY-EIGHT

JOHNNIE

Once the nurse checked Kendall out and placed a call to her doctor, Johnnie left Roxanne in Kendall's room, watching over her as she slept. Kendall looked at peace, though her face was drawn. But her hair, always so vibrant, stood out against the white of the sheets. To Johnnie, she was as beautiful as ever.

A part of him still felt doubt about the future of their marriage. He hoped this was the wakeup call they both needed.

Johnnie couldn't begin to express his gratefulness that Kendall had survived. Since Digger had rushed him to the hospital to be at her side, Johnnie hadn't left. Earlier today, Mortician had delivered Johnnie's Navigator, visited Kendall—though she hadn't awakened yet—then returned to Hortensia with Val, who'd followed Mortician to the hospital.

Having his SUV at his disposal came in handy now. Once he slid into the driver's seat and started the engine, he texted Christopher to let him know Kendall had awakened.

In response, Christopher sent a thumbs-up.

At first, Christopher and Megan's absence had outraged him, until Johnnie had discovered the reason why. He and Christopher had kept in contact via text, neither of them willing to leave their women to check on the other's wife.

Johnnie set his phone aside, opened his glove compartment, checking for extra bullets. If he needed them. He hadn't decided how he'd kill Emily.

Discovering Kendall's heartache over bullshit texts sent ice cold rage through him. He had one goal in mind. If he had to spend the rest of his life hunting Emily down, he would.

Enough was enough. Emily should've been killed ages ago. He was so fucking disappointed in himself that he hadn't come to that conclusion before then. Turning his radio to his favorite country station, Johnnie whistled to a couple of songs as he drove to Emily's place.

When he arrived, he found a parking spot, grabbed the extra bullets for the Glock he carried at all times, then headed up the iron steps to her second-floor apartment.

The neighborhood was run-down and riddled with signs of lawlessness. Graffiti scrawled on buildings. A corner store where men loitered. The scent of piss and alcohol ruining the air. Loud music and raucous laughter rising all around him.

The thin door allowed him to hear the heavy breathing emanating from the other side. He hated to be a spoilsport, of course, but some fucking things couldn't be helped.

Adrenaline pouring through him, Johnnie kicked the door in, satisfied when it flew open underneath the pressure of his boots. Emily, naked and flushed, jumped off the lap of a motherfucker.

"Who the fuck are—?"

The shot to his head stopped the fucker cold. Emily screamed and scrambled to her feet, tripping backwards.

"Johnnie! What are you doing?" she cried, terror in her eyes. "You k-killed him."

"Oh, I'm sorry," Johnnie said cordially. "Did I? Maybe, he isn't dead."

Firing three more times in quick succession, Johnnie shot the nameless motherfucker until he was also faceless, wild with bloodlust, appeased at Emily's sobs and pleas.

"I'm calling the cops," Emily cried, grabbing her cell phone from the table that stood in front of the sofa where the unrecognizable corpse slumped.

Johnnie reached her in three strides and yanked the phone from her hand, grabbing her throat. Her nudity seemed poetic justice. She'd leave the world in the same fucking way she came in.

"Why the fuck did you lie to Kendall?" he asked, not truly interested in her answer. He didn't give a fuck about her reasons.

"I don't know what you mean," Emily gasped out, attempting to pry his hand from around her neck. "What did I lie to Kendall about?"

"Fuck you," he snarled through clenched teeth, shaking her. "You showed her those fucking phony texts."

"I don't know what you're talking about. I swear! Just c-calm down and talk to me."

"You're a goddamn liar," he said, losing patience. The club's policies were not to harm or kill women. *That* was the reason he was talking to her, trying to wring a confession from her.

He still intended to kill her, so who gave a fuck about a confession.

Shoving his gun back into his pocket, Johnnie wrapped both hands around Emily's neck and met her terrified gaze. She struggled for a couple of minutes, until the effects of oxygen deprivation claimed her. Her eyes rolled back in her head and she went limp. He released her and let her smack the floor.

He wasn't sure if she twitched or if he imagined the movement. Not wanting Emily alive to ever torture Kendall again, he drew his gun, stood over her, and fired two shots into her head, smiling at the spray of blood.

His task done, Johnnie took Emily's phone from where it had fallen. He'd bring it to Stretch so they could find the messages Kendall spoke of. After collecting the spent shell casings, Johnnie walked out of the apartment and closed the half-broken door behind him. He made it back to his SUV, started the engine, and backed out of his spot.

A popular song started playing on the radio. Tapping his fingers on the steering wheel, Johnnie whistled, and headed back to the hospital to be at Kendall's side.

~

CHRISTOPHER

Hands shoved into his pockets, Christopher stared at Axel as he lay in the omnibed, a combination incubator and radiant warmer that helped his frail, little body stay alive, along with all types of tubes, drips, and monitors. He wasn't allowed to hold his son and the baby had a host of medical problems, yet he was a micro-preemie, too small and fragile to undergo any procedures.

His boy might have lifelong complications all because Christopher wanted Megan pregnant. Yeah, she'd gotten filled with his kid before his dick snip flip, but, maybe, the results would've been the same even if it had been afterwards.

There'd been a reason he'd gotten the fucking snip in the first fucking place. He hadn't been able to rest because he'd grown more and more concerned each time she got pregnant. Then he'd had the bright goddamn idea to change his fucking mind.

His girl and his kid was paying for it.

Johnnie was suffering too because of Christopher. He shouldn't have played the games he had with Kendall. He shouldn't have rewarded her with a house or a law firm or anything. He should've fucking made her disappear and been done with it. Then, he wouldn't have had to hear Johnnie's screams of grief. He wouldn't have felt a smidgeon of guilt. Not for Kendall but for Johnnie.

And Axel.

And Megan.

All for Christopher's sins.

"Prez?"

A moment after Slipper called him, the scent of the man hit his nose. It was fucking funny that he hadn't paid attention to the mother-fucker's smell the past two days. Now, though, the rancid fuckhead had the odor of skunk pussy. Bear dick. Fish ass. Some un-fucking-fathomable aroma that made Christopher want to punch the fuck out of Slipper.

"Ima go back to my girl room," he growled. "Stay the fuck away from her, Slipper. I ain't wantin' you to smother Megan from your goddamn stink."

Slipper's bloodshot eyes lit up. "Meggie wake?"

"No."

"Oh." Slipper drew his bushy brows together. "You want me to go take a shower before I tell you about Krag?"

"My fuckin' nose would really fuckin' appreciate that shit, but since I wanna know why the fuck this motherfucker ain't got his ass up here yet, Ima fuckin' give you a pass. Just remember to wash your fuckin' ass when you get home."

Slipper nodded. "You got it, Prez."

"Talk, motherfucker."

"Me and my boy, Orange, was wondering the same thing. Krag and those boys Meggie's guards. They need to be here. We decided to investigate. We went to the club and found those motherfuckers there. At the fucking bar, Prez."

Christopher grunted. "I guess Ima give the motherfuckers a pass this time. They was probably drinkin' to get over them bein' so upset about Megan."

"No, Outlaw," Slipper said with a shake of his head. "They was laughing at the way she'd gone into seizures. They was saying they hoped she died, so they wouldn't have to bitch sit her anymore. They said they didn't know what had gotten into you, giving them the duties to guard your cumbag."

Christopher stared at Slipper, the rage suffusing him making sweat pop out.

"Where them motherfuckers at now?"

Slipper shrugged.

Drawing in a deep breath to control his anger, Christopher gazed through the window at Axel again. He needed to check on Megan, then he'd deal with those almost-dead motherfuckers.

"Don't say nothin' to them, Slipper," Outlaw instructed. "Ima handle it."

"The way they was talking about Meggie was such a shame."

Gritting his teeth, Christopher raised his head. "Yeah, it fuckin' was. Thank you for comin' to me about this."

"We like Meggie."

"I know, brother," Christopher responded, so wound up that his fucking eye jumped.

He stared at Axel a moment longer, then walked in the direction of the elevators. Once he reached Megan's floor, he went to her room, pulled the chair close to her, then laid his head against her thigh. She had almost as many tubes as Axel, and it broke Christopher's heart.

She'd had low platelets, a swollen liver, and sky-high blood pressure. She had so many other ailments that he couldn't remember them all. Delivery of the baby was the most effective way to get her back to normal, but she'd also needed a transfusion and doses of magnesium sulfate. Since delivering Axel, Megan's pressure had dropped but it was still elevated. She was still in as much danger as their son.

How many times had Megan been in this position and how many times it was because of his actions or something he was involved in?

Long before he'd met Megan, he'd had his share of injuries. They'd be taken care of at the clubhouse or in the back room of a doctor's office whose staff was in their back pocket. When Christopher started the medical lab, he also felt it was of the utmost importance to build relationships with the local hospital. Couldn't make money if doctors didn't send patients to the labs for piss, shit, and blood samples.

Hortensia General had been the logical choice to build the closest ties with, although the club also associated with other hospitals in surrounding towns. If Christopher had known what an important role the place would play in his family life, he would've doubled his yearly donations.

Fuck, if he'd known how much motherfucking time he'd spend there, he would've had a goddamn suite built just for them.

Fingers glided through his hair and Christopher stilled, afraid he was imagining her touch. He felt the same light caress again.

Sitting up, he gazed in his wife's direction. Groggy blue eyes stared at him.

"Megan," he whispered, praying he wasn't dreaming.

Unable to talk because of the ventilator, she nodded.

He reached over and pressed the nurse's button, wanting to kiss and hug her, but knowing he couldn't.

She might've been just a slip of a thing, but she was a fighter, and for that, Christopher was grateful.

Megan

Three days later, Christopher walked into Meggie's room and stopped in his tracks.

"The ventilator gone," he whispered, emotion playing across his handsome face.

"Hey, you," she said hoarsely, smiling at him, though it hurt to talk.

He'd been gone no more than ten minutes. It seemed as if he'd just left when the nurse came in to remove the tube. She'd probably been gone about two minutes before he'd walked back in.

She hadn't had a chance to ask about her baby. Or what had happened to her. Or if she could have more kids. She didn't know how long she'd been out. But before she bombarded her husband with questions, she enjoyed the feel of his lips against her own, dry ones.

Pulling away, he stared at her in awe, caressing her cheek. He lowered the bed railing and on the edge, wrapping his arms around her.

"Megan, baby, I'm so sorry. All the shit that happened all my fault."

Memories of Patrick hit her, and she drew in a deep breath, tears rushing to her eyes. "Our baby died," she managed around sobs.

"Huh...No! No, baby," he said with gruffness, combing hair behind her ears. "No, Axel got a long fuckin' battle, but he a fighter just like his Ma."

"Axel?" Meggie asked.

Hesitating, Christopher nodded. "I ain't even able to hold the lil' motherfucker, so he probably ain't knowin' his name yet if you wanna change it. I just..." His voice trailed off and he shrugged.

Her tough, strong Christopher had such a vulnerable streak in him, sometimes still expecting to be rejected by someone he loved.

"I know you like those fuckin' 'R' names. I coulda call his lil' ass Ratchet, but motherfuckers might be thinkin' the wrong reason we gave him that name. Not a lot of motherfuckers know a ratchet a fuckin' tool."

Meggie placed her lips over his. "I love it," she croaked. "Axel is perfect."

Nodding, he looked at her again and then grinned. "You sure?"

She nodded.

"I want to see him," Meggie said.

"Okay, baby. Lemme get your nurse and see what she say."

"Okay." She stopped him before he walked out. "Christopher?"

"Yeah, baby?"

"I love you. Thank you for being such a good dad and the best husband a girl could ever have."

"It's all cuz of you, Megan," he told her quietly.

She sniffled. "You're my everything."

"Just like you mine, baby," he told her and walked out, leaving Meggie thankful to be alive and happy that her baby had survived.

CHRISTOPHER

Walking into Kendall's room, Christopher felt like a pussy for the tears he'd almost shed when he'd found Megan with her ventilator gone. And her words to him touched his heart and soul. *She* was his heart and soul.

Megan had to wait a day before she saw Axel. She also needed pain meds because her throat was hurting. But she'd improved so much in just a matter of days that Christopher was grateful. Although she didn't yet know about Kendall, he intended to tell her soon.

Right before Megan dozed off, he said he had a run to make, and kissed her bye. He'd gotten two miracles with the lives of Megan and Axel, so he decided to clear the air with Kendall.

Finding her asleep, he studied her. Without makeup and with all she'd been through, her face looked pulled-down, but harmless. Seeing her now made it hard to believe she'd been the bitch who'd gotten into more shit than he wanted to remember.

She shifted and groaned, opening her eyes. When she realized he stood next to her bed, she started then shrank back.

"Hey, Kendall," he greeted.

"Hi," she told him, wary.

Before he went on, Johnnie walked in and stopped. "I was trying to get here before you did, Christopher."

He shrugged. "Under-fuckin-standable."

"How's Megan?"

"What's wrong with Meggie?" Kendall asked.

"She gettin' better, now," Christopher said. Everyone had come to visit his girl by now, except her motherfucking guards. And now he knew why. "She been awake for three days. Finally able to breathe on her own. Axel fightin' too."

"Who's Axel?" Kendall asked.

"Our new boy."

"Meggie had another baby?" Shock was clear in Kendall's voice.

"Yeah," Christopher answered.

"I suppose you summoned me here so you can tell us together that Kendall won't be welcomed back on club premises," Johnnie guessed, looking as devastated as he sounded.

"Sit down, Johnnie," Christopher ordered.

Without question, Johnnie complied.

"I'm not gettin' into how I fuckin' feel about you, Kendall," Christopher started. "We all fuckin' know. No matter how the fuck my ass been tryin' these last coupla days, I still hate you."

Johnnie shot to his feet. "Get the fuck out of here with that bullshit, Christopher. Kendall doesn't need to be subjected to your torture. She's too vulnerable."

"Sit down, assfuck," Christopher demanded with irritation, glaring in Johnnie's direction until he sat down. "Just cuz *I* hate Kendall ain't meanin' you do. As a matter of fuckin' fact, I ain't ever realized how much you fuckin' love her until she tried to fuck herself up." Ignoring Johnnie's glower, Christopher looked at Kendall. "If you ain't made it, I ain't too sure Johnnie wouldna shot the fuck outta himself. He love you and I love him, so I wanna get some shit straight with you."

Kendall swallowed. "Wh-what?"

Looking from Johnnie to Kendall as he spoke, Christopher said, "My ass the motherfucker who set John Boy up to meet Emily. And you was right. The house was fuckin' bugged."

"How dare you, Christopher?" Johnnie snarled.

"Don't fuckin' start, Johnnie. You fuckin' lucky Megan had Kendall on her goddamn No-Kill list. Otherwise, I wouldna went through all these goddamn games and woulda just shot the fuck outta her."

"Christopher—"

Raising his hand, he indicated Johnnie shut the fuck up. "You want my ass to go through all the shit Kendall done that woulda got other motherfuckers fucked up sixteen times over? Do you?" he demanded when neither of them said a word. "Don't lemme bring up my woman and my kid."

"Your woman and kid?" Johnnie seethed. "What about mine? Do I have to overlook what they need because you're so fucking determined that Megan be happy at everyone else's expense?"

"How that shit new to you?" Christopher snapped. "Your ass should be fuckin' happy cuz it's cuz of Megan Kendall ain't dead."

"By your hand," Johnnie spat.

"*Directly* by my hand," Christopher supplied, wondering when this motherfucker would catch on.

Johnnie's eyes widened, then narrowed. "What the fuck are you saying? You wanted Kendall to commit…" His voice trailed off and he stared at Christopher, shock, pain, and anger crossing his face. "You told me you weren't seeking revenge," he shouted. "You lied to me."

"No the fuck I ain't. I lied to *Megan*. I ain't wanted her to discover the truth."

"Get out," Johnnie said coldly. "This is the last fucking straw. You've pushed me too fucking far. You claim you love me, yet you almost ruined my life because of your hatred for Kendall."

"No, that's fuckin' because you a stupid motherfucker and she a dumb bitch."

"Fuck off! I'm never going to forgive you."

A sliver of hurt passed through Christopher, but he ignored it. The only person in the world who forgave him almost anything was his Megan. Just because he and Johnnie had always been so close, Christopher shouldn't have expected the same from him.

He shrugged. "Your fuckin' choice. As long as I got my girl, I got every-fuckin-thing I need." He looked at Kendall, surprised to find she wasn't giving him one of her bitchy glares. "Johnnie ain't want nothin' to do with Emily, Kendall. I was payin' her to pressure him into startin' something with her. He ain't fucked her or nothin'. He love *you*. I hope you love his ass e-fuckin-nuff to straighten the fuck up."

"I do," she said quietly. "We…he's committing me."

"You goin' back to a psycho camp?"

Johnnie growled.

Kendall nodded. "For at least six months. We'll be working on our marriage and our parenting skills. We have a long road ahead of us. I hope we can make it through."

Christopher shrugged.

"I knew…I knew you wouldn't let my actions go unanswered," Kendall admitted. "And I know you're sorry."

He paused. Kendall had had such a fucked-up childhood, starting with her old man's death. Her ma hadn't liked her, and Emily had bullied her. He understood that, even sympathized with her. But Kendall blamed every-fucking-body for what happened to her, instead of pointing the fucking finger at the two motherfuckers that wreaked all the havoc. She made excuses, thought it was her fucking right, to do what the fuck she wanted to and not have fucking consequences. He was willing to let bygones be bygones and give her a fresh start—although he hoped Megan kept her distance. However, for all Kendall's past sins and the way he'd addressed them...*Nope, I ain't sorry for any-fuckin-thing I did to you. I re-fuckin-gret the emotional toll it took on John Boy.*

"How fucking kind of you," Johnnie sneered.

Christopher ignored him and stayed focused on Kendall. "I hope now you get some fuckin' help and behave." How many fucking times had he said the same goddamn thing to her?

"Leave, Christopher," Johnnie ordered.

"I understand you offended on behalf of your woman."

"Oh, you admit she's my woman now and not a cunt?"

"I'm about to fuckin' call *you* the cunt, motherfucker," Christopher barked.

Johnnie got to his feet and stalked to Christopher, standing nose-to-nose with him. "Emily's dead, Christopher. I've already told Kendall, now I'm telling you. *I* killed her."

"Why the fuck—?"

"Why?" Johnnie interrupted before Christopher got his full question out. "Because she spoofed my goddamn phone number and showed Kendall phony fucking texts. Not only that, Stretch found a to-do list to get to Megan and kill her!"

"What the fuck you said?"

"It doesn't matter," Johnnie snapped. "Emily's games led *my wife* to try to take her life. *Your* fucking games."

Annoyance rose in Christopher and a sense of anger that he hadn't gotten his hands-on Emily. "Back the fuck up, John Boy. I don't know why the fuck you so fuckin' furious at my ass. I ain't got a fuckin' thing to apologize to neither of you motherfuckers for. Kendall got you fuckin' shot. Knocked the fuck out. Maybe, if *your* fuckin' ass knew how to handle her, *my* fuckin' ass wouldna had to step the fuck in."

"Are you fucking kidding me?" Johnnie spat.

"Nope. Even if you think my ass need to apologize for your woman tryna kill herself, I ain't agreein', so fuck you. You follow club rules. You stay the fuck outta club business if you not a member. You leave my woman in peace. You keep your fuckin' hands off lil' kids. Or you fuckin' die. Case fuckin' closed. That shit not new to you or your bitch, Johnnie."

He drew himself up. For a moment, sadness replaced the anger, then he stiffened and glared at Christopher. "Leave," he ordered again. "We don't want you here."

"Have it your fuckin' way, motherfucker," Christopher said, heading out. At the door, he stopped. "Ain't botherin' to threaten neither of you motherfuckers no more. All the fuck I can say is if Kendall fuck up a-fuckin-gain, *run*."

With that, he walked away, not telling them if it ever came to that they had better hope, he never, *ever* fucking found them. If there ever was a next time, justice would be swift and decisive.

After summoning the members to emergency church, Christopher headed to the clubhouse. Johnnie's presence surprised Christopher. He wondered if Johnnie was there to resign from the club, given his self-righteous indignation. Krag, Talbot, Webster, and Pete were there and that was the important thing.

"Ain't keepin' you motherfuckers long," Christopher started after calling the meeting to order. "Any assfuck I choose to guard my woman got the fuckin' right to decline. If you ain't likin' the position, you gonna make her miserable and that ain't ever gonna fuckin' fly." He walked from behind the podium, and went to the table where those four motherfuckers sat. "I picked you motherfuckers cuz y'all old-timers. Knew Big Joe. Boss loved the fuck outta Megan, so I thought it woulda been a honor."

Krag gave Christopher a half-smile. "We enjoy every moment we spend with your precious wife, Outlaw."

Webster, Talbot, and Pete sniggered. Slipper wasn't known to lie, but just the subtle hint of arrogance from the soon-to-be maggot chips told Christopher of the man's truthfulness.

"Fuck, Prez," Digger grumbled. "I got my good jeans on."

"Is there a problem, Outlaw?" Krag asked calmly.

"Nope," Christopher answered, drawing his nine with the hollows. "Not no more, motherfucker."

He shot all four motherfuckers in the head, unaffected at the gushes of blood, or the ensuing silence. Sticking his gun back into the inside pocket of his cut, Christopher lit a cigarette and took a few puffs before he walked back to the podium, ignoring Digger's scowl.

"When I come to you to watch my woman, de-fuckin-cide if you like livin' with your brain in your head or outside the motherfucker."

"You not surviving if you don't have a brain in your head, Outlaw," Digger protested.

"You sure, fool?" Mortician called. "You've done fine without one in your fucking head all these goddamn years."

"Ha, ha, ha," Digger said, flipping the room at large off at all the laughter rising up.

"Get the dead motherfuckers outta here," Christopher ordered.

"Where you want us to put them?" Val asked.

"Wherever the fuck you make those motherfuckers fit."

"I got a new solution I want to try to see how effective it is to dissolve bodies," Mortician said, lighting his own cigarette.

"You can use one of them for your experiment," Johnnie added. "We had all our tools ready for Knox and never got to use them. I was a little disappointed."

"In that case, John Boy, your ass welcome to move the motherfuckers," Digger said. "I won't get my good jeans ruined."

"We got four dead motherfuckers," Christopher said. "You four assfucks each move a body."

"All we need is barrels rolled in here if we do it my way," Mortician explained. "Stuff the motherfuckers in there, then roll the barrels to the meatshack. We don't even have to bring them inside."

Christopher shrugged. "Whatever the fuck you think best." He turned to the other brothers, whose expressions ranged from completely fucking terrified to shook-up to indifference. "Meetin' adjourned," he announced, then headed to his bike, anxious to see his girl.

"Christopher?"

At Johnnie's call, Christopher mounted his bike but didn't start it.

Holding out his hand, Johnnie met Christopher's gaze. "We've been a team our whole lives," he began. "You're my family. I can't just turn away from you and pretend you don't exist."

Christopher smiled and slammed his hand into Johnnie's, then drew him into a bear hug. "I love you, motherfucker."

"I love you too, you fucking psycho stalker Wildman."

Chuckling, Christopher started his bike, gave Johnnie a two-finger salute and sped off, acknowledging his relief that he and John Boy had cleared the air.

CHAPTER FIFTY-NINE

Roxy

After all the drama of the past three months—hateful sons, engagement rings with bad ju-ju, forced living arrangements, secret rendezvous, sadity bitches, low-down bitches, uppity bastards, scheming motherfuckers, *stupid motherfuckers,* larcenous priests, riding lessons, new tattoos, murder, suicide attempts, new engagement rings, and dangerous pregnancies—it all came down to this. The night before the wedding at the Harrington estate to enjoy the dinner after their rehearsal at Father Wilkins' church.

Joan and Hal, Knox's parents, hadn't made the drive to Hortensia for the practice ceremony. Not that it surprised Roxy, although she knew Knox had been a little disappointed.

News crews and helicopters had dogged them from the clubhouse to the church and then to the mansion. Knox had seemed unfazed, but the attention had made Roxy more than a little nervous. She wasn't used to such public scrutiny.

The street leading up to the gate where Harrington House was located—Roxy had just found out tonight the motherfucker had a name—had been blocked off with uniformed police officers only allowing residents and guests to the rehearsal dinner in. Because her momma and other two daughters were in town, Knox hired a limousine, so he could enjoy their company without the distraction of driving.

After a meeting, it was decided the entire family would have limousines, and divided the occupants by households—Caldwell, Donovan, Taylor, Banks, Banks, and, of course, Knox and Roxy's.

Extra staff had been hired to direct the cars on where to turn to make it up the hill to reach the valet area. Butlers in gold and lavender had met them each step of the way as they were guided to the Grande Salon, where a flutist and pianist awaited them. The room was like a scene from a fairytale, where no expense had been spared. Hanging crystal and wisteria dripped from the ceilings. Each table had huge arrangements of white roses, pristine white tablecloths and gleaming crystal.

"We got to sit at different tables?" Val asked before Knox's parents had a chance to welcome them.

"No the fuck we not," Pearllene announced, leaning heavily on her cane as she crossed the room. "Come on, Rissa, Lex, let's fix this shit."

"Momma—" Roxy started, trying and failing to catch her mother's hands.

Sniggering as her kin started pulling out chairs, Mortician, Digger, Outlaw, Val, and Johnnie joined them in ruining the setup.

"What are you people doing?" Joan screamed. "Stop this instant before I have you thrown out of my house."

"Mother," Knox called, then winked at Roxy, "it's fine. I happen to agree with them. Come on, Cam."

Shocked, Roxy watched as her man and his best friend joined the other guys to place the tables together in two rows of two. The beautiful arrangements were placed against one of the walls, out of the way.

"If I'd wanted it this way, I would've gotten long, rectangle tables," Joan huffed.

"Dear, don't worry yourself," Hal advised. "Knox wants it this way."

"Joan, I thought I heard your cry of distress," Charlotte Redding announced, breezing into the room on Brooks's arm.

"What the fuck is she doing here?" Johnnie demanded. "I thought I told you to stay the fuck away."

Joan lifted her chin. "Yes, well, considering this is my house, sir, I can invite whoever I want. Charlotte is my friend, therefore, she's on my guest list."

Narrowing his eyes, Johnnie drew his gun from his cut. "Not if I shoot the fuck out of her."

"Johnnie!" Roxy yelled, rushing forward as Brooks jumped in front of his wife.

"Boy, what the fuck is your goddamn problem?" Pearllene demanded, hitting Johnnie on the side of the head with her purse."

"Give me that shit, motherfucker," Alexia demanded, yanking the gun from Johnnie's hand. Her dyed blonde hair was outstanding against her milk chocolate skin.

Outlaw stepped forward and snatched the Glock away from Alexia. Once he emptied it of bullets, he slammed it against Johnnie's chest.

"I ain't allowin' you to mar this fuckin' dinner with fuckin' brains and blood all over the fuckin' place."

"Yeah, Johnnie," Digger said, waving Bunny over, having chosen his spot. "That would delay dinner and I'm hungry."

"You stay fucking hungry," Mortician complained.

"What do you mean *delay* dinner, Digger?" Carissa called. "That would've ruined the shit. Personally, I couldn't eat nothing if I saw a bitch killed."

Outlaw's whistle stopped the arguing. "E-fuckin-nuff. Let's sit the fuck down, so dinner can fuckin' start." He pointed to the musicians who were aghast. "If one of you motherfuckers play the fuckin' bullshit I fuckin' know you intendin' to play, Ima break your fuckin' fingers."

"Omigod, Christopher!"

Meggie had healed completely and Axel, now three months old, had another week, at most, to stay in the hospital before he was released. He was small for his age, but hadn't been harmed during the trauma of his birth.

"Hal!" Joan cried. "Do something."

Outlaw crooked his finger at Meggie. Once she got to her seat and sat, he slid her forward.

"Knox, come and see your groom cake," Outlaw demanded.

Knox's eyes widened. "You got me a groom cake?"

"My ass the bride family. Ain't I'm supposed to do that?"

"Don't worry, Mort," Digger said. "I got you covered."

Outlaw searched the room.

"The cakes are in the kitchen," Joan said tightly.

"Bring them motherfuckers out *here*. What the fuck good they doin' in the goddamn kitchen?"

"So no one would see them," Joan snapped.

"The whole point of a fucking groom cake is for the shit to be seen *before* getting cut," Pearllene said.

Digger pointed at her. "What she said."

"Oh, for God's sake!" Joan cried. "Do any of you have class?" She drew herself up and glared at Pearllene. "How old are you, madame?"

Laughing nervously, Roxy rushed forward as Pearllene growled, "old enough to say what the fuck I want."

"Let me help you to your seat, Momma," Roxy said, grabbing her mother's arm and turning her toward a chair.

"This the table you're sitting at, huh, baby?" Pearllene asked.

"Of course," Roxy declared, squeezing her mother's shoulder.

"The cakes are on the way," Hal announced as he returned to the salon. He placed his hand at the small of Joan's back and guided her to the same table that Pearllene sat at.

By the time everybody had seated themselves, two members of the kitchen staff each wheeled in a silver cart, containing cakes. Before Roxy had a chance to see Knox's, he and Outlaw blocked her view by standing in front of the cart.

Just as Mortician's cake registered with Roxy, Carissa nudged her girlfriend, Liza, and screamed with laughter. "We know who the chocolate dick cake for!" she howled.

"Did you have to make the motherfucker squirt cum?" Roxy asked, torn between amusement and annoyance.

Joan threw stares of death to them, her dress and jewelry understated compared to the ostentatious display of wealth—lost wealth—Charlotte displayed.

All the women were in various styles of white dresses, the color being Joan's request. She'd demanded the men wear suits. Of course, Mortician and the rest of them didn't comply because, according to them, they'd made enough concessions by agreeing to wear the fucking monkey suits for the wedding.

Outlaw sauntered back to his table, while Knox stepped aside to reveal his cake. It was a golden money bag with a glittering dollar sign designed into the front, dripping coins and Benjamins. It leaned against a "bottle" of Knox's favorite whisky and sat next to an open "wooden" humidor filled with cigars, a badge, and a motorcycle. The cake was a true masterpiece, with each segment so realistic she found it hard to believe it had started out as simple flour.

"Okay, the grooms-to-be saw the fucking cakes," Digger said. "Can we eat now?"

"There will be nothing served until my musicians start to play," Joan answered with smugness.

"Aww, fuck." Digger looked at Outlaw. "If Johnnie ruining the dinner for a minute by shooting Charlotte, you going to do the same thing. Can't you plug your fucking ears with cigarettes and let the motherfuckers play?"

"I got some weed paper," Val offered. "That might be better, Outlaw."

Meggie glared between them. "He won't need those, Val," she said primly. "He won't kill the flutist or pianist, so it's fine for them to play." She sniffed. "Right, Christopher?"

Outlaw scowled at her, but Meggie didn't back down. "Fuck, Megan, you lil' pain-in-the-ass motherfucker, fine. Let the ear-hurtin' motherfuckers play. But you might gotta give me an extra cock suck to calm me the fuck down."

"Can we eat please?" Digger demanded, before Meggie had a chance to respond.

Joan stood. "I'll ring the kitchen to bring out the first course."

"What is this shit?" Pearllene demanded, holding her fork in the air. Squid-ink covered linguine hung limply from the utensil.

"Try it, Momma. It's good," Roxy encouraged.

Her look skeptical, Pearllene sniffed it, then shoved it under her gentleman friend's nose. "Taste this, Hamish. It smell like my chooney after you fucked it. Tell me if it taste like it."

"Jesus Christ," Knox breathed, laying his fork against the plate as Roxy prayed the ground opened up and squished her like a fucking bug.

Digger spat the noodles back onto the plate and glared at Pearllene. "I'm not interested in eating nothing that smell like your pussy," he grouched. "Now if it was Bunny..."

"Shut up, Mark," Bunny ordered.

"Miss Pearllene, you sure is right," Hamish said. "Taste a lot like your chooney."

"Since when you started calling MeMe *Miss Pearllene*, Hamish?" Carissa demanded. She looked at Liza. "You ever heard him call her that, bae?"

"He got to add miss to my goddamn name from now on. If I got to pay for a motherfucker plane ticket, then that motherfucker got to put a title to address me."

"Goddamn, you ruthless, old woman," Mortician said, then smirked at Hamish. "Bet your ass sorry you didn't hitch a ride on Sloane private jet."

Hamish shrugged. "Had a roof to finish."

"My Hamish a roofer," Pearllene announced proudly.

"I don't take many jobs no more," Hamish confessed. "After that fifth fall and I broke my leg again, I decided to be real selective, so my cash kind of low nowadays."

"As long as you got money for your Viagra, you just fine," Pearllene reassured him.

"Can we leave?" Knox begged, his face flaming.

Too embarrassed to speak, Roxy nodded.

Pearllene got to her feet, using her cane to brace herself. "You two not going nowhere until I toast you."

"That comes after the cake," Charlotte inserted. "And only if you're invited."

"Did I ask your ass, lady?" Peallene demanded. "And they hearing my toast whether they like it or not. If I hadn't pushed Roxanne out my pussy, she wouldn't—"

"Okay!" Roxy cried, jumping to her feet and holding her hands up. "We get the point. "Just get on with the toast."

Pearllene smiled. "Thank you, baby."

Grabbing her glass of wine, she raised it, beaming between Knox and Roxy, and Mortician and Bailey.

"Mortician, you a better grandson to me than the motherfucker that got my blood running through his veins. You got me out of a scape or two with no questions asked. When I call you for something, you never say it's a problem. You just get it done. Because I'm Bailey MeMe, I'm yours, too. Thank you for looking after all of us so good and being the fine man you are. Congratulations on renewing your vows and the new baby that'll be coming in late fall." Pearllene blew a kiss to Bailey. "MeMe love you, Bailey."

Bailey stood and went to Pearllene, hugging her tightly. "I love you, too, MeMe," she said, then released her and stepped aside so Mortician could take her place.

"Come here, old woman," he said gruffly, bending down and hugging her.

Pearllene's hearty laugh filled Roxy with joy.

"Chile, if I was just two hours younger, I think I'd have to give up the chooney to you," Pearllene said around chuckles.

Rolling his eyes, Mortician released her. "Two hours ago your ass was still the same age."

"Boy, don't make me stick my foot up your ass. You know that was just me showing my wit."

"Yeah, man, okay."

Allowing Bailey to guide him away, Mortician offered Pearllene a last glower then took his seat.

"Roxanne, my precious baby," Pearllen started, aiming her raised glass in their direction. "Oooo, wait, shit. I forgot to drink on Mortician and Bailey toast. Rectifying that immediately, she smiled again and resumed her position. "Roxanne, my precious baby, I never, ever thought your ass would be marrying a fourth goddamn time, but since you are, I'm so happy for you. This time, I hope you get the shit right. I'm about tired of you finding the wrong motherfuckers."

"Knox isn't the wrong man," Roxy said with reassurance.

"Congratulations, baby," Pearllene said, not responding to Roxy's statement as she turned to Knox. "I heard you haven't got pussy from Roxanne in months, so I hope you not sticking you dick in no other bitch."

"Of course I'm not!" Knox said with indignation as Joan started to sob.

"Can you shut your momma up?" Pearllene asked.

"Oh, Joan, I understand," Charlotte soothed, pushing out of her chair and rushing to Joan, guiding her to her feet. "Come. Let's retire to the ladies' room to calm you down."

"Momma, that was a beautiful toast," Roxanne said once Joan and Charlotte were gone.

"Sit down. I'm not finished."

"Fuck." Huffing out a breath, Roxy drained her wine glass.

"I got a little advice about bacon grease."

"Oh, fuck no!" Roxy jumped to her feet as the distant sound of sirens reached her. "Don't even say it, Momma."

"Wait, I wanna hear," Outlaw said.

"No the fuck you don't," Roxy snapped.

"Roxanne right, Prez," Digger said. "I happen to like bacon and, if this conversation going in the direction I think it is, I won't ever be able to chew on fried pig again."

"I didn't say a fucking thing about bacon," Pearllene said with a sniff. "I said bacon *grease*."

"You not getting the grease if you don't fry the goddamn bacon," Mortician huffed.

A loud bang prevented a response. The boys all jumped to their feet, drawing their weapons and inserting themselves of front of their wives. Hamish slid under the table, then yanked Pearllene down. Knox stood in front of Roxy, drawing a weapon of his own, while Cam mirrored his actions with Jordan.

"Drop your weapons!" an official-sounding voice commanded. *"Now!"*

When the guys complied and raised their hands, a sinking feeling dropped into Roxy's stomach. Standing, she saw members of SWAT aiming rifles in the direction of the tables.

"What is the meaning of this, officer?" Hal demanded. "I'm Hal Harrington and this is my home where we are hosting a private event!"

"I'm Lieutenant Mitchell, sir," one of the officers said. "We're here to arrest Knox Harrington on charges of gun smuggling."

CHAPTER SIXTY

Knox

With Outlaw not wanting to leave either Megan or Axel, and Amfinger pressuring Knox to step in to see the deal through, Knox had talked Outlaw into giving into Amfinger's demands. He'd pointed out that Bailey was pregnant, so Mortician wouldn't want to leave, and Johnnie was busy helping Kendall, getting counseling of his own, and working on his marriage. Although Outlaw could've chosen any of the club members to go in his place, Amfinger said he'd be more comfortable negotiating with someone familiar to him. Outlaw, wrapped up in his family's crisis, had agreed.

After weeks of exchanges in the midst of riding lessons, completing his tattoos, and fittings, they'd reached a conclusion two weeks ago when Knox traveled to California to deliver suitcases filled with cash, in exchange for a truckload of light arms. Knox didn't know how to drive a semi, so Cash had ridden into town to save the day.

While Cash drove the truck back to Hortensia, Knox had to ride the motorcycle.

"If you fuck up my ride, I'm going to fuck you up," Cash had warned.

Knox's prevailing thought had been, *in for a pound, in for a penny*, so he'd snatched Cash's helmet and told the man not to worry. At the time, he never would've admitted how nervous he'd been. His motorcycle skills had progressed tremendously since the first lesson, but he wasn't sure how he'd fare riding hundreds of miles.

As it turned out, he'd been just fine. It took three, grueling days to get back to the club. At night, Cash insisted they find a place to sleep. He hadn't expected to rough it outside, but that's what they'd done.

Once they arrived back at the club, Knox wasn't sure what had become of the guns, so how he'd ended up arrested for smuggling, while everyone else was released, he had no idea. It had been doubly humiliating because of the news crews and, then, seeing a few friends from the force when he'd arrived at the police station to be booked in.

Sitting in the holding cell, burning with anger and embarrassment, Knox decided he needed to rethink the ceremony to Roxanne, due to take place, in less than twenty hours.

Roxy

Out of her mind with worry, Roxy directed the limousine driver to go to the police station where Knox was being held. The boys wanted her to pile into one of the limousines with all of them and head back to the club, but Roxy wouldn't have been able to rest, so she declined. The guys were going exchange limousines for bikes, while the women would stay behind at the club.

She couldn't imagine what was happening. Knox had left for a business trip a couple of weeks ago. She hadn't questioned him, but now, she wondered if he'd gone on behalf of the club.

Knox knew how to stick his nose into biker business if it suited him. When she'd discovered his role in Kendall's downward spiral, she'd been mad as hell. She'd stopped talking to him for two days, until Outlaw told her Knox wouldn't have participated if he hadn't threatened him if he didn't assist.

"Why the fuck didn't Knox tell me that?"

"Cuz I told the motherfucker I'd rip his fuckin' tongue out if he opened his fuckin' mouth."

She wasn't sure if Outlaw's explanation made sense. The man had too many resources to demand Knox's help, but she hadn't pointed that out. Instead, she and Knox had had a nice, long talk, where he promised he'd never fuck over one of her babies again.

Gunfire shattered the limo's windshield, striking the driver in the head. Blood splashed onto her and the car veered off the road.

Roxy screamed, terrified, slamming into the seat in front of her and then crashing backwards as the loud noise of the car running into a tree filled the air.

Immediately, smoke poured from under the ruined hood, flooding the air vents. Ignoring her dizziness and how banged up she felt, Roxy tried to open the doors on either side of her, but neither would budge.

The first lick of flame rose in the night. Knowing she needed to keep calm, Roxy decided not to bother with kicking the doors in. She held her breath to block out the horrendous fumes, then braced herself on her elbows, using both feet and all her might to break the window glass. She'd expended almost all of her energy by the time the glass finally shattered. The flames were crawling from under the hood, beginning to consume the dashboard.

Choking and knowing she had to launch herself out as soon as she broke the glass completely, since oxygen would only feed the fire, Roxy used her shoulder to finish the glass. Shards of glass stabbed into her, but she didn't care. She knew she was alive. Face-first, Roxy shoved herself through the broken glass, landing hard on the ground. Refusing to give in, Roxy crawled as far away as she could from the burning car, seeking refuge in foliage as the first explosion rocked the ground.

A moment later, she managed to get to her feet and limp forward. One of her heels had broken, so she took both shoes off and tossed them away, wishing her phone hadn't gotten blown up. But the fire behind her was growing and before the entire forest started to burn, she needed to get help.

The rustle of leaves alerted her to movement. Fuck, she hoped that wasn't a goddamn wild animal.

The bright fire illuminated the area, so when a man she hadn't seen in years stepped in front of her and raised a rifle, she knew who it was immediately.

Joyner Amfinger.

Knox

Arriving back at the club at five o'clock in the morning, Knox followed Brooks into the main room, finding a beehive of activity. Although Megan and Pearllene sat at Outlaw's table, Zoann, Ophelia, Bailey, Carissa, Alexia and Bunny were serving food.

Knox wanted to go to his room and sleep. He wanted to talk to Roxanne, see her face, and hug her. As embarrassed as he was, he decided not to make the mistake of calling off their wedding. He'd lose her forever this time and he'd never forgive himself.

"You did what I'm payin' your ass for, huh, Brooks?" Outlaw called.

"Yes," Brooks answered, not smiling. He'd been quiet during the entire ride back to the clubhouse, for which Knox was grateful. He hadn't felt like talking.

"You okay, Knox?" Outlaw asked.

"Except for being tired from all the bullshit, I'm excellent," Knox answered, scrubbing a hand over his face. "I'm too exhausted to demand an explanation from you about why I was the only one arrested."

"Ain't givin' a fuck if you was wide the fuck awake, ain't got a explanation to give you. This shit as much a mystery to me." He indicated everyone behind him. "But we fuckin' findin' out."

"Knox, why did you leave Momma outside?" Bailey asked, walking up to him, Outlaw, and Brooks.

Knox frowned. "Roxanne isn't here?"

"What the fuck that mean?" Mortician demanded, joining them. "You fucking see her here?"

"Your woman went down to the station to wait for Brooks to get his ass there," Digger said from where he stood at the bar.

All eyes turned to Brooks. Horror dropping into his face, he shook his head. "I've not seen Roxanne," he managed.

A thoughtful expression crossed Outlaw's features. "Bailey, you ever hear of a motherfucker name Joyner Amfinger?" he asked.

"How do you know that evil fuckhole?" Alexia demanded.

Staring at Outlaw, Bailey nodded, unease creeping into her face, while Knox's stomach sank.

"Joyner Amfinger is Creighton's minion," she answered in a faint voice. "He does anything and everything Duke's father tells him to do." She swallowed. "Why?"

Knox staggered back, the horror overcoming him almost knocking him off his feet.

"Amfinger got a fuckin' record?" Outlaw pressed.

"Cretin's a lawyer," Pearllene called. "And connections. All anybody would ever see in public records is his ass being a gun dealer or some shit."

Carissa snorted. "Amfinger wish he had the balls or the brains to do shit like that. It's Creighton. All Creighton."

"Call that motherfucker cretin like the goddamn heathen he is," Pearllene demanded. "He met a Jessica Rabbit-looking heifer at one of the strip clubs he owns. Which, by the way, is also the basis for his drug operation."

"Roxanne knew what Creighton was up to?" Johnnie demanded.

"Yeah. I found the evidence in her house," Pearllene answered. "She never told me. In all the years since her divorce, she never once mentioned it. I think she thought if she just pushed it away, it would go away. But diseased-brain motherfuckers keep turning up. Creighton not going nowhere."

"Oh, yeah, the fuck he is," Outlaw declared. "As soon as I get my fuckin' hands on him, him, Amfinger, and the fuckin' guns gonna be blown the fuck up."

"No!" Knox said. "We can't kill them. Let the law take care of them."

"For fuckin' real, assfuck?" Outlaw demanded. "If you get to the motherfucker before my ass, have him arrested. Otherwise, fuck you. We gotta figure where the fuck Roxanne at. What happen to Aintfinger and Cretin can be fuckin' debated later. Stretch, get a bead on Amfinger phone. If we find him, we find her."

Knox debated on whether or not to do it his way or Outlaw's way. Then, Knox remembered Outlaw was part of Roxanne's close-knit family, which meant Knox was to. Therefore, he'd stick with them and hope when the time came for retribution he'd be able to look the other way.

Roxy

Tied to a chair with a gag in her mouth, Roxy glared as Joyner circled her. The tight clothes he wore and the highness of his hair made him look like a caricature of a man. Except he was more than fucking real.

"Would you like to hear how Knox's ex-wife pleaded for her life? Begged me not to kill her." Joyner laughed as tears began to stream down Roxy's face. "Don't know why I did it?" He shrugged. "Oh, that's right. Lassoing Knox in was taking too long and it annoyed me. I'd been holed up in a shitty little town, with a warehouse full of guns, expecting the job to be easy. I never expected that biker, Outlaw, to be so suspicious."

Stopping in front of Roxanne, he thumped her forehead so hard that her neck snapped back. Trying to speak but failing, Roxy kicked his shin.

Joyner groaned and slapped her cheek. "Don't test me, woman! I still haven't gotten back home to my women. I've been stuck at this motel with suitcases filled with money, waiting for a chance to get Knox. We finally decided to put our plans into motion tonight, when your daughters told your son they were heading this way for wedding celebrations. Tomorrow, would've been your turn. Then, you ended up in a limo by yourself and we expedited the plan." He smiled. "And here we are."

She was dizzy and cut-up. The white dress she intended to preserve for prosperity as part of her wedding ensemble, was torn and stained with blood—hers and the limo driver's.

A knock came on the door. Rubbing his hands together, Joyner grinned at her, then went to the door and looked through the peephole.

"Our guests have arrived," he announced, unlocking the door and opening it.

Of all the people she expected to see, Creighton and Duke would've been the last two she'd guessed. Her son had gotten taller since the last time she'd seen him. But seeing her boy with two of the vilest men she'd ever known sent tears to her eyes. Being with them meant he was against her.

"I have a fine son," Creighton announced, smiling.

At one time, she thought he'd been so handsome when he strolled into the office where she'd worked part-time as a receptionist. Within weeks of meeting, he'd proposed to her. A year later they'd married, and ten months after that Duke was born.

"Pity you're his mother," Creighton finished, glaring at her. Coming closer, he slapped her across the face.

For a moment, Roxy thought she saw anger flash across Duke's face, but it must've been a trick of her wooziness and pain.

"What kind of a stupid bitch are you?" Creighton demanded. "Leaving *evidence* of my dealings in your house where your low-class, miserable daughters could find them and tell my son." He straightened to his full height, then sidled a glare at Duke. "Who then took it upon himself to confront me?"

"You tried to have MeMe killed, Dad!" Duke said. "That's why I confronted you."

Unable to talk, Roxy grunted through her gag, shocked at the news. "There were two bikers who saved her. Mortician and another dude," Duke said.

"And made two of my men disappear," Creighton said. He walked to Duke and turned so they faced each other. The same type of blow he gave to Roxy, he hit Duke with.

Roxy kicked her legs, trying to get words out, while Duke grabbed his jaw.

"Because of you, I've been living a nervous existence for months," Creighton continued, pacing in front of Roxanne. "So Amfinger and I devised a little plan. Frame Knox Harrington. Humiliate him. Maybe, find a few bogus charges to add in if I found the right prosecutor. His life ruined. Your life ruined. Yet knowing you still had information that could destroy me didn't sit right. I realized I had to neutralize the threat. Get rid of you, and that old biddy you call a mother wouldn't last long after your death. Or, if she lingered for more than a week or two, take care of her as well. I have special plans for Alexia and Carissa. Bailey, though, will present a problem because of her husband."

Through her haze, Roxy thought she heard the rumble of motorcycles. Again, it must've been merely her imagination. The guys couldn't rescue her because they wouldn't be able to find her. Her purse with the tracking device and her phone with the tracking app were gone.

Blearily, she watched Joyner hand Creighton a gun. He aimed it at her head.

"Dad!" Duke cried, situating himself in front of Roxy. "I can't allow you to kill my mama. I've done everything you told me to do! Let her live for me."

A moment of silence before the report of a gun. Duke crumpled to the floor.

Tears rushing to her eyes, Roxy screamed, the sound muted because of the material in her mouth.

Creighton raised the gun again. Before he fired, the door was kicked in. Outlaw shot the gun out of Creighton's hand, while Mortician fired on Joyner, blowing one side of his face away.

Val, Johnnie, and Digger parted ways to allow Knox to rush

through. He slid to a halt at first glance of her, the hand holding the gun slackening at his side. His eyes widened and his mouth dropped open. She felt bloody, beaten, and swollen. If she saw herself, she'd probably stare like that, too.

"Roxy, baby," Knox cried, "who did this to you?"

"Duke, you little motherfucker," Mortician yelled.

Knox pulled the gag from Roxy's mouth.

"Don't hurt him," she screamed. "Creighton shot him. Duke was trying to protect me!"

"Protect you from being shot?" Knox asked in a strangely calm voice.

"Yes!"

He stared at her, then focused on Creighton. "You were going to kill her?"

"Not going to," Creighton snarled. "I *will*. I'm going to dance in her blood."

"No, the fuck you not, son," Mortician growled, going for his gun again.

Knox still held the weapon. Before Mortician drew, Knox aimed at Creighton's head and opened fire.

He stood still and silent for a long moment, then clenched his jaw, shoved the gun into his waistband, and rushed to Roxy. Once he freed her, he lifted her into his arms and carried her away. Still not speaking a word.

CHAPTER SIXTY-ONE

Knox

H e'd gotten very little rest because, after finding Roxanne at seven in the morning, he'd taken Roxanne to the hospital, while the guys got Duke there. While Knox was happy all of this had taken place on the outskirts of Hortensia, where the club had pull, that didn't help timewise.

Duke had been shot in the side. Emergency surgery had removed the bullet. Once Roxanne was seen to and released, she rushed up to her son's room in ICU. By then, it was noon, with their wedding taking place in five hours.

Knox was happy to see them makeup. Duke's treatment of her had been weighing on her for months. To think, it had all been orchestrated by his father. This crusade had begun before Roxanne's cancer. Creighton thought she'd succumb to the disease, so he'd backed off. Instead, she'd survived and then met Knox.

Duke was too afraid to go to his grandmother, sisters, or mother, so he went along with Creighton's schemes, convinced his father had so much power that he'd destroy anyone Duke confided in. Creighton also swore to Duke if it came to that type of destruction, he'd tie the boy up and make him watch as Creighton murdered Roxanne.

Knox hadn't intended to kill the man. Outlaw had surprised Knox and said he'd leave all motherfuckers alive, until they heard them out, because he had a debt to pay because his newest child and his wife were both alive.

At first, Knox hadn't known why Mortician had killed Joyner. Later, he'd discovered the asshole had pulled a weapon out. Seeing it, Mortician fired.

Discovering Joyner had murdered Callie made Knox wish Mortician had taken that bastard to the meatshack and tortured him for a while.

Outlaw recovered the club's money and now had possession of the cash he'd paid for the guns and the weapons themselves. The fire department had extinguished the blaze before it grew too out-of-control. Along with the limousine—and the body inside—an abandoned cabin had burned along with fifty acres of forest.

Given all that had happened, Knox thought the wedding would be postpone two or three days. Instead, the start time had been pushed from five in the afternoon to eight in the evening. His mother's private secretary had contacted all the guests to inform them of the changed time.

Somehow, it had all worked out. Except he hadn't slept in over a day. Neither had Roxanne. On top of that, she'd been injured.

"Well, Mr. Harrington, you look the worse for wear," Father Wilkins remarked as the bridal party marched down the aisle. He looked ridiculous wearing a cut over his priestly garb, but Knox kept his opinion to himself.

"C'mon, bruh," Digger said to the priest. "Don't start this. This a high-class function. Even Knox momma decided to come. If she can behave, you can."

"Lest I remind you, you're in my church."

Mortician glowered at him. "Lest I remind *you*, you got a lot of cash from my wife. Not a motherfucker alive more larcenous than you."

"It is not larceny, Mortician," Father Wilkins said. "It's looking out for one's self."

"Well, when one's self finds one dead don't be fucking surprised," Mortician retorted.

Father Wilkins looked at Mortician over the top of his glasses, but snapped his mouth shut.

Five minutes later, the wedding march began and the guests got to their feet. Mortician beamed as Johnnie marched Bailey down the aisle. Unable to wait, he met them halfway and transferred Bailey's hand from Johnnie's arm to his own, walking her to the altar.

Roxanne appeared, holding onto Outlaw as she limped down the aisle, banged and bruised but gorgeous and alive.

Outlaw stopped at the edge of the altar and lifted a brow at Father Wilkins.

"This where you say who the fuck give this woman," Outlaw said.

"She been given too many times for that bullshit, Outlaw," Pearl-lene called from the audience.

"Ain't movin' until this motherfucker say it," Outlaw said stubbornly.

"This is ridiculous," Knox said, annoyed. He glared at the priest. "Would you just say it so the wedding can commence?"

"My dear friends and family," his mother began, suddenly standing from her seat. "Please don't let these people be a reflection of me and my Hal. My Knox might be a lost cause—"

"Really, Mother?" Knox called, glaring at the back of her head.

"Sit down, Joan," his father said around a cough.

"Here, take her, Knox," Outlaw called. "The lil' motherfucker said it while your ma was actin' just as bad as us."

Kissing Roxanne's hand, Knox guided her to the altar. When the priest got to their vows, Roxanne halted the ceremony, stood and summoned Grant, who'd been sitting in the row with Meggie, Outlaw, and most of their children. Rebel, CJ, and Diesel had been members of the wedding party.

"Yes, ma'am?" Grant said when he walked up to Roxy.
"Come here, sugar," she said, guiding Grant to stand next to Knox. "I don't ever intend to take the place of your ma," she started, "but I

want you to know the ring your Daddy is putting on my finger means the three of us are family. You can come to me with anything, at any time, and I'll be right there for you. I will love and cherish you as if you were my own son and help you to keep your Mama's memory alive."

A tear slid down Grant's cheek, and he nodded, sniffling. Roxanne swiped it away, then kissed the top of his head. "Stand next to your Uncle Cam while me and your daddy finish our vows."

He started to follow her directions, then stopped and hugged her. "I love you, Roxy."

"And I love you, Grant," she whispered back.

"I love both of you," Knox said gruffly. He looked at the priest. "Bind me to the woman, man, because this is the beginning of the rest of my life."

EPILOGUE

One Month Later...

Roxy

Wearing thigh high boots to protect her skin from the hot pipes and exposed metal of Knox's bike—she wore a short, leather skirt—Roxy held onto Knox as he leaned into a curve in the road with ease. It had been a hard-won victory to get her interfering-ass son-in-law off her back, so she could hop on the back of Knox's bike. For a solid week, Mortician demanded Knox ride with a passenger wherever he went.

Although it annoyed Knox, he understood Mortician's concern. Instead of arguing, Knox complied.

He pulled into a clearing and rode behind a copse of trees. Pushing the kickstand down and planting his booted feet firmly onthe ground, Knox killed the engine, removed his helmet, and hung it on one of the two hooks, that he paid to have installed on each side of the handlebars. The boys refused to disgrace a bike in such a manner, and Knox insisted on the convenience of the hooks.

Without prompting from Knox, Roxy got to her feet, removed her own helmet, and hung it on the other hook, then she turned to him and met his gaze.

She smiled. "Mr. Harrington," she murmured.

Grinning, Knox raised her left hand to his lips and kissed her ring finger. "Mrs. Harrington."

Her pink princess cut diamond on the engagement ring Knox had bought specifically for her sparkled, seeming to reflect how she felt and what her life had become—a warm, bright place gleaming with love and laughter. She and her son had made up. She had a child in her life again that she was partly responsible for. Bailey would give her another grandchild soon. Harley and Lou were two of the most beautiful kids in the world. Her mother and Hamish were still going strong, and Carissa and Alexia were now both in relationships.

Outlaw, Meggie, and their kids were once again the rollicking bunch that brought joy to her heart. Johnnie and Kendall both had a long road ahead of them, but they were working on themselves individually, as parents, and as a couple. Bunny and Ophelia were both pregnant again. Val had brought a pot-bellied pig home and, somehow, got Zoann to agree to keep it as a pet. Diesel had gone off to college, while Cam and Jordan were also increasing their family by adopting newborn twins.

Knox placed his arm around her waist and pulled her closer. "The guys told me there's nothing in the world like bike sex."

Roxy brushed his lips with her own, then slipped her tongue into his mouth to deepen it. She didn't want to answer that.

Besides, he was right. The naughty thought made her giggle. "You have the most joyous laughter, Roxanne," he told her, sliding backward to give her room to climb in front of him.

She settled her legs on each side of Knox and leaned back against the handlebars. "Thank you. Guess what I *don't* have?"

Knox lifted a brow. "What might that be?"

"Panties on," she cooed, sliding her skirt up partially.

"Fuck! For real?"

She blinked at how like Outlaw Knox sounded, and burst into laughter.

"What can I say? The man grows on you," he said, knowing what she found so funny without her saying it."

"I told you those boys were good people."

"They are, and I'm lucky to know them." He snapped his finger as if a thought had just occurred to him. "That reminds me. I have something to show you."

He removed a sheet of paper from the inside of his leather jacket pocket, then held it out to her. When Roxy opened it, she saw measurements for a plot of land.

"What's this?"

"The acreage I purchased from the club to build our house on. It's at a diagonal from Bailey and Mortician."

Roxy gasped. They'd discussed housing for the past month. On the overnight honeymoon, in between very hot and intense fucking, they'd talked about where to live. So far, they remained in her quarters, but it was hard to host her entire family there.

"Oh my God!" Roxy breathed. "Knox!"

"There's no way I can take you or Grant away from our family. They live there, we live there. Case closed."

Laughing through her tears, Roxy launched herself into his arms. "I love you."

He slipped his hand under her skirt. "I love you, too, sweetheart," he said, cupping her pussy. "Now, straddle me and show me just how much."

Overflowing with contentment, Roxy was more than happy to comply.

The End

Dear Reader,

It has been quite an amazing journey that I've gone on since first meeting Christopher "Outlaw" Caldwell, his brothers, and the women they love. The twists and turns they've taken me on has been as surprising to me as they have to you, in some cases.

Out of all the books, Misrule has been, by far, the hardest to write. I started in February 2018 and didn't finish it until summer 2019. I had two cancer scares, my mother went through an angiogram because of heart problems, her vertigo returned, my computers died on me...you get the picture. Each time, I sat down to immerse myself in writing another crisis arose. But I was determined to get it written and I finally got it completed. I truly hope you enjoyed my finished product. It has been a long time coming. My sense of accomplishment is similar to what I felt when I finished Misled. That was a milestone for me and so is Misrule.

Thank you for going on this crazy ride with me. Without you, none of this would be possible. You can visit the Death Dweller boys any time at

https://www/deathdwellersmc.com

For everyone who is wondering—YES! There will be a second generation. As Outlaw would say *Ain't Nothin' but a Thing! Case fuckin' closed!*

Kat

ALSO BY KATHRYN C. KELLY

Phoenix Rising Rock Band Series

Inferno

Incendiary

Inflame

Death Dwellers MC Series

Misled

Misappropriate

Misunderstood

Misdeeds

Misbehavior

Misjudged

Misguided

Misalliance

Misconduct

A Very Christopher Christmas

Misfit

Mistrust

Misgivings

Outlaw's Dictionary

Death Dwellers: The Complete Series

An Outlaw Valentine

Dirty Boys Studio Series

Dirty Boy

Other Titles

All My Tomorrows

Dangerous

Riveted

Pink: Hot 'N Sexy for a cure: The
Books for Boobies 2015 Anthology

When Clubs Collide

Desire Me

ABOUT KATHRYN C. KELLY

In her dreams, Kathryn C. Kelly is a flirtatious biker babe with the rumble of a hog between her legs and a shirtless bad boy wrapped in her arms. Kathryn and her bad ass biker boy spend their evenings tossing back great scotch (Chivas Regal) and fighting over who is better at Cards against Humanity (she is, obviously.)

In her reality, Kathryn is a native New Orleanian who has survived Hurricane Katrina and breast cancer. Now she's hoping to survive three lively girls. While not playing Wonder Mom, Kathryn can be found putting all those dreams into the pages of her next Death Dwellers Motorcycle Club novel.